NOBODY LIVES FOR EVER

A cloud hung over James Bond as he negotiated the Bentley Mulsanne Turbo through the streets of Ostend at the start of a well-earned spell of leave in Rome. He had a worrying assignment in the Klinik Mozart, in the mountains south of Salzburg.

The two bronchial attacks May, his Scottish housekeeper, had suffered had thrown 007 into a paroxysm of concern. Her convalescence had done something to ease his mind, but nothing to still May's caustic tongue. If she refused to co-operate, she might not see her next birthday.

An incident on board the cross-Channel ferry had made him unaccountably jumpy. The search for the two youngsters who seemed to have gone overboard made him check his 9mm ASP automatic and spare ammunition clips behind the dashboard and to withdraw the Concealable Operations Baton in its soft leather case.

M's advice to be 'especially careful' seemed to be justified when, just hours after disembarking, the first grisly move in a bewildering game of cat-and-mouse was made, with Bond as the prey. What could be the purpose behind the personal vendetta of an assailant Bond failed to identify?

Bond realises there is, quite literally, a price on his head. Never have his defence mechanisms been more sorely tested.

FOR SPECIAL SERVICES

'John Gardner has got the 007 formula down pat.
But not too pat . . . he manages to create suspense
and spring a few surprises'

Financial Times

ICEBREAKER

'One of his best yet in his 007 mode'

The Listener

Also by the same author,
and available from Coronet:

James Bond Titles
Licence Renewed
For Special Services
Icebreaker
Role of Honour

Other Thrillers
The Nostradamus Traitor
The Garden of Weapons
The Quiet Dogs
The Werewolf Trace

About the Author

John Gardner was educated in Berkshire and at St John's College, Cambridge. He has had many fascinating occupations and was variously a Royal Marine Officer, a stage magician, theatre critic, reviewer and journalist.

He is the creator of the *Moriarty Journals*, the *Boysie Oakes* series and the *Herbie Kruger* trilogy, which has been favourably compared to le Carré's Smiley series.

John Gardner was commissioned by Glidrose, the company to which Ian Fleming assigned the copyright in his James Bond stories, to update the series and bring a slightly older Bond into the 1980s. The first of his Bond books, LICENCE RENEWED, was an immediate success, the *Daily Telegraph* passing the verdict that 'Ian Fleming would not be displeased'. It was quickly followed by FOR SPECIAL SERVICES, ICEBREAKER, which the *Standard* claimed was 'just as enjoyable as the originals', and ROLE OF HONOUR.

NOBODY LIVES FOR EVER

John Gardner

CORONET BOOKS
Hodder and Stoughton

**For Peter and Peg
with affection**

Copyright © Glidrose Publications Ltd 1986
First published in Great Britain by
Jonathan Cape Ltd and Hodder and Stoughton Ltd in 1986
Coronet early export edition 1986
Coronet open market edition 1987

British Library C.I.P.

Gardner, John, *1926–*
Nobody lives for ever.
I. Title
823′.914[F]   PR6057.A629

ISBN 0 340 39860 4

Printed and bound in Great Britain for
Hodder and Stoughton Paperbacks, a
division of Hodder and Stoughton Ltd.,
Mill Road, Dunton Green, Sevenoaks,
Kent (Editorial Office: 47 Bedford
Square, London, WC1B 3DP) by
Richard Clay Ltd.,
Bungay, Suffolk.

CONTENTS

1	The Road South	1
2	The Poison Dwarf	13
3	Sukie	23
4	The Head Hunt	35
5	Nannie	47
6	The Nub	63
7	The Hook	76
8	Under Discipline	93
9	Vanmpire	109
10	The Mozart Man	119
11	Hawk's Wing and Macabre	133
12	England Expects	145
13	Good Evening, Mr Boldman	153
14	Frost-free City	163
15	The Price for a Life	179
16	Going Down Tonight	189
17	Shark Island	199
18	Madame Awaits	213
19	Death and Destruction	231
20	Cheers and Applause	241

1

THE ROAD SOUTH

JAMES BOND SIGNALLED late, braked more violently than a Bentley driving instructor would have liked, and slewed the big car off the E5 motorway and on to the last exit road just north of Brussels. It was merely a precaution. If he was going to reach Strasbourg before midnight it would have made more sense to carry on, follow the ring road around Brussels, then keep going south on the Belgian N4. Yet even on holiday, Bond knew that it was only prudent to remain alert. The small detour across country would quickly establish whether anyone was on his tail, and he would pick up the E40 in about an hour or so.

Lately there had been a directive to all officers of the Secret Service, advising 'constant vigilance, even when off duty, and particularly when on leave and out of the country'.

He had taken the morning ferry to Ostend, and there had been over an hour's delay. About half-way into the crossing the ship had stopped, a boat had been lowered, and had moved out, searching the water in a wide circle. After some

1

forty minutes the boat had returned and a helicopter appeared overhead as they set sail again. A little later the news spread throughout the ship. Two men overboard, and lost, it seemed.

'Couple of young passengers skylarking,' said the barman. 'Skylarked once too often. Probably cut to shreds by the screws.'

Once through Customs, Bond had pulled into a side street, opened the secret compartment in the dashboard of the Bentley Mulsanne Turbo, checked that his 9mm ASP automatic and the spare ammunition clips were intact, and taken out the small Concealable Operations Baton, which lay heavy in its soft leather holster. He had closed the compartment, loosened his belt and threaded the holster into place so that the baton hung at his right hip. It was an effective piece of hardware: a black rod, no more than fifteen centimetres long. Used by a trained man, it could be lethal.

Shifting in the driving seat now, Bond felt the hard metal dig comfortably into his hip. He slowed the car to a crawl of 40k.p.h., scanning the mirrors as he took corners and bends, automatically slowing again once on the far side. Within half an hour he was certain that he was not being followed.

Even with the directive in mind, he reflected that he was being more careful than usual. A sixth sense of danger or possibly M's remark a couple of days ago?

'You couldn't have chosen a more awkward time to be away, 007,' his chief had grumbled, though Bond had taken little notice. M was noted for a grudging attitude when it came to matters of leave.

'It's only my entitlement, sir. You agreed I could

take my month now. If you remember, I had to postpone it earlier in the year.

M grunted. 'Moneypenny's going to be away as well. Off gallivanting all over Europe. You're not . . . ?'

'Accompanying Miss Moneypenny? No, sir.'

'Off to Jamaica or one of your usual Caribbean haunts, I suppose,' M said with a frown.

'No sir. Rome first. Then a few days on the Riviera dei Fiori before driving across to Austria – to pick up my housekeeper, May. I just hope she'll be fit enough to be brought back to London by then.'

'Yes . . . yes.' M was not appeased. 'Well, leave your full itinerary with the Chief-of-Staff. Never know when we're going to need you.'

'Already done, sir.'

'Take care, 007. Take special care. The Continent's a hotbed of villainy these days, and you can never be too careful.' There was a sharp, steely look in his eyes that made Bond wonder whether something was being hidden from him.

As Bond left M's office, the old man had the grace to say he hoped there would be good news about May.

At the moment, May, Bond's devoted old Scottish housekeeper, appeared to be the only worry on an otherwise cloudless horizon. During the winter she had suffered two severe attacks of bronchitis and seemed to be deteriorating. She had been with Bond longer than either cared to remember. In fact, apart from the Service, she was the one constant in his not uneventful life.

After the second bronchial attack, Bond had

insisted on a thorough check-up by a Service-retained doctor with a Harley Street practice, and though May had resisted, insisting she was 'tough as an auld game bird, and not yet fit for the pot', Bond had taken her himself to the consulting rooms. There had followed an agonising week, with May being passed from specialist to specialist, complaining all the way. But the results of the tests were undeniable. The left lung was badly damaged, and there was a distinct possibility that the disease might spread. Unless the lung was removed immediately and the patient underwent at least three months of enforced rest and care, May was unlikely to see her next birthday.

The operation was carried out by the most skilful surgeon Bond's money could buy, and once she was well enough, May was packed off to a world-renowned clinic specialising in her complaint, the Klinik Mozart, in the mountains south of Salzburg. Bond telephoned the clinic regularly and was told that she was making astonishing progress.

He had even spoken to her personally the evening before, and he now smiled to himself at the tone of her voice, and the somewhat deprecating way she had spoken of the clinic. She was, no doubt, reorganising their staff and calling down the wrath of her Glen Orchy ancestors on everyone from maids to chefs.

'They dinna know how to cook a decent wee bite here, Mr James, that's the truth of it; and the maids canna make a bed for twopence. I'd no employ any the one of them – and you paying all this money for me to be here. Yon's a downright waste, Mr James.

4

A *crinimal* waste.' May had never been able to get her tongue round the word 'criminal'.

'I'm sure they're looking after you very well, May.' She was too independent to be a really good patient.

Trust May, he thought. She liked things done her way or not at all. It would be purgatory for her in the Klinik Mozart.

He checked the fuel, deciding it would be wise to have the tank filled before the long drive that lay ahead on the E40. Having established that there was nobody on his tail, he concentrated on looking for a garage. It was after seven in the evening, and there was little traffic about. He drove through two small villages and saw the signs indicating proximity to the motorway. Then, on a straight, empty, stretch of road, he spotted the garish signs of a small filling station.

It appeared to be deserted and the two pumps unattended, though the door to the tiny office had been left open. A notice in red warned that the pumps were not self-service, so he pulled the Mulsanne up to the Super pump and switched off the engine. As he climbed out, stretching his muscles, he became aware of the commotion behind the little glass and brick building. Growling, angry, voices could be heard, and a thump, as though someone had collided with a car. Bond locked the car using the central locking device and strode quickly to the corner of the building.

Behind the office was a garage area. A white Alfa Romeo Sprint, stood in front of the open doors. Two men were holding down a young woman on the bonnet. The driver's door was open and a handbag lay ripped open on the ground, its contents scattered.

'Come on,' one of the men said in rough French, 'where is it? You must have some! Give.' Like his companion, the thug was dressed in faded jeans, shirt and sneakers. Both were short, broad shouldered, with tanned muscular arms – rough customers by any standards. Their victim protested, and the man who had spoken raised his hand to hit her across the face.

'Stop that!' Bond's voice cracked like a whip as he moved forward.

The men looked up, startled. Then one of them smiled. 'Two for the price of one,' he said softly, grabbing the woman by the shoulder and throwing her away from the car.

The man facing Bond held a large wrench, and clearly thought Bond was easy prey. His hair was untidy, tight and curly, and the surly young face already showed the scars of an experienced street fighter. He leaped forward in a half crouch, holding the wrench low. He moved like a large monkey, Bond thought, as he reached for the baton on his right hip.

The baton, made by the same firm that developed the ASP 9mm pistol, looked harmless enough – fifteen centimetres of non-slip, rubber-coated metal. But, as he drew it from its holster, Bond flicked down hard with his right wrist. From the rubber-covered handle sprang a further, tele-scoped twenty-five centimetres of toughened steel, which locked into place.

The sudden appearance of the weapon took the young thug off guard. His right arm was raised,

clutching the wrench, and for a second he hesitated. Bond stepped quickly to his left and swung
the baton. There was an unpleasant cracking noise,
followed by a yelp, as the baton connected with the
attacker's forearm. He dropped the wrench and
doubled up, holding his broken arm and cursing
violently in French.

Again Bond moved, delivering a lighter tap this
time, to the back of the neck. The mugger went on
his knees and pitched forward. With a roar, Bond
hurled himself at the second thug. But the man had
no stomach for a fight. He turned and started to run;
not fast enough, though, for the tip of the baton
came down hard on his left shoulder, certainly
breaking bones.

He gave a louder cry than his partner, then raised
his hands and began to plead. Bond was in no mood
to be kind to a couple of young tearaways who had
attacked a virtually helpless woman. He lunged
forward, and buried the baton's tip into the man's
groin, eliciting a further screech of pain which was
cut off by a smart blow to the left of the neck, neatly
judged to knock him unconscious but do little
futher damage.

Bond kicked the wrench out of the way, and
turned to assist the young woman, but she was
already gathering her things together by the car.

'You all right?' He walked towards her, taking in
the Italianate looks – the long tangle of red hair, the
tall, lithe body, oval face and large brown eyes.

'Yes. Thank you, yes.' There was no trace of
accent. As he came closer, he noted the Gucci
loafers, very long legs encased in tight Calvin Klein
jeans, and a silk Hermes shirt. 'It's lucky you came

7

along when you did. Do you think we should call the police?' She gave her head a little shake, stuck out her bottom lip and blew the hair out of her eyes.

'I just wanted petrol.' Bond looked at the Alfa Romeo. 'What happened?'

'I suppose you might say that I caught them with their fingers in the till, and they didn't take kindly to that. The attendant's out cold in the office.'

The muggers, posing as attendants, had apologised when she drove in, saying the pumps out front were not working. Could she take her car to the pump around the back? 'I fell for it, and they dragged me out of the car.'

Bond asked how she knew about the attendant?

'One of them asked the other if he'd be okay. He said the man would be out for an hour or so.' There was no sign of tension in her voice, and as she smoothed the jungle of hair, her hands were steady. 'If you want to be on your way, I can telephone the police. There's really no need for you to hang about you know.'

'Nor you,' he said with a smile. 'Those two will also be asleep for some time. The name's Bond, by the way. James Bond.'

'Sukie.' She held out a hand, the palm dry and the grip firm. 'Sukie Tempesta.'

In the end, they both waited for the police, costing Bond over an hour and half's delay. The pump attendant had been badly beaten and required urgent medical attention. Sukie did what she could for him while Bond telephoned the police. As they waited they talked and Bond tried to find out more about her, for the whole affair had begun to intrigue him. Somehow, he had the impression that she was holding out on him. But, however cleverly he phrased his questions, Sukie managed to sidestep with answers that told him nothing.

There was little to be gleaned from observation. She was very self-possessed, and could have been anything, from a lawyer to a society hostess. Judging by her appearance and the jewellery she wore, she was well off. Whatever her background, Bond decided that Sukie was certainly an attractive young woman, with a low-pitched voice, precise economic movements and a reserved manner that was possibly a little diffident.

One thing he did discover quickly was that she spoke at least three languages, which pointed to both intelligence and a good education. As for the rest, he could not even discover her nationality, though the plates on the Sprint were, like her name, Italian.

Before the police arrived in a flurry of sirens, Bond had returned to his car and stowed away the baton – an illegal weapon in any country. He submitted to an interrogation, and was asked to sign a statement. Only then was he allowed to fill up his car and leave, with the proviso that he gave his whereabouts for the next few weeks, and his address and telephone number in London.

Sukie Tempesta was still being questioned when he drove away, feeling strangely uneasy. He recalled the look in M's eyes; and began to wonder about the business on the ferry.

Just after midnight, he was on the E25 between Metz and Strasbourg. He had again filled the tank, and drunk some passable coffee at the French frontier. Now the road was almost deserted, so he spotted the tail lights of the car ahead a good four kilometres before overtaking it. He had set the cruise control at 110k.p.h., after crossing the frontier, and so sailed past the big white BMW, which appeared to be pottering along in the fifties.

Out of habit, his eyes flicked to the car's plates and the number registered in his mind as did the international badge D, which identified the car as German.

A minute or so later, Bond became alert. The BMW had picked up speed, moving into the centre lane, yet remaining close to him. The distance varied between about five hundred to less than a hundred metres. He touched the brakes, switched back from cruise control and accelerated. One hundred and thirty. One hundred and forty! The BMW was still there.

Then, with about fifteen kilometres to go before the outskirts of Strasbourg, he became aware of another set of headlights directly behind him in the fast lane, and coming up at speed.

He moved into the middle lane, eyes flicking between the road ahead and the mirror. The BMW had fallen back a little, and in seconds the oncoming lights grew, and the Bentley was rocked slightly as a little black car went past like a jet. It must have been touching 160k.p.h., and in his headlights Bond could get only a glimpse of the plates, which were splattered with mud. He thought they must be Swiss, as he was almost certain that he had caught sight of a Ticino Canton shield to the right of the rear plate. There was not enough time for him even to identify the make of the car.

The BMW remained in place for only a few more moments, slowing and losing ground. Then Bond saw the flash in his mirror: a brutal crimson ball erupting in the middle lane behind him. He felt the Bentley shudder under the shock waves and watched in the mirror as lumps of flaming metal danced across the highway.

Bond increased pressure on the accelerator. Nothing would make him stop and become involved at this time of night, particularly on a lonely stretch of road. Suddenly he realised that he felt oddly shaken at the unexplained violence which appeared to have surrounded him all day.

At one-eleven in the morning, the Bentley nosed its way into Strasbourg's Place Saint-Pierre-le-Jeune and came to a standstill outside the Hotel Sofitel. The night staff were deferential. Oui, M. Bond . . . Non, M. Bond. But certainly they had his reservation. The car was unloaded, his baggage whipped away, and he took the Bentley himself to the hotel's private parking.

The suite proved to be almost too large for the overnight stay, and there was a basket of fruit, with the compliments of the manager. Bond did not know whether to be impressed or on his guard. He had not stayed at the Sofitel for at least three years.

Opening the minibar, he mixed himself a martini. He was pleased the bar stocked Gordon's and a decent vodka, though he had to make do with a simple Lillet vermouth instead of his preferred Kina. Taking the drink over to the bed, Bond selected one of his two briefcases – the one that contained the sophisticated scrambling equipment. This he attached to the telephone and dialled

Transworld Exports (the Service Headquarters' cover) in London.

The Duty Officer listened patiently while Bond recounted the two incidents in some detail. The line was quickly closed, and Bond, tired after the long drive, took a brief shower, rang down for a call at eight in the morning, and stretched out naked under the bedclothes.

Only then did he start to face up to the fact that he was more than a little concerned. He thought again of that strange look in M's eyes; then about the Ostend ferry and the two men overboard; the girl – Sukie – in distress at the filling station, and the appalling explosion on the road. There had been too many incidents to be mere coincidence, and a tiny suspicion of menace started to creep into his mind.

2

THE POISON DWARF

BOND SWEATED THROUGH his morning workout – the
twenty slow pushups with their exquisite lingering
strain; then the leg lifts, performed on the stomach;
and lastly the twenty fast toe-touches.

Before going to the shower, he called room
service and gave his precise order for breakfast:
two thick slices of wholewheat bread, with the
finest butter and, if possible, Tiptree Little Scarlet
jam or Cooper's Oxford marmalade. Alas, Mon-
sieur, there was no Cooper, but they had Tiptree. It
was unlikely they could supply De Bry coffee, so
after detailed questioning he settled for their
special blend. While waiting for the tray to arrive,
he took a very hot shower, followed by another
with the water freezing cold.

A man of habit, Bond did not normally like
change, but he had recently altered his soap,
shampoo and cologne to Dunhill Blend 30, as
he liked their specially masculine tang – and
now, after a vigorous towelling, he rubbed the
cologne into his body. Then he slipped into his
silk travelling Happi-coat to await breakfast,

which came accompanied by the local morning papers.

The BMW, or the débris that was left, seemed to be spread across all the front pages, while the headlines proclaimed the bombing to be everything from an atrocious act of urban terrorism to the latest assassination in a criminal gang war that had been sweeping France over the last few weeks. There was little detail, except for the information given by the police, that there had been only one victim, the driver, and that the car had been registered in the name of Conrad Tempel, a German businessman from Freiburg. Herr Tempel was missing from his home, so they presumed he was among the fragments of the motor car.

While reading the story, Bond drank his two large cups of black coffee without sugar, and decided that he would skirt Freiburg later that day, after driving into Germany. He planned to cross the frontier again at Basle. Once in Switzerland, he would make his way down to Lake Maggiore in the Ticino Canton and spend a night in one of the small tourist villages on the Swiss side of the lake. Then he would make the final long run into Italy and the lengthy sweat down the autostradas to Rome. He would spend a few days with the Service's Resident and his wife, Steve and Tabitha Quinn.

Today's drive would be less taxing. He did not need to leave until noon, so he had a little time to relax and look around. But first there was the most important job of the day, the telephone call to the Klinik Mozart, to enquire after May.

He dialled 19, the French 'out' code, followed by the 61 which would take him into the Austrian system, then the number. Doktor Kirchtum came on the line almost immediately.

'Good morning, Mr Bond. You are in Belgium now, yes?'

Bond told him politely that he was in France, would be in Switzerland tomorrow, and in Italy the following day.

'You are burning a lot of the rubber, as they say.' Kirchtum was a small man, but his voice was loud and resonant. At the clinic he could be heard in a room long before he arrived. The nurses called him *das Nebelhorn*, the Foghorn.

Bond asked after May.

'She still does well. She orders us around, which is a good sign of recovery.' Kirchtum gave a guffaw of laughter. 'I think the chef is about to cash in his index, as I believe you English say.'

'Hand in his cards,' Bond said, smiling to himself. The Herr Doktor, he was sure, made very studied errors in colloquial English. He asked if there was any chance of speaking to the patient, and was told that she was undergoing some treatment at the moment and would not be able to talk on the telephone until later in the day. Bond said he would try to telephone again during his drive through Switzerland, thanked the Herr Doktor, and was about to hang up when Kirchtum stopped him.

'There is someone here who would like a word with you, Mr Bond. Hold on. I'll put her through.'

To Bond's surprise, he heard the voice of M's P.A., Miss Moneypenny, speaking to him with that hint of affection she always reserved for him.

'James! How lovely to talk to you.'

15

'Well, Moneypenny. What on earth are you doing at the Mozart?'

'I'm on holiday, like you, and spending a few days in Salzburg. I just thought I'd come up and see May. She's doing very well, James.' Moneypenny's voice sounded light and excited.

'Nice of you to think of her. Be careful what you get up to in Salzburg, though, Moneypenny – all those musical people looking at Mozart's house and going to concerts . . .'

'Nowadays all they want is to go and see the locations used in *The Sound of Music*,' she replied, laughing.

'Well, take care all the same, Penny. I'm told those tourists are after only one thing from a girl like you.'

'Would that you were a tourist, then, James.'

Miss Moneypenny still held a special place in her heart for Bond. After a little more conversation Bond again thanked her for the thoughtful action of visiting May.

His luggage was ready for collection, the windows were open and the sun streamed in. He would take a look around the hotel, check the car, have some more coffee and get on the road. As he went down to the foyer he realised how much he needed a holiday. It had been a hard, tough year, and for the first time Bond wondered if he had made the right decision. Perhaps the short trip to his beloved Royale-les-Eaux would have been a better idea.

A familiar face slid into the periphery of his vision as he crossed the foyer. Bond hesitated, turned and gazed absently into the hotel shop window, the better to examine the reflection of a man sitting near the main reception desk. He gave no sign of having seen Bond, as he sat casually glancing through yesterday's *Herald Tribune*. He was short, barely four feet two inches. Neatly and expensively dressed, he had the look of complete confidence characteristic of so many small men. Bond always mistrusted people of short stature, knowing their tendency to over-compensate with ruthless pushiness, as though it were necessary to prove themselves.

He turned away, having made his identification. The face was known well enough to him, with thin, ferret-like features and the same bright, darting eyes as the animal. What, he wondered to himself, was Paul Cordova – or the Rat as he was known in the underworld – doing in Strasbourg? Bond knew there had been a suggestion some years ago that the K.G.B., posing as a United States Government agency, had used him to do a particularly nasty piece of work in New York.

Paul, the Rat, Cordova was an enforcer – a polite term for a killer – for one of the New York Families, and his photograph and record were on the files of the world's major police and intelligence departments. It was part of Bond's job to know faces like this, even though Cordova moved in criminal rather than intelligence circles. But Bond did not think of him as the Rat. To him, the man was the Poison Dwarf. Was his presence in Strasbourg another 'coincidence'? Bond wondered.

He went down to the parking area, checked the Bentley carefully, and told the man on duty that he would be picking it up within half an hour. He refused to let any of the hotel staff move the car.

Indeed, there had been a certain amount of surliness on his arrival because he would not leave the keys at the desk. On his way out, Bond could not fail to notice the low, black, wicked-looking Series 3 Porsche 911 Turbo. The rear plates were mud-spattered, but the Ticino Canton disc showed clearly. Whoever had raced past him on the motorway just before the destruction of the BMW was now at the hotel. Bond's antennae told him that it was time to get out of Strasbourg. The menacing small cloud had grown a shade larger.

Cordova was not in the hotel foyer when he returned. On reaching his room. Bond put through another call to Transworld Exports in London, again using the scrambler. Even on leave it was his duty to report on the movements of anyone like the Poison Dwarf, particularly so far away from his own patch.

Twenty minutes later, Bond was at the wheel of the Bentley, heading for the German border. He crossed without incident, skirted Freiburg, and by afternoon again crossed frontiers, at Basle. After a few hours' driving he boarded the car train for the journey through the St Gotthard Pass, and by early evening the Bentley was purring through the streets of Locarno and on to the lakeside road. Bond passed through Ascona, that paradise for artists, both professional and amateur, and on to the small and pleasing village of Brissago.

In spite of the sunlight and breathtaking views of clean Swiss villages, and towering mountains, a sense of impending doom remained with Bond as he travelled south. At first he put it down to the odd events of the previous day and the vaguely disconcerting experience of seeing a New York Mafia hood in Strasbourg. Yet, as he neared Lake Maggiore, he wondered if this mood could be due to a slightly dented pride. He felt distinctly annoyed that Sukie Tempesta had appeared so self-assured, calm and unimpressed by his charm. She could, he thought, at least have shown some sort of gratitude. Yet she had hardly smiled at him.

But when the red-brown roofs of the lakeside villages came in sight, Bond began to laugh. Suddenly his gloom lifted and he recognised his own pettiness. He slid a compact disc into the stereo player and a moment later the combination of the view and the great Art Tatum rattling out *The Shout* banished the darkness, putting him into a happier mood.

Though his favourite part of the country lay around Geneva, Bond also loved this corner of Switzerland that rubbed shoulders with Italy. As a young man he had lazed around the shores of Lake Maggiore, eaten some of the best meals of his life in Locarno, and once, on a hot moonlit night, with the waters of Brissago alive with lamp-lit fishing boats, in the very ordinary little hotel by the pier, had made unforgettable love to an Italian countess.

It was to this hotel, the Mirto du Lac, that he now drove. It was a simple family place, below the church with its arcade of cypresses, and near the pier where the lake steamers put in every hour. The *padrone* greeted him like an old friend, and Bond was soon ensconced in his room, with the little balcony looking down to the forecourt and landing stage.

Before unpacking Bond dialled the Klinik

Mozart. The Herr Direktor was not available and one of the junior doctors told him politely that he could not speak to May because she was resting. There had been a visitor and she was a little tired. For some reason the words did not ring true. There was a slight hesitation in the doctor's voice which put Bond on the alert. He asked if May was all right, and the doctor assured him that she was perfectly well, just a little tired.

'This visitor,' he went on, 'I believe a Miss Moneypenny . . .'

'This is correct.' The doctor was the one who sounded most correct.

'I don't suppose you happen to know where she's staying in Salzburg?'

He did not. 'I understand she is coming back to see the patient tomorrow,' he added.

Bond thanked him and said he would call again. By the time he had showered and changed, it was starting to get dark. Across the lake the sunlight gradually left Mount Tamaro, and lights went on along the lakeside. Insects began to flock around the glass globes, and one or two couples took seats at the tables outside.

As Bond left his room to go down to the bar in the corner of the restaurant, a black Series 3 Porsche 911 crept quietly into the forecourt and parked with its nose thrust towards the lake. Its occupant climbed out, locked the car and walked with neat little steps back the way he had driven, up towards the church.

It was some ten minutes later that the people at the tables and in the hotel bar heard the repeated piercing screams. The steady murmur of conversation faded as it became obvious the screams were not part of some lighthearted game. These were shrieks of terror. Several people in the bar started towards the door. Some men outside were already on their feet, others were looking around to see where the noise was coming from. Bond was among those who hurried outside. The first thing he saw was the Porsche. Then a woman, her face white and her hair flying, her mouth stretched wide in a continuous scream, came running down the steps from the churchyard. Her hands kept going to her face, then wringing the air, then clutching her head. She was shouting, '*Assassinio! Assassinio!*' – Murder – as she pointed back to the churchyard.

Five or six men got up the steps ahead of Bond and clustered round a small bundle lying across the cobbled path, shocked into silence at the sight that confronted them.

Bond moved quietly to the perimeter of the group. Paul, the Rat, Cordova lay on his back, knees drawn up, one arm flung outwards, his head at an angle, almost severed by a single deep slash across the throat. Blood had already spread over the cobbles.

Bond pushed through the gathering crowd and returned to the lakeside. He had never believed in coincidences. He knew that the drownings, the affair at the filling station, the explosion on the motorway, and Cordova's appearance, here and in France, were linked, and that he was the common denominator. His holiday was shattered. He would have to telephone London, report, and await orders.

Another surprise awaited him as he entered the hotel. Standing by the reception desk, looking as elegant as ever in a short blue-tinged leather outfit, probably by Merenlender, stood Sukie Tempesta.

3

SUKIE

'JAMES BOND!' The delight seemed genuine enough, but with beautiful women you could never be sure.

'In the flesh,' he said as he moved closer. For the first time he really saw her eyes: large, brown with violet flecks, oval, and set off by naturally long, curling lashes. They were eyes, he thought, that could be the undoing or the making of a man. His own flicked down to the full, firm curve of her breasts under the well-fitting leather. She stuck out her lower lip, to blow hair from her forehead, as she had done the day before.

'I didn't expect to see you again.' Her wide mouth tilted in a warm smile. 'I'm so glad. I didn't get a chance to thank you properly yesterday.' She bobbed a mock curtsey. 'Mr Bond, I might even owe you my life. Thank you very much. I mean *very* much.'

He moved to one side of the reception desk so that he could watch her and at the same time keep an eye on the main doors. Instinctively, he felt danger close at hand. Danger by being close to Sukie Tempesta, perhaps.

23

Outside the commotion was still going on. There were police among the crowd and the sound of sirens floated down from the main street and the church above. Bond knew he needed his back against a wall all the time now. She asked him what was going on, and when he told her she shrugged.

'It's commonplace where I spend most of my time. In Rome, murder is a fact of life nowadays, but somehow you don't expect it here in Switzerland.'

'It's commonplace anywhere.' Bond tried his most charming smile. 'But what are you doing here, Miss Tempesta – or is it Mrs, or even Signora?'

She wrinkled her nose prettily and raised her eyebrows. 'Principessa, actually – if we have to be formal.'

Bond lifted an eyebrow. 'Principessa Tempesta.' He dropped his head in a formal bow.

'Sukie,' she said with a wide smile, the large eyes innocent, yet with a tiny tinge of mockery. 'You must call me Sukie, Mr Bond. Please.'

'James.'

'James.' And at that moment the *padrone* came bustling up to complete her booking. As soon as he saw the title on the registration form everything changed to a hand-wringing, bowing comedy, causing Bond to smile wryly.

'You haven't yet told me what you're doing here,' he continued, over the hotel keeper's effusions.

'Could I do that over dinner? At least I owe you that.'

Her hand touched his forearm and he felt the

natural exchange of static. Warning bells rang in his head. No chances, he thought, don't take chances with anybody, particularly anyone you find attractive.

'Dinner would be very pleasant,' he replied before once more asking what she was doing here on Lake Maggiore.

'My little motor car has broken down. There's something very wrong, according to the garage here – which probably means all they'll do is change the plugs. But they say it's going to take days.'

'And you're heading for?'

'Rome, naturally.' She blew at her hair again.

'What a happy coincidence.' Bond gave another bow. 'If I can be of service . . .'

She hesitated briefly. 'Oh, I'm sure you can. Shall we meet for dinner down here in half an hour?'

'I'll be waiting, Principessa.'

He thought he saw her nose wrinkle and her tongue poke out like a naughty schoolgirl as she turned to follow the *padrone* to her room.

In the privacy of his own room, Bond telephoned London again, to tell them about Cordova. He had the scrambler on, and as an afterthought asked them to run a check on both the Interpol computer and their own, on the Principessa Sukie Tempesta. He also asked the Duty Officer if they had any information about the BMW's owner, Herr Tempel of Freiburg. Nothing yet, he was told, but some material had been sent to M that afternoon.

'You'll hear soon enough if it's important. Have a nice holiday.'

Very droll, thought Bond as he packed away the

scrambler, a CC500 which can be used on any telephone in the world and allows only the legitimate receiving party to hear the caller *en clair*. Each CC500 has to be individually programmed so that eavesdroppers can hear only indecipherable sounds, even if they tap in with a compatible system. It was now standard Service practice for all officers out of the country, on duty or leave, to carry a CC500, and the access codes were altered daily.

There were ten minutes to spare before he was due to meet Sukie, though Bond doubted she would be on time. He washed quickly, rubbing cologne hard into face and hair, and then put on a blue cotton jacket over his shirt. He went quickly downstairs and out to the car. There was still a great deal of police activity in the churchyard, and he could see that a crime team had set up lights where Cordova's body had been discovered.

Inside the car he waited for the courtesy lights to go out before he pressed the switch on the main panel, revealing the hidden compartment below. He checked the 9mm ASP and buckled its compact holster in place underneath his jacket, then secured the baton holster to his belt. Whatever was going on around him was dangerous. At least two lives had already been lost – probably more – and he did not intend to end up as the next cadaver.

To his surprise, Sukie was already at the bar when he got back into the hotel.

'Like a dutiful woman, I didn't order anything while I waited.'

'I prefer dutiful women.'

Bond slid on to the bar stool next to her, turning

26

it slightly so that he had a clear view of anyone
coming through the big glass doors at the front.
'What will you drink?'

'Oh no, tonight's on me. In honour of your
saving *my* honour, James.'

Again her hand slightly brushed his arm, and he
felt the same electricty. Bond capitulated.

'I know we're in Ticino, where they think grappa
is good liquor. Still, I'll stick to the comic drinks. A
Campari soda, if I may.'

She ordered the same, then the *padrone* bustled
over with the menu. It was very *alla famiglia*, very
semplice, he explained. It would make a change,
Bond said, and Sukie asked him to order for them
both. He said he would be difficult and change the
menu around a little, starting with the *Melone con
kirsch*, though he asked them to serve his without
the kirsch. Bond disliked any food soused in
alcohol.

'For the entrée, there's really only one dish,
pasta excepted, in these parts, you'll agree?'

'The *coscia di agnello*?'

She smiled as he nodded. In the north these
spiced chops were known as 'lamm-Gigot'. Here,
among the Ticinese, they were less delicate in taste,
but made delicious by the use of much garlic. Like
Bond, Sukie refused any vegetables, but accepted
the plain green salad which he also ordered,
together with a bottle of Frecciarossa Bianco, the
best white wine they appeared to supply. Bond had
taken one look at the champagnes and pronounced
them undrinkable, but 'probably reasonable for
making a dressing', at which Sukie laughed. Her
laugh was, Bond thought, the least attractive thing

about her, a little harsh, maybe not entirely genuine.

When they were seated Bond wasted no time in offering to help her on her journey.

'I'm leaving for Rome in the morning. I'd be very pleased to give you a lift. That is, if the Principe won't be offended at a commoner bringing you home.'

She gave a little pout. 'He's in no position to be offended. Principe Pasquale Tempesta died last year.'

'I'm sorry, I . . .'

She gave a dismissive wave of the right hand. 'Oh, don't be sorry. He was eighty-three. We were married for two years. It was convenient, that's all.' She did not smile, or try to make light of it.

'A marriage of convenience?'

'No, it was just convenient. I like good things. He had money; he was old; he needed someone to keep him warm at night. In the Bible, didn't King David take a young girl – Abishag – to keep him warm?'

'I believe so. My upbringing was rather Calvinistic, but I do seem to recall the Lower Fourth sniggering over that story.'

'Well, that's what I was, Pasquale Tempesta's Abishag, and he enjoyed it. Now I enjoy what he left me.'

'For an Italian you speak excellent English.'

'I should. I *am* English. Sukie's short for Susan.' There was the smile again, and then the laugh, a little more mellow this time.

'You speak excellent Italian then.'

'And French, and German. I told you that yesterday, when you were trying to ask subtle questions, to find out about me.'

She reached forward, putting out a hand to cover his as it lay on the table beside his glass.

'Don't worry, James, I'm not a witch. But I can spot nosey questions. Comes from the nuns, then living with Pasquale's people.'

'Nuns?'

'I'm a good convent-educated girl, James. You know about girls who've been educated in convents?'

'A fair amount.'

She gave another little pout. 'I was pretty well brainwashed. Daddy was a broker – all very ordinary: home counties; mock Tudor house; two cars; one scandal. Daddy was caught out with some funny cheques and got five years in an open prison. Collapse of stout family. I'd just finished at the convent, and was all set to go to Oxford. That was out, so I answered an ad in *The Times* for a nanny, with a mound of privileges, to an Italian family of good birth: Pasquale's son, as it happened. It's an old title, like all the surviving Italian nobility, but with one difference. They still have property and money.'

The Tempestas had taken the new English nanny into the family as one of their own. The old man, the Principe, had become a second father to her. She became very fond of him, so when he proposed a marriage – which he described as *comodo* as opposed to *comodita* – Sukie saw a certain wisdom in taking up the offer. Yet even in that she showed shrewdness, careful to ensure that the marriage

would in no way deprive Pasquale's two sons of
their rightful inheritance.

'It did, to some extent, but they're both wealthy
and successful in their own right, and they didn't
object. You know old Italian families, James.
Papa's happiness, Papa's right, respect for
Papa . . .'

Bond asked how the two sons had achieved
success, and she hesitated for a fraction too long
before going on airily.

'Oh, business. They own companies and that
kind of thing – and, yes, James, I'll take you up on
your offer of a ride to Rome. Thank you.'

They were half-way through the lamb when the
padrone came hurrying forward, excused himself
to Sukie, and bent to whisper that there was an
urgent telephone call for Bond. He pointed towards the bar, where the telephone was off the
hook.

'Bond,' he said quietly into the receiver.

'James, you somewhere private?' He recognised
the voice immediately. It was Bill Tanner, M's
Chief-of-Staff.

'No. I'm having dinner.'

'This is urgent. Very urgent. Could you . . . ?'

'Of course.' He put down the receiver and went
back to the table to make his apologies to Sukie. 'It
won't take long.' He told her about May being ill in
the clinic. 'They want me to ring them back.'

In his room he set up the CC500 and called
London. Bill Tanner came on the line straight
away.

'Don't say anything, James, just listen. The
instructions are from M. Do you accept that?'

30

'Of course.'

He had no alternative if Bill Tanner said he was speaking for the Chief of the Secret Service.

'You're to stay where you are and take great care.' There was anxiety in Tanner's voice.

'I'm due in Rome tomorrow, I . . .'

'Listen to me, James. Rome's coming to you. You, I repeat *you*, are in the gravest danger. Genuine danger. We can't get anyone to you quickly, so you'll have to watch your own back. But stay put. Understand?'

'I understand.' When Bill Tanner spoke of Rome coming to him, he meant Steve Quinn, the Service Resident in Rome. The same Steve Quinn Bond had planned to stay with for a couple of days. He asked why Rome was coming to him.

'To put you fully in the picture. Brief you. Try to get you out.' He heard Tanner take a quick breath at the other end of the line. 'I can't stress the danger strongly enough, old friend. The Chief suspected problems before you left, but we only got the hard intelligence in the last hour. M has flown to Geneva and Quinn is on his way there to be briefed. Then he will come straight to you. He'll be with you before lunch. In the meantime, trust nobody. For God's sake, just stay close.'

'I'm with the Tempesta girl now. Promised her a ride to Rome. What's the form on her?' Bond was crisp.

'We haven't got it all, but her connections seem clean enough. Certainly not involved with the Honoured Society. Treat her with care, though. Don't let her get behind you.'

'I was thinking of the opposite, as a matter of

fact.' Bond's mouth moved into a hard smile, tinged with a hint of cruelty.

Tanner told him to keep her at the hotel. 'Stall her about Rome, but don't alert her. You really don't know who are your friends and who your enemies. Rome will give you the full strength tomorrow.'

'We won't be able to leave until late morning, I'm afraid,' he told Sukie, once back at the table. 'That was a business chum who's been to see my old housekeeper. He's passing through here tomorrow morning, and I really can't miss the chance of seeing him.'

She said it did not matter. 'I was hoping for a lie-in tomorrow anyway.' Could he detect an invitation in her voice?

They talked on and had coffee and a *fine* in the neat dining room, with its red and white checked tablecloths and gleaming cutlery, the two stolid north Italian waitresses attending the diners as though serving writs instead of food.

Sukie suggested they should sit at one of the tables outside the Mirto, but Bond made the excuse that it could be uncomfortable.

'Mosquitoes and midges tend to congregate around the lights. You'll end up with that lovely skin blotched. It's safer indoors.'

She asked what kind of business he was in, and he gave her the usual convincing if vague patter, which she appeared to accept. They talked of towns and cities they both enjoyed, and of food and drink.

'Perhaps I can take you to dinner in Rome,' Bond suggested. 'Without wanting to seem ungrateful,

I think we can get something a little more interesting at Papa Giovanni's or the Augustea.'

'I'd love it. It's a change to talk to someone who knows Europe well. Pasquale's family are very Roman, I'm afraid. They don't really see much further than the Appian Way.'

Bond found it a pleasant evening, although he had to make some effort to appear relaxed after hearing the news from London. Now he had to get through the night.

They went up together, with Bond offering to escort Sukie to her room. They reached the door, and he had no doubts as to what should happen. She came into his arms easily enough, but when he kissed her she did not respond, but kept her lips closed tight, her body rigid. So, he thought, one of those. But he tried again, if only because he wanted to keep her in sight. This time she pulled away, gently putting her fingers to his mouth.

'I'm sorry, James. But no.' There was the ghost of a smile as she said, 'I'm a good convent girl, remember. But that's not the only reason. If you're serious, be patient. Now, goodnight, and thank you for the lovely evening.'

'I should thank *you*, Principessa,' he said with a touch of formality.

He watched as she closed her door, then went slowly to his own room, swallowed a couple of Dexedrine tablets and prepared to sit up all night.

4

THE HEAD HUNT

STEVE QUINN WAS a big man, tall, broad, bearded and with an expansive personality, not the usual sort to get a responsible undercover position in the Service. They preferred what they called 'invisible men' – grey people who could vanish into a crowd. 'He's a big, bearded bastard,' Steve's wife, the petite blonde Tabitha, was often heard to remark.

Bond watched from behind his half-closed shutters as Quinn got out of a hired car and walked towards the hotel entrance. A few seconds later, the telephone rang and Mr Quarterman was announced. Bond told them to send him up.

Quinn was inside with the door locked almost before the knock had died in the air. He did not speak immediately, but went straight to the window and glanced down at the forecourt and the lake steamer which had just docked. The sheer beauty of the lake usually took the tourists' breath away when they disembarked, but this morning the loud yah-yahing of an English woman's voice could be heard, even in Bond's room, saying, 'I wonder what there is to see here, darling.'

Bond scowled, and Quinn gave a tiny smile, almost hidden by his beard. He looked at the remains of Bond's breakfast and mouthed noiselessly, asking if the place was clean.

'Spent the night going over it. Nothing in the telephone, or anywhere else.'

Quinn nodded. 'Okay.'

Bond asked why they could not have flown Geneva up to him.

'Because Geneva's got problems of his own,' said Quinn, his finger stabbing out towards Bond. 'But not a patch on your problems, my friend.'

'Talk, then. The Chief met you for a briefing?'

'Right. I've done what I can. Geneva doesn't like it, but two of my people should be here by now to watch your back. M wants you in London – in one piece if possible.'

'So, there is someone on my tail.' Bond sounded unconcerned, but pictures of the shattered car on the motorway and Cordova's body lying in the churchyard flashed through his mind.

Quinn lowered himself into a chair. He spoke in a near whisper.

'No,' he said, 'you haven't got some*one* on your tail. It seems to us that you've got just about every willing terrorist organisation, criminal gang and unfriendly foreign intelligence service right up your rectum. There's a contract out for you. A unique contract. Somebody has made an offer – to coin a phrase – none of them can refuse.'

Bond gave a hard, half-smile. 'Okay, break it to me gently. What am I worth?'

'Oh, they don't want all of you. Just your head.'

Steve Quinn filled in the rest of the story. M had

received a hint about two weeks before Bond went on leave. 'The Firm that controls South London tried to spring Bernie Brazier from the Island,' he began. In other words, the most powerful underworld organisation in South London had tried to get one Bernie Brazier out of the high security prison at Parkhurst, on the Isle of Wight. Brazier was doing life for the cold blooded killing of a notorious London underworld figure. Scotland Yard knew he had carried out at least twelve other murders, although they could not prove it. In short, Bernie Brazier was Britain's top mechanic, a polite name for hired killer.

'The escape was bungled. A real dog's breakfast. Then after it was all over, friend Brazier wanted to do a deal,' Quinn continued, 'and, as you know, the Met don't take kindly to deals. So he asked to see somebody from the sisters.'

He spoke of their sister organisation, M.1.5. This had been refused, but the details were passed to M, who sent their toughest interrogator to Parkhurst Prison. Brazier claimed he was being sprung to do a job that threatened the country's security. In return for giving them the goods, he wanted a new identity and a place in the sun, with money to singe if not actually to burn.

Bond remained oddly detached as Quinn described the nightmarish scene. He knew the devil incarnate in M would promise the world for hard intelligence, and that in the end he would give his source the minimum. So it had been. Two more interrogators had gone to Parkhurst and had a long talk with Brazier. Then M had taken the trip himself to make the deal.

'And Bernie told all?' he finally asked.

'Part of it. The rest was to come once he was nicely tucked away in some tropical paradise with enough birds and booze to give him a coronary within a year.' Quinn's face went very hard. 'The day after M's visit they found Bernie in his cell – hanged with piano wire.'

From outside came the sound of children playing near the jetty, the toot of one of the lake boats, and far away the drone of a light aeroplane. Bond asked what they had got from the late Bernie Brazier.

'That you were the target for this unique contract. A kind of competition.'

'Competition?'

'There are rules, it appears, and the winner is the group that brings your head to the organisers – on a silver charger, no less. Any bona fide criminal, terrorist, or intelligence agency can enter. They have to be accepted by the organisers. The starting date was four days ago, and there's a time limit of three months. The winner gets ten million Swiss.'

'Who in heaven's name . . . ?' Bond started.

'M discovered the answer to that less than twenty-four hours ago, with the help of the Metropolitan Police. About a week back, they pulled in half of the South London mob, and let M's heavy squad have a go. It paid off, or M's paying off, I don't quite know which. I do know that four major London gangland chiefs are pleading for round the clock protection, and I guess they need it. The fifth laughed at M and walked out of the slammer. I gather they found him last night. He was not in good health.'

When Quinn went into the details of the man's demise, even Bond felt queasy. 'Jesus . . .'

'. . . Saves.' Quinn showed not a shred of humour. 'One can but hope He's saved that poor bastard. Forensic say he took an unconscionable time a-dying.'

'And who's organised this grisly competition?'

'It's even got a name, by the way.' Quinn sounded off-hand. 'It's called the Head Hunt. No consolation prizes, just the big one. M reckons that around thirty professional killers went through the starting gate.'

'Who's behind it?'

'Your old friends the Special Executive for Counterintelligence, Terrorism, Revenge and Extortion – SPECTRE; in particular, the successor to the Blofeld dynasty, whom you've had one nasty brush with already, M tells me . . .'

'Tamil Rahani. The so-called Colonel Tamil Rahani.'

'Who will be the late Tamil Rahani in a matter of three to four months. Hence the time limit.'

Bond was silent for a minute. He was fully aware of how dangerous Tamil Rahani could be. They had never really discovered how he had managed to take over as Chief Executive of SPECTRE, which seemed always to have kept its leadership within the Blofeld family. But certainly the inventive, brilliant strategist, Tamil Rahani, had become SPECTRE's leader. Bond could see the man now – dark-skinned, muscular, radiating dynamism. He was a ruthless, internationally powerful leader.

He recalled the last time he had seen Rahani,

drifting by parachute over Geneva. His great forte as a commander was that he always led from the front. He had tried to have Bond killed about a month after that last meeting. Since then there had been few sightings, but 007 could well believe this bizarre competition was the brain-child of the sinister Tamil Rahani.

'Are you implying the man's on his way out? Dying?'

'There was a sudden escape by parachute . . .' Quinn did not look him in the eyes.

'Yes.'

'I'm told that he jarred his spine on landing. This set off a cancer affecting the spinal cord. Apparently six specialists have seen him. There is no hope. Within four months, Tamil Rahani's going to be the late Tamil Rahani.'

'Who's involved, apart from SPECTRE?'

Quinn slid a hand down his dark beard, 'M's working on it. A lot of your old enemies, of course. For starters, whatever they call the former Department V of the K.G.B., these days – what used to be SMERSH . . .'

'Department Eight of Directorate S: K.G.B.,' Bond snapped.

Quinn went on as though he had not heard: '. . . Then practically every known terrorist organisation, from the old Red Brigade to the Puerto Rican F.A.L.N. – the Armed Forces for National Liberation. With ten million Swiss francs as the star prize you've attracted a lot of attention.'

'You mentioned the underworld.'

'Of course – British, French, German, at least three Mafia Families and, I fear, the Union Corse.

Since the demise of your ally, Marc-Ange Draco, they've been less than helpful . . .'

'All right!' Bond stopped him sharply.

Steve Quinn lifted his large body from the chair. There was none of the visible effort that might be expected from a man of his size, just a fast movement, a second between his being seated and standing, with one large hand on Bond's shoulder. 'Yes. Yes, I know, this is going to be a bitch.' He hesitated. 'There's one more thing you ought to know about Head Hunt . . .'

Bond shook off the hand. Quinn had been tactless in reminding him of the special relationship he had once nurtured between the Service and the Union Corse, an organisation that could be even more deadly than the Mafia. Bond's contacts with the Union Corse had led to his marriage, followed quickly by the death of his bride, Marc-Ange Draco's daughter.

'What other thing?' he snapped. 'You've made it plain I can't trust anybody. Can I even trust you?'

With a sense of disgust, Bond recognised the truth of the last remark. He could trust nobody, not even Steve Quinn, the Service's man in Rome.

'It's to do with SPECTRE's rules for Head Hunt.' Quinn's face was expressionless. 'The contenders are restricted to putting one man in the field – one only. The latest information is that already four have died violently, within the past twenty-four hours – one of them only a few hundred metres from where we're sitting.'

'Tempel, Cordova and a couple of thugs on the Ostend ferry.'

'Right. The ferry passengers were representatives from two London gangs – South London and the West End. Tempel had links with the Red Army Faction. He was an underworld-trained hood and a bar-room politician trying for the rich pickings in the politics of terrorism. Paul Cordova you know about.'

All four, Bond thought, had been very close indeed when they were murdered. What were the odds on that being a coincidence? Aloud, he asked Quinn what M's orders were.

'You're to get back to London as quickly as you can. We haven't the manpower available to look after you loose on the Continent. My own people will see you to the nearest airport and then take care of the car . . .'

'No.' Bond spat the word. 'I'll get the car back. Nobody else is going to take care of it for me – right?'

Quinn shrugged. 'Your funeral. You're vulnerable in that car.'

Bond was already moving about the room finishing his packing, yet all the time his senses were centred on Quinn. Trust nobody: right, he would not even trust this man.

'Your boys?' he said. 'Give me a rundown.'

'They're out there. Look for yourself.' Quinn nodded in the direction of the window. He crossed to the long shutters and peered through the louvred slats. Bond placed himself just behind the big man.

'There,' said Quinn, 'the one standing by the rocks, in the blue shirt. The other's in the silver Renault parked at the end of the row of cars.'

It was a Renault 25 V6i, not Bond's favourite

kind of car. If he played his cards properly he could outrun that pair with ease.

'I want information on one other person,' he said as he stepped back into the centre of the room, 'an English girl with an Italian title . . .'

'Tempesta?' There was a sneer on Quinn's lips. Bond nodded.

'M doesn't think she's part of the game, though she could be bait. He says you should take care. His words were "Exercise caution." She's around, I gather.'

'Very much so. I've promised to give her a lift to Rome.'

'Dump her!'

'We'll see. Okay, Quinn, if that's all you have for me, I'll sort out my route home. It could be scenic.'

Quinn nodded and stuck out his hand, which Bond ignored. 'Good luck. You're going to need it.'

'I don't altogether believe in luck. Ultimately I believe in only one thing – myself.'

Quinn frowned, nodded and left Bond to make his final preparations. Speed was essential, but his main concern at this moment was what he should do about Sukie Tempesta. She was there, an unknown quantity, yet he felt she could be used somehow. As a hostage, perhaps? The Principessa Tempesta would make an adequate hostage, a shield even, if he felt sufficiently ruthless. As though by telepathy, the telephone rang and Sukie's mellow voice came on the line.

'I was wondering what time you wanted to leave, James?'

'Whenever it suits you. I'm almost ready.'

She laughed, and the harshness seemed to have gone. 'I've nearly finished packing. I'll be fifteen minutes at the most. Do you want to eat here before we leave?'

Bond said he'd prefer to stop somewhere on the way, if she did not mind. 'Look, Sukie, I've got a small problem. It might involve a slight detour. May I come and talk to you before we go?'

'In my room?'

'It would be better.'

'It could also cause a small scandal for a well brought up convent girl.'

'I can promise you there'll be no scandal. Shall we say ten minutes time?'

'If you insist.' She was not being unpleasant, just a little more formal than before.

'It is rather important. I'll be with you in ten minutes.'

Hardly had he put down the telephone and snapped the locks on his case, when it rang again.

'Mr Bond?' He recognised the booming voice of Doktor Kirchtum, Direktor of the Klinik Mozart. He seemed to have lost some of his ebullience.

'Herr Direktor?' Bond heard the note of anxiety in his own tone.

'I'm sorry, Mr Bond. It is not good news . . .'

'May!'

'Your patient, Mr Bond. She is vanished. The police are here with me now. I'm sorry not to have made contact sooner. But she is vanished with the friend who visited yesterday, the Moneypenny lady. There has been a telephone call and the police wish to speak to you. She has been, how do you say it? Napped . . .'

44

'Kidnapped? May kidnapped, and Money-penny?'

A thousand thoughts went through his head, but only one made sense. Someone had done his homework very well. May's kidnapping could just possibly have been associated with Moneypenny's, who was always a prime target. What was more probable, however, was that one of the Head Hunt contenders wanted Bond under close observation, and how better than to lead him in a search for May and Moneypenny?

5

NANNIE

ALL THINGS considered, Bond thought, Sukie Tempesta showed that she was an uncommonly cool lady. He dropped the Happi-coat on to the bed, ready to pack later, and caught sight of his naked body in the long mirror. What he saw pleased him, not in any vain way, but because of his obvious fitness: the taut muscles of his thighs and calves, and the bulge of his biceps.

He had showered and shaved before Quinn's arrival, and now he dressed as he worked out a viable plan to deal with Sukie. He put on casual slacks, his favourite soft leather moccasins and a Sea Island cotton shirt. To hide the 9mm ASP, he threw on a battledress-style grey Oscar Jacobson Alcantara jacket. He placed his case and the two briefcases near the door, checked the gun, and went quickly downstairs, where he settled both his own and Sukie's accounts. He then went straight up to her room.

Sukie's Gucci luggage stood in a neat line near the door, which she opened to his knock. She was back in the Calvin Klein jeans, this time with a black silk shirt which looked to Bond like Christian Dior.

Gently he pushed her back into the room. She did not protest, but said simply that she was ready to leave. Bond's face was set in a serious mask, which made her ask, 'James, what is it? Something's really wrong, isn't it?'

'I'm sorry, Sukie. Yes. Very serious for me, and it could be dangerous for you too.'

'I don't understand . . .'

'I have to do certain things you might not like. You see, I've been threatened . . .'

'Threatened? How threatened?' She continued to back away.

'I can't go into details now, but it's clear to me – and others – that there's a possibility you could be involved.'

'Me? Involved with what, James? Threatening you?'

'It *is* a serious business, Sukie. My life's at risk, and we met in rather dubious circumstances . . .'

'Oh? What was dubious about it? Except for those unpleasant young muggers?'

'It seemed as though I came along at a fortunate moment, and that I saved you from some unpleasantness. Then your car breaks down, conveniently near where I'm staying. I offer you a lift to Rome. Some might see it as a set-up, with me as the target.'

'But I don't . . .'

'I'm sorry, I . . .'

'You can't take me to Rome? Her voice was level. 'I understand, James. Don't worry about it,

I'll find some way, but it does present me with a little problem of my own . . .'

'Oh, you're coming with me, maybe even to Rome eventually. I have no alternative. I have to take you, even if it's as a hostage. I must have a little insurance with me. You'll be my policy.'

He paused, letting it sink in, then, to his surprise, she smiled and said, 'Well, I've never been a hostage before. It'll be a new experience.'

She looked down and saw the gun in his hand.

'Oh, James! Melodrama? You don't need that. I'm on a kind of holiday anyway. I really don't mind being your hostage, if it's necessary.' She paused, her face registering a fascinated pleasure. 'It could even be exciting, and I'm all for excitement.'

'The kind of people I'm up against are about as exciting as tarantulas, and lethal as sidewinders. I hope what's going to happen now isn't going to be too nasty for you, Sukie, but I have no other option. I promise you this is no game. You're to do everything I say, and do it very slowly. I'm afraid I have to ask you to turn around – right around – with your hands on your head.'

He was looking for both a makeshift weapon and one more cunningly concealed. Sukie wore a small cameo brooch at the neck of her shirt. He made her unpin the brooch and throw it gently on to the bed, where her shoulder bag lay. Then he told her to take off her shoes.

He kept the cameo; it looked safe, but he knew technicians could do nasty things with brooch pins. He performed the entire examination deftly with one hand, while he held the ASP well back in the other. The shoes were clean, as was her belt. He apologised for the indignity, but her clothes, and person, were the first priorities. If she carried nothing suspicious he could deal with the luggage later, making sure it was kept out of harm's way until they stopped somewhere. He emptied the shoulder bag on to the bed. The usual feminine paraphernalia spilled out over the white duvet – including a cheque book, diary, credit cards, cash, tissues, comb, a small bottle of pills, crumpled Amex and Visa receipts, a small Cacharel Anaïs spray, lipstick and a gold compact.

He kept the comb, some book matches, a small sewing kit from the Plaza Athénée, the scent spray, lipstick and compact. The comb, book matches and sewing kit were immediately adaptable weapons for close-quarter work. The spray, lipstick and compact needed further inspection. In his time Bond had known scent sprays to contain liquids more deadly than even the most repellent scent, lipsticks to house razor-sharp curved blades, propellants of one kind or another, even hypodermic syringes, and powder compacts that were miniature radios, or worse.

Sukie was more embarrassed than angry about having to strip. Her body was the colour of rich creamed coffee, smooth and regular, the kind of tan you can get only through patience, the right lotions, a correct regimen of sun, and nudity. It was the sort of body that men dreamed of finding alive and wriggling in their beds.

Bond went through the jeans and shirt, making sure there was nothing inserted into linings or stitching. When he was satisfied, he apologised again, told her to get dressed and then call the concierge. She was to use his exact words, saying that the luggage was ready in her room and in Mr Bond's. It was to be taken straight to Mr Bond's car.

Sukie did as she was told. As she put down the receiver, she gave a little shake of the head. 'I'll do exactly what you tell me, James. You're obviously desperate, and you're also undoubtedly a professional of some kind. I'm not a fool. I like you. I'll do anything, within reason, but I too have a problem.' Her voice shook slightly, as though the whole experience had unnerved her.

Bond nodded, indicating that she should tell him her problem.

'I've an old school friend in Cannobio, just along the coast . . .'

'Yes, I know Cannobio, a one-horse Italian holiday resort. Picturesque in a touristy kind of way. Not far.'

'I'm afraid I told her we'd pick her up on our way through. I was meant to meet her last night. She's waiting at that rather lovely church on the lakeside – the Madonna della Pietà. She'll be there from noon onwards.'

'Can we put her off? Telephone her?'

Sukie shook her head. 'After I arrived with the car problems, I telephoned the hotel where she was supposed to be staying. That was last night. She hadn't arrived. I called her again after dinner, and she was waiting there. They were fully booked. She was going in search of somewhere else. You'd said we might be late setting off so I just told her to be at the Madonna della Pietà from twelve noon. I didn't think of getting her to call back . . .'

She was interrupted by the *padrone* himself, arriving to collect the luggage.

Bond thanked him, said they would be down in a few minutes, and turned his mind to the problem. There was a big distance to cover, whatever he did. His aim was to get to the Klinik Mozart, where there would be a certain amount of police protection because of the search for May and Moneypenny. He had no wish to go into Italy at all, and from what he could recall of the centre of Cannobio, it was the perfect place for a set-up. The lakeside road and the front of the Madonna della Pietà were always busy, for Cannobio was a thriving industrial centre as well as holidaymakers' paradise. The square in front of the church was ideal territory for one man, or a motorcycle team, to make a kill. Was Sukie, knowingly or not, putting him on the spot?

'What's her name, this old school friend?' he asked, sharply.

'Norrich.' She spelled it out for him. 'Nannette Norrich. Everyone calls her Nannie. Norrich Petrochemicals, that's Daddy.'

Bond nodded. He had already guessed. 'We'll pick her up but she'll have to go along with my plans.' He took her firmly by the elbow, to let her know he was in charge.

Bond knew that the trip to Cannobio would hold him up for only an hour, thirty minutes there, and another thirty back, before he could head off towards the frontier, and Austria. If he took the risk, it would mean two hostages rather than one, and he could position them in the car to make a hit more difficult. There was also comfort in the thought that it was only his head that would gain the prize. Whoever struck would have to do it on a lonely stretch of road, or during a night stop. It was easy enough to sever a human head. You did not even have to be very strong. A flexi-saw – like a bladed garrotte – would do it in no time. What would be essential to accomplish the task was a certain amount of privacy. Nobody would have a go in front of the main church in Cannobio, beside Lake Maggiore.

Outside, the *padrone* stood, at the rear of the British racing green Mulsanne Turbo, waiting patiently with the luggage. From the corner of his eye, Bond spotted Steve Quinn's man, who had been standing above the rocks, begin to saunter casually back along the cars towards the Renault. He did not even look in Bond's direction, but kept his head down, as though searching for something on the ground. He was tall, with the face of a Greek statue that had been exposed to much time and weather.

Bond contrived to keep Sukie between himself and the car, reaching forward from behind her to unlock the boot. When the luggage was stowed, they shook hands with the *padrone* with due solemnity, and Bond escorted Sukie to the front passenger side.

'I want you to fasten the seatbelt, then keep your hands in sight on the dashboard,' he said with a smile.

At the end of the line of cars the Renault's engine started up. Bond settled in the driving seat of the Bentley.

'Sukie, please don't do anything stupid. I

promise that I can act much faster than you. Don't make me do anything I might regret.'

She smiled coyly. 'I'm the hostage. I know my place. Don't worry.'

They backed out, headed up the ramp and seven minutes later crossed the Italian frontier without incident.

'If you haven't noticed, there's a car behind us.' Sukie's voice wavered slightly.

'That's right.' Bond smiled grimly. 'They're babysitting us, but I don't want that kind of protection. We'll throw them off eventually.'

She nodded.

He had told her that Nannie would have to be handled carefully. She should not be told anything except that she could go on to Rome under her own steam. Plans had changed and they had to get to Salzburg in a hurry. 'Leave it to her. Let her make up her own mind. Be apologetic, but try to put her off. Follow me?'

There was a lot of activity going on around the Madonna della Pietà when they arrived. Standing by a small suitcase, looking supremely elegant, was a very tall young woman with hair the colour of a moonless night, pulled back into a severe bun. She wore a patterned cotton dress which the breeze caught for a second, blowing it against her body to reveal the outline of long, slim thighs, rounded belly and well-proportioned hips. She grinned as Sukie called her over to the passenger side of the car. 'Oh, how super! A Bentley. I adore Bentleys.'

'Nannie, meet James. We have a problem.'

She explained the situation, just as Bond had instructed her. All the time, he watched Nannie's

calm face – the rather thin features, the dark grey
eyes peering out brightly, through granny glasses,
full of intelligence. Her eyebrows were unfashion-
ably plucked, giving the attractive features a look
of almost permanent sweet expectation.

'Well, I'm easy,' Nannie said in a low-pitched
drawl, giving the impression that she did not
believe a word of Sukie's tale. 'It's a holiday after
all – Rome or Salzburg, it matters not. Anyway, I
adore Mozart.'

Bond felt vulnerable out in the open, and could
not allow the chattering to continue long. His tone
implied urgency.

'Are you coming with us, Nannie?'

'Of course. I wouldn't miss it for the world.'
Nannie had the door open, but Bond stopped her.

'Luggage in the boot,' he said a little sharply,
then very quietly to Sukie, 'Hands in sight, like
before. This is too important for games.'

She nodded and placed her hands above the
dashboard, as Bond got out and watched Nannie
Norrich put her case into the boot.

'Shoulder bag as well, please.' He smiled his
most charming smile.

'I'll need it on the road. Why . . .'

'Please, Nannie, be a good girl. The problems
Sukie told you about are serious. I can't have any
luggage in the car. When the time comes, I'll check
your bag and let you have it back. Okay?'

She gave a curious little worried turn of the head,
but did as she was told. The Renault, Bond
noticed, was parked ahead of them, engine idling.
Good, they thought he planned to go on through
Italy.

'Nannie, we've only just met and I don't want you to get any ideas, but I have to be slightly indelicate,' he said quietly. There were a lot of people around, but what he had to do was unavoidable. 'Don't struggle or yell at me. I have to touch you, but I promise you, I'm not taking liberties.'

He ran his hands expertly over her body, using his fingertips and trying not to make it embarrassing for her. He talked as he went through the quick frisk. 'I don't know you, but my life's at risk, so if you get into the car you're also in danger. As a stranger you could also be dangerous to me. Do you understand?'

To his surprise, she smiled at him. 'Actually, I found that rather pleasant. I don't understand, but I still liked it. We should do it again sometime. In private.'

They settled back in the car and he asked Nannie to fasten her seat belt as there would be fast driving ahead. He started the engine again and waited for the right amount of space in the traffic. Then he put the Bentley into reverse, spun the wheel, banged at the accelerator and brake, and slewed the car backwards into a skid, bringing the rear around in a half circle. He roared off, cutting in between a creeping Volkswagen and a truck load of vegetables – much to the wrath of the drivers.

Through the mirror he could see that the Renault had been taken by surprise. He increased speed as soon as the Bentley was through the restricted zone, and began to take the bends and winds of the lakeside road at a dangerous speed.

At the frontier he told the guards that he thought they were being followed by brigands, making

much of his diplomatic passport, which he always
carried for emergencies. The *carabinieri* were
suitably impressed, called him *Eccellenza*, bowed
to the ladies, and promised to question the occupants of the Renault with vigour.

'Do you always drive like that?' Nannie asked
from the rear. 'I suppose you do. You strike me as a
fast cars, horses and women kind of fellow. Action
man.'

Bond did not comment. Violent man, he thought,
concentrating on the driving and leaving Sukie and
Nannie to slip into talk of schooldays, parties and
men.

There were some difficulties on the journey,
particularly when his passengers wanted to use
women's rooms. Twice during the afternoon they
stopped at service areas, and Bond positioned the
car so that he had a full view of the pay telephones
and the women's room doors. He let them go one at
a time, making pleasantly veiled threats as to what
would happen to the one left in the car should the
other do anything foolish. His own bladder had to
be kept under control. Just before starting the long
mountainous drive into Austria, they stopped at a
roadside café and had some food. It was here that
Bond took the chance of leaving the other two
alone.

When he returned they both looked entirely
innocent and even seemed surprised when he took
a couple of benzedrine tablets with his coffee.

'We were wondering . . .' Nannie began.

'Yes?'

'We were wondering what the sleeping arrangements are going to be when we stop for the night.

I mean, you obviously can't let us out of your sight . . .'

'You sleep in the car. I drive. There'll be no stopping at hotels. This is a one-hop run . . .'

'Very Chinese,' Sukie muttered.

'. . . and the sooner we get to Salzburg, the sooner I can release you. The local police will take charge of things after that.'

Nannie spoke up, level-voiced, the tone almost one of admonition. 'Look, James, we hardly know one another, but you have to understand that, for us, this is a kind of exciting adventure – something we only read about in books. It's obvious that you're on the side of the angels, unless our intuition's gone seriously wrong. Can't you confide in us just a little? We might be more help to you if we knew some more . . .'

'We'd better get back to the car,' Bond said flatly. 'I've already explained to Sukie that it's about as exciting as being attacked by a swarm of killer bees.'

He knew that Sukie and Nannie were either going through a transition, starting to identify with their captor, or were trying to establish a rapport in order to lull him into complacency. To increase his chances of survival he had to remain detached, and that was not easy with two young women as attractive and desirable as they were.

Nannie gave a sigh of exasperation, and Sukie started to say something, but Bond stopped her with a movement of his hand.

'Into the car,' he ordered.

They made good time on the long drag up the twisting Malojapass and through St Moritz, finally

58

crossing into Austria at Vinadi. Just before seven-thirty, having skirted Innsbruck, they were cruising north-east along the A12 autobahn. Within the hour they would turn east on the A8 to Salzburg. Bond drove with relentless concentration, cursing his situation. So beautiful was the day, so impressive the ever-changing landscape that, had things been different, this could have been a memorable holiday indeed. He searched the road ahead, scanning the traffic, then swiftly checked his speed, fuel consumption and the temperature of the engine.

'Remember the silver Renault, James?' said Nannie in an almost teasing voice from the rear. 'Well, I think it's coming up behind us fast.'

'Guardian angels,' Bond breathed. 'The devil take guardian angels.'

'The plates are the same,' Sukie said. 'I remember them from Brissago, but I think the occupants have changed.'

Bond glanced in the mirror. Sure enough, a silver Renault 25 was about eight hundred metres behind them. He could not make out the passengers. He remained calm; after all, they were only Steve Quinn's people. He pulled into the far lane, watching from his offside wing mirror.

He was conscious of a tension in the two girls, like game that has sensed the hunter. Fear suddenly seemed to flood the interior of the car, almost tangibly.

The road ahead was an empty, straight ribbon, with grassland curving upwards on either side to outcrops of rock and pine and fir forests. Bond's eyes flicked to the wing mirror again, and he saw the concentration on the face of the Renault's driver.

The low red disc of the sun was behind them. Perhaps the silver car was using the old fighter pilot tactic – out of the sun . . . As the Bentley swung for a second, the crimson fire filled the wing mirror. The next moment, Bond was pressing down on the accelerator, feeling the proximity of death.

The Bentley responded as only that machine can, with a surge of power effortlessly pushing them forward. But he was a fraction late. The Renault was almost abreast of them and going flat out.

He heard one of the women shout and felt a blast of air as a rear window was opened. He drew the ASP and dropped it in his lap, then reached towards the switches that operated the electric windows. Somehow he realised that Sukie had shouted for them to get down, while Nannie Norrich had lowered her window with the individual switch.

'On to the floor!'

He heard his own voice as his window slid down to the pressure of his thumb on the switch and a second blast of air began to circulate within the car. Nannie was yelling from the rear, 'They're going to shoot', and the distinctive barrel of a pump-action sawn-off Winchester showed for a split second from the rear window of the Renault.

Then came the two blasts, one sharp and from behind his right shoulder, filling the car with a film of grey mist bearing the unmistakable smell of cordite. The other was louder, but farther away, almost drowned by the engine noise, the rush of wind into the car and the ringing in his own ears.

The Mulsanne Turbo bucked to the right as though some giant metal boot-tip had struck the rear with force; at the same time there was a rending clattering noise, like stones hitting them. Then another bang came from behind him.

He saw the silver car to their left, almost abreast of them, a haze of smoke being whipped from the rear where someone crouched at the window, with the Winchester trained on the Bentley.

'Down, Sukie!' Bond yelled. It was like shouting at a dog, he thought, his voice rising to a scream as his right hand came up to fire through the open window. He aimed two rounds accurately at the driver.

There was a lurching sensation and a grinding as the sides of the two cars grated together, then drifted apart again, followed by another crack from the rear of the car.

They must have been moving at 100 k.p.h., and Bond knew he had almost lost control of the Bentley as it swerved across the road. He touched the brakes and felt the speed bleed off as the front wheels mounted the grass verge. There was a sliding sensation, then a rocking bump as they stopped. 'Get out!' Bond shouted. 'Out! On the far side! Use the car for cover!'

When he reached the relative safety of the car's side he saw Sukie had followed him, and was lying as though trying to push herself into the earth. Nannie, on the other hand, was crouched behind the boot, her cotton skirt hitched up to show a stocking top and part of a white suspender belt. The skirt had hooked itself on to a neat, soft leather holster, on the inside of her thigh, and she held a small .22 pistol in a two-handed grip, pointing across the boot.

'The law are going to be very angry,' Nannie shouted. 'They're coming back. Wrong side of the motorway.'

'What the hell . . .' Bond began.

'Get your gun and shoot at them,' Nannie laughed. 'Come on, Master James, Nannie knows best.'

6

THE NUB

OVER THE LONG snout of the Bentley, Bond saw the silver Renault streaking back towards them, moving up the slow lane in the wrong direction, causing two other cars and a lorry to career across the wide autobahn to avoid collision. He had no time to go into the whys and wherefores of how he had missed finding Nannie's gun.

'The tyres,' she said coolly. 'Go for the tyres.'

'*You* go for the tyres,' Bond snapped, angry at being given instructions by this woman. He had his own method of stopping the car, which was now almost on top of them.

In the fraction before he fired, a host of thoughts crossed his mind. The Renault had originally contained a two-man team. When it reappeared there were three of them: one in the back with the Winchester, the driver and a back-up who seemed to be using a high-powered revolver. Somehow the man in the back had disappeared and the one in the passenger seat now had the Winchester. The driver's side window was open and in a fanatical act of lunacy, the passenger seemed to be leaning across the driver to fire the Winchester as they came up to the Mulsanne Turbo, which was slewed like a bleached whale just off the hard shoulder of the road.

Bond was using the Guttersnipe sighting on the ASP, the three long bright grooves that gave the marksman perfect aim by showing a triangle of yellow when on target. He was on target now, not aiming at the tyres, but at the petrol tank. The ASP was loaded with Glaser Slugs, prefragmented bullets, containing No. 12 shot suspended in liquid Teflon. The impact from just one of these was devastating. It could penetrate skin, bone, tissue or metal before the mass of tiny steel balls exploded inside their target. The Slugs could cut a man in half at a few paces, remove a leg or arm, and certainly ignite a petrol tank.

Bond began to take up the first pressure on the trigger. As the rear of the Renault came fully into his sights, he squeezed hard and got the two shots away. He was conscious of the double crack from his left. Nannie was giving the tyres hell. Then several things happened quickly. The nearside front tyre disintegrated in a terrible burning and shredding of rubber. Bond remembered thinking that Nannie had been very lucky to get a couple of puny .22 shots so close to the inner section of the tyre.

The car began to slew inwards, toppling slightly as though it would cartwheel straight into the Bentley, but the driver struggled with wheel and brakes and the silver car just about stayed in line, running fast and straight towards the hard shoulder, hopelessly doomed. At the same time as the tyre disintegrated, the two Glaser Slugs from the ASP scorched through the bodywork and into the petrol tank.

Almost in slow motion, the Renault seemed to continue on its squealing, unsteady course. Then, just as it passed the rear of the Bentley, a long, thin sheet of flame, like natural gas being burned off hissed from the back of the car. There was even time to notice that the flame was tinged with blue before the whole rear end of the Renault became a rumbling, irregular, growing crimson ball.

The car began to cartwheel, a burning, twisted wreck, about a hundred metres beyond the Bentley, before the noise reached them: a great hiss and whump, followed by a screaming of rubber and metal as it went through its spectacular death throes.

Nobody moved for a second, then Bond reacted. Two or three cars were approaching the scene, and he was in no mood to be involved with the police at this stage.

'What kind of shape are we in?' he called.

'Dented, and there are a lot of holes in the bodywork, but the wheels seem okay. There's a very nasty scrape down this side. Stem to stern.'

Nannie was the other side of the car. She unhitched her skirt from the suspender belt, showing a fragment of white lace as she did so. Bond asked Sukie if she was okay.

'Shaken, but undamaged, I think.'

'Get in, both of you,' said Bond crisply. He dived towards the driving seat, conscious of at least one car containing people in checked shirts and sun hats cautiously drawing up near the burning wreckage.

He twisted the key almost viciously in the ignition and the huge engine throbbed into life. He knocked off the main brake with his left hand, slid into drive and smoothly took the Mulsanne back on to the autobahn.

The traffic was still light, giving Bond the opportunity to check the car's engine and handling. There was no loss of fuel, oil or hydraulic pressure; he went steadily up through the gears and back again. The brakes appeared unaffected. The cruise control went in and came out normally, and the damage to the coachwork did not seem to have affected either the suspension or handling.

After five minutes he was satisfied that the car was relatively undamaged, though he did not doubt there was a good deal of penetration to the bodywork from the Winchester blasts. The Bentley would now be a sitting target for the Austrian police, who were unlikely to be enamoured of shoot-outs between cars on their relatively safe autobahns – particularly when the participants ended up incinerated. He needed to reach a telephone quickly and alert London, to get them to call the Austrian police off. Bond was also concerned about the fate of Quinn's team. Or could that have been his team, turned rogue hunters for the Swiss millions? Another image nagged at his mind – Nannie Norrich with the lush thigh exposed and the expertly handled .22 pistol.

'I think you'd better let me have the armoury, Nannie,' he said quitely, hardly turning his head.

'Oh, no, James. No James. No, James, no,' she sang, quite prettily.

'I don't like women roving around with guns,

especially in the current circumstances, and in this car. How in heaven's name did I miss it anyway?'

'Because, while you're obviously a pro, you're also something of a gentleman, James. You failed to grope the inside of my thighs when you frisked me in Cannobio.'

He recalled her flirtatious manner, and the cheeky smile. 'So I suppose I'm now paying for the error. Are you going to tell me it's pointing at the back of my head?'

'Actually it's pointing towards my own left knee, back where it belongs. Not the most comfortable place to have a weapon.' She paused. 'Well, not *that* kind of a weapon anyway.'

A sign came up indicating a picnic area ahead. Bond slowed and pulled off the road, down a track through dense fir trees, and into a clearing. Rustic tables and benches stood in the centre. There was not a picnicker in sight. To one side a neat, clean, telephone box in working order awaited them.

Bond parked the car near the trees, ready for a quick getaway if necessary. He cut the engine, unfastened his seat belt, and turned to face Nannie Norrich, holding out his right hand, palm upwards.

'The gun, Nannie. I have to make a couple of important calls, and I'm not taking chances. Just give me the gun.'

Nannie smiled at him, a gentle, fond smile. 'You'd have to take it from me, James, and that might not be as easy as you imagine. Look, I used that weapon to help you. Sukie's given me my orders and I am going to co-operate. I can promise you, had she instructed otherwise, you would have known it very soon after my joining you.'

'Sukie's ordered you?' Bond felt lost.

'She's my boss. For the time being, anyway. I take orders from her, and . . .'

Sukie Tempesta put a hand on Bond's arm. 'I think I should explain, James. Nannie *is* an old school friend. She is also President of NUB.'

'And what the devil's the NUB?' Bond was cross now.

'Norrich Universal Bodyguards.'

'What?'

'Minders,' said Nannie, still very cheerful.

'Minders?' For a second he was incredulous.

'Minders, as in people who look after other people for money. Minders. Protectors.' Nannie began again: 'James, NUB is an all-women outfit, staffed by a special kind of woman. My girls are highly trained in weaponry, karate, all the martial arts, driving, flying – you name it, we do it. Truly we're good, and we have a distinguished clientèle.'

'And Sukie Tempesta is among that clientèle?'

'Naturally. I always try to do that job myself.'

'Your people didn't do it very well the other evening in Belguim.' Bond heard the snarl in his voice. 'At the filling station. I ought to charge commission.'

Nannie sighed. 'It was unfortunate . . .'

'It was also my fault,' added Sukie. 'Nannie wanted to pick me up in Brussels, when her deputy had to leave. I said I'd get home without any trouble. I was wrong.'

'Of course you were wrong. Look, James, you've got problems. So has Sukie, mainly because she's a multimillionaire who insists on living in Rome for most of the year. She's a sitting duck. Go and make your telephone calls and just trust me. Trust me. Trust NUB.'

Eventually Bond shrugged, got out of the car and locked the two women in behind him. He took the CC500 from the boot and went over to the telephone booth. He made the slightly more complex attachments to link up the scrambler to the pay telephone. Then he dialled the operator, and placed a call to the Resident in Vienna.

The conversation was brief, and ended with the Resident agreeing to square with the Austrian police. He even suggested that a patrol meet Bond at the picnic area, if possible including the officer in charge of the May and Moneypenny kidnapping. 'Sit tight,' he advised. 'They should be with you in about an hour.'

Bond hung up, dialled the operator again, and within seconds was speaking to the Duty Officer at the Regent's Park Headquarters in London.

'Rome's men are dead,' the officer told him flatly. 'They were found in a ditch shot through the back of the head. Stay on the line. M wants a word.'

A moment later he heard his Chief's voice, sounding gruff. 'Bad business, James.' M called him James only in special circumstances.

'Very bad, sir. Moneypenny as well as my housekeeper missing.'

'Yes, and whoever has them is trying to strike a hard bargain.'

'Sir?'

'Nobody's told you?'

'I haven't seen anyone to speak to.'

There was a long pause. 'The women will be

returned unharmed within forty-eight hours in exchange for you.'

'Ah,' said Bond, 'I thought it might be something like that. The Austrian police know of this?'

'I gather they have some of the details.'

'Then I'll hear it all when they arrive. I understand they're on their way. Please tell Rome I'm sorry about his two boys.'

'Take care, 007. We don't give in to terrorist demands in the Service. You know that, and you must abide by it. No heroics. No throwing your life away. You are not, repeat *not* to comply.'

'There may be no other way, sir.'

'There's always another way. Find it, and find it soon.' M closed the line.

Bond unhooked the CC500 and walked slowly back to the car. He knew that his life might be forfeit for those of May and Moneypenny. If there was no other way, then he would have to die. He also knew that he would go on to the bitter end, taking any risks that may resolve his dilemma.

It took exactly one hour and thirty-six minutes for the two police cars to arrive. While they waited, Nannie told Bond about the founding of Norrich Universal Bodyguards. In five years she had established branches in London, Paris, Rome, Los Angeles and New York, yet never once had she advertised the service.

'If I did, we'd get people thinking we were call girls. It's been a word-of-mouth thing from the start. What's more, it's fun.'

Bond wondered why neither he nor the Service had ever heard of them. NUB appeared to be a well kept secret within the close-knit circles of the ultra-rich.

'We don't often get spotted,' she told him. 'Men out with a girl minder look as though they're just on a date; and when I'm protecting a woman we make sure we both have safe men with us.' She laughed. 'I've seen poor Sukie through two dramatic love affairs in the last year alone.'

Sukie opened her mouth, her cheeks scarlet with fury, but at that moment the police arrived. Two cars, their klaxons silent, swept into the glade in a cloud of dust. There were four uniformed officers in one car and three in the other, with a fourth in civilian clothes. The plain-clothes man unfolded himself from the back of the second car and thankfully stretched out his immense length. He was immaculately dressed, yet his frame was so badly proportioned that only an expert tailor could make him even half presentable. His arms were long, ending with very small hands that seemed to hang apelike almost down to his knees. His face, crowned with a head of gleaming hair, was too large for the oddly narrow shoulders. He had the apple cheeks of a fat farmer and a pair of great jug-handle ears.

'Oh, my God.' Nannie's whisper filled the interior of the Bentley with a breath of fear. 'Show your hands. Let them see your hands.' It was something Bond had already done instinctively.

'Der Haken!' Nannie whispered.

'The hook?' Bond hardly moved his lips.

'His real name's Inspektor Heinrich Osten. He's well over retirement age and stuck as an inspector, but he's the most ruthless, corrupt bastard in

Austria.' She still whispered, as though the man who had now started to shamble towards them could hear every word. 'They say nobody's ever dared ask for his retirement because he knows too much about everyone – both sides of the law.'

'He knows you?' Bond asked.

'I've never met him. But he's on our files. The story is that as a very young man he was an ardent National Socialist. They call him Der Haken because he favoured a butcher's hook as a torture weapon. If we're dealing with this joker, we all need spoons a mile long. James, for God's sake don't trust him.'

Inspektor Osten had reached the Bentley and now stood with two uniformed men on Bond's side of the car. He stooped down, as though folding his body straight from the waist – reminding Bond of an oil pump – and waggled his small fingers outside the driver's window. They rippled, as though he were trying to attract the attention of a baby. Bond opened the window.

'Herr Bond?' The voice was thin and high-pitched.

'Yes. Bond. James Bond.'

'Good. We are to give you protection to Salzburg. Please to get out of your car for a moment.'

Bond opened the door, climbed out and looked up at the beaming polished-apple cheeks. He grasped the obscenely small hand, outstretched in greeting. It was like touching the dry skin of a snake.

'I am in charge of the case, Herr Bond. The case of the missing ladies – a good mystery title, *ja*?'

There was silence. Bond was not prepared to laugh at May's or Moneypenny's predicament.

'So,' the inspector becamse serious again. 'I am pleased to meet you. My name is Osten. Heinrich Osten.' His mouth opened in a grimace which revealed blackened teeth. 'Some people like to call me by another name. Der Haken. I do not know why, but it sticks. Probably it is because I hook out criminals.' He laughed again. 'I think, perhaps, I might even have hooked you, Herr Bond. The two of us have much to talk about. A great deal. I think I shall ride in your motor so we can talk. The ladies can go in the other cars.'

'No!' said Nannie sharply.

'Oh, but yes.'

Osten reached for the rear door and tugged it open. Already a uniformed man was half helping and half pulling Sukie from the passenger side. She and Nannie were dragged protesting and kicking to the other cars. Bond hoped Nannie had the sense not to reveal the .22. Then he realised how she would act. She would make a lot of noise, and in that way obtain legal freedom.

Osten gave his apple smile again. 'We shall talk better without the chatter of women, I think. In any case, Herr Bond, you do not wish them to hear me charge you with being an accessory to kidnapping and possibly murder, do you?'

7

THE HOOK

BOND DROVE with exaggerated care. For one thing,
the sinister man who now sat next to him appeared
to be possessed of a latent insanity which could
explode into life at the slightest provocation. Bond
had felt the presence of evil many times in his
life, but now it was as strong as he could ever recall.
The grotesque Inspektor Osten smelled of something else, and it took time to identify the old-
fashioned bay rum which he obviously used in large
quantities on his thatch of hair. They were several
kilometres along the road before the silence was
broken.

'Murder and kidnapping,' Osten said quietly,
almost to himself.

'Blood sports,' Bond answered placidly. The
policeman gave a low, rumbling chuckle.

'Blood sports is good, Mr Bond. Very good.'

'And you're going to charge me with them?'

'I can have you for murder,' Osten chuckled.
'You and the two young women. How do you say in
England? On toast, I can have you.'

'I think you should check with your superiors

before you try anything like that. In particular your own Department of Security and Intelligence.'

'Those sulking, prying idiots have little jurisdiction over me, Mr Bond.' Osten gave a short, contemptuous laugh.

'You're a law unto yourself, Inspektor?'

Osten sighed. Then, 'In this instance I am the law, and that's what matters. You have been concerned for two English ladies who have disappeared from a clinic . . .'

'One is a Scottish lady, Inspektor.'

'Whatever,' he raised a tiny doll's hand, the action at once dismissive and full of derision. 'You are the only key, the linking factor in this small mystery; the man who knew both victims. It is natural, then, that I must question you – interrogate you – thoroughly regarding these disappearances . . .'

'I've yet to learn the details myself. One of the ladies is my housekeeper . . .'

'The younger one?' The question was asked in a particularly unpleasant manner, and Bond replied with some asperity.

'No. Inspektor, the elderly Scottish lady. She's been with me for many years. The younger lady is a colleague. I think you should forget about interrogations until you hear from people of slightly higher status . . .'

'There are other matters – bringing a firearm into the country, a public shoot-out resulting in three deaths and great danger to innocent people using the autobahn . . .'

'With respect, the three men were trying to kill me and the two ladies who were in my car.'

Osten nodded, but with reservation. 'We shall see. In Salzburg we shall see.'

Casually, the man they called the Hook leaned over, his long arm stabbing forward, like a reptile, the tiny hand moving deftly. The inspector was not only experienced, Bond thought: he also had a highly developed intuition. Within seconds, he had removed both the ASP and the baton from their holsters.

'I am very uncomfortable with a man armed liked this.' The apple cheeks puffed out like a balloon into a red shiny smile.

'If you look in my wallet, you'll find that I have an international licence to carry the gun,' Bond said, tightening his hands grimly on the wheel.

'We shall see,' Osten gave another sigh and repeated, 'In Salzburg we shall see.'

It was late when they reached the city, and Osten began to direct him peremptorily – left here, then right and another right. Bond caught a glimpse of the River Salzach, and the bridges crossing it. Behind him the Hohensalzburg castle, once the stronghold of the prince-archbishops, stood flood-lit on its great mass of Dolomite rock, above the old town and river.

They were heading for the new town, and Bond expected to be guided towards the police head-quarters. Instead, he found himself driving through a maze of streets, past a pair of modern apartment blocks and down into an underground car park. The two other cars, which they had lost on the outskirts of the city, were waiting, neatly parked with a space between them for the Bentley. Sukie sat in one, Nannie in the other.

A sudden uneasiness put Bond's senses on the alert. He had been assured by the Resident that the police were there to get him safely into Salzburg. Instead he was faced with a very unpleasant and probably corrupt policeman, and an apparently prearranged plan to bring them to a private building. He had no doubt that the car park belonged to an apartment block.

'Lower my window,' Osten spoke quietly.

One of the policeman had come over to Osten's side of the Bentley, and another stood in front of the vehicle. The second man had a machine pistol tucked into his hip, the evil eye of the muzzle pointing directly at Bond.

Through the open window, Osten muttered a few sentences of command in German. His voice was pitched so low, and his odd high-piping Viennese German so rapid that Bond caught only a few words: 'The women first', then a mutter, 'separate rooms . . . under guard at all times . . . until we have everything sorted out . . .' He ended with a question, which Bond did not catch at all. The answer, however, was clear.

'You are to telephone him as soon as possible.'

Heinrich Osten nodded his oversized head repeatedly, like a toy in a rear car window. He told the uniformed man to carry on. The one with the machine pistol did not move.

'We sit quietly for a few minutes.' The head turned towards Bond, red cheeks puffed in a smile.

'As you have only hinted at charges against me, I think I should be allowed to speak to my Embassy in Vienna.' Bond clipped out the words, as though they were parade ground orders.

'All in good time. There are formalities.' Osten sat supremely calm, his hands folded as though in complete command of the situation.

'Formalities? What formalities?' Bond shouted. 'People have rights. In particular, I am on an official assignment. I demand to . . .'

Osten gave the hint of a nod towards the policeman with the machine pistol. 'You can demand nothing, Mr Bond. Surely you understand that. You are a stranger in a strange land. By the very fact that I am the representative of the law, and you have an Uzi trained on you, you have no rights.'

Bond watched Sukie and Nannie being hustled from the other cars. They were kept well apart from one another. Both looked frightened. Sukie did not even turn her head in the direction of the Bentley, but Nannie glanced towards him. In an instant the message was clear in her eyes. She was still armed and biding her time. A remarkably tough lady, he thought: tough and attractive in a clean-scrubbed kind of way.

The women disappeared from Bond's line of vision, and a moment later Osten prodded him in the ribs with his own ASP.

'Leave the keys in the car, Mr Bond. It has to be moved from here before the morning. Just get out, showing your hands the whole time. My officer with the Uzi is a little nervous.'

Bond did as he was bid. The nearly deserted underground park felt cool and eerie, smelling of gasoline, rubber and oil.

The man with the machine pistol motioned to him to walk between the other cars to a small exit passage, and towards what appeared to be a brick wall. Osten made a slight movement, and Bond caught sight of a flat remote control in his left hand. Silently a door-sized section of the brickwork moved inwards and then slid to one side, revealing steel elvator doors. Somewhere in the car park an engine fired, throbbed and settled as a vehicle made its exit.

The elevator arrived with a brief sigh, and Bond was signalled to enter. The three men stood without speaking as the lift cage made its noiseless upward journey. The doors slid open and again Bond was ushered forward, this time into a passageway lined with modern prints. A second later they were in a large, luxurious apartment. The carpets were Turkish, the furnishings modern, in wood, steel, glass and expensive fabrics. On the walls were paintings and drawings by Piper, Sutherland, Bonnard, Gross and Hockney. From the enormous open-plan room, plate-glass windows led to a wide balcony. To the left, an archway revealed the dining area and kitchen. From lower arches ran two long passages with gleaming white doors on either side. A police officer stood in each of these as though on guard. Outside a floodlit Hohensalzburg could be seen before Osten ordered the curtains to be closed. Light blue velvet slid along soundless rails.

'Nice little place you have for a police inspector,' Bond said.

'Ah, my friend. I wish it were mine. I have only borrowed it for this one evening.'

Bond nodded, trying to indicate this was obvious, if only because of the style and elegance.

He turned to face the inspector, and began speaking rapidly. 'Now, sir. I appreciate what you've told me, but you must know that our Embassy and the department I represent have already given instructions as to my safety, and received assurances from your own people. You say I have no right to demand anything, but you make a grave error there. In fact I have the right to demand everything.'

Der Haken looked at him glassy-eyed, then gave a loud chuckle. 'If you were alive, Mr Bond. Yes, if you were still alive you would have the right, and I would have the duty to co-operate if I were also alive. Unhappily we are both dead men.'

Bond scowled, just beginning to appreciate what Osten intended.

'The problem is actually yours,' the policeman continued. 'For you really are a dead man. I am merely lying – what is the phrase? Lying doggo?'

'A little old-fashioned, but it'll do.'

Osten smiled and glanced around him. 'I shall be living in this kind of world very shortly. A good place for a ghost, yes?'

'Enchanting. And what kind of place will I be haunting?'

Any trace of humanity disappeared from the policeman's face. The muscles turned to hard rock, and the glassy stare broke and splintered. Even the apple cheeks seemed to lose colour and become sallow.

'The grave, Mr Bond. You will be haunting the cold, cold grave. You will be nowhere. Nothing. It will be as though you had never existed.' His small hand flicked up so that he could glance at his wrist watch, and he turned to the man with the Uzi, sharply ordering him to switch on the television. 'The late news will be starting any moment. My death should already have been reported. Yours will be announced as probable – though it will be more than probable before dawn. Please sit down and watch. I think you'll agree that my improvisation has been brilliant, for I only had a very short time to set things up.'

Bond slumped into a chair, half his mind on the chances of dealing with Osten and his accomplices, the other half working out what the policeman had planned and why.

There were commercials on the big colour screen. Attractive Austrian girls standing against mountain scenery told the world of the essential value of a sun barrier cream. A young man arrived hatless from the air, climbed from his light aircraft and said the view was *wunderschön* but even more *wunderschön* when you used a certain kind of camera to capture it.

The news graphics filled the screen and a serious-faced brunette appeared. The lead story was about a shooting incident on the A12 autobahn. One car carrying tourists had been fired at and had crashed in flames. The pictures showed the wreckage of the silver Renault surrounded by police and ambulances. The young woman, now looking very grave, appeared again. The horror had been compounded by the death of five police officers in a freak accident as they sped from Salzburg to the scene of the shooting. One of the police cars had gone out of control and was hit broadside on by the other. Both cars had skidded into woodland and caught fire.

There were more pictures showing the remains of the two cars. Then Inspektor Heinrich Osten's official photograph came up in black and white, and the newscaster said the Austria had lost one of her most efficient and long-serving officers. The inspector had been travelling in the second car and had died of multiple burns.

Next Bond saw his own photograph and the number plate of the Bentley Mulsanne Turbo. He was said to be a British diplomat, travelling on private business, probably with two unidentified young women. He was wanted for questioning regarding the original shooting incident. A statement from the Embassy said he had telephoned appealing for help, but they feared he might have been affected by stress and run amok. 'He has been under great strain during the last few days,' a bland Embassy spokesman told a television reporter. So, the Service and Foreign Office had decided to deny him. Well, that was standard. The car, diplomat and young women had disappeared and there were fears for their lives. The police would resume the search at daybreak, but the car could easily have gone off one of the mountain roads. The worst was feared.

Der Haken began to laugh. 'You see how simple it all is, Mr Bond? When they find your car smashed to pieces at the bottom of a ravine sometime tomorrow, the search will be over. There will be three mutilated bodies inside.'

The full impact of the inspector's plan had struck home.

'Mine will be without its head, I presume?' Bond asked calmly.

'Naturally,' Der Haken said with a scowl. 'It seems you know what's going on.'

'I know that somehow you've managed to murder five of your colleagues . . .'

The tiny hand came up. 'No! No! Not my colleagues, Mr Bond. Tramps, vagrants. Scum. Yes, we cleaned up some scum . . .'

'With two extra police cars?'

'With the two original cars. The ones in the garage are fakes. I have kept a pair of white VWs with detachable police decals and plates for a long time in case I should need them. The moment arrived suddenly.'

'Yesterday?'

'When I discovered the real reason for the kidnapping of your friends – and the reward. Yes, it was yesterday. I have ways and means of contacting people. Once I knew about the ransom demand I made enquires and came up with . . .'

'The Head Hunt.'

'Precisely. You're very well informed. The people offering the large prize gave me the impression that you were in the dark – that is correct, in the dark?'

'For a late starter, Inspektor, you seem to be well organised,' said Bond.

'Ach! Organised!' The polished cheeks blossomed with pride. 'I have spent most of my life being ready to move at short notice – with ways, means, papers, friends, transport.'

Clearly the man was very sure of himself, as well he might be, with Bond captive in a building high above Salzburg, his own territory. He was also expansive.

'I have always known the chance of real wealth and escape would come through something big like a blackmail or kidnap case. The petty criminals could never supply me with the kind of money I really need to be independent. If I was able to do a private deal, in, as I have said, a blackmail, or kidnap, case, then my last years were secure. But I never in my craziest dreams expected the riches that have come with you, Mr Bond.' He beamed like a malicious child. 'In my time here I have made sure that my team had the proper incentives. Now they have a great and always good reason for helping me. They're not really uniformed men, of course. They are my detective squad. But they would die for me . . .'

'Or for the money,' Bond said coldly. 'They might even dispose of you for the money.'

Der Haken laughed shortly. 'You have to be up early in the morning to catch an old bird like me, Mr Bond. They could try to kill me, I suppose, but I doubt it. What I do not doubt is that they will help me to dispose of you.' He rose. 'You will excuse me, I have an important telephone call to make.'

Bond lifted a hand. 'Inspektor! One favour! The two young women are here?'

'Naturally.'

'They have nothing to do with me. We met entirely by chance. They're not involved, so I ask you to let them go.'

Der Haken did not even look at Bond as he muttered, 'Impossible', and strode off down one of the passageways.

The man with the Uzi smiled at Bond over the barrel, then spoke in bad English. 'He is very clever, Der Haken, yes? Always he promises us one day there will be a way to make us all rich. Now he says we will sit in sunshine and luxury soon.' Like as not, Osten would see his four accomplices at the bottom of some ravine before he made off with the reward – if he ever got the reward. In German he asked how they had concocted a plan so quickly.

Der Haken's team had been working on the kidnapping at the Klinik Mozart. There were a lot of telephone calls. Suddenly the inspector disappeared for about an hour. He returned jubilant. He had brought the whole team to his apartment and explained the situation. All they had to do was catch a man called Bond. The accident was simple to stage. One they had him, the kidnapping would be over – only there was a bonus. The people who owned this very apartment would see that the women were returned to the clinic and pay a huge sum for Bond's head.

'The Inspektor kept calling in to headquarters,' the man told him. 'He was trying to find out where you were. When he discovered, we left in the cars. We were already on the way when the radio call told us you were waiting off the A8. There had been a shooting and a car was destroyed. He thinks on his feet, the Inspektor. We picked up five vagrants, from the worst area of the town, and drove them to the place where we keep the other cars. The rest was easy. We had uniforms with the cars; the vagrants were drunk and easy to make completely unconscious. Then we came on to pick you up.' He was not certain of the next moves in the game, but knew his chief would get the money.

At that moment Der Haken strode back into the room.

'It is all arranged,' he said, smiling. 'I am afraid I shall have to lock you in one of the rooms, like the others, Mr Bond. But only for an hour or two. I have a visitor. When my visitor has gone we will all go for a short drive into the mountains. The Head Hunt is almost over.'

Bond nodded, thinking to himself that the Head Hunt was not almost over. There were always ways. He now had to find a way quickly to get them all out of Der Haken's clutches. The grotesque inspector was gesturing with the ASP, indicating that Bond should go down the passageway on the right. Bond took a step towards the arch, then stopped.

'Two questions. Last requests, if you like . . .'

'The women have to go,' Osten said quietly. 'I cannot keep witnesses.'

'And I would do the same in your shoes. I understand. No, my questions are merely to ease my own mind. First, who were the men in the Renault? They were obviously taking part in this bizarre hunt for my head. I'd like to know.'

'Union Corse, so I understand.' Der Haken was in a hurry, agitated, as though his visitor would arrive at any moment.

'And what happened to my housekeeper and Miss Moneypenny?'

'Happened? They were kidnapped.'

'Yes, but how did it take place?'

Der Haken gave a snarl of irritation. 'I haven't got time to go into details now. They were kidnapped. You do not need to know anything else.' He gave Bond a light push, heading him in the direction of the passage. At the third door on the right Der Haken stopped, unlocked it and almost threw Bond inside. He heard the key turn and the lock thud home.

Bond found himself in a bright bedroom with a modern four poster, more expensive prints, an armchair, dressing table and built-in wardrobe. The single window was draped with heavy cream curtains.

He moved quickly, first checking the casement window, which looked out on to a narrow section of balcony at the side of the building – almost certainly part of the large main terrace. The glass was thick, unbreakable, and the locks were high-security and would take time to remove. An assault on the door was out of the question. There was a deadlock on it that wouldn't be easy to break without a lot of noise, and the only tools he had hidden on him were small. At a pinch he might just do the window, but what then? He was at least six storeys above ground. He was also unarmed and without any climbing aids.

He checked the wardrobe and dressing table; every drawer and cupboard in the room was empty. As he did so, a door bell sounded from far away in the main area of the apartment. The visitor had arrived – Tamil Rahani's emissary, he supposed; certainly someone of authority in SPECTRE. Time was running out. It would have to be the window.

Oddly for a policeman, Osten had left him with his belt. Hidden almost undetectably between the thick layers of leather was the long, thin multi-purpose tool, made like a very slim Swiss Army knife. Fashioned in toughened steel, it contained a whole set of minute tools – screwdrivers, picklocks, even a tiny battery and connectors which could be used in conjunction with three small explosive charges, the size and thickness of a fingernail, hidden in the casing.

The Toolkit had been designed by Major Booth-royd's brilliant assistant in Q Branch, Anne Reilly, know to everyone at the Regent's Park Headquarters as Q'ute. Bond silently blessed her ingenuity as he now set to work on the security locks screwed tightly into the casement frame. There were two, in addition to the lock on the handle, and it took about ten minutes to remove the first of these. At this rate of progress, there was at least another twenty minutes' work – possibly more – and Bond guessed he didn't have that kind of time at his disposal.

He worked on, blistering and grazing his fingers, knowing the alternative of trying to blow the deadlock on the door was a futile exercise. They could cut him down almost before he could reach the passage.

From time to time he stopped, listening for any noise coming from the main room in the apartment. Not a sound reached him, and he finally disposed of the second lock. All that remained was the catch on the handle, and he had just started to work on it when a blaze of light came on outside. Somebody had switched on the balcony lights and one was on the wall just outside this bedroom window.

He could still hear nothing. The place probably had some soundproofing in the walls, while the windows were so toughened that little noise from outside would seep through. After a few seconds, his eyes adjusted to the new light, and he was able to continue his attack on the main lock. Five minutes passed before he managed to get one screw off. He stopped, leaned against the wall and decided to have a go at the lock mechanism itself, which held down the catch and handle.

He tried three different picklocks before hitting on the right one. There was a sharp click as the bar slid back. A glance at his Rolex told him the whole business had taken over forty-five minutes. There could be very little time left, and he still had no firm plan in mind.

Quietly Bond lifted the handle and pulled the window in towards him. It did not squeak, but a chill blast of air hit him and he took several deep breaths to clear his head. He stood, ears straining for any sound that might come from the main terrace round the corner to his right.

There was only silence.

Bond was puzzled. Time must now be running out for Der Haken. It had long been obvious that one of the competitors was watching, waiting for the moment to strike, carefully taking out the opposition as he went along. Der Haken had arrived, unexpectedly, on the scene. He was the wild card, the joker – the outsider who had suddenly solved SPECTRE's problems. He would have to move fast to ensure his reward.

Carefully, making no noise, Bond eased his way through the window and pressed against the wall. Still there was no sound. Cautiously he peered round the corner of the building to the wide terrace, high above Salzburg. It was furnished with lamps, huge pots filled with flowers and white-painted garden furniture. Even Bond took in a quick, startled breath as he looked at the scene. The lamps blazed and the panorama of the new and old towns twinkled as a beautiful backdrop. The furniture was neatly arranged – as were the corpses.

Der Haken's four accomplices had been laid out in a row between the white wrought-iron chairs, each man with the top of his head blown away, the blood stippling the furnishings and walls, seeping out over the flagstones set into the thick concrete balcony.

Above the huge sliding windows leading to the main room pots of scarlet geraniums hung on hooks embedded in the wall. One of these had been removed and in its place was a rope with a small reinforced loop. A long, sharp butcher's hook was threaded through the loop, and on its great spike Der Haken himself had been hung.

Bond wondered when he had last witnessed a sight as revolting as this. The policeman's hands and feet were tied together, and the point of the hook had been pushed into his throat. It was long enough to have penetrated the roof of the mouth, and to re-emerge through the left eye. Someone had taken great trouble to see that the big, ungainly man had suffered slowly and unremittingly. If the old Nazi stories were true, then whoever had done this wanted Inspektor Heinrich Osten's death to be seen as poetic justice.

The body, still dripping blood, swung slightly in the breeze, the neck stretching almost visibly as it moved. What was left of the face was contorted in horrible agony.

Bond swallowed and stepped towards the window. At that moment there came a grotesque background sound, mingling with the creaking of rope on hook. From across the street, a group of rehearsing musicians began to play. Mozart, naturally; Bond thought it was the sombre opening of the Piano Concerto No. 20, but his knowledge of Mozart was limited. Then farther down the street a jazz trumpeter, a busker probably, started up. It was an odd counterpoint, the Concerto mingling with the 1930s' *Big House Blues*. Bond wondered if it were mere coincidence.

8

UNDER DISCIPLINE

BOND NEEDED TIME to think, but standing there on the terrace amidst the carnage was not conductive to concentration. It was now three o'clock in the morning. Apart from the music floating up from below, the city of Salzburg was silent – a glitter of lights, with the outline of mountains showing pitch black against the dark navy sky.

The lights were still on in the main room as he entered. There was no sign of a struggle. Whoever had blown away Der Haken and his crew must have operated very quickly. There would have been more than one to deal with those five men. And whoever had carried out the executions would have been trusted, at least by Osten. Bloodstains could be seen on the wall between the two archways, and there were more traces on the deep pile cream carpet. On one of the tables his ASP and baton lay in full view. Bond checked the weapon, which was still loaded and unfired, before returning it to the holster. He paused, weighing the baton for a moment before slipping it into the cylindrical holder still attached to his belt.

Then he went over and closed the windows, Der Haken's body bumping heavily against the glass, and found the button which operated the curtains, blotting out the gruesome sight on the terrace.

He had moved from the balcony quickly, knowing that whoever had finished off the policemen could still be in the apartment. Drawing the ASP, Bond began a systematic search of the flat. The door out to the lift appeared to have been secured from the outside, and three of the rooms were also firmly locked. One was the guest room he had recently vacated, the other two, he deduced, contained Sukie and Nannie. There was no response from either room when he knocked, and no sign of keys.

Two things worried Bond. Why, with his quarry under lock and key in this very apartment, had not his adversary used the opportunity to kill him on the spot? One of the Head Hunt competitors appeared to be playing a devious game and eliminating any other competitor who had come near the prize. Who were the most likely people to be running this kind of interference? The obvious choice was SPECTRE itself. It would be just their style to mount a competition with a fabulous price on the victim's head, and then step in at the last moment to reap the reward. That would be the most economic way to have your cake and eat it.

But if SPECTRE were responsible for knocking out the opposition, they surely would have disposed of him by now? Who could be left in the game? Perhaps one of the unsympathetic espionage organisations? If so, Bond's first choice would be the current successors to his old enemy, SMERSH.

Since he had first encountered this devious arm of the K.G.B., SMERSH (an acronym for *Smiert Spionam*: Death to Spies) had undergone a whole series of changes. For many years it had been known as Department Thirteen, before becoming completely independent as Department V. In fact, Bond's Service had allowed all but their inner circle to go on referring to Department V long after it too had disappeared.

What had happened was very much the concern of the Secret Intelligence Service, who had been running an agent of their own, Oleg Lyalin, deep within Department V. When Lyalin defected in the early 1970s, it took a little time for the K.G.B. to discover he had been a long-term mole. After that Department V had suffered a purge which virtually put it out of business.

Even Bond had not been informed until relatively recently that his old enemies were now completely reformed under the title Department Eight of Directorate S. Was this new K.G.B. operations unit now the likeliest dark horse in the race for his head?

In the meantime, there were very pressing problems. Check out the rooms which he thought contained Nannie and Sukie; and do something about getting out of the apartment block. The Bentley Mulsanne Turbo cannot be called the most discreet of vehicles. Bond reckoned that, with the alert still on, he could get about half a kilometre before being picked up.

Searching Der Haken's swinging body was not pleasant, but it did yield the Bentley keys, but not those to the guest bedrooms or to the elevator.

The telephone was still working, but Bond had no way of making a clandestine call. Carefully he dialled the direct number for the Service Resident in Vienna. It rang nine times before a befuddled voice responded.

'It's Predator,' Bond said quickly, using his field cryptonym. 'I have to speak clearly, even if the Pope himself has a wire on your telephone.'

'Do you realise it's three in the morning? Where the hell are you? There's been an almighty fuss. A senior Austrian police officer . . .'

'And four of his friends were killed,' Bond interrupted.

'They're out looking for you . . . How did you know about the policeman?'

'Because he didn't get killed . . .'

'What?'

'The bastard was doubling. Set it up himself.'

'Where are you?' The Resident now sounded concerned.

'Somewhere in the new town, in a very plush apartment block, together with five corpses and, I hope, the two young ladies who were with me. I haven't a clue about the address, but there's a telephone number you can work from.' He read out the number on the handset.

'Enough to be going on with. I'll call you back as soon as I get something sorted out, though I suspect you're going to be asked a lot of questions.'

'The hell with the questions, just let me get out to the clinic and on with the job. Quickly as you can.'

Bond closed the line. He then went to the first of the two locked rooms and banged hard on the door. This time he thought he could hear muffled grunts coming from inside. The deadlock would have to be dealt with by brute force, whatever the noise.

In the kitchen he found a sharp, heavy meat cleaver, with which he demolished a section of door round the lock. Sukie Tempesta lay on the bed, bound, gagged, and stripped to her plain underwear.

'They took my clothes!' she shouted angrily when he got the ropes untied and the gag off.

'So I see,' Bond said with a smile as she reached for a blanket.

He went across to the other room, where he succeeded in breaking in more quickly. Nannie was in the same situation, only she looked as though she bought her underwear from Fredericks of Hollywood. It was always the plain-looking ones, Bond thought, as she yelled,

'They took my suspender belt with the holster on it.'

At that moment the telephone started to ring. Bond lifted the receiver.

'Predator.'

'A very senior officer's on the way with a team,' the Resident said. 'For heaven's sake be discreet, and tell only what is absolutely necessary. Then get to Vienna as fast as you can. That's an order from on high.'

'Tell them to bring women's clothes,' Bond snapped, giving a rough estimate of the sizes.

By the time he was off the telephone he could hear squeals of delight from one of the bathrooms, where the clothes had been found bundled into a cupboard. Sukie came through fully dressed but, almost blatantly, Nannie appeared doing up her stockings to her retrieved suspender belt, which still had holster and pistol in place.

'Let's get some air in here,' Sukie said, advancing towards the windows. Bond stepped in front of her, saying that he would not advise even opening the curtains, let alone the windows. Quietly, he explained why and told them to stay in the main room. Then he made his own way behind the drapes to let air into the room.

The doorbell rang violently. After shouted identifications, Bond explained in German through the closed door that he could not get it open from inside. He heard sets of keys rattling as they were tried in the lock before the seventh worked and the door swung open to admit what seemed like half the Salzburg police force, headed by a smart, authoritative, grey-haired man whom the rest treated with great respect. He introduced himself as Kommissar Becker. The investigative team got on with their job on the terrace while Becker talked to Bond. Sukie and Nannie were led away by plain-clothes men, presumably to be questioned separately elsewhere.

Becker had a long patrician nose and kindly eyes. He knew the score and came quickly to the point.

'I have been instructed by our Foreign Ministry and Security Departments,' he began in almost unaccented English. 'I understand that the Head of the Service to which you belong has also been in touch. All I want from you is a detailed statement. You will then be free to go. But, Mr Bond, I think it would be advisable for you to be out of Austria within twenty-four hours.'

'Is that official?'

Becker shook his head. 'No, not official. It is merely my own opinion. Something I would advise. Now, Mr Bond, let us take it from the top as they say in musical circles.'

Bond recounted the story, omitting all he knew about Tamil Rahani and SPECTRE's Head Hunt. He passed off the shoot-out on the autobahn as one of those occupational hazards that can befall anyone involved in his kind of clandestine work.

'There is no need to be shy about your status,' Becker said with an avuncular smile. 'In our police work here in Austria, we come into contact with all kinds of strange people, from many walks of life – American, British, French, German and Russian – if you follow me. We are almost a clearing house for spies, only I know you don't like to use that word.'

'It is rather old-hat.' Bond found himself smiling back. 'In many ways we are an outdated tribe and a lot of people would like to see us consigned to the scrap heap. Satellites and computers have taken over much of our work.'

'It is the same with us,' the policeman said with a shrug. 'However, nothing can replace the policeman on the beat, and I'm sure there is still a need for the man on the ground in your business. It is the same in war also. However many tactical or strategic missiles appear over the horizon the military needs live bodies in the field. Here we are geographically placed at a dangerous crossroads. We have a saying especially for the NATO powers. If the Russians come, they will be in Vienna for breakfast; but they will have their afternoon tea in London.'

With a detective's knack of moving from a digression back to the mainstream of questioning, Becker asked about the motives of Heinrich Osten – Der Haken – and Bond gave him a word by word account of what had passed between them, again leaving out the core of the business concerning the Head Hunt.

'He has apparently been looking for a chance to line his pockets, and get away, for many years.'

Becker gave a wry smile. 'It doesn't surprise me. Der Haken, as most people called him, had an odd hold over the authorities. There are still many folk, some in high office, who recall the old days, the Nazis. They remember Osten all too well, I fear. Whoever brought him to this unpleasant end has done us a favour.' Again, he switched his tack. 'Tell me, why do you think the ransom has been set so high on the two ladies?'

He tried his innocent expression. 'I don't really know the terms of the ransom. In fact, I have yet to be told the full story of the kidnapping.'

Becker repeated his wry smile, this time wagging a finger as though Bond were a naughty schoolboy. 'Oh, I believe you know the terms well enough. After all, you were in Osten's company for some time after the reports of his death. I took over the case last night. The ransom is you, Mr Bond, and you know it. There's also the little matter of ten million Swiss francs lying, literally, on your head.'

Bond made a gesture of capitulation. 'Okay, so the hostages are being held against me, and your colleague found out about the contract, which is worth a lot of money . . .'

'Even if you had been responsible for his death,'

Becker cut in, 'I don't think many police officers, either here or in Vienna, would go out of their way to charge you – Der Haken being what he was.' He lifted an inquisitorial eyebrow. 'You didn't kill him, did you?'

'You've had the truth from me. No, I didn't, but I think I know who did.'

'Without even knowing the details of the kidnapping?' Becker enquired sagely.

'Yes. Miss May – my housekeeper – and Miss Moneypenny are bait. As you say, it's me they want. These people know I will do everything I can to rescue the ladies, and that in the last resort I'd give myself up to save them.'

'You are prepared to give your life for an elderly spinster and a colleague of uncertain age?'

'Also a spinster,' Bond said with a smile. 'The answer is yes, I would do that – though I intend to do it without losing my head.'

'My information is, Mr Bond, that you have many times almost lost your head over . . .'

'What we used to call a bit of fluff?' Bond smiled again.

'That is an expression I do not know – bit of fluff.'

'Bit of fluff, piece of skirt – young woman,' Bond explained.

'Yes. Yes, I see, and you are correct. Our records show you as a veritable St George slaying dragons to save young and attractive women. This is an unusual situation for you. I . . .'

Bond cut in sharply, 'Can you tell me what actually happened? How the kidnap took place?'

Kommissar Becker paused as a plain-clothes officer came into the room and there was a quick exchange. The officer told Becker that the women had been questioned. Becker instructed him to wait with them for a short time. The team on the balcony were also completing their preliminary investigation.

'Inspektor Osten's case notes are somewhat hazy,' the Kommissar said. 'But we do have a few details, of his interviews with Herr Doktor Kirchtum of the Klinik Mozart, and others.'

'Well?'

'Well, it appears that your colleague, Miss Moneypenny, visited the patient twice. After the second occasion she telephoned the Herr Direktor asking permission to take Miss May out – to a concert. It seemed a pleasant and untaxing suggestion. The doctor gave his consent. Miss Moneypenny arrived as arranged in a chauffeur driven car. There was another man with her.'

'There is a description?'

'The car was a BMW . . .'

'The man?'

'A silver BMW, a Series 7. The chauffeur was in uniform, and the man went into the clinic with Miss Moneypenny. The staff who saw them said he was in his mid-thirties, with light hair, and was well dressed, tall and muscular.'

'And Miss Moneypenny's behaviour?'

'She was a little edgy, a tiny bit nervous. Miss May was in good spirits. One nurse noticed that Miss Moneypenny treated her with great care. The nurse said it was as though your Miss Moneypenny had nursing experience. She also had the impression that the young man knew something about medicine. He stayed very close to Miss May the whole time.' The policeman drew in breath through his teeth. 'They got into the BMW and drove off. Four hours later, Herr Doktor Kirchtum received a telephone call saying they had been abducted. You know the rest.'

'I do?' Bond asked.

'You were told. You started out towards Salzburg. Then there were the shoot-out and your unpleasant experience with Inspektor Osten.'

'What about the car? The BMW?'

'It has not been sighted, which means that either it was out of Austria very quickly with the plates changed and maybe a respray, or it's hidden away somewhere until all goes quiet.'

'And there's nothing else?'

It was as though the Kommissar was holding something back, uncertain whether to speak. He did not look at Bond but towards the men on the balcony, taking their photographs and measurements.

'Yes. Yes, there is one other thing. It was not in Osten's notes, but they had it on the general file at headquarters.'

He hesitated again, and Bond had to prompt him. 'What was on file?'

'At 15.10 on the afternoon of the kidnapping – that is, around three hours before it took place – Austrian Airlines received a last-minute booking from the Klinik Mozart. The caller said they had two very sick ladies who had to be transported to Frankfurt. There is a flight at 19.05, OS 421, which arrives at Frankfurt at 20.15. That evening there were few passengers so the booking was accepted.'

'And the ladies made the flight?'

'They went first class. On stretchers. They were unconscious, and their faces were covered with bandages . . .'

A classic K.G.B. ploy, thought Bond. They had been doing it for years. He recalled the famous Turkish incident, and there had been two at Heathrow.

'They were accompanied,' Kommissar Becker continued, 'by two nurses and a doctor. The doctor was a young, tall, good-looking man with fair hair.'

Bond nodded. 'And further enquiries showed that no such reservation had been made from the Klinik Mozart.'

'Exactly.' The Kommissar raised his eyebrows. 'One of our men followed up the booking on his own initiative. Certainly Inspektor Osten did not instruct him to do it.'

'And?'

'They were met by a genuine ambulance team at Frankfurt. They transferred on to another flight, the Air France 749, arriving in Paris at 21.30. It left Frankfurt on schedule, at 20.25. The ambulance people just had time to complete the transfer. We know nothing about what happened at the Paris end, but the kidnap call was placed to Doktor Kirchtum at 21.45. So they admitted the abduction as soon as the victims were safely away.'

'Paris,' Bond repeated absently. 'Why Paris?'

As though in answer to his question, the telephone began to ring. Becker himself picked it up and said nothing, but waited for an identification on the line. His eyes flicked towards Bond, betraying signs of alarm.

'For you,' he mouthed quietly, handing over the mouthpiece. 'The Herr Doktor Kirchtum.'

Bond took the handset and identified himself. Kirchtum's voice still held its resonance, but he was obviously a very frightened man. There was a distinct tremor in his tone, and there were pauses between his words, as though he was being prompted.

'Herr Bond,' he began, 'Herr Bond, I have a gun . . . They have a gun . . . It is in my left ear, and they say they will pull the trigger if I don't give you the correct message.'

'Go on,' Bond said calmly.

'They know you are with the police. They know you have been ordered to go to Vienna. That is what I must first tell you.'

So, Bond thought, they had a wire on this telephone and had listened to his call to the Resident in Vienna.

Kirchtum continued very shakily. 'You are not to tell the police of your movements.'

'No. Okay. What am I to do?'

'They say they have booked a room for you at the Goldener Hirsch . . .'

'That's impossible. You have to book months ahead . . .'

The quaver in Kirchtum's voice became more pronounced. 'I assure you, Herr Bond, for these people nothing is impossible. They understand you have two ladies with you. They say they have a room reserved for them also. It is not the fault of the ladies that they have been . . . have been . . . I'm sorry, I cannot read the writing . . . Ah, have been implicated. For the time being these ladies will stay at the Goldener Hirsch, you understand?'

'I understand.'

'You will stay there and await instructions. You will tell the police to keep away from you. You will on no account contact your people in London, not even through your man in Vienna. I am to ask if this is understood?'

'It is understood.'

'They say, good, because if it is not understood, Miss May and her friend will depart, and not peacefully.'

'It is *understood*!' Bond shouted in the mouthpiece.

There was a moment's silence. 'The gentlemen here wish to play a tape for you. Are you ready?'

'Go ahead.'

There was a click at the other end of the line. Then Bond heard May's voice, unsteady, but still the same old May.

'Mr James, some foreign friends of yorn, seem to hae the idea that I can be afeard easy. Dinna worry aboot me, Mr Jam . . .' There was a sudden slap as a hand went over her mouth, then Moneypenny's voice, thick with fear, sounded as clear as if she were standing behind him. 'James!' she cried. 'Oh, God, James . . . James . . .'

Suddenly an unearthly scream cut into his ear – loud and terrified, and obviously coming from May. It made Bond's blood run cold. It was enough to place him in the power of those holding the two women captive, for it would take something truly terrifying to make tough old May scream like that. Bond was ready to obey them to the death.

He looked up. Becker was staring at him. 'For pity's sake, Kommissar, you didn't hear any of that conversation.'

'What conversation?' Becker's expression did not change.

9

VAMPIRE

SALZBURG WAS CROWDED – a large number of American citizens were out to see Europe before they died, and an equally large number of Europeans were out to see Europe before it completely changed into Main Street Common Market. Many thought they were already too late, but Salzburg, with the ghost of Mozart, and its own particular charm, did better than most.

The hotel Goldener Hirsch holds up exceptionally well, especially as its charm, comfort and hospitality reaches a long arm back through eight hundred years.

They had to use one of the festival car parks and carry their luggage to the Goldener Hirsch, where it stands in the traffic-free centre of the old town, close to the crowded, colourful Getreidegasse with its exquisite carved window frames and gilded wrought iron shop signs.

'How in the name of Blessed St Michael did you get reservations at the Goldener Hirsch?' asked Nannie.

'Influence,' Bond said soberly. 'Why St Michael?'

'Michael the Archangel. Patron saint of body-guards and minders.'

Bond thought grimly that he needed all the help the angels could provide. Heaven alone knew what instructions he would receive within the next twenty-four hours, or whether they would be in the form of a bullet or a knife.

Before they left the Bentley, Nannie cleared her throat.

'James,' she began primly, 'you said something a while back that Sukie finds offensive, and doesn't make me happy either.'

'Oh?'

'You said we'd only have to bear with you for another twenty-four hours or so.'

'Well, it's true.'

'No! No, it isn't true.'

'I was accidentally forced to involve you both in a potentially very dangerous situation. I had no option but to drag you into it. You've both been courageous, and a great help, but it couldn't have been fun. What I'm telling you now is that you'll both be out of it within twenty-four hours or so.'

'We don't want to be out of it,' Nannie said calmly.

'Yes, it's been hairy,' Sukie began, 'but we feel that we're your friends. You're in trouble, and . . .'

'Sukie's instructed me to remain with you. To mind you, James, and, while I'm at it, she's coming along for the ride.'

'That just might not be possible.' Bond looked at each girl in turn, his clear blue eyes hard and commanding.

'Well, it'll just have to become possible.' Sukie was equally determined.

'Look, Sukie, it's quite likely that I shall be given instructions from a very persuasive authority. They may well demand that you're left behind, released, ordered to go your own sweet way.'

Nannie was just as firm. 'Well, it's just too bad if our own sweet way happens to be the same as your own sweet way, James. That's all there is to it.'

Bond shrugged. Time would tell. It was possible that he would be ordered to take the women with him anyway, as hostages. If not, there should be an opportunity to leave quietly when the time came. The third option was that it would all end here, at the Goldener Hirsch, in which case the question would not arise.

'I might need some stamps,' Bond said, quietly, to Sukie as they approached the hotel. 'Quite a lot. Enough for a small package to the U.K. Could you get them? Send a few innocuous postcards by the porter, and collect some stamps at the same time if you would.'

'Of course, James,' she answered.

The Goldener Hirsch is said by many to be the best hotel in Salzburg – enchanting, elegant and picturesque, even if rather self-consciously so. The staff are dressed in the local Loden and the rooms are heavy with Austrian history. Bond reflected that his room could have been prepared for the shooting of *The Sound of Music*.

As the porter left, closing the door discreetly behind him, Bond heard Kirchtum's warning again clear in his head: 'You will . . . await instructions . . . You will on no account contact your people in

London.' So, for the time being at least, it would be folly to telephone London, or even Vienna and report progress. Whoever had fixed the bookings would also have seen that his telephone was wired somewhere in the network outside the hotel. Even using the CC500 would alert them to the fact that he was making contact with the outside world. Yet he must keep Headquarters informed.

From his second briefcase Bond extracted two minute tape recorders, checked the battery strength and set them to voice activation. He rewound both tapes and attached one machine with a sucker microphone the size of a grain of wheat to the telephone. The other he placed in full view, on top of the minibar.

Fatigue had caught up with him. He had arranged to meet the others for dinner that evening in the famous snug bar around six. Until then, they had agreed to rest. He rang down for a pot of black coffee and a plate of scrambled eggs. While he waited, Bond examined his room and the small, windowless bathroom. There was a neat shower protected by solidly built sliding glass doors. He approved, and decided to have a shower later. He was hanging his suits in the wardrobe when the waiter arrived with freshly brewed strong coffee and the eggs cooked to perfection.

When he had eaten he placed the ASP near at hand, put the DO NOT DISTURB sign on the door and settled into one of the comfortable armchairs. Eventually he fell into a deep sleep and dreamed that he was a waiter in a continental café, dashing between the kitchen and the tables as he served M,

Tamil Rahani, the now-deceased Poison Dwarf, and Sukie and Nannie. Just before waking he took tea to Sukie and Nannie with a huge cream cake, which disintegrated into sawdust as soon as they tried to cut it. This appeared not to concern either of them, for they paid the bill, each one leaving a piece of jewellery as a tip. He went to pick up a gold bracelet when it slipped, falling with a heavy crash on to a plate.

Bond woke with a start, convinced the noise was real, yet he heard only street noises drifing in through his window. He stretched, uncomfortable and stiff after sleeping in a chair, and glanced at the stainless steel Rolex on his wrist. He was amazed to see that he had slept for several hours. It was almost four-thirty in the afternoon.

Bleary-eyed with sleep, he went to the bathroom, turned on the lights and opened the tall doors to the shower. A strong hot shower followed by an icy one, then a shave and change of clothes would freshen him up.

He began to run the shower, closed the door and started to strip. It crossed his mind that whoever had told him to await orders were taking their time. If he had been manipulating this kidnap, he would have struck almost as soon as his victim had registered at the hotel, getting his quarry out in the open while he was still in bad shape from a night without sleep.

Naked, he went back into the bedroom for the ASP and the baton, which he placed on the floor under a couple of hand towels, just outside the shower. Then he tested the temperature and stepped under the spray. He closed the sliding door and began to soap himself, rubbing his body vigorously with a rough flannel.

Drenched with the hot spray, and exalting in a sense of cleanliness, he altered the settings on the taps, allowing the water to cool quickly until he stood under a shower of almost ice-cold water. The shock hit him, as though he had walked out into a blizzard. Feeling thoroughly revitalised, he turned off the water and shook himself like a dog. Then he reached out to open the sliding door.

Suddenly he was on the alert. He could almost smell danger near by. Before he touched the door handle the lights went out, leaving him disorientated for a second, and in that second he missed the handle, though he heard the door slide open a fraction and close again with a thud. He knew he was now not alone. There was something else in the shower with him, which brushed his face and then went wild, thudding against his body and the sides of the shower.

Bond scrabbled desperately for the door with one hand, flapping the flannel about his face and body with the other to ward off the creature confined with him in the shower. But when his fingers closed over the handle and pulled, the door would not move. The harder he tugged the more vicious the creature's attacks became. He felt a clawing at his shoulder, then his neck, but managed to dislodge it, still hauling on the door, which refused to budge. The thing paused for a moment, as though in preparation for a final assault.

Then he heard Sukie's voice, far away, bright, even flirtatious.

'James? James, where on earth are you?'

'Here! In the bathroom! Get me out, for heaven's sake!'

A second later, the lights went on again. He was aware of Sukie's shadow in the main bathroom. Then he saw his adversary. It was something he had come across only in zoos, and never one as big. Hunched on top of the shower head crouched a giant vampire bat, its evil eyes bright above the razor-toothed mouth, its wings beginning to spread in another attack. He lunged at it with the flannel, shouting,

'Get the shower open!'

The door began to slide open. 'Get out of the bathroom, Sukie. Get out!' Bond wrenched back the door as the bat dived.

He fell sideways into the bathroom, slamming the shower door closed as he did so. He rolled across the floor, making straight for the weapons under the towels.

Although he knew that a vampire cannot kill instantly, the thought of what it could inject into his bloodstream was enough to make Bond feel nauseous. And he had not been quick enough, for the creature had escaped with him into the bathroom. He shouted again to Sukie to close the door and wait.

In the space of two heartbeats all he knew of the vampire bat – even its Latin name, the *Desmodus rotundus* – flashed through his mind. There were three varieties. Usually they hunted at night, creeping up on their prey and clamping on to a hairless part of the body with incredibly sharp canine teeth. They sucked blood, at the same time pumping out saliva to stop the blood clotting. It was the saliva that could transmit disease – rabies and other deadly viruses.

This bat was obviously a hybrid and would be carrying some particularly unpleasant disease in its saliva. The lights of the bathroom had completely disorientated it, though it obviously needed blood badly and would fight to sink its teeth into Bond's flesh. Its body was about twenty-seven centimetres long, while the wingspan spread a good sixty centimetres – over three times the length of a normal member of the species.

As though sensing Bond's thoughts, the huge bat raised its front legs, opening the wings to full span and gathered its body up for the fast attack.

Bond's right hand flicked downwards, clicking the baton into its open position. He smashed the weapon hard in the direction of the oncoming creature. His aim succeeded more by luck than judgment, for bats, with the radar-like senses, can usually avoid objects. Probably the unnatural light had something to do with its slow reflexes, for the steel baton caught it directly on the head, throwing it across the room, where it struck the shower doors. With a stride Bond was over the twitching, flapping body and like a man demented he hit the squirming animal again and again. He knew what he was doing, and was aware that fear played no small part in it. As he struck the shattered body time after time his thought were of the men who had prepared such a thing as this especially to kill him – for he had little doubt that the saliva of this vampire bat contained something which would bring a fast, painful death.

When he had finished, he dropped the baton in

the shower, turned on the spray and walked into the bedroom. He had some disinfectant in the small first aid kit which was now Q Branch standard issue.

He had forgotten about his nakedness.

'Well, now I've seen everything. Quits,' said Sukie, unsmiling, from the chair in which she waited.

There was a small pistol, similar to the one Nannie carried, in her right hand. It was pointing steadily midway between Bond's legs.

10

THE MOZART MAN

SUKIE LOOKED HARD at Bond, and then down at
the gun. 'It's a pretty little thing, isn't it?' She
smiled, and he thought he could detect relief in her
eyes.

'Just stop pointing it at me. Put on the safety
catch and stow it, Sukie.'

She broadened the smile. 'Same goes for you,
James.'

Suddenly Bond became aware of his nakedness,
and grabbed at the hotel towelling robe as Sukie
fitted the small pistol into a holster attached to her
white suspender belt.

'Nannie fixed me up with this. Just like hers.' She
looked up at him, primly pulling down her skirt. 'I
brought your stamps, James. What was going on in
the bathroom? For a horrible moment I thought
you were having real trouble.'

'I was having trouble, Sukie. Very unpleasant
trouble, in the shape of a large hybrid vampire bat,
which is not a creature you usually come across in
Europe, and especially not in Salzburg. Somebody
prepared this one for me.'

119

'A vam*pire bat*?' Her voice rose in astonishment. 'James! It could have . . .'

'. . . probably killed me. It was almost certainly carrying something even more lethal than rabies or bubonic plague. How did you get in, by the way?'

'I knocked but there was no reply.' She laid the little strip of stamps on the table. 'Then I realised the door was open. It wasn't until I heard the noises coming from the bathroom that I switched on the light. Someone had jammed the shower door with a chair. Actually, I thought it was a practical joke – it's the kind of thing Nannie gets up to – until I heard you shout. I kicked the chair out of the way and moved like lightning.'

'And then waited in here with a loaded gun.'

'Nannie's teaching me to use it. She seems to think it's necessary.'

'And I think it's really necessary for you both to get out of this but thinking won't make it happen. Would you like to do me another favour?'

'Whatever you wish, James.'

Her attitude was suspiciously soft, even yielding. Bond wondered if a girl like Sukie Tempesta would have the guts to handle a dangerous hybrid vampire bat. On balance, he thought, the Principessa Tempesta was perfectly capable of such an act.

'I want you to get me some rubber gloves and a large bottle of antiseptic.'

'Any particular brand?' She stood up.

'Something very strong.'

After Sukie had left on her errand, Bond retrieved the small bottle from the first aid kit and rubbed antiseptic over every inch of his skin. To counteract the strong antiseptic smell he applied cologne. Then he started to dress.

He was concerned about disposing of the bat's corpse. Really it should be incinerated, and the bathroom ought to be fumigated. Bond could hardly go to the hotel manager and explain the circumstances. Plenty of antiseptic, a couple of the hotel plastic carriers and a quick visit to the waste-disposal unit, then hope for the best, he thought.

He put on his grey Cardin suit, a light blue shirt from Hilditch and Key of Jermyn Street, and a white-spotted navy blue tie. The telephone rang and as Bond picked it up he glanced at the tape machine. He saw the tiny cassette begin to turn as he answered curtly.

'Yes.'

'Mr Bond? Is that you, Mr Bond? It was Kirchtum, breathing heavily and obviously very frightened.

'Yes. Herr Direktor. Are you all right?'

'Physically, yes. They say I am to speak the truth and tell you what a fool I've been.'

'Oh?'

'Yes, I tried to refuse to pass any further instructions to you. I told them they should do this job themselves.'

'And they did not take too kindly to that.' Bond paused, then added for the sake of the tape, 'Particularly as you had already told me I must come with the two ladies to the Goldener Hirsch, here in Salzburg.'

'I must now give you instructions quickly, they say, otherwise they will use the electricity again.' The man sounded on the verge of tears.

'Go ahead. Fast as you like, Herr Doktor.'

Bond knew what Kirchtum was talking about – the brutal, old, but effective method of attaching electrodes to the genitals. Outdated methods of persuasion were often quicker than the drugs used by more sophisticated interrogators nowadays. Kirchtum spoke more rapidly, his voice high-pitched with fear, and Bond could almost see them standing over him, a hand poised on the switch.

'You are to go to Paris tomorrow. It should take you only one day. You must drive on the direct route, and there are rooms booked for you at the George Cinq.'

'Do the ladies have to accompany me?'

'This is essential . . . You understand? Please say you understand, Mr Bond . . .'

'I . . .' He was interrupted by an hysterical scream. Had the switch been pulled for encouragement? 'I understand.'

'Good.' It was not the doctor speaking now, but a hollow, distorted voice. 'Good. Then you will save the two ladies we are holding from a most unpleasant, slow end. We shall speak again in Paris, Bond.'

The line went dead, and Bond picked up the miniature tape machine. He ran the tape back and replayed it through its tiny speaker. At least he could get his information to Vienna or London. The final echoing voice on the line might also be of some small help to them. Even if the men terrorising Kirchtum at the Klinik Mozart had used an electronic 'voice handkerchief', there was still the chance that Q Branch might take an accurate voice print from it. At least if they could make some identification, M would know which particular organisation Bond was dealing with.

He went over to the desk and removed the tiny cassette from the tape machine, nipping off the little plastic safety lug to prevent the tape from being accidentally recorded over. He addressed a stout envelope in M's cover name as Chairman of Transworld, at one of the safe Post Office box numbers, folded the cassette into a sheet of hotel writing paper, on which he had written a few words, and sealed the envelope. Guessing the weight of the package, he added stamps.

He had just finished this important chore when a knock at the door heralded Sukie's return. She carried a brown paper sack containing her purchases, and appeared inclined to stay in the room until Bond firmly suggested that she join Nannie and wait in the snug bar for him.

The job of cleaning up the bathroom, wearing the rubber gloves and using almost the entire bottle of antiseptic which Sukie had brought him took fifteen minutes. Before completing the job he added the gloves to the neat, sinister parcel containing the remains of the vampire bat. He was as sure as he could be that no germs had entered his system.

While he worked, Bond thought of the possibilities regarding the perpetrator of this last attempt on his life. He was almost certain that it was his old enemy, SMERSH – now Directorate S's Department Eight of the K.G.B. – who were holding Kirchtum, and using him as their personal messenger. But was it really their style to use such a thing as a hybrid vampire bat against him?

Who, he wondered, would have the resources to work on the breeding and development of a weapon so horrible? It struck him that the creature must have taken a number of years to be brought to its present state, and that indicated a large organisation, with funds and the specialist expertise required. The work would have been carried out in a simulated warm forest-like environment, for, if his memory was correct, the species' natural habitats were the jungles and forests of Mexico, Chile, Argentina and Uruguay.

Money, special facilities, time and zoologists without scruples: SPECTRE was the obvious bet, though any well-funded outfit with an interest in terrorism and killings would be on the list, for the creature would not have been developed simply as a one-off to inject some terrible terminal disease into Bond's bloodstream. The Bulgarians and Czechs favoured that kind of thing, and he would not even put it past Cuba to send some agent of their well-trained internal G-2 out into the wider field of international intrigue. The Honoured Society, that polite term for the Mafia, was also a possibility – for they were not beyond selling the goods to terrorist organisations, as long as they were not used within the borders of the United States, Sicily or Italy.

But, when the chips were down, Bond plumped for SPECTRE itself – only, once more during this strange dance with death, someone had saved him, at the last moment, from another attempted execution, and this time it was Sukie, a young woman met seemingly by accident. Could she be the truly dangerous one?

He sought out the kitchens and with a great deal of charm explained that some food had been left accidentally in his car. He asked if there was an incinerator and a porter man was summoned to lead him to it. The man even offered to dispose of the bundle himself, but Bond tipped him heavily and said he would like to see it burned.

It was already six-twenty. Before going to the bar he made a last visit to his room and doused himself in cologne to disguise any remaining traces of the antiseptic.

Sukie and Nannie were anxious to hear what he had been doing, but Bond merely said they would be told all in good time. For the moment they should enjoy the pleasanter things of life. After a drink in the snug bar, they moved to the table which Nannie had been sensible enough to reserve and dined on the famous Viennese boiled beef dish called *Tafelspitz*. It was like no other boiled beef on earth, a gastronomic delight, with a piquant vegetable sauce, and served with melting sautéed potatoes. They had resisted a first course for it is sacrilege to decline dessert in an Austrian restaurant. They chose the light, fragile *Salzburger soufflé*, said to have been created nearly three hundred years ago by a chef in the Hohensalzburg. It arrived topped by a mountain of *Schlag*, rich whipped cream.

Afterwards they went outside among the strolling window-shoppers in the warm air of the Getreidegasse. Bond wanted to be safe from bugging equipment.

'I'm too full,' said Nannie, hobbling with one hand on her stomach.

'You're going to need the food with what the night has in store for us,' Bond said quietly.

'Promises, promises,' Sukie muttered, breathing heavily. 'I feel like a dirigible. So what's in store, James?'

He told them they would be driving to Paris.

'You've made it plain that you're coming with me, whatever. The people who are giving me the run-around have also insisted that you're to accompany me, and I have to be sure that you do. The lives of a very dear friend, and an equally dear colleague are genuinely at risk. I can say no more.'

'Of course we're coming,' Sukie snapped.

'Try and stop us,' added Nannie.

'I'm going to do one thing out of line,' he explained. 'The orders are that we start tomorrow – which means they expect us to do it in daylight. I'm starting shortly after midnight. That way I can plead that we did start the drive tomorrow, but we might get a jump ahead of them. It's not much, but it may just throw them off balance.'

It was agreed that they would meet by the car on the stroke of midnight. As they started to retrace their steps towards the Goldener Hirsch, Bond paused briefly by a letter box set into the wall and slid his package from his breast pocket to the box. It was neatly done, in seconds, and he was fairly certain that even Sukie and Nannie did not notice.

It was just after ten when he got back to his room. By ten-thirty the briefcases and his bag were packed, and he had changed into casual jeans and jacket. He was carrying the ASP and the baton as usual. With an hour and a half to go, Bond sat down and concentrated on how he might gain the initiative in this wild and dangerous death hunt.

So far, the attemps on his life had been cunning. Only in their early encounters had someone else stepped in to save his life, presumably in order to set him up for the final act in the drama. He knew that he could trust nobody – especially Sukie since she had revealed herself as his saviour, however unwitting, in the vampire bat incident. But how could he now take some command over the situation? Suddenly he thought of Kirchtum, held prisoner in his own clinic. The last thing they would expect would be an assault on this power base. It was a fifteen minute drive out of Salzburg to the Klinik Mozart and time was short. If he could find the right car, perhaps it was just possible.

Bond left the room and hurried downstairs to the reception desk to ask what self-drive hire cars were immediately available. For once, he seemed to be making his own luck. There was a Saab 900 Turbo, a car he knew well, which had only just been returned. A couple of short telephone calls secured it for him. It was waiting only four minutes' walk from the hotel.

As he waited for the cashier to take his credit card details, he walked over to the internal telephones and rang Nannie's number. She answered immediately.

'Say nothing,' he said quietly. 'Wait in your room. I may have to delay departure for an hour. Tell Sukie.'

She agreed, but sounded surprised. By the time he returned to the desk, the formalities had been completed.

Five minutes later, having collected the car from a smiling representative, Bond was driving skilfully out of Salzburg on the mountain road to the south, passing in the suburbs the strange Anif water-tower which rises like an English manor house from the middle of a pond. He continued almost as far as the town of Hallein, which had begun as an island bastion in the middle of the Salzach and which has been made famous as the birthplace of Franz-Xavier Gruber, the composer of *Stille Nacht, Heilige Nacht*.

The Klinik Mozart stands back from the road, about two kilometres on the Salzburg side of Hallein, the seventeenth-century house screened from passing view by woods.

Bond pulled the Saab into a lay-by. He switched off the headlights and the engine, put on the reverse lock and climbed out. A few moments later he had ducked under the wooden fencing and was moving carefully through the trees, peering in the darkness for his first sight of the clinic. He had no idea how the security of the clinic was arranged; neither did he know how many people he was up against.

He reached the edge of the trees just as the moon came out. There was light streaming from many of the large windows at the front of the building, but the grounds were in darkness. As his eyes adjusted, Bond tried to pick up movement across the hundred metres of open space that separated him from the house. There were four cars parked on the wide gravel drive but no sign of life. Gently he eased out the ASP, gripping it in his right hand. He took the baton in his left and flicked it open, ready for use.

Then he broke cover, moving fast and silently, remaining on the grass and avoiding the long drive up to the house.

Nothing moved and there was not a sound. He reached the gravel forecourt and tried to remember where the Direktor's office was situated in relation to the front door. Somewhere to the right, he thought, remembering how he had stood at the tall windows when he had come to arrange May's admission, looking out at the lawns and the drive. Now he had a fix, for he recalled that they were french windows. There were french windows immediately to his right showing chinks of light through the closed curtains.

He eased himself towards the windows, realising with thudding heart that they were open and muffled voices could be heard from inside. He was close enough actually to hear, if he concentrated, what was being said.

'You cannot keep me here for ever – not with only three of you.' It was the Direktor's voice that he recognised first. The bluffness had disappeared, and was replaced by a pleading tone. 'Surely you've done enough.'

'We've managed well enough so far,' another voice said. 'You have been co-operative – to a point – Herr Direktor, but we cannot take chances. We shall leave only when Bond is secure and our people are far away. The situation is ideal for the short-wave transmitter; and your patients have not suffered. Another twenty-four, maybe forty-eight hours will make little difference to you. Eventually we shall leave you in peace.'

'*Stille Nacht, Heilige Nacht,*' a third voice

chanted with a chuckle. Bond's blood ran cold. He moved closer to the windows, the tips of his fingers resting against the open crack.

'You wouldn't . . .' There was trembling terror in Kirchtum's voice, not hysterical fear, but the genuine terror that strikes a man facing death by torture.

'You've seen our faces, Herr Direktor. You know who we are.'

'I would never . . .'

'Don't even think about it. You have one more message to pass for us when Bond gets to Paris. After that . . . Well, we shall see.'

Bond shivered. He had recognised a voice he would never have thought, in a thousand years, he would hear in this situation. He took a deep breath and slowly pulled, widening the crack between the windows. Then he moved the curtains a fraction to peer into the room.

Kirchtum was strapped into an old-fashioned desk chair with a circular seat, made of wood and leather, and with three legs on castors. The bookcase behind him had been swept clean and books replaced by a powerful radio transmitter. A broadshouldered man sat in front of the radio, another stood behind Kirchtum's chair, and the third, legs apart, faced the Direktor. Bond recognised him at once, just as he had known the voice.

He breathed in through his nose, lifted the ASP and lunged through the windows. There was no time for hesitation. What he had heard told him that the three men constituted the entire enemy force at the Klinik Mozart.

The ASP thumped four times, two bullets

shattering the chest of the man behind Kirchtum's chair, the other two plunging into the back of the radio operator. The third man whirled around, mouth open, hand moving to his hip.

'Hold it there, Quinn! One move and your legs go – right?'

Steve Quinn, the Service's man in Rome, stood rock still, his mouth curving into a snarl as Bond removed the pistol from inside his jacket.

'Mr Bond? How . . . ?' Kirchtum spoke in a hoarse whisper.

'You're finished, James. No matter what you do to me, you're finished.' Quinn had not quite regained his composure, but he made a good attempt.

'Not quite,' said Bond smiling, but without triumph. 'Not quite yet, though I admit I was surprised to find you here. Who are you really working for, Quinn? SPECTRE?'

'No.' Quinn gave him the shadow of a smile. 'Pure K.G.B. First Chief Directorate, naturally – for years, and not even Tabby knows. Now on temporary detachment to Department Eight, your old sparring partner, SMERSH. Unlike you, James, I've always been a Mozart man. I prefer to dance to good music.'

'Oh, you'll dance.' Bond's expression betrayed the cold, cruel streak that was the darkest side of his nature.

11

HAWK'S WING
AND MACABRE

JAMES BOND WAS not prepared to waste time. He
knew, to his cost, the dangers of keeping an enemy
talking. It was a technique he had used to his own
advantage before now, and Steve Quinn was quite
capable of trying to play for time. Crisply, still
keeping his distance, Bond ordered him to stand
well away from the wall, spread his legs, stretch out
his arms and lean forward, palms against the wall.
Once in that position, he made Quinn shuffle his
feet back even further so that he had no leverage
for a quick attack.

Only then did Bond approach Quinn and frisk
him with great care. There was a small Smith &
Wesson Chief's Special revolver tucked into the
waistband of his trousers, at the small of his back.
A tiny automatic pistol, an Austrian Steyr 6.35mm
was taped to the inside of his left calf, and a wicked
little flick knife to the outside of his right ankle.

'Haven't seen one of these in years,' said Bond as
he tossed the Steyr on to the desk. 'No grenades
secreted up your backside, I trust.' He did not

smile. 'You're a damned walking arsenal, man. You should be careful. Terrorists might be tempted to break into you.'

'In this game, I've always found it useful to keep a few tricks up my sleeve.'

As he spoke the last word, Steve Quinn let his body sag. He collapsed on to the floor and in the fraction of a second flip-rolled to the right, his arm reaching towards the table where the Steyr automatic lay.

'Don't try it!' Bond snapped, taking aim with the ASP.

Quinn was not ready to die for the cause for which he had betrayed the Service. He froze, his hand still raised, like an overgrown child playing the old game of statues.

'Face down! Spreadeagled!' Bond ordered, looking around the room for something to secure his prisoner. Keeping the ASP levelled at Quinn, he sidled behind Kirchtum, and used his left hand to unbuckle the two short and two long straps obviously designed to restrain violent patients. As he moved he continued to snap orders at Quinn.

'Face right down, eat the carpet, you bastard, and get your legs wider apart, arms in the crucifix position.'

Quinn obeyed, grunting obscenities. As the last buckle gave way, Kirchtum began to rub the circulation back into his arms and legs. His wrists were marked where the hard leather thongs had bitten into his flesh.

'Stay seated,' Bond whispered. 'Don't move. Give the circulation a chance.'

Taking the straps, he approached Quinn with his

gun hand well back, knowing that a lashing foot could catch his wrist.

'The slightest move and I'll blow a hole in you so big that even the maggots will need maps. Understand?'

Quinn grunted and Bond kicked his legs together, viciously hitting his ankle with the steel-capped toe of his shoe so that he yelped with pain. While the agony was sweeping through him, Bond swiftly slid one of the straps around Quinn's ankles, pulled hard and buckled the leather tightly.

'Now the arms! Fingers laced behind your back!'

As though to make him understand, Bond knocked the right wrist with his foot. There was another cry of pain, but Quinn obeyed, and Bond secured his wrists with another strap.

'This may be old-fashioned, but it'll keep you quiet until we've made more permanent arrangements,' Bond muttered as he buckled the two long straps together. He fastened one end of the elongated strap around Quinn's ankles, then brought the rest up around his neck and back to the ankles. He pulled tightly, bringing the prisoner's head up and forcing the legs towards his trunk. Indeed it was a method old and well tried. If the captive struggled he would strangle himself, for the straps were pulled so tightly that they made Quinn's body into a bow, with the feet and neck as the outer edges. Even if he tried to relax his legs, the strap would pull hard on the neck.

Quinn let out a stream of obscene abuse, and Bond, enraged now at discovering an old friend to be a mole, kicked him hard in the ribs. He took out

135

a handkerchief and stuffed it into Quinn's mouth with a curt, 'Shut up!'

For the first time Bond had a real chance to look around the room. It was furnished in solid nineteenth-century style – a heavy desk, the book-cases rising to the ceiling, the chairs with curved backs. Kirchtum still sat at the desk, his face pale, hands shaking. The big, expansive man had turned to terrified blubber.

Bond went over to the radio, stepping over the books that had been swept off the shelves. The radio operator was slumped in his chair, the blood dripping on to the carpet bright against the faded pattern. Bond pushed the body unceremoniously from the chair. He did not recognise the face, twisted in the surprised agony of death. The other corpse lay sprawled against the wall, as though he was a drunk collapsed at a party. Bond could not put a name to him, but had seen the photographs in the files – East German, a criminal with terrorist leanings. It was amazing, he thought, how many of Europe's violent villains were turning into merce-naries for the terrorist organisations. Rent-a-Thug, he thought, as he turned to Kirchtum.

'How did they manage it?' he asked blandly, seemingly drained by the knowledge that Quinn had sold out.

'Manage?' Kirchtum appeared to be at a loss.

'Look – ' Bond almost shouted before realising that Kirchtum's English was not always perfect, and could have deserted him in his present state. He walked over and laid an arm on the man's shoulder, speaking quietly and sympathetically. 'Look, Herr Doktor, I need information from you

very quickly, especially if we are ever to see the two
ladies alive again.'

'Oh, my God.' Kirchtum covered his face with
his big, thick hands. 'It is my fault that Miss May
and her friend . . . Never should I have allowed
Miss May to go out.' He was near to tears.

'No. No, not your fault. How were you to know?
Just calm yourself and answer my questions as
carefully as you can. How did these men manage to
get in and hold you here?'

Kirchtum let his fingers slide down his face. His
eyes were full of desolation. 'Those . . . those
two . . .' He gestured at the bodies. 'They came as
repair men for the *Antenne* – what you call it? The
pole? For the television . . .'

'The television aerial.'

'*Ja*, the television aerial. The duty nurse let them
in, and on to the roof. She thought it good, okay.
Only when she was coming to me did I smell a
mouse.'

'They asked to see you?'

'In here. My office, they ask. Only later I find
they had been putting up *Antenne* for their radio
equipment. They lock the door. They threaten me
with guns and torture. Tell me to put the next
doctor in charge of the clinic. To say I would
be occupied in my study on business matters for
a day or two. They laughed when I had to say
"tied up". They had pistols. Guns. What could I
do?'

'You do not argue with loaded guns,' Bond
agreed, 'as you can see.' He nodded to the corpses.
Then he turned to the grunting, straining Steve
Quinn. 'And when did this piece of scum arrive?'

137

'The same night, later. Through the windows, like you.'

'Which night was that?'

'The day after the ladies disappeared. The two in the afternoon, the other at night. By that time they had me in this chair. All the time they had me here, except when I had to perform functions . . .' Bond looked surprised, and Kirchtum said he meant natural functions. 'Finally I refused to give you messages on the telephone. Until then they had only threatened me. But after that . . .'

Bond had already seen the bowl of water and the large crocodile clips wired up to a socket in the wall. He nodded, knowing only too well what Kirchtum must have suffered.

'And the radio?' he asked.

'Ah, yes. They used it quite often. Twice, three times a day.'

'Did you hear anything?' Bond looked at the radio. There were two sets of earphones jacked into the receiver.

'Most of it. They wear the earphones sometimes, but there are speakers there, see.'

Indeed, there were two small circular speakers set into the centre of the system. 'Tell me what you heard.'

'What to tell? They spoke. Another man spoke from far away . . .'

'Who spoke first? Did the other man call them?'

Kirchtum thought for a moment. 'Ah, yes. The voice would come with a lot of crackling.'

Bond, standing beside the sophisticated high frequency transmitter, saw that the dials were glowing and heard a faint hum from the speakers.

He noted the dial settings. They had been talking to someone a long way off – anything from six hundred to six thousand kilometres away.

'Can you remember if the messages came at any specific times?'

Kirchtum's brow creased, and then he nodded. '*Ja*. Yes, I think so. In the mornings. Early. Six o'clock. Then at midday . . .'

'Six in the evening and again at midnight?'

'Something like that, yes. But not quite.'

'Just before the hour, or just after, yes?'

'That is right.'

'Anything else?'

The doctor paused, thought again, and then nodded. '*Ja*. I know they have to send a message when news comes that you are leaving Salzburg. They have a man watching . . .'

'The hotel?'

'No. I heard the talk. He is watching the road. He is to telephone when you drive away and they have to make a signal with the radio. They must use special words . . .'

'Can you remember them?'

'Something like the package is posted to Paris.'

That sounded par for the course, Bond thought. Cloak and dagger. The Russians, like the Nazis before them, read too many bad espionage novels.

'Were there any other special words?'

'Yes, they used others. The man at the other end calls himself Hawk's Wing – I thought it strange.'

'And here?'

'Here they call themselves Macabre.'

'So, when the radio comes on, the other end

139

says something like, "Macabre this is Hawk's
Wing . . .""

'Over.'

'Over, yes. And, "Come in Hawk's Wing."'

'This is just how they say it, yes.'

'Why haven't any of your staff come to this
office, or alerted the police? There must have been
noise. I have used a gun.'

Kirchtum shrugged. 'The noise of your gun
might have been heard from the windows, but the
windows only. My office is soundproofed because
sometimes there are disturbing noises from the
clinic. This is why they opened the windows here.
They opened them a few times a day for the
circulation of air. It can get most heavy in here with
the soundproofing. Even the windows are soundproofed with the double glaze.'

Bond nodded and glanced at his watch. It was
almost eleven forty-five. Hawk's Wing would be
making his call at any time, and he had already
figured that Quinn's man would be stationed
somewhere near the E11 autobahn. In fact he
probably had all exit roads watched. Nice and
professional. Far better than just one man at the
hotel.

But he was now playing for time. Quinn had
stopped twisting on the floor, and Bond was
already beginning to work out a scheme that would
take care of him. The man had been in the game a
long time, and his experience and training would
make him hard to crack, even under ideal interrogation conditions; violence would be counter-
productive. There was, he knew, only one way to
get at Stephen Quinn.

He went over and knelt beside the trussed figure.
'Quinn,' he said softly, and saw the hate in the sidelong, painful glance. 'We need your co-operation.'

Quinn grunted through the makeshift gag. It was
clear that in no way would Quinn co-operate.

'I know the telephone is insecure, but I'm calling
Vienna for a relay to London. I want you to listen
very carefully.'

He went over to the desk, lifted the receiver and
dialled 0222–43–16–08, the Tourist Board office in
Vienna, where he knew there would be an answering machine at this time of night. He held the
receiver away from his ear so that Quinn would at
least hear a muffled answer. When it came, Bond
put the receiver very close to his ear, simultaneously
pressing the red button.

'Predator,' he said softly. Then, after a pause,
'Yes. Priority for London to copy and action
soonest. Rome's gone off the rails.' He paused
again, as though listening. 'Yes, working for Centre. I have him, but we need more. I want a snatch
team at Flat 28, 48 Via Barberini – it's next to the
J.A.L. offices. Lift Tabitha Quinn and hold for
orders. Tell them to alert Hereford and call in one
of the psychos if M doesn't want dirty hands.'

Behind him, he heard Quinn grunting, getting
agitated. A threat to his wife was the only thing that
would have any effect.

'That's right. Will do. I'll run it through you, but
termination, or near termination may be necessary. I'll get back within the hour. Good.' He put
down the instrument. When he knelt again beside
Quinn, the look in the man's eyes had changed;
hatred was now edged with anxiety.

'It's okay, Steve. Nobody's going to hurt you. But, I'm afraid it could be different with Tabby. I'm sorry.'

There was no way that Quinn could even suspect a bluff, or double bluff. He had been in the Service for a long time himself, and was well aware that calling in a psycho – the Service name for their mercenary killers – was no idle threat. He knew the many ways his wife could suffer before she died. He had worked with Bond for years and was sure 007 would show no compunction in carrying out the threat.

Bond continued, 'I gather there will be a call coming through. I'm going to strap you into the chair in front of the radio. Make the responses fast. Get off the air quickly. Feign bad transmission if you have to. But, Steve, don't do anything out of line – no missing out words or putting in "alert" sentences. I'll be able to tell, as you know. Just as you'd be able to detect a dodgy response. If you do make a wrong move, you'll wake up in Warminster to a long interrogation and a longer time in jail. You'll also be shown photographs of what they did to Tabby before she died. That I promise you. Now . . .'

He manhandled Quinn into the radio operator's chair, and adjusted the straps from the strangulation position, binding him tightly into the chair. He felt confident, for the fight appeared to have gone out of Steve Quinn. But you could never tell. The defector might well be so indoctrinated that he could bring himself to sacrifice his wife.

At last he asked if Quinn was willing to play it straight. The big man just nodded his head sullenly, and Bond pulled the gag from his mouth.

'You bastard!' Quinn said in a hoarse, breathless voice.

'It can happen to the best of us, Steve. Just do as you're told and there's a chance that both of you will live.'

As he was speaking, the transmitter hummed and crackled into life. Bond's hand went out to the receive and send switch, set to Receive. A disembodied voice recited the code:

'Hawk's Wing to Macabre. Hawk's Wing to Macabre. Come in Macabre.'

Bond nodded to Quinn, clicked the switch to Send, and for the first time in years prayed.

12

ENGLAND EXPECTS

'MACABRE, HAWK'S WING, I have you. Over.'

Steve Quinn's voice sounded too steady for Bond's liking, but he had to let him go through with it. The voice at the distant end crackled through the small speakers.

'Hawk's Wing, Macabre, routine check. Report situation. Over.'

Quinn paused for a second, and Bond allowed the muzzle of the ASP to touch him behind the ear.

'Situation normal. We await developments. Over.'

'Call back when package is on its way. Over.'

'Wilco, Hawk's Wing. Over and out.'

There was silence for a moment as the switch was clicked to the Receive position again. Then Bond turned to Kirchtum, asking if it all sounded normal.

'It was usual,' he said with a nod.

'Right, Herr Doktor. Now you come into your own. Can you get something that will put this bastard to sleep for around four or five hours, and make him wake up feeling reasonable – no slurred speech or anything?'

'I have just the thing.'

For the first time, Kirchtum smiled, easing his body painfully from the chair and hobbling towards the door. Half-way there he realised he was wearing no shoes or socks and limped back to retrieve them. He put them on and slowly left the room.

'If you have by any chance alerted Hawk's Wing, you know that Tabby won't last long once we've found you out. You do everything by the book, Quinn, and I'll do my best for you as well. But the first person to be concerned about is your wife. Right?'

Quinn glared at him with the hatred of a traitor who knows he's cornered.

'This applies to your information as well. I want straight answers, and I want them now.'

'I might not have the answers.'

'You just tell me what you know. We'll know the truth from fiction in the long run.'

Quinn did not reply.

'First, what's going to happen in Paris? At the George Cinq?'

'Our people are going for you. At the hotel.'

'But you could have got me here. Enough people have tried already.'

'Not my people. Not K.G.B. We banked on you coming down here after May and Moneypenny. Yes, we organised the kidnap. The idea was for us to take you on from here. Getting you to Salzburg was like putting you into a funnel.'

'Then it wasn't your people who had a go in the car?'

'No. One of the competition. They took out the Service people. None of my doing. You seem to have had a guardian angel all the way. The two men I put on to you were from the Rome Station. I was to burn them once they saw you safely into Salzburg.'

'And send me on to Paris?'

'Yes, blast you. If it were anyone else but Tabby, I'd . . .'

'But it is Tabby, we're thinking about.' Bond paused. 'Paris? Why Paris?'

Quinn stared steadily into Bond's eyes. The man did know something more. 'Why Paris? Remember Tabby.'

'The rules are it's to be Berlin, Paris or London. They want your head, Bond, but they want to see it done. We were out to claim the reward and just taking your head wasn't enough. My instructions were to get you to Paris. The people there have orders to pick you up, and . . .'

He stopped, as though he'd already said enough.

'And deliver the package?'

There was fifteen second's silence.

'Yes.'

'Deliver it where?'

'To the Man.'

'Tamil Rahani? The head of SPECTRE?'

'Yes.'

'Deliver it where?' Bond repeated.

No response.

'Remember Tabby, Quinn. I'll see Tabby suffer great pain before she dies. Then they'll come for you. Where am I to be delivered?'

The silence stretched for what seemed to be minutes.

'Florida.'

'Where in Florida? Big place, Florida. Where? Disney World?'

Quinn looked away. 'The most southern tip of the United States,' he said.

'Ah.' Bond nodded.

The Florida Keys, he thought. Those linked islands that stretch 150 kilometres out into the ocean. Bahai Honda Key, Big Pine Key, Cudjoe Key, Boca Chica Key – the names of the most famous ones flicked through his mind. But, the southernmost tip – well, that was Key West, once the home of Ernest Hemingway, a narcotics route, a tourist paradise, with a sprinkling of islands outside the reef. Ideal, thought Bond. Key West – who would have imagined SPECTRE setting up its headquarters there?

'Key West,' he said aloud, and Quinn gave a small, ashamed nod. 'Paris, London or Berlin. They could have included Rome and other major cities. Anywhere they could get me on to a direct Miami flight, eh?'

'I suppose so.'

'Where exactly in Key West?'

'That I don't know. Honestly, I just do not know.'

Bond shrugged as though to say it did not matter.

The door opened and Kirchtum came in. He was smiling as he flourished a kidney bowl covered with a cloth.

'I have what you need, I think.'

'Good,' said Bond, smiling back, 'and I think I have what I need. Put him out, Herr Doktor.'

Quinn did not resist as Kirchtum rolled up his sleeve, swabbed a patch on the upper right arm and slid the hypodermic needle in. It took less than ten seconds for his body to relax and the head to loll over. Bond was already busy with the straps again.

'He will have a good four to five hours' sleeping. You are leaving?'

'Yes, when I've made sure he can't get away once he wakes up. One of my people should arrive here before then, to see that he gets the telephone call from his watcher and relays it on to his source. I have to arrange that. My man will use the words, "Ill met by moonlight." You reply, "Proud Titania." Got it?'

'This is Shakespeare, the *Summer Midnight Dream, ja*?'

'*A Midsummer Night's Dream, ja,* Herr Doktor.'

'So, summer midnight, midsummer night's what's the difference?'

'It obviously mattered to Mr Shakespeare. Better get it right.' Bond smiled at the bear-like doctor. 'Can you deal with all this?'

'Try me, Herr Bond.'

Five minutes later, Bond was heading back to the Saab. He drove fast to the hotel. In his room he called Nannie to apologise for keeping them waiting.

'There's been a slight change of plan,' he told her. 'Just stand by. Tell Sukie. I'll be in touch soon. With luck, we'll be leaving within the hour.'

'What the hell's going on?' Nannie sounded peeved.

'Just stay put. Don't worry, I won't leave without you.'

'I should jolly well think not,' she snapped, banging down the receiver.

Bond smiled to himself, opened up the briefcase containing the CC500 scrambler and attached it to the telephone. Though he was, to all intents and purposes, on his own, it was time to call from some limited assistance from the Service.

He dialled the London Regent's Park number, knowing the line would be safe now he had taken out the team at the clinic, and asked for the Duty Officer who came on almost immediately. After identifying himself, Bond began to issue his instructions. There was information he wanted relayed fast to M, and on to the Vienna Resident. He was precise and firm, saying that there was only one way to deal with the matter – his way. Otherwise they could lose the chance of a lifetime. SPECTRE had made themselves into a sitting target, which only he could smash. His instructions had to be carried out to the letter. He ended by repeating the hotel number and his room and asked for a call-back as quickly as possible.

It took just over fifteen minutes. M had okayed all Bond's instructions and the operation was already running from Vienna. A private jet would bring in a team of five – three men and two women. They would wait at Salzburg airport for Bond who should get clearance for a private flight to Zurich on his Universal Export passport B. Bookings were made on the Pan American Flight 115 from Zurich to Miami, departing at 10.15 local time. Bond thanked the Duty Officer and was about to close the line when he was stopped.

'Predator.'

'Yes?'

'Private message from M.'

'Go on.'

'He says, "England expects". Nelson, I suppose – "England expects that every man will do his duty.'

'Yes,' Bond replied irritably. 'I do know the quotation.'

'And he says good luck sir.'

He knew he would need every ounce of luck that came his way. He unhooked the CC500 and dialled Nannie's room.

'All set. We're almost ready for the off.'

'About time. Where are we going?'

'Off to see the Wizard.' Bond laughed without humour. 'The Wonderful Wizard of Oz.'

13

GOOD EVENING,
MR BOLDMAN

'JAMES. James you're going the wrong way. You left the Bentley in the car park to the left. Remember?'

'Don't tell the whole world, Sukie. We're not using the Bentley.'

On his way back, after parking the Saab, he had made a quick detour, and used the old trick of sticking the Bentley's keys up the exhaust pipe. It was not as safe as he would have liked, but it would have to do. Now they were lugging their suitcases to the Saab.

'Not . . .' There was an intake of breath from Nannie.

'We have alternative transport,' Bond said crisply, his voice sharp with authority.

His plan to outflank SPECTRE depended entirely on caution and timing. He had even considered ditching Sukie and Nannie, leaving them in the hotel. But, unless he could isolate them, it was a safer course to take them along. They had already shown their determination to remain with him anyway. Dumping them now was asking for trouble.

'I hope your American visas are up to date,'

Bond said, once they had packed everything into the car and he had started the engine.

'American?' Sukie's voice rose in a petulant squeak.

'Visas not okay?'

He edged out of the parking place and began to negotiate the streets that would take them on to the airport road.

'Of course they are!' Nannie sounded cross.

'I haven't a thing to wear,' Sukie said loudly.

'Jeans and a shirt will do where we're going.'

Bond smiled as he turned on to the Innsbruck road. The *Flughafen* sign was illuminated for a second in his headlights.

'Another thing,' he added. 'Before we leave this car you'll have to stow your hardware in one of my cases. We're heading for Zurich, then flying direct to the States. I have a shielded compartment in my big case and our weapons will have to go in there. From Zurich we'll be on commercial airlines.'

Nannie began to protest and Bond quickly cut her short. 'You both decided to stay with me on this. If you want out, then say so now and I'll have you taken back to the hotel. You can have fun going to all those Mozart concerts.'

'We're coming, whatever,' Nannie said firmly. 'Both of us. Okay. Sukie?'

'You bet your sweet . . .'

'As arranged, then.' Bond could see the *Flughafen* signs coming up fast now. 'There's a private jet on its way for us. I shall have to spend some time with the people who will be arriving on it. You cannot be in on that, I'm afraid. Then we take off for Zurich.'

In the airport car park, Bond opened up the hatchback and unzipped his folding Samsonite case. Q Branch had taken it apart and fitted a sturdy extra zipped compartment in the centre. This was impervious to all airport surveillance and Bond had found it invaluable when travelling with airlines not allowing him to carry a personal weapon.

'Anything you should not be carrying, ladies, please.'

He held out a hand while both Sukie and Nannie hoisted their skirts and unclipped from their suspender belts the identical holsters carrying automatic pistols. When the case had been returned to the luggage compartment, he ushered them back into the car.

'Remember, you're unarmed. But as far as I can tell, there's no danger. The people who are on my trail should have been diverted. I shall be with the airport manager.'

He told them he would not be long, and then walked towards the airport buildings. The airport manager had been alerted and was treating the arrival of the executive aircraft as a normal routine matter.

'They are about eighty kilometres out, and just starting their approach,' he told Bond. 'I believe you need a room for a small conference while the aircraft is being turned around.'

Bond nodded, apologising for the inconvenience of having the airport opened at this time of night.

'Just be grateful the weather is good,' the manager said with an uncertain smile. 'It's not possible at night if there is a lot of cloud.'

They went out on to the apron, and Bond saw that the airport had been lit for the arrival. A few minutes later he spotted the flashing red and green lights creeping down the invisible path of the approach to the main runway. In a few seconds the little HS 125 Exec jet, bearing no markings but a British identification number, came hissing in over the threshold. It touched down neatly and pulled up with a sharp deceleration. The pilot had obviously used Salzburg before and knew its limits. The aircraft was brought to a standstill by a 'batsman' using a pair of illuminated batons.

The forward door opened and the gangway was unfolded. Bond did not recognise the two women, but was glad to see that at least two of the men coming down the steps were people he had worked with before. The more senior was a bronzed, athletic young man called Crispin Thrush, with Service experience almost as varied as Bond's.

The two men shook hands, and Crispin introduced him to the other members of the team as the manager led them to a small, deserted conference room. Coffee, bottles of mineral water, and note pads were set out on a circular table.

'Help yourselves,' Bond said as he looked around at the team. 'I think I'll go and wash my hands.' He jerked his head at Crispin, who nodded and followed him from the room out into the airport car park. They spoke in lowered voices.

'They briefed you?' Bond asked.

'Only the basics. Said you'd put the flesh on it.'

'Right. You and one of the other chaps take a rented Saab – the one with the two girls in it, over there – and go straight up to the Klinik Mozart. You've got the route?'

Thrush nodded. 'Yes, they gave us that. And I was told something almost unbelievable . . .'

'Steve?'

He nodded again.

'Well, it's true. You'll find him there, sleeping off some dope the clinic's Director, Doktor Kirchtum, gave him. You'll find Kirchtum a godsend. Quinn and a couple of heavies have been holding him there.'

He went on to explain that there was some cleaning up to be done, and Quinn was to be made ready to take a telephone call from the K.G.B., man watching the road for the Bentley. 'When he makes his radio report, listen to him and watch him, Crispin. He's a rogue agent, and I've no need to tell you how dangerous that can be. He knows all the tricks and I've only got his co-operation because of threats against his wife . . .'

'They pulled Tabby in, I understand. She's stashed in one of the Rome safe houses. Gather the poor girl's a bit confused.'

'Probably doesn't believe it. He says she had no idea that he'd defected. Anyway, if the whole team will fit into the Saab, you'd better drop your two girls, and the other lad off at the Goldener Hirsch. If we keep it short in the conference room, you can get the Bentley team on their way. The car will be spotted, so make sure you've got time to get settled into the clinic, with Quinn awake, before the Bentley leaves. Their watcher will take it for granted that I'm in it, with my companions, heading for Paris. That should throw them for a while.'

157

He told Crispin where the Bentley could be found, with the keys in the exhaust, and the route the team should take to Paris. Once the messages had been passed on, Crispin and his man were to get Steve Quinn to Vienna by the fastest means possible.

'Tickets. With the Resident's compliments.'

Crispin reached into his jacket and pulled out a heavy, long envelope. Bond slid it unopened into his breast pocket, as they began walking slowly back to the conference room. They stayed there for less than fifteen minutes, drinking coffee and improvising a business meeting concerning an export deal in chocolate. Eventually Bond rose.

'Right, ladies and gentlemen. See you outside, then.'

He had already arranged that Sukie and Nannie would not even see the team that had flown in. He used some charm to get a man to remove their luggage from the Saab, and now he briskly ushered them into the airport building, where the manager was waiting for them. He joined them a few minutes later, having passed on the Saab keys to Crispin, and wished the new team good luck.

'M's going to boil you in oil if this goes wrong,' Crispin said with a grin.

Bond cocked an eyebrow, sensing the small comma of hair had fallen over his right temple. 'If there's anything left of me to boil.'

As he said it, Bond had a strange premonition of an unsuspected impending disaster.

'V.I.P. treatment.' Sukie sounded delighted when she saw the executive jet. 'Just like the old days with Pasquale.'

Nannie simply took it in her stride. Within minutes they were buckled into their seat belts, whining down the runway and lifting into the black hole of the night. The steward came round with drinks and sandwiches, then discreetly left them alone.

'So, for the umpteenth time, where are we going, James?' Sukie asked as she raised her glass.

'And what's more to the point, why?' said Nannie, sipping her mineral water.

'The where is Florida. Miami first, and then on south. The why's more difficult.'

'Try us,' Nannie said with a smile, peering over the top of her granny glasses.

'Oh, we've had a rotten apple in the barrel. Someone I trusted. He set me up, so now I've set him up, arranged a small diversion so that his people think we're all on the way to Paris. In fact, as you can see, we're travelling in some style to Zurich. From there we go by courtesy of Pan American Airlines to Miami. First class, of course, but I suggest we separate once we reach Zurich. So here are your tickets, ladies.'

He opened the envelope given him by Crispin and handed over the long blue and white folders containing the Zurich – Miami flight reservations made out in their real names, the Principessa Sukie Tempesta and Miss Nannette Norrich. He held back the Providence and Boston Airlines tickets that would get them from Miami to Key West. For some reason he sensed it was better not to let them know the final destination until the last minute. He also glanced at his own ticket to check it was in the name of Mr J. Boldman, the alias used on his B passport, in which he was described as a company director. Everything appeared to be in order.

They arranged to disembark separately at Zurich, to travel independently on the Pan Am flight and to meet up again by the Delta Airlines desk in the main building at Miami International.

'Get a Skycap to take you there,' Bond advised them. 'The place is vast and you can easily get lost. And beware of legal panhandlers – Hare Krishna, nuns, whatever, they're . . .'

'Thick on the ground,' finished Nannie. 'We know, James, we've been to Miami before.'

'Sorry. Right, we're set then. If either of you have second thoughts . . .'

'We've been over that as well. We're going to see it through,' said Nannie firmly.

'To the bitter end, James.' Sukie leaned forward and covered his hand with her own. Bond nodded.

He caught sight of the pair at Zurich having a snack in one of the splendid cafés that seem to litter that clean and pleasant airport. Bond drank coffee and ate a croissant before checking in for the Pan Am flight.

On the 747, Sukie and Nannie were seated right up in the front, while Bond occupied a window seat some way behind on the starboard side. Neither gave him a second look. He admired the way Sukie had so quickly picked up field technique; Nannie he almost took for granted, for she had already shown how good she could be.

The food was reasonable, the flight boring, the movie violent and cut to ribbons. It was hot and crowded when they landed at Miami International, soon after eight in the evening. Sukie and Nannie were already at the Delta desk when he reached it.

'Okay,' he greeted them. 'Now we go through Gate E to the P.B.A. departures.'

He handed them the tickets for the final flight.

'Key West?' queried Nannie.

'The Last Resort, they call it,' said Sukie, laughing. 'Great. I've been there.'

'Well, I want to arrive . . .'

The ping-pong of an announcement signal interrupted him. He opened his mouth to continue, expecting it to be a routine call for some departure, but the voice mentioned the name Boldman.

'Would Mr James Boldman, passenger recently arrived from Zurich, report to the information desk opposite the British Airways counter. Mr Boldman, please.'

Bond shrugged. 'I was going to say that I wanted to arrive incognito. Well, that's my incognito. There must be some development from my people. Wait for me.'

He pressed his way through queues of people and baggage waiting to be checked in. At the information desk a blonde with teeth in gloss white and lips in blood red batted her eyelids at him.

'Can I help y'awl?'

'Message for James Boldman,' he said, and saw her glance behind his left shoulder and nod.

The voice was soft in his ear, and unmistakable.

'Good evening, Mr Boldman. Nice to see you.'

Steve Quinn pressed close as Bond turned. He could feel the pistol muzzle hard against his ribs, and knew his face to be etched with surprise.

'How nice for us to be meeting again, Mr – what do you call yourself now – Boldman?' Doktor

Kirchtum stood on his right, his big face moulded into what appeared to be a big smile of welcome.

'What . . .' Bond began.

'Just start walking quietly out of the exit doors over there.' Quinn's smile didn't change. 'Forget your travelling companions and the P.B.A. flight. We're going to Key West by a different route.'

14

FROST-FREE CITY

THE AIRCRAFT WAS very quiet in flight. Only a low
rumbling whine from the jets was audible. Bond,
who had managed no more than a quick look
before boarding, thought it was probably an Aero-
spatiale Corvette, with its distinctive long nose.
The interior was decorated in blue and gold, with
six swivel armchairs and a long central table.

Outside there was darkness, with only the occasional pin of light flashing in the distance. Bond
guessed they were now high over the Everglades,
or turning to make the run in to Key West across
the sea.

The initial shock of finding himself flanked by
Quinn and Kirchtum had passed very quickly. One
learned to react instantly in his job. In this situation
he had no option but to go along with Quinn's
instructions: it was his only chance of survival.

There had been a moment's hesitation when he
first felt the gun pressing into his ribs. Then he
obeyed, walking calmly between the two big men
who kept close beside him, as though making a
discreet arrest. Now he was really on his own. The

other two had their tickets to Key West, but he had told them to wait for him. They also had all the luggage, and his case contained the weapons – Nannie's two little automatics, the ASP, and the baton.

A long black limousine with tinted windows stood parked directly outside the exit. Kirchtum moved forward a pace to open the rear door, bent his heavy body and entered first.

'In!' Quinn prodded Bond with the gun, almost pushing him into the leather-scented interior and quickly following him so that he was sandwiched between the two men.

The motor was started before the door slammed shut, and the vehicle pulled smoothly away from the kerb. Quinn had the gun out now – a small Makarov, Russian made and based on the German Walther PP series design. Bond recognised it immediately, even in the dim glow thrown into the car from the airport lights. By the same light he could see the driver's head, like a large, elongated coconut, topped with a peaked cap. Nobody spoke, and no orders were given. The limousine purred on to a slip-road which, Bond guessed, led to the airport perimeter tracks.

'Not a word, James,' Quinn whispered, 'on your life, and on May's and Moneypenny's as well.'

They were approaching large gates set into a high chain-link fence.

The car stopped at a security shed and Bond heard the electronic whine as the driver's window was lowered. A guard approached. The driver offered him a clutch of identity cards and the guard muttered something. The nearside rear window slid down and the guard peered in, looking at the cards in his hand and then glancing in at Quinn, Bond and Kirchtum.

'Okay,' he said at last in a gravel drawl. 'Through the gate and wait for the guide truck.'

They moved forward and stopped, lights dipped. Somewhere ahead of them there was a mighty roar as an aircraft landed, its reverse thrust blanketing all other sounds. Dimmed lights appeared as a small truck performed a neat turn in front of them. It was painted with yellow stripes and a red light revolved on the canopy. The rear carried a large 'Follow me' sign.

Keeping behind the truck, the car moved slowly past aircraft of all types – commercial jets being loaded and unloaded, large piston-engined aeroplanes, freighters, small private craft, the insignias ranging from Pan Am, British Airways, and Delta to Datsun and Island City Flying Service. They made for an aircraft that stood apart from the rest near a cluster of buildings on the far side of the field, pulling up so close that Bond thought for a moment they might touch the wing.

For large men, Quinn and Kirchtum moved fast. Like a well-drilled team, Kirchtum left the car almost before it had come to a standstill, while Quinn edged Bond towards the door, so that he was constantly covered from both sides. Once in the open, Kirchtum kept a steel grip on his arm until Quinn was out. Using an arm-lock, they forced him up the steps and into the aeroplane. Quinn's pistol was now in full view as Kirchtum hauled in the steps and closed the door with a solid thud.

'That seat.' Quinn indicated with the pistol. Kirchtum placed handcuffs on each of Bond's wrists, which he then attached to small steel D-rings in the padded arms of the seat.

'You've done this before,' Bond said, smiling. There was no edge in showing fear to people like this.

'Just a precaution. It would be foolish to be forced to use this once we're airborne.'

Quinn stood clear, the pistol levelled, as Kirchtum looped shackles around Bond's ankles, and secured them to similar steel D-rings on the lower part of the seat. The engines rumbled into life and seconds later they were moving. There was a short wait as they taxied in line, then the little jet swung on to the runway, burst into full life and roared away, climbing fast.

'I apologise for the deception, James.' Quinn was now relaxed and leaning back in his seat with a drink. 'You see, we thought you might just visit the Mozart, so we stayed prepared – even with the torture paraphernalia on show, and the Herr Doktor looking like an unwilling victim. I admit to one serious error: I should have ordered my outside team to move in after you entered. However, these things happen. The Doktor was excellent in his role of frightened captive, I thought.'

'Oscar nominee.' Bond's expression did not alter. 'I hope nothing nasty is going to happen to my two lady friends.'

'I don't think you need bother yourself about them,' said Quinn, smiling happily. 'We sent them a message that you would not be leaving tonight. They think you're joining them at the Airport

Hilton. I expect they're waiting there for you now. If they do get suspicious, I'm afraid they won't be able to do much about it. You have a date around lunchtime tomorrow with what the good old French revolutionaries called Madame La Guillotine. I shall not be there to witness it. As I told you, we have orders only to hand you over to SPECTRE. We take the money and see to the release of May and Moneypenny – you can trust me over that. They will be returned unopened. Even though it would have been useful to interrogate Moneypenny.'

'And where is all this going to take place?' Bond asked, his voice betraying no concern about his appointment with the guillotine.

'Oh, quite near Key West. A few miles off shore. Outside the reef. Unfortunately our timing isn't brilliant – we'll have to hole up with you until dawn. The channel through the reef is not the easiest to navigate, and we don't want to end up on a sandbar. But we'll manage. I promised my superiors I would hand you over and I like to keep my promises.'

'Especially to the kind of masters you serve,' Bond replied. 'Failure isn't exactly appreciated in the Russian service. At best you'd be demoted, or end up running exercises for trainees; at worst it would be one of those nice hospitals where they inject you with Aminazin – such a pleasant drug. Turns you into a living vegetable. I reckon that's exactly how you'll end up.' He turned to Kirchtum. 'You too, Herr Doktor. How did they put the arm on you?'

The doctor shrugged.

'The Klinik Mozart is my whole life, Mr Bond.

167

My entire life. Some years ago we had – how do I put it? A financial embarrassment . . .'

'You were broke,' Bond said placidly.

'So. *Ja*. Broke. No funds. Friends of Mr Quinn – the people he works for – made me a very good offer. I could carry on my work, which has always been in the interests of humanity, and they would see to the funds.'

'I can guess the rest,' Bond cut in. 'The price was your co-operation. The odd visitor to be kept under sedation for a while. Sometimes a body. Occasionally some surgery.'

The doctor nodded sadly. 'Yes, all those things. I admit that I did not expect to become involved in a situation like the present one. But Mr Quinn tells me I shall be able to return with no blot on my professional character. Officially I am away for two days. A rest.'

Bond laughed. 'A rest? You believe that? It can only end up with arrest, Herr Doktor. Either arrest, or one of Mr Quinn's bullets. Probably the latter.'

'Stop that,' Quinn said sharply. 'The doctor has been a great help. He will be rewarded, and he knows it.' He smiled at Kirchtum. 'Mr Bond is using an old, old trick, trying to make you doubt our intentions, attempting to drive a wedge between us. You know how clever he can be. You've seen him in action.'

Again the doctor nodded. '*Ja*. The shooting of Vasila and Yuri was not funny. That I did not like.'

'But you were also clever. You gave Mr Quinn some harmless injection . . .'

'Saline.'

'And then you must have followed me.'

'We were on your track very quickly,' Quinn said flatly as he glanced towards the window. Outside there was still darkness. 'But you changed my plans. My people in Paris were supposed to deal with you. It took some very fast and fancy choreography to arrange this, James. But we managed.'

'You did indeed.'

Bond swivelled his seat, leaning forward to see out of the window. He thought there were lights in the distance.

'Ah.' Quinn sounded pleased. 'There we are. Lights – Stock Island and Key West. About ten minutes to go, I'd say.'

'And what if I make a fuss when we land?'

'You won't make a fuss.'

'You're very confident.'

'I have an insurance. Just as you had with me, because of Tabitha. I really do believe you will do as you're told to secure the release of May and Moneypenny. It's the one chink in your armour, James. Always has been. Yes, you're a cold fish; ruthless. But you're also an old-fashioned English gentleman at heart. You'd give your life to save a defenceless woman and this time we're talking of two women – your own ageing housekeeper and your Chief's Personal Assistant, who has been hopelessly devoted to you for years. People you care for most in the world. Of course you'll give your life for them. Unhappily, it's in your nature. Unhappily, did I say? I really meant happily – for us, happily.'

Bond swallowed. Deep down inside he knew that Steve Quinn had played the trump card. He was right. 007 would go to his own death to save the lives of people like May and Moneypenny.

'There's another reason why you won't make a fuss.' It was hard to detect Quinn's smile under that bushy beard, and it did not show in his eyes. 'Show him, Herr Doktor.'

Kirchtum lifted a small case which lay in the magazine rack between the seats. From it he drew out what looked like a child's space gun made of clear plastic.

'This is an injection pistol,' Kirchtum explained. 'Before we land I shall fill it. Look, you can see the action.'

He drew back a small plunger from the rear, lifted the barrel in front of Bond's face and touched the tiny trigger. The instrument was no more than seven centimetres long, with about five for the butt. As he touched the trigger, a hypodermic needle appeared from the muzzle.

'An injection is given in 2.5 seconds.' The doctor nodded gravely. 'Very quick. Also the needle is very long. Goes easily through cloth.'

'You show the least sign of making a fuss, and you get the needle, right?'

'Instant death.'

'Oh, no. Instant facsimile heart attack. You'll come back to us within half an hour, as good as new. SPECTRE want your head. In the final resort, we would kill you with a power tool. But we'd rather deliver your whole body alive and intact. We owe Rahani a few favours, and the poor man hasn't long to live. Your head is his last request.'

A moment later the pilot came on the intercom system to ask for seatbelts to be fastened and cigarettes extinguished. He announced that they would be landing in about four minutes. Bond watched out of the window as they dropped towards the lights. He saw water and tropical vegetation interspersed with roads and low buildings coming up to meet them.

'Interesting place, Key West,' mused Quinn. 'Hemingway once called it the poor man's St Tropez. Tennessee Williams lived here too. President Truman established a little White House near what used to be the Naval Base and John F. Kennedy brought the British P.M., Harold Macmillan, to visit it. Cuban boat people landed here, but long before that it was a pirates' and wreckers' paradise. I'm told it's still a smugglers' heaven, and the U.S. Coastguard operates a tight schedule out of here.'

They swept in over the threshold and touched down with hardly a bump.

'There's history in this airport as well,' Quinn continued. 'First regular U.S. mail flight started from here; and Key West is both the beginning and end of Highway Route One.' They rolled to a halt, then began to taxi towards a shack-like hut with a veranda. Bond saw a low wall with faded lettering: 'Welcome to Key West the Only Frost-Free City in the United States'.

'And they have the most spectacular sunsets,' Quinn added. 'Really incredible. Pity you won't be around to see one.'

The heat hit them like a furnace as they left the aircraft. Even the mild breeze felt as if it was blowing from an inferno.

The departure from the jet was as carefully

organised as the boarding, with Kirchtum close enough to use his deadly little syringe at any moment, should Bond alert their suspicion.

'Smile and pretend to talk,' muttered Quinn, glancing towards the veranda where a dozen or so people were waiting to welcome passengers off a newly arrived P.B.A. flight. Bond scanned the faces, but recognised nobody. They passed through a small gate in the wall beside the shack, Quinn and Kirchtum pushing him towards another sleek dark automobile. In a few moments, Bond was again seated between the two men. This time the driver was young, in an open-necked shirt and with long blond hair.

'Y'awl okay?'

'Just drive,' Quinn snapped. 'There's a place arranged I understand.'

'Sure thing. Git y'there in no time.' He drew out on to the road, turning his head slightly. 'Y'awl mind if'n I have some music playin'?'

'Go ahead. As long as it doesn't frighten the horses.'

Quinn was very relaxed and confident. If it had not been for Kirchtum, tense on the other side, Bond would have made a move. But the doctor was wound up like a hair trigger. He would have the hypo into 007 if he moved a muscle. A burst of sound filled the car, a rough voice singing, tired, cynical and sad:

> There's a hole in Daddy's arm,
> Where all the money goes . . .

'Not that!' cracked Quinn.

'Ah'm sorry. I kinda like rock and roll. Rhythm and blues. Man, it's good music.'

'I said not that.'

The car went silent, the driver sullen. Bond watched the signs – South Roosevelt Boulevard, a restaurant alive with people eating, Martha's. There were wooden, clapboard houses, white with fretted gingerbread decorations along the porches and verandas; lights flashing – Motel; No vacancy. Lush tropical foliage lined the road, with the ocean on their right. They appeared to be following a long bend taking them away from the Atlantic. Then they turned suddenly at a sign to Searstown. Bond saw they were in a large shopping area.

The car pulled up beside a supermarket alive with late shoppers and an optometrist's. Between the two lay a narrow alley.

'It's up there. Door on the right. Up above the eye place, where they sell reading glasses. Guess y'awl want me to pick you up.'

'Five o'clock,' Quinn said quietly. 'In time to get to Garrison Bight at dawn.'

'Y'awl goin' on a fishin' trip, then?'

The driver turned round and Bond saw his face for the first time. He was not a young man, as Bond had thought, despite the long blond hair. Half his face was missing, sunken in and patched with skin grafts. He must have sensed Bond's shock for he looked at him straight with his one good eye, and gave an ugly grimace.

'Don't you worry about me none. That's why I work for these gentlemen here. I got this brand new face in Nam, so I thought I could put it to use. Frightens the hell outa some folks.'

'Five o'clock,' Quinn repeated, opening the door.

The routine did not vary. They had Bond out, along the alley, through a door and up one flight of stairs in a few seconds. They had brought him to a bare room. In it were only two chairs and two beds, flimsy curtains and a noisy air-conditioning unit. Again they used the handcuffs and shackles, and Kirchtum sat close to Bond, the hypodermic in his hand, while Quinn went out for food. They ate melon and some bread and ham, washing it down with mineral water. Then Quinn and Kirchtum took turns in guarding Bond, who, resigned, fell asleep with exhaustion.

It was still dark when Quinn shook him awake. He stood over Bond in the bare, functional little bathroom as he tried to fight off the grogginess of travel. After about ten minutes they led him downstairs to the car.

There were few signs of life so early in the morning. The sky looked hard and grey, but Quinn said it was going to be a beautiful day. They came to North Roosevelt Boulevard, then passed a marina on their left with yachts and big powered fishing boats moored. Water appeared on the right as well. Quinn pointed.

'That's where we'll be heading. The Gulf of Mexico. The island's out on the far side of the reef.'

At the Harbour Lights restaurant sign Bond was hustled out of the car, along the side of the sleeping restaurant and down on to the marina quayside. A tall, muscular man waited beside a large, powered fishing boat with a high laddered and skeletal superstructure above the cabin. The engines were idling.

Quinn and the captain exchanged nods, and they pushed Bond aboard and down into the narrow cabin. Once more the handcuffs and shackles were put on. The noise of the engine rose, and Bond could feel the swell as the craft started out from the quayside, cruising into the marina and under a bridge. As the boat picked up speed, Kirchtum grew calmer. He put away the hypodermic. Quinn joined the captain at the controls.

Five minutes out, they had really started to make way, the boat rolling slightly and bounding, slapping hard down into the water. Everyone appeared to be concentrating on the navigation, and Bond began to think seriously about his predicament. They had spoken of an island outside the reef, and he wondered how long it would take them to reach it. He then concentrated on the handcuffs realising that there was little he could do to be out of them. Unexpectedly, Quinn came down into the cabin.

'I'm going to gag you and cover you up.' Then he spoke to Kirchtum and Bond just made out what he was saying. 'There's another fishing boat to starboard . . . appears to be in some kind of trouble . . . The captain says we should offer to help . . . they could report us. I don't want to raise suspicion.'

He pushed a handkerchief into Bond's mouth and tied another around it, so that, for a moment he thought he would suffocate. Then, after checking the shackles, Quinn threw a blanket over him.

In the darkness, Bond listened. They were slowing, rolling a little, but definitely slowing.

Above he heard the captain shouting, 'You in trouble?' Then, a few seconds later, 'Right, I'll come aboard, but I have an RV. May have to pick you up on the way back.'

There was a sharp bump, as though they had made contact with the other boat, and then all hell broke loose. Bond lost count after the first dozen shots. There were the cracks of hand guns followed by the stutter of a machine pistol; then a cry, which sounded like Kirchtum, and thumps on the deck above. Then silence, until he heard the sound of bare feet descending into the cabin.

The blanket was hauled back roughly and Bond tried to turn his head widening as he saw the figure above him. Nannie Norrich had her small automatic in one hand.

'Well, well, Master James, we do have to get you out of some scrapes, don't we?' She turned her head. 'Sukie, it's okay. He's down here, trussed up and oven-ready by the look of it.'

Sukie appeared, also armed. She grinned appealingly.

'Bondage, they call it, I believe.'

She began to laugh as Bond let off a stream of obscenities which were completely incomprehensible from behind the gag. Nannie wrenched at the handcuffs and shackles. Sukie went aloft again, returning with keys.

'I hope those idiots weren't friends of yours,' said Nannie. 'I'm afraid we had to deal with them.'

'What do you mean, "deal"?' Bond spluttered as

the gag came away. She looked so innocent that his blood ran cold.

'I'm afraid they're dead, James. All three of them. Stone dead. But you must admit, we were clever to find *you*.'

15

THE PRICE FOR
A LIFE

BOND FELT AN ODD sense of shock that two relatively
young women had brought about the carnage he
saw on the deck, yet could remain buoyant, even
elated, as though killing three men was like swatting flies in a kitchen. He also realised that he was
suffering from a certain amount of resentment – he
had taken the initiative, he had been duped by
Quinn and Kirchtum, he had fallen into their
quickly devised trap. Yet he had not been able to
effect his own escape. These mere women had
rescued him, and he felt resentful – a peculiar
reaction when he should have been grateful.

Another, almost identical powered fishing boat
bearing the name *Prospero* lay alongside, rising,
falling and gently bumping against their vessel.
They were well outside the reef. In the far distance
little low mounds of islands rose from the sea. The
sky was turning from pearl to deep blue as the sun
cleared the horizon. Quinn had been right. It was
going to be a beautiful day.

'Well?'

Nannie stood near him, looking around while Sukie appeared to be busying herself on the other boat.

'Well what?' Bond asked flatly.

'Well, weren't we clever to find you?'

'Very.' He sounded sharp, almost angry. 'Was all this necessary?'

'You mean blowing away your captors?' The expression sounded strange coming from Nannie Norrich. She flushed with anger now. 'Yes, very necessary. Can't you even say thank you, James? We tried to deal with it peacefully, but they opened up with that damned Uzi. They gave us no option.'

She pointed towards their boat and the nasty jagged row of holes in the hull, abaft the high skeleton superstructure above the cabin.

Bond nodded, muttering his thanks.

'You were, indeed, very clever to find me. I'd like to hear more about that.'

'And so you shall,' Nannie said waspishly, 'but first we really have to do something about this mess.'

'What weapons are you carrying?'

'The two pistols from your case – your stuff's back at the hotel in Key West. I had to force the locks, I'm afraid. I couldn't work out the combinations, and we were fairly desperate by then.'

'Any extra fuel around?'

She pointed past Kirchtum's slumped corpse in the stern well. 'A couple of cans there. We've got three aboard our boat.'

'It's got to look like a catastrophe,' Bond said with a frown. 'What's more, they mustn't find the bodies. An explosion would be best – preferably when we're well out of the area. It's easy enough to do, but we must have some kind of fuse, and that's what we haven't got.'

'But we do have a signal pistol. We could use the flares.'

Bond nodded. 'Good. What's the range – about a hundred metres? You go back with Sukie and get the pistol and flares ready. I'll do what's necessary here.'

Nannie turned away, sprang lightly on to the guard rail, and jumped aboard their boat, calling cheerfully to Sukie.

Bond then set about his grim task, still preoccupied with the recent turn of events. How did they manage to find him? How could they have been in the right place at the right time? Until he had answers that satisfied him, he could not trust either of the young women.

He searched the boat carefully, assembling everything that might be useful on the deck – rope, wire and the strong lines used for bringing in sharks and swordfish. All the weapons he threw overboard, except for Quinn's automatic, a prosaic Browning 9mm, and some spare clips.

Then came the grisly job of moving the bodies into the stern well. Kirchtum, already there, only needed turning over, which Bond managed to do with his feet; the captain's body stuck in the wheelhouse door, and he had to tug hard to get it free. Quinn was the most difficult to move, for the bloody decapitated remains had to be dragged along the narrow gap separating cabin from guard rail.

He placed the corpses in a row directly over the fuel tanks and lashed them loosely together with fishing line. He then went forward again and gathered as much inflammable material as he could find – sheets and blankets off the four cabin bunks, cushions, pillows and even pieces of rag. These he piled up well forward, weighting them with life jackets and heavier equipment. One piece of coiled rope he left near the bodies.

He transferred himself to the other boat, where he found Sukie standing in the wheelhouse with Nannie close behind her on the steps leading down to the cabin. Nannie was holding the bulbous flare projector by the muzzle.

'There it is. One flare pistol.'

'Plenty of flares?'

She pointed to a metal box containing a dozen stumpy cartridges, each marked with its colour: red, green or illuminating. Bond picked out three of the illuminating flares.

'These should do us.'

He rapidly gave them instructions, and Sukie started the engines while Nannie cast off all but one rope amidships.

Bond returned to the other boat to make the final preparations. He dragged the rope near the bodies to the pile of material, secured it underneath and gently played it out back to the stern wall, laying it alongside the inlets to the fuel tanks. He went forward again with one of the emergency fuel cans and saturated first the material, then, shuffling backwards towards the corpses, he ran plenty of the liquid over the rope.

He opened the second can to dowse the human

remains in fuel, unscrewed the main fuel cap and lowered the saturated rope into the tank.

'Stand by!' he yelled.

He ran from the stern well, mounted the guard rail and was aboard the other boat just as Nannie let go of the rope amidships. Sukie slowly eased open the throttle and they pulled away, gently turning stern-on to the other boat.

Bond positioned himself aft of the superstructure, slid a flare into the pistol, checked the wind and watched the gap slowly widen between the two craft. At around eighty metres he raised the pistol high and fired an illuminating flare in a low, flat trajectory. The flare hissed right across the bows of the other boat. Bond had already reloaded and taken up another position. This time, the fizzing white flare performed a perfect arc, leaving a thick stream of white smoke behind it, to land in the bows. There was a second's pause before the material ignited with a small *whumph*. The flames were carried straight along the rope fuse towards the fuel tanks, and the bodies.

'Give her full power and weave as much as possible!' Bond shouted to Sukie.

The engine note rose, bows lifting, almost before he had finished giving the order. Rapidly they bounced away from the blazing fishing boat.

The corpses caught alight first, the stern well sending up a crimson flame and then a dense cloud of black smoke. They were a good two kilometres away when the fuel tanks went up – a great roaring explosion with a dark red centre, ripping the boat apart in a ferocious fireball. For a few moments there was the smoke and a rising cascade of débris, then nothing. The water appeared to boil around what little remained of the powerful fishing launch, then it settled, steamed for a few seconds, and flattened. The shock waves hit the rear of their boat a second or two after the explosion. There was a slight burn on the wind, which they felt on their cheeks.

At five kilometres there was nothing to be seen, but Bond remained leaning againt the superstructure, gazing in the direction of the small, violent inferno.

'Coffee?' Nannie asked.

'Depends how long we're staying at sea.'

'We hired this boat for a day's fishing,' she said. 'I don't think we should raise suspicion.'

'No, we'll even have to try and fish. Is Sukie okay at the wheel?'

'Sukie Tempesta turned and nodded, smiling.

'She's sailed boats all her life.' Nannie gestured towards the steps leading below. 'There's coffee on . . .'

'And I want to hear how you managed to find me,' Bond said, staring at her steadily.

'I told you. I was minding you, James.'

They were now seated on the bunks in the cramped cabin, facing each other. They nursed mugs of coffee as the boat rolled and the sea thudded against the hull. Sukie had reduced power and they seemed to be performing a series of gentle, wide circles.

'When Norrich Universal Bodyguards take it upon themselves to look after you, you get looked after.'

Nannie had her long legs tucked under her on the

bunk, and had unpinned her hair so that it fell, dark and thick, to her shoulders, giving her face an almost elfin look, and somehow making the grey eyes softer and very interesting. Take care, Bond thought, this lady has to explain herself, and she had better be convincing.

'So I got looked after.' He did not smile.

She explained that as soon as he had been paged at Miami International she had left Sukie with the luggage and followed him at a discreet distance.

'I had plenty of cover – you know how crowded the place was – but I saw the routine. I'm experienced enough to know when a client is being pulled.'

'But they took me away by car.'

'Yes. I got its number and then made a quick call – my little NUB has a small branch here, and they put a trace on the limo. I said I'd call them back if I needed assistance. After that I called the flight planning office.'

'Resourceful lady.'

'James, in this game you have to be. Apart from the scheduled flights to Key West there was one private exec jet that had filed a flight plan. I took down the details . . .'

'Which were?'

'Company called Société pour la Promotion de l'Écologie et de la Civilisation . . .'

SPEC, Bond thought. SPEC. SPECTRE.

'We had about six minutes to catch the P.B.A. flight to Key West, so I gambled that we'd make it just before the private flight.'

'You also gambled on my being on board the SPEC jet.'

185

She nodded. 'Yes, and you were. If you hadn't been, I would have had egg on my face. As it happened, we were off the aircraft a good five minutes before you came along. I even had time to hire a car, send Sukie to book into the hotel and follow you to that shopping centre in Searstown.'

'And then what?'

'I hung around.' She paused, not looking at him. 'To be honest, I didn't really know what to do. Then, like a small miracle, the big bearded guy came out and went straight to the telephone booth. I was only a few paces away and I've got good eyesight. Don't be fooled by the spectacles. I watched him punch out a number and talk for a while. When he went to the supermarket I slipped into the booth and dialled the number. He had called the Harbour Lights restaurant.'

There was a street guide in the little rented Volkswagen, and the Harbour Lights was easy enough to find. 'As soon as I got inside I realised it was a fishing and sailing place, full of bronzed, muscular men renting boats, and themselves to sail them. I just asked around. One man – the one who went up in smoke just now – mentioned that he had been hired for an early start. He'd had a bit to drink and even told me what time he was leaving, and that he had three passengers.'

'So you hired another powered fishing launch.'

'That's right. I told the captain I didn't need help. Sukie can navigate the trickiest waters blindfold and with her hands tied. He took me down to this boat, made a pass and got the push. But he did show me the charts, and told me about the currents and channels, which are not easy. He talked about

186

the reef, the islands and the drop-off into the Gulf
of Mexico.'

'So you went back to Sukie at the hotel . . .'

'And poured over the charts half the night. We
got down to Garrison Bight early and were outside
the reef when your boat came out. We watched you
on the radar. Then we positioned ourselves near
enough to your course, stopped the engines and
started firing distress flares. You know the rest.'

'You tried the soft approach, but they opened up
with the Uzi.'

'To their cost.' She cocked her head, and gave a
sigh. 'Lord, I'm tired.'

'You're not alone. And what about Sukie?'

'She seems happy enough. She always is with
boats.' Nannie put down her empty coffee mug and
started slowly to undo the buttons of her shirt. 'I
really think I'd like to lie down, James. Would you
like to lie down with me?'

'What if we hit a squall? We'll be thrown all over
the place.' Bond leaned forward to kiss her gently
on the mouth.

'I'd rather meet a swell.' Her arms came up
around his neck, drawing him towards her.

Later, she said that she'd rarely been thanked so
well for saving somebody's life.

'You should do it again sometime.'

Bond kissed her, running one hand over her
naked body.

'Why not now?' asked Nannie with an implike
grin. 'It seems a fair price for a life.'

16

GOING DOWN TONIGHT

'AS FAR AS I can tell, there are three islands outside
the reef that are privately owned and have some
kind of building on them.' Sukie's finger roamed
around the chart of the Key West vicinity.

It was early afternoon, and they were hove to
with fishing lines out. Four large red snapper had
come their way, but nothing big – no sharks or
swordfish.

'This one here,' said Sukie, indicating an island
just outside the reef, 'is owned by the man who
built the hotel where we're staying. There's
another to the north, and this one,' her finger
circled a large patch of land, 'just on the shelf,
before you reach the drop-off. The continental
shelf suddenly drops down from 270 metres to over
600. Great fishing water around the drop-off.
There have been treasure seekers by the dozen in
the area too.' She prodded the island on the map.
'Anyway, it looked very much as though that was
where you were heading.'

Bond peered closer to see the name. 'Shark
Island,' he said. 'How cosy.'

'Someone seems to think so. I asked around the hotel last night. A couple of years ago a man who called himself Rainey, Tarquin Rainey, bought the place. The boy at the hotel is from an old Key West family and knows all the gossip. He says this fellow Rainey is a mystery man. He arrives by private jet and gets ferried out to Shark Island by helicopter, or by a launch which belongs to the place. He's also a bit of a go-getter. People who build on the islands usually take a lot of time; it's always difficult getting the materials taken out to them. Rainey had his place up in the space of one summer and the island landscaped in the second summer. He's got tropical trees, gardens, the lot. They're very impressed, the people in Key West, and it takes a great deal to impress them, particularly as they claim to be a republic. The Conch Republic.'

She pronounced it 'Konk'.

'Nobody's seen him?' Bond asked, knowing that tha alias Tarquin Rainey could not be a coincidence. The man had to be Tamil Rahani, which meant Shark Island was SPECTRE property.

'I believe a few people have had glimpses of him – at a distance. Nobody's encouraged to get near him, though. Apparently some people have approached Shark Island by boat and been warned away, politely, but very firmly, by large men in fast motor boats.'

'Mmmmm.' Bond thought for a few moments, then asked Sukie if she could navigate to within a couple of kilometres at night.

'If the charts are accurate, yes. It'll be slow going, but it's possible. When did you want to go?'

'I thought perhaps tonight. If that's where I was

being taken, it's only common courtesy for me to call on Mr Rainey at the earliest possible opportunity.'

Bond gazed steadily first at Sukie and then at Nannie, both of whom looked very dubious about the idea.

'I think we should head back to Garrison Bight now,' he went on. 'See if you can keep the boat for a couple of days longer. I'll get myself a few bits and pieces I'm going to need. We could have a look around Key West – see and be seen. We'll set out for Shark Island at about two in the morning. I won't put you in danger, that I promise. You simply wait off shore and if I don't return by a certain time, you get the hell out and come back tomorrow night.'

'Okay by me,' said Sukie as she got to her feet.

Nannie just nodded. She had been quiet since they had come back on deck. Occasionally she would shoot warm glances in Bond's direction.

'Right. Let's get the lines hauled in,' he said decisively. 'We said at two. In the meantime, there's a great deal to be done.'

The local police were at Garrison Bight when they returned, checking on the boat hired by Steve Quinn. There had been a report from another power boat which had seen a plume of smoke, and from a naval helicopter that had spotted wreckage. They had seen it themselves an hour or so after Quinn's boat had exploded and had even waved to it, knowing they were well away from Quinn's vessel.

Nannie went ashore and talked to the police, while Sukie staying in sight on deck and Bond remained in the cabin. After half an hour Nannie returned, saying that she had charmed the pants off the cops and had hired the boat for a week.

'I hope we're not going to need it that long,' Bond said with grimace.

'Better safe than sorry, as we nannies say.' She poked her tongue out before adding, 'Master James.'

'I've had enough of that little joke, thank you.' He sounded genuinely irritated. 'Now, where are we staying?'

'There's only one place to stay in Key West,' Sukie put in. 'The Pier House Hotel. You get a wonderful view of the famous sunset from there.'

'I've a lot to do before sunset,' Bond said sharply. 'The sooner we get to this – what's it called? Pier House – the better.'

As they set off in the hired Volkswagen, Bond suddenly felt very naked without a weapon of any kind. He sat next to Nannie, with Sukie, who had been here before, squeezed into the back giving an occasional commentary.

To Bond, the place was an odd mixture of tourist resort garishness and pockets of great beauty, with areas of luxury which spelled money. It was hot, palm trees shimmered and moved in the light breeze, and they passed numerous clapboard gingerbread houses, which were bright and well painted, their yards and gardens filled with the colour of sub-tropical flowers. Yet well-kept houses could be adjacent to rubbish tips. The sidewalks were in fine order in one street, in the next cracked, broken or almost non-existent.

At an intersection, they had to wait for an

extraordinary-looking train – a kind of model railroad engine built on to a diesel-powered jeep, which pulled a series of cars full of people under striped awnings.

'The Conch Train,' Sukie informed them. 'That's the way tourists get to see Key West.'

Bond could hear the driver, all done out in blue overalls and peaked cap, going through a litany of the sights and their history as the train wound its way around the island.

They finally turned into a long street of wood and concrete buildings, which appeared to house nothing but jewellery, tourist junk and art shops, interspersed with prosperous-looking restaurants.

'Duval,' announced Sukie. 'It goes right down to the ocean – to our hotel in fact. It's great at night. There, that's the famous Fast Buck Freddie's Department Store. And there's Antonia's, a great Italian restaurant. Sloppy Joe's Bar was Ernest Hemingway's favourite haunt when he lived here.'

Even if Bond had not read *To Have and Have Not* he could not now have escaped knowing that Hemingway had lived in Key West. There were souvenir T-shirts and drawings of him everywhere, and Sloppy Joe's Bar proclaimed it loudly, not just from an inn sign but also on a tall painted legend on the wall.

As they reached the bottom of Duval, Bond saw what he was looking for and noted that it was a very short walk from the hotel.

'You're already registered, and your luggage is in your suite,' Nannie told him, as she parked the car. They hustled him through the light main reception area furnished in bamboo and through an enclosed courtyard where a fountain played on flowers and the tall wooden statue of a naked woman. Above, large fans revolved silently, sending a down draught of cool air.

He followed them down a passage and out into the gardens, along twisting flower-bordered pathways, with a pool deck to the left. Beyond, a line of wood and bamboo bars and restaurants ran beside a small beach. The pier the hotel was named after stretched out over the water on big wooden piles.

The building appeared to be U-shaped, with gardens and pool in the centre of the U. They entered the main hotel again at the far side of the pool and took the elevator up one floor to two adjacent suites.

'We're sharing,' said Sukie, inserting her key into one of the doors. 'But you're right next to us, James, in case there's anything we can do for you.'

For the first time since they had met, Bond thought he could detect an invitation in Sukie's voice. He certainly saw a small angry flash in Nannie's eyes. Could it be that they were fighting over him?'

'What's the plan?' Nannie asked, a little sharply.

'Where's the best place to watch this incredible sunset?'

She allowed him a smile. 'The deck outside the Havana Docks bar, or so they tell me.'

'And at what time?'

'Around six.'

'The bar's in the hotel?'

'Right over there.' She waved a hand vaguely in the direction from which they had come. 'Above the restaurants, right out towards the sea.'

'Meet you both there at six, then.'

Bond smiled, turned the key in his door and disappeared into a pleasant and functional, if not luxurious, suite.

The two briefcases stood with his special Samsonite folding case in the middle of the room. It took Bond less than ten minutes to complete his unpacking. He felt better with the ASP hidden away under his jacket, and the baton at his waistband.

He checked the rooms carefully, made certain the window catches were secure, then quietly opened the door. The corridor was deserted. Silently he closed the door, making his way quickly to the elevator and back down into the gardens, using an exit to the car park which he had noticed on the way through. It was hot and humid outside.

At the far end of the parking lot stood a low building called the Pier House Market, with access from both the hotel and Front Street. Bond went straight through, pausing for a moment to look at the fruit and meat on sale, then on Front Street he turned right and crossed the cracked and lumpy road, walking fast to the corner of Duval. He passed the shop he really wanted to visit and bought some faded jeans, a T-shirt free of tasteless slogans and a pair of soft loafers in a male boutique. He also selected an over-priced short linen jacket. For anyone in Bond's job, a jacket or blouse was always necessary to hide the hardware.

He came out of the boutique and made his way back to the place he had spotted from the car. It had a walk-in front with a dummy clad in Scuba gear out on the sidewalk. The sign read 'Reef Plunderers' Diving Emporium'. A bearded salesman tried to sell him a three and a half hour snorkelling trip on a dive boat predictably called *Reef Plunderer II*, but Bond said he was not interested.

'Captain Jack knows all the best places to dive along the reef,' the salesman protested limply.

'I want a wet suit, snorkelling mask, knife, flippers and undersea torch. And I shall need a shoulder bag for the lot,' Bond told him in that effectively quiet but firm tone.

The salesman looked at Bond, took in the physique under the lightweight suit and the hard look in the icy blue eyes.

'Yes, siree. Sure. Right,' he said, leading the way to the rear of the shop. 'Gonna cost a ransom, but you sure know what y'awl're after.'

'That's right.' Bond did not allow his voice to rise above the almost whispering softness.

'Right,' the salesman repeated. He was dressed to look like an old salt, with a striped T-shirt and jeans. A gold ring hung piratically rather than fashionably from one ear. He gave Bond another sidelong look and began to collect the equipment from the back of the store. It was more than a quarter of an hour before Bond was completely satisfied. He added a belt with a waterproof zipper bag to his purchases, and then paid with his Platinum Amex Card, made out in the name of James Boldman.

'Guess I'll have to just run a check on this, sir, Mr Boldman.'

'You don't have to, and you know it.' Bond gazed at the man with ice-cold eyes. 'But if you're about to make telephone calls, I'm going to stand next to you. Right?'

'Right. Right,' the pirate salesman repeated, leading the way to a tiny office at the back of the store. 'Yes, sir-bub. Yes, siree.' He picked up the telephone and dialled the Amex number. The card was cleared in seconds. It took another ten minutes for the purchases to be stowed away in the shoulder bag. As he left, Bond put his mouth very close to the pierced ear with the ring in it.

'Tell you what,' he began. 'I'm a stranger in town, but now you know my name.'

'Sure.' The pirate gave him a trapped look.

'If anyone else gets to know I've been here except you, Amex and myself, I shall come back cut that ring from your ear and then do the same job on your nose, followed by a more vital organ.' He dropped his hand, fist clenched, so that it lay level with the pirate's crotch. 'You understand me? I mean it.'

'I already forgot your name, Mr ... er ... Mr ...'

'Keep it like that,' said Bond as he strode off.

He made his way back to the hotel at the more leisurely pace of the people thronging the street. Back in his suite, he lugged the CC500 from its briefcase, hooked it to the telephone and put in a quick call to London. He did not wait for a response, but gave them his exact location, saying he would be in touch as soon as the job was completed.

'It's going down tonight,' he finished. 'If I'm not in touch within forty-eight hours, look for Shark Island, off Key West. Repeat, it's going down tonight.'

It was a very apt phrase, he thought, as he changed into his newly acquired clothes. The ASP and baton were in place, so he no longer felt naked, but, surveying himself in the mirror, he thought he would blend in nicely with the tourist scene.

'Going down tonight,' he said softly to himself. Then he left for the Havana Docks bar.

17

SHARK ISLAND

THE DECK in front of the Havana Docks bar at the Pier House is made of wooden planks, raised on several levels and has metal chairs and tables arranged to give visitors the impression that they are on board a ship at anchor. Globe lights on poles stand at intervals along the heavy wooden guard rails. It is perhaps the best vantage point in Key West, from which to watch the sun setting over the sea.

The deck was crowded and there was a buzz of lighthearted chatter. The lights had come on, attracting swarms of insects around the globes. Someone was playing *Mood Indigo* on the piano. The rails were lined with tourists eager to capture the sunset with their cameras.

As the clear sky turned to a deeper navy blue, so an occasional speedboat crossed in front of the hotel, while a light aircraft buzzed a wide circuit, its lights flashing. To the left, along the wide Mallory Square which fronts on to the ocean, jugglers, conjurers, fire eaters and acrobats performed amid a crush of people. It was the same on every fine night, a celebration of the day's end and a look towards the pleasures the night might bring.

James Bond sat at a table and gazed out to sea past the two dark green humps of Tank and Wisteria Islands. If he had any sense he would be on a boat or aeroplane moving out, he thought. He was fully aware of the danger close at hand. There could be no doubt that Tarquin Rainey was Tamil Rahani, Blofeld's successor and that this could well be his last chance to smash SPECTRE once and for all.

'Isn't this absolutely super,' said Sukie delightedly. 'There really is nothing like it in the whole world.'

It was not clear whether she was talking about the huge shrimps they were eating with that very special tangy, hot red sauce, their Calypso Daiquiris, or the beautiful view.

The sun appeared to grow larger as it dropped slowly behind Wisteria Island, throwing a huge patch of blood-red light across the sky.

Above them, a U.S. Customs helicopter clattered its way, running from south to north, red and green lights twinkling on and off as it turned, heading towards the naval air station. Bond wondered if SPECTRE had become involved in the huge drug traffic which was reported to pass into America by this route – landing on isolated sections of the Florida Keys, to be taken inland and distributed. The Navy and Customs kept a very close eye on places like Key West.

A cheer went up, echoed from the crowd further up the coastline on Mallory Square, as the sun finally plunged into the sea, filling the whole sky with deep scarlet for a couple of minutes before the velvet darkness took over.

'What's the deal, James?' Nannie asked in almost a whisper.

They drew together, their heads lowered over the seafood. He told them that until midnight, at least, they should all be seen around.

'We'll stroll out into town, have dinner somewhere, and then come back to the hotel. Afterwards I want us each to leave separately. Don't use the car, and keep an eye out for anyone following you. Nannie, you're trained in this kind of thing so you can brief Sukie, tell her the best way to avoid suspicion. I have my own plans. The most important thing is that we rendezvous at Garrison Bight, aboard *Prospero*, around one in the morning. Okay?'

Bond noticed a small furrow of concern between Nannie's eyes. 'What then?' she asked.

'Has Sukie looked at the charts?'

'Yes and it's not the easiest trip by night.' Sukie's eyes were expressionless. 'It's a challenge, though. The sandbars are not well marked and we'll have to show a certain amount of light to begin with. Once we're beyond the reef it's not too bad.'

'Just get me to within a couple of kilometres of the island,' Bond said with a hint of authority, looking straight into her eyes.

They finished their drinks and rose to leave, sauntering casually from the deck. At the door to the bar, Bond paused and asked the others to wait for a moment. He went back to the rails and looked down into the sea. Earlier he had noticed the hotel's little pull-start speed boat making trips close to the beach. It was still there, tied up between the wooden piles of the pier. Smiling to himself, he rejoined Sukie and Nannie, and they went through the bar, where the pianist was now playing *Bewitched*. A small dance floor had been set up on the beach, and a three-man combo had started to pound out rhythms. The paths were lit by shaded lamps, and people were still swimming, diving into the floodlit pool, laughing with pleasure.

They strolled, arms linked – one on each side of Bond – down Duval, looking at shop windows and peering into the restaurants, all apparently full to capacity. A crowd stood in front of the light grey, English-looking church, staring across the road at half a dozen youngsters who were breakdancing to the music of a ghetto-blaster in front of Fast Buck Freddie's Department Store.

Eventually, they retraced their footsteps and found themselves in front of Claire, a restaurant that looked both busy and exceptionally good. They walked up to the maître d', who was hovering by a tall desk in the small garden outside the main restaurant.

'Boldman,' said Bond. 'Party of three. Eight o'clock.'

The maitre d' consulted his book, looked troubled and asked when the booking had been made.

'Yesterday evening,' Bond said with conviction.

'There seems to be some error, Mr Boldman . . .' the bemused man retorted, a little too firmly for Bond's liking.

'I reserved the table specially. It's the only night we can make this week. I spoke to a young man last night and he assured me I had the table.'

'Just one moment, sir.' The maître d' disappeared into the restaurant and they could see him in agitated conversation with one of the waiters. Finally he came out, smiling. 'You're lucky, sir. We've had an unexpected cancellation . . .'

'Not lucky,' Bond said with his jaw clenched. 'We had a table reserved. You're simply giving us our table.'

'Of course, sir.'

They were shown to a corner table in a pleasant white room. Bond took a seat with his back to the wall and a good view of the entrance. The table-cloths were paper, and there were packets of crayons beside each plate. Bond doodled, drawing a skull and crossbones. Nannie had sketched something vaguely obscene, in red. She leaned forward.

'I haven't spotted anyone. Are we being watched?'

'Oh yes,' Bond said with a knowing smile as he opened the large menu. 'Two of them, working each side of the street. Possibly three. Did you notice the man in a yellow shirt and jeans, tall, black and with a lot of rings on his fingers? The other's a little chap, dark trousers, white shirt, with a tattoo on his left arm – mermaid being indecent with a swordfish, by the look of it. He's across the street now.'

'Got 'em,' Nannie said as she turned to her menu.

'Where's the third?' asked Sukie.

'An old blue Buick. Big fellow at the wheel, alone and cruising. Not easy to tell, but he's been up and down the street a lot. So have others, but he was the only one who didn't seem to take any interest in people on the sidewalks. I'd say he was the backup. Watch out for them.'

A waiter appeared and took their order. They all chose Conch chowder, the Thai beef salad and, inevitably, Key lime pie. They drank a Californian champagne, which slightly offended Bond's palate. They talked constantly, keeping off their plans for the night.

When they were out on the street again, Bond told them to be wary.

'I want you both there, on board and with nobody on your backs, by one o'clock.'

As they walked west towards the Front Street intersection, the man in the yellow shirt kept well back on the other side of the street. The tattooed man let them pass him, then overtook them and let them pass again before they got back to the Pier House. The blue Buick had cruised by twice, and was parked outside the Lobster House, almost opposite the main entrance to the hotel.

'They have us well staked out,' Bond murmured as they crossed the street and walked up the drive to the main entrance. There they made a great show of saying goodnight.

Bond was taking no chances. As soon as he got to his room he checked the old, well-tried traps he had laid. The slivers of matchstick were still wedged into the doors of the clothes cupboards and the threads on the drawers were unbroken. His luggage was also intact. It was ten-thirty, time to move. He doubted if SPECTRE's surveillance team would expect anyone to make a move before the early hours. He had not let the others know that he had slipped the spare charts from *Prospero* inside his jacket before they left the boat that afternoon. Now he spread them out on the round glass table in the centre of his sitting room and began to study the course from Garrison Bight to Shark Island, making notes. When he was satisfied that he had all the compass bearings correct, and a very good idea of how he could guide a boat to within safe distance of the island, Bond began to dress for action.

He peeled off the T-shirt and wriggled into a light black cotton rollneck from his case. The jeans were replaced by a pair of black slacks, which he always packed. Next, he took out the wide belt which had been so useful when Der Haken had him locked up in Salzburg. He removed the Q Branch Toolkit and spread the contents out on the table. He checked the small explosive charges and their electronic connectors, adding from the false bottom of his second briefcase four small flat packets of plastique explosive, each no larger than a stick of chewing gum. Into the inner pockets of the belt he fitted four small lengths of fuse, some extra thin electric wire, half a dozen tiny detonators, a miniature pin-light torch, not much larger than the filter of a cigarette – and one other very important item.

Together the explosives would not dispose of an entire building, but they could be useful with locks or door hinges. He buckled on the belt, threading it through the loops on his trousers, then opened up the shoulder bag which contained the wet suit and snorkelling equipment. Sweating a little, he struggled into the wet suit and clipped the knife into place on the belt. The ASP, two spare magazines, the charts and the baton he put into the waterproof pouch threaded on to the belt. He carried the flippers, mask, underwater torch and snorkel in the shoulder bag.

Leaving the suite, he kept inside the hotel for as long as possible. There was still a great deal of noise coming from the bars, restaurant and makeshift dance floor and he finally emerged through an exit on the ocean side of the festivities.

Squatting down with his back against the wall, Bond unzipped the shoulder bag and pulled on the flippers, then slowly edged himself towards the water. The music and laughter were loud behind him as he climbed over the short stretch of rock marking the right-hand boundary of the hotel bathing area. He washed the mask out, slipped it on and adjusted the snorkel. Grasping the torch, he slid straight down into the water. He swam gently round the metal shark guard which protected swimmers using the hotel beach. It took about ten minutes to find the thick wooden piles under the Havana Docks bar deck, but he surfaced only a couple of metres from the moored motor boat.

Any sound he made clambering aboard would not have been heard above the noise coming from the hotel, and once inside the neat little craft, he could quickly check the fuel gauges with the pin-light torch. The beach staff were efficient and the tank had been filled, presumably ready for the next morning's work.

He cast off using his hands to manoeuvre the speed boat from under the pier. He then allowed it to drift, occasionally guiding it with the flat of his hand in the water, heading north, into the Gulf of Mexico, silently passing the Standard Oil pier.

The boat was about a kilometre and a half out

when Bond switched on the riding lights. He moved aft to prime and start the motor. It fired at the first pull, and he had to scramble quickly forward and swing himself behind the wheel, one hand on the throttle. He opened up, glancing down at the small luminous dial on the compass, and silently thanked the Pier House for the care they took in keeping the boat in order.

Minutes later, he was cruising carefully along the coast, fumbling with the pouch to pull out the charts and take his first visual fix. He could not risk running the speed boat at anywhere approaching its full speed. The night was clear, and the moon was up, but Bond still had to peer into the dark water ahead. He spotted the exit point from Garrison Bight and began negotiating the tricky sandbars, cruising slowly, occasionally feeling the shallow draught of the boat touch the sand. Twenty minutes later he cleared the reef and set course for Shark Island.

Ten minutes passed, then another ten, before he caught a glimpse of lights. Soon afterwards he cut the engine and drifted in towards shore. The long dark slice of land stood out against the horizon, twinkling with lights from buildings set among trees. He leaned over, washed out his mask again, took up the torch, and, for the second time that night, dropped into the sea.

He remained on the surface for a while, judging that he was a couple of kilometres off shore. Then he heard the drumming of engines and saw a small craft rounding the island to his left, searching the waters with a powerful spotlight. Tamil Rahani's regular patrol, he thought. There would be at least two boats like this keeping a constant vigil. He took in air and dived, swimming steadily but conserving energy against any emergency.

He surfaced twice on the way in, to discover the second time that they had found the speed boat. The patrol craft had stopped and voices drifted over the water. He was less than a kilometre from shore and he was concerned now about the possibility of meeting sharks. The island would hardly be named after the creatures were they not known to haunt its vicintiy.

Suddenly he came up against the heavy wire mesh of shark guard, around sixty metres from the beach. Clinging on to the strong metal, he could see lights shining brightly from picture windows in a large house. There were floodlights in the grounds. Looking back, he saw the spotlight from the patrol boat and heard its engine rise again. They were coming to look for him.

He heaved himself up on to the metal bar that topped the protective fence. One flipper caught awkwardly in the mesh, and he lost a few precious seconds disentangling himself before finally lowering his body into the water on the far side.

Again, he dived deep, swimming a little faster now that he was almost there. He had gone about ten metres when instinct warned him of danger: something was close by in the water. Then the bump jarred his ribs, throwing him to one side.

Bond turned his head and saw swimming beside him, as though keeping station with him, the ugly, wicked snout of a bull shark. The protective fence was not there to keep the creatures out but to make sure that an island guard of sharks remained close inshore – the favourite hunting ground of the dangerous bull shark.

The shark had bumped him but had not attempted to turn and attack, which meant that it was either well fed or had not yet sized up Bond as an enemy. He knew his only salvation was to remain calm, not to antagonise the shark, and certainly not knowingly to transmit fear – though he was probably doing that at the moment.

Still keeping pace with the shark, he slid his right hand down to the knife handle, his fingers closing around it, ready to use the weapon at a second's notice. He knew that on no account must he drop his legs. If he did that, the shark would recognise him immediately as prey, and the bull shark could move like a racing boat. The most dangerous moment lay ahead, and not very far ahead, when he reached the beach. There Bond would be at his most vulnerable.

As he felt the first touch of sand under his belly, he was aware of the shark dropping back. He swam on until his flippers began to churn sand. In that moment, he knew the shark was behind him, probably even beginning to build up speed for the strike.

Later Bond thought he had seldom moved as quickly in water. He gave a last mighty push forward, bringing his feet down, then he raced for the beach, in an odd splay-footed, hopping run made necessary by the flippers. He reached the surf and rolled to the left just in time. The bull shark's snout, jaws wide and snapping, broke through the foaming water, missing him by inches.

Bond continued to roll, trying to propel himself

forward, for he had heard of bull sharks coming right out of the water to attack. Two metres up the beach, he lay still, panting, feeling his stomach reel with a stab of fear.

Instantly his subconscious told him to move. He was on the island, and heaven alone knew with what other guardians SPECTRE had surrounded their headquarters. He kicked off the flippers and ran forward, crouching, to the first line of palms and undergrowth. There he squatted to take stock. First he had to dump the mask, snorkel and flippers. He pushed them under some bushes. The air was balmy and the sweet smell of night-blooming tropical flowers came to his nostrils.

He could detect no sounds of movement coming from the grounds, which were well-lit and laid out with paths, small water gardens, trees, statues and flowers. A low murmur of voices came from the house. It was built like a pyramid lifted high above the ground on great polished steel girders. He could make out three storeys, each with a metal balcony running around the whole of the building. Some of the large picture windows were partly open, others had curtains drawn across them. On top of the building a forest of communications aerials stretched up like some avant-garde sculpture.

Gently, Bond reached into the waterproof pouch and drew out the ASP, slipping off the safety catch. He was breathing normally now, and using the trees and statues for cover he moved stealthily and silently towards the huge modern pyramid. As he got closer, he saw there were several ways into the place. A giant spiral staircase running up through the centre and three sets of metal steps, one on each side, which zig-zagged from one balcony to the next.

He crossed the last piece of open ground and stood to listen for a moment. The voices had ceased; he thought he could hear the patrol boat, far out to sea. Nothing else.

Bond began to climb the open zig-zagging stairs to the first level, his feet touching the fretted metal noiselessly, his body held to the left so that his right hand, clutching the ASP, was constantly ready. Standing on the first terrace, he waited, his head cocked. Just ahead of him there was a large sliding picture window, the curtains only partially drawn, and one section open. He crossed to the window and peered in.

The room was white, furnished with glass tables, soft white armchairs, and valuable modern paintings. A deep pile white carpet covered the floor. In the centre was a large bed, with electronic controls that could adjust any section to any angle, to improve the comfort of the patient who now lay in it.

Tamil Rahani was propped up with silk-covered pillows, his eyes closed, and his head turned to one side. Despite the shrunken face with skin the colour of parchment, Bond recognised him immediately. On their previous meetings, Rahani had been smooth, short and dapper, attractive in a military kind of way. Now the heir to the Blofeld fortune was reduced to this human doll, dwarfed by the seductive luxury of the high-tech bed.

Bond slid open the window, and stepped inside. Moving like a cat to the end of the bed, he gazed down on the man who controlled SPECTRE.

Now I can have him, he thought. Now, why not? Kill him now and you may not ruin SPECTRE, but at least you'll decapitate it – just as its leader wants you decapitated.

Taking a deep breath, Bond raised the ASP. He was only a few steps from Rahani's head. One squeeze of the trigger and it would be obliterated, and he could be away, hiding in the grounds until he found a way to get off the island.

As he began to squeeze the trigger, he thought he felt a small gust of air on the back of his head.

'I don't think so, James. We've brought you too far to let you do what God's going to do soon enough.' The voice came from behind him.

'Just drop the gun, James. Drop it, or you'll be dead before you can even move.'

He was stunned by the voice. The ASP fell with a noisy thump to the floor and Tamil Rahani stirred and groaned in his sleep.

'Okay, you can turn around now.'

Bond turned to look at Nannie Norrich, who stood in the window, an Uzi machine pistol held against her slim hip.

18

MADAME AWAITS

'I'M SORRY IT had to be like this, James. You lived up to your reputation. Every girl should have one.'

The grey eyes were as cold as the North Sea in December, and the words meant nothing.

'Not as sorry as I am.' Bond allowed himself a smile which neither the muzzle of the Uzi, nor Nannie Norrich deserved. 'You and Sukie, eh? You really did take me in. Is it private enterprise, or do you work for one of the organisations?'

'Not Sukie, James. Sukie's for real,' she replied flatly. Any feelings she might have had were well under control. 'She's in bed at the Pier House. I slipped her what the old gumshoe movies would call a Mickey Finn – a very strong one. We had coffee on room service after we left you. And I provided a service of my own. You'll be long gone by the time she wakes up. If she does wake up.'

Bond glanced at the bed. The shrunken figure of Tamil Rahani had not moved. Time. He needed time. Time for some fast talking, and a little luck. He tried to sound casual.

'Originally, a Mickey Finn was a laxative for horses. Did you know that?'

'She took no notice. 'You look like a black Kermit the Frog in that gear, James. It doesn't suit you, so – very slowly – I want you to take it off.'

Bond shrugged. 'If you say so.'

'I do, and please don't be foolish. The tiniest move and I won't hesitate to take your legs off with this.' The muzzle of the Uzi moved a fraction.

Slowly, and with a certain amount of difficulty, Bond began to take off the wet suit. All the time, he tried to keep her talking, picking questions with care.

'You really did have me fooled, Nannie. After all, you saved me several times.'

'More than you know.' Her voice was level and emotionless. 'That was my job, or at least the job I said I'd try to do.'

'You wasted the German – what was his name? Conrad Tempel – on the road to Strasbourg?'

'Oh, yes, and there were a couple before that who had latched on to you. I dealt with them. On the boat to Ostend.'

Bond nodded, acknowledging that he knew about the men on the ferry. 'And Cordova – the Rat, the Poison Dwarf?'

'Guilty.'

'The Renault?'

'That took me a little by surprise. You helped a great deal, James. Quinn was a thorn in the flesh, but you helped again. I was simply your guardian angel. That was my job.'

He finally pulled off the wet suit, standing there in the black slacks and rollneck.

What about Der Haken? The mad cop.'

Nannie gave a frosty smile. 'I had some help there. My own private panic button – Der Haken was briefed; he thought I was a go-between for himself and SPECTRE. When he had outlived his usefulness, Colonel Rahani sent in the heavy mob to dispose of him. They wanted to take you as well, but the Colonel let me carry on – though there was a penalty clause: my head was on the block if I lost you after that. And I nearly did, because I was responsible for the vampire bat. Lucky for you that Sukie came along to save you when she did. But that gave me a hard time with SPECTRE. They've been experimenting with the beasts here. It was meant to give you rabies. You were a sort of guinea pig, and the plan was to get you to Shark Island before the symptoms became apparent. The Colonel wants your head, but he wanted to see the effect of the rabies before they shortened you, as they say.'

She moved the Uzi again. 'Let's have you against the wall, James. The standard position, feet apart, arms stretched. We don't want to find you're carrying any nasty little toys, do we?'

She frisked him expertly, and then began to remove his belt. It was the action of a trained expert, and something Bond had dreaded. 'Dangerous things, belts,' she said, undoing the buckle, then unthreading it from the loops. 'Oh, yes. This one especially. Very cunning.' She had obviously detected the Toolkit.

'If SPECTRE has someone like you on the payroll, Nannie, why bother with a charade like this competition – the Head Hunt?'

'I'm not,' she said curtly. 'Not on the payroll, I

215

mean. I entered the competition as a freelance. I've done a little work for them before, so we came to an arrangement. They put me on a retainer, and I stood to get a percentage of the prize money if I won – which I have done. The Colonel has great faith in me. He saw it as a way of saving money.'

As though he had heard talk of himself, the figure on the bed stirred.

'Who is it? What . . . Who?'

The voice, so commanding and firm the last time Bond had heard it, was now as wasted as the body.

'It's me, Colonel Rahani,' said Nannie respectfully.

'The Norrich girl?'

'Nannie, yes. I've brought you a present.'

'Help . . . Sit up . . .' Rahani croaked.

'I can't at the moment. But I'll press the bell.'

Bond, leaning forward, hands spread against the wall, heard her move, but knew he had no chance of taking precipitate action. Nannie was fast and accurate at the best of times. Now, with her quarry cornered, her trigger finger would be very itchy.

'You can stand up now, James, slowly,' she said a couple of seconds later.

He pushed himself from the wall.

'Turn around – slowly – with your arms stretched out and feet apart, then lean back against the wall.'

Bond did as he was told, regaining a full view of the room just as the door to his right opened. Two men entered with guns in their hands.

'Relax,' Nannie said softly. 'I've brought him.'

They were the usual SPECTRE specimens, one fair-haired, the other balding; both big muscular men with wary eyes and cautious, quick movements.

The fair one smiled. 'Oh, good. Well done, Miss Norrich.' His English bore the trace of a Scandinavian accent. The bald one merely nodded.

They were followed by a short man, dressed casually in white shirt and trousers, his face distorted by the right corner of his mouth, which seemed permanently twisted towards the right ear.

'Dr McConnell,' Nannie greeted him.

'Aye, so it's you, Mistress Norrich. Ye've brought yon man the Colonel's always raving about, then?'

His face reminded Bond of a bizarre ventriloquist's dummy as he spoke in his exaggeratedly Scottish accent. A tall, masculine-looking nurse plodded in his wake, a big, raw-boned woman with flaxen hair.

'So, how's ma patient, then?' McConnell asked as he stood by the bed.

'I think he wants to see the present I've brought for him, doctor.' Nannie's eyes never left Bond. Now she had him, she was taking no chances.

The doctor gave a signal to the nurse, who moved towards the white bedside table. She picked up a flat black control box the size of a man's wallet, attached to an electric cable that snaked under the bed. She pressed a button and the bedhead began to move upwards, raising Tamil Rahani into a sitting position. The mechanism made no more than a mild whirring noise.

'There. I said I'd do it, Colonel Rahani, and I did. Mr James Bond, at your service.' The smallest hint of triumph could be detected in Nannie's voice.

There was a tired, wheezing cackle from Rahani

as his eyes focused. 'An eye for an eye, Mr Bond. Apart from the fact that SPECTRE has wanted you dead for more years than either of us would care to recall, I have a personal score to settle with you.'

'Nice to see you in such a bad way,' Bond said with icy detachment.

'Ah! Yes, Bond,' Rahani croaked. 'On the last occasion we met, you caused me to jump for my life. I didn't know then that I was jumping to my death. The bad landing jarred my spine, and that started the incurable disease from which I am now dying. Since you've caused the downfall of previous leaders of SPECTRE and decimated the Blofeld family, I regard it as a duty, as well as a personal privilege, to see you wiped from the face of the earth – hence the little contest.' He was rapidly losing strength, each word tiring him. 'A contest which was a gamble with the odds in SPECTRE's favour, for we took on Miss Norrich, a tried and true operator.'

'And you manipulated other contestants,' Bond said grimly. 'The kidnapping, I mean. I trust . . .'

'Oh, the delightful Scottish lady, and the famous Miss Moneypenny. You trust?'

'I think that's enough talking, Colonel,' said Dr McConnell, moving closer to the bed.

'No . . . no . . .' Rahani said, scarcely above a whisper. 'I want to see him depart this life before I go.'

'Then ya will, Colonel.' The doctor bent over the bed. 'Ye'll have to rest a while first, though.'

Rahani tried to speak to Bond, 'You said you trust . . .'

'I trust both ladies are safe, and that, for once,

SPECTRE will act honourably and see they are returned in exchange for my head.'

'They are both here. Safe. They will be freed the moment your head is severed from your body.'

Rahani seemed to shrink even smaller as his head sank back on to the pillows. For a second Bond relived the last time he had seen the man, over the Swiss lake – strong, tough, outclassed – yet leaping from an airship to escape Bond's victory.

The doctor looked around at the hoods. 'Is everything prepared? For the . . . er . . . the execution? He did not even glance at Bond.

'We've been ready for a long time.' The fair man gave his toothy smile again. 'Everything's in order.'

The doctor nodded. 'The Colonel hasn't got long, I fear. A day, maybe two. I have to give him medication now, and he will sleep for about three hours. Can you do it then?'

'Whenever.' The balding man nodded, then gave Bond a hard look. He had stony eyes the colour of granite.

The doctor signalled to the nurse and she started to prepare an injection.

'Give the Colonel an hour, he'll no be disturbed by being moved then. In an hour ye can move the bed into . . . what d'ye call it? The execution chamber?'

'Good a name as any,' the fair-haired man said. 'You want us to take Bond up?' he asked Nannie.

'You touch him and you're dead. I know the way. Just give me the keys.'

'I have a request.' Bond felt the first pangs of fear, but his voice was steady, even commanding.

'Yes? What is it?' asked Nannie almost diffidently.

219

'I know it'll make little difference, but I'd like to be sure about May and Moneypenny.'

Nannie looked across at the two armed guards and the fair one nodded, and said, 'They're in the other two cells. Next to the death cell. You can manage him by yourself? You're sure?'

'I got him here, didn't I? If he gives me any trouble I'll take his legs off. The doctor can patch him up for the headectomy.'

From the bed, where he was administering the injection, McConnell gave a throaty chuckle. 'I like it, Mistress Norrich – headectomy, I like it verra much.'

'Which is more than can be said for me.' Bond sounded very cool. At the back of his mind he was already doing some calculations. The mathematics of escape.

The doctor chuckled again. 'If ye want tae get a head, get a Nannie, eh?'

'Let's go.' Nannie came close to prodding Bond with the Uzi. 'Hands above the head, fingers linked, arms straight. Go for the door. Move.'

Bond walked through the door and into a curving passage with a deep pile carpet and walls of sky blue. The passage, he reckoned, ran around the entire storey, and was probably identical to others on the floors above. The great house on Shark's Island, though externally constructed as a pyramid, seemed to have a circular core.

At intervals along the passage were alcoves in Norman style, each containing an *objet d'art* or painting. Bond recognised at least two Picabias, a Duchamp, a Dali and a Jackson Pollock. Fitting, he thought, that *spectre* should invest in surrealist artists.

They came to elevator doors of brushed steel, curved to fit the shape of the passage. Nannie ordered him to lean back with his hands against the wall again, while she summoned the elevator. It arrived as soundlessly as the doors slid open. Everything appeared to have been constructed to ensure constant silence. She ushered him into the circular cage of the elevator. The doors closed and although he saw Nannie press the second floor button. Bond could hardly tell whether they were moving upwards or down. Seconds later the doors opened again, on to a very different kind of passage – bare, with walls which looked like plain brick, and a flagstone floor that absorbed the sound of every footstep. The curved passage was blocked off at either end.

'The detention area,' Nannie explained. 'You want to see the hostages? Okay, move left.'

She stopped him in front of a door that could have been part of a movie set, made of black metal, with a heavy lock and a tiny Judas squint. Nannie waved the Uzi.

From what he could see, the interior appeared to be a comfortable but somewhat spartan bedroom. May lay asleep on the bed, her chest rising and falling and her face peaceful.

'I understand they've been kept under mild sedation,' Nannie said with just a glimmer of compassion in her voice. 'They take only a second or two to be wakened for meals.'

She ushered him on, to a similar room where he saw Moneypenny on a similar bed, relaxed and apparently sleeping, like May.

Bond drew back and nodded.

'I'll take you to your final resting place, then, James.'

Any compassion had disappeared. They went back the way they had come, this time stopping before not a door but an electronic dial pad set into the wall. Nannie again made him take up a safe position against the wall as she punched out a code on the numbered buttons. A section of wall slid back, and Bond was ordered forward.

His stomach turned over as they entered a large, bare room with a row of deep comfortable chairs, like exclusive theatre seats, set along one wall. There was a clinical table and a hospital Gurney trolley, but the centrepiece, lit from above by enormous spots, was a very real guillotine.

It looked smaller than Bond had expected, but that was probably due to the French Revolution movies filming the instrument from a low angle, with the blade sliding down between very high, grooved posts. This instrument stood barely two metres high, making it look like a model of all the Hollywood representations he had seen.

There was no doubt that it would do the job. Everything was there, from the stocks for head and hands at the bottom, and an oblong plastic box to catch them once dismembered, to the slanting blade waiting at the top between the posts.

A vegetable – a large cabbage, he thought – had been jammed into the hole for the head. Nannie stepped forward and touched one of the upright posts. He did not even see the blade fall, it came down so fast. The cabbage was sliced neatly in two and there was a heavy thud as the blade settled. It was a macabre and unnerving little episode.

'In a couple of hours or so . . .' Nannie said brightly.

She allowed him to stand for a minute, to take in the scene. Then she pointed him towards a cell door at the far side of the chamber, similar to those in the passage. It was directly in line with the guillotine.

'They've done it quite well, really,' said Nannie, almost admiringly. 'The first thing you'll see when they bring you out will be Madame La Guillotine.' She gave a little laugh. 'And the last thing too. They'll do you proud, James. I understand that Fin is to do the honours, and he's been instructed to wear full evening dress. It'll be an elegant occasion.'

'How many have received invitations?'

'Well, I suppose there are only about thirty-five people on the whole island. The communications people and guards will be working. Ten, possibly thirteen if you count me, and should the Colonel want the hostages present, which is unlikely . . .'

She stopped abruptly, realising that she was giving away too much information. Quickly she regained her composure. It did not matter if he knew or not. In two hours the blade would come thudding down, separating Bond's head from his body in a fraction of a second.

'Into the cell,' she said quietly. 'Enough is enough.' As he passed through the door she called, 'I suppose I should ask if you have a last request.'

Bond turned and smiled. 'Oh, most certainly, Nannie, but you're in no condition to supply it.'

She shook her head. 'I'm afraid not, my dear James. You've had that already – and very pleasant it was. You might even be pleased to hear that Sukie was furious. She's absolutely crazy about you. I should have brought her along. She would have been glad to comply.'

'I was going to ask you about Sukie.'

'What about her?'

'Why haven't you killed her? You're a pro. You know the form. I would never have left someone like Sukie lying around, even in a drugged stupor. I'd have made sure she was silenced for good and all.'

'Maybe I have killed her. The dosage was near lethal.' Nannie's voice dropped, sounding slightly sad. 'But you're quite right, James. I should have made certain. There's no room for sentiment in our business. But . . . well, I suppose I held back. We've been very close, and I've always managed to hide my darker side from her. You need someone to like you, when you do these kind of things: you need to be loved, or don't you find that? You know, when I was at school with Sukie – before I discovered men – I was in love with her. She's been good to me. But you're right. When we've finished with you, I shall have to go back and finish her too.'

'How did you manage to engineer that meeting between Sukie and me?'

Nannie gave a tiny explosion of laughter. 'That really was an accident. I was playing it very much by ear. I knew where you were because I'd stuck a homer on your Bentley. I had it done on the boat. Sukie really did insist on making that part of the journey alone, and you *did* save her. I was going to set up something, depending where you were staying because I knew you were heading towards

Rome, as she was. It's funny, but the pair of you played right into my hands. Now, anything else?'

'Last requests?'

'Yes.'

Bond shrugged. 'I have simple tastes, Nannie. I also know when I'm beaten. I'll have a plate of scrambled eggs and a bottle of Tattinger – the '73, if that's possible.'

'In my experience, anything's possible with SPEC-TRE. I'll see what I can do.'

She was gone, the cell door slamming shut with a heavy thump. The cell was a small room, bare but for a metal bed covered with one blanket. Bond waited for a moment before going to the door. The flap over the Judas squint was closed, but he would have to be quick and careful. The silence of the place was against him; someone could be outside the door without his even knowing it.

Slowly, Bond undid the waistband of his slacks. Very rarely did he leave things to chance these days. Nannie had removed his belt and found Q Branch's Toolkit. The extra piece of equipment he had taken from his briefcase back at the Pier House had been the spare one he now needed. The black slacks were also made by Q Branch, and contained hidden compartments stitched into the waistband. They were well nigh undetectable. It took him just over a minute to remove the equipment from its secure hiding places. At least he knew there was a fair chance of his being able to release the cell door so that he could get as far as the execution chamber. After that, who knew?

He reckoned he had half an hour before they brought the food. In that time he must establish whether he could open the cell door. For the second time in a matter of days he went to work with the picklocks.

Unexpectedly, the cell lock was simple, a straightforward mortice that could be manipulated easily by two of the picks. He had it open and closed again in less than five minutes. Opening it the second time, he pushed at the cell door and walked out into the execution chamber. It was eerie, with the guillotine standing there in the centre of the room. He began a reconnaissance, and soon discovered he could find the main door only because he remembered roughly where it was located. It was operated electronically and fitted so well into the wall that it appeared to be part of it. If he placed the explosives correctly he might just do it, but the chances of finding the right position to blow the electronic locks would be more a matter of luck than judgment.

He returned to the cell, locked the door behind him and pushed the Toolkit out of sight under the blanket. He realised that the chances of blowing the execution chamber door were remote.

Bond racked his brains in an attempt to come to some resolution. He even considered destroying the guillotine itself. But he knew that this would be a hopeless act of folly, and a waste of good explosives. They would still have him, and there was more than one way of separating a man from his head.

The food was brought to him by Nannie herself, with the balding guard in attendance, the knuckles of his hands white as he grasped the Uzi.

'I said nothing was impossible for SPECTRE,'

Nannie said without smiling as she indicated the Taittinger.

Bond simply nodded, and they left. As the cell door was closing, he felt he had been given one tiny morsel of hope. He heard the balding man mumble to Nannie,

'The old man's sleeping. We're going to bring him through now.'

Rahani was to be brought up in good time, so that he could wake from his medication already in position. As long as the nurse did not stay with him. Bond might just do it. The idea now formed in his mind as he ate the scrambled eggs and drank the champagne. He was glad he had asked for the '73. It was an excellent year.

He thought he could hear sounds from the other side of the door and he put his ear hard against the metal, straining to catch the slightest noise. Almost by intuition, he knew there was somebody approaching the door.

Quickly Bond stretched himself on the bed, still alert for any sound, until he was sure that he heard the Judas squint move back and then into place again. He counted off five minutes, then took out the Toolkit, leaving the explosives and detonators hidden for the time being. For the second time, he went to work on the lock. When the door swung open he found the chamber in darkness but for the glow of a bedside lamp, by which he could just see Tamil Rahani's electronically operated bed.

He crossed the chamber swiftly. Rahani lay silent and sleeping. Bond touched the control pad for the bed, discovered that its wire came from below the mattress, and followed it under the bed.

What he saw gave him hope, and he crossed back to the cell to fetch the Toolkit, explosives and pinlight torch.

He slid quickly under the bed on his back, and in the darkness sought out the small electronic sensor box which moved the bedhead up and down to raise and lower Rahani. The cable ran to a switching box, bolted more or less centrally on to the underside of the bed. From it a power lead was laid to a mains plug in the wall. Wires ran from the switching box to the various sensors which adjusted each section to different angles. He was interested in the wires which connected the switching box to the bedhead sensor. Stretching forward cautiously, Bond turned off the power switch in the wall and then began to work on the slim bedhead sensor wires.

First he cut them and trimmed off about a centimetre of their plastic coating. Then he collected together every piece of plastic explosive he had managed to bring in. This he moulded to the edge of the sensor, finally inserting an electronic detonator, its two wires hanging loose and short from the plastique.

All that remained now was to plait together the wires as before, only this time adding a third wire to each pair – the wires from the detonator. In the Toolkit there was a minute roll of insulating tape no wider than a single book match. It took a little time, but he succeeded in insulating one set of wires from the others, thereby making sure that no bare wire could touch another by somebody moving the bed.

Finally, he gathered up all the contents of the

Toolkit, turned on the mains power again and returned to the cell. He locked the door with the picks and once more hid the Toolkit.

The relatively small amount of explosives should be detonated the moment anyone pressed the control buttons to raise the bedhead. When – and he had to admit if – his device worked, he would have to move like lightning. Now he could only wait and hope.

It seemed like an eternity before he heard, quite suddenly, the key in the cell door. The fair-haired guard call Fin stood there in full evening dress and white gloves. Behind and to his right the balding man – also in tails – carried a heavy silver dish. They were going to do this in style, Bond thought. His head would be presented to the dying Tamil Rahani on a silver charger, in imitation of the old legends and myths.

Nannie Norrich appeared from behind the balding man and for the first time Bond saw her, under the glare of the lights, probably in her true persona. She wore a long dark dress, her hair loose and her face so heavily made up that it looked more like a tartish mask than the face of the charming woman he thought he had known. Her smile was a reflection of ugly perversity.

'Madame La Guillotine awaits you, James Bond,' she said.

He squared his shoulders and stepped into the chamber, quickly taking in the entire scene. The sliding doors were open, and he saw something he had missed before – a small shutter in the wall next to them, now open and revealing a dial pad identical to the one in the passage.

Two more big men had joined the party and were standing just inside the door, each with the familiar stony expression, one carrying a hand gun, the other an Uzi. Another pair, also with hand guns, were positioned near Rahani's bed, as were Dr McConnell and his nurse.

'She awaits you,' Nannie prompted, and Bond took a further step into the room. It hasn't worked, he thought. Then he heard Rahani's voice, weak and thin from the bed.

'See . . .' he whined, 'must see. Raise me up.' And again, stronger, 'Raise me up!'

Bond's eyes flickered round the group once more. The nurse reached for the control.

He saw as if in close-up her finger press the button that would raise the bedhead. Then hell and confusion exploded in the room.

19

DEATH AND DESTRUCTION

FOR A FEW seconds, Bond could not be certain that
he had heard an explosion, though he was aware of
a great blast of scorching air pushing him backwards. After the flash it was as though somebody
had clapped cupped hands over his ears.

Time stood still. Everything took on a dreamlike
quality, the scene apparently enacted in slow
motion. In reality, events were moving at high
speed and two thoughts were repeated over and
over in Bond's mind – survive, and save May and
Moneypenny.

He saw the remains of Rahani's bed blazing in
the far corner to his right. There was nothing left of
Rahani himself. Pieces of him had been spattered
over the doctor, the nurse and the two guards who
had been standing close to the explosion. He was
aware of the doctor suddenly pitching forward into
the fire where the centre of the bed had been. The
nurse stood petrified, her head back, clothes ripped
from her burned body. From her mouth came a
drawn-out, strangled scream before she too fell
towards the fire.

The two guards had been lifted up and hurled across the room, one towards the guillotine, the other with one arm half-severed and flapping, towards the man with the Uzi stationed by the door. He was knocked back against the door, his arm jerking forward so that the Uzi skated across the floor to land just in front of the guillotine, on the opposite side to Bond. The fourth guard appeared to be unhurt but dazed, his hand limp. He let go of his pistol and it slid, spinning towards Bond.

Bond had stepped back into the cell as the nurse reached for the control. In spite of the ringing in his ears, and the dazzle in his eyes, he had been shielded from the blast. Now, still unable to see or hear properly, he stepped out automatically from the cell and stood like a man mesmerised, staring at the pistol sliding towards him. Then he flung himself at the weapon and was on his belly, hand grasping at the pistol, rolling and firing as he rolled, first at the remaining guard near the door, then at Fin and the balding man. Two rounds apiece, in the approved service fashion.

He heard the shots as tiny pops in his ears and knew he had scored with each round. The guard by the door went spinning backwards. Fin's white evening shirt was suddenly patterned with blood. The balding man sat splay-legged on the floor clutching his stomach, a surprised look on his face.

Bond span round, looking for Nannie. She was making a dive for the Uzi on the far side of the guillotine. She took the shortest route, her body flat on the ground, arms reaching across the stocks. He saw her hands close on the weapon just as he flung himself towards the guillotine, his arms lifted, and struck the projecting lever.

Even through his deafness, Bond heard the appalling thud and the awful scream as the blade sliced through Nannie's arms. He was conscious of the spurting blood, the never-ending scream and the fact that the fire was now pouring out thick, dark smoke. He paused only to grab the Uzi and shake off the detached arms with their hands clamped around the weapon. It took two hard shakes to free them from the machine pistol. Then he was outside in the passageway, which was also rapidly filling with smoke.

Turning, Bond looked at the electronic locking pad set into the wall. It seemed to be a simple numerical device, but then he saw that the bottom row contained red buttons and was marked 'Time lock'. There was a small strip of printed instructions below them: *Press Time button. Press Close. When doors shut press number of hours required. Then press Time button again. Doors will remain inoperable until period of time set has elasped.*

His fingers stabbed at the Time, then Close buttons. The doors slid shut. He pressed Two . . . Four . . . Time. Everyone in the execution chamber was either dead or dying anyway. Putting the doors on a twenty-four hour time lock just might hold back the fire. Now for the hostages.

As he ran for the cell containing May, alarm bells began to ring. Bond could hear them well enough. Either the fire had set them off, or someone still with strength left had activated them from inside the death chamber.

He reached the door of the first cell, looking

around wildly for any sign of a key. There were no keys. Standing well to one side Bond fired a burst from the Uzi, not at the metal lock but at the topmost hinge and the area around it. Bullets whined and ricocheted in the passage, but they also threw out great splinters of wood and Bond saw the door sag as the top part of the frame gave way. He turned the Uzi on to the lower hinge, gave it two fast bursts and leaped to one side as the slab of metal detached itself from the wall, hesitated, then fell heavily to one side.

May cowered back on her bed, eyes wide with fear, looking as though she was trying to push her body through the wall.

'It's okay, May! It's me!' he yelled.

'Mr James! Oh, my God, Mr James!'

'Just hang on there,' Bond shouted at her, realising he was raising his voice too high because of his temporary deafness. 'Hang on while I get Moneypenny. Don't come out into the passage until I tell you!'

'Mr James, how did . . .' She began, but he was away, up the passage to the next cell door, where he repeated the process with the Uzi. The passage appeared to be filling fast with smoke.

'It's okay, Moneypenny,' he shouted breathlessly. 'It's okay. It's the white knight come to take you off on the pommel of his saddle, or something like that.'

She looked grey with fear, and was shaking badly.

'James! Oh, James. I thought . . . they told me . . .'

She rushed to him and threw her arms around his

neck. Bond had to disentangle himself firmly from his Chief's Personal Assistant. He almost dragged her into the passage and pointed her towards May's cell.

'I'll need your help with May, Penny. We've still got to get out of here. There's a fire blazing along the passage and unless I'm mistaken, quite a number of people who don't really want to see us leave. So for God's sake, don't panic. Just get May out of here as quickly as you can, then do as I tell you.'

As soon as he saw her respond, he ran through the thickening smoke towards the elevator doors. *Never use elevators in the event of fire.* How many times had he seen that warning in hotels? Yet now there was no alternative. Like it or not, there appeared to be no other way out of the passage.

He got to the curved steel doors and jabbed at the button. Perhaps others were making their escape from the floors above by the same method. Maybe the mechanism had already been damaged. He could now hear the roaring of fire along the passage, behind the doors of the execution chamber.

Reaching out, Bond touched the curved metal doors and found them distinctly warm. He waited, jabbing again at the button, then checked the Uzi and the automatic pistol. The automatic was a big Stetchkin with a twenty round magazine, and he had only loosed off six shots. He tucked the almost empty Uzi under his left arm, holding the Stetchkin in readiness.

Moneypenny came slowly along the passage supporting May, just as the elevator doors opened to reveal four men in dark combat jackets. Bond took in the surprised looks and the slight movement as one of them began to reach towards a holster at his hip.

His thumb flicked the Stetchkin from single shot to automatic, and he turned his hand sideways – for the Stetchkin has a habit of pulling violently upwards on automatic fire. If turned sideways it would neatly stitch bullets from left to right. Bond fired a controlled six rounds and the four men were littering the floor of the elevator. He held up a hand to stop Moneypenny bringing May any closer. Quickly he hauled the bodies out of the cage, jamming one of them across the doors to keep them from closing while he performed the task.

In less than thirty seconds he was ushering May and Moneypenny towards the lift. It was rapidly becoming very hot, and as soon as they were inside he pressed the Down button, keeping his finger on it for five or six seconds. When the doors next opened, they were facing the curved passage leading to Tamil Rahani's room.

'Slowly,' he warned May and Moneypenny, 'take care.'

A burst of machine gun fire rattled in the distance. It crossed Bond's mind that something odd was now going on. A fire was obviously blazing above them, yet they would be the only targets for any of SPECTRE's people left on the island. Why then was there shooting going on that was not directed at them?

The door to Rahani's room was open. There was a violent burst of fire from within. Slowly Bond edged into the doorway. Two men dressed in dark combat jackets, like those in the elevator, manned a heavy machine gun set up near the big picture windows. They were firing down into the gardens. Beyond them Bond could see helicopters, their lights blinking red and green, hovering over the island. A star shell burst high in the night sky, and three sharps cracks followed by splintering glass left him in no doubt that the house itself was coming under attack.

He hoped that the men out there were on the side of the angels as he stepped into the room and placed four bullets neatly into the necks of the two machine gunners.

'Stay in the passage! Stay down!' he shouted back to May and Moneypenny.

There was a moment's silence. Then Bond heard the unmistakable sound of boots clanking up the metal steps leading to the terrace balcony. Holding the pistol low, he called to those he could now see outside the window. 'Hold your fire! Escaping Hostages!'

A burly officer of the U.S. Navy, brandishing a very large revolver, appeared at the window, followed by half a dozen armed naval ratings. Behind them he saw the white, frightened face of Sukie Tempesta, who cried out.

'It's them. It's Mr Bond and the people they were holding to ransom!'

'You Bond?' snapped the naval officer.

'Bond, yes. James Bond.' He nodded.

'Thank the Lord for that. Thought you were a gonner. Would have been but for this pretty little lady here. We've gotta move it, fast. This place will go up like a fired barn in no time.'

The leathery-faced man reached out, grasped Bond's wrist and propelled him towards the balcony, while three of his men hurried forward to help May and Moneypenny.

'Oh, James! James, it's so good to see you.' He had been thrown almost straight into the arms of the Principessa Sukie Tempesta and, for the second time in a matter of minutes, Bond found himself being kissed with an almost wild, skidding passion. This time he was in no hurry to break away.

Bond asked breathlessly what had happened as they were hustled through the gardens to the small pier. No sooner were they aboard than the coastguard cutter drew away, gathering speed. They looked back at the island. Other launches and cutters were circling, as were more helicopters, rattling their way around and keeping station with each other, some shining spotlights down into the beautifully laid out gardens.

'It's a long story, James,' Sukie said.

'Jesus!' said one of the coastguard officers through clenched teeth as the great pyramid that had been SPECTRE's headquarters spouted flame from the top of the structure, like an erupting volcano.

The helicopters had started to turn away, one making a low pass over the cutter. May and Moneypenny sat in the bows, being tended by a naval doctor. In the weird light from the Shark Island fire they both looked feverish and ill.

'She'll blow any minute,' the coastguard officer muttered and almost as he said it the building appeared to rise out of the island and hover for a second, surrounded by a sheet of dancing flame.

Then it exploded in a flash of such dazzling intensity that Bond had to turn his head away.

When he looked again, the air seemed to be filled with burning fragments. A pall of smoke hung across the little hump that had been Shark Island.

He wondered if that was really the end of his old, old enemy, SPECTRE, or whether it would ever rise again, like some ungodly phoenix from the ashes of the death and destruction which he, James Bond, had caused.

20

CHEERS AND APPLAUSE

SUKIE TOLD HER story once the cutter was inside the reef, and the sounds of waves, wind and engines grew less, so that she did not have to shout.

'At first I couldn't believe my eyes – then, when Nannie made the telephone call, I knew,' she said.

'Just take it a step at a time.' Bond was still shouting as the ringing in his ears had not yet gone.

When Sukie and Nannie had left Bond the previous evening, Nannie had ordered coffee from room service.

'It arrived while I was in the bathroom touching up my face, so I told her to pour it,' Sukie told him.

She had left the door open, and in the mirror she saw Nannie put something in her cup from a bottle. 'I couldn't believe she was really up to no good, in fact I nearly taxed her about it. Thank goodness I didn't. I remember thinking she was trying to do me a good turn and keep me out of danger. I've always trusted her – she's been my closest friend since schooldays. I never suspected there was anything like . . . well . . . She was a very faithful friend you know, James. Right up until this.'

'Never trust a faithful friend,' Bond said with a wry smile. 'It always leads to tears before bedtime.'

Sukie had dumped the coffee and feigned sleep. 'She stood over me for a long time, lifted my eyelids and all that sort of thing. She used the telephone in the room. I don't know who she spoke to, but it was quite clear what she was up to. She said she was going to follow you. She thought you might try and make it to the island without us. "I've got him, though," she said. "Tell the Colonel I've got him."

'I stayed put for a while, in case Nannie came back – which she did, and made another call. Very fast. She said you'd taken the hotel motor boat and that she was following. She told them to keep a watch for you, but that you were her prisoner and she didn't want anyone else to take you. She kept saying she'd get you to the Colonel in one piece. He could divide you. Does that make sense?'

'Oh, a great deal of sense.'

Bond thought of the guillotine blade smashing down and removing Nannie Norrich's arms.

'Terrible,' he said, almost to himself. 'Really terrible. You know, I quite liked her – even grew fond of her.'

Sukie stared at him, but said nothing, as the cutter entered the small naval base harbour.

'And who's paying for all this luxury? That's what I want to know.' May was obviously well recovered.

'The Government,' said Bond, smiling at her. 'And if they don't, then I shall.'

'Well, it's a wicked waste of good money, keeping us all here in this verra expensive hotel. Ye ken how much it's costing here, Mr James?'

'I ken very well, May, and you're not to worry your head about it. We'll all be home soon enough, and this'll seem like a dream. Just enjoy it, and enjoy the sunset. You've never seen a Key West sunset, and it's truly one of God's miracles.'

'Och, I've seen sunsets in the Highlands, laddie. That's good enough for me.' Then she appeared to soften. 'It's guy kind of you though, Mr James, for getting me fit and well once more. I'll say that. But, oh, I'm longing for ma kitchen again, and looking after you.'

It was two days after what the local newspaper called 'The Incident on Shark Island' and they had all been released as fit from the naval hospital that afternoon. Now May sat with Sukie and Bond on the deck in front of the Havana Docks bar at the Pier House Hotel. The sun was just starting its nightly show and the place was crowded. Again Sukie and Bond were eating the huge, succulent shrimps with little bowls of spicy sauce and drinking Calypso Daiquiris. May spurned both, making do with a glass of milk, about which she loudly expressed her hope that it was fresh.

'Lord, this really is the place where time stood still.' Sukie leaned over and kissed Bond lightly on the cheek. 'I went into a shop on Front Street this afternoon and met a girl who came here for two weeks. That was nine years ago.'

'I believe that is the effect it has on some people.'
Bond gazed out to sea, thinking it was the last place
he would want to stay for nine years. Too many
memories were crowded in here – Nannie, the nice
girl who had turned out to be a wanton and ruthless
killer; Tamil Rahani, whom he had really met for
the last time; SPECTRE, that dishonourable society
willing even to cheat others of promised prizes for
Bond's head.

'Penny for them?' Sukie asked.

'Just thinking that I wouldn't like to stay here for
ever, but I wouldn't mind a week or two – perhaps
to get to know you better.'

She smiled. 'I had the same thought. That's
why I arranged for your things to be brought up to
my suite, dear James.' The smile turned into a
grin.

'You did what?' Bond's jaw dropped.

'You heard, darling. We've got a lot of time to
make up.'

Bond gave her a long, warm look and watched
the sky turn scarlet as the sun dropped behind
the islands. Then he glanced towards the doors
of the bar to see the ever-faithful Moneypenny
striding in their direction and beckoning to
him.

He excused himself and went over to her. 'Signal
from M,' she said, shooting dagger-like glances in
Sukie's direction.

'Ah.' Bond waited.

'"Return soonest. Well done. M."' Moneypenny intoned.

'You want to return home soonest?' he asked.

She nodded, a little sadly and said that she could

understand why Bond might not wish to leave just yet.

'You could perhaps take May back,' he suggested.

'I booked the flight as soon as the signal came in. We leave tomorrow.' Efficient as ever.

'All of us?'

'No, James. I realised that I would never be able to thank you as I'd like to – for saving my life, I mean . . .'

'Oh, Penny, you mustn't . . .'

She put a hand up to silence him. 'No, James. I've booked a flight for May and myself. I've also sent a signal.'

'Yes?'

'"Returning immediately. 007 still requires remedial treatment that will take about three weeks."'

'Three weeks should do just nicely.'

'I thought so,' she said and turned, walking slowly back into the hotel.

'You actually had my stuff moved into your suite, you hussie?' Bond asked, once he had returned to Sukie.

'Everything you bought this afternoon – including the suitcase.'

Bond smiled. 'How can we? I mean, you're a Principessa – a Princess. It wouldn't be right.'

'Oh, we could call the book something like *The Princess and the Pauper*.' She grinned again – wickedly, with a dash of sensuality.

'I'm not a pauper, though,' said Bond, feigning huffiness.

'The price here could fix that,' Sukie said,

245

laughing, and at that moment the whole air and sky around them became crimson as the sun took its dive for the day.

From Mallory Square, where crowds always watched the sunset, you could hear the cheers and applause.

"Come in, Miss Summers, I've been waiting for you."

Dazed, Delia walked into an elegant, sun-filled office. Her worst nightmare had come true. Here was Craig Locksley. And now she knew that this meeting had always been inevitable. She'd been a fool to think she could escape him.

"Good morning, Mr. Locksley. I'm here from Orchid Cosmetics and—and—" Her confident manner faded. "I don't understand any of this. How can you possibly be here?"

"My partners have brilliant ideas, but not a lot of business sense. I provide that."

"I…get the picture," she said slowly.

"No, you don't. Your ideas of blindness come out of the nineteenth century. I have a computer that talks to me, a first-rate secretary and a mind that remembers everything."

"Everything?"

"Everything…."

From boardroom...to bride and groom!

Dear Reader,

Welcome to the latest book in our MARRYING THE
BOSS miniseries, which features some of your favorite
Harlequin Romance® authors bringing you a variety of
tantalizing stories about love in the workplace!

Falling for the boss can mean trouble, so our gorgeous
heroes and lively heroines all struggle to resist their
feelings of attraction for each other. But somehow love
always ends up top of the agenda. And it isn't just a
nine-to-five affair.... Mixing business with pleasure
carries on after hours—and ends in marriage!

Happy reading!

The Editors

Look out next month for a further novel in our
MARRYING THE BOSS series:
The Boss and the Baby by Leigh Michaels
Harlequin Romance

Beauty and the Boss
Lucy Gordon

Harlequin Books

TORONTO • NEW YORK • LONDON
AMSTERDAM • PARIS • SYDNEY • HAMBURG
STOCKHOLM • ATHENS • TOKYO • MILAN
MADRID • WARSAW • BUDAPEST • AUCKLAND

To The Guide Dogs for the Blind Association
with thanks for their help.

ISBN 0-373-15794-0

BEAUTY AND THE BOSS

First North American Publication 1999.

Copyright © 1997 by Lucy Gordon.

Printed in U.S.A.

CHAPTER ONE

'DELIA, DARLING!' The photographer advanced with his arms outstretched. 'Every time I see you, you're more beautiful. If only I could get some pictures of *you*, instead of those so-called models.'

Laughing, Delia tossed her mane of glorious black hair over her shoulder. 'Dear Max, you say that every time we meet.'

'I bet I'm not the only one who says it, either.'

It was true that Delia constantly received compliments about her looks. As assistant publicity director of Orchid Cosmetics she had the whole range of the firm's products at her disposal, but that was only part of the story.

Nature had made Delia gorgeous. She had large, dark eyes set in delicate, regular features, perfect skin and wavy black hair. Her body was tall and slender, with long, silky legs that short skirts showed off to perfection. She wasn't in the least vain about her beauty, but she knew that other people responded to it in a way that made them easy to deal with, and she'd unconsciously come to take this for granted.

Max snapped away busily at the models that had been hired to show off Orchid's new range. 'It's going to come out looking great,' he told her. 'The camera loves every lipstick and blusher, every grain of powder.'

'I hope you're right. Everyone's holding their breath about the new lines.'

Max dropped his voice. 'I hear that the publicity campaign has hit a few rough patches. Apparently the advertising agency you're using isn't up to scratch.'

'Hush!' she murmured, looking around. 'You know I can't tell tales out of school, Max.'

'Sweetie, the tales are telling themselves all over London. Lombard's is a rotten agency, and Brian won't admit it because he chose them. Not that he's exactly boasting about that. Has he managed to offload the blame onto you yet?'

Delia laid a finger over her lips, but what Max said was true. Brian Gorham, chief publicity director of Orchid, had insisted on Lombard's and was distancing himself from the choice now. It was taking all Delia's skill to sidestep his attempts to put her in the firing line, but she was determined not to let him succeed. Brian would be retiring soon, and her heart was set on his job. She knew she was young for such a promotion, but her adventurous spirit had risen to the challenge. Her motto was Nothing ventured, nothing gained.

At last they were finished. The models, make-up experts and hairdressers began scurrying around in haste to leave the studio. Max sealed his films. 'Can I drive you home?' he asked Delia.

'No, thanks. I've just bought a new car and it's the love of my life.'

'That has a melancholy sound. Don't you ever long to love something warmer than a car?'

'You mean a man?' Delia asked with a chuckle. 'Whatever for? Cars are better. They don't argue and I get my own way all the time. Bye.'

The session had run late and it was dark as she made her way to the car park. Even in the dim light her new vehicle was perfect. Delia gazed adoringly at its sleek lines before sliding into the driver's seat. It had cost her more than she could afford, but it was worth it for the sense of achievement it gave her.

Despite what she'd said to Max it was only partly true that she prized her car above her boyfriend. For the past three months she'd been dating Laurence Davison, a handsome, youngish merchant banker. She was fond of him, but she hadn't fallen in love. Perhaps it was because he admired her looks too obviously, while seeming oblivious to the rest of her. It made her wonder if he saw her only as a status symbol.

She thought of Maggie, currently visiting her, with a heart of gold and a plain face, who'd said with the frankness of long friendship, 'Delia, if there's one thing about you that gets up my nose it's your ingratitude.'

'Ingratitude?' Delia had echoed, startled. 'Whatever do you mean by that?'

'I mean that if I looked like you I'd count my blessings, not witter on about wanting to be loved for myself.'

A few minutes into her journey Laurence called her on her mobile phone. Delia answered and pulled in to the side. She always felt safer that way.

'Just finished,' she said. 'On my way home now.'

'Meet me for supper?'

'Not tonight,' she said regretfully. 'I've got a report to write when I get home.'

'Did you really have to attend this photography session?' he asked. 'Couldn't you have stayed in the office and worked on your report?'

'Maybe,' she conceded reluctantly. 'But I really needed to be sure those pictures were just right. I've got to prove I'm good enough for that job.'

'Which means I'm not going to see you tonight,' he said peevishly.

'I'll make it up to you. Tomorrow?'

'I'll give you a call,' he said, and hung up abruptly.

There were a few more calls she needed to make. Leaving the car, she took the mobile to a small greasy spoon around the corner, ordered tea, and dialled the first number. By the time she'd finished she'd been there for half an hour. As she turned the corner outside she saw signs of a small commotion. A police car was a few feet from her own vehicle, and a large policeman was trying to placate the driver of a juggernaut. Both turned as Delia approached.

'Are you the owner of this car?' the policeman demanded.

'I am.'

'I've had a complaint.'

'About *me*?' Delia's voice was a masterpiece of innocent bewilderment.

'Yes, about you, from inside the factory whose gate your car is blocking. They work through the night, and their trucks need to get in and out.'

'I've got a home to go to,' the juggernaut driver said bitterly. 'And I'd like to dump this stuff and go to it, *if* no one minds.'

'Oh, goodness, I'm terribly sorry. How could I have been so thoughtless?' She smiled at the driver. 'I'll move at once.'

He gulped, taking in her breathtaking smile and large, glowing eyes. 'If you wouldn't mind, miss,' he said unsteadily.

'Don't go far,' the policeman said. 'I want a word.'

When she'd got out of the juggernaut's way she returned and gazed up to where the driver was now sitting in the cab. 'I do hope you forgive me.'

'Yeah—well, I may have been a bit hasty. No hard feelings, then, miss?'

'None at all.' She turned her head on one side in an angle she knew flattered her. He gulped again and turned his vehicle into the gate, narrowly missing the side.

The policeman snorted. 'That's all very well, Miss Summers—'

'How do you know my—? Oh, hello, Sergeant Jones. I remember now, we've met before.'

'Several times,' he agreed.

'Be fair,' she pleaded. 'I've never hurt anyone, and I'm completely sober. Why don't you get the Breathalyser out, and I'll prove it?'

'Just a minute. Your licence, please.'

Delia produced it at once.

'How about that Breathalyser?' she said as he studied it.

'All in good time.'

'But when I think of the burglars you could be apprehending, and all I want to do is blow into your little machine, and you won't let me—'

'Miss Summers,' he said patiently, 'you've got the wrong script. *I'm* supposed to say, "Will you blow into this, please?" And *you're* supposed to say, "Yes, Sergeant!" You *don't* direct me here and there like a shepherd with an awkward sheepdog.'

She looked at him with wide, hurt eyes. 'Is that what I was doing? I'm really sorry.'

'Just blow into the machine,' he said patiently.

She did so and he studied the crystals intently, although both of them knew that the result would be negative.

'I never drink when I drive,' she declared truthfully. 'I don't know why you waste your time with me.'

He regarded her wryly. Detecting the hint of a twinkle far back in his eyes, Delia gave him the full benefit of her glorious smile. The sergeant breathed hard.

'I ought to charge you with causing an obstruction—'

'But you're not going to, are you? Not really.'

'Get out of here,' he said. 'And don't let me have to talk to you again.'

'Bless you!' She blew him a kiss.

'And that's enough of that,' he told her. 'Or I'll book you for trying to corrupt a police officer.'

He turned away, followed by her delightful chuckle, but before he reached the police car something made him stop and look back. 'Miss Summers!'

'Yes, Sergeant?'

'A word of advice. Be careful who you try it on. One day you'll meet a guy who's proof against it.'

'They don't live that long,' she told him cheerfully.

'You'll meet him. I just wish I could be there to see it.' He gave her a friendly gesture of salute and got back into his car.

His words reminded Delia of her mother, who'd often said the same thing as she watched her daughter growing up enchanting men left, right and centre—starting with her father. It was a family legend how John Summers hadn't really wanted children, but had fallen under his baby daughter's spell on the first day.

Delia could remember being held up so that she could look directly into John's eyes, shining with adoration. 'Just wait till you're grown up!' he'd said. 'You're going to be a real heart-breaker. The boys'll be standing in line.'

It had happened just as he'd predicted. From wrapping John around her little finger it had been a short step to doing the same with every other man she met. Why not? It was so easy.

Delia might have become a spoilt brat. She was saved from that fate by a kind heart and a sense of the ridiculous. But she'd lived for twenty-four years in a world that was enchanted by her looks, and she knew nothing else.

After school she'd taken beauty courses and business courses, and had finally gone to work in the publicity department of a small cosmetics company. She'd learned her trade very thoroughly, and after two years she'd moved on to Orchid, a firm that had once dominated the cosmetics market, but then slumped when its image didn't keep up with the times.

It was thrilling. The whole firm was being reorganised. New products had been invented, and everything repackaged to look bright and modern. As assistant publicity director Delia was in the thick of the struggle to market Spring Dew for the teen market, Summer Bloom for the young-to-middle-aged customer, and Autumn Glow for the older woman. After three years things were going well, she reflected, but there was still much to do. She was so preoccupied with her thoughts that she failed to notice that her speed was creeping up and up.

Suddenly she realised what was happening. She stared in horror at the speedometer, only for a moment, but that moment was enough to cause disaster. In taking her eyes from the road she'd missed an approaching bend. She slammed on the brakes, wrenching frantically at the wheel. The car turned too sharply, and skidded around the bend with a shriek of tyres. Delia fought for control but she couldn't straighten the vehicle up again. Before she knew what was happening she'd mounted the pavement, and there was a sickening thump as she hit something.

At last she managed to stop, and was instantly out of the car and running back, praying desperately.

A man was on his knees, reaching out to a shape that lay slumped in front of him. Delia's heart lurched at the stillness of that shape. The man was calling a name in a desperate voice.

'Are you hurt?' she asked breathlessly, flinging herself down beside him.

'No, I'm fine,' he said quickly. 'But *she's* hurt—Jenny!—*Jenny!*'

Then Delia saw the dog lying there. She

was a golden Labrador, a lovely animal
with a large head and pale, silky fur. But
she was frighteningly still.

'Oh, heavens!' Delia whispered. 'What
have I done?'

'Is she dead?' the man asked raggedly.
Is she dead?'

Delia put her hand over Jenny's heart,
and for the first time noticed that she was
wearing the harness of a guide dog. Startled,
she looked at the man and realised that his
eyes were blank as he reached desperately
for the animal.

To her great relief Delia could feel a
heartbeat. 'She's alive,' she said, pulling
herself together. 'If we get her to a vet
quickly she'll be all right.' She was trying
to reassure herself. Jenny's immobility
scared her.

'Stay here,' she said. 'I'm going to fetch
my car.'

She eased the car near to him and opened
the rear door. He rose, gathering the dog
carefully in his arms. Jenny whimpered.

'Here,' Delia said, guiding him to the
door. 'A little more to the right—let me
hold her while you get in.'

No,' he said with soft vehemence. He

added raggedly, 'She's uneasy with strangers.'

But Delia understood his real meaning. After what she'd done he didn't want her touching Jenny. She closed the door after them and quickly got into the driving seat.

'Tell me where to go,' she said.

He gave her the name of his vet, and the night telephone number, which she called. 'We'll be there in ten minutes,' she informed the vet.

'Who am I to expect?' he asked.

'What's your name?' she asked her passenger.

'Craig Locksley,' he said in a hoarse voice. 'Tell them it's Jenny.'

'Mr Locksley is bringing Jenny.'

She was practically functioning on automatic as she drove. If she'd allowed herself to think she would have been consumed by guilt. She'd been speeding, however unintentionally, and through her own carelessness she'd knocked down a guide dog. The sight of Jenny drooping in her master's arms had almost overcome her. She'd pulled herself together so that she could be of some use, and now she was fighting to keep calm.

Don't let her die, she prayed silently.

To her relief they arrived to find a door already open and the vet standing waiting for them. He and a nurse brought a trolley out to the car, lifted Jenny onto it and hurried in. Craig Locksley stood by the car, looking desperate.

'Can I help you get inside?' Delia asked.

'*No, thank you!*'

'But—'

'I know the layout of this place,' he said coldly. 'All you can do for me is get out of the way. In fact, leave altogether. There's nothing further for you to do.'

She stood aside and he made his way carefully to the door. Apparently he really did know the layout, because he turned in the right direction. Delia followed him inside to the brightly lit room where Jenny lay on the table. The vet was removing the harness and talking to Craig Locksley.

'A car, you say? Any idea how fast it was travelling?'

'Yes,' Delia said, and told him what had happened.

The vet pursed his lips. 'Bad,' he said. 'All right, it's best if you two wait outside. I'll do what I can.'

The man reached out to touch Jenny. At that moment she came round and raised her head to lick him. The love and trust between them was almost tangible.

'It's all right, old girl,' he whispered against her golden fur. 'I'm here.'

Jenny caressed his face with her tongue, and thumped her tail feebly. Delia looked away to hide the fact that her eyes had suddenly blurred.

'Is there somewhere I can clean up?' she asked, and the nurse guided her to the little washroom.

She was grimy from having knelt in the road. As she washed she found she was shaking. What she'd done was bad enough, but to it was added the contempt in the man's voice when he'd rejected her services. She couldn't blame him, but it was vital to speak to him again, and make him understand that she wasn't as bad as he thought.

She found him sitting in the waiting room, his head leaning back against the wall, his eyes closed. He was younger than she'd first supposed, probably in his early thirties, with a lean face that was set in a harsh look of grief and despair. She had no chance to study him further because when he heard her he sat up, immediately alert.

'I told you to go,' he said sharply. 'Nobody needs you here.'

'But—I have responsibilities, Mr Locksley. I've caused you injury—at least you must let me tell you my name, and give you my insurance details.'

He turned his head, and although she knew he couldn't see her the look of scorn he flung in her direction made her flinch.

'And what is your insurance company going to do if my friend dies?' he demanded harshly. 'Bring her back to life?'

'Your—friend?'

'You'd probably call her just a dog. What would you know about it? For seven years Jenny has given me her love and her unquestioning loyalty. She spends her life controlling her natural instincts so that she can put me first. She keeps me safe. She's there in the night. She's honest and she's *warm*.' His voice was husky.

'I'm sorry,' she faltered.

'To hell with you!' he raged. 'You're sorry! You took that bend at an insane speed—yes, I knew you were speeding long before you arrived. I could hear it. Jenny heard it. She wouldn't step into the road, but then you mounted the pavement, so she didn't have a chance. She put herself between me and your car—' He stopped and shuddered. Delia watched him in horror. 'Now she's probably dying,' he resumed after a moment. 'And you're *sorry*.'

Delia was silent. There was nothing to say in the face of so much anguish.

'Well, go on,' he sneered. 'Aren't you going to recite the next bit?'

'What—?'

'Your smooth speech about how you'll cover all the vet's bills. After all, you're a very prosperous woman. Cars that hum as sweetly as yours cost a fortune. So you'll pay my bills and think that settles it.'

'No,' she said quickly. 'At least—of course I will, but I'm not so insensitive as to say it now. You said it, not me. Why can't you give me a chance?'

'How much chance did Jenny have?'

'She won't die—I'm sure she won't. I saw a mass of advanced equipment in the vet's surgery—and there's so much they can do these days—'

'You know nothing about it,' he said flatly. 'Words to make yourself feel better won't help Jenny.'

'No, they won't. I'm sorry, I was just—'

'I know what you were trying to do. Please go now.'

'No,' she said with sudden resolution. 'This concerns me too. I'm staying until I know how she is.'

'And if I say I don't want you to, that makes no difference, does it? You've decided, and that's it, because you're the kind of woman who always does what she wants.'

'You know nothing about the kind of woman I am.'

'I would have said I know quite a lot, and none of it does you credit,' he said with bitter irony. 'You have a very high opinion of yourself. You drive fast because you expect the world to get out of your way. And you have an impatient face.'

Hot anger sprang to her lips, but she forced it back. 'Mr Locksley, I don't want to be offensive, but you don't know what my face looks like,' she said.

'Your voice is impatient. If your face doesn't reflect it yet, it soon will.'

No one had spoken to Delia like that for as long as she could remember. Whatever her mistakes she'd always been able to win swift forgiveness. But not from this man. Her beauty, the magic talisman she'd always relied on, meant nothing to him.

'I know you're angry with me,' she tried

again. 'But I did my best to put it right. I got Jenny here as fast as I could.'

'Yes, I appreciate that you're not a hit-and-run driver,' he responded in a tone of cool dismissal. 'There are plenty of people who'd simply have driven off. Just as there are plenty of people who wouldn't have hit her in the first place.'

It was hopeless. She couldn't win against his implacable judgement. Delia rose and walked out of the waiting room, unable to bear his rage and contempt. It was better to wait outside until she knew Jenny's fate.

There was a chill in the night air, but she was hardly aware of it. She felt as if she'd had a blow in the stomach. It was like becoming another person, one who could actually do something as terrible as this. She wanted to protest that this other self wasn't really her. But it was. She hated the sensation, and she wasn't sure she could cope with it.

The door opened behind her and he stood there.

'What are you doing out here?' he demanded.

'How did you—?'

'For pity's sake! It's not a conjuring trick! I didn't hear your car leave, but I could still hear your footsteps. When you stormed off I thought you'd gone for good.'

'I didn't storm off,' she protested. 'I left to relieve you of my hated presence.'

'Come inside and stop being melodramatic,' he snapped.

Having invited her in, he showed no further interest in her, but sat with his hands clasped between his knees, staring sightlessly into space. Delia found herself trying to study him without being too obvious about it, just as she would have done with a sighted person. He seemed intensely aware of everything about him, and she couldn't help feeling that if she looked at him he would know.

Craig Locksley was a handsome man: tall, with wide shoulders and an athletic build. He had dark, brilliant eyes that showed no sign of blindness. His face was lean, with vivid features and a wide, shapely mouth. There was sensitivity in that mouth, but also bitterness, she thought. She wondered how it looked when he laughed. Or did he never laugh? Had the bitterness so invaded his soul that there was no room for tenderness or joy?

She had some sort of answer a moment later, when there was the shrill of a mobile phone. He took a phone from his pocket. 'Yes?' he asked sternly.

The next moment his face had relaxed into a smile. 'Hello, darling,' he said warmly. 'Are you having a good time?'

Delia tried not to listen, but in the quiet waiting room it was impossible to avoid hearing. The man's face was transformed by love.

'I know I'm usually at home by now,' he said, 'but Jenny and I took our walk a little late tonight... Yes, she's fine...and I'm fine... No, of course I don't want you to hurry home...give my love to them both... Bye.'

As soon as he'd finished his face altered dramatically, revealing the strain of putting on a bright front when the truth was tearing him apart. Delia wondered who 'darling' was, and why he was so protective of her.

At that moment the door to the surgery opened, and the vet appeared. Jenny's fate seemed to be written all over his weary face.

'That's that,' he said heavily.

CHAPTER TWO

THEY both froze in horror, while the dreadful finality of 'That's that' tolled like a death knell.

'One of the toughest jobs I've ever done,' the vet said. 'But it's finished now, and she's very strong, despite not being as young as she was.'

Delia stared, hardly daring to hope. 'You mean—?'

'She's not out of the woods yet, but she's got through the worst. Now it's just a question of waiting.'

Craig was very pale and seemed to be holding himself in check with great control. 'Thank you,' he said with an effort. 'Thank you.'

'Go home now,' the vet advised him.

'Yes,' he said unsteadily. 'I'd better go in case Alison calls the house phone and finds me out. I haven't told her—I let her think everything was fine. I don't know how I'll explain if—'

'It probably won't happen,' the vet said firmly.

'But you can't be sure, can you?' Delia asked.

'Not yet. She's got a good chance, but she has some nasty injuries. Shall I call you a cab?'

'There's no need,' Delia said. 'I'll drive Mr Locksley home.'

He left the surgery with her. Not until they were well out of the vet's hearing did he say curtly, 'I'll get myself home. Goodnight.'

'Won't you please let me drive you?' she begged.

'It's quite unnecessary, thank you. I'm very familiar with these roads.'

He strode off down the road, moving so easily that Delia thought he might really manage alone. But suddenly he stopped. She saw him turn and reach out, feeling the hedge on one side of him, and a lamppost on the other. It was obvious that he'd become disorientated.

Delia caught up in the car, and got out to confront him. 'Mr Locksley, I'm sorry for all I've done, but I am simply not going to abandon you to walk home alone. Please get into my car. You don't have to forgive me, or even talk to me. Just don't add more damage to what I've already caused.'

He steadied himself against the lamppost. His whole attitude spoke of tension and anguish. Delia ventured to touch him, but he stiffened at once and she snatched her hand back. She opened the rear door, letting it click as audibly as she could.

'The car's just in front of you,' she said. 'The door's open. All you have to do is get in.'

Now she could hear herself as he obviously heard her—an impatient woman who gave orders. No doubt his poor opinion of her was reinforced.

He stood motionless for so long that she thought he would refuse, but at last he reached out. When he was sure it was the rear door he'd found, he got in. Delia bitterly appreciated his manoeuvres to make sure he didn't have to sit next to her.

'Can I have your address, please?' she asked as she got into the driving seat. When he'd given it she added, 'Shall I call your home in case they're worried about you?'

'There's nobody there.'

'You live alone?'

'No, I don't live alone—if it's any concern of yours. I live with my daughter, but she's away visiting her grandparents, thank goodness.'

After a few minutes she turned into a tree-lined street. His home surprised her. She'd pictured a small, neat flat, adapted for a blind person, but he lived in a large Victorian house, set back from the road. It looked rambling and comfortable.

'Thank you,' he said, getting out. 'Goodnight.'

'Not yet,' she said firmly. 'I'm going to fix you a stiff drink.'

He took a long, exasperated breath. 'Is there any way of getting rid of you?'

'Yes,' she said with spirit. 'Let me come in and see that you're all right. Try to believe that I'm really sorry. Talk to me for a while. Then I'll leave quietly.'

'Very well! On those terms.'

He was a different man in his own domain. He climbed the four steps to the front door and put the key in the lock without hesitating. At his signal Delia passed in front of him into the house and turned just in time to see him stand aside for an unseen presence. He checked himself with a sharp breath, and Delia's hand flew to her mouth as she realised that he'd instinctively made room for Jenny. But Jenny wasn't there. She was lying sedated in a darkened room, fighting for her life. He remembered it too, and his face had a withered look.

'Come in,' he said curtly.

He flicked on the light switches and showed her into a large room that looked like a library. Books lined two of the walls. A third wall was covered in posters, and the fourth was taken up by a huge bay window. A desk in the corner held a computer that Delia could see was state-of-the-art. In the centre of the room was a leather sofa. There were a couple of leather armchairs and several very large cushions scattered about. The colour scheme was autumnal, a mixture of brown, orange, biscuit and tan that was both warm and restful.

He made his way to the drinks cabinet in the corner and poured himself a stiff brandy.

'None for you,' he declared. 'You've got to drive home. You'd better have a hot drink. You've had a shock. Tea or coffee?'

'Coffee, please. Can I help?'

'Thank you, but I know my way around my own kitchen.' He left the room.

After a moment she followed him. The kitchen was bright and modern, with every possible gadget. He moved as easily as a

sighted man, putting his hand on precisely
placed objects. Some of the containers made
her smile. They were shaped like comic an-
imals, and struck a strange note with this
stern man.

'Most of this is my daughter's doing,' he
said, hearing her approach. 'It was her idea
to use the animal containers. I protested a
bit, but I can always tell exactly what I've
got hold of, from the feel. The bear is sugar,
the squirrel is tea, and the penguin is coffee.
Take this inside.'

He handed her the tray and signalled for
her to move on. His manner was authoritative, even brusque, and Delia had the feeling this wasn't just because he could relax
in his own home. Instinct told her that this
was the real Craig Locksley. His earlier hesitation had simply been due to his disorientation. Nature had designed him to command.

'Put the tray on that low table,' he said,
'and sit in the armchair by the lamp.'

'What difference does it make where I
sit?' she demanded, becoming a bit nettled.

'It's a question of acoustics,' he said, settling himself on the sofa. 'For some reason
they're clearer in that precise spot.'

'You mean it's your equivalent of turning a lamp onto my face?' she said wryly.

He gave a sudden grin, and it transformed him. 'Exactly,' he said. 'You must allow me my occasional small advantages.'

A moment later he proved how sharp his hearing was. Delia's attention was taken by a photograph on the table. She turned it towards her, the frame making a faint scratching noise. At once he said, 'That's my daughter, Alison. She's ten.'

Delia was immediately drawn to the impish little girl who sat with her arm flung around a beaming Labrador.

'The dog with her—' she began.

'Yes, that's Jenny. Alison adores her. That's why I didn't tell her anything when she called me tonight.'

The accusation hung in the air between them. To fend it off, Delia said quickly, 'She's lovely.' This was stretching the facts rather. The child looked intelligent and full of personality, but her face wasn't conventionally pretty, although it had promise for later.

'Yes, she is lovely,' he answered. 'But how would you *know*?'

'Well—I can see—' she stammered.

'Yes, you can see, but how do you know?

How do you think *I* know? I've been blind
for years. I haven't seen her since she was
small, but I know that she's beautiful. Her
heart is kind and gentle. Her soul is loving.
She has grace and compassion.'

'Things that you don't believe I know
anything about?' Delia challenged.

He was silent.

'What about your wife?' Delia asked
when she couldn't bear it any longer.

His mouth tightened. 'I'm divorced,' he
said curtly.

'And now Alison looks after you?'

'*I* look after *her*,' Craig snapped. 'Just
like any other father.'

'I'm sorry,' Delia said, mortified. 'Everything I say seems to be wrong.'

'Only because you're looking at life the
wrong way,' he said.

'I obviously don't look at it in your way,'
she said. 'How can I? You live in a different
kind of world—'

'No,' he interrupted her. 'I live in the
same world that you do. But it reaches me
in different ways. Drink your coffee. I make
very good coffee.'

The abrupt change of subject disconcerted her. While she sipped the excellent

coffee he said, 'You'd better tell me about yourself. What's your name?'

Evidently he was a man who'd never heard the word 'please', she thought.

'My name is Delia Summers,' she began.

'You sound as if you're in your twenties,' he said, with a question in his tone.

'Yes, I am.'

'Does the car belong to you?'

'When I've finished paying the instalments, yes.'

'Then you're successful in your job. What is it?'

'I'm the assistant publicity director for Orchid Cosmetics.'

'And you want your boss's job.'

'Don't tell me you can hear that as well?' she said with an edge in her tone.

'Of course. Why not? Ambition is a quality that comes across very clearly. You're efficient, and you know where you're going.'

'Except when I drive,' Delia added with a sigh.

'I purposely didn't say that. Go on about yourself. What do you look like?'

'I'm tall, slim. I have very long legs, long black hair and dark blue eyes.'

He gave a faint grin. 'And you're used to men telling you that you're beautiful.'

'That was a guess,' she insisted.

'No, it wasn't. You listed your assets lovingly. You're proud of them. From your footsteps I'd say you have high heels to set off those legs that you couldn't resist telling me were *very* long. You're probably wearing a short skirt as well so that everyone can see and admire them.'

'I have to look my best in my job,' Delia said. 'Otherwise I wouldn't be much of an advertisement for Orchid Cosmetics.'

As she said this she instinctively put her head on one side as she'd done with the truck driver. It emphasised her long neck, and made her hair swing free in glorious curves. It was most effective when combined with a half smile and a direct look through her heavy lashes. It was her automatic response when dealing with a man she wanted to win over, and it was basically as innocent as a puppy wagging its tail for approval. But when she found herself doing it now a wave of self-disgust went through her.

She glanced nervously at Craig Locksley, who seemed to know everything without being told. Would he detect her foolish attempt to charm him with her beauty, and despise her even more for it?

'Go on,' he said. 'Why have you stopped talking?'

'There's nothing more to say about me.'

'Strange. You might have told me if you're married, and whether you have children. But it never crossed your mind, did it?'

'Why don't *you* tell *me*?' she asked tensely. 'I'm sure something in my voice has already given you the answer.'

'You have no children. In fact you have no responsibilities to anyone but yourself.'

'Now there you're wrong. I have a lot of responsibility in my job—'

'Job,' he said impatiently. 'I'm talking about human responsibility—people. You've never borne a child or even cared for one. You've never loved another creature more than yourself.'

'Who would have thought my voice revealed so much?' Delia said after a little silence. If only she could get out of here, away from this man who disliked and disapproved of her. But to go now would feel like running away, and she was no quitter.

'Your choice of job reveals a great deal more,' he observed. 'But then, if you find the surface of life so agreeable, it's natural to choose to work with surfaces.'

'Well, surfaces matter,' she retorted. 'Not to you, perhaps, but to the rest of us. Of course women want to be pretty. Why blame them for it? Why not blame the men who put a premium on beauty?'

'Not all men,' he countered sharply.

'But how many are like you?'

'Not many are blind,' he agreed. 'But plenty of the sighted ones know that Shakespeare was right when he said, A fair face will wither...but a good heart is the sun and the moon. That's *Henry V* in case you want to look it up.'

'Thank you,' she said angrily. 'How kind of you to enlighten my ignorance. Now let me enlighten yours. These sensitive male creatures, looking into people's souls, are figments of your imagination. Most men look at a woman's face and figure.'

'I dare say you'd know about that,' he said affably. 'Beauty is quite a weapon, isn't it?'

'Yes,' she said defiantly.

'Tell me, have you ever had to face up to anything in your entire life? Or have those very long legs and black hair always taken care of things for you?'

'I've had enough of this,' she said angrily. 'The accident was my fault, but it doesn't entitle you to make glib judgements about me. You don't believe it, but I'm really sorry. I'd do anything to undo what I've done. Oh, I know what you're thinking—'

'Do you?'

'Yes—that it can't be undone, and I'm just trying to make myself feel better—'

'Am I as hard as that?' he murmured.

Delia hardly heard him. She'd held herself in check, but now the shock and strain were getting to her. She set her cup down sharply, jumped up and began to stride restlessly about the room.

'You don't have to tell me,' she told him. 'I know it's true. I hate myself, but what can I *do*? I'm not really the kind of person who does things like this— Oh, yes, it's easy to claim that afterwards, isn't it?'

'Is that another of the things I was going to say?' he asked wryly.

'Perhaps you're right. Perhaps I *am* this kind of person—stupid and selfish, and oblivious to everyone except myself. But I don't mean to be. I'd give anything to put the clock back to just before it happened—'

It was suddenly too much for her. She

heard her voice wobble and tried to fight back the tears, but she couldn't blot out the sense of horror. She stood with her arms crossed over her breast, fighting for control.

He was on his feet, moving the two steps towards her, taking hold of her. She tried to push him away, furious with herself for yielding to weakness, but his hands were strong. He put one arm firmly around her shoulder.

'Come and sit down,' he said.

'No, just leave me—I'll be all right—'

'I said, sit down, and don't argue.' He pulled her down onto the sofa beside him. 'That's better,' he said firmly. 'Come on, there's no need for you to cry.'

'I'm not—crying,' she said in a gasping voice.

'You sound on the verge of hysterics.'

'I'm *not*,' she said fiercely. 'How dare you say that?'

Her mind kept playing and replaying the moment of the collision, the sight of Jenny lying on the ground, the way her body had drooped when he'd raised her. It came to an end, went back to the beginning and started again.

'No!' she said huskily. 'Not again. *Please*—I didn't mean to—'

She couldn't say any more. She was heaving with sobs that wouldn't be forced back. She tried to pull out of his arms but he drew her closer while the storm of anguish raged within her. His movements were neither rough nor gentle. They were simply matter-of-fact. But his chest was broad and firm, and a curious sense of comfort began to steal over her. He despised her, but the power of his arms seemed to promise that the world could be a safe place after all.

'What did you mean—not again?' he asked.

'I keep seeing what happened—I try not to—my mind keeps going over and over it. If you only knew—'

'But I do. My mind does exactly that, and I can't escape by looking at my surroundings. It won't last. You're in a state of shock, but it'll pass soon enough.'

'You think I'm pretty shallow, don't you?'

'Let's say I don't think you're used to having to deal with unpleasantness. Now you've got to, and it's far more of a shock to you than anything you've done.'

'That isn't true,' she protested hotly.

'Isn't it? Well, maybe I'm wrong about you.'

'But you don't think so?' she demanded, stung by his dismissive tone.

He shrugged. 'Does it really matter? We met by accident, and we'll forget each other in an hour. Why should either of us care about the other's opinion?'

'No reason at all,' she said in a muffled voice.

'You're not still crying, are you? Now that's enough.' He spoke in a bracing voice, and produced a clean handkerchief, which he used to dry her cheeks. His brilliant eyes seemed to be focused directly on her. Despite their lack of expression it was almost impossible to believe that he couldn't see.

Delia felt confused. Men had studied her face before, with delight. But there was no admiration in this man's eyes. There was nothing at all. And yet...

She saw the moment when his attention was arrested. His movements slowed, and he seemed to forget what he'd started out to do. He dropped the handkerchief, and began to explore her features with his fingers. She held her breath as he softly touched her eyes, her nose, her mouth. He seemed to be lost in a dream. The strength and warmth of his hands affected her strangely. At last an almost imperceptible sigh broke from him. He lowered his hands.

'I apologise,' he said harshly. 'I had no right to do that without asking you first. Forgive me.'

'It's all right,' she said, trying to speak normally. 'I just hope you discovered what you wanted to know.'

'A good deal. You have splendid bone structure, and delicate, regular features. It's a good beginning.'

'A beginning?'

'It creates the superficial appearance of beauty, but it won't last long if you go on destroying it the way you're doing.'

This was such a let-down after what had just happened that Delia replied angrily, 'That's nonsense. I have the whole of Orchid Cosmetics to choose from, and I use everything necessary to take care of my looks.'

'Ah, yes,' he said ironically. 'Moisturisers, and softening creams, and skin food— things you put on at night and take off in the morning, and other things that you put on in the morning and take off at night. Do you really think I meant *that*?'

'Now look—'

'No, you look! Or, more importantly, feel. Put your finger tip between your eyebrows. Feel the little frown-line there. All the wrinkle removers in the world aren't going to erase that line as long as you're busy deepening it every day.

'You don't laugh enough, not really laugh. You smile politely, but you don't let yourself go with spontaneous laughter. That would make your face lighter, because it takes fewer muscles to laugh than to frown. Did you know that? Come down from your pedestal and join the rest of the world. Then perhaps the line will start to fade.'

'Well, you've got a nerve—'

'Why, because I dare to criticise you? Perhaps if you'd heard more of the harsh truth about yourself my friend might not be lying at death's door. You live in a world of surfaces, and mostly you arrange them to your own satisfaction.'

'I'm not listening to another word,' Delia said angrily. 'This is all speculation. You don't know half of the things about me that you pretend to know—'

'How can you tell what I know and don't know? Can you get behind my useless eyes and sense what's there? If you could, you might have a shock. I don't understand beauty as you mean it. What I understand best is the inner truth that lies hidden in everything.'

'Perhaps you don't judge people's inner truth as accurately as you think,' she said tensely. 'You're so sure you know *my* inner truth. Impatient and domineering. Isn't that how you see—imagine me?'

'You can say the word "see",' he told her wryly. 'I won't fall apart.'

'But that's how you think of me, isn't it?' she insisted. 'Impatient and domineering?'

'Impatient and unhappy,' he said quietly.

'Nonsense! I'm not unhappy.'

'I think a lonely woman is always unhappy.'

'What about a lonely man?' she threw at him.

'I wouldn't know. I'm not lonely. I have my daughter to love. But who do you love?'

'I don't love anyone,' Delia said with a touch of defiance. 'But I have plenty who love me.'

'So why are you lonely?'

'I've told you, I'm *not*.'

'Then why do you sound haunted and desperate?'

'You imagined that, and I'm not continuing this conversation. You know nothing about me. *Nothing.*'

She pulled away from him and got hastily to her feet. As she moved away he reached out for her.

'Wait!' he cried.

'I'm leaving my card on the desk beside your computer. Please let me know how much I owe you for Jenny's care. Now it's time I was going.'

'Not yet.'

'It's very late and I have a lot to do when I get home,' Delia said brightly. She wanted to run far away from this place, from this man with his eyes that saw nothing and everything.

'You can't go like this,' he said, rising to his feet. *'Delia!'*

Only later would she realise that he'd used her first name for the only time that night. All she could think of at that moment was escaping him. She almost ran to the front door, and the next moment she was out in the street.

CHAPTER THREE

'AND I couldn't bear the thought that I'd done a thing like that.'

'It probably wasn't your fault at all,' Laurence said soothingly.

'Of course it was. I was speeding, and that poor dog—'

'I thought guide dogs were supposed to protect their owners,' Laurence said coolly and with the merest hint of boredom. 'It couldn't have been doing its job properly.'

'Jenny isn't an "it". She's a she. I mounted the pavement—'

'Waiter, another bottle of wine.'

'I'm sorry if I've been boring you,' Delia said stiffly.

'Let's just say that I'm more interested in telling you how beautiful you are tonight. Of course, that's always true—'

'But what do you mean when you say it, Laurence? That my features are regular and my nose straight? Is that all beauty is?'

'I beg your pardon?' he said blankly.

'Shouldn't it have something to do with what's inside?'

He kissed her hand. 'Who cares for what's inside? I'll settle for the exquisite exterior.'

Delia frowned. 'Perhaps that's what he meant,' she murmured.

'Who?'

'Never mind.' She checked herself hastily. 'It's just that I've been doing some thinking.'

'I know you have,' he said with a sigh. 'When you're not fretting about this fellow and his wretched dog you're going off at philosophical tangents about inner meaning. You never used to be like this.'

'I know. I feel as if I'm never going to be the same person again.'

They were sitting in a very expensive restaurant in the heart of London's Mayfair. Laurence liked to show Delia off in luxurious surroundings. Tonight she was wearing an olive-green silk dress that displayed her smooth, perfect shoulders, and about her neck was a ruby pendant. Heads had turned as they'd entered, and other men had regarded Laurence with envy. It was the kind of evening they'd often spent together in perfect harmony. But tonight something was wrong.

In fact, something had been wrong every night for the last month. As Delia had driven away from Craig's house she'd felt relieved to think that he was growing distant, fading into nothing. But when she'd reached home he'd seemed to be there, waiting for her. Her exquisite apartment, her carefully chosen possessions had all looked different, as though a man who couldn't see had changed the lighting.

Next day she'd called the vet, and discovered, to her heartfelt relief, that Jenny was still holding on. But her attempt to pay the bills had been turned down. The receptionist had explained that Craig Locksley had insisted on paying every penny himself. He'd even gone to the lengths of leaving firm instructions that the vet mustn't take any money from her.

And that was no more than I expected, Delia thought wryly.

Since then she'd called twice more, and gathered that Jenny was out of danger and recovering slowly. Now, she'd thought, she really would be able to put it behind her.

A crisis at work was demanding all her attention. Gerald Hedwin, the firm's managing director, had cancelled the contract with Lombard's, the disastrous agency, and quietly made it clear to Delia that he knew Brian was to blame.

But Brian had fought back at a big publicity meeting. He'd arrived with a smooth young man called Mark, whom he'd introduced as his nephew, 'seconded to the department'. It was the first Delia had heard of it. During the meeting Brian had lost no chance to push Mark forward, and it had been clear that he had him lined up as his successor.

Mark's appearance was smooth, like his ideas and his presentation. The managing director had seemed impressed. Only Delia had been troubled by a certain slick coldness about the young man.

'For a new advertising agency we could do a lot worse than look at Calloways,' Mark said. 'They're aggressive and go-getting, and some of their recent results have been very impressive. Norrington Groceries have recently doubled their turnover, and they ascribe it to the brilliant campaign Calloways mounted.'

He thrust a folder across the table at Mr Hedwin, who studied it, giving small grunts of agreement. Delia saw Mark and Brian exchange gleeful looks. A glance at the folder showed her that the work was excellent, but she was dismayed at the way she'd been deliberately sidelined.

'Actually I'd have liked to bring them on board before,' Brian said, 'but they couldn't take us. They're very much in demand. But Mark has connections in the firm and he's been pulling strings for us.'

'Well done, Mark,' Mr Hedwin said, beaming.

Delia could see the job slipping away from her, unless she could come up with something good.

'Well, if that's everything—' Mr Hedwin began to say.

'Actually, there is one more thing,' Delia said quickly. 'I think I've found a new approach. I'd like to write some leaflets to be distributed with our goods—'

Brian laughed patronisingly. 'Tips on how to put on lipstick, the latest technique for blusher and foundation. Good solid stuff, of course, but hardly original.'

'I didn't mean just make-up techniques,' Delia said. 'I'm talking about *inner* beauty—the true beauty of the heart that creams and lotions can never replace.'

'Once women start thinking along those lines, who needs us?' Mark demanded.

'They do, if we tackle it properly,' Delia said at once. 'Look, we all know that a good complexion starts with a good diet. If a woman is eating the wrong things creams won't give her a perfect skin. Beauty comes from within physically, but also spiritually.'

'But who's interested?' Mark objected. 'Women make up to attract men, because they realise that men care most about their looks.'

'Actually,' Delia retorted, 'there are plenty of men who know that Shakespeare was right when he said, "A fair face will wither...but a good heart is the sun and the moon."' She saw that Mark was looking taken aback, and added casually, 'That's *Henry V* in case you want to look it up.'

'Shakespeare, eh?' Mr Hedwin mused. 'I like it. It's classy. Go on.'

'No lotion will keep wrinkles at bay in someone who's constantly frowning,' Delia said, warming to her theme. 'Did you know that it takes more muscles to frown than to smile? We've already put out advisory leaflets on health and diet. I'd like to write some about improving your appearance with a beautiful nature.'

'Fine,' Mr Hedwin said, 'but how are you going to translate this into extra sales?'

Delia gave him her best confident smile. 'By the way I write them.'

'Then let me see something soon.'

'I worked really hard on those leaflets,' Delia told Laurence now, as they sat over their coffee and liqueurs. 'And they came out well.'

'So what's wrong?' Laurence asked, for something in her tone proclaimed her dissatisfaction.

'It's him,' she said restlessly. 'Craig Locksley. The whole thing came from him, and I didn't even see it until it was too late.'

'You discussed the leaflets with him?'

'No, I mean all that stuff about inner beauty was his. I thought I'd been so original, and I was just parroting him.'

She didn't add that the real shock had been the discovery that she hadn't dismissed him from her mind at all. He'd been there, silently haunting her, all the time.

'Well, that's how to succeed in this world,' Laurence said comfortably. 'Take something from everyone you meet. I shouldn't have to tell *you* that.'

'Meaning that I'm a taker?' Delia asked, shocked. 'Just a taker, not a giver?'

'Hey, steady on. I only meant that you've always had that beautiful head screwed on right.'

Delia smiled mechanically. Somehow she couldn't enjoy compliments any more, and this particular compliment made her uneasy. Soon afterwards she announced that she had a headache and asked Laurence to take her home.

When her door was safely locked behind her she stripped and showered, trying to disperse something that seemed to cling to her from the restaurant. It was an atmosphere of heat and over-indulgence, of senses gorged on food, wine and the promise of heedless pleasure. It was familiar, and it had never troubled her before. But tonight she needed to wash it away.

She thought about her recent success. She'd written the leaflets in a blaze of inspiration. The words had poured out:

You've made a good start by choosing Orchid's Skin Lotion, but watch yourself in the mirror as you rub it in. Are you frowning over the troubles of the day? Forget them. Bickering with your husband will only increase the lines you're trying to banish. Forgive him if he didn't put the rubbish out. Concentrate on the kind things he's done for you. You'll be happier, and you'll be helping Orchid to help you.

There were six leaflets, each one written like that, with a subtle twist that made inner beauty appear no more than an aid to Orchid Cosmetics. The result had been so good that Mark had looked dismayed, and Brian had tried to rubbish them, until he'd realised Mr Hedwin was delighted, whereupon he'd swiftly changed tack.

So for the moment Delia was riding high, but her pleasure was spoilt by the thought of what Craig Locksley would say if he knew how she'd misrepresented his thoughts.

She couldn't banish the memory of his face that night, or the feel of his arms holding her. There'd been no tenderness, no offer of comfort. But she'd taken comfort, nonetheless, from the power that seemed to flow from him. None of the other men she knew made her feel as safe as she'd felt in those few blinding moments. This man, who didn't bother to hide his contempt, had shown her what was missing in her glittering life. He'd called her lonely, and she'd denied it. But the accusation had touched a nerve.

She'd half hoped he might contact her about Jenny's progress, but there'd been only silence. He'd wiped her from his mind, and the thought left an aching hollow inside her.

Mr Hedwin summoned her next morning. 'We've hired Calloways,' he said triumphantly.

Delia said the right things. Mark's choice of advertising agency was a setback for her, but she mustn't let it show.

'I want you to see their managing director in an hour,' he went on, 'to discuss all the publicity we currently have in train. You'll find him well informed.'

Calloways had a prestigious address in the heart of London's Mayfair, in a street of elegant stone buildings. Some had been turned into shops selling exotic antiques that bore no price tags, because anyone who needed to ask couldn't afford them. There were a couple of estate agents offering apartments priced in the millions. The rest simply bore brass plates. Calloways was one of these.

A receptionist directed her to the office of the managing director. His door was slightly ajar. Delia blinked at the name on the door plate. For a moment she'd thought she'd read 'Craig Locksley'. She pulled herself together. It was time she stopped brooding on him. She was beginning to see him everywhere.

Then a cool voice that she remembered called, 'Come in, Miss Summers. I've been waiting for you.'

Dazed, Delia walked into an elegant, sunfilled office. Her worst nightmare had come true. Here was Craig Locksley, waiting for her. And now she knew that this meeting had always been inevitable. She'd been a fool to think she could escape him.

'Good morning, Mr Locksley. I'm here from Orchid Cosmetics and—and—' Her confident manner faded. 'I don't understand any of this. How can you possibly be here?'

'My partners have brilliant ideas but not a lot of business sense. I provide that.'

'I—get the picture,' she said slowly.

'No, you don't. Your ideas of blindness come out of the nineteenth century. I have a computer that talks to me, a first-rate secretary and a mind that remembers everything.'

'Everything?'

'Everything I want it to remember.'

'You didn't remember to call me about Jenny.'

'I didn't forget. I didn't think it necessary.'

'Didn't the vet tell you I kept calling him to check her progress?'

For the first time she had him at a disadvantage. 'No,' he said after a moment. 'Nobody mentioned that.'

'I was worried about her, and so glad that she was all right. Is she here with you?'

'No, she's not up to that yet.'

Craig's secretary looked in. 'Joe and Peter say they're ready when you are.'

'Then we'll be right along. They're my partners, the Calloway brothers,' he explained to Delia. 'You'll be mostly dealing with them, but I wanted to meet you first.'

'To enjoy the joke of making a fool of me?' Delia said coolly.

'No. I wanted to find out if you still struck me in the same way as last time.'

'And do I?' she couldn't help asking.

'Don't rush me. I'll tell you later.'

'Mr Locksley, I'm here professionally. We'll both conduct our business better if we leave personal considerations out of it, and forget we ever met before.'

'You're quite right, Miss Summers.

Business first and last. Let's go.' He led her confidently along the corridor to a huge, well-lit office. There were two desks, two powerful computers and a great deal of paper strewn about. He introduced her and said, 'I've got some calls to make. I'll be back later.'

The Calloway brothers were in their forties, both bald, plain and charming. Delia found them delightful, and soon realised that, as Craig had said, they were the creative brains behind the firm's brilliant advertising concepts. They cheerfully admitted that they had only the vaguest idea about money, which was why the firm had been floundering before Craig had taken it by the scruff of the neck. He'd called in debts, renegotiated loans and launched an attack on expenses that left everyone reeling.

'Including us,' Peter Calloway said, sighing. 'He's a hard taskmaster.'

'But he saved us,' Joe chimed in. 'And he keeps us safe. Can you imagine that?'

'Yes,' Delia murmured to herself. 'I can.'

'We couldn't do without him. You don't want to be fooled by his blindness. Our bank manager's terrified of him. He says that Craig always acts as though he's doing the bank a favour.'

Delia laughed, but the words 'he keeps us safe' echoed in her head. Craig Locksley presented an even greater impression of strength than he had before.

They talked for a couple of hours. The brothers were full of terrific ideas for Orchid, and Delia began to relax. They were equally complimentary about her work, especially the leaflets.

'Nice original stuff,' Peter Calloway said. 'That's why we asked your boss if we could deal with you.'

'That—was your idea, then?'

'Actually Craig suggested it. I'm not sure how he knew you'd written them, but he seems to know everything without being told. By the way, he wants you to drop in again before you go.'

She found Craig Locksley dictating letters into a machine. He stopped when she knocked.

'I've had lunch served,' he said, indicating a trolley. 'Perhaps you'd take over.'

She served up the chicken salad and crusty rolls, setting a plate beside him on the desk. He drew in a breath and seemed to be concentrating.

'Is something wrong?' Delia asked with

a slight edge to her tone. 'My voice? My shoes? Do tell me.'

'Your perfume. It's wrong for you.'

'Really?' she said coolly.

'It's obviously expensive, but it doesn't suit your style.'

'I've set the coffee near your elbow,' she said. Not for the world would she have given him the satisfaction of asking what her style was.

He waited a moment, then a grin spread over his face. It had a derisive quality, as if he was calling her a coward for ducking his challenge.

'It was you who wrote those leaflets, wasn't it?' he demanded abruptly.

'Yes,' she said, trying not to sound as self-conscious as she felt.

He made a wry face. 'You didn't really understand a word I said that night, did you? It was just grist to the cosmetics mill.'

He didn't seem angry, more disappointed, as though she'd merely confirmed his poor opinion.

'It wasn't like that,' she protested. 'I—I didn't do it cynically.'

'But you did it.'

'I had to. It's easy for you to sit there and judge—'

'I'm not judging you. I admire your shrewdness. You wasted no time going for the jugular, and that's how to get ahead.'

'It's *my* jugular that's being gone for.' Delia defended herself. 'My boss has brought his nephew into the department at the last moment, and he's trying to manoeuvre him into the top job.'

'Which, of course, cuts across your manoeuvring.'

'I've worked very hard to earn that job. Brian's trying to give Mark an easy ride, and I'm blowed if I'll let them get away with their little tricks.'

'So you tried a few little tricks of your own,' Craig said, amused. 'Well done. A display of sincerity is the cleverest trick in the book.'

Delia bit her lip. There seemed no way past his irony.

'By the way,' he added, 'I haven't quite concluded negotiations with your boss. Tell him that my final price will be ten per cent more than he's offering.'

He thrust some figures towards her. Delia stared.

'He'll never agree to that,' she said at last.

Craig grinned like a pirate about to overrun a captured vessel. 'He'll agree when he compares the quality with what he can get from Lombard's,' he said.

'We'll see.' At once Delia drew in her breath, shocked at herself. 'I'm sorry.'

'Don't be,' he snapped. 'Talk to me as though I was a normal man, because although you may not think it that's what I am.'

Before Delia could answer a young, disapproving voice from the doorway said, *'Daddy!'*

The girl from the photograph came into the office. She had an intelligent face and a cheeky smile. She had her father's dark, brilliant eyes. But, unlike his, they showed her the world. The look she gave Delia was thorough and appraising.

'Don't take any notice of Daddy,' she said cheerfully. 'He's just acting like a bear because he's lost without Jenny.'

'I'm not lost,' Craig growled.

Alison smiled at him. It was an adult smile, protective and understanding. 'No, Daddy,' she said gently.

'And don't say, "No, Daddy," like that,' he growled. 'You don't have to humour me.'

'No, Daddy.'

At last he gave a reluctant grin. 'You're a cheeky monkey.'

Alison beamed. 'Yes, Daddy.'

'Miss Summers, this is my daughter, Alison. Alison, this is Delia Summers, from Orchid Cosmetics.'

Instantly the child's face was eager. Delia guessed she was just beginning to be interested in her appearance, and found make-up an entrancing new world.

'Are you a model?' she asked, thrilled. 'I mean, do you wear Orchid make-up so that everyone can see how terrific it is?'

'I work in the publicity department,' Delia explained.

'But they let you use everything you want?'

'Anything I want,' Delia confirmed.

Alison sighed wistfully. 'I wish I was pretty like you. I keep looking in the mirror, hoping I'll be pretty today, but it never happens.'

'But you won't discover it that way,' Delia said. 'Nobody looks pretty staring in the mirror. It's something other people see.'

'Not me,' Alison said despondently. 'My face is just wrong. Everything about it is wrong.'

'But it hasn't finished developing yet,'

Delia argued. 'Wait until you're older and it'll start to look right.'

'But isn't there something I could put on it to make it right *now*?' Alison asked anxiously.

Delia couldn't resist giving Craig an impish look to see how he reacted to this heresy in his own family. Then she checked herself with a little gasp of dismay. Suddenly she felt frighteningly helpless. She had an armoury of weapons to win a man round, but they were all useless with him.

Is that all I am? she thought with horror. A collection of tricks with nothing inside?

'You don't need to put things on your face at your age,' she said quickly. 'But here—' She reached into her bag for a tiny cologne spray she always kept with her. 'Dab a little of this on behind your ears.'

'*Perfume!*' Alison said, thrilled.

'Not perfume,' Delia hastened to say with one eye on Craig. 'Just cologne. Use it sparingly.'

She might as well have saved her breath. Delighted with her very first cosmetic, Alison began spraying it around enthusiastically.

'Keep that away from me,' Craig said

sharply. 'You shouldn't be using that muck at your age.'

Alison quietened at once, but instead of being upset at her father's unreasonable harshness, like any other child, she said quietly, 'Sorry, Daddy.' Again the hint of protectiveness was there.

He sighed. 'No, *I'm* sorry,' he said. 'I shouldn't have barked at you. Come here.'

He reached out a hand, which Alison grasped at once, and gave her a fierce hug. It was clear that she was used to coping with her father's problems. Before leaving the circle of his arms she said in a stage whisper, 'You ought to say sorry to Miss Summers too.'

'I'll be dam—what for?' he demanded. 'And don't say I'm like a bear, because I'm the most kindly man alive.'

This time Delia and Alison laughed together. To Delia's delight and surprise Craig actually looked sheepish. 'Well, maybe I'm not in the best of moods,' he conceded.

'It's not Daddy's fault,' Alison explained. 'It's because he hasn't got Jenny, his guide dog. So I have to look after him specially. But she'll be home next week, and then I'm going camping.'

'I see,' Delia said slowly, conscious that she was entering a minefield.

Alison nodded earnestly. 'She got knocked down by some stupid driver who was going too fast. Daddy says she's the sort of woman who does everything too fast, and causes a lot of harm, because she doesn't think. I hate people like that, don't you?'

'Yes,' Delia said heavily. 'I do.' It took all her courage to add, 'I'm afraid—I'm afraid the driver was me.'

The brightness drained out of Alison's face, leaving only puzzlement behind. 'What do you mean?' she asked, as if unwilling to believe it.

It was even harder to say it again, but Delia forced herself. 'I was driving the car. I hit Jenny.'

A moment ago she'd been almost a heroine to Alison. Now the child's delight was wiped out, replaced not by anger but by shock. Delia clenched her hands, finding that Alison's disillusionment was just as painful as Craig's dismissiveness.

'I'm very sorry,' she said. 'I didn't mean to do it...' Oh, the useless words, when the deed was done!

'Of course you didn't,' Alison said politely. 'It must have been an accident. Daddy, I think I'll go and see Uncle Joe now.'

'All right, but don't get in his way,' he said gently.

Alison spoke politely to Delia. 'Goodbye. It's been so nice meeting you.'

No child should have to be as controlled as this, Delia thought sadly. It would be better if she yelled at me.

When Alison had gone she turned on Craig. 'You could have stopped that conversation instead of letting me walk into it,' she said angrily.

'Spare you, you mean?' he demanded. 'Why should I? I ask no quarter and I give none.'

'Evidently. But it's a little hard on a child.'

'I didn't create that situation,' he insisted. 'I just didn't see it coming. Besides, I never expected you to admit it. That took courage.'

'I think I'll go,' Delia said. 'It was kind of you to offer me lunch, but if I stay we'll start saying unprofessional things to each other.'

'*Start* saying?'

'Good day, Mr Locksley. As you said

earlier, I'll be dealing mostly with your partners, so I'm sure there won't be any need for us to meet again.'

Craig listened as her heels clicked on the marble floor of the corridor, fading into the distance. His face was expressionless. After a moment Alison returned. She went and stood quietly beside him, twining her fingers in his. He gripped her hand tensely.

'Did she really knock Jenny down?' Alison asked.

'I'm afraid so.'

'It's strange. She's not a bit the way you talked about her.'

'Why don't *you* describe her to *me*?' Craig asked.

'She's tall and slim, and ever so pretty. I mean, really pretty, not just because of the make-up. I wish my eyes were like hers—sort of big, and dark blue, with black lashes.' She sighed wistfully. 'Then I could be a siren.'

'Is that today's ambition?' he asked. 'Last week it was a vet.'

'Well, I could be a siren too.'

'Is Miss Summers a siren?'

'We-ell...' Alison considered. 'She's got a gorgeous smile.'

'Yes,' he murmured, too softly for her to hear. 'I know.'

CHAPTER FOUR

'HEY, look at that super-sexy man!'

Delia turned in smiling protest at her office junior's frank comment. But her smile died when she saw the man in Helen's sights.

Craig Locksley had just entered the reception area, with Alison. Delia was too surprised to protect herself against his impact, and the uncontrollable agitation about her heart was alarming.

'You shouldn't say things like that,' she reproved Helen. 'He might hear you.'

'But he *is* sexy,' Helen protested in a lower voice. 'Don't you think so?'

'Have you got those books I asked for? Very well, take them to my office and I'll be there in a moment.'

They were in a corridor. Delia had come looking for Helen to discover why she was taking so long, and had encountered her just where there was a good view of Reception.

Delia heard the receptionist say, 'I'll tell Mr Gorham that you're here.'

'I'm a little early for my appointment,' Craig said.

So Brian had made an appointment with Craig and had told her nothing about it, Delia mused. She was angry but not surprised. In the two weeks since her visit to Calloways Brian had several times insinuated Mark into meetings where he didn't belong, always managing to sideline Delia.

Alison waved at Delia, giving her a beaming smile. At least the child had forgiven her about Jenny, she thought with relief. She hurried forward and received an exuberant greeting.

'Good afternoon, Mr Locksley. Hello, Alison, it's nice to see you again. How's Jenny?'

'She's ever so much better, but not quite right yet,' Alison said. 'So Daddy said I could come here with him, if I promised not to pester you to let me see things, and of course I'm not going to.'

Craig was grinning, and it transformed him. 'I might have known you'd find a way around it, you little wretch,' he said.

'But honestly, Daddy, I didn't pester. I didn't even *ask*, did I, Miss Summers?'

'No, you didn't. You managed it beautifully without asking.' The three of them
laughed together.

Brian appeared, full of effusive greetings.
'Craig! Wonderful! My office is this way.'

At once Alison put herself in front of her
father so that he could rest his hand naturally on her shoulder. Her face was grave
and concentrated as she led him to the door
of Brian's office. Delia went too, but at the
last moment Brian blocked her way.

'I'll send for you if I need you,' he said,
flashing a brilliant, insincere smile. Delia
had no choice but to step back, but not before she'd seen Mark inside the office.

'So you and I can go and look around,'
she told Alison.

Delia took her first to the laboratory
where new products were tested to make
sure they looked and smelled right. Next
they visited the salon where members of the
public volunteered to be guinea pigs for
Orchid's own beauty school. Delia provided
Alison with a shiny bag, bearing Orchid's
name and glamorous logo, and began to fill
it with samples of products. She knew Craig
would be annoyed if the child started painting her face, so the samples were mostly
moisturisers, bath gels, talcum powders and

various skin-care products. But Delia added one very pale pink lipstick in answer to a beseeching look. Then she held a finger over her lips. Alison made the same gesture, nodding in conspiracy.

Helen appeared, looking urgent. 'Mr Gorham wants you in the meeting.'

Delia handed Alison over into Helen's care and hurried to Brian's office. He smiled when she entered but she could sense a tinge of annoyance in his manner.

'Mr Locksley felt you should join us since you were the last to deal with him, although I don't really feel— However, you're here now. I understand that you knew about this proposal to increase the price. You should have told me.'

Delia gasped. 'But I did, Brian. I told you the same day, and you said—'

'I don't think so. I don't *think* so, Delia. I would have remembered that. It's very awkward being faced with something like this at the last moment.'

Delia ground her teeth to stop herself saying something very impolite. She had the feeling that Craig Locksley could follow every charged undercurrent, and was enjoying it.

'It seemed only fair to let you see what

you were paying for before we finalised the price,' he observed. 'This work is as good as you'll ever get.'

Delia went through the folder he'd brought, and was thrilled with it. The Calloway brothers had excelled themselves with a campaign that was vivid, beautiful and imaginative. Even with an extra ten per cent, they were getting full value for money.

Brian tried to hold out. 'Shall we say an extra five per cent?' he asked jovially.

'No, let's say an extra ten, because that's what it's worth,' Craig said, unruffled.

Brian turned to his nephew. 'What do you think, Mark?'

'It's excellent work,' Mark said, as if giving the matter great consideration, 'but I feel an extra five would be generous. Money's a little tight in the department at the moment—'

'Only because you wasted so much of it on Lombard's,' Craig observed. 'They raised the price twice, and you paid up, hoping they'd deliver the goods eventually. But they never did.'

'I think you've been misinformed,' Mark said defensively. 'We started from a low base with Lombard's and increased it *once*, I believe—'

'Twice,' Craig repeated, and gave the precise figures and dates. 'The details were all over town,' he added, by way of explanation. 'With Calloways you're buying the best, but the best costs.'

The haggling went on. Brian occasionally deferred to Mark, but pointedly excluded Delia. It was obvious that she was here only because Craig had insisted on it, and Brian was furious. This was a mistake. Temper was putting him at a disadvantage, while Craig coolly stood his ground. Mark yapped obediently in his uncle's wake.

'Why don't we ask your deputy for an opinion?' Craig asked at last, slightly stressing the words 'your deputy'. Delia's alert eyes caught the instinctive turn of Brian's head in Mark's direction, before he remembered that his deputy was Delia.

'I think this is superb,' she said. 'It's exactly the campaign Orchid needs.'

'Would you agree that it follows the lines discussed at your meeting with Joe and Peter?' Craig asked her.

'Perfectly. They seem to have read my mind.'

'I'll tell them you said that. They'll be flattered because they were very enthusiastic about working with you. Joe said he'd seldom met anyone who understood what she was talking about so well.'

'We're all agreed that Calloways is the best,' Brian said in a tight voice. 'That's why Mark went to such lengths to secure the firm for us. I said at the time that we could trust his instinct, and I'm glad you've come round to that point of view, Delia.'

Delia saw a faint, derisive grin on Craig's face, and knew it wasn't directed at her. He was a receiver, fine-tuned to pick up the subtlest waves, and he understood everything that was going on in this room. That was why he'd given her a boost, playing Brian and Mark at their own game.

'Well, gentleman,' he said, 'do we have a deal or not? If not, I have to be moving on.'

'We'll have to let you know,' Brian hedged.

'You can let me know right now. I have no more time to waste.'

'Look, this has been sprung on us—'

'No, Miss Summers reported my terms to you two weeks ago. You know my price. If I don't hear from you by this evening I shall conclude that the whole deal's off. Good day, gentlemen.'

Craig rose to his feet and made a slight

turn. What happened next happened so fast that it was over before Delia realised what she'd done. Craig had forgotten that Jenny wasn't with him. He reached out for the dog, didn't find her, and paused, shocked and confused. Delia was close enough to tug his sleeve in the right direction without being seen by the other two. He gave no sign of recognition, but walked without further help to the door.

'Perhaps you'll be kind enough to reunite me with my daughter, Miss Summers?' he said.

'Certainly.' She managed to guide him unobtrusively until they were out of the door, then he tucked his hand into her arm.

'Thank you,' he said quietly, and she didn't have to ask what for.

She was coming to terms with her own action, with the fact that she'd instinctively taken Craig's side against the firm in helping him to leave the room with dignity. But she'd been full of admiration for the way he'd got the better of Brian and Mark.

'Alison's been doing the grand tour,' she said. 'I'll send Helen a message to bring her back. How about some coffee in the meantime?'

She guided him into her pleasant office and towards the leather sofa.

'Thank you,' he said again. 'Not just for helping me in there but for being so discreet about it. I appreciate you played it down for your own reasons, but thank you anyway.'

'What do you think my own reasons were, Mr Locksley?'

'It wouldn't have looked good if your boss had seen you giving me a gesture of support, would it?'

'No, it wasn't that,' she said quickly. 'I didn't want to see your exit ruined. I'd had so much fun watching you wipe the floor with them.'

Craig grinned, and it was the grin of an adventurer who'd brought off a risky enterprise. Delia remembered Helen saying, 'Look at that super-sexy man!' That was what you would think if you saw Craig Locksley for the first time, she realised. Not, Look at that blind man! or, Look at that helpless man! No, it would be his vibrant male attractiveness that would strike you first.

'Now I've met that pair, I forgive you for the pamphlets,' he said with a touch of unconscious arrogance. 'Uncle Brian really is determined to squeeze you out and hand the plum job to his little nephew on a plate, isn't he?'

'Exactly,' she said warmly. 'And why should I just lie down and let them get away with it? If there's a superb candidate for that job, someone better than me, I'll give in gracefully and work as their deputy. But Mark is being wormed in by intrigue.'

'And you're being nudged out by intrigue. By the way, I hope you appreciated my cunning in getting you brought in?'

'Yes, I did. Now it's my turn to thank you.' She chuckled. 'They were as mad as fire, and when you kept on about my meeting with Joe and Peter I thought Brian was going to explode.'

'How did Mark look at that moment?' Craig asked appreciatively.

'Like a little boy who'd seen a bigger boy snatch his lollipop.' They laughed together.

'You should get that job,' Craig said. 'You're more intelligent than either of them, and more responsive. You know how to take good advice.'

'Do I? How do you know?'

'I told you two weeks ago that your perfume didn't suit your style. I'm glad you took some notice. This new one is much better. It's lighter. It has a dancing quality. It's witty.'

In a moment Delia was flooded by self-consciousness. It was almost a relief that he couldn't see the blush rising to cover her face. This was ridiculous, she told herself. Why should she be as awkward as a school-girl because of a half-joking compliment? Yet she was completely, uncontrollably glad. In the same moment came the instinct to hide her feelings from his all-seeing inner eye.

'Actually, I was due for a change,' she said casually. 'It's my job to try out the company's products. That's all, although naturally I'm glad you like it. I'll make sure your appreciation is fed into our market research programme.'

He smiled, half to himself. 'I wonder what your market research programme would make of the thoughts going through my head at this moment?'

'Perhaps you should tell me,' she suggested lightly. Her heart had begun to beat with rapid insistence.

For a moment she thought he would answer her, but then he said, 'Not now. Alison may arrive at any minute. Or there may be a message from your boss to say he's agreed to my terms.'

Delia felt absurdly disappointed. It made her say coolly, 'Or perhaps a message to say just the opposite.'

'No, he won't do that,' Craig said calmly. 'He can't afford to. I've got him cornered, and he knows it.'

A moment ago Delia had been in charity with him. Now she found his arrogant assurance insufferable. 'You don't suffer from a lack of confidence, do you, Mr Locksley?'

'Of course not! What would be the point?'

'What indeed?' she echoed wryly.

'While we're still alone, there's something I've been meaning to say to you. It's an apology for some of the things I said to you the night we met. I'm sorry if I went for you. Like you, I had thoughts that I couldn't erase. I needed to lash out, and you were handy.'

'Don't apologise,' she said at once. 'Who else should you lash out at but me?'

'I was angry—not entirely with you. Just—angry. I didn't expect it to hit you that way.'

'Neither did I. I'm usually so calm and

collected. But then I don't usually do harm to people, or dogs.'

'I believe you,' he said quietly.

'And Jenny's really going to be all right? I thought you'd have her back by now.' To her alarm he hesitated. 'What is it? Hasn't she recovered?'

'Physically she's fine. But she was very shaken up and it's taking time for her nerves to settle down. I had a guide-dog trainer working with her for a few days. Jenny's all right indoors but she gets very unhappy if she's taken onto the road.'

'Oh, no! You mean she might never be her old self again?'

'It's possible. But she's gone back to the training centre for a while, and a few weeks there will probably put her right.'

'But suppose she's not?' Delia asked frantically. 'I never thought of anything like this. Oh, God, what have I done?'

'Delia, stop it!' Craig said firmly. 'It's too soon to panic. If there's one thing being blind has taught me it's not to anticipate trouble. Jenny will come home. I just hope it's soon. I hate having to rely on Alison.'

A thought struck Delia. 'Wasn't Alison supposed to be at camp by now?'

'Yes, she was.'

'And you kept her at home to look after you? That's monstrous!'

'Will you stop making glib judgements?' Craig demanded. 'I didn't keep her at home. I don't want her making sacrifices for me, but I couldn't force her to leave. We had a huge row about it. I laid down the law, ordered her to obey me. But I might as well have saved my breath.'

'Where's your fatherly authority?'

'It's easy to talk. My so-called fatherly authority got me precisely nowhere.'

'But that's nonsense. She's ten years old. You should simply have insisted.'

'I'd like to hear you trying to change my daughter's mind. She's as stubborn as a donkey.'

'I wonder where she gets that from.'

He gave a bark of laughter. 'OK. She gets it from me. That's how I understand her so well.'

'You could have made her go if you'd really wanted to,' Delia insisted. Her anger was out of all proportion to the situation and her feeling for Alison. Craig evidently realised this, for he turned his head in her direction, as if to catch a note in her voice more clearly. 'She'll have to be serious and responsible soon enough,' Delia said. 'Must she start now? Isn't she entitled to some freedom?'

'Certainly she is,' he said coldly. 'I'm a burden on her. I know it, and don't need reminding.'

'I didn't mean—'

'Do you think I *like* this situation, knowing that my daughter loses out on the pleasures of childhood because of me?' he demanded with a touch of bitterness. 'Listen, I can hear her voice. See if you can talk her round. You won't find it so easy.'

Alison came in, carrying her shiny bag of goodies. Her face told the story of her wonderful morning, and Delia guessed she didn't have many treats. Her overgrown sense of responsibility got in the way, and her father let it happen. She noticed how Alison gave him a quick, concerned glance before letting her youthful eagerness overflow. Well, this time, Delia thought crossly, she would force him to put his daughter first.

'I've had the most lovely time,' Alison said eagerly. 'Thank you *ever* so.'

'What have you been doing, darling?' Craig asked.

'I've been everywhere. And I've seen how they make things and—'

She bubbled on for several minutes. Many fathers would have been bored, but Delia had to give Craig full marks for listening with an appearance of interest. He even asked sensible questions.

Delia poured Alison an orange juice, and said, 'I was wondering why you weren't at camp. I know you were looking forward to it.'

'Jenny's not home yet,' Alison explained.

'But does that mean you can't go? Your father knows the way around the house—'

'And I've got an excellent secretary during the day,' Craig supplied.

'So you see,' Delia said, 'he'll be fine.'

'You don't understand,' Alison said simply. 'I can't leave Daddy alone. I just can't.'

'That's nonsense,' Craig said edgily. 'I'm a grown man and I don't need looking after.'

Alison caught Delia's eye and silently mouthed, 'He *does*.' There was a look of mulish obstinacy around her mouth that so exactly mirrored her father's that Delia almost laughed.

As if the subject were now closed Alison brought her bag over to Delia's desk and said calmly, 'Look at the lovely talcum powder they gave me.'

Then, quick as a flash, she seized a pen, scribbled something on a sheet of paper and pushed it over to Delia. It read, 'Daddy has terrible, black moods when he's alone.' Delia read it and nodded in silent comprehension.

'But why does it have to be you who stays?' she asked. 'Don't you have any family?'

'I don't need anyone,' Craig repeated.

Neither of the other two took any notice of this.

'Well, there's Grandma and Grandpa— my mother's parents,' Alison explained. 'But it can't be them because Grandma changes everything around in the kitchen, and she drives Daddy mad fussing. And Grandpa tells the same fishing stories over and over.'

'That would be unbearable even for a man who could see,' Delia agreed sympathetically.

'It would be unbearable even for a man who was interested in fishing,' Craig growled. 'Which I'm not. How many times do I have to say that I'll be fine on my own? Alison, you will get yourself off to camp, and that's an order.'

'Daddy, we've been through all this,'

Alison said in an uncannily adult voice. 'I thought I'd made it plain.'

'Yes, you did, and now *I'm* making myself plain. I'm calling the camp to say you'll be there this evening.'

This time Alison said nothing, but simply sat with her hands folded and the stubborn look about her mouth again. Evidently Craig could interpret the silence because he said furiously, 'And don't sit there looking at me like that.'

'Like what, Daddy?'

'Like you are doing. Do you think I can't hear the expression on your face?'

'No, Daddy, I know you can. That's why I don't need to say I'm not going.'

'Thus demolishing my reputation with Miss Summers. She thinks this is all my fault.' He glared at Delia. 'Well, I hope you know better now.'

Afterwards she wasn't sure if she'd already made her decision, or was still inching towards it, but something made her say, 'OK, there's a problem. But there's also a solution.'

'Then you tell us what it is,' Craig said.

'All right, I will. I'll stay with you.'

'*You?*' His astonishment was unflattering but Delia refused to be disconcerted.

'Yes, me. I won't change things round, or talk too much, or fuss. I'll be like Jenny, just *being* there.' She appealed to Alison. 'How does that sound?'

'That would be wonderful!' Alison breathed. 'I know Daddy would be all right with you, and then I could go to camp. Oh, thank you, *thank you*.'

Craig's protest died on his lips. Alison's joy had got through to him, and there was no way he could spoil it for her now. Delia read everything in his face.

'You won't find me so bad,' she said lightly. 'I'll stay out of your way and not speak unless I'm spoken to.'

Alison giggled and smothered it quickly.

'You find something funny?' Craig growled.

'No, Daddy, honestly.' The child composed her features.

'You haven't left me much choice between you,' he said.

'Does that mean you say yes?' Alison pleaded.

'If I do, will you go to camp?'

'Oh, *yes*.'

'Then I agree. Thank you, Miss Summers.' His tone was polite but Delia felt the words were wrenched out of him.

'Where is the camp?' she asked.

He told her. It was only about twenty miles away.

'I'll drive her down this evening as soon as I finish work,' Delia offered, but then saw Alison shaking her head vigorously, and raised her eyebrows in a silent question.

'Can you come home first so that I can show you your room?' Alison asked. Then she mouthed, 'And explain things.'

'You're giving Miss Summers a great deal of trouble—' Craig began, but Delia interrupted him quickly.

'I think it's much better if I come home first. Now, why don't you call the camp and tell them Alison will be there today?'

He did so while Alison danced about the room, singing, 'I'm going to camp, I'm going to camp.'

Delia's internal phone rang. It was Brian. 'Is Locksley still here?' he demanded.

'Yes, he's with me now.'

'Then bring him back to my office. We're going to have to pay his price. It's too late to negotiate. It's a pity you didn't tell me about it earlier.'

'I *did* tell you—' she began to say furiously. But Brian had hung up.

'Will you please return to Mr Gorham's

office?' she said. 'He's going to pay your price.'

'Of course.'

'People always do what Daddy wants,' Alison said cheekily.

'That's rich, coming from you,' Craig informed her with a grin. 'Miss Summers, just give me a few minutes, and we'll go straight home so that you can pack.'

'I'll come as soon as I've finished work,' she promised.

CHAPTER FIVE

ALISON was waiting at the window as Delia drove up. The next moment she was pulling the door open and eagerly taking her by the hand to lead her straight upstairs.

She'd given Delia a corner room that was sunny and pleasant, with plenty of space. She watched as Delia unpacked, oohing and aahing over her clothes.

Craig greeted her briefly then returned to his computer while Alison showed her the secrets of the kitchen, and stressed again the importance of never moving anything by so much as a quarter of an inch.

'You won't actually have to do any housework,' she explained like a solemn little professor. 'Mrs Gage does that. She comes in to clean every day, except weekends. The car collects Daddy each morning and brings him home in the evening. During the day his secretary, Alexandra, looks after him, and he gets home at about seven.'

'And that's when I've got to be here?'

Alison nodded. 'He can do all the practical things for himself,' she said in a lowered voice, 'but when he's on his own he minds terribly about being blind. You see, he wasn't always blind. He can remember how things should look and he—well, he just *minds*. When he's going through a bad time I've seen him put his arms round Jenny and hug her ever so tight. But it's all right,' she added as if a thought had struck her. 'You don't have to hug Daddy. Just talk to him, and let him hear you moving about.'

She gave Delia a list that had obviously been prepared with care. It concerned Craig's habits, the fact that he rose early and went to bed late, and didn't like talking at the table. Delia read it thoroughly.

'What are you two whispering about?' Craig demanded, appearing in the kitchen doorway.

'Nothing, Daddy. I was just telling Miss Summers where to find things. Oh, yes, and coffee.' She turned back to Delia. 'Daddy likes it very strong—'

'That's enough,' Craig snapped. 'For heaven's sake stop mother-henning me. I don't need all this fuss.'

There was a silence, during which Alison's eyes were suspiciously bright.

Then she said, 'I'll get my things,' and rushed past her father.

'That was a rotten thing to do,' Delia said furiously. 'You made her cry. Why can't you accept her help graciously?'

'Because I don't want anyone's help,' he said savagely, and turned away.

Alison reappeared with her suitcase, having regained her composure. 'We're off now,' she said brightly. 'Goodbye, Daddy.'

'Aren't I allowed to come in the car with you?'

'Are you sure you're not too busy?' she said wistfully.

Craig touched her cheek. 'I'm never too busy for you, chicken,' he said. 'Besides, I expect you've got a load of last-minute instructions to give me.'

He sat with her in the back seat, holding her hand and listening meekly while Alison lectured him about safety precautions. Delia had to admit that when Craig did something he did it properly. He was trying to atone for his bear-like behaviour, and was obviously succeeding. Alison's tears were forgotten and she was as happy as a lark.

They arrived just after eight o'clock. There was still a warm sun by which to see the white-painted wooden huts set under the

trees. Everywhere there were girls of
Alison's age. Some of them bounced over
to them, greeting her eagerly. They were
followed by the camp superintendent, a
pleasant, middle-aged woman who calmed
the riot and introduced herself as Miss
Jeffries.

'I'm so glad Alison was able to join us,
Mr Locksley,' she said. 'If you'll both come
to my office we can have a cup of tea and
complete the formalities.'

Delia waited for Alison to take Craig's
arm, but instead the child stood back,
watching her. She understood. Alison
wanted to see her perform her duties, so that
she would know her father was in safe
hands. Delia guided Craig's hand so that he
could clasp her arm.

She concentrated all her mental energy
on anticipating his needs, but he knew how
to manage better than she did. As they approached the hut that did duty as an office
she murmured, 'Here we are,' and felt his
fingers tighten on her arm. To her relief he
climbed the three steps with confidence.

Inside, Miss Jeffries indicated a couple of
chairs. Delia said, 'Why don't you sit *here*?'
scraping the chair slightly against the floor
so that the noise would direct him.

'There are a couple of papers for you to sign, giving Alison into our care,' Miss Jeffries explained. 'Who will sign?'

'I will,' Craig said immediately.

Delia put the pen in his hand, and guided his fingers to the space. To her relief he wrote his name firmly. Alison looked cheerful, as if a weight had been lifted off her mind.

Craig said goodbye to his daughter, and stayed where he was while Delia went to Alison's hut and saw her exchanging eager greetings with other girls. When she was satisfied, she left.

As she drove home he said, 'Thank you. You managed it beautifully.'

'Alison was watching,' Delia told him. 'One false step from me and she'd have insisted on coming back.'

'She really wanted to go to that camp, didn't she? Much more than I realised.'

'She's a little girl. It's natural that she wants to be with other children. It's a lovely camp. I saw tennis courts and a swimming pool.'

'You sound as if you'd like to be there yourself,' he said with a grin.

'Of course not. I just think it's nice for her.'

'No, there was a longing note in your voice.' When she didn't answer he said, 'What is it? Did I hit a nerve?'

'Well, maybe I was thinking of a trip I missed when I was a child,' she admitted reluctantly.

'Is that why you got so defensive on Alison's behalf?'

'Perhaps.'

'Tell me about it.'

'Goodness, there's nothing to tell,' she said lightly. 'It's too trivial to talk about.'

To her relief he didn't press the subject, and for the rest of the journey they talked about inconsequential things.

Delia didn't make the mistake of trying to guide him when they reached home. As before, he managed the steps easily and put his key in the lock.

'I could do with a coffee,' she suggested.

'Then I'll make you one. After that we have things to talk about.'

'Don't worry,' she said as he moved around the kitchen. 'I promise not to get in your way.'

'That's not exactly—' He broke off as the telephone rang, and picked up the receiver on the kitchen wall. 'Hello, darling.'

So it was Alison. Delia watched as Craig's smile grew tense.

'Of course I got home safely. Miss Summers is a very good driver...yes, she's here.' He held out the receiver. 'She wants to talk to you.'

Alison sounded full of relief when she heard Delia. 'I just wanted to make sure everything was all right.'

'Everything's fine,' Delia assured her. 'You get on with your holiday, and enjoy yourself.'

At last the little girl was reassured. Delia passed her back to her father, then rescued the coffee which was about to perk.

'Did I make it right?' she asked as Craig sipped it. 'Very strong.'

'It's perfect,' he said in a tight voice, 'but I think I should make it plain that the farce stops here.'

'I beg your pardon?'

'I pretended to fall in with this outrageous idea because otherwise Alison wouldn't have gone. But I never had any intention of carrying it through, and now she's safely at the camp, I want you to leave.'

'But I can't!' Delia said, angry and astonished. 'I promised her—'

'Miss Summers, I'm trying to keep my temper, because I'm very aware of what you did for my daughter, and believe me I'm grateful. But if you think the two of us can share a roof then you must be out of your mind. I may be blind, but I can't stand being treated as a cripple at the best of times—and with you of all people!'

Delia set down her cup sharply. 'Mr. Locksley, let me make my position plain. I'm not doing this for you, but for Alison, who's getting a rough deal. Left to myself I'd rather jump off a cliff than spend one moment with a man who has all the charm and graciousness of a wire-wool scraper. As for being under the same roof, if there were ten thousand other people under the same roof I would still feel your presence as an irritant.'

'That being the case, you'll have no difficulty in doing as I wish and departing.'

'But what about Alison? If she telephones she'll expect to find me here.'

'She just did, and you *were* here. She won't call again tonight because Miss Jeffries will insist she goes to bed.'

'And tomorrow night?'

'I'll work late and call her from the office. Don't worry, I'll find ways to cover your absence.'

'At least let me drop in here for an hour on my way home—'

'No,' he said fiercely. 'Don't you understand? *No*.'

'If you put it that way, no, I don't understand. It's beyond me how any man can be so pigheaded and self-righteous, and so *emotionally* blind. You pride yourself that your inner eye can see things that the rest of us miss. But you've never tried to see things from Alison's perspective. If you had, you'd show her a little more patience and kindness. But you can only think of what it's like for you. And being physically blind is no excuse for that.'

She ran upstairs and began to pack her clothes in a fury. She wasn't only angry with him but with herself too. She'd genuinely made her offer for Alison's sake, but now she could see that the thought of spending some time with him had appealed to her. In their enforced closeness she might have found something she was seeking. She couldn't put a name to it, but her instincts told her the answer lay with this difficult man. But in the light of his cruel rejection her thoughts seemed like ridiculous, school-girl dreams.

Normally she was a meticulous packer, taking care of her things. But now she shoved them in anyhow and slammed the case shut, longing to get away from here.

Craig was standing in the hall as she went down. She departed without speaking to him. She was afraid that her voice might betray her emotion. Besides, what was there to say?

Back in her own flat, in her own bed, Delia was just nodding off to sleep when the phone by her bed rang.

It was Craig, sounding uncharacteristically hesitant. 'I'm sorry if I woke you.'

'Not really. What's wrong?'

'Alison called a few minutes ago.'

Delia sat up in bed. 'But it's nearly eleven o'clock. You said they wouldn't let her call again.'

'Apparently it's camp policy never to prevent a child calling home, at any time of the night or day. She was worried that you weren't here. I told her you'd gone home to fetch something you'd forgotten. But—' he seemed to be having difficulty with the words '—she's calling back in an hour. If you're not here she's quite capable of returning tomorrow.' There was a silence, in which Delia was almost sure she could hear the sound of Craig grinding his teeth. 'I know you think I behaved unforgivably—'

'Think?'

'All right. I did behave unforgivably, but for Alison's sake I'm asking you to return.'

'For how long? Just long enough to fool her? Because I won't be part of that.'

'No, it wouldn't work. I see that now.'

'The original deal?'

'The original deal.'

'And you'll stick to it as you promised?'

This time she was sure he ground his teeth. 'I'll stick to it,' he said, sounding desperate. 'Will you come back, *please*?'

'Yes, I will. For Alison's sake we'll just have to put up with each other.'

A few minutes later, dressed and repacked, Delia emerged from her room. Maggie, the friend who was staying with her for a few weeks, called from the kitchen, 'Come and have some tea before you go.'

Delia gratefully accepted a cup. 'How did you know I was going?'

'Elementary, my dear Watson. I was

eavesdropping. He's really got under your skin, hasn't he?'

'I'm doing it for his daughter,' Delia explained, a trifle stiffly.

'Sure you are.' Maggie eyed her spooning sugar into her cup. 'I think I hate you most when you do that,' she said affably. 'It never puts so much as an ounce on you. Why can't you get fat like the rest of us? Or at least spotty.'

'It's a pity I can't,' Delia mused. 'That might make him approve of me.'

'I thought you didn't care about his opinion.'

'I don't,' Delia said firmly.

Craig was obviously listening for her because he opened the door as she drew up. By the time she was out of the car he'd descended the steps. 'Let me take your case,' he said.

'I can manage.'

'Delia, it's my eyes that are useless, not my arms. Give me your case.'

She set it down by his feet. He carried it all the way to her room without missing a step, and she followed. Once there he seemed awkward. 'It was good of you to come back,' he said politely. 'I assure you I appreciate it.'

Delia gazed at him in dismay. 'This will be impossible if you're going to talk to me like that,' she said.

'Like what?'

'Like *that*! It's awful.'

'I thought I was perfectly polite.'

'You were. That's what I can't stand. It doesn't sound like you. I preferred you growling at me. After all, I can always growl back. But if you're going in for frigid courtesy I'm out of here.'

Craig gave a reluctant grin. 'Am I as bad as that?'

'Dreadful,' she said frankly. 'But that's all right. I can cope with dreadful. It's when you start trying to say the right thing I get confused.'

'It's going to be a great few days,' he agreed wryly.

'It's gone midnight,' Delia said. 'I can't believe Alison is really going to call now, so I—there's the phone!'

'Answer it quickly.'

She hurried down and snatched up the phone. 'Hello?'

'It's really you,' Alison said eagerly. 'I

thought—well, you know—that you might not be there.'

'Of course I'm here,' Delia said brightly. 'I promised, didn't I?' The sight of Craig coming into the room made her add, 'Daddy promised too, and you know he always keeps his word.' Craig made a wry face in her direction. 'But you shouldn't be out of bed at this time.'

'I'll go back to bed now. Honestly. Are you all right, settled in and everything?'

'I'm really comfortable. You did a great job.'

'What did you forget?'

'What?'

'Daddy said you went home for something you'd forgotten.'

'Oh, that.' Delia collected her wits frantically. 'There was another suitcase with a special dress I need to wear tomorrow.'

'Daddy didn't seem to know what it was.'

'Of course not. He's a man. What do they know?'

Alison gave a conspiratorial giggle. 'Is he standing there glaring at you?'

'He certainly is.'

'Can I talk to him?'

She handed the receiver to Craig and listened while he bid his daughter goodnight. At last he hung up and said, 'I think we convinced her. Thank you. I don't know what I'd have done if you'd refused to help me.'

'I never would have refused.'

'No, you play fair. I'll give you that.'

'I'd like to make myself some tea.'

'I'll make it.'

'There's no need. You don't have to prove to me—'

'I'm not. I just don't want you blundering about in my kitchen until you've learned where everything goes. If you put things down in the wrong place, I'm lost.'

'I know. Alison told me, and you snarled at her for it.'

'OK, I give in. You make it.'

She made tea carefully, replacing everything in its exact place. When she'd finished he felt around the pots and gave a grunt of approval.

'Do I get top marks?' she asked.

'We-ll, you put the squirrel back a quarter of an inch out.'

'I *what*?'

He grinned. 'Only joking. Well done. I'll let you pour.'

As she did so he explained, 'I have groceries delivered, always the same. We stocked up this afternoon, and Alison put everything in its right place, so you won't have to worry about that. Are you hungry?'

'I've just realised that I am.'

He put two slices of bread into the toaster. While they waited she said, 'Perhaps you'd better explain my duties to me.'

'You mean Alison hasn't?' he asked with a smile.

'She said a car collects you in the mornings and brings you back.'

'That's right. There's no need for you to hurry back, as long as you're here when Alison calls.'

'Alison will call early, to make sure I'm not cutting corners,' Delia mused. 'And she'll call again, late, to make sure I haven't gone out and left you alone.'

'I'm afraid you're right. It's going to be pretty much a prison sentence for you.'

'I'll manage, as long as you don't bite my head off too often.'

As he buttered the toast he asked, 'And what will it do for your career to be leaving work on the dot every night? Don't kid yourself that Mark won't notice and make capital out of it.'

'You let me worry about Mark. I've said I'll do this and I will.'

His expression became gentler. 'You're doing all this for my daughter?'

And for you, she thought. To spend time with you, and see your face soften towards me like that. Maybe you'll get to like me, and smile at me sometimes. I know I'm taking a risk, but something is happening to me that's never happened before. It makes me nervous, but I have to go forward.

'What is it?' he asked suddenly. 'What are you thinking?'

'I—nothing. This toast is very good.'

'You wouldn't tense up like that because of the toast. The air was jagged. You were having thoughts you couldn't tell me.'

To her dismay Delia felt herself blushing furiously. Could he discern that too?

'I have a lot of thoughts that I can't tell you, because they're not your business,' she said firmly. 'And I resent being interrogated.'

'Just as long as you and Alison aren't cooking something up that I don't know about.'

She relaxed. He wasn't on the right track after all.

The phone rang. 'I don't believe it,' Craig

said. 'It can't be that little imp again.' He snatched the phone up. 'Yes?' Then a black scowl came over his face. He rapped out, 'Yes, she's here.' He handed the receiver to Delia. 'A man for you.'

'Hello?'

'So there you are,' came a familiar voice.

'*Laurence?* Whatever are you doing, calling me at this hour?'

'I tried your apartment and your friend told me what you were up to.'

'Can I just—?'

'Are you raving mad?' he interrupted her. 'If ever there was a time when you needed to give all your attention to your work this is it. And what are you doing? Playing Florence Nightingale.'

'I'm not playing, Laurence. I'm trying to put right a wrong.'

'You've taken leave of your senses. This is your big chance and you're risking it. You have to look out for yourself in this life.'

Recently Delia might have thought the same. Now it was like listening to another language. She floundered, at a loss for words. She was fond of Laurence. Once she'd even thought that fondness might turn into love. But suddenly he seemed irrelevant to what was happening in her heart.

'I can't talk now,' she said in a low voice. 'I'll call you from work in the morning.'

'I'm only thinking of you, you know.'

'I know, and it's nice of you. But please, Laurence, don't call me here.'

'Tomorrow morning, then. Bye.'

Delia hung up quietly, and looked around, hoping Craig wouldn't have overheard too much. But to her relief he was already halfway up the stairs. He called, 'Goodnight,' over his shoulder, and went on to his room.

CHAPTER SIX

THE next evening was enlivened by a visit from Craig's sister, Grace. She was a robust, outspoken woman with a grating voice, but a no-nonsense attitude that Delia found appealing.

'Heaven help you!' she declared when she got Delia on her own. 'Being shut up with my brother is my idea of hell. Of course I should have offered to do it myself, but my boss is sending me abroad tomorrow.' Grace was a high-ranking civil servant attached to the diplomatic corps.

'Actually there's another reason,' she confided. 'Craig can't stand having me around. Says it makes him want to chuck things.'

'That's not very nice of him,' Delia said, aghast.

'Don't worry,' Grace hooted cheerfully. 'He has the same effect on me. Anyway, he's never very nice, as I expect you've already discovered.'

'He's certainly not sweetness and light.'

'Well, to be fair to him, he was a lot better before he went blind. Are you making coffee? Fine. I like mine strong.' She closed the kitchen door and settled herself at the table.

'How long has he been blind?' Delia asked.

'Only about seven years. It hit him terribly hard because he'd always been a high achiever. It was expected in our family. If you didn't come first it meant you just weren't trying. He was a businessman, a financial wizard, and an athlete on the side. On the day he married Philippa he seemed to have everything a man could want. He was crazy about her, and she was considered quite a catch. She turned out to be a cold-hearted little schemer, but she had great looks. Not as brilliant as yours, but enough to knock their eyes out.'

'How did he lose his sight?'

'Hurt himself in the gym. Fell off the parallel bars and landed on his head. When he woke up, he was blind.'

'How terrible!'

'For a while it destroyed him. He went into a black depression. At first they weren't sure it was permanent, and Philippa played

the loyal wife to perfection. "We'll fight
this together, darling," and so forth. But
when she realised that this was how it
would always be she changed her tune. She
didn't fancy being shackled to a blind man.
I think she married him for money and an
exciting life, and suddenly the money dried
up and it wasn't exciting any more. She left
him for a man called Frank Elward, taking
Alison.

'Oddly enough, that was the thing that
jerked Craig back to life. He knew Elward
was a nasty bit of goods, with criminal
friends. Craig said he wasn't going to let
his daughter be raised in that atmosphere,
and he took them to court. Of course,
Philippa used his blindness against him,
said he couldn't cope with a child. But
Craig was armed with some very unpleasant
information about Elward. And he won.

'He even offered to take Philippa back,
rather than part her from Alison. But for all
Philippa's prattle about loving her baby she
chose Elward. After that Craig really got
going. He learned Braille, got a guide dog,
which he'd refused before. He studied every
technique for overcoming the obstacle of
his blindness. Then he went out and conquered the world again.'

'I'm glad you told me all this,' Delia said slowly. 'Now I know why he seems to be fighting all the time.'

'He is. And he can't win, because at heart he wants to believe that he isn't blind. He almost defeats it, but he can't come to terms with it, and he's filled with anger and frustration.'

The next moment she put a finger to her lips. She'd heard Craig's footsteps outside.

'I hope you're not talking about what I think you are,' he growled, opening the door.

'You mean you?' Grace asked robustly. 'Forget it. Why should anyone want to talk about you?'

'If you're telling Delia that I'm a monster of tyranny and ingratitude, you needn't bother. She's already discovered that.'

Though brother and sister had scarcely a good word to say to each other Delia noticed that they hugged each other with real affection when Grace left. She left with a wave, saying, 'Goodbye, Delia. I hope you're still alive at the end of your ordeal.'

'Be off with you,' Craig called, grinning.

After a few days Delia found she'd slipped into Craig's routine easily. They were polite to each other at breakfast, except for a tense moment one morning when she carelessly left the coffee in the wrong place. But she soon learned where everything went, and made no more mistakes.

She would reach his home in the evenings to find that he'd already started to prepare supper. She suspected that he did this deliberately, to underline his independence, and was sure of it when he asked her opinion of the food with a sardonic expression. She was able to praise it honestly. He was an excellent cook. Delia came to understand that in this, as in everything else, he felt the need to excel.

Alison always called soon after supper, and for her sake they would sound cheerful and friendly. The child was having a wonderful time, and Delia was glad of whatever instinct had prompted her to take on the care of this prickly man.

There were times when Craig seemed barely to know she was there, which was disconcerting to a woman used to the attention of men. If she could have known how hard it was for him to assume an indifferent front her heart might have been lighter.

For Craig her presence was as much of a strain as he'd feared. Every fibre of him was

aware of her. With the super-developed
senses of the blind man he knew each tiny
movement she made. If they were in the
same room he would hear her soft
breathing, and know exactly how far away
from him she was. Her light movements
told him of her gracefulness. He would try
not to picture it, try not to imagine her slim,
elegant body, because that way lay madness. But he couldn't shut down his imagination, which loved to dwell on her.

Often her perfume would reach him. It
was usually the one he'd told her he liked,
but always something light and flowery.
Occasionally she wore no perfume at all,
and that was almost worse, because then he
had the scent of *her*, warm, womanly, elusive.

He'd once been glad not to have been
born blind, because at least he could remember how things looked. But now he felt
it would almost be better not to know about
the beauty of a woman, to have no way of
picturing her. He might have suffered less.
But to be always in the presence of loveli-
ness, to know its separate components without seeing how they made one perfect
whole—this was torture. The darkness had
never been so terrible.

The more he felt her presence as a desirable woman, the more conscious he was of his blighted condition. He'd feared this and tried to send her away. It had been almost a relief when Alison had forced him to bring her back. But the relief had been short-lived. Laurence had called. Laurence, the boyfriend. There was bound to be one, of course, and he could only be grateful to have learned about him at the start.

He could still hear her voice that first night, low and urgent. 'I can't talk now...I'll call you from work in the morning...please, Laurence, don't call me here.'

Pity, he thought with loathing. Be kind to the blind man from on high, and feel good about it. Real life is somewhere else. At one time...

He wouldn't let himself think about the past, when he'd been a whole man, and could have made her want him. He would go insane if he thought about that.

One evening Delia came home to find no evidence of Craig. Usually he was in the kitchen, and would sing out to her that coffee was ready and dinner was coming up soon. But tonight there was no sign of him. She'd just decided that he would be home late when she heard an unusual sound from the rear of the house. It consisted of creaking, thumping, and someone breathing heavily. Worried in case he'd injured himself, she hurried through to a back room she'd never seen before, and opened the door. Then she stopped on the threshold, thunderstruck by the sight that met her eyes.

It was a wide, sunny room, equipped as a gymnasium. Everything was here: weights, machines and more traditional equipment—a vaulting horse, parallel bars, climbing ropes. And there, working on the parallel bars, was Craig.

He was almost naked, covered only in a pair of black, very brief briefs. They were made of some shiny material, and clung to him damply, hiding almost nothing. Craig's whole body glistened from the vigour of his workout. Delia had always guessed that he was athletically built, but now she saw it for herself. His shoulders were broad and powerful, the arms muscular. There wasn't an ounce of fat on him, from his smooth chest to his flat stomach and lean hips. Everywhere was taut and full of force.

Craig was so absorbed in what he was doing that he hadn't heard her enter. Delia knew she shouldn't watch him while he was unaware. But admiration held her rooted to the spot. His movements were smooth and confident as he placed his hands with practised ease in the right places on the bars, swinging back and forth swiftly and gracefully.

She held her breath as he whirled, somersaulting off the bars and returning to them with his body facing the opposite direction. His face was fierce with concentration, and she guessed it was no accident that he'd chosen the equipment from which he'd had his fall. The bars were an enemy that had injured him, and now he had to prove himself their master.

He twisted, swung, did handstands. The light from the windows caught every bead of perspiration, bathing him in a golden glow. He was beautiful, she thought. Not just handsome, but beautiful in a magnificent way. Every line of him spoke of authority. Many of his moves would have been dangerous in less assured hands, but he never faltered.

As Delia's gaze was fixed on the broad, powerful shoulders, the thighs thick with muscles, she suddenly found her mind possessed by shameless, wanton thoughts. She blushed at the images that were conjured up as he twisted and turned. She'd thought of herself as cool and level-headed where men were concerned. She knew that she inspired their sensual fantasies, but no man had ever sent her own thoughts rioting. Until this moment.

Now there seemed no way of controlling the brazen ideas that chased through her head. The blush seemed to be spreading from her face throughout her whole body, so that she felt hot all over, and every inch of her was alive to him.

He began to go faster, trying things which made her want to cry out a warning. But she kept quiet. He would never forgive her if he knew she'd watched him. As he made his final somersault off the bars she backed quietly out of the room and closed the door.

She went straight to the kitchen and tried to think of mundane things, but he was there with her, in her consciousness, over-powering her with his presence, filling her with a yearning need that made thought im-possible. She took a deep breath and sat down abruptly. Her hands were shaking. So was the rest of her.

'I've got to pull myself together,' she

said firmly. 'This is nonsense. Where's the recipe book? I'll try something new.'

But the words swam together. Delia tried harder to concentrate.

Craig came into the kitchen half an hour later, fully dressed.

'I'm making supper tonight,' she told him. 'I'm trying out a brand-new recipe, so be warned.'

'Fine.' He gave her a smile. His workout had left him in a good mood.

'I thought you were out,' Delia said. 'There was no sign of you when I came in. Have you been busy?'

'Working in my room,' he said quickly. 'I've got a big meeting the day after tomorrow. Alex, my secretary, should be calling.'

Delia made some suitable reply. Her thoughts were out of control again. They persisted in looking through his clothes at the nearly naked magnificence she'd seen in the gym.

'What book are you taking the recipe from?' he asked. 'No, don't tell me. Let's see if I can find out.'

He ran light fingers along the spine and outer edge of the book. 'It feels like one of my old ones,' he said cheerfully. 'I used it to teach Alison. She read it out and I explained what— Hang on! Why are you reading it upside down?'

'I'm not,' she said frantically.

'Yes, you are. There's a tear in the cover, just here. I know the shape. But it's at the bottom.' He gave a hilarious grin. 'How come you didn't even notice it was upside down?'

'I—I was daydreaming,' she said. 'I've—got a lot on my mind.'

'Delia,' he said, puzzled, 'you sound half-witted.' His eyes gleamed with humour and he grasped her shoulders firmly. His sudden touch, the nearness of his face were so unnerving in the midst of her turbulent thoughts that she jumped.

'What's the matter?' he asked in a gentler voice. 'You're shaking. Did I startle you?'

'Yes—yes, you did,' she gabbled.

'This isn't like the cool, efficient Miss Summers.'

'I'm not always cool and efficient,' she protested. 'Sometimes—my thoughts just get—carried away.'

To her intense relief he let her go. 'I can see supper's going to be very interesting. Perhaps I should take a stomach powder first.'

'Forget new recipes,' she said briskly. 'It's going to be ham and eggs.'

'Fine by me.' He left the kitchen, chuckling. Delia breathed out hard. Then a slow smile spread over her face at the sound of his laughter. It was a good sound.

Over supper he teased her some more, but she'd recovered her poise and gave as good as she got. It was a merry meal. He even managed to laugh when he spilt his coffee over himself.

While he was upstairs changing, the phone rang. Delia answered it, expecting to hear Alison. 'Hello?'

'Craig, please.' The young woman on the other end sounded slightly superior.

'I'm afraid he's not here. Can I help? Or can I get him to call you back?'

'This is Alexandra Mason, his personal assistant. I'm in the north, doing a report for Craig. I've called to say that it'll take longer than I thought and I won't be back until Friday.'

'Does he know where to call you?' Delia asked.

Miss Mason named a hotel, but added, 'I have to go out at once, so he may miss me.'

When Craig appeared Delia said, 'Your personal assistant called.'

'I don't have one.'

'Alexandra Mason.'

He grinned. 'Oh, I see. Alex is my secretary. She keeps hinting to be called personal assistant because she thinks it sounds more important, but so far I've turned a deaf ear. She's very efficient, but she's only been with me a short time, and there's something about her I'm still not quite sure of. What did she want?'

'To say she can't get back until Friday. The report you asked for is taking longer than expected.'

His grin faded. 'Damn! I knew it might take an extra day, but not that long.'

'I've got the number of her hotel, but she said she was going straight out.'

She read him the number and he dialled it, but sure enough Alexandra was missing.

'Can you manage without her that long?' Delia asked.

'I can get one of the other secretaries—there are several that I've used before, for routine work. But the day after tomorrow I'm going to a shareholders' meeting of—' He named a company that had been much in the news for its complacent management and highly paid board. 'I'm going to make life very uncomfortable for some fat-cat di-

rectors who want to award themselves huge
pay rises. That's where I really needed her.
She knows the figures and the background.
I can't take a clerk from the office pool for
that. It wouldn't be fair.'

Delia thought quickly. She had some
leave due to her. 'I'll do it,' she said.

'*You?*' His emphasis wasn't flattering.

'Why not? I'm really quite bright, whatever you think.'

'I'm sure you are, but it wouldn't be easy
to take this over at the last minute. I'm very
demanding—'

'No, really?'

He grinned. 'You've no idea how bad I
can be. It's tough. You need to be on the
ball the whole time.'

'And you don't think a bimbo like me
can manage it? Thanks.'

'Delia, I'm not trying to be insulting—'

'No, just managing it without trying,' she
said lightly.

'It's the day after tomorrow. You'd have
to take time off work.'

'Then I'll take it. I'm due for some leave.
You don't want to miss your meeting, do
you?'

'No, I damn well don't. But what about
the dreaded Mark?'

'Even the dreaded Mark can hardly do much in one day. I'll be there. Just brief me.'

'Fine. In that case, let's start now.'

Under his direction she called up certain files on his computer.

'These figures show that the firm has made huge profits recently,' he explained, 'but at a dreadful cost. They're predators, buying up smaller firms, closing them down and throwing out the employees. But they still manage to produce the goods. And how? Because they import them cheaply from countries which use child slave labour.'

'But that's wicked,' Delia exploded.

'Yes, it is. What's more, the chairman who's been responsible for this is about to retire and award himself a bonus of a million. He ought to be in gaol, not wallowing in money.'

'Can the shareholders stop it?'

'In theory, yes. In practice it's going to be very hard. The big institutions who own shares will vote with the board, because the members of their boards are all planning the same thing. You scratch my back, I'll scratch yours. The small shareholders find it hard to make an impact because they're not organised, and they haven't got a voice.'

'And you're going to be the voice?'

'I've been writing round to as many as I can, and if they're given a strong lead it may be enough to block this proposal, and get the whole nasty business out in the open. But we need everything at our fingertips. Suppose I ask you for the up-to-date facts about—' He named an aspect of the company's work. 'Which file would you call up?'

After a moment's thought she got it right. She got the next one even faster. The third one she made a mess of.

'No,' he said irritably. 'You'll have to do better than that. I don't want you making me look an idiot in there. Perhaps we'd better forget the whole idea.'

'We will not,' Delia said firmly. 'I'll get it right.'

They worked for three hours. At the end of it her head was aching but she was exhilarated because she'd mastered the problem. Even Craig had to admit, 'You're getting it. Not bad at all.' Which she took to be praise of a high order.

'OK, just transfer those files onto the laptop, make sure it has fresh batteries, and we're in business. And don't glare at me like that.'

'I won't ask how you know.'

He smiled wryly. 'It was written all over the air. Hate! Hate!'

'Not hate,' she protested. 'Actually I rather enjoyed it, even though you *are* the world's worst tyrant.'

'You call *that* tyranny? You've seen nothing yet.'

She threw up her hands, crying, 'I believe it. I believe it.' They laughed together.

Next day she made sure that all her work was up to date, left Helen properly briefed, and cleared it with Brian for her to take a day off.

'That's fine,' he said genially. 'You've been working very hard. I expect you feel the need of a nice restful day.'

'I get the feeling that restful is the last thing it's going to be,' Delia said cheerfully.

In this she was proved right. Craig insisted on leaving very early the next morning, to be there before the rush for seats. The meeting was to be held in a cinema.

'It was the only place they could find big enough,' Craig confided as she drove through the London traffic. 'The original venue was much smaller, but then they got all these acceptances, and had to revise their plans.'

'Because of you?'

'Let's say that it was after I contacted the other shareholders that the cinema was booked.' Whatever he might say, his whole being radiated confidence in his own effectiveness.

Because they were early Delia managed to park the car close to the cinema. They walked the short distance back and were almost the first waiting for the doors to open. After that the queue lengthened rapidly.

'A lot of people have turned up,' she told him.

'Good. The more the merrier. I'll give those swine a run for their money.'

He would, too, she thought. There was a fierce light in his blind eyes. This was a man to be reckoned with, even perhaps to be feared. There would be no prisoners taken today.

At last the outer doors opened. Craig tucked his arm into Delia's.

'Smooth tiled floor, no steps,' she said. 'The door to the auditorium is about twenty feet away.' He stepped forward with apparent ease until they neared the door.

Here they encountered a problem Delia

hadn't anticipated. It was a shareholders-only meeting, and she had no shares.

'Sorry, no journalists,' the steward said firmly.

'I'm not a journalist,' Delia said.

'Hmm. How do I know that? The press isn't allowed in this meeting, but your lot will try anything.'

'She's my eyes,' Craig said. He explained his blindness and his need of her in a quiet, almost meek voice that made Delia shoot a suspicious glance at him. The steward yielded. After giving Craig an identification tag to wear on his shoulder, and pointedly refusing one to Delia, he allowed them both in.

'I could hardly believe that was you talking,' she murmured as they went to their seats.

He grinned. 'I can act the blind man as well as anyone, in a just cause,' he said without irony. 'Get as near the front as you can, and make sure I have an aisle seat.'

'We're coming to steps,' she told him. 'They're shallow and broad, which is awkward because you can't get into a rhythm. *Now*. Then two steps forward, and down.'

He managed the tricky width, his hand tucked in her arm.

'We're here now. Aisle seats.'

'You go in first, so that I'm on the outside.' When they'd seated themselves he said, 'Look around and tell me what you see.'

'It's filling up fast. At this rate it'll be standing room only.'

At last every seat was taken. Lights went up on the stage and seven men trooped on to take their seats behind a long table. Delia described them.

'The one in the middle is fat and jowly, with white hair.'

'That's the chairman, Leabridge. Is there one built like a string bean with dark hair and a mouth like a trap?'

'Yes, just next to him.'

'The company secretary, Derham. I believe he's behind the labour policy. Leabridge is a buffoon and Derham manipulated him. Now he wants him out so that he can take over, so he's trying to grease his path with money.'

'The chairman's getting up,' Delia said.

'Ready for battle?'

'You bet!'

Delia was fired with excitement. Then she felt a strange sensation in her right hand. For a moment she almost thought Craig had squeezed it, but when she looked his head was turned towards the stage, as though he wasn't aware of her.

CHAPTER SEVEN

AT FIRST very little happened. There was a round of self-congratulatory speeches. Craig sat quietly, waiting for them to finish. Then, when Derham rose, he was on the alert.

Derham's speech was carefully crafted so that the increases he was proposing were almost lost in the verbiage. But Delia, watching Craig, knew that he missed nothing.

At last Derham said, 'Perhaps we could vote on this straight away.'

There was a rumble of agreement from the hall, but Craig broke into it, standing up and facing the platform. 'Before we vote,' he said in a voice pitched to carry, 'there are a few points I think we should consider.'

Derham controlled his irritation at being held up and managed an expression of polite interest. 'I'm sure we would all be interested in hearing your points,' he said.

'You've proposed some very large bonuses for yourselves, and particularly for

Mr Leabridge,' Craig said. 'Do you really think the company's recent behaviour justifies this?'

'The company's recent performance has been excellent—' Derham began.

'I didn't say performance,' Craig interrupted him. 'I said *behaviour*.'

'Then I can't imagine what you mean. Profits have never been better—'

'Profits for the board and shareholders perhaps, but the men and women thrown onto the scrap heap haven't got much to celebrate.'

There was a warning in his tone but Derham failed to heed it. 'Regrettably, in the modern industrial age it's been necessary to streamline, to require more work from the employees—'

'But you don't use employees, do you?' Craig said dangerously. 'You use child slaves in countries where you can't be called to account. You're making a fortune on the backs of infants, some as young as six, who live night and day in factories, half starving, and working a fourteen-hour day.'

Leabridge leapt to his feet. 'That is totally false,' he shouted. 'A fabrication got up by a spiteful press.'

A murmur had risen in the hall, but in the

face of such a categorical denial it faded.
Delia had a moment of apprehension.
Surely Craig couldn't have made a mistake.

Then she looked at his face and saw in it
an expression of pure delight that reassured
her. By denying the charge so completely
the chairman had walked right into Craig's
trap.

'Mr Chairman,' he said, 'you have told a
barefaced lie in front of two thousand people. And I'm going to prove it's a lie. Your
own internal documents confirm it.'

He turned so that he faced the audience,
and began to reel off facts and figures, refusing to be silenced, charging on like a
juggernaut in the face of protests from the
platform. He named meetings, listed those
present. He seemed to have an uncanny
knowledge of who had said what.

Delia didn't have to wait for him to instruct her. She could think ahead, deduce
what he needed, and have the relevant file
open before his signal. But she was only
back-up. He had it all in his head.

A faceless young man who seemed to act
as an aide to the chairman jumped to his
feet. 'Those are private company matters,'
he spluttered. 'They're confidential—'

'Not any more, they aren't,' Craig cried,

and the audience roared with laughter. Before it had quite died away he was back in his stride, mowing the opposition down like wrath from heaven.

'As if the present position wasn't bad enough,' he roared, 'there are plans to close yet another factory and move the manufacturing process to a more 'accommodating' country.'

He named the country and detailed some of its abuses. 'The president of that state lives by pocketing backhanders. In return for the right sum he'll provide land, buildings, slave labour, and police who turn a blind eye when children die at the machines. Just how much have you greased his palm so far this year? It wouldn't be a million, would it?'

He was drowned out by shouting, but only for a moment. When he raised his voice it altered, becoming gravelly and powerful. The audience quietened, dominated less by his volume than by the sheer force of his personality.

'Every year that this company has slipped further into the moral mud, its directors have awarded themselves huge bonuses, share options, and anything else their greedy little hearts desire. Now the chairman seeks to smooth his exit with gold. Not so much a golden handshake, more like a golden kick in the rear.'

Leabridge was on his feet again, pale and furious to the point of incoherence. 'You have no right to—nothing is decided—discussions—I will not necessarily be leaving—'

'You will if I have anything to do with it,' Craig informed him, to a round of applause.

After that, the argument moved into a different area and things got extremely technical. Craig needed her help even more now. It took all Delia's concentration to keep up with his demands, calling up files, giving him the necessary information. The men on the platform grew more flustered. They tried to shut Craig up and pass on, but by now the crowd was on his side.

Once, when he'd repeatedly demanded facts against the evasions from the platform, the chairman said, 'I think we've given quite enough time to this matter, and should now pass on to something else.'

'Not so fast!' Craig cried.

'This subject is now closed,' Leabridge intoned, letting his gaze rove around the cinema. 'Any other questions? If not I take it we can—'

'I've got a question.' Delia jumped to her feet.

The chairman regarded her with something like relief. 'Yes, madam? What is it?'

'This,' she said, and proceeded to repeat Craig's last question, word for word. There was laughter and applause, but then someone noticed Delia's lack of a tag.

'Are you a shareholder? If not you shouldn't be on your feet—most irregular— No, I won't listen to you.'

An elderly lady got to her feet. She looked pink and frail, but her words dispelled that illusion. '*I* am a shareholder,' she said firmly, 'and I want a proper answer to the last question.'

'So do I,' someone called. Another voice was raised, then another, and soon the whole audience was baying for the answer nobody on the platform wanted to give.

A man behind Craig tugged his arm. His identification tag gave his name as Selsdon, and proclaimed him a representative of block shareholders—the ones Craig had said would support the increases for their own greedy motives. It seemed he was right because Selsdon hissed, 'Cut it out for Pete's sake! This will do a lot of damage.'

'Delia?' Craig rapped out.

'Selsdon,' she said, reading. 'Here to represent—' She gave the name of the company.

Craig nodded as though his suspicions had been confirmed. 'Damage to whom?' he demanded of Selsdon.

'All of us. Who wants to rock the boat?'

Craig gave a wolfish, piratical grin. 'I do. And I'm going to keep rocking this particular boat until it capsizes. I advise you to jump ship before your company's name is mud.' His turned his back contemptuously on Selsdon, who sat there, fuming.

The crowd was still calling for an answer. Under cover of the noise Craig demanded some details from the files, and when Delia hesitated he snapped, 'Hurry up! We haven't got all day.'

'Yes, sir!'

He seethed with impatience while she tapped at the laptop, finally locating what he wanted. His thanks was a perfunctory grunt, but she felt no resentment. She was thrilled with what he was doing, caught up in the drama, overwhelmed by her admiration for him.

He returned to the fray. The chairman tried to make some sort of reply, got hopelessly bogged down and changed tack.

'This is all very fine and noble,' he sneered at Craig, 'but none of these grand principles have stopped you benefiting as a shareholder, I notice.'

'I bought shares in this company as the only way I could get into shareholder meetings,' Craig snapped. 'I've had one dividend, which I refuse to make use of. It stays in a separate bank account while I try to find a home for it. I've tried to give it to charity, but when I tell them the facts no self-respecting charity will touch it with a barge pole. *Who touches pitch will be defiled.*' His last words were a roar which had the audience cheering.

Delia looked around. Most of the people there were the small shareholders, whose incomes might be affected, yet they were with him, swayed by the force of his honest indignation.

'I propose we vote to deny these monstrous increases,' he cried. 'I further propose a vote of no confidence in this board, and a vote for a total review of its policy.'

The chairman made a dismissive movement, but voices were raised, seconding

Craig. At last he had to give in, and the voting started.

'Note down the numbers,' Craig instructed Delia. 'Make certain they're dead accurate.'

Behind them Selsdon was in a rage. 'What the hell am I supposed to do now?' he demanded. 'I've got my instructions from head office. Support the board. But you've made them look immoral. My company's got a good name. It doesn't like being associated with anything dubious.'

'You'll have to follow your conscience,' Craig said ruthlessly. 'Always assuming you and head office can locate it. Hunt about a bit.' Selsdon cast him a look of loathing.

In the end Selsdon faced both ways at once, refusing the vote of no confidence but denying the increases and agreeing to a review of policy. It seemed that a lot of the other company representatives did the same for Craig lost the no-confidence proposal but won the other two. The faces on the platform were pale and strained. The crowd was jubilant. Craig sat back in his seat with a look of grim satisfaction.

Delia turned to him with a glowing face, longing to meet his eyes and exchange the knowledge of their teamwork, and their victory. But there was only blankness there. He was cut off from her admiration and she felt a sudden bitterness, not for herself, but for him. It was so unfair.

Impulsively she seized his hand. 'You did it,' she cried.

He didn't respond in words, but she felt a slight pressure, and this time it was unmistakable. Then he quickly withdrew his hand.

The meeting ended very soon after that. The members of the board couldn't get out fast enough.

'I don't know how I'm going to explain this to head office,' Selsdon muttered.

Somehow Delia got Craig through the mêlée and out to where she'd parked the car. It was hard because everyone wanted to talk to him, slap him on the back, and she guessed that he found it a strain to have these things coming out of the darkness. At last they were safely in the car.

'Home?' she asked.

'Nope.' He gave her an address which she recognised as that of a national paper, and dialled a number on the car phone. 'Jack? We're on our way.' The exhilaration of victory was still in his voice.

'It's a pity you didn't win the no-confidence vote as well,' she sympathised.

'That was inevitable. I only put it in to give the company representatives a minor victory to take back to their head offices. Without that they might have voted down one of the other two, and they were the really important ones.'

'You've got a Machiavellian mind,' she chuckled.

'Thank you,' he said, rightly taking this as a compliment.

Jack turned out to be a battered newshound who'd been on red alert, waiting for Craig's call, seething with frustration at being excluded from the meeting himself. He tapped away eagerly on his computer as Craig tossed out fact after fact, occasionally appealing to Delia for information.

'That's a great story,' Jack said at last. 'Now, a bit about you—'

'No,' Craig said at once. 'This is about the scandal of fat cats living off the suffering of children—'

'And the man who stopped them in their tracks,' Jack protested. 'It's great human interest—'

But Craig was already rising. 'I've given you your story, Jack,' he said firmly. 'If you dare turn me into a circus freak I'll come back here and make you sorry you were born.'

'All right, all right. Look in tomorrow's paper.' He caught his breath. 'That is—'

'Fine. I'll *look*,' Craig said severely. 'Delia, let's go!'

He was quiet on the home journey, but by the time they arrived his mood had improved. Later, he let her cook the supper, and while she was at work he entered the kitchen bearing two glasses of champagne. 'You've earned it,' he said, handing one to her. 'Was I very hard on you?'

'Awful,' she said without rancour. She mimicked him. ''Hurry up! We haven't got all day.''

Craig grinned. 'That's what Alison calls ''Daddy being a bear.'''

'Not a bear, a lion. You had them all scuttling for cover.'

'I did, didn't I?' he said with grim satisfaction.

'Let's drink to you.' She clinked his glass.

'No, to us. You were wonderful. When you stood up to ask a question I could have wrung your neck for letting them off the hook. Then, when I realised what you were really doing, I could have—well—'

You could have kissed me, she thought. Is that what you were going to say? Her eyes were drawn to his generous, mobile mouth with its firm lips, and she saw them tighten, as though the same idea had occurred to him, only to be rejected. There was a slight flush on his face.

'Anyway, you were marvellous,' he said.

Reluctantly she let it go. Perhaps her moment would come later. It would be useless to try to urge this prickly man to do anything he wasn't sure about. It had always been so easy to make other men do what she wanted, but with Craig it was a whole new territory.

'Supper's almost ready,' she said. 'I'm just about to serve up.'

'Great! I'm famished.' He sounded relieved.

The meal was riotous as they relived their triumph. Afterwards he insisted on helping with the washing up, drying dishes and putting them away accurately.

By the time they returned to the living room he'd mellowed enough to tell her some funny stories about the fights he got involved in, and evidently enjoyed.

'People like we met today don't know how to deal with my blindness, and I make use of that,' he admitted.

'But you hate being perceived as blind.'

'Yes, I do. I won't let Jack use me for 'human interest' fodder, but I'll do what I have to for the sake of those children, even it if means playing up to ignorant preconceptions. What do my problems matter?'

Delia began to laugh.

'What's so funny?'

'That chairman as he scuttled off the platform. And the others chasing him. They all gave you a look of sheer hatred as they went, but they were scared too.'

'That's what I like to hear,' he announced triumphantly.

But even as he said the words the light died from Craig's face, to be replaced by a look of melancholy. He took a deep, shuddering breath. Delia watched him in anguish. By now she was attuned to his mind and could follow what had happened. Tonight he'd made light of his blindness, pretending to use it cynically for his own ends. But it was all a front, and behind it was a wilderness of darkness and despair. His humour was a defence, but the enemy was always waiting to pounce. As it had pounced now.

She couldn't bear it. Tears sprang to her eyes and she reached for him. 'Craig,' she whispered.

He stiffened as she touched his face, and his voice was hard. 'It's all right, Delia. I'm fine.'

'You're not,' she cried passionately. 'Why must you pretend? It's all an act, isn't it? You don't want anyone to know how much you're hurting—'

'But I'm not hurting.' Suddenly he slammed his glass down. 'Damn you, stop this! Who the hell do you think you are?'

'But I only want to help you—'

'You did help me, today, when I wanted it. That kind of help I need, but not what you're offering now. Tears and pity—' A tremor went through him. 'I'm going to bed.'

He rose quickly and strode out into the hall. But his anger had confused him. He missed his footing on the bottom step, stumbled, clutched the bannister and fell on the steps. Delia flew to help him.

'Don't touch me!' he shouted.

She stayed where she was, a foot away from him, scared to move or even speak

while Craig was mentally thrashing around
in his private nightmare.

'If you know what's good for you, don't
come near me,' he said at last in a shaking
voice. 'Do you hear? *Where are you?*'

'I'm here,' she said quickly. 'I'm not
coming any closer. I'm going right away
from you. I promise.'

She took a few steps back, and watched
unhappily as he picked himself up, located
the bannister with his hand and began to
climb the stairs. She couldn't move until the
door of his room had closed behind him.
Then she stumbled back to the sofa and collapsed on it, her head in her hands, rocking
back and forth in anguish.

She knew the truth about herself at that
moment, and it was dreadful. Beneath a
pretty face she was nothing, just a vacuum.
Because when the man who increasingly
touched her heart needed help she was useless to him. There was nothing in her that
could make him reach out to her in his pain,
and take comfort from her presence. There
was nothing of value in her at all. She'd
suspected it for a long time, but she knew
it now.

She lay awake half the night, trying not to
shiver at the thoughts that had risen up to

taunt her. But Craig had forced her to face
the terrible truth that she'd avoided for
years. She wondered how she could endure
staying in this house, where there was nowhere to hide from herself.

All at once she sat up, wondering if she
was imagining things, or if she really could
hear shouting from along the corridor. The
next moment there was a crash. Delia leapt
out of bed and rushed to Craig's room.
When she snapped the light on she could
see that his bedside radio lay on the floor.
Craig himself was standing in the middle of
the room, reaching out around him in a
frantic effort to find some firm object. He
wore only pyjama trousers, and his bare
chest heaved with his distress.

'Craig!' she cried.

He turned to her. His face was livid.
'Where am I?' he demanded. *'Where the
hell am I?'*

'Keep still.' She took his hand and he
seized her convulsively.

'I had a bad dream,' he gasped. 'I must
have got up while I was still asleep—I've
lost my bearings—'

'It's all right. Put your hand on my shoulder.'

She guided his hand around her shoulders and put her free arm about his waist. He was trembling violently and without thinking what she was doing she instinctively slipped her other arm about him as well, holding him firmly in a gesture of consolation. His grip tightened and he clung onto her like a drowning man with a straw. Delia felt herself pressed against him, absorbing the heat from his body, and she was suddenly very aware of how little she was wearing. Her low-cut nightdress was made of the sheerest silk, so that there was almost nothing between her nakedness and his.

He sensed it in the same moment. She felt his sudden tension as his hands brushed against her skin with its gossamer covering. Before, he'd only touched her face. Now he was finding her slim shape, its elegant curves, its seductiveness.

Time seemed to stop. Delia was intensely aware of every part of him at the same moment. She'd admired his body in the gym, but only at a distance. Being held close to it was an experience that left her trembling. She could feel the hard, lean length of him pressed against her, and with it was the unmistakable intimation that he'd discovered her as a woman.

Delia's head swam with the intensity of the feelings that coursed through her. If he'd found her as a woman, she'd found him as a man, and with a completeness that was almost shocking. They'd been careful, treating each other with caution. Yet this had been waiting all the time, ready to come alive when their guards were down. Now it was too late. She wanted him. She wanted everything. She wanted his lips on her mouth, his arms about her body. She wanted him in her bed, caressing her, claiming her.

Craig began moving his hands tentatively, letting his fingers trace a soft line down her cheek, her long neck, over the curves and valleys of her shape, causing tremors of unbearable excitement to go through her. Until now her body had existed for others to gaze at and appreciate, but now suddenly it existed for herself. It had been created so that this one man could bring it to joyful life.

He was only stroking her gently, but his lightest touch affected her more than another man's kiss would have done. Half-unconsciously she pressed against him, lifting her face so that her warm breath caressed his skin. She moved her fingers lightly on his naked back, not drawing him closer but sending him soft messages of intimacy. In another moment he would surely tighten his arms and kiss her.

But then she saw Craig's face. It was desperate. Something that to her was a joyful revelation was, to him, a terrible weakness. He wanted her, but he didn't *want* to want her. He would fight his desire like an enemy.

At last a shudder went through him and his hands dropped. The battle was over and he'd won, at a terrible cost to them both. He wanted to pretend it hadn't happened, and if she seemed aware of his 'weakness' he would never forgive her.

'Come with me,' she forced herself to say. 'Your bed is over here.'

Slowly she guided him, letting him feel the edge of the bed against his legs. He snatched his hands away from her and sat, feeling around for the cabinet, the bedhead, anything that was familiar.

Delia picked up the radio and tried not to let her voice shake with the strength of her emotion. 'You must have lashed out in your dream, and knocked the radio onto the floor. I heard the crash.'

'Did you—hear anything else?'

'Yes, I heard you shout. That must have been the dream.'

'I owe you an apology,' he said politely. 'I was very rude to you tonight.'

Her heart sank at his formal tone. She longed to assure him she didn't mind his rough behaviour, but he would interpret that as being patronising.

'You were pretty rotten,' she agreed. 'But it doesn't worry me any more.'

He gave an awkward grin. 'How about making me a cup of tea? I don't think I could manage it myself right now.'

When she returned with a tray of tea and two cups, she'd covered herself with a dressing gown. Craig had put on a pyjama jacket and dressing gown, and was sitting in a chair. She poured his cup and set it by his elbow. He thanked her, said something by way of small talk and she answered in the same vein. She knew that he was re-establishing their relationship on a prosaic footing, with the distance between them increased by the moment of blazing awareness that had caught them both.

Delia looked around her, taking in the details of his room. It was spartan, almost bleak. The unusually large bed was made of pine, as was the wardrobe and dressing table. Against the far wall she saw something that made her catch her breath sharply.

'What is it?' Craig demanded at once.

'Nothing, I—it's just—the dog basket—it's so sad and empty.'

'Yes,' he said heavily. 'Not that Jenny spends much time in it. Mostly she sleeps on the bed. Guide dogs are trained not to, but Jenny and I decided to ignore that bit. We like being together. That's why the bed's so wide. She just takes the space she wants and leaves me to make do with the rest. I got tired of clinging onto the edge so I bought one big enough for three.'

The next moment a glance of sadness crossed his face, as though he was thinking of the lonely nights without the warm, comforting presence.

'But you'll have her back soon, won't you?' she asked urgently.

It seemed a long time before he said, 'I don't know. If she can't overcome her fear of traffic I'll have to have another dog. But I don't want another. I want *her*.' His voice shook.

'Another dog wouldn't be the same,' he went on after a moment. 'Jenny and I have years of trust and love that we've built up. We knew from the very first moment that we were right for each other.' He gave a forced laugh. 'I guess that sounds pretty sentimental.'

'No. Why shouldn't you love her when she's so good to you? But surely she'll get her nerve back, with rest and retraining?'

'She's eight years old. That's elderly for a dog. It may simply be too much of a struggle for her. I'm going to visit her at the training centre this weekend. Maybe that will help. I don't know.'

'That's fine,' Delia said eagerly. 'I'm looking forward to meeting her properly.'

After an awkward silence Craig said, 'My usual driver is going to take me. There's no need to trouble you.'

Delia drew in a slow breath, wondering if she would ever get used to the pain of being snubbed. 'You mean you don't want me around Jenny, don't you?' she asked in a mortified voice.

'Delia, don't take it personally—'

'How else can I take it? Don't you realise that the last time I saw Jenny she was lying unconscious in the vet's surgery? I can't get that picture out of my mind. But perhaps I'd be able to if I saw her looking well. I might begin to feel less of a monster. But as far as you're concerned I'm still beyond the pale, aren't I?'

'Don't be silly,' he said roughly. 'I don't mean that at all. I may have had a few uncharitable thoughts about you at first, but we're past that now. I didn't think you'd want to come—'

'Of course I do. I want— Oh, *hell*!' She set down her cup sharply and rested her forehead in her hands. The words she wanted to say wouldn't come. He would probably think them stupid.

After a moment she felt the light touch of his fingers on her hair. 'Delia? Are you all right?'

'Yes, I'm all right,' she said gruffly. She wanted to take hold of one of his hands, turn her head and rub her cheek against it. But she resisted the temptation.

'Does this really mean so much to you?'

'More than you'll ever know. You see, I want—I want to ask Jenny to forgive me,' she whispered.

'All right,' he said after a moment. 'In that case—I'll be glad if you'll come with me.'

CHAPTER EIGHT

JACK had done them proud. The story that
appeared in next morning's paper was calculated to make the chairman and board
shake in their shoes. Delia read it to Craig
over breakfast.

'Are you sure he hasn't put in anything
sickening about me?' Craig demanded suspiciously.

'He hasn't even mentioned that you're
blind,' Delia reassured him.

'Good. Then I hope I've started a riot.
With any luck their shares will be plunging
in an hour.' He grinned. 'I feel ready for a
good day.'

'So do I.' She drank her coffee and
looked out of the window. 'Your driver's
here. I must dash.'

She reached the office to find Helen urgently awaiting her arrival. 'Brian called a
meeting yesterday afternoon,' she said. 'He
came in here looking for you.'

'I told him I was taking a day's leave. I suppose Mark was at this meeting?'

'And Mr Gorham. Brian told him he simply couldn't imagine where you were.'

'Then I think I'll have a word with Brian,' Delia seethed, and headed along the corridor.

But Brian was all prepared. 'Delia, I'm so sorry. Of course you did tell me you were going to be absent, and I—somewhat reluctantly—agreed.'

'You never said anything about being reluctant,' she protested.

'I think I did. I *think* I mentioned that there was a lot of work on at the moment, and it wasn't really convenient. But it's no matter. You're here now, and I'm sure you'll soon catch up. Mark will fill you in about our meeting yesterday.'

Delia bit back the hot words that sprang to her lips. It could do no good now. For the next hour she had to endure the mortification of being briefed by Mark at his most insufferable.

The one pleasure the day held was that of watching the news on her office television. The story was growing by the minute and the shares were diving, as Craig had predicted. Leabridge, panic-stricken, was backtracking and announcing policy reviews every five minutes.

Brian looked into her office at the end of the day. 'I'd like you to read through these papers,' he said, placing them on her desk. 'They're rather important, so you won't mind if I call you about them tomorrow, during the day.'

'But tomorrow is Saturday. I'm sorry, Brian, but I'm busy all day.'

'Indeed. Indeed. I should have thought that in view of— However, as you say, it's Saturday, and of course your personal life is your own.'

'I beg your pardon?'

'A beautiful young woman doesn't want to spend all her life working. I'm sure there's a boyfriend in the picture somewhere. Love has its claims.'

'I'll read the papers on Sunday and see you first thing Monday morning,' Delia said stiffly.

'I'm afraid you'll be seeing me sooner than that. Tomorrow evening is the P.R. Associates dinner. Remember?' Brian said, whisking them away. 'Don't let the papers trouble you. Mark and I can manage.'

Delia watched him go, realising that she'd handed him and Mark a victory. But she had no choice. Tomorrow she was taking Craig to visit Jenny, and nothing was more important than that.

Craig told her more about Jenny as they drove to the centre.

'She was given to me by The Guide Dogs for the Blind Association. They train a young dog for about eight months until it knows all the things it has to do, like stopping, starting, waiting at kerbs, judging distances. But the hard part is matching a dog with the right owner.

'I went to stay for a month in the place we're going to now. When I'd settled into my room I heard the door open and close again. The next moment there was fur brushing against my hand, and a cold nose pressing against my cheek. I felt her all over, and her tail was wagging like mad. She was beautiful. I knew at once that we were perfect together, and so did she.

'When we started working as a team everything went right. That doesn't always happen. Some teams have to work a long time before they get it right. But we were completely in tune at once. Since then she's been part of my life; not just my eyes, but my friend. I can tell her things I wouldn't tell anyone else.' He said this simply, genuinely.

At last they turned into a quiet road. The training centre was a collection of low buildings. Craig directed her to the right one from memory. When they were inside he said, 'We have to find Hilda Mullins' office. Let's see if I can remember the way.'

He managed it at first, but then became lost. 'Curse it!' he said fretfully. 'I was so sure I could— What was that?' A bark had reached them from around the corner. 'That's Jenny,' he said excitedly.

'Craig,' she protested, laughing. 'There must be so many dogs here.'

'No, it's *her*. I'd know her bark if there were a million others. Hilda said she'd have her in her office, ready for me. Follow that bark.'

It was coming more insistently now, infused with a note of agitated delight.

'Perhaps she heard your voice,' Delia said, making her way around the corner. The excitement was getting to her too.

At last she found the door and knocked. A pleasant voice from inside said, 'Come in.'

Hilda was a middle-aged woman with a warm smile. She rose at once, but her greeting was lost in the commotion made by a yellow Labrador, who scurried forward, her tail going nineteen to the dozen, and was enfolded in Craig's arms. Her delight was reflected on his face as he patted her, scratched her head and murmured in her ear.

When at last the two had finished greeting each other Craig straightened up and said to Delia, 'This is Jenny.'

She took a deep breath and leaned down. To her relief Jenny didn't back away from her, but looked up with soft brown eyes. On the night of the accident Delia had noticed in passing that this was a lovely dog, but now she could see just how lovely. She was a pale honey colour, with a broad head, thick silky fur and an expression of benevolence. Delia had last seen her lying unconscious on the surgery table. Now Jenny was bright, friendly and apparently confident. It seemed impossible that anything could still be wrong with her, and Delia dropped to her knees and embraced her with relief.

'I'm sorry,' she whispered. 'I'm so sorry.'

Jenny placed her chin confidingly in Delia's hand, looking slightly puzzled, as if wondering what there was to be sorry about.

Of course, she'd seen only the car, not the driver, Delia thought. But still she was passionately thankful at what felt like a gesture of forgiveness.

Over tea Hilda explained Jenny's problems.

'Most of the time she seems fine. She can do everything as she used to, including walking in the street, sometimes. But then suddenly she'll get a panic attack at the kerb.'

'I'm afraid that's my fault,' Delia confessed. 'I was driving the car that struck her.' She forced herself to continue. 'I mounted the pavement. She didn't have a chance.'

Hilda hesitated briefly, but her voice was still friendly as she asked, 'Do you have the same car today?'

'Yes.'

'Then we can see how she reacts to it. But first I think Mr Locksley should work with her, so that they can get used to each other again.'

When Craig bent down to fix her harness on Jenny gave a beaming grin, as if saying that this was how things were supposed to be. They all went outside, and Delia watched with Miss Mullins as the two of them went through their paces. Jenny performed everything asked of her with quiet authority.

'Now let's see her take you between us,' Hilda said to Craig. 'Delia, will you stand just inside this doorway, and I'll do the same on the other side, so there's just a narrow gap between us? Craig, the doorway is just in front of you. See if she'll take you through.'

'Forward,' Craig commanded.

Jenny considered, then sat down.

'Forward,' Craig repeated.

Jenny didn't budge.

'Well done!' Hilda cried.

'It's good that she disobeyed?' Delia asked.

'With you crowding that doorway, the gap must be too small for me,' Craig explained. 'Jenny knows exactly how wide my shoulders are, and if there's no room she won't move. Well done, girl. You remembered that perfectly.'

The grounds were set up with tests for going round obstacles, and even a simulated street, with helpers driving vehicles. Jenny sailed through everything.

'Shall we try it with my car?' Delia said.

Craig went to stand with Jenny on the

edge of the kerb. Delia got behind her wheel and began to drive forward slowly. As she drew close she saw Craig's lips move in the command, 'Forward.' Jenny studied the road, then stayed motionless. There was no doubt that she'd seen the car, but beyond becoming rooted to the spot she didn't re-act. Craig reached down and touched her, and Delia just had time to notice his smile as she went past.

'How was it?' she asked eagerly when she'd run back.

'Fine. She didn't shake or show any signs of distress,' Craig said jubilantly. 'We're getting there, Jenny. You'll soon be home.'

He knelt down to pet the dog, who received his caresses ecstatically. Delia watched them with delight.

Hilda was more restrained. 'It's fine,' she said, 'but that was the easy bit. It'll be much harder on the roads.'

'I know.' Craig straightened up. 'I'll take her out now, while she's doing so well.'

'Perhaps I'd better come with you, just in case,' Hilda suggested.

'I'll go,' Delia said at once.

'You can leave me in Delia's safe hands,' Craig said wryly. 'If there are any problems, she'll bring me back. But there won't be any. Jenny's her old self, aren't you, girl?'

Jenny gave a bark of agreement, and the three of them set off cheerfully for the gate. Delia kept her distance from the other two, thrilled at how perfectly they were working again. A weight was lifting from her conscience.

They left the entrance behind, heading for the main road. As they turned into it Craig called, 'There's a big set of traffic lights just here. I'm going to tell her to cross.'

Delia didn't answer. She was watching Jenny, troubled by a change that had come over the dog. She was walking normally, but suddenly her tail had drooped.

At the edge of the pavement they halted. Craig pressed the button that worked the lights, and listened for the sound that would tell him it was safe to cross. At last it came.

'Come on, Jenny,' he said. 'Let's show 'em. Forward.' But Jenny didn't move. 'Forward,' Craig said again, louder.

When there was no response he spoke to Delia. 'Is there something coming? Is that why she's refusing?'

'All the traffic has stopped at the lights,' Delia said.

He bent to touch the dog, and immediately felt what was wrong. Jenny was shivering so violently that Delia could see it from a few feet away. Craig was very pale.

'All right,' he said quietly. 'Back.' He gave a slight tug on the harness and Jenny stepped back from the edge of the pavement. 'I guess we'd better give this up,' he said heavily.

Jenny gave a soft whimper, and at once his hand was on her head, caressing her gently. 'All right, girl. Not your fault.'

They returned in silence. Hilda received them sympathetically. She said little while Craig consoled Jenny. The dog responded, rubbing her head against his hand, but she looked drained and miserable. She'd failed at the work to which her whole life had been dedicated. Above all she'd failed her beloved master, and her sadness and confusion were there in her eyes.

'It's too soon to give up hope,' Hilda said gently. 'We'll keep her here for a while, and hope it comes back to her.'

There was a silence. In the end it was Delia who asked, 'And if it doesn't?'

'It will,' Craig said at once.

'I'm sure it will,' Hilda said. 'But if not I'm afraid you'll have to have another dog.'

'And give up Jenny?' Craig asked in a strained voice.

'What would happen to her?' Delia asked. 'She wouldn't be put down?'

'Certainly not,' Hilda said firmly. 'We never put down healthy dogs, just retire them to new homes.'

'I won't let her go to strangers,' Craig said at once. 'She'd hate it. She knows she belongs with me.'

Hilda thought for a moment. 'You don't live alone, do you? My notes say you've got a daughter, and someone who comes in every day.'

'That's right.'

'And quite a large house and garden. You could cope with two dogs.'

'You mean I could keep her as a pet?' Craig asked eagerly.

'Possibly. It's not ideal, but it sometimes works.'

A sick feeling was overtaking Delia as she listened. 'But what would Jenny do during the day?' she asked. 'She's used to coming to work with you, and being with you all the time. She'd have to be left behind—like a reject.'

Craig turned his head in her direction, a

quizzical look on his face. 'That's a bit melodramatic, isn't it?' he said.

'Perhaps. I just think she'd feel it when
you left the house with another dog wearing
her harness.'

'We'll do everything we can to get her
confidence back,' Hilda said. 'But she's not
young. This may be the best compromise.
Don't worry about it for the moment.'

It was time to go. Craig held out a hand
to Jenny who came to him eagerly.

'Goodbye, old girl,' he murmured. 'I'll
come again soon. Be good.'

He gave her a final pat, and went to the
door. Jenny looked after him, a bewildered
expression on her face. A soft whimper
broke from her throat as she realised Craig
was leaving her behind. True to her training,
she didn't try to follow, or protest. She
merely sat there forlornly as her master
went away.

Craig didn't seem to want to talk as they
drove home, and Delia was glad. She was
full of misery—a feeling that started with
Jenny's fate but went beyond it.

She made them both a light meal when
they got in, but then sat staring at her plate.

'What is it?' Craig asked at last. 'You've

been quiet ever since we left the centre. Is it Jenny? She's going to be fine.'

'No, she isn't,' Delia said fiercely. 'Not if she's relegated to second-best because she couldn't measure up. It'll break her heart. You can't let her—you don't understand.' Her voice was becoming thick with tears as she struggled to find the words. 'You didn't see her face as you left, but I did and—oh, God, what have I done?' She broke down and wept unrestrainedly.

Craig was thunderstruck. He'd heard her weep once before, on the first night, but that had been a reaction from overstretched nerves. Her grief for the suffering of another creature was something different.

After a moment he stroked her hair with gentle fingers. 'Don't cry, Delia. It'll come right.'

'Suppose it doesn't?' she asked huskily. 'How will she bear it?'

'But Jenny's a dog. You don't know what she's feeling.'

'I do. I saw it in her eyes, and—I know. It happened to me, and I *know*.'

'What do you mean, it happened to you?'

'I—I can't explain.'

'Yes, you can. Tell me.'

When she didn't answer he took a firm

hold of her and drew her to her feet, propelling her into the living room and towards the sofa. 'Now, you're going to tell me what's upsetting you,' he insisted. 'And we'll see what can be done about it.'

'All right, I'll tell you. I know you despise me as a vain, shallow woman who thinks of nothing but her looks and the admiration she can get.'

'I don't despise you—'

'It's been more like a curse to me, right from the start. From the moment I was old enough to understand words I heard about nothing but my looks. My father was so proud of me—no, of *them*. I've got a sister, a year younger. She's bright and clever, and nice-looking, but he didn't give her half as much attention as me, because I was *the family beauty*.' Delia said the last words in a scathing tone that made Craig turn his head sharply to catch every nuance of her voice.

'Go on,' he said.

'It was fine at first, being Daddy's darling, able to wrap him round my little finger. But he became obsessive. I was a child model because that was what he wanted.'

'What about your mother?'

'She wasn't happy but my father just

steamrollered over her. He was the one who came to photographic shoots with me. He loved basking in all the attention. I ended up with a crowded schedule and no time to be young.'

'That's why you got so annoyed for Alison?'

'Yes. There were so many childish pleasures I missed out on because he'd booked me in somewhere. He took on far too many engagements and I got exhausted. One day, when I couldn't take any more, I threw a screaming tantrum right in the middle of a shoot. Nobody would hire me again, and he was furious with me.'

Her voice became husky. 'After that I wasn't his pride and joy any more. He just lost interest in me. He discovered that my sister could act. He had contacts by then, and he used them to push her into commercials, so after that she had all his attention. I used to watch them go off together— do you see…?'

'Yes,' he said softly. 'I see.'

'I'd thought he really loved me, that I was special to him. But I wasn't—not really…'

Craig listened to the silence. When it wasn't broken he reached for her. His hands touched her shoulder and he tensed when he felt it shaking.

'Are you still crying?' he asked in wonder.

'No—no—it's just—I've started remembering things I've tried not to think of for years.'

'Your father really stopped loving you for a reason like that?'

'It wasn't *me* he loved. It was my face, and the exciting life it could give him. For a while I hated my own looks. I played them down, tried to hide them. But then I started to grow up, and realised that looks could have their advantages, so I began making the best of myself, only this time I did it for me.

'Oh, there are a thousand ways. There are smiles, and turns of the head, and glances through your lashes. And men get dizzy looking at you and forget they were going to give you a parking ticket, or they let you jump the queue. It's easy and it's cheap, and soon your whole life is like that, and there's nothing else...'

'Why are you so hard on yourself?' he asked gently. 'Is it because I was hard on you?'

'You had every right to be,' she cried. 'Everything you said about me is true.'

'Nothing I said about you that night is true. I spoke in anger, and I didn't know you then.'

'You knew me better than anyone,' she said with self-condemning bitterness. 'You were the one person I couldn't fool.'

'Delia, don't talk like this. Don't make yourself out to be a monster just because you got a little confused.'

Craig had reached out his hand. Delia clung to it as though it were her salvation, trying to sort out her thoughts. She'd told him part of the story, but there were no words to express the bewildered anguish of discovering that the father she'd adored had loved her for the most superficial reasons—which meant he hadn't really loved her at all. His later indifference had filled her with fear in case other men should also learn her terrible secret—*that she was worthless inside.*

She'd polished up the glossy surface so that nobody could see beneath it. But then she'd met Craig, to whom the surface meant nothing. He'd judged her harshly, reviving the demons that haunted her. If only she could find the way to explain it all to him.

But perhaps the man whose blind eyes saw so much would know without words.

'I'm glad you told me all this,' he said at last. 'Now I know why your face was so tense and haunted when we first met. But that seems a long time ago.'

'And—now?' she asked breathlessly.

'Now it's different: gentle and kind, the way nature meant it to be.'

'But how can you know? You've never touched my face since that night, when you told me all the things that you disliked about it.'

'I didn't dislike it. I was just troubled that it was being spoiled by something wrong inside you. But since then I've heard echoes in your voice—kindness and compassion, and—other things. I know you're good and lovely inside because you turned your own pain into care for my daughter. I know your features are softer, and your eyes glow. If I touched your face now I'd find it truly beautiful, as I understand beauty.'

'Why don't you?' she whispered.

He gave a sigh that was half a shudder. 'Because it would make me want you too much.'

'Would that be so bad?'

'Yes. You know—you are not for me.'

She whispered, 'I am, if you want me.'

He was silent and still racked by indecision. Delia drew his fingers up and laid them against her cheek. A tremor went through him. He would have pulled away from her, but he was helpless. Slowly he began to touch her face.

Her eyes were large, fringed with heavy, silky lashes. Her eyebrows too were heavy. He could guess how they dominated her face, giving it dramatic impact. With one finger he traced her straight, delicate nose with its precisely perfect length.

Her mouth was a revelation, wide and generously curved. He'd imagined it like that, thought of how it would feel to kiss it, and now the temptation to do so was tormenting him.

Delia hardly dared to move but her heart was beating wildly. Ever since the night she'd heard him calling and had gone to him, she'd longed for Craig to touch her.

At the back of her mind had been the half-conscious hope that his perception of her beauty would bring him too under her spell, and she would feel safe again, in a world where she understood the rules.

But as his fingers drifted softly across her features she knew that she was deluding

herself. His touch did something magical to
her, something no other man's touch had
ever done, and she wanted it to go on happening. Inside her everything was dissolv-
ing into warmth and happiness. If only she
could stay like this with him for ever.

The feel of his fingers, tracing the outline
of her lips, was devastating. Tremors went
through her. Only half knowing what she
did, she placed her hands at either side of
his face, holding them there for a moment
before drawing his head closer to hers.

Craig groaned as he felt the last of his
control drain away. All his wiser instincts
warned him he was doing something he
would regret, but nothing in the world could
have stopped him. He'd fought his desire
too long, and he couldn't fight it any longer.

Her lips burned him. They were soft and
yielding, warm with promise, suggesting
everything, making him want everything.
All caution was forgotten. He was filled
now with awareness of her, only of her. He
moved his mouth over hers, tasting her
sweetness.

'Delia...' His murmur of her name was
almost inaudible, yet she heard it and
thrilled to the wondering note she sensed
there. She couldn't answer because his kiss

had deepened, become hungry, as though all his pent-up desire and emotion had broken out at last.

Their constraint was falling away, leaving only a man and a woman, in each other's arms because they were in each other's hearts, and Delia rejoiced as she felt herself coming home at last.

But the next moment she felt him stiffen in resistance. Then she felt his hands, firm on her shoulders, pushing her away reluctantly, but insistently.

'Craig...' she protested softly.

'You shouldn't have done that, Delia. It's not kind to torment me.'

'Do you really think that's what I was doing? Playing with you, just to prove that I have some sort of power? Craig, you can't believe me capable of that. You *can't*.'

He gave a groan. 'No—not that. But you don't know what it's like in the dark. You don't understand how everything lovely becomes a torment because it's always taken away.'

'But I'm not going away,' she said, putting her arms about his neck and laying her lips on his again. 'I want this, Craig,' she murmured. 'I want *you*.'

Now he didn't resist, but drew her back

into the circle of his arms. She came eagerly, offering up everything she had or was to this man whose hold on her heart was so painful, yet so strong. It was like being kissed for the first time, a revelation of what a kiss could be, and this time nothing was going to prevent her claiming her love.

CHAPTER NINE

THE shrill of the doorbell shattered their dream. It was a cruel interruption, and for a moment they clung together, trying to believe it wasn't happening. But the loud ringing came again, unrelenting, offering no escape.

'Whoever's there isn't going to go away,' Delia sighed. 'Let's hope it's someone I can put off.'

But the man who stood outside was Laurence, wearing evening rig and an irritated expression.

'Whatever are you doing here?' Delia gasped.

'What are *you* doing here? Why aren't you at home, waiting for me to collect you, as we arranged?'

'Oh, heavens!' Delia's hand flew to her mouth as memory returned. 'That!'

'Yes, that.' Laurence brushed past her into the house. 'Only one of the most important evenings in your calendar. And you forgot all about it, didn't you?'

She had indeed forgotten about the annual dinner given by the Public Relations Associates. It was held at a top West End hotel, and was a gathering of all the most notable names in the business. Delia always made a point of attending, knowing that she would make vital contacts. But tonight it had gone right out of her head.

'Who is it?' Craig called.

Reluctantly Delia allowed Laurence to pass her. He marched confidently into the house and headed straight for the room where Craig had risen from the sofa. He was pale but composed. Delia introduced the two men. Craig held out his hand, but instead of simply shaking it naturally Laurence set down the large suitcase he was carrying and encased Craig's hand in both of his, shaking it earnestly.

'I'm really delighted to meet you,' he said in a slow, hushed voice that suggested he was talking to a mental incompetent, and which Delia knew would infuriate Craig. 'Delia's told me so much about you.'

He released Craig's hand and said, 'Won't you sit down?' as though this were his own house instead of Craig's.

Craig ignored the suggestion. 'What's happened, Delia?'

'Nothing for you to worry about,' Laurence broke in before she could speak. 'A small contretemps that Delia and I can easily put right. There's no need for you to be concerned.'

'Delia?' Craig asked sharply.

'I forgot I was supposed to be going to some function tonight. I'm sorry, Laurence, but it went right out of my head. Will you mind very much going without me?'

'There's no need for that,' Laurence assured her with irritating smoothness. 'We've just got time if you hurry.'

'I haven't got a suitable dress here.'

'So I anticipated. That's why I collected one from your flat.' He opened the suitcase and pulled out a slinky red creation with a great deal of glitter.

Delia was too distracted to notice Craig's slight stiffening at the news that Laurence was in a position to enter her flat and go through her clothes. 'I'm sorry I forgot, really I am,' she said. 'But I simply can't come now.'

'Nonsense. You must. Think of the useful people you'll meet.'

'Naturally you'll go, Delia,' Craig said

quietly. 'I won't hear of you missing it. I'm only sorry I was the cause of you forgetting.'

She looked at him in despair. How could he send her away at a moment like this, when together they'd come so close to the gate of heaven? Did it mean nothing to him?

'Hurry up and get changed,' Laurence urged, holding out the dress.

'Not into that,' Delia said, regarding it with horror. How could she ever have worn such a deliberately provocative creation, so skin-tight, so low-cut over the bosom, so high-slit up the side? She'd bought it at a time when she'd regarded her looks as no more than a useful asset, and now the man who'd taught her better was standing there, every line of his body tense. Luckily he couldn't see the vulgar garment, but how much could he guess?

'What's wrong with it?' Laurence demanded peevishly.

'It's not—suitable,' she hedged. She threw him a frantic glance to make him stop this, but either Laurence didn't see it or he didn't understand it.

'Why isn't it suitable?' he persisted.

'... tight and—and low in the front.

I need something more demure.' Delia lowered her voice, but Craig's sharp ears still caught every word.

Laurence gave a crack of laughter. 'Demure? For that lot? They don't know what demure is. This dress is perfect: a bit low-cut perhaps, but you can afford that. If you've got it, flaunt it, I say. You've never minded flaunting it before.'

Delia felt herself going hot with shame. It was like seeing her previous self paraded before her. 'I want to get something else,' she said, trying to sound firm.

'Darling, you haven't got the time,' Laurence said with the kind of patience that was really impatience. 'We'll only just make it if we leave now.'

'Go and change, Delia,' Craig said quietly. 'I'm sure the dress will look charming on you.'

'Craig,' she appealed to him, 'you don't know what it's like.'

'I can imagine,' he said quietly.

Snatching the garment from Laurence, she ran up the stairs.

'Can I get you a drink?' Craig asked calmly.

'Thanks. Just a ginger ale, if you h

Got to be careful when I'm driving Delia. Precious cargo. Know what I mean?'

'Exactly,' Craig said in a voice that gave nothing away.

'Perhaps I'd better pour it.'

'Thank you, I know my way around my own drinks cabinet.' Craig touched the bottles until he found the right one, and filled a glass.

'Hey, you got it just right,' Laurence said admiringly. 'Wish I knew how you do that. Dead clever.'

Out of sight Craig clenched his hands until the knuckles were white, but his voice was cool and emotionless. 'You're too kind,' he said. 'I've trained myself to do a good deal. I can even eat without help.'

Laurence stared, then light dawned and he gave a guffaw. 'That was a joke, right? Very good. Very good. Well, so this is where Delia's been shutting herself away from the world. Not a bad little place, I must say. Not bad at all. Of course, my Delia's got an overgrown conscience. Oh, yes. She was very cut up about what happened. Anything she could do to put it right, and all that. Mind you, I doubt if she really then—well, anyway...'

voice was hard. 'If you're suggesting that I pressured her you've made a big mistake.'

'No, no, I never meant that,' Laurence said in a voice that was supposed to be soothing, but which grated on his listener like metal on glass. 'But she's a bit impetuous. Take tonight, for instance. The annual dinner of PR Associates. A big night for her, and what happens? She forgets it, and that's not like Delia. Getting on in the world is the only thing that matters to her.'

'You do her an injustice. These things are only on the surface. Underneath is the real Delia, a gentle, beautiful woman.'

Laurence laughed. 'Well, we all know she's beautiful. Hey, how did *you* know?'

'It doesn't matter,' Craig said quietly. 'I know.'

At last they heard her footsteps, making a slight click that told Craig she'd changed into high heels. Of course she would, he thought. Only high heels would go with that tight-fitting, low-cut dress that he was picturing so painfully.

'I won't be long,' she said to Craig.

'Nonsense,' he said quickly. 'You must stay late and make as many contacts as you can. I won't hear of you throwing your chances away.'

'They'll all want to meet my girl,' Laurence declared. Delia wished he'd stop calling her his, in front of Craig. Then something even worse happened.

'Before we leave, you must put this on,' Laurence declared, opening a flat box. 'I bought it to go with that dress. It's a ruby necklace,' he added kindly, for Craig's benefit.

'I can't take it; it's much too expensive,' Delia protested.

'You're worth all the money in the world,' he stated. 'Naturally I bought the best for you.' He was fixing it around her neck as he spoke. 'It looks great,' he announced. 'Nice and heavy, and V-shaped. It follows the line of your cleavage, and it'll knock their eyes out.'

Delia felt as if she was moving through a nightmare. She managed a mechanical smile, and Laurence, taking this as encouragement, gave her a noisy kiss.

'Mmm, who'll have the biggest beauty on his arm tonight?' he murmured against her neck.

'Laurence, please...' she whispered ve-
~~tly.~~

~~d~~ to be shy, darling.'

~~te~~ you should leave quickly,'

Craig broke in. It was impossible to tell from his voice what he was feeling. 'Goodnight, Delia.'

'Alison hasn't called yet,' she said in final protest.

'When she does I'll explain to her. I'm sure she won't begrudge you an evening's enjoyment.' He turned and walked away, leaving Delia looking after him in helpless anguish.

When Laurence had eased his gleaming car into the traffic a few minutes later he said, 'I can't believe you actually forgot, especially considering what might hang on it.'

'Hang on it?'

'Don't tell me you've forgotten that too. The award, for Pete's sake! You had enough to say about it when you were putting in your entry.'

'No, I hadn't forgotten,' she said quickly. It would have been useless to try to make him understand how far away it all seemed. The Associates had its own awards scheme, and Delia had entered the New Product category with a promotion she'd done on a new Orchid line the previous year. Mark had entered the same category with some work he'd done in his previous employment. So they were in direct competiti

Once that would have seemed terribly important.

'I don't think your flatmate likes me,' Laurence was saying. 'She let me in, but very reluctantly.'

'I'm surprised Maggie let you go through my wardrobe.'

'She didn't. I described the dress I wanted and she fetched it. I made the right choice, too. You look stunning, Delia. Delia?'

'Sorry. I was miles away.'

'I said you look stunning. Exactly like I expect my girl to look.'

'Thank you, Laurence. I'm glad you feel I do you credit.'

The hotel ballroom had been designed to suggest a palace, with gilt and cream decor, heavy brocade curtains and glittering chandeliers. Laurence and Delia were among the last to arrive. Nearly a thousand people were there, dressed to the nines, drinking, talking, laughing too loud at each other's familiar jokes.

'We've just got time for one drink before ___' Laurence declared.

'___ve a mineral water,' Delia said.

'___ what you usually—'

'Just a mineral water, please.'

'Suit yourself. I hope you're not going to spoil this evening by sulking. You ought to thank me for keeping an eye out for you.'

'I know you meant it kindly, Laurence—'

'Well, you might try sounding a little more friendly. Isn't that your boss over there?'

Gerald Hedwin had seen her and was coming across, a young, pretty girl on his arm. He introduced her as his daughter Nora, and there were general greetings, during which he studied her appearance with approval.

'You really do Orchid proud,' he said, beaming. 'I was a bit concerned when you were late. Might be our big night, you know. Pity if you weren't there.'

Laurence gave her a sidelong glance of triumph. Delia tried to be grateful, although she felt as though shackles were being hung onto her. But she smiled and said the right things. It was almost a relief when Brian hurried across with Mark trotting at his heels. They glanced hurriedly from herself to Mr Hedwin, trying to calculate what they'd missed.

'It's the clash of the Titans tonight,' Brian remarked jovially. 'Delia and Mark.

Rumour says that it's between you two. Well, it's all good for Orchid.'

'I must confess to crossing my fingers for Delia,' Mr Hedwin said. 'Mark's entry is work he did outside, but hers was an Orchid campaign.'

'Yes, of course, of course.' Brian recovered himself hastily. 'Delia's campaign was excellent. I said so at the time when she asked my advice on a few little points...'

'Did I?' Delia asked pointedly. 'I think you were on vacation, and didn't return until it was all done.'

'Oh, yes, but we wrapped it up together. I'm sure you recall that.'

Mr Hedwin's eyes gleamed with malicious enjoyment at this exchange. He stopped a passing waiter and handed glasses around. 'Here's to both of you,' he said. 'And may the best person win.'

As they threaded their way to the table Laurence murmured, 'It looks like you've got it in the bag.'

'What do you mean?'

'That was a damage-limitation exercise going on back there. Didn't you realise?'

She hadn't, but now it was obvious. Brian thought she'd won and had been trying to claim a share of her glory. Delia took a deep breath and forced herself to concentrate on what was happening now. She'd dreamed of moments like this.

The room was dominated by a raised dais on which stood a long table for the guests of honour. Behind it was a huge blow-up of the statuette that was given to each award winner.

Circular tables filled the body of the room, with eight places at each. Delia knew most of her companions, at least slightly. The dinner was excellent, the talk good, and she found the others giving her glances of appraisal. After the toasts the president of the society rose to start the ceremony.

After a few minor awards the president beamed and said, 'And now for that part of the contest that is most eagerly awaited every year. Youth is the lifeblood of our profession, and the spotting of new talent is one of the...'

Brian was looking at Delia anxiously from his nearby table. Mark was drumming his fingers on the table.

'...seven campaigns entered, all of them excellent...'

Delia tried to let nothing show in her expression.

'...very hard decision...'

Mr Hedwin was looking at the ceiling in apparent unconcern.

'By a unanimous vote, the winner was— *Ms Delia Summers for her excellent promotion of Vital by Orchid.*'

Applause washed over Delia as she rose and made her way up the steps. She'd forgotten to prepare a speech, just in case, but suddenly her head was clear. She was aware of everything, including Mr Hedwin cheering, Brian clapping politely, but looking ready to spit feathers. Mark forced a smile, but appeared on the verge of tears.

The noise died away. 'Ladies and gentlemen, I can't tell you what this means to me, and I should like to thank...'

Once she'd begun it was easy to go on. She managed a couple of witticisms that drew genuine laughter, and praised Orchid products for 'being so good that they promote themselves'. Light bulbs flashed, and she returned to her seat amid applause. It was over.

There were more awards. She sat through them with an air of attentiveness, clapped and cheered in the right places. But she was functioning on automatic.

'Come on, darling,' Laurence chivvied. 'You ought to be dancing with joy.'

Only a few weeks ago she would have been. Once, she'd have been delighted with that shiny statuette, and the annoyance of Brian and Mark would have been all part of an enjoyable game. But none of it mattered beside the memory of a man who'd sent her away when she longed only to be in his arms. What did Craig think of her now? What would he tell Alison if she called? Please, she thought, let the evening end soon!

When the award ceremony was finally over Nora Hedwin approached their table, ostensibly to congratulate Delia, although her eyes constantly strayed to Laurence's handsome profile. Her father asked Delia for a dance. 'I'm proud of you,' he said as they twirled the floor. 'It's good for the firm to have an award winner, and I was impressed by your speech.' His voice became confidential. 'Between you and me, Brian's as sick as a parrot at your success. You know what he's up to, don't you?'

'Trying to grease Mark into his job when he leaves.'

'That's right. Of course, Mark is good, and maybe he'll get the job, maybe he won't. I just thought you'd like to know that I'm fully aware of the scheming, and I'm not entirely sold on Mark. Everything's still to play for.'

'Thank you for telling me,' Delia said politely.

What was Craig doing now? Could she slip away to call him?

'But you haven't sewn it up yet,' he continued. 'I've always been impressed by your commitment, Delia. First in the office, last out. Now you dash off at the first chance, and I often feel that your mind is elsewhere.'

'But surely my work hasn't suffered?' she asked quickly. 'I work right through lunch.'

'Yes, but you're playing into Mark's hands if he's there and you aren't. Still, enough of that. I know I only have to drop a hint. Now let's enjoy ourselves.'

Delia smiled brightly and said something appropriate. After that she had to dance with Brian, and listen to his insincere compliments. Mark followed, and his efforts to cover his chagrin provided some light relief.

'I'm delighted for you to have your little moment of glory,' he purred.

'But you'd have been even more delighted to have it yourself?' she said sweetly.

'My dear girl, I only entered to make up the numbers. They were pitifully small in that category. Which rather takes the gilt off the gingerbread, but I don't want to spoil your night.'

'On the contrary, you're making my night,' she assured him. 'Don't be spiteful, Mark. It suits you only too well.'

His lips tightened, but he was too wise to challenge her further.

Laurence was missing when she returned to the table, and she saw him dancing smoochily with Nora. Delia couldn't blame him. The girl's blatant admiration must have come as sweet balm after her own awkwardness. She had another coffee and refused further invitations to dance.

Laurence returned, full of apologies for his 'neglect', and she smiled warmly. After all, she owed him something for protecting her interests.

'It's done you good to get out,' he observed. 'I don't know how you stand it cooped up with the cripple.'

Delia stiffened. '*What* did you say?'

'All right, all right. One isn't supposed to say crippled. Visually challenged. Blind as a bat. What's the difference? He's still leeching on you.'

'How dare you say such a thing?' Delia flashed. 'Craig isn't a cripple. He spends his life fighting not to depend on people—'

'Oh, yes? That's why you're in his house, is it?'

'I'm there because I chose to be. I forced him to accept me for his little girl's sake. Craig is a strong, independent man and—and ten times the man you are.'

'Oh, come on, darling! Defending him's one thing, but that's going a bit far, isn't it? If you ask me, he's making the most of the situation.'

'What do you mean by that?'

'Having you around, attending to his every whim. I wouldn't mind a gorgeous handmaid, I can tell you.'

'You're incurably vulgar, Laurence. As for my being gorgeous—he's blind.'

'He knows you're a looker, though. He told me.'

'*What*? What did he say?'

'Oh—some nonsense!'

'What did he say?' Delia asked in agony. 'Tell me. I must know.'

'I told him how much it mattered to you to get on in the world, and he started on about how I was doing you an injustice. He said underneath was the real Delia—gentle and beautiful—or something like that. I can't remember. Hey, where are you going?'

Delia had risen quickly and gathered up her things. 'Goodnight, Laurence. Thank you for bringing me; I'm sorry I can't stay any longer. And please take this back.' She unclasped the ruby necklace. 'It was kind of you, but I can't accept it. No, don't come with me. I'll get a taxi.'

'But you can't just dash off like— What about this?' Laurence held up her award, but he was talking to empty air.

and beautiful—or something like that, I
can't remember. Hey where are you going?

Delia had risen quickly and gathered up
her things. "It's time I was going. Thank
you for bringing me. I'm sorry I can't stay
any longer. And please lock this door." She

CHAPTER TEN

EXCEPT for the lamp over the front door,
the house was dark when Delia let herself
in. She could hear nothing. Craig must have
gone to bed. It was a relief not to have to
face him, yet it would have been nice if
he'd waited up for her.

She climbed the stairs, moving quietly so
as not to disturb him. But her way led past
the door of his bedroom, standing open, and
she sensed a faint movement within. She
glanced inside.

The curtains were drawn back and there
was a little light from the window, by which
she could just make out Craig. He was sitting on the bed with his head bent, his face
buried in the silk scarf Delia had worn earlier that day. He looked like a man seeking
refuge.

She was shocked by the sight of him.
Before, she'd known only Craig's
strength—all he'd allowed her to know. But

now his defences were down because he thought there was no one to see him.

He raised his head, and she nearly cried out at the sight of his ravaged face. There was the truth that he hid from the world. Beneath the efficiency and cool irony he was tortured to the point of madness. But was it only his blindness, or was there something more? The compulsive movement of his fingers in her scarf, the way he held it to his face, inhaling her perfume, suggested another possibility, one that made Delia's heart leap. If only…

But then he crumpled the scarf and tossed it aside. He buried his head in his hands, tearing at his hair like a man possessed, while a groan broke from the depths of him.

'Craig,' she said softly. 'Craig—don't. There's no need.'

His head jerked up at the sound of her voice. His face was full of horror. He would have risen from the bed, but Delia went to him, dropping down on one knee and taking his face between her hands. He grew very still.

'Why?' she asked him urgently. 'Why this?'

'You should have told me,' he said

fiercely. 'Damn you! Why couldn't you have been honest with me?'

'I don't know what you mean.'

'I mean this little game you've been playing. It looks like kindness, but it's actually the worst kind of cruelty. Be nice to the poor sightless fool. Make him think he means something to you. Then go away feeling like Lady Bountiful.

'Or is it worse than that? Did you set out to drive me crazy? Does it make you feel good to know that I can't stop thinking about you, night or day? I can't work properly because I'm wondering about you. When you're there I want to know if you're looking at me, and what you think of what you see.

'I had to be your fool, didn't I, like all the others? It was just a test of technique. I can't be impressed with your more obvious assets, so I was a harder nut to crack. What a challenge! But you rose to it, triumphantly.'

'Stop it,' she cried in anguish. 'How dare you speak to me like that? What have I done to deserve it? I didn't want to go out. You forced me to.'

'I hope you had an enjoyable time,' he said stiffly.

'No, I had a rotten time. I was thinking about you.'

'You mean worrying about me, don't you? Like Alison?'

'Craig, what's happened to you? You were so different before—I felt we were really getting close—'

'Close?' he echoed derisively. 'How close can we be when you're in love with another man?'

'I'm not in love with any other man.'

'Maybe you don't have to be in love with him to live with him. Or is it one of those modern arrangements where you each have the key to the other's flat? It makes no difference. You should have told me the situation between you and that man. I suspected something when he called you that first night, but not this.'

'The "situation" between Laurence and me is that he's my "ex"—insofar as he was ever anything. But he doesn't have a key to my flat, and never did.'

'Yet he managed to get in and go through your wardrobe.'

Light dawned. 'Oh, Craig, you fool.' She could hardly keep the laughter out of her voice. It was laughter of relief and joy as much as amusement.

'Don't laugh at me, damn you! *Don't laugh.*'

'I'm not really. Craig, I swear I don't love Laurence. I live alone, but just now I've got a friend staying with me. She let him in.'

He was tense, like a man who feared to believe good news, lest he wake and find it a dream. 'He knew what dress to go for,' he said warily.

'He's seen me in it before. It's vulgar. I didn't mind that then but I do now. It's all over between him and me. There never was very much, and he met a girl tonight who really admires him. Craig, please forget about Laurence.'

'If only I could,' he murmured longingly.

'You must. He isn't between us. You're the one I—the one I love.' It took all her courage to utter the words.

'Don't say that if it isn't true,' he said hoarsely.

'It *is* true. I don't know when it began. Somehow it just happened. By the time I realised, it was too late.' She tried to read his face, but it showed nothing, and her heart sank. 'If you don't love me...' she began in a faltering voice.

She got no further. His arms tightened

around her, crushing her against him, and his mouth was on hers. He kissed her urgently, seeking the answers to questions he couldn't ask. She gave him those answers with all her heart. At last he was casting away his barriers of suspicion, revealing himself to her, in a way she'd hardly dared hope for.

She knew now why her heart had been cool for so many years. She'd been waiting to meet the one man who could set it on fire. Now it had happened and her life was beginning. She gave herself up to him freely, gladly, wanting only to be his.

His lips moved insistently on hers. His hands roved over her, seeking out her shape. The feel of her slender body inflamed him. The tight dress lovingly emphasised every curve and valley, exciting his imagination.

'I was sure you were his,' he murmured. 'I wouldn't let myself think of you—'

'I've thought about you from the first moment. I tried not to. I disliked you, but I couldn't get you out of my mind.' The last words were muffled as she laid her lips once more against his.

He seemed to hesitate, as though waiting to know what he should read into this. But her soft mouth was persuasive, sending him messages he couldn't ignore. 'Craig,' she whispered. 'Craig…'

'Is this what you want?' he asked, drawing her closer.

'Yes,' she whispered. 'This is what I want…'

He burned as if with fever. There was hunger in his embraces. 'Don't do this unless you mean it,' he begged.

Delia slipped her hand behind her back and pulled down the zip that held the skintight dress in place. He heard the soft rasping sound, felt her rise to her feet, taking his hands and placing them on the dress. A slight pull and it slipped down easily. Her slip followed and soon there was nothing between his eager hands and her naked body. He sighed, burying his face against her flesh, inhaling its sweet aroma of womanly warmth and desire. Then her heart was beating wildly close to his ear, and the sound gave him courage to take the next step into the strange, mysterious world that her love promised.

He rose to face her, enjoying her soft movements as she peeled away his clothes. He half feared the moment of nakedness, when she would have the advantage of sight, but it was gone in an instant. It felt right to discard all barriers, and free their mutual passion.

He took her in his arms gently, thrilling to the feel of her skin against his own. He'd once thought he could guess how she looked, but she was a revelation, more delicately built than he'd imagined. Her breasts were small and rounded, each one fitting his cupped hand as if made for it. Against his own size and strength she was almost lost, and a new feeling of protectiveness filled him as he slowly drew her down on the bed beside him.

Delia gave herself up to his caresses gladly, but with a feeling almost of awe. She'd craved this moment, but now that it was here she had no idea where it would lead. With every tender touch he took her further into a new dimension, where she could forget herself. Her insides seemed to dissolve, no longer flesh but pure sensation, where every feeling evoked its opposite. There was joy, but it was of the bittersweet kind, and hope blended with fear. Alongside an adventurous longing to explore these new realms was an instinct to hurry back to the safety she'd once known.

But it was too late for that. She no longer

knew herself. The once proud woman had turned into someone who would put her hand gladly into her lover's and say, 'Lead me.'

His embrace grew stronger, as if he'd discovered what he needed to know, and all was well. The darkness was no hindrance to him now. He could claim the woman his heart desired as much as his flesh without fear, because with every touch, every softly whispered word she told him how willingly she made the gift.

At the moment of their perfect union he felt flooded by a kind of peace that he hadn't known for seven years. The world was a new place where everything was possible, because she loved him.

At last Delia felt herself become completely his, as she'd longed to be. To her wonder and delight it was everything she'd dreamed of. His prickly shell had been discarded and he gave himself to her as totally as he claimed her. And he gave everything, not merely his passion but also his pain and his need. He wanted more than her love. He wanted her comfort. He would never ask for it in words, because he couldn't. But he could entreat it in the urgency of his kiss, in the way his arms enfolded her body, as though protecting a long-lost treasure. Most of all, he told her what she needed to know when he finally fell asleep with his head on her breast.

Slowly Delia opened her eyes. But her blissful smile faded at the sight of Craig, sitting on the edge of the bed, his head buried in his hands.

'Craig?'

He reached out for her, but his head was still bent. 'What is it?' she asked in dismay. 'What's wrong?'

'I had no right to do that,' he groaned. 'I swore that I wouldn't—and yet—' He could say no more. Somehow his peace had deserted him. It might still be there, somewhere, but it was a new-born infant that must be constantly nourished to survive. When he'd found himself alone again in his own head he'd realised that the path was still rocky.

'You swore not to make love to me?' Delia echoed. 'Why?'

'Because I'm the man I am. What chance would we have?'

She pulled herself up in bed and threw her arms around him. 'The chance we give ourselves. If we love each other anything is possible.'

'Do you want to hear me say I love you?' he asked gruffly. 'All right, I'll say it. I love you. I love everything about you. Not just your beauty, but your honesty and courage, and your compassion.' He gave a brief, self-mocking laugh. 'Another good resolution gone.'

'If you resolved not to love me, that was a *bad* resolution,' Delia said strongly.

'And what can I offer you? A life shackled to a man who's full of demons and suspicion, who's likely to yell at you because sometimes he—just—can't—cope.' He said the last words with his hands clenched.

'But you do a great job of coping,' she said, pleadingly.

'Only on the outside. Inside—' He checked himself, on the verge of revealing to her what he'd never discussed with another living soul.

'Inside, you have only the darkness,' she said softly.

He reached for her, startled by the precision with which she'd voiced his thought. The sighted didn't understand that when you were blind the darkness was everywhere, not just in your eyes. But *she* knew.

At last he relaxed enough to lean back against the pillows, one arm behind his head, the other holding her close. 'I wish we'd met years ago,' he said, 'when I was a real man.'

'I have no complaints on that score,' Delia murmured demurely, and he gave a crack of laughter.

'Thank you, but that wasn't what I meant. When I had my eyes I was a *man*. I was in charge. I could go out and make the world dance to my tune.'

'You don't do so badly now,' she observed. 'But I'd love to know what you were like in those days.'

'I expect my sister told you about our family. You had to achieve. Nothing else counted. It can be tough on a child, and I've never pressurised Alison that way. But I thrived on it.'

'I can imagine,' she said, nestling against him and dropping a tender kiss on his chest. 'Go on.'

'I felt like a king. I made a success of business, married a woman all the other men had wanted and we had a wonderful baby. Everything worked out as I'd planned. I was in control. And then—' a shudder went through him '—I discovered that my control was an illusion. One fall, and it was all taken away from me. I was left groping about helplessly in the dark—an object of derision, most of all to myself.'

'Derision?' she said, aghast. 'Surely people didn't—?'

'Some hid it better than others. Gillian, my mother-in-law, always disliked me. She thought me aggressive and bumptious, which I suppose I was. She fought me for custody of Alison. She said a "helpless man" had no right to raise her grandchild. Luckily the court found my wife's lover as disgusting as I did, and when they learned that he was always welcome in Gillian's house—in fact she'd introduced them—they let me keep Alison. But I've tried to keep contact with my in-laws for Alison's sake, and to be a normal father to her, and not accept her help more than I have to.'

'For her sake—or yours?' Delia asked gently.

'For hers of course. Well, perhaps a little for mine too. I feel uneasy when she mothers me. And it isn't fair to Alison.'

'Is it fair to her to reject her love?'

'I never reject her love.'

'Perhaps you don't mean to, but I think it comes across to her like that. She enjoys

looking after you. She loves you terribly,
Craig, and that's how she shows it. And
when you reject her care you hurt her.'

'I'm just trying to give her a little normal,
childhood freedom.'

'Of course, but don't push her away. I've
seen her expression when she's doing something for you.'

'So have I. It's in her voice: very kind
and wise, like a nanny.'

'Maybe you're not listening closely
enough. You haven't picked up her happiness when she feels necessary to you. It's
Alison's nature to care. She'll probably become a doctor, or one of those lawyers who
only ever work for the defence. Anything
where she can help people. If only you
could tell her sometimes that you need her.'

He didn't answer this, but his grip on her
hand tightened, and Delia understood. From
the start he'd felt his blindness as a humil-
iation, and had fought to prove himself as
good a man as any other.

But he'd overdeveloped one side of himself—the tough, need-nobody side—while
his capacity for tenderness was in danger of
withering because he was afraid to show it.
Even their love was something he'd felt as
a weakness, and not yielding to weakness

was important to him. There were so few
parts of his life where he felt in control.

'Never mind that now,' she said, drawing
him close. 'We have so much to learn about
each other. And it's Sunday. We don't have
to go into work...'

They spent the day loving and talking. He
insisted on doing the cooking, but now it
was different. He was no longer proving
himself, but performing a loving service for
his lady. For the first time she heard him
give a full-bodied laugh. He could even
make jokes.

'You've given me a real problem,' he
said as they lay together on Sunday evening. 'What am I going to do about
Alexandra?'

'Your personal assistant—sorry, secretary?'

'The very one. She stayed in the north on
purpose so that I'd be without her at the
meeting. It's her way of showing me how
much I need her, so that I'll promote her. I
won't stand for blackmail, so I was going
to fire her.'

'But?'

'If she hadn't let me down you wouldn't

have come with me, and we might not have discovered each other in time.'

'In time?'

'Soon it might have been too late for me. My defences were growing every day.'

'It doesn't make any difference,' she promised. 'No matter how thick they grew I'd have found a way in, less for your sake than for mine. I need you so much.'

'You—need me?'

'You're the only man who's ever seen me properly.'

This time he didn't ask what she meant, but held her tightly. At last he said, 'So I really owe Alexandra a debt of gratitude.'

'What are you going to do?'

He grinned. 'I think I'll promote her instead—for services rendered. Delia, my love...'

But as she was snuggling up to him blissfully the phone rang. 'Alison,' they announced together.

'I adore my daughter,' Craig said, groaning, 'but she has a lousy sense of timing.' He lifted the bedside receiver and said, 'Hello, darling?'

Delia could hear Alison's voice clearly as she asked the question that was always top of her list.

'I'm fine,' Craig said instinctively, but then added quickly, 'Except for missing you.'

Alison sounded anxious. 'Isn't Miss Summers looking after you properly?'

'Yes—of course she is—but—' Craig signalled to Delia wildly for help. She placed her hand over the mouthpiece and whispered, 'But it's not the same as having my girl.'

Craig repeated the words, hoping Alison hadn't heard enough to be suspicious. Instead her voice was filled with almost painful eagerness as she asked. 'Do you really miss me, Daddy?'

'More than you'll ever know, darling. Especially at breakfast, when you usually read bits out of the paper to me. And in the evening, when you usually come dashing in—and the daft programmes you watch on TV, and—' Delia whispered again '—the way you kiss me goodnight, and so many things.'

'Do you want me to come home?'

'Don't you dare. You stay and enjoy yourself. I just want you to know that I'm thinking about you, all the time.'

Delia slipped away. Craig needed to talk to his daughter alone, and tell her what was in his heart, if he could. It might be too much to ask, all at once, but he'd made a start.

Without her, Craig found that the words were harder, but he was touched by Alison's eager question. 'Do you really miss me, Daddy? Really and truly?'

'Really and truly,' he promised. The ecstatic little sigh that reached him down the phone line was a revelation. It meant that much to her! And he hadn't known.

He tried again. He was awkward, but she drank up every encouraging word like a desert thirsting for a few drops of water. By the time they hung up Alison was completely happy. Craig lay there, feeling guilty that he'd been too self-absorbed to read his daughter's heart.

But it wasn't too late. Truly Delia had come to him 'in time'. But perhaps only just.

He called her name, wanting to reach out to her in passionate gratitude, and suddenly she was there beside him, in his arms.

CHAPTER ELEVEN

ON THE night before Alison was due back Craig arrived home early and set himself to make a special supper for Delia. He had a new recipe and wanted to surprise her.

The last week had been the happiest of his life, not just in the years since his blindness, but of his whole life. He'd thought himself happy when he'd married Philippa, but looking back he recognised that he'd always known something was amiss, that one day she would coolly betray him. Now, looking into Delia's heart, he knew he'd found the perfect woman: warm, loving, and with a pure truth of the heart that would never fail him.

He'd prided himself on his inner eye, which he'd believed saw everything. But Delia had shown him the things he'd missed in his spiritual blindness. She'd seen the danger with Alison, and taught him how to avoid it. For that she would have not only his love but also his eternal gratitude.

She'd also revealed to him the danger within himself, the subtle twisting that bitterness that had caused in his character. In her arms he'd felt his nature become straight again. Bitterness was something that could be conquered, because she was there.

He smiled as he found himself thinking of Philippa as his *first* wife, which meant that he was planning a second. But, while his subconscious had decided that he must marry Delia, his reason drew back.

To him their love represented risk. He was used to an ordered world where things were always in the same place. Now this woman who was like no other had invited him to step into the unknown with her. In that new place nothing would be familiar, but infinite joy would reward the brave man.

But was he a brave man? He'd never doubted it before. His steely courage had brought him through hell. Now, faced with the ultimate challenge, he was uncertain. Suddenly nothing was in its familiar place.

He'd talked it all over with himself many times, trying to be sensible. But how could a man be sensible with the memory of her lips and hands, and the generous outpour-

ings of her heart? Every day his doubts
grew fainter. Perhaps this very evening,
when he was holding her hand and picturing
how she looked in the candlelight...

The phone rang when he was at an awkward moment in the cooking. Craig cursed,
and turned the gas down before he answered.

'Hello?'

'I have to talk to Delia urgently,' came
Laurence's brusque voice.

'She's not here. Can I get her to call you
back?'

'When will she be in? This is important.'

'I'm expecting her in about half an hour,'
Craig said, trying not to be annoyed by the
other man's rudeness.

'Tell her to call me at once. *At once*. Are
you sure you understood that?'

'Quite sure,' Craig said coldly. 'I'm
blind, not brain-dead.'

'Well, I sure as hell don't know where
your wits have been wandering recently,'
Laurence snapped. 'You have a lot to answer for.'

'Perhaps you'd like to tell me what that
means?'

'She's lost that job. It's going to Mark
Gorham. I told her this would happen if she

wasted her time on you. She should have been in there fighting, not letting it go by default. Now it's too late. I hope you're pleased with yourself.'

'Have you finished?' Craig asked in an iron-hard voice.

'I'll just say this. Delia was wide awake before you got your claws into her, making her feel guilty. Why the hell should she throw her life away on your problems? Just tell her to call me.' Laurence hung up.

Delia arrived back half an hour later, to find Craig on the leather sofa, his head thrown back. She leaned down and kissed him, but he barely responded.

'There was a message for you to call Laurence,' he said.

'Laurence? But that's all over.' Delia laughed. 'And I know he's not pining for me because he consoled himself pretty fast with Nora Hedwin.'

'Just call him,' Craig said.

Laurence answered at once. 'What's up, Laurence?'

'I warned you that you'd lose that job if you weren't careful, but would you listen?'

'Mr Hedwin is still considering—'

'That's what you think. Mark has been privately told that it's his. Nora told me.'

Delia turned so that she had her back to Craig, and spoke in a low voice. 'How certain is Nora about this?'

'Dead certain. I'd say you had only yourself to blame, but I think the real blame lies elsewhere—'

'That's enough,' she said quietly. 'Thank you for letting me know.' She hung up, feeling as if she'd had a blow in the stomach. Laurence had warned her. Craig had warned her. Now it had happened, and the injustice hurt. Not as much as it once would have done, but it hurt.

She looked at him, lying with his head back against the sofa, and a fierce urge to protect him made her resolve to keep silent. She put her head up and walked over to him.

'Well?' Craig asked.

'Nothing much,' she said cheerfully. 'Just Laurence making a fuss about trivia, as usual.'

'I wouldn't call it nothing that Mark has stabbed you in the back over that job.'

Delia drew in her breath. She'd been too upset to consider what Laurence might have told Craig.

'I only meant that it's not important,' she said lightly.

'Not important?' There was a warning note in Craig's voice.

'Not the end of the world. There are other jobs.'

'But you wanted this one. And you've lost it. And you didn't tell me. And I know why. You were being 'kind'. Don't tell the blind man the damage he's done in case he feels useless—or worse.'

'No,' she said frantically. 'It wasn't like that. What did Laurence say to you?'

'Only the truth—that I destroyed your chances.'

'You didn't. Mark and Brian just intrigued too cleverly—'

'And you let them get away with it. Why the devil did you take the risk?'

'Because I love you,' she said passionately. 'Because I wanted to be with you more than anything else—'

'Because you wanted to *look after* me,' he interrupted. 'You're very generous.'

Delia took a sharp breath. 'If you don't know the difference between love and pity then our time together has been wasted. Didn't it mean anything to you?'

'You'll never know how much it meant,' he said harshly. 'But I've been living in a fool's paradise. I batten on people and destroy their lives. I try not to, but it happens anyway. Alison, and now you. I damage everyone, and I can't take that any more.'

'Craig, please,' she cried frantically. She could see her new-found happiness slipping away, and she was terrified that she couldn't stop it. 'Can't you understand what you've done for me? You made me believe that I have some value, apart from my looks. For the first time in my life I feel worth something. Not my face, *me*. And you did that.'

'Then I'm glad. At least I gave you something good to set against the harm. But I won't let you risk yourself for me again.'

'Whether I get this job or not doesn't matter, not like it used to—'

'But it *will* matter again, and very soon. What will be in your eyes then, Delia, that I'll never see? This man lost me everything, because he's maimed and useless. I threw my chances away for him, and he selfishly let me.'

'*No!*' she cried.

'Do you think I could endure life wondering what you're thinking, tortured because I can't see your feelings in your eyes?'

'What about last night?' she burst out. 'And the other nights when we lay together in the darkness—you couldn't see me then, and I couldn't see you. But you didn't need sight to know my heart. If you don't know by now that I love you—if you don't love me—'

'You don't need to ask me that,' he said. 'Yes, I love you—enough to send you away before my blindness ruins your life.'

'It doesn't matter,' she cried. 'It's you I love, what you *are*. I can't leave you—don't ask me to. We could have so much...'

He found his way towards her, and took hold of her arms, firmly but gently. 'But we couldn't.' he said. 'The poison is in me. If I were a better man, perhaps I could overcome it. For a while I thought I had. But the reality is always there, waiting to catch us. Whatever we could have had is a "might have been", and it must stay that way.'

'Why have you so little faith in me?' she demanded in agony.

'Not in you. In myself. For both our sakes you should go at once.'

'No, I've got to be here when Alison gets home.'

'That's tomorrow. It's best if she knows nothing about this.'

'So we smile and shake hands as if noth-

ing has happened?' she asked, horrified.
'And we part "good friends"?'

His face was already withered with suffering. 'What else can we do?' he asked
quietly.

The campers were returning by coach. Craig
came with her to the coach station and they
endured the journey in silence. It had all
been said.

Alison jumped from the coach and flung
herself against her father with an eagerness
that made him gasp. They all laughed at that
and the moment was eased. On the way
home she chattered about the wonderful
time she'd had.

Delia had her bags packed and was ready
to leave at once, but Alison promptly vetoed
this plan. 'I want to give you your present,'
she said. 'Oh, you *must* wait.'

She'd bought Delia a charming print of
wild flowers. Her gift to her father was a
heavy piece of wood that she herself had
whittled down into the rough shape of an
owl. She guided his hands over it, indicating various features, letting him feel the
varnish. Craig smiled and thanked her
warmly. Delia watched them, glad that he'd

at least managed to take this step, and even more glad that Alison suspected nothing.

But misery was clouding her perceptions, and she failed to notice Alison's quick glance between them.

At last she could get away. Alison had bounded upstairs to unpack, and Craig came with Delia to the car.

'Goodbye, Delia,' he said quietly.

'I can't believe it's going to end like this,' she whispered.

'Perhaps it hasn't. Maybe one day—maybe even soon—' He took a sharp breath as if dismayed at what he was saying.

'What do you mean by that, Craig?'

'Nothing. I'm talking nonsense.'

'You sound as if you hoped for something.'

'I tell you it was nothing,' he said angrily. 'I never hope. Hope just destroys you. Remember that.' He turned abruptly and went back into the house. Delia watched him go, wondering how anything could hurt so much and still leave her standing.

Delia expected to be given the bad news about the job at once, but day followed day and nothing happened except that Mark vanished and was seen no more. At last she

received the summons and went to Mr
Hedwin's office. Brian too was there, with
a smile fixed on his face by sheer force.

'Congratulations,' Mr Hedwin said, extending his hand to her as soon as she appeared. 'You've just been appointed
Orchid's new chief publicity director.' He
added, slightly too firmly, 'Brian is as
pleased as I am.'

'Delighted,' Brian murmured, his eyes
glassy.

It appeared that he was to leave in two
weeks' time, much earlier than Delia had
expected. 'I should have retired last year,
but Mr Hedwin particularly requested me to
stay,' he explained loftily. 'But now my
successor has been chosen I feel that the
time has come to lay down the burdens.'

So Brian had stayed on to smooth Mark's
path, and now that he'd failed he was jumping ship. He confirmed this indirectly as
they returned to their own offices. 'I ought
to congratulate you, my dear Delia, but I
find I really can't do it,' he said spitefully.

'I understand how you feel, Brian.'

'I doubt that. Honest competition is one
thing, but sneaking in by the back way is
something I dislike.'

'Then why did you try to sneak Mark in

by the back way? Was that honest competition?'

'It was a sight more honest than getting your friends to pull strings for you.'

Delia stared. 'Nobody pulled strings for me, Brian.'

'Oh, please, don't pretend you didn't know what was going on.'

'I thought Mark had got it—'

'He had, until you got Craig Locksley to go into action for you.'

Her heart lurched at the mention of Craig's name, but she was still puzzled. 'What has he got to do with this? He's not a member of the firm.'

'But he's very important to Orchid right now. When he told Hedwin that you were the only one he could deal with, it went a long way, as you knew it would.'

'I swear I didn't know—'

'Oh, please,' Brian interrupted disdainfully. 'I detest affectations of innocence. I just hope your victory doesn't turn sour in your mouth.'

'You mean you hope it does,' Delia replied with spirit.

He shrugged. 'Either way, we shall soon be out of each other's hair.'

He stalked off, closing his door sharply

behind him. Delia was left trying to come to terms with the shattering discovery. Craig had intervened to help her. For a moment her heart glowed. He was thinking of her.

But, of course, he'd done it for the sake of his own pride. Some of her elation died as she recalled his bitterness at her loss, and how he'd blamed himself. Now he'd put things right. That was all there was to it.

Several times she almost called Craig to thank him, but drew back. When at last she dialled his work number, his secretary informed her that he was away for a few days. She called his home and heard his answering machine. Perhaps he'd taken a holiday with Alison. She never tried again. He'd dismissed her so finally, and this last gesture was merely tying up ends. He didn't want to hear from her.

The only other thread of contact she could maintain with him was the story of the child-labour firm. Craig had achieved everything he'd wanted. When the shares had gone into their final nosedive the board had given in and reversed its policy. The foreign factories were being closed down, and factories at home were re-opening. Leabridge and Derham had both announced early retirement, 'due to ill health', and departed without bonuses.

Brian was making her life as awkward as possible. Several times she asked him to talk to her and hand over the reins in an orderly manner. He promised, but the meetings were always delayed. Then, abruptly, he pronounced himself too ill to work further, and was never seen at Orchid again. So Delia was thrown in at the deep end, with no help from Brian at all. The files were full of things he'd concealed from her, and at first she was all at sea, as he'd obviously intended.

Luckily Brian's secretary was a tower of strength. Even so, Delia worked all hours, determined to succeed despite obstacles. She was first in the office and last out. On Saturday morning she went in until lunchtime, and when she left she was carrying a heap of files.

As she drove home her mind was racing with thoughts of the work she would do that afternoon. By day she always kept her mind running on something, to stop it lingering on Craig. That would come late at night, when she was alone in bed, and he could no longer be shut out. All the way up in the lift she was mentally drafting letters. But then the lift reached her floor, the doors opened, and Delia saw something that wiped all else from her mind.

'*Alison!*'

The child had been sitting beside Delia's front door. Now she jumped up eagerly and went straight into her arms. 'I'm so glad you've come,' she said in a muffled voice. 'I've been waiting and waiting. I was afraid I'd have to go without seeing you.'

There were a thousand questions to be asked, but Delia held them back until they were inside. Alison looked pale and unhappy.

'What is it?' Delia asked urgently. 'Is something wrong with your father? Did he send you?'

'No, Daddy doesn't know I'm here. I told him I wanted to get in touch with you, and he said not if I knew what was good for me.'

Delia sighed. How like the old Craig that sounded! 'But you came anyway?'

'Yes, because I may not know what's good for me, but I *do* know what's good for Daddy. Much better than he does.' Alison paused as though trying to summon up courage, took a deep breath and said, 'Miss Summers, are you and Daddy in love?'

'Yes, we are,' Delia said simply.

Alison sighed, as though the difficult part had been accomplished. 'I thought so. When I came home you were barely speaking to each other. The air was absolutely *jagged*,' she said dramatically. 'People don't get like that unless they mind terribly about each other.'

Delia gave a wan smile. 'Terribly,' she said. 'At least, I do. I thought he did too, but then he sent me away.'

Alison nodded. 'Daddy can be awfully silly sometimes,' she confirmed.

'He was convinced it was his fault I lost my promotion. But I got it anyway. It seems he had something to do with that.'

'I thought so,' Alison said wisely. 'I knew I had to get here somehow. I asked Grandma to bring me, but she said, 'Nonsense,' so I'm afraid I had to tell her a whopper. She thinks I'm at the cinema with a friend.'

Delia steered her into the kitchen and put on the kettle. 'Your grandmother? Is she staying with you?'

'Yes. I hate it.'

'I thought you liked her. Didn't you stay with her a while back?'

'That's my other granny: Daddy's

mother. This is Grandma Gillian, and she's always cross because the court gave me to Daddy. She keeps making little barbed remarks about him not being able to look after me properly, but he *does*. I'm stuck with her until he gets out of hospital.'

'Oh, Alison, no! You mean he's ill?'

'Not ill. He's had an operation on his eyes. He's been trying to decide for weeks, and he made up his mind very suddenly.'

'You mean—he might be able to see again?' Delia could hardly get the words out.

'It's about a thirty per cent chance,' Alison said, sounding very knowledgeable. 'He's trying not to count on it.'

Pain and happiness warred within Delia. So much was happening to Craig, and she wasn't there to share it because he didn't want her. He'd sent her away because he wouldn't tie her to a blind man. If he regained his sight there might be hope for them. But he hadn't sought her help in his most crucial hour. Could any love survive that bitterness?

She began setting out cups, acting and speaking mechanically to cover her inner turmoil. 'Would you like something to eat?'

'Oh, please!' Alison said at once.

'Grandma's been taking lessons in nouvelle cuisine, and she's practising on me. Last night she served up something she said was soup, but it looked as though she'd just done the washing up in it. Honestly, sometimes I get desperate for egg and chips.'

'Egg and chips coming up!'

Slice the potatoes, she thought. Focus on them, think only of the food. Don't think that he doesn't want you. Heat up the chip pan. He doesn't even need you. Break the eggs. Concentrate. Maybe that will ease the pain.

'Why did he spend weeks deciding?' she asked at last. 'Why not jump at it at once?'

'I think it's because this is his one hope,' Alison said slowly. 'If it doesn't work, he'll have no hope left. That might be even harder than being blind.'

Delia nodded, accepting the child's opinion. Alison understood her father like no one else.

'This is smashing,' she said a few minutes later as she tucked into the food. 'I wish you were there instead of Grandma.'

'What about—?' Delia stopped delicately.

'My mother was just going on holiday,' Alison said woodenly.

'With Mr Elward?'

'No, he was over ages ago. It's Roy now—oh, no, he was last year. Now it's Joe—or somebody. I forget.'

'I see,' Delia said gently.

'It doesn't matter,' Alison said with a touch of defiance. 'I've got Daddy.' But then she added wistfully, 'I wish you two could have got it together. It would have been so nice.'

Delia squeezed her shoulder. 'Is there any news of Jenny?' she asked after a while.

'Oh, yes.' Alison brightened. 'We've got Jenny back, but she still can't go out in traffic, and I don't suppose she ever will now. If this operation doesn't work Daddy's going to need another guide dog. Jenny will just be a pet.'

'She'll hate that.'

'Oh, yes, she will,' Alison agreed at once. 'She's used to being really needed. She always looked so proud when her harness went on. She'll mind terribly if she's left behind while another dog does her work. I give her plenty of love to make her feel better. Grandma says Jenny's getting old and it would happen anyway. But that's different.'

'Yes, that's honourable retirement,' Delia

agreed. 'Jenny's going to feel she's failed. Oh, Alison, I'm so sorry. This is all my fault!'

'Is it?'

'I knocked her down.'

'I'd forgotten that. You just seem like a friend now. I can talk to you like no one else. Much better than Grandma. Better than Daddy sometimes.'

'Your father isn't an easy man.'

'No,' Alison said with feeling, and they smiled at each other like conspirators.

'When did all this happen?'

'About a week after you left. Daddy was very, very quiet. And then he suddenly began talking about the operation, asking me what I thought. Then he said he'd talk to the doctor about it again. He even asked me to go to the doctor with him. He's never, ever done that before.'

'I'm glad you were there.'

'So am I. He thought about it for a few more days, and then he said, "All right. We'll give it a try." He went into hospital a week ago. He came through the operation terribly well.' But the next moment the child's strong façade cracked, and there were tears in her eyes. 'Oh, Miss Summers,

you've got to visit him. You've simply got
to.'

'Darling, I want to. But if he doesn't
want me—'

'He does, I know he does, but he won't
say so. He's lonely and unhappy and—and
scared. He'd be cross if he heard me say
that, but I know he is. I try and try, but he
won't talk about the worst, even to me, because he thinks I'm a child. He can't even
have Jenny in the hospital, so he's all alone
in the dark—' She dropped her knife and
fork and rubbed her eyes, while tears
poured down her cheeks.

At once Delia took her in her arms and
the little girl sobbed unrestrainedly. 'I don't
know what to do for him. Please, you must
come and help.'

Did she dare to do this? Her heart longed
to see Craig again, and wouldn't it be worth
the risk? If she could only tell him how
much she loved him, surely then he'd understand, and open his arms to her?

'All right, Alison. I'll come with you.'

CHAPTER TWELVE

WHEN they were in the hospital corridor, Alison said, 'You come into Daddy's room with me, and don't say anything just at first. I'll tell Daddy, and then—you'll see. Everything will be all right.' She almost skipped the last few feet.

Delia held her breath as Alison opened the door slowly and the room came into view. There was the foot of the bed, then the coverlet with one hand lying on it, the sheet, and then the whiteness of the pillow. She bit her lip, trying not to cry out her distress. Craig's eyes were covered in bandages, and what was visible of his face was very pale. But what really tore at Delia was his stillness. It spoke eloquently of dread and despair.

It took all her self-control not to rush forward and put her arms about him, but she knew that was the last thing she must do. She had no place here unless Craig himself wanted her.

Suddenly he turned his head on the pillow. 'Is someone there?'

'It's me, Daddy.' Alison hurried forward as he held out his arms to her.

Delia stayed where she was, her heart hammering. Suppose his sixth sense were to tell him she was in the room? But he was absorbed in his daughter.

'I've been listening for you,' he said. 'But I didn't hear you. I must have been asleep.'

'You should put your radio on, so that you don't sleep too much in the day,' Alison lectured him gravely. 'Otherwise you won't sleep at night.'

'I know.' He touched her face. 'You always have good advice for me.'

'And you never take it.'

'I will in future.'

'Promise?'

'Promise. Now tell me what you've been doing. How are you managing with Grandma?'

Alison cast a look at Delia, who put a finger over her lips. Not yet. Alison nodded and began to talk about the nouvelle cuisine. Craig managed to laugh. He held on tightly to his daughter.

Delia kept very still, longing to put her

arms around the man she loved, and promise him that she would be there for ever. But she must be patient.

'What else?' Craig asked. 'Tell me everything.'

Alison took a deep breath. 'I went to see Miss Summers.'

Craig was very silent for a moment. 'Why did you do that?' he asked at last.

'I needed to. I can't talk to Grandma. She doesn't understand, and Miss Summers does.'

Craig seemed to relax. 'If you did it for yourself, that's all right. Is she well, enjoying her new job?' He might have been asking about a stranger.

'She's working terribly hard, even on Saturdays.'

'Well, it's nice that she got what she wanted.'

'But she didn't,' Alison said, pleadingly. 'She wants you. You know she does. Just like you want—'

'That's enough,' he said sternly. 'There are some things we can't discuss. I suppose you told her about this?' He indicated his bandages. 'I wish you hadn't, but knowing you I'm sure you did.'

'Yes, and she wants to come and visit you.'

'Of course she does. She's a nice, kind person, but I—well, let's just say it's not a good idea. You can tell her I'm fine, but don't want any visitors—except you.' His arms tightened in a convulsive hug. '*You* stay with me,' he said, almost fiercely. 'I need you.'

Alison snuggled up to him, her face blissful. Delia watched them sadly. She knew she'd achieved something for the two people she loved. With her help they'd found each other. But there was no place for her. She backed quietly out of the room.

Because Alison kept in touch Delia was able to follow everything that happened to Craig. She knew the day he went home from hospital, still wearing bandages.

'The doctor wasn't keen but Daddy was desperate to be home,' Alison told her, having dropped in for a chat the day after Craig arrived home. 'So the doctor said yes, as long as he had a nurse.'

'What's the nurse like?'

'Not too bad. Her name's Vera. She tried to order Jenny off the bed at first, but Daddy said that was where Jenny belonged, and

Vera backed down. Grandma's going home tomorrow.'

'I expect your grandfather will be glad to have her back.'

'Actually he said she should stay as long as she felt she was needed.' Alison gave a giggle. 'I don't think he likes drinking washing-up water either.'

'Is Jenny any better?'

Alison shook her head. 'But it doesn't matter just now. Daddy likes to have her with him all the time. I play with her in the garden, but when the game's finished she goes straight back to him.'

'And what about you?'

Alison's smile told Delia what she wanted to know. 'He talks to me more now,' Alison said simply.

Delia smiled warmly, but her exclusion was very painful. Craig had found the way to reach out to his daughter, and his need of Jenny was greater than ever. But he refused to turn to the woman who loved him. She was shut out, pressing her face against the glass.

Day followed day, with no word from him. When he'd been home a week Delia could stand it no longer. One night, at about eleven o'clock, she got into her car and drove over to his house, parking some distance away. She walked back, entering his drive quietly, and going to a place under the trees, from which she could look up at his window.

She heard a rustling from the bushes and she stepped back. But it was only Jenny, having her final outing before going to bed. She stood still, sniffing the air, then turned and trotted over to Delia. She dropped to her knees, petting the dog, who received her embraces willingly.

'You remember me, don't you?' Delia said, and felt the rasp of Jenny's tongue in confirmation.

'How is he?' she whispered. 'Does he ever talk to you about me? Are you helping him to cope? Oh, why can't you speak?' She hugged Jenny fiercely, as Craig hugged her, trying to reach him just a little.

Then she heard the front door opening. Before she could back away Craig himself came out onto the step. In the dim light from the porch lamp she could just see that he was in pyjamas and dressing gown, with bandages over his eyes.

'Jenny,' he called.

The dog hurried over to him and he bent to pat her. 'Why were you so long, old girl?' he asked gently. 'Didn't you know I missed you?'

Suddenly he straightened up, all his senses alert. Delia held her breath, wondering if she dared reveal herself. Would it really do harm if she stepped forward and called his name? Wouldn't he be glad, after all?

'Is anyone there?' he called. Jenny gave a soft whine. 'What is it, girl? Is there someone?'

He listened again. Delia stayed silent. Her heart was aching, but the risk was too great.

Then he did something that almost broke her resolve. He leaned against the doorpost as if whatever was supporting him had suddenly given way. For a moment he dropped his face into his hands. Jenny pawed at him, whimpering. At last he straightened up and patted her.

'Come on, Jenny,' he said softly. 'Let's go inside and get to bed.'

Alison, in a dressing gown, was waiting for him at the top of the stairs. 'Are you all right, Daddy?'

'What are you doing out of bed at this hour?'

'I just came to make sure you were safely in.'

He touched her shoulder, smiling. 'You're like a mother hen with an awkward chick.'

'Someone needs to mother-hen you,' she said wisely. 'You look terrible. Let me see you safely in bed.'

Once he would have told her sharply that he needed no help. But his heart understood more now, and he simply said, 'Thank you, darling.'

She settled him and pulled the bedclothes up with difficulty, since Jenny was already in position.

'Shove over,' Craig ordered her. 'This is my bed too.'

Jenny moved half an inch. Craig waited until his daughter had kissed him and departed before he wrapped an arm around the dog. 'You felt it, didn't you?' he murmured to her. 'So did I. But we were both wrong.'

Standing below, Delia saw the light in his room go off. Now she knew he was alone up there with his terrible private darkness, clinging onto his last hope. But not needing her. She stayed motionless, watching the window, for an hour. Then she went home.

Two days to go before the bandages came off. One day. On the evening before, Alison rang.

'The doctor's coming at eleven o'clock tomorrow morning,' she said. 'Daddy said he wanted it to happen at home. I'll call you straight after. Or perhaps—perhaps Daddy will.'

'Perhaps,' Delia said, trying to believe it.

She couldn't concentrate on her work. Her mind was with Craig, knowing that this day would bring the fulfilment of his dreams or the dashing of his last hope. And with it would go every last hope of her own.

But hadn't her hope already died? If Craig asked her back into his life only because he'd regained his sight it would only be second-best. She would return to him, because she loved him too much to refuse. But the knowledge that he'd chosen to go through his crisis without her would always be there, poisoning what ought to be beautiful. They would share a crippled love, with something permanently missing. And how long could it last?

She couldn't help counting the hours. All of life had become focused on the approaching moment.

'Aren't you going to bed?' Maggie eventually asked.

'I will in a minute.'

'You've said that twice before. You can't sit watching that clock all night.'

When Maggie had gone to bed Delia tried to read a book, but the words danced. What was he doing now? Could he manage to sleep? Or was he lying awake, listening to the ticking of the clock, knowing that in a few hours his life would begin—or end?

The shrill of the phone brought her sharply upright. She snatched up the receiver. 'Hello?'

'Delia?' said the voice she'd feared never to hear again.

'*Craig,*' she whispered.

He sounded different. All the confidence had gone from his voice. 'You don't mind my calling you so late?'

'No—no, I'm glad you did. How are you?'

'Not so good. There are things that— well, I gather Alison's told you.'

'You mustn't be angry with her,' Delia said quickly.

'I'm not. I thought—you'll laugh at this, but I even thought you might come to me.'

'I wanted to, but you made it clear that you didn't need me.'

'I've needed you every moment since you went away. There hasn't been a time when I wasn't thinking of you, longing for you. And now more than ever—' His voice shook. 'Come now, Delia,' he said huskily. 'Come to me tonight. I can't stand it alone. I'm—afraid.'

'Wait for me,' she said breathlessly. 'I'm coming.'

She was out of the house in seconds. When she pulled into his drive she could already see Craig standing at the door, listening with painful eagerness. Another moment and she was in his arms.

'I was afraid you wouldn't come,' he said against her mouth. 'After I drove you away I thought there was no hope.'

'I never really went away,' she said. 'In my heart I was always with you. Kiss me, my love…kiss me…'

He responded fiercely. The feel of his lips on hers after the long, aching weeks was so good that she felt giddy. How could there be so much joy in the world?

He drew her inside, keeping his arms around her, as though afraid that she would vanish.

'You're really here, aren't you?' he asked urgently. 'You won't disappear?'

'I'm here for as long as you want me.'

'That'll be for ever. For ever and ever. I've thought so much about when the bandages come off tomorrow—if I can see you—and Alison. To live a normal life, with you as my wife—'

'And if you can't see, will you send me away again?' she asked.

'Never in this life,' he said fervently. 'I thought I was strong enough to survive without you. But I'm not.'

'Craig, will you marry me? Will you promise to marry me whatever happens, in darkness or in light?'

'In darkness or in light,' he promised. 'In the darkness I'll need you more than ever. But while you're with me there will be no darkness.'

He led her to the top of the stairs and into his room. They discovered each other as lovers, but now everything was different. They'd been through the fire and learned that they couldn't survive apart. For him, especially, the discovery was like a flash of lightning over his black landscape, showing past and future. He knew that his future must be with her, whatever else might happen.

He made love to her like a man still trying to believe in his own blessings, half fearful of losing them, half triumphant that his faith had been justified. Other lovings had been full of passion. This one was full of tenderness as they consoled and reassured each other, not knowing if the day would bring heaven or hell, but ready for both, together.

Afterwards there was the warmth of his arms about her, and the infinite peace of lying together, knowing that they had come home to each other for ever.

While they lay together, there was a soft thump and the bed trembled as they were joined by a third presence that settled itself across Craig's legs. They both reached out and felt the silky fur. Two brown eyes gleamed in the darkness, watching them both contentedly, before closing. In minutes all three of them were asleep.

At dawn Delia awoke. Craig was lying with his arm thrown over her, as though seeking refuge. Jenny had settled in the crook of his knees and was snoring. Delia kissed him and slid out of bed. In the closet she found a light dressing gown, and slipped it on so that she could sit at the window.

The darkness had turned to grey, and the scene outside was getting lighter by the moment. She thought of the coming day and what it would mean for so many people. If the worst came to the worst she wouldn't let Craig fall into the old melancholy pattern. She would use all her love and strength to make his life worth living.

For Alison it might mean a normal childhood at last, free of the responsibilities she'd assumed too young. But I'll make sure she has that anyway, Delia thought.

Even Jenny had something to lose or gain. If Craig could see again she would remain the only dog. If he couldn't, she'd suffer the heartbreak of becoming second-best.

It was seven o'clock. Delia realised that she must leave Craig's room. Alison would be up and about soon, and no doubt she would check on her father. She'd said she wanted Delia back, but how would she react to finding her here without warning?

But it was already too late. Even as Delia rose from the window seat the door handle turned and a small, tousled head appeared. It halted suddenly, and Alison's eyes met

Delia's for a long moment, then a slow
smile of delight crept over her features. Her
face was full of a silent question. Delia nodded, returning her smile. Silently Alison put
a finger over her lips and backed out of the
room.

The doctor arrived at ten minutes to eleven.
Craig was downstairs, dressed in sweater
and trousers and trying to appear cheerful.
But his face was dreadfully pale.

Alison went to sit beside him on the sofa
and took his hand in hers. He squeezed it
and turned a valiant smile in her direction.
Even Jenny seemed to know that something
momentous was about to happen, and settled at her master's feet, looking up anxiously.

In a tense silence the doctor began to un-
wind the bandages. It seemed to go on for
ever, but at last the final bandage fell away.
Craig's eyes stayed closed, and Delia knew
that he dreaded opening them, in case his
final hope died.

She sat on his other side, and took his
hand in hers. 'Come on, darling,' she whispered. 'Take the bull by the horns.'

At last Craig's eyes opened. His head
was bent, and nobody could see his face. It

was impossible to tell whether he saw or not.

Then a faint smile came over his face. He seemed to focus his attention on Alison's hand, holding his on the left, and Delia's, doing the same on the right. Slowly he raised them to hold them against his face.

For a moment Delia misunderstood. Her heart lurched painfully at what she believed was a gesture seeking comfort. Then his head went up and she saw his smile, broad now, and telling everything.

'Craig?' she said, almost unable to speak. 'Craig, tell me.'

'It's all right,' he said in an awed voice.

Alison gave a shriek of delight that reached the ceiling, and flung her arms about his neck, crying, 'Daddy, Daddy.' Jenny gave a bark.

Craig hugged his daughter back eagerly. 'I can see you, chicken,' he said. 'Let me look at you better.'

She drew back so that he could study her face. 'You're smashing,' he said.

'And Jenny? Isn't she smashing too?'

He looked down at the golden head, the chin resting on his knee. 'Jenny's everything I hoped she would be,' he said.

While he was speaking he kept a tight

hold of Delia's hand. Once he glanced at her briefly and she understood the message. There was so much for them to say that couldn't be said now.

They held themselves in check while the doctor gave instructions about future care, which they barely heard. Alison showed him to the door, then tactfully vanished.

Craig took Delia's face between his hands, and looked deeply. Her shining eyes and trembling lips touched his heart more than words could have done.

'I knew,' he said simply. 'All the time I knew you'd look like this. I knew the beauty of your eyes, because I knew your heart. And I'd found your lips for myself...' He brushed his own against them gently. 'But mostly I knew that your face would tell me that you love me. And as long as it says that you will always be beautiful.'

'Even when I'm old and grey?' she asked.

'Until the end of time,' he said softly. 'And that's the greatest beauty in the world.'

Harlequin® Historical

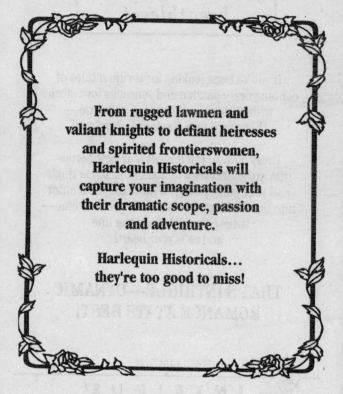

From rugged lawmen and
valiant knights to defiant heiresses
and spirited frontierswomen,
Harlequin Historicals will
capture your imagination with
their dramatic scope, passion
and adventure.

Harlequin Historicals...
they're too good to miss!

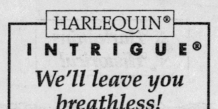

TRINITY

DAVE BARA

Acknowledgments

I'd like to thank my editor at Baen, Tony Daniel, and his publisher, Toni Weisskopf, for their faith in me and in *Trinity*. It is always gratifying to see your work and your career given a second chance, another bite at the apple, as it were. Writing is a hard business, and I encourage all of you out there working to break in to keep writing, keep taking your shot at the stars.

I would also like to acknowledge the hard work of my agent, Paul Stevens of the Donald Maass Literary Agency, (and all the people there) in making *Trinity* a reality.

Onward and upward,

Dave

❇ **PROLOGUE** ❇

Captain Jared Clement of the Rim Confederation Navy gunship *Beauregard* contemplated his tactical screen. He was alone in his cabin, as was his habit before battle, concentrating and formulating his upcoming strategy.

The tactical screen showed him no love. The fleet of 5 Suns Alliance Navy ships approaching his position over the planet Argyle, and its space station of the same name, had left their positions around the planet Shenghai in the nearby Kemmerine system over thirty-eight light-hours ago. The ships had accelerated impossibly fast, well over twenty-five *g*s, and had reached a velocity so close to light speed as to be insignificant in its difference in just thirty minutes. Normally acceleration at that speed could only be accomplished by unmanned vessels or weapons. Any human crew would be left as bloody splatters against the walls of the ships, unless there was some mitigating technology perhaps, he suspected, a new propulsion system aboard the 5 Suns Navy vessels.

Clement had heard rumors of inertial dampening technology being developed by the 5 Suns, some sort of projectors that literally distorted space in front of an accelerating ship by pushing out leading gravity waves. Humankind had been pushing at the limits of light speed for decades, and this "rumored" technology was extremely promising. So much so that Clement was fairly sure he was watching it in action for the first time on the tactical screen right in front of him.

Just a light-hour earlier the attacking formation had split into three groups, one each setting course for the three inhabited planets, Helios, Ceta, and Argyle, of the weak orange dwarf Rim star. They were close enough now that Clement could count their numbers: five light cruisers for each of Ceta and Helios, but fifteen reserved for him at Argyle. He'd made no secret of where he was stationed. Now he regretted that decision.

He'd beaten the 5 Suns Navy enough times in the ongoing conflict that it was clear they were going out of their way to finish him and the *Beauregard* off as quickly and efficiently as they could. As a former 5 Suns Navy officer himself, he was undoubtedly high on their hit list, as was his crew, he reminded himself. And he wasn't willing to sacrifice them, especially not his XO, who happened to be his former lover, and a native of the planet Helios. Commander Elara DeVore had broken off their relationship when he'd been named captain of the *Beauregard*, a move he had agreed with from a professional standpoint, if not a personal one. She in turn had agreed to follow him to his new command, but only if they broke off the relationship. It was a high price to pay, but he knew he needed her on his ship. She was still, for him, the most extraordinary woman he had ever met, but the rules were the rules, and Clement had reluctantly accepted her decision more than two years ago. Oh, there had been women since then, but none like Elara DeVore, not even close.

He fingered the rim of his whiskey glass as he tried to work out some kind of tactical strategy that gave them a fighting chance. He could find none. He wanted a drink now, badly, but he repressed the impulse. Alcohol was his personal demon, one he had learned to accept, but he didn't have to like it.

In response to the approaching flotilla, the Rim Confederation Navy had only their famous gunships. Clement had four here at Argyle, and there were three each at the other planetary defense stations. It wasn't enough. But it was all they had left. Clement himself had been in charge of the development plans on the gunships, so they were practically designed for him and his style of fighting. The Rim Navy had lost many ships in the last two years, including all of their capital ships in a mistaken attempt to take the space station at the nearby Kemmerine star. For the record, Clement had been against that move, thinking it was likely to sharpen the 5 Suns Navy's fighting edge. Regrettably, he'd been right. But the "Admirals" in charge of the Rim Navy (former commanders and captains with the 5 Suns Navy before the war) had made their plans and as a good soldier Clement had done his best during the attack.

The only ships to escape Kemmerine that day had been his gunships and a pair of battered destroyers, both of which had to be scuttled on the return trip. It had been a bad day for the Rim, if not a personal victory for him and his tactics. They'd made him Fleet Captain then (he had turned down the offered rank of Admiral) and he'd spent most of the last year preparing the Rim Navy for the inevitable: a full-scale invasion by the 5 Suns. It now appeared this was the day they had dreaded.

This had all the signs of an end-game maneuver by the 5 Suns Navy, and looking at his tac board, it seemed likely it would succeed despite his best efforts. He contemplated the situation, and briefly considered surrender, but his orders had been clear from Fleet headquarters: fight until you could fight no more. The order was tinted with the likelihood that those admirals were facing the noose for treason soon, but Clement was too good a sailor to do other than what he was ordered to do.

Just then he got the com chime from his bridge and he responded quickly. "Report, XO," he said.

"Enemy flotilla is decelerating rapidly, estimate eleven minutes until they are able to engage us on the battlefield," she said. He was amazed at the rapid deceleration he was witnessing, but not surprised. The rumored inertial dampening tech was on full display.

"Eleven minutes? Christ, I find myself longing for the old days when you had a couple of hours to prep for the battlefield," he said.

"Those days are gone, sir," she replied, the alarming tone of her voice indicating her desire for him to take control of the situation and start giving orders. He decided he should heed her. He shut down his display and got up to take the nine steps from his cabin to the bridge, a path he might be taking for the last time.

"Order the fleet to accelerate to 0.25 g, maneuvering

thrusters only, 0.000086 inclined to the ecliptic. Get us some distance from Argyle Station. Hopefully, that will make them have to adjust their course," he said as he hit the mechanism and the doors to his cabin parted.

"What about the station? Are we leaving it undefended?" He paused to reconsider.

"No. Tell Captain Cormack to hold back the *Antietam*, but his orders are not to fight if he is outnumbered. If we don't give them multiple targets with our gunships they *might* leave the station intact. Might," he said.

"Understood, sir."

A few short steps later and he was on his bridge. The main tactical display showed the glowing dots of the incoming 5 Suns flotilla. The screen was rimmed with a pulsating red light, indicating danger, something Clement already knew.

"Status," he ordered, standing in front of his tactical station. Each of his bridge crew in turn gave their updates.

"Fifteen 5 Suns Navy light cruisers coming in hot, sir. They're still decelerating, but estimate they will be at zero within two minutes. Then they will have to shift their flight path to intercept us," reported DeVore. "It will take about five minutes more for them to catch us on our current course, using conventional thrusters."

"I don't think we can count on that, XO, based on what I saw of their crossing speed."

"The gravity wave technology?"

"Possibly. I just don't know if they can use it effectively on a short-range battlefield."

"How long do we continue our burn, sir?" The question came from Mika Ori, the *Beauregard*'s pilot.

"We don't, Lieutenant. As soon as they reach zero acceleration I want us moving at forty-five degrees to their position. If they precalculated our course based on our current burn they'll have to reconfigure. Give them something to think about," Clement said.

"Looking for the best ground to fight on, sir?" asked Ivan Massif, Ori's husband and the *Beauregard*'s navigator. Clement eyed the tall, lanky man.

"Regrettably, there is no 'best ground' in this area of space, Ivan. We'll make two of the forty-five-degree pivots, three minutes apart, then we take our chances."

"We're going to attack?" said DeVore. Clement gave her an annoyed look.

"This is most likely our last battle, Commander. I wouldn't want it any other way, giving them one last bloody nose."

"But—"

"Commander," he said, beckoning her to come to his station. She did, reluctantly. He looked into her dark brown eyes, searching for understanding in them, but finding only confusion. He was always an enigma to her, he knew, and that's what had probably made their relationship work for as long as it did. "XO," he started in a whispered voice, "if they come after us, then perhaps they'll go easier on the other ships. I'm hoping this maneuver will save lives."

"But not ours," she replied, equally quiet. He looked away from her.

"I'm the Fleet Captain," he said. "I'm the prize they want."

"What about the rest of us?"

He gave her a silent nod of affirmation. "I'll do the best I can," he whispered. And the conversation was over. She returned to her console, and he continued taking reports.

Thirty seconds from the 5 Suns fleet reaching zero point, he sent out a private com to his navigator and pilot, giving them specific time and instructions on the two burns and the attack vector. Each pinged him with confirmations. They understood. He wouldn't have to give the orders verbally.

The 5 Suns fleet reached zero deceleration, just one hundred kilometers from Argyle Station in a precision maneuver his ships could never emulate. Three light cruisers immediately broke off from the main fleet and accelerated toward the station and the *Antietam*.

The rest, twelve ships, started burning their thrusters toward the stationary Rim gunships. He was outnumbered four to one—not bad odds, considering. He looked down at his tac board.

Now, he thought, just as Mika Ori gunned the engines. Perfect.

They'd been engaged with the 5 Suns Navy cruisers for more than fifteen minutes, and so far, so good. Clement had them scrambling to defend their positions, but he still had one surprise left in his hand of cards. One his crew had practiced, but never executed in battle.

"Inverted C dive, now!" demanded Clement of his pilot.

"Full C dive, aye, sir!" said Mika Ori. She slammed the *Beauregard*'s chemical infusion drive to the wall, accelerating the ship to over six gravities as they started their dive, pulling them away from the 5 Suns Navy cruiser formation. At this speed, on a crowded battlefield, it had never been tried. The chances of hitting a slice of metal or even colliding with a full ship were high, but Clement believed his ship could carry out the maneuver—and after all, he was her designer. He knew how much she could take, beyond what the specs said.

Some would have called a max-thruster inverted "C" in battle a suicide move. Not Clement. He'd built his ship for just this kind of off-the-books performance. The burn took the *Beauregard* away from the battlefield in a tight curve, from under the main plane of battle and then up through the battlefield again before his ship dropped back "down" on the enemy from above. No enemy commander would have tried it in one of the clunky 5 Suns Navy cruisers. Hell, no enemy ship could have likely carried it out.

He strained against his acceleration couch, his body squirming inside his g-force dampening suit. The suit at least partially compensated against the forces of inertial gravity. Clement and the rest of his suited bridge crew could still move, just not nimbly or quickly.

He watched on his tactical board as the 5 Suns Navy ships hardly reacted at all. Certainly, no one dared to chase the *Beauregard*, and most probably thought he was trying to escape. The Rim Confederation Navy was outgunned in this particular encounter, but the *Beauregard* had a way of evening things up. She was faster, better shielded, and carried enough ordnance to make any 5 Suns Alliance Navy cruiser's day miserable. And the 5SN relied almost exclusively on their midsized light cruisers to fight the RCN.

The *Beauregard* reached the apex of its dive (relative to the ecliptic of the Argyle system and the battlefield) and kept burning, powering through the lower arc of the inverted C-curve maneuver. "Cut the engines," ordered Clement as they reached their max speed of one hundred seventy-five kilometers per second, completing their acceleration and driving back down to the battlefield, nearly ten thousand kilometers distant now. At that speed, they would be back on the invading fleet in slightly less than a minute.

"Prep the scatter mines," ordered Clement through his pressure suit's com system.

"We're ready," came the response from his engineer, Hassan Nobli, via the com from his engine room. What they were ready with was more than two hundred mobile metal mines armed with 0.10 kiloton charges that would be released over the battlefield as the *Beauregard* swept through the multitiered 5 Suns fleet formation. The result would be potentially devastating to the 5 Suns light cruisers, a cloud of death unleashed on the battlefield, enveloping everything in its path. Clement had used these weapons only once before, at the Battle of Kemmerine as a means for his gunships to escape the 5 Suns fleet. But in that case the scatter mines had been used as a rear-guard action while his deployed gunships sped away from the battlefield. They'd never been used in such a high-speed maneuver before.

"I'm detecting unusual EM activity from four of the 5 Suns Alliance cruisers," came a warning from DeVore.

"Specify, XO," said Clement.

"I can't, sir. I'm reading heightened electromagnetic

activity on four ships, as I said, sir. Uncertain as to what it means. We still have time to break off the attack and reform with the other gunships," she said.

Clement thought for a moment, looked up at his tactical board one last time and said, "No. Maintain course and speed."

No one said anything, least of all DeVore. They had all learned to trust their captain, his instincts and intuitions. They had been fighting together in a civil war for autonomy from the 5 Suns Alliance for the most distant planets in 5 Suns space, the Rim Confederation. But this battle was the biggest of the entire war, a game-ending play by the 5 Suns Navy to finish the costly four-year-old conflict which had seen both sides pushed to their limits.

They had seconds now before the *Beauregard* pierced the positions of the 5 Suns Navy cruisers at blinding speed. Clement watched on his tactical board as the 5SN ships finally began to scramble, looking to get out of range of the gunship's suicide dive. Near Argyle Station itself, Clement watched the desperate battle between the Rim Navy's remaining gunships and the 5SN cruisers, a battle the Rim Confederation Navy was losing. This was his biggest play ever, and it *had* to work.

"Captain!" came DeVore's warning, a second after Clement saw it. Four 5SN cruisers had formed up in a flat square, a full kilometer on each side, right in the *Beauregard*'s descending path. They were sacrificing those cruisers . . . but to what end?

At the speed the *Beauregard* was traveling the metal from the mines would rip through the hulls of the cruisers on kinetic energy alone. But these weapons, which

Clement had a hand in creating, were designed to be more powerful than anything else that had been used in the war to date, containing their own propulsion systems and the exploding ordnance.

At ten seconds to contact he ordered the scatter mines released. They swarmed out and accelerated away from the *Beauregard*, as they were designed to do, seeking out their targets. The four 5 Suns Alliance Navy cruisers didn't stand a chance against them.

At five seconds to contact he saw their play. An orange-tinted EM field, looking like a waving, beaded carpet, extended between the four ships, forming a perfect one-kilometer-square blanket of electron-charged plasma. The *Beauregard* had no chance to evade it, no hope of changing course or decelerating to avoid contact.

The scatter mines slammed into the four battle cruisers with devastating effect, sending showers of sparks and flame out into the eternal night of space. For a moment Clement thought they were delivered, but then he saw the awful truth: four probes that were detached from the cruisers had kept the plasma blanket as a fully charged closed circuit.

The *Beauregard* impacted the plasma, and Clement's world exploded. The bridge arced and flamed with static energy. It seemed like everything was on fire, including some of the crew. He opened his mouth to give orders but nothing came out, nothing comprehensible at least. His ship rattled and rocked, rolling uncontrollably through space, spinning and decelerating at a frightening clip. The crew were pinned to their acceleration couches again, some of them burning in place. His com filled with their

Dave Bara

screams of agony and shouts for help. It was an eternity until Clement was strong enough to escape his couch and grab a fire extinguisher. He put out three fires, two of them on members of his crew, charred bodies now, while the rest of the survivors did the same. It was true Hell.

He pulled off his helmet and his lungs filled with the acrid smell of burned flesh and burning equipment. Only a few systems were left operating on the ship, one of them the tactical board. He looked around the bridge. Of his nine bridge officers only himself, DeVore, Mika Ori and Ivan Massif, had survived.

"Show me," he said to DeVore. She brought up the tactical board.

The four 5SN cruisers spreading the plasma blanket had been destroyed, cut to pieces. Two others were damaged to less than fifty percent tactical efficiency. The rest of the flotilla, six operating cruisers, was intact and closing in on the *Beauregard*. The remaining Rim gunships had fled, trying to protect Argyle Station. The *Antietam* was adrift, with heavy damage, knocked out of the battle and sinking into the gravity well of the planet Argyle itself, where she would no doubt burn up. There were nine active cruisers now against just three working gunships, a three-to-one advantage for the 5 Suns Navy, and the *Beauregard* itself was finished, that much was obvious.

"What did they hit us with?" asked DeVore.

"Some kind of electron-charged plasma weapon. Our own speed through the battlefield displaced enough energy to magnify the blanket's effect a hundredfold. We're done," Clement said.

"If they'd kept to standard tactics we should have gotten half their fleet, at least," said Ori.

"Yes, we should have," said Clement. "But they anticipated our move."

"How?" asked Ori. Clement shook his head.

"Only one way I can think of. They knew what our plan was and how we were going to execute it." Clement promised himself he would find out who had betrayed him and his crew, and one day enact revenge.

He went to the tactical board again and checked his ship's course and speed, and the status of the remainder of the Rim Confederation fleet. The *Beauregard* was rapidly decelerating. The remaining gunships protecting Argyle itself were in the process of surrendering. Argyle Station had already fallen. If this scene was being repeated at Ceta and Helios then not only was the battle over, the war was too.

"We should consider surrendering," stated DeVore.

"Should we?" said Clement, then he turned to Ori. "Mika, can you give me one-quarter speed on the chemical thrusters?" She nodded.

"I'll try, sir."

The *Beauregard*'s thrusters groaned and moaned but eventually she started moving again at the pilot's command. They had been drifting in the general direction of Argyle 4, a twenty-kilometer-wide rock that passed as a moon of Argyle. Clement set his direction there.

"What are you doing?" asked DeVore.

"We may be beaten but we're still Rim Confederation Navy. They want my ship for a trophy. The *Beauregard* has kicked more 5 Suns Navy ass in this system than any other ship we've had in the entire war. They'll want her so they can scrape her insides for every bloody secret she has. But I'm not going to let them," he said, defiant.

"You're scuttling her?" said DeVore.

"I am," he replied without looking up from his board.

"But sir—"

"They're not getting their grubby hands on my ship, Elara!" he snapped. "All of you to the rescue pods, that's an order," Clement said, then he sounded the general alarm, and called down to Hassan Nobli, his closest friend on the ship, besides DeVore, of course. "Get off the ship, Nobli. I'm going to scuttle her."

"If you're going down with her I am too!" insisted Nobli through the com.

"Evac now, Hassan. That's an order. That alarm is for you too." There was a moment's silence, then Nobli said, "Aye, sir. It's been a pleasure serving with you."

"It damn well hasn't, and you know it. We were never close. You were only my friend for the drinking," he said.

"Understood, sir," came Nobli's reluctant reply, indicating he had absorbed his cover story for the 5 Suns Navy interrogations that would likely follow their capture.

Clement cut the line.

The evacuations aboard the rest of the ship started almost immediately. When he was satisfied the bulk of the surviving crew was free of the ship and the rest would surely be gone in the next few minutes, he personally fired the thrusters a second time on a collision vector toward Argyle 4.

"Mika, Ivan, off with you," he said. "I don't need anyone to help me fly my ship into an asteroid."

"I want to stay with you, sir," Ori protested. Clement shook his head.

"Not possible. Now get to a pod and get off my ship, both of you. That's an order." *And probably my last as captain of this ship*, he thought. Ori and Massif saluted sharply and then they were off to one of the three bridge escape pods. One of them was damaged beyond repair, but Clement watched as they boarded another pod and a second later they were gone. There was one rescue pod left with a capacity of two people.

Alarms blared as the emergency lights flickered amongst the still burning fires and system circuit overloads. Clement looked around his smashed bridge. DeVore came up and wrapped her arm in his, taking hold of his hand.

"I don't know what you're thinking, but you are *not* going to go down with this ship," she said to him. He looked at her. A loyal comrade, his most trusted advisor, his lost love, and his friend. He smiled weakly.

"No, I'm not," he admitted. He checked the vector of the *Beauregard* one more time, satisfied she would meet her end on Argyle 4 and not fall into the hands of the 5SN, then he let DeVore lead him by the hand to the last escape pod. He unlocked it and pushed her through, then, after a moment's hesitation, he stepped off of his Rim Confederation Navy command for the last time and into the rescue pod. This, he was sure, would be his last commission, in any navy.

They both strapped in and Clement donned his helmet again before he switched on the IFF beacon that would identify them to the enemy. In his final act as captain, he hit the activation button and the rescue pod explosively accelerated away from the *Beauregard*. He felt the pain of loss, of losing his ship, but also a sense of relief that the long, uphill climb was finally over. He was embarrassed that he felt that way.

Six minutes of silence later he watched his ship crash onto the surface of Argyle 4, scraping a scar across its already ugly face. Four minutes after that and they were in the shadow of a 5 Suns Alliance Navy light cruiser.

"So what happens now?" asked DeVore. Clement shook his head.

"It doesn't matter," he said. "We've lost. And I'll become a ghost. We'll all become ghosts of this war." DeVore squeezed his hand.

"No," she said, "some of us won't."

✷ 1 ✷

11 Years Later

Jared Clement held up his normal end of the bar, just like every night, drinking his Argyle whiskey, straight, and watching the propaganda that passed for "news" on the Argyle Station monitors. According to the 5 Suns Alliance News Network, crop yields had just broken records on the planet below the orbiting space station, but Clement knew better. That was one of the reasons he preferred to stay aboard a well-stocked space station instead of on the bleak landscape of the planet Argyle itself. The people below, almost two million of them, were mostly starving, and everyone around here knew it. Hell, more than a decade ago, Clement had fought, and lost, a war over it. Not that any of that mattered now.

The real truth was that the relatively well-off world of Ceta, where he was born, had upped their food shipments to Argyle just to stave off the starvation of a handful of the colonists below. Crop yields on Argyle were lower than at any time in the last two decades, and even though the 5 Suns Alliance had promised increased food aid to the

17

three worlds of the former Rim Confederation as a promise made for ending their civil war with an armistice, that support had never come. What aid that did get sent was skimmed and sold on the black market by 5 Suns Alliance administrators, with a sizeable kickback to the Rim Worlds Governor-General to look the other way. It was the same kind of issue that had started the uprising, but nowadays people in the Rim just seemed to have no belly for the fight anymore. They were too busy trying to survive.

As a war veteran though, Clement had a better deal than most. He hadn't been forced by conscription back into the 5 Suns Alliance Navy, nor exiled on Ceta or Argyle itself. And he used his vet status and a meager pension (really, just a buyoff from the 5SA to keep the peace) as a means to stay in space and serve in the merchant marine. He'd managed to squeak out a pretty good subsistence as a reliable ship captain and sometimes pilot. It wasn't much, but despite the drinking he'd proven reliable enough to keep an apartment on the station, and most merchant sailors had stopped giving him stick for being a "dirty rebel" years ago. Most, in fact, rarely even recognized him anymore. He had become a nobody to the 5 Suns, and that's the way he wanted to keep it. He'd lost enough in the goddamned war, his ship, friends, and even a lover. Rebellion wasn't even a word in his vocabulary anymore.

He'd chosen Argyle as his base because it was the best of the Rim stations, and the main port where the 5 Suns Navy offloaded all of their best contraband for reselling. In retrospect, it had been a wise choice. There was (almost) always good booze and even some delicacies from the Core Planets that came through the station, like oysters and shellfish and even the occasional blue lobster. It made life a bit more interesting anyway.

He flipped his index finger at the barkeep, another grizzled veteran of the war whose name he'd forgotten, as a signal to hit him with another shot of the whiskey. The barkeep did as instructed, then said, "one more," and held up his own index finger just to emphasize the point. Clement had set himself a drink limit at the bar to keep from falling into financial chaos. Six shots a night was all he would allow himself. Tonight though, that limit was looking dubious. These days, since the war, drinking was his only solace and alcohol usually his only companion.

The 5 Suns Alliance news had now turned to sports, specifically the Super-Rugby Final between Voyagers and Holy Sacrament from the Core Worlds of the two main-sequence inner suns, those being Colonus A and B. The planets Santos, Carribea, and Freehold orbited Colonus A, with Atlas and Columbia orbiting B. Clement forgot which planet which team was from, but he was pretty sure he used to be a Voyagers fan when he was a kid. Either that or he hated them. He couldn't actually remember.

Clement downed his fifth shot. It was now nearly certain the barkeep was watering down the whiskey. He barely had a buzz on, and it was getting near midnight.

Word was he might have a job coming up as a Class VI freighter pilot, but that wasn't for two more weeks. Plenty more shots to go between now and then, and that was fine with Clement. The war had taken all of the ambition out of his system, in more ways than one.

The 5 Suns shipping syndicates liked hiring him because of his reputation for being fast and efficient, and also his ability to avoid troublesome Tax Compliance patrols. He was a good pilot, using a combination of speed, stealth, and sometimes just brute power to avoid trouble with the authorities. Everything he'd learned had been from watching his pilot in the war, Mika Ori. She was magnitudes of scale better than he was. Absently, he thought about contacting her and her husband, Ivan Massif. It had been over three years since their last communication. Heck, maybe they were divorced. He let that thought slide out of his mind with the whiskey . . .

"Captain Clement," came the voice from over his shoulder. It was female, and pleasant, but still, Clement had to decide if he wanted to turn around. Ultimately, he decided he didn't.

"There is no 'Captain Clement,' lady, hasn't been for many years. My name's Jared, and I can tell from your voice that whatever you came here to ask me, the answer is no." He signaled the barkeep and was dutifully rewarded with a shot glass. The woman came around his shoulder and leaned in on the bar, looking toward him and getting in his personal space to the point where he had to pay attention to her. Unable to avoid her further, Clement relented and looked at her.

She was a pretty woman of Asian descent, in her late twenties he guessed, and all made up in a 5 Suns Alliance Navy commander's rank uniform. Her hair hung short and straight with a full run of bangs across her forehead with no part. He decided *she* looked serious enough, even if *he* wasn't.

"By the rules of the Treaty of Argyle you're still allowed the honoraria of your Rim Confederation Captain's rank, even if you're retired, Mr. Clement," she said, pointedly avoiding using his rank this time. For his part, Clement looked away and contemplated ordering one more shot.

"You know, I think you're the highest-ranking navy officer I've seen since my war parole ended," he deadpanned. She humored him.

"And how long ago was that?"

"About nine years," Clement said. "I did nine months in navy confinement after the armistice, forced to give up my tactical secrets to your navy, was separated from my crew after the war ended, then had supervised parole for another two years to make sure I was firmly compliant and not thinking about restarting an old conflict. Not the best of times. And you're reminding me of them now."

"I really don't know that much about the war, or its aftermath, Mr. Clement. All of that was over well before I joined the 5 Suns Alliance Navy." She leaned in a bit closer, as if she were examining his face. It still had some of the glow of youth. The short-cropped and buzzed hair had a hint of gray at the temples and he had his share of weathered wrinkles on his forehead and crow's feet, though not in abundance. It certainly was the face of a man who had been through some difficult times in life.

Clement made a squinty face of disapproval at her. "Don't you have to study navy history anymore? Hell, I did when I was in the 5SN."

She nodded, humoring him. "We do. But now we have peace again, and everyone gets along like they're supposed to," she said.

Clement twirled his empty shot glass on the bar and eyeballed the commander, then signaled for the barkeep to fill his last shot. She watched as Clement's shot glass was filled.

"You're new to the Rim, aren't you, Commander?" he said sarcastically. She smiled before continuing, and it looked pleasant on her face.

"As a matter of fact, yes. This is my first time in the Rim Sector. I've spent most of my career in the Kemmerine Sector apart from a short stint at Colonus Sector on Atlas," she said. Colonus Sector was the richest part of 5 Suns Alliance space, where the two main-sequence G-type stars that formed the core of exo-Sol human civilization revolved around each other in an eighty-year dance. The three outlying orange K-type stars that completed the 5 Suns Alliance all had habitable planets, but the three outlier worlds of the Rim were by far the poorest, not being blessed with nearly the natural resources that the five worlds that spun around Colonus A and B had. Clement smiled.

"You're practically wet behind the ears, Commander. What did you say your name was?"

"I didn't, but if you must know it's Tanitha Yan. Commander Tanitha Yan."

"Tanitha? Odd name for a Chinese girl from New Hong Kong on Shenghai," commented Clement. She blushed just a bit and then sat down on the empty stool next to him.

"How did you know what city I was from?" she asked. He smiled.

"I'm pretty good with my colonial accents. Yours is very

slight, but I was still able to make it out," he said. "From what I know of the culture on your world, I'm guessing that most of your friends were no doubt more interested in being socialites, but you joined the 5 Suns Navy, Tanitha. I wonder why?"

She shrugged. "My father was a professor," Commander Yan offered. "My mother stayed at home. I guess you could say I was privileged. Compared to almost anyone on the Rim worlds I'm sure you'd think me rich and spoiled. But I wanted to do something on my own, away from my surroundings and my parent's protection. When the navy needed recruits, I agreed to join the officer corps right out of college, but I wasn't given anything. I got where I am on merit, Mr. Clement."

He nodded. "Fair enough. Now tell me how you got that name again, Tanitha?"

Again the shrug. "It's just a westernized name I took over my given name when I went to school. My parents thought it would be easier for me growing up on a split colony," she said.

"Well, the French and Chinese have gotten along so well over the centuries," Clement deadpanned, referring to the early colonial wars that broke out on her home planet. "So now you have to tell me because I must know. What was your given name?"

She blushed again and her face took on a lovely pink tone. "Xiu Mei," she said. Now Clement laughed openly and loudly.

"Xiu Mei? Do you know what that means?" he said. She gave a nod of her head as she turned even more pink.

"Yes."

"Beautiful Plum!" He looked at her, laughing as she smiled, embarrassed. "Well you certainly are all that, Miss Yan. But now that I've had my fun with you, why don't you tell me why you're here talking to me?"

"I would prefer that to be done in private, Mr. Clement," Yan said. Clement downed his last shot.

"Well, I'm a very private man, Miss Yan; I don't open my door to just anyone."

Now she got a serious look on her face. "The proposal I have for you will be well worth your time, I would think. And it comes from the highest of authorities."

"I'm not much on authority these days, especially when it comes from the 5 Suns Alliance Navy," he said.

"You're going to want to hear this proposal, believe me," she replied. The look on her face was firm and serious.

He shrugged. "My time isn't free," Clement said flatly.

"Name your price," she said quickly.

Clement looked to the barkeep. "Argyle Select Scotch, single malt," he said, "and unopened." The last was to verify that it wasn't watered down.

"You're over your limit," protested the bartender, not wanting to give up a bottle of his highest-quality booze at any price. Clement looked to Yan and back.

"I'll have the bottle," he said. "She's buying." The bartender looked to Yan, who nodded. Reluctantly he pressed a key on his register and a biometric scanner flashed across her eyes and debited the listed amount for the scotch, which was much higher than its real commercial value. The bartender took the bottle off his rack and slid it across the bar to Clement, who took it with a practiced ease and a nod, and then slid a two-crown tip the other way. Then he stood to leave.

"You'll have fifteen minutes to convince me in my cabin, Miss Yan. Then I kick you out," he said.

"Fair enough," she replied, standing as well, "but I hope you don't think my 'convincing' will be with anything but words."

"Oh, I have no doubt of that. Besides, I would never dream of asking such a thing of an obvious lady like yourself. Now, if you'd like to follow me . . ." He gestured toward the door of the bar with a broad sweep of his hand. Yan said nothing, but stepped past him and into the adjoining corridor, which was full of general station riffraff.

They both went silent as they walked, Yan observing in her staid, military way and Clement walking casually, cradling the unopened bottle of scotch. They arrived at his cabin on C deck and he keyed in the door code, the security system scanning Yan for weapons as she passed the threshold.

"You're not the trusting type, are you, Mr. Clement?" she commented.

"Just something I learned from your kind during the war," he said.

"I was fifteen," she replied, "during your war."

Yan entered and surveyed the room. It was small, barely more than a studio, but he had a porthole view of the station's stem and the dusty planet Argyle below. There was a small desk, entertainment complex, separate bathroom and a divider for his bed, a small sofa, and a reclining chair which Clement promptly sat down in, likely his favorite spot, she decided. It was neat and clean, and showed the care of a former military man who was deep on discipline if not entirely flowing in crowns and luxury.

"So what's your assessment of my lifetime of accomplishments?" he said, capping the scotch and pouring into two drinking glasses. Yan looked around one more time, then started in.

"Despite your rather shaggy outward appearance, which I suspect is a false front, underneath you are disciplined and thoughtful. You don't need for much, and you don't want much, but you seem to be a man who is ready at any time to take advantage of an opportunity if it comes your way, and I would guess you've been expecting it to come your way for a while now," she said.

He contemplated her from over the rim of his glass. "And now, coincidentally, you're here. Thanks for the psychoanalysis, by the way," he said.

Yan sat down on the sofa facing him and picked up her glass of the scotch. She looked to a bookcase in the entertainment complex. One display panel had his military medals, some 5SN and some Rim Confederation, a pair of old conventional field glasses in a glass box, and...a photo of his former command crew on the *Beauregard*. She pointed to the photo.

"You feel like you let them down." It was a simple statement, followed by a simple answer.

"I did, which is why I can't imagine why anyone in the 5 Suns Navy would want to talk to me," he said.

"And yet here I am, representing that very same navy, and someone of special importance in it. Someone who knows your military record very well."

Clement sat deeper into his chair, crossing his legs and resting them on the table in a show of disinterest. "So tell me your proposal, Miss Yan," he said as he took a small drink of his scotch, which was damn good compared to the swill in the station bar.

"Aren't you curious who it's from?" she asked. He shook his head.

"If it's a shit job I won't care to know, so you'd best be out with it," he said.

Yan settled in a bit, then addressed him in an almost formal way. "The Fleet Admiral of the 5 Suns Alliance Navy for the Kemmerine Sector wants to offer you a command," she said simply. Kemmerine was the nearest 5 Suns Alliance sector to the Rim. Its single star was one of the orange K types, but much more powerful than Argyle, with six planets in the system, two habitable, one of which was Yan's home world of Shenghai. The other was called New Paris.

"Why?" he said, skeptical and taking another drink.

"Because the mission is dangerous. Because it requires a ship commander of exceptional ability and experience, and the Fleet Admiral doesn't feel she has anyone who fits that description under her command," Yan said.

"*Her* command?" said Clement, intrigued. "I can't think of too many women who have that kind of respect for me."

Yan looked at him, eyes unwavering. A smile crossed her face. "Elara DeVore does," she said.

That shocked him. Hearing her name was like a bolt of lightning through his nervous system. It took all of his efforts to control himself, to try and not show Yan the very tender button she had just pushed. He thought long and hard before he spoke again.

"I haven't seen or heard from Elara DeVore since the war ended, and that was eleven years ago. We were split up, all of my crew, into different POW camps while the peace treaties were being negotiated. And now you're telling me that she's a 5 Suns Alliance Navy *Fleet Admiral*?" he finally said, his voice raising more than he wanted it too.

"Yes," said Yan, "in command over the entire Kemmerine Sector. And she wants you to undertake a very special mission. That's why I'm here."

Clement said nothing. After another long silence between them, Yan stood to leave. "I see you're a bit stunned by this news. I understand. But I'll need to give her an answer. Shall I tell her it's a no?" Clement looked to the bottle, then up at Yan.

"Not yet," he said.

Yan got a look of frustration on her face. "I leave Argyle station at 1000 hours tomorrow, Mr. Clement. I'll come by here in the morning at 0800. If you're going with me to Kemmerine, you'll be ready. If you aren't ready, then I'll know your answer," she said.

Clement poured into his glass again, saying nothing.

Yan went to the door, but turned back one last time. "They said you were the best captain in the Rim Confederation fleet. They must be wrong, because I don't see that man here now. I just see someone who's lost inside of a bottle," she said.

Clement glared at her, holding back his rising anger. "Maybe you're right," he said. "Maybe that man doesn't exist anymore. Maybe the man that Elara DeVore wants never existed. Maybe he's a myth."

Yan's face gave away nothing. "Perhaps he is. At any rate, what I see now is just useless Rim Confederation trash," she said, using a nearly forgotten war slur. "But I want you to know, if you don't take this job, then it falls to me, and I can't wait to go on this mission for my commanding officer." At that she opened the door to leave. Clement's voice stopped her.

"And what happens to you if I do take the mission?"

"Then I will be your executive officer," Yan said.

Clement looked at her with disdain. "The hell you will," he said.

"Well, you've made your position clear. I hope you enjoy holding up your end of the bar here on Argyle. See you at 0800. Or not." Then she stepped through the door and it shut swiftly behind her.

And Clement was left alone with his bottle of scotch.

✵ 2 ✵

Yan buzzed in at Clement's door at precisely 0800. To her surprise the door slid open immediately. She stepped in and looked around the room. It was completely cleaned, almost spotless, in fact. The bed had been made up in military cut and a single open duffel bag sat at the foot of it. She turned again and noticed that the bottle of scotch was still on the table from the night before. It looked like it hadn't been touched since she'd left. The drinking glasses were cleaned and put back in their cabinet. Water was running in the bathroom.

"Just give me one more minute," said Clement from behind the partly open bathroom door. Yan just stood in place waiting. After a few seconds Clement emerged from the bathroom in attire that could only be described as military in fashion, separate pants and a jacket cut tightly around his body. He was in fine shape for a man of his age, which Yan realized she didn't actually know.

The jacket and pant cuffs were rimmed with black, while the main material was a dark heather gray. After a moment Yan realized what she was looking at: it was Clement's Rim Confederation Navy captain's uniform with all the rank and adornments removed.

Clement was rubbing his freshly shaven face with a towel. His hair was clean and swept back. In short, to Yan, he looked like a million bucks.

"I doubt that outfit will be warmly received at Kemmerine Station," she said.

Clement put the towel back in his bathroom and took one last look in the mirror. "It's all I have," he said.

"I doubt that," she replied. And she was right. Clement was clearly making a statement. He looked at her and shrugged.

"Once a navy man, always a navy man," he said.

"Yes, but, wrong navy," said Yan.

"Depends on how you look at it, I guess," he replied, smiling sarcastically at her. With that he picked up his duffel, zipped it up, and slung it over his shoulder. "Ready when you are, Commander."

Yan eyed him, doubtful of his quick turnaround from the station drunk to spritely military man, but for lack of any other evidence, she was forced to accept the man before her at face value. She turned to leave. She had to admit to herself that he cleaned up very nicely. As they walked out the door of his cabin Yan glanced one more time at the wall. Although his navy medals were still there, the photo of his crew was gone. No doubt he was taking it with him. She made a mental note of that.

After he had locked his cabin door with a security code they made the trek to the military docks together mostly in silence, just the necessary chatting between them. When they arrived in the military section of the station almost all personnel were in 5 Suns Navy uniforms. Clement's choice of attire certainly stood out and got more than a few second looks and glares from the 5 Suns sailors.

They approached a security checkpoint and the young ensign behind the podium asked for identity cards. Yan produced hers and was quickly processed through. The ensign took a lot more time with Clement, looking at him and his clothing with disdain.

Clement's card identified him as a commercial spacer and pilot, and the red rim around the card identified him as former combatant and possible security risk. The security officer took full advantage of this, having Clement remove all the contents from his duffel bag and even take off his jacket so they could check the lining. Yan stood by watching this impatiently as they waved a variety of detection devices over him. Finally, after ten minutes of exams, she stepped in.

"I think that's enough, Ensign. I know security is your job but this man is under my jurisdiction for the duration of the flight to Kemmerine and at the station after we arrive. I'm convinced he'll be no trouble," she said.

"I'm glad to hear that, *Commander*, but I still have my job to do and the trash here is even wearing the colors of the RCN," the ensign protested. The 5 Suns Alliance Navy favored navy blues with red trim and gold adornments, an ugly color combination in Clement's mind, colors he had come to hate over the years for what they represented. Colors he himself had once worn.

"I'd like you to pass him through now, *Ensign*, and that's an order," said Yan.

"But Commander, I am well within my rights—"

"Yes you are, Ensign. But my orders override your

rights in this matter. Now clear him." The threat in her voice was obvious. Reluctantly the young officer did as she requested. Clement took back his ID and then gathered up his belongings, strewn all over the deck, and went to a nearby bench to repack.

Yan took the opportunity to lean in and speak with the security officer privately.

"One last thing," she said. "You may want to watch who you call trash around here. I know it's a popular name to call the old rebels, but I feel I should tell you that if all goes as planned, that 'trash' may be someone you'll have to salute soon. Very soon."

The ensign nodded, gave her a "yes, sir," and then resumed his duties without another word.

Yan went over to Clement, who was just zipping the duffel bag back up. "Everything in order?" she asked.

Clement nodded as he threw the duffel back over his shoulder. "Of course."

The two of them started walking down the corridor together toward their waiting ship.

"You enjoyed that, didn't you?" she asked.

Clement smiled. "Oh, Commander Yan, you have no idea," he said.

Their transport was a fast frigate called the *Bosworth*. They both locked down in acceleration couches for a five-g acceleration that lasted forty minutes, after which the couches disconnected and the cabin assumed a smooth and comfortable one g cruising attitude. Kemmerine Station was nine hours away at their current speed.

It was Yan that started in on the conversation.

"So how close were you and Fleet Admiral DeVore?" she asked casually.

The answer was anything but casual for Clement. "I'm not sure you want to know that answer, Commander," he said back, casually shuffling through a navy travel brochure, hoping to warn her off.

"But what if I do?"

Clement stopped his paper-shuffling and looked at her. For all the world she seemed like a naive girl thrust into a position above her skill level by the benefit of having a wealthy or influential family. It would never have happened in the old days of the 5 Suns Navy, when Clement was a green middie. He had to earn his way to the top of the ladder, and he did that, getting his own command in just six years. But inopportune timing on a trip home from his station in the Virginis Sector had caught him on the wrong side of the line when the war started. It only took a couple of days of seeing what was really happening on Ceta—the starvation, the exploitation—for him to give up his 5SN blues for Rim Confederation Navy grays.

Yan waited patiently for Clement to answer.

He stared at her, uncertain that he would answer, when suddenly the words were coming out of his mouth, almost as if it was against his own will. "Elara DeVore was the love of my life," he said. "We fought side by side for four years. I lost two other ships in battle and she still followed me to the *Beauregard*."

"That was your last command? The one where you scuttled your ship rather than let the 5SN have her?"

Clement nodded. "We were betrayed, by someone

close, someone inside. I've never figured out who. But I'll have a special dagger for him if I ever figure it out."

"That's a long time to carry a grudge," said Yan.

He looked at her again, trying to determine whether she was the simple girl she appeared to be, or something more. Clement smiled, as a cover for his emotions.

"The dagger is only metaphorical," he said, more casual. "I'm not sure I could ever use it even if I found out who the traitor was. War makes for strange bedfellows, Yan. I wouldn't put it past the Confederation Council for giving us up. We were going to lose anyway, that was obvious by the winter of 2504, but the 5 Suns Alliance and their Navy wanted my hide."

"Because you had beat all of their best rising stars, in every battle. And you left them all alive to spread the word about how badly they were beaten by the rube gray coat from the backwater planet," she said.

Clement nodded.

"And Elara DeVore?"

Again Clement smiled. "A dark and comely girl from Helios," he said, "full of brash ideas and seething anger at the 5 Suns Alliance. A great tactician, a leader, a combat fighter, tall, lithe . . . everything a soldier boy dreamed of."

"But after the war—" Clement's look made her stop mid-sentence. Then just as quickly, he continued with the story.

"After I scuttled the *Beauregard* I never saw Elara again. I don't blame her, I would have stayed away from me too. But now, to find out she's a 5 Suns Navy Fleet Admiral . . ." He trailed off.

Yan stayed silent, then Clement looked at her and said,

"You never forget a woman like that." And with that he turned away from her, and Yan knew the conversation was over.

Clement tried his best to snooze through the trip to Kemmerine, but it would only come in fits and starts. Yan, for her part, just took a sleeping pill and nodded off for five hours of timed rest. There was really nothing more for them to talk about until they met with Fleet Admiral DeVore.

Thoughts of Elara DeVore were enough to keep him from fully resting, but that didn't matter to Clement. His body clock was on Argyle time and it was the middle of the day for him anyway. Yan was almost certainly on a different sleeping schedule, Shenghai having a twenty-six-hour (and change) planetary rotation, and Kemmerine Station kept the same clock, at least it had when Clement was in the 5SN. He reset his watch to Kemmerine time and saw that it would be 2130 hours local time when they arrived, just enough time to catch dinner and hit the station pubs before bed.

Clement gently shook Yan awake when the twenty-minute docking toll chimed.

"What? What time is it?" she asked. Clement looked at his watch.

"Almost 2100."

She sat up quickly. "Argyle time or Kemmerine time?"

"Kemmerine," he said. "Just early enough to get unpacked and catch some dinner. You know a good restaurant on the station?"

Yan smiled. "I know about ten," she said.

Clement nodded. "Impressive."

"What's your pleasure? New Hong Kong cuisine or French Colonial?"

They both made Clement's mouth water. There was nothing like that cuisine on Argyle Station, something he had often lamented. "Let's try New Hong Kong," he said.

"All right. Always a favorite of mine."

"And a navy pub for a drink after."

Yan eyed him skeptically. "Now, wait a minute. You're going to mix with navy sailors? In *that* uniform? That sounds like trouble to me."

"You of all people should know that I'm trouble by now, Yan," he said. She started to say something else, but he cut in. "I promise I'll be good and not start any fights."

"Can I trust you?" she said.

He shrugged. "You'll have to, unless you want to put a guard on me," he teased.

"That's an option," she replied, smiling back at his charm despite herself. Then the *Bosworth*'s captain came on the com and asked them to activate their couches again for deceleration.

"Don't let me down, Clement," said Yan.

Clement smiled as the couch safety glass closed over him. "I wouldn't dream of it."

After arriving at Kemmerine Yan followed Clement to his room, an outside berth with a large view window of Shenghai. The view was spectacular; the green glow of the planet was nothing like looking at the poor, dull beige worlds of the Rim. The cabin, or rather stateroom, was much more than Clement had expected, a full suite with a large bedroom and, of all things, a bathtub. It was clear that Fleet Admiral DeVore was using her power and influence to put a full high press on him. Once he got his duffel contents stowed he came back into the living area to find Yan had a gift for him. It was a 5 Suns Navy commander's uniform with rank stripes but no bars and stars to identify him as a full member of the navy.

"I thought after yesterday's fun that you might be done with your little protest about a war that's been over for a decade," she said.

Clement looked at the navy blue uniform with gold and red piping and crinkled up his nose in a distasteful look. "I'd still prefer to wear my Rim grays," he said. Yan laid the uniform over a chair.

"Not to meet the Fleet Admiral you won't. I want to avoid any more conflicts like that security guard yesterday."

"You see, that's the difference between you and me, Yan. I don't consider yesterday to be a conflict in any way."

Yan picked up the uniform and gently pushed it at him. "Please?" she said sarcastically, dipping her head slightly but keeping her eyes on him, like a young girl trying influence her boyfriend.

"Maybe," Clement said, "as long as I get to pick where we eat."

"That would be fine."

He looked disdainfully at the uniform one more time. "All right then, Commander, you win. We'll play it your way." Then he took the uniform from her and made his way to the bathroom to dress in private.

They got dinner at what Clement would definitely call

a restaurant, not a pub. Linen tablecloths were not prevalent in Argyle Station pubs. Kemmerine was huge, more than twice the size he remembered it from his navy days. There were at least fifty navy ships and maybe twice as many tourist ships, merchants and private yachts docked at its many spider-webbed ports. The deck they were on had a view of Shenghai below and seemed exclusively for leisure, with shops, restaurants, and even a film theater. No doubt the sailor's pubs were somewhere less savory, but at least on this deck the 5 Suns Alliance was showing off for the tourist classes.

Clement gently swirled his tea in his cup before taking a last sip. On the expansive table was the scattered remains of their meal. Clement couldn't remember the last time he ate so well. An automated busboy swung by and cleaned their table of dishes while Clement contemplated the view of the planet below.

"You seem satisfied with your dinner," said Yan.

He smiled. "I am. We have nothing like this on Argyle. Blue crab and lobster . . ."

"Well, you didn't have to pick up the check, you know. The navy has been quite generous with my expense account."

"I know, Yan, but the fact is there isn't much to spend your money on at Argyle. And besides, you've been a gracious host so far. It's the least I could do."

She smiled at that. "You're a man of contradictions, Clement."

He shrugged. "It's been a while since I've been out with a proper lady. Why don't we just say I needed the practice?"

Yan shifted in her chair. "Practice for meeting Elara DeVore again?" she probed.

"Maybe," he said, then put down his teacup and stretched. "Time for a walk to see the sights?" he suggested.

"You seriously mean to go get a drink at a navy pub? And cause a ruckus?"

"Me?" he demurred. "I wouldn't dare. I'm here at the behest of Fleet Admiral DeVore. No ruckusing for me."

"I'm sure."

He stood and pulled her chair out for her, like a gentleman would. His attitude toward her had certainly warmed since Argyle. Yan wondered if it was because of his proximity to Elara DeVore, or for other reasons.

They made their way through the atrium, glancing in at both formal and casual diners as they shared a meal, a bottle of wine, or something stronger.

"I wonder," started Clement.

"Yes?"

"I wonder how many of these patrons, no doubt on their way to or from someplace exciting, are having an illicit tryst, or hiding some secret from their wives or husbands, perhaps meeting a beau on a secret rendezvous," he said.

"That's fairly melodramatic, don't you think? This is a military station after all. Constant observation. I doubt too many get away with things like that here."

Clement acted surprised. "You think so? I find the thought kind of romantic, personally."

Yan smiled at that, thinking it over. "One drink, Clement." Then she held up her finger to him. "One."

"Lead the way," he said.

They made their way down the escalator, and after a few minutes of sticking their heads in several crowded bars full of 5 Suns Navy sailors, they settled on a dark but warm looking place called The Battered Hull. Appropriately named, Clement thought.

They came in and sat down at an open table, Clement ordering them both a glass of the local sailor's ale from the bartender. You could always tell the quality of a place by its basics. It was a good sign if they took care of their sailors. An auto waiter served them their glasses of a dark brown ale and they clinked glasses, with Clement taking a deep drink of his. It was damn good.

"My compliments to The Battered Hull," he said.

"Mine too," said Yan, then she looked around the bar. "I don't think I've ever been in here." The crowd was a mix of noncoms and middies, and occasionally their significant others in civilian dress. Yan was the only officer in the place, and Clement stood out because of his 5 Suns officer's uniform and accompanying lack of rank. They were getting plenty of steely-eyed glances from the crowd.

"Are we sticking out like a sore thumb?" he inquired.

"Yes. I'm beginning to think this was a bad idea," she said. Clement shrugged.

"Just finish your ale and we can get out of here, then," he said. Looking around the bar he noticed a group of four middies at a booth that were giving him more than the occasional light glance. One in particular, a blond male, was motioning quite vigorously to his companions.

"Uh oh," said Clement, smiling at Yan.

"What?"

"I may have been outed." He nodded toward the booth.

Yan observed them for a moment. "Does trouble *always* have a way of finding you?" she said.

He shrugged again. "Just comes with the territory, I guess."

Then the game was up. All four middies, three men and one young woman, vacated their booth and made their way toward Clement and Yan. They gathered around the high table, standing and resting their ales with him and Yan. It was the blond one who spoke first.

"I have a bet with my friends here," he started. "I think I know you. I saw your pictures in my military history classes."

"And just who *do* you think I am?" said Clement to the middie, not backing down.

"I'm betting you're Captain Jared Clement of the Rim Confederation Navy. You fought in the War of the 5 Suns. You were the Scourge of the 5 Suns Alliance fleet," he said, as if it were a matter of fact, or a title.

Clement took another drink of his ale. "And what did you bet?"

"Pardon, sir?" said the middie.

"What did you bet on me being this 'Scourge of the Fleet' character?"

"I have to pick up the tab if I'm wrong, or Tsu here does if I'm right," he said, nodding toward a tall Asian middie.

"And what if you're only half right?" said Clement, taking another drink. Yan watched the interplay closely.

"I don't understand, sir," the middie said. Clement

looked at the four young faces, all of them wore a determined look; they were going to succeed, none of them doubted it. He went from one to the other to the next until he had their full attention.

"You're half right, Middie, because I am Jared Clement, but I'm not a captain, and there's no such thing as the Rim Confederation Navy anymore."

"I knew it!" said the middie, then turned to his friends, demanding that they pay up in navy silver crowns. This caused quite a reaction in the bar, and Yan leaned in close.

"Now you've done it," she said.

"Started a ruckus? Maybe," he whispered back.

When the horse trading in silver was over, the middies turned back to Clement, and many other patrons of The Battered Hull were watching their table intently.

"Would you tell us a war story?" asked the blond middie.

Clement hesitated. "War is nothing to trifle about, son. People live and die every day, and some never heal from losing their friends. If I start bragging in here about how I got the better of the 5 Suns Alliance and their navy I might find myself spaced out the nearest garbage port," he said.

"Well done," whispered Yan in his ear, then she assumed her disinterested commanding-officer pose.

"Please, sir?" asked the middie again, and then there were nods all around.

"Well . . ." started Clement, leaning back and catching Yan's eye. She was not amused. "Maybe just one story."

Again the nods. Yan covered her face with her hand. Clement started in.

"The first thing you lads and lasses have to understand about the war was that it was over before it began," he said in a loud enough voice to be heard by several nearby tables. Yan assumed that was what he wanted. "And by that I mean there was never any doubt about the outcome. The 5 Suns Alliance had far too many resources and far too many navy ships for the Rim planets to have a chance at winning, so the war strategy from the beginning was one of pure defense. You have to remember the seeds of the war were that the Rim planets are poor, and that's still true. They're the furthest from the Colonus core twins—they don't get much light, so it's hard to grow food—and the soil on those planets is shit anyway. Livestock doesn't take much to the climates on Ceta or Argyle; Helios is a bit warmer, but try living in the warm glow of an orange K-type star for a while . . . it's not easy."

"So if the war was not winnable then why did you fight it?" asked the young female middie, an African girl by complexion.

"That's a good question, Middie. When I signed up for the navy, the *5 Suns Alliance* Navy mind you, I was helping fill a quota for my home planet of Ceta. The navy needed recruits constantly, just like now, to fulfill their end of the bargain, which was food, tech, and industrial assistance for the Rim colonies. Unlucky for me, one day I found myself on leave visiting my parents on Ceta. The conditions at home were horrible, food was scarce, and so was everything else—medicine, fuel, electrical power. I was sending back half my paycheck every month to my family but the fact was there was nothing to buy with it. Most of the food assistance was being hijacked by the

Governor-General and his lackeys and sold for a profit on the black market, and the 5 Suns Alliance government was looking the other way. Unfortunately, the navy was the government's enforcement arm. I wasn't home for two days when there was a riot in Ceta City and the Governor-General was run out of town and into hiding in a secret bunker. I was called back to my command, but when I got to the spaceport my shuttle was already gone—hell, the whole 5 Suns Navy had bugged out. There were some merchants and local navy personnel that stayed and tried to form a navy for defense of the Rim. After two weeks of laying low back at home they finally contacted me and asked if I'd join the cause. On my way back to the city I saw why the revolution had come; people were starving in the streets. I gave away all my rations on the way in, and when I got to the base, I decided to join up with the Rim. I had to do something.

"Within a week they had me in command of a forty-year-old destroyer named *Benfold* that the 5 Suns had left behind in the Argyle docks. I had half a crew, thirty sailors instead of sixty. We trained for a few days, expecting the 5SN to be back and end the rebellion any time. Then I got called to a meeting where men who had been commanders in the 5SN were calling themselves Admirals, and they told me they had a plan but no ship captain to carry it out. They wanted to attack first, give the 5 Suns Alliance government a bloody nose, and they wanted to know how well I knew the Virginis sector. Since I'd been stationed there I really couldn't lie to them, so they armed up that old destroyer and put me in charge of a stealth mission, a rearguard maneuver, to knock out 5SN supply lines and communications. So I went, and when we got there the 5 Suns Navy was not expecting us."

The middies were entranced now, and Clement held their attention in the palm of his hand. He continued, "We coasted in for seven hours after our deceleration burn. Without a heat signature from our engines we were practically invisible to their scans. One by one we started to knock out the local ansible network, taking down random satellites as we went on an approach vector. It made it look like they were experiencing a system failure rather than a pending assault. They had no idea a Rim Navy ship could get to them as deep into space as the Virginis sector.

"The station was only guarded by three corvettes. Their primary ships had been sent off to Kemmerine or were out on patrol, looking for the Rim Navy. I used conventional tactical missiles to knock out the first two of the corvettes, taking them completely by surprise, but the third one got its only energy cannon locked on to us. I had just enough momentum left for a thruster burn to make for the station. The corvette commander must have been very young, because he used his thrusters to keep spinning his ship and keep me in firing range the whole way in. He splattered volley after volley at us, missing by a few hundred yards every time, but we had the advantage of speed and that kept him from hitting us. Eventually we passed behind the station itself, which in those days had no defenses of its own, and started our turn back toward him. His next three volleys hit the station instead of us. Again he used his thrusters to try and turn, but by then we had him in our sights. One missile finished the job. We docked, raided the food storage section of Virginis Station, and stole their best booze. The station personnel were terrified of us. They thought the war would stay very far away, but we brought it home to them, and that concept scared the shit out of them."

Clement shrugged then. "Looking back at it now, it wasn't much of a tactical victory, but it had the effect of diminishing 5 Suns Navy morale, which was almost better than taking the station would have been. We snuck out of there as fast as we could, avoiding 5SN patrols the whole way home. When I got back to Argyle, I was the first hero of the Rim Confederation Navy and the war, like it or not."

"And how many 5 Suns Alliance Navy sailors did you kill in your sneak attack?" asked the female middie, pointedly. All eyes turned to Clement then, measuring how he would react.

"I have no way of knowing. Corvettes used to carry a crew of eighteen in those days. The one thing I will say in my defense is that in those early days of the war we never sought to destroy the enemy ships. Hell, the 5 Suns Navy wasn't our enemy, the corrupt 5 Suns Alliance government was. We targeted the propulsion sections of the corvettes only, to knock them out, not destroy them, but they were too small and they were destroyed. The war was fought that way all the way up to the Battle of Columbia," Clement said, then he took another drink of his ale.

"What changed the rules of engagement at Columbia?" asked the Asian middie, Tsu.

Clement thought about that before answering. "We started making our own ships, better ships than before, better than the 5 Suns Navy even had. I got the gunship

Beauregard and she was almost untouchable. But our leaders forgot they were fighting for survival, not victory. We got too close to winning, we became a real threat to the 5 Suns Alliance government, and then one of our ships took out an unarmed troop transport with two thousand 5 Suns Alliance soldiers on board. After that, it was mayhem. No quarter, and our little war of independence turned into a war of attrition we had no chance to win."

"They say you personally extended the war for two years with your tactics," said the blond middie.

"Well, I don't know about *that*," replied Clement, "but I do know we fought hard to win every engagement, and we had more than our share of successes. Hell, the Virginis sector government surrendered to us after our surprise attack, but we never had any intention of taking it over. It was just a hit and run. It was just our three little worlds, fighting to survive. We thought the 5 Suns government might leave us alone. We weren't really offering much to the other worlds in the 5 Suns Alliance, and we took more than we gave. My parents relied on subsidies to grow wheat and corn but it was all we could do to survive eating our own food and never shipping anything to the Core worlds. But they came after us anyway, and that was that." Clement downed the rest of his ale, and Yan followed suit.

"Thank you, gentlemen," Clement said to the middies, then started to leave.

The blond one piped up one last time. "Sir, if I may ask, why are you here on Kemmerine? And why are you wearing a navy uniform with no rank?"

Yan leaned in at this. "No, you may not ask, Middie,

now off with the lot of you," she said forcefully, like an angry mother, with a wave of her hand. And at that they were all gone back to their booth. Clement turned to walk out of The Battered Hull, and all eyes were on him as casual conversation resumed around them.

"Satisfied?" asked Yan as they made their way back to the escalator. Clement shrugged.

"No," he said, and they walked on in silence.

A few minutes later they were back at Clement's cabin door. He turned to Yan. "Want to come in?"

"Why?" she said.

"You look a little 'peaked,'" he said.

"What does 'peekt' mean?"

"Peek-ed." Clement smiled as he unlocked his cabin door. "It's just something my mother used to say to me when I was sick. It means you look a bit pale, that's all."

"I'm not sick," protested Yan. Then her hand went to her forehead. Clement's smile got a bit bigger.

"Are you sure?" Clement asked.

"Goddamn sailor's ale," said Yan, then she wobbled just a bit. Clement took her by the waist, to steady her at first, then pulled her in close. "I think I'm gonna—" At that Clement hustled her into his room and got her to the toilet just in time. He left her alone with the bathroom door shut for a few minutes until she reemerged, still unsteady but with a bit more color in her face.

"Thank you," she said, then sat down on the couch, far apart from him.

"You're welcome. I called down to the navy concierge, and they're sending up a female MP to escort you back to your room," he said.

Yan glanced at him from under the hand covering her eyes. "Thank you again."

The MP arrived and Yan departed without another word. As Clement shut the door behind her, he turned back, contemplating his empty stateroom.

Clement was up by 0730, showered, ate, and was ready to go by 0815. Yan showed up right on time at 0830. Their meeting with Admiral DeVore was on the military side of the station, a good twenty-minute tram ride from the cabin decks to the Admiral's office.

Yan was pleased that Clement was ready, smiling at him as he left his cabin, and walked side by side with him to the tram station, just a few hundred meters away. She said nothing about the previous night, and Clement was gentleman enough not to bring it up.

Once on the tram with the bustling uniformed crowd heading to their morning stations though, things changed.

"About last night," Yan started as they sat together as the high-speed tram accelerated toward the navy wing of Kemmerine Station, tugging gently against the artificial gravity generated by the station. Clement held up a hand.

"No need to bring it up, Commander. It was my fault."

Yan hesitated, then, "I don't remember much, goddamned sailor's ale, but I'd like to know if I . . . if we . . . I remember being inside your cabin?"

"Just to puke. Nothing happened, Yan."

Yan laughed uncomfortably. "I really can't remember."

Clement brooded, then decided he owed her more. "You seemed to warm to me after our dinner and the storytelling at The Battered Hull, and despite my best efforts, you were very attractive to me in that moment. A proper soldier, but also a woman. But I realized I was being influenced by the ale and a memory from my past, not by anything you said or did."

Yan looked at him. "Elara DeVore?"

Clement did not reply. He didn't have to.

The tram hummed to a stop a few minutes later and about half the car emptied out, going to the main service section of the navy stockyards. Mostly they appeared to be technicians and professionals, no doubt higher ranking staff and the like. The tram continued on to the next stop and the emptying process repeated itself. There were only a handful of officers left on the tram now, some of whom glanced at the 5 Suns Navy commander and her unranked companion in curiosity. Clement, for his part, kept his eyes focused straight ahead, only pausing to glance out at the docks when he saw an interesting ship or some repair work going on. Kemmerine Station was a very big and busy place.

Finally, the tram made its final stop at what could only be the station's main administration complex. Clement and Yan made their way out of the tram and onto a broad and wide deck. A large office tower took up most of the far end of the complex, with huge view windows to either side looking down on the ships below. Clement imagined that the top office in the tower would have a panoramic view of the whole shipyards. That would be the office, undoubtedly, of Fleet Admiral Elara DeVore.

Yan led him through a promenade where fleet officers were chatting and conferring in groups, large and small. Clement wondered what kind of work would justify this bustle of activity. It was almost what you would expect during the preparation for a large military operation. They made their way through the busy crowd and inside the tower to an elevator, which took them up five stories.

The elevator opened onto a bright office area with two large hardwood doors, undoubtedly the Fleet Admiral's office. It was the only office on the entire top floor of the tower. Yan made her way to a long reception desk where a man with the 5 Suns Navy rank of lieutenant sat behind a full security station. Clement, for his part, held back while Yan checked them in. The lieutenant called him over and handed him a security badge, which he attached to his uniform. They were both pointed to a waiting area where they sat down, presumably to wait on the Admiral. Clement checked his watch: 0900 on the dot. It wasn't like the Elara DeVore he knew to be late.

He and Yan sat together in silence for what seemed a long time, but when Clement looked at his watch again, only five minutes had passed. His heart was beating faster and he was twitching his leg in nervous activity. Yan noticed, but said nothing. Finally the door to the Admiral's office opened up and a short and small man in captain's rank uniform came through from the other side and went straight to Yan, who stood.

"The Admiral is ready now," he said. Clement glanced at his watch, which said 0908 hours. Then the captain turned to Clement and extended his hand. "I'm Captain Craig Wilcock," he said formally. Clement stood and shook his hand.

"Jared Clement." Wilcock nodded and then turned quickly as Clement and Yan followed the captain through the reception doors. A long way down the office toward the windows there was a desk, and Clement could see there was someone sitting at it, but he couldn't make out the face well. They walked across the office past a large conference sitting area, a small kitchen, and some cubicles for technicians and the staff, before arriving at the Admiral's desk.

Elara DeVore was busy dictating notes on a pad, her head turned partly away from her guests, saying nothing to them for a few moments as she spoke quietly into the com. Captain Wilcock waited with what seemed unending patience. Clement just felt annoyed as they all stood, waiting, Yan and Wilcock at attention. Clement had his hands clasped behind his back, taking a more casual stance. He reminded himself he wasn't in the military anymore, least of all the 5 Suns Alliance Navy.

He looked at Elara. From the side her hair was cut shorter than she used to wear it, in a regulation style, and although her uniform was well-adorned, it wasn't overly garish for a high-ranking Fleet Admiral. Her skin was still a gentle olive, but lighter than he remembered, indicating perhaps that she spent much of her time now in space, and not on any planet like her hot home world of Helios. That planet's proximity to the Rim's sun had darkened her skin in her youth when he knew her the first time. Her face seemed free of wrinkles, and she looked every bit of ten years younger than what Clement knew her age to be, forty-two standard years. Eventually she finished her pad entries, and looked up.

They say the eyes are the window to the soul, and when Clement looked into the eyes of his former lover for the first time in eleven years, he saw why. The brightness, the enthusiasm of her youth was still there, every bit of it.

Clement exhaled as Fleet Admiral DeVore stood and came around the desk, a deep and warm smile on her face. He held out his hand to her.

"Don't be ridiculous," she said, and waved his hand away as she gave him a firm hug that lingered a bit, like old friends that had been apart too long. Still in Clement's arms, DeVore looked over to Yan.

"Thank you for bringing him here, Tanitha," she said. Yan nodded.

"Of course, Admiral."

"Have you been well, Jared?" DeVore asked.

"Well, I'm not an Admiral, if that's what you mean," he deadpanned. DeVore stepped away and made her way back around to her side of the desk.

"Was he hard to convince?" she asked Yan.

Now Yan smiled. "Not once I mentioned your name, ma'am."

DeVore laughed and gestured to two chairs. "Please sit," she said. He and Yan both did, and then she just looked at Clement, smiling. She turned to their escort. "That will be all for now, Captain Wilcock." He nodded and left the office without another word. DeVore turned back to him and Yan. "Jared Clement. I swear, the years have just made you even more handsome," she said.

"Yan has already tried flattery on me, Admiral. It didn't work," said Clement in mock seriousness.

"I'll keep that in mind. I don't suppose Yan here has shared why I asked you to come today?"

Clement shook his head. "No, Admiral, she hasn't," he said. Despite the warm hug, Clement was still all business. At that, DeVore got up again and went toward the conference area.

"Follow me, please," she said. Clement did so, watching every tug on her uniform as she walked. Her body was certainly more mature than he remembered, but every bit as enticing. Yan, a step behind him, gently nudged him to get his attention back on business. Presently DeVore motioned to a set of conference chairs and Yan and Clement sat down.

"What I'm about to show you now is classified, and even if you don't accept my offer, I do expect you to keep this presentation secret, on your honor as a former navy sailor and as a gentleman," DeVore said.

Clement nodded his assent and DeVore fired up the viewing screen. After a few seconds the panel lit up, revealing a 3D map of 5 Suns Alliance space. Before she started speaking though, she slid a thin electronic pad across the desk to Clement.

"What's this?" he asked.

"A military NDA. Just a written guarantee of your honor as a gentleman," she said. Clement slid it back.

"I'm not in the military," he said.

DeVore sent it back to him a second time as Yan watched the interchange, noting the undoubted chemistry between them, and the underlying competition.

"It will only be relevant if you choose to re-enlist," she said. Clement at least looked at it this time, then pulled up an attached pen and signed without really reading it. A glowing red sensor lit up next to his signature and he pressed his left thumb to it. The print stayed on the pad. "Thank you," said DeVore, then put the paper to one side before continuing.

"What I'm sure you know as a matter of course is that the planets of the 5 Suns Alliance have been in an uneasy peace since the War of the 5 Suns. Oh, there's no imminent danger of violence breaking out again, and there are no more war criminals, but the dangers that faced humanity during that war face us again today. Essentially, we have two billion people on eleven planets, facing much the same population problem as Earth faced before the Exodus, three hundred years ago. The problem here in the Alliance is that our worlds are not nearly so fertile as Mother Earth," she started. "Our projections are that within a decade the Rim worlds, where you and I were born, will face starvation on a widespread scale."

"They already do in many places on Ceta and Argyle," interrupted Clement. "I'm not as sure about Helios."

"Oh, there are food shortages there as well," said DeVore. "Scattered, but becoming more systemic. The Rim worlds should probably never have been colonized, but you can't stop pioneers and libertarian free thinkers from trying to make a paradise of their own."

"Yes, well, this is all very good information, Admiral, but it's planetary economics, and I'm a spaceship captain," said Clement. "Or at least I was." Yan gave him a concerned look at his tone, but said nothing.

"I understand. If you'll allow me to continue?"

"Of course."

"We expect the Rim economies to collapse in the next few years, and there won't be enough aid available from the other worlds to save them. Our models indicate the Kemmerine worlds will soon follow with their own collapse within a decade, brought down by millions of refugees from the Rim planets. Then Virginis within another decade, and so on, so that within thirty years the five central worlds of Colonus Sector will be in danger themselves, both from a starving populace seeking to emigrate and the possibility of wars over resources. It's a cascading-failure event just waiting to happen," she said.

"If you'd been home in the last eleven years you'd see that it's already started," said Clement. DeVore gave him an impatient look.

"What makes you think I haven't?"

"With all due respect, Admiral, the woman I commanded aboard the *Beauregard* had a deep olive complexion, like a native of Helios would. You don't look like you've been in the sun, of any planet, much in the last eleven years."

Now impatience turned to anger on DeVore's face. "So, you're judging me now?"

Clement shook his head. "No, Admiral. I'm merely stating that if you'd been home recently, you would probably have found that your cascading-failure event has already begun," said Clement in an even tone.

"Ever the rebel, aren't you, Clement?" said DeVore.

"Better than being a sellout," he snapped in reply.

DeVore opened her mouth to retaliate when Yan

stepped in before any more damage could be done. "Perhaps now would be a good time to focus on the proposed mission," she said.

"I'm not sure the captain here is up to it anymore," said DeVore in an angry tone. "Maybe I've made a mistake."

"Perhaps you're right, Admiral. And maybe I was never going to accept your proposal anyway." He stood to leave and Yan stood with him. "Maybe all I ever wanted was to have my curiosity about where you disappeared to for eleven years sated, and maybe that's already been done. You sold out to the enemy."

"There is no enemy anymore, Clement, that's what you fail to see. It's fine with me if you want to back out," said DeVore. "You always took too many chances for my taste. You were bound to hit rock bottom at some point, and now I see that you're there."

Yan jumped in again, trying to save the mission. "Wait. Clement, you've come all this way, and you're going to leave before you even hear what the mission is? And with respect to the Admiral, how many times in the last six months have I heard you say there was only one commander for this mission, and that's Jared Clement? I can leave the room now if you two want to hash out your personal anger at each other, but I'd much rather stay and hear the rest of the mission briefing," she said. DeVore looked to Yan, surprised at her take-charge tone, and then glared at Clement, who finally relented and sat back down. Yan followed suit. The tension between them was obvious, as was the connection that had brought them together. After a few tense moments of silence, DeVore sat down and continued on with the briefing.

"So we've stated the problem. And now it's time to discuss the proposed solution," she said. "Four years ago we started a program using unmanned probes, a program to develop a high-speed interstellar drive that could get us to new star systems much faster than the old-generation ships that we used to found our colonies. As part of that program we sent out probes to a number of nearby star systems using different kinds of experimental FTL technologies. Most of them we lost contact with almost instantly, others kept sending us data but never made it to their destinations. But one of those probes went out, completed its survey, and came back within a very quick, and very surprising, time frame. In short, Clement, we think we've broken the light-speed barrier," DeVore said.

Now Clement was intrigued. He sat forward in his chair. "You *think* you've broken the light-speed barrier? What does that actually mean?"

DeVore nodded to Yan, who took over the briefing for the technical details. "It's called LEAP, Liquid Energy Absorption Propulsion. Essentially, it's a quantum-fluid drive," she started.

"Well that just rolls right off the old tongue," said Clement.

"Please listen," replied Yan, perturbed at his sarcasm. "LEAP is based on a centuries-old concept called an Alcubierre drive. Basically, when the drive is activated, a ship or probe creates a bubble of warped space around the vessel that contracts in front of the ship and expands behind the ship. The ship itself doesn't actually move within the bubble, but rather 'surfs' on a 'wave' of 'liquefied' space generated by the LEAP drive within the bubble. The bubble moves, but the ship doesn't. Normal space-time is warped around the ship. Essentially, it creates a quantum-fluid environment that allows for movement through normal space at faster-than-light speed."

"To warp space as you describe would take an enormous amount of power," stated Clement, skeptical. "What do you use to power the thing?"

DeVore cut in here. "An antimatter annihilation reactor."

"A what?" said Clement.

Yan took over again. "Basically, the power we need is created by containing a matter/antimatter interaction within a closed vacuum. We accelerate quantum particles until they become unstable enough to create a singularity, which in turn generates an antimatter particle. That particle is then dropped into the reactor vacuum chamber where it is bombarded by an equal particle of normal matter. The resulting collision annihilates both particles inside the chamber and releases tremendous amounts of energy that takes on a quantum-liquid state. The energy is then channeled from the reactor and through the LEAP drive components to provide the power we need for creating and maintaining the bubble and running the drive."

"So essentially you're creating an antimatter micro-universe and then destroying that same universe every second to drive your ship?" asked Clement.

"Essentially," said Yan. "Only it happens a lot more often than once a second."

"How often?" Clement asked.

"About one hundred fifty million times per second, we estimate."

Clement looked at the two women. "That's insane," he said.

DeVore shrugged. "It works, and we can control it. As to the specifics of it, I leave that to the scientists. The navy just does the sailing, Clement."

"You said that this probe went out, completed its survey, and came back quickly. How quick are we talking here, and how far did it go?"

"It went to a star system 11.5 light-years from here, completed a full survey of the system for five days, and then returned to the station in seventy-three total days, roundtrip," said Yan. "That's about one hundred ten times the speed of light, if you were wondering."

"I was," said Clement. He leaned back in his chair again. "Has this LEAP drive ever been tested with humans on board? I mean what about radiation, g-forces, acceleration, and the like? I wouldn't want to just be a blood spatter on the wall once it starts accelerating."

"Again," said Yan, "the ship itself wouldn't actually be accelerating, just the bubble around the ship, therefore no corresponding g-forces or inertia."

"So it would be like accelerating at one g the whole way?"

"Like sitting in your living room, or the local bar," said Yan.

"I have to admit I'm intrigued," said Clement. "But—"

"We've refitted a prototype ship with the LEAP drive. It has successfully made the round trip, unmanned, three times with no discernable effects that could be harmful to humans. Now the time has come for a human crew to make the journey," said DeVore.

"So you need a new captain and a crew," said Clement.

DeVore nodded. "And now you know why you're here."

Clement thought about it.

"So only one more question: How does all this relate to the planetary-economics lesson earlier?"

"And that's the real question," said DeVore, warming to the interchange now that she had engaged Clement's curiosity. "This new system is a red dwarf, not unlike the dim K-type stars of Argyle or even Virginis. There are five rocky planets and two dwarf gas planets, and three of the rocky worlds are habitable with abundant water, gentle temperatures, and comfortable oxygen/nitrogen atmospheres. However, in addition to those beneficial conditions, each habitable world has more natural resources than all of 5 Suns Alliance space put together. Minerals like platinum, gold, silver, chromium, natural gas, petroleum, and so on. In short, all three planets are like a paradise, just waiting for us to colonize them."

"And solve your overpopulation problems with conscripts from the Rim planets," said Clement.

DeVore nodded. "They would be the first colonists. Others would follow, trained professionals from throughout the 5 Suns Alliance. You have to admit, Clement, it's better to move the Rim populations than to let them die and bring down our whole civilization."

"You realize you're talking about forcibly moving nearly 4.4 million people."

"No one will be forced, Clement," DeVore said. "The

lure of these new worlds should far outweigh the prospects of starvation on the Rim. And eventually we'll open up these worlds for general migration. The 5 Suns planets will survive and flourish, and so will the new colonies."

"Plus, you'll need workers," he replied.

DeVore nodded, and the conversation stopped.

"We call the system Trinity," interjected Yan after a few moments. "In many ways, it's like the divine has intervened for us. These three planets are the jewels in the crown. They will save humanity."

DeVore put up a representation of the Trinity system. There were two inner rocky worlds that were uninhabitable, one with atmosphere, one without; three blue/green middle worlds with water and atmosphere; and two outer planets, both gas "giants," at least in comparison to the inner five worlds. The three habitable planets on the visual display all had names: Alphus, Bellus, and Camus, going from the inside out. The fourth planet in the system, Bellus, was the largest of the three and had a notable moon.

DeVore looked at Clement. "So you've seen the mission. What do you think?"

Clement took in a deep breath and exhaled. "I think I'm going to have to see this miracle ship of yours, Admiral."

DeVore smiled.

Twenty minutes later the three of them plus Captain Wilcock were on their way down an elevator to the station dockyards.

"You can see it from here," said DeVore, pointing out

the glass windows of the elevator to a specific ship. What Clement could see was a small section of the hull and a large ring around the rear third of the ship. It was obviously a prototype; it looked nothing like the standard navy ships in dock, nor any of the commercial vessels. It did, however, have a main fuselage that was a familiar shape, but modified by several attached cylindrical tubes and the ring.

"Is that ring the LEAP drive emanator?" Clement asked.

"It is," said Yan. "You have a sharp eye."

"For spaceships I do, yes."

"The ring is connected by four tubular pylons that translate the reactor power to the drive components, making it go."

"How long does it take for the bubble to form once you activate the drive?"

"About thirty seconds," said Yan.

"And when it's fully formed?"

"Then off you go, instantly."

The elevator moved out of visual range of the prototype and they descended into a large, wide hallway that was filled with dock personnel scurrying to and from their assignments. There were two oversized beltways that carried large components, such as engine drive components, to either side of a pair of sliding sidewalks. The sidewalks were also full of people in work coveralls moving and connecting to other walkways leading throughout the dock. It was an impressive sight.

"I see the 5 Suns Navy has spared no expense on these dockyards," said Clement.

"I am a bit proud of it myself, I have to admit," said DeVore. She was clearly gauging his reaction to everything she was showing him, and liking what she saw.

The elevator settled and they stepped out into the scurry and bustle, making their way straight forward toward the far end of the station. There was little talk among their party of four, but DeVore had to deal with plenty of salutes from uniformed officers heading the other way. The utility and technical workers were apparently exempt from this protocol, especially if they were moving some sort of equipment. Clement surmised they were probably civilian contractors.

Eventually they turned right onto a new slideway that had large metal doors, emblazoned with the identifier "DOCK 19" in exceptionally large lettering looming over it. The scene was enhanced by two fully armed station security guards with cobra rifles at the ready. At their arrival at the dock they stepped off the slideway and then went in through a side door after being scanned by the security team. Wilcock pulled open the door and said, "This way." Clement let the two ladies go in first and then followed them through.

He was far more impressed by the sight of the prototype than he thought he would be. It was big, as big as an old 5 Suns Alliance Navy light cruiser or even a Rim Navy gunship. She looked like she could carry over a hundred crew, easily. She had the look of gleaming silver chrome about her, which gave her a certain grace as she hung above them in her antigravity dry dock.

Her fuselage caught his attention most, though. Forward of the drive ring and support pylons she had very

similar lines to a Rim Confederation gunship, much like
the one he'd commanded at the end of the war. Aft of the
ring and pylons, though, she was much bulkier, seeming
to carry a great deal of her mass to the rear. The constructs
there looked like boat pontoons, six of them, attached to
the main body of the ship. DeVore gestured for them to
go up an inclined gantry walkway and into the ship, and
Clement did so.

Once inside they were in a broad cargo hold, but it
reminded Clement of where the enlisted crew's quarters
would be on a Rim gunship. In fact, the layout, to his
naked eye, was almost exact.

"Is there a problem, Jared?" asked DeVore.

He looked around some more. "No, Admiral, just a bit
of déjà vu," he said.

She said nothing to that and they continued upward a
couple more decks via a central gangway and stairs,
Clement looking right and left as they went. The Admiral
had to stop multiple times to return salutes from
uniformed officers who were overseeing maintenance and
installations on the prototype. It had all the look of a rush
job for an imminent departure.

As DeVore and Wilcock led the way ahead, Yan caught
up to Clement and spoke softly as he scanned the ship's
innards. "You're looking squirrely, Clement. Something
bothering you?" she said.

He nodded. "This just all seems so familiar. I'd swear
this was a Rim Confederation gunship, at least the main
fuselage is."

"I've never been on a Rim Confederation gunship, so
I wouldn't know. I did hear that the main hull was salvage,

refurbished and repurposed for this mission," said Yan.

"Salvage? Hmm, as I recall we surrendered a half dozen fully functioning gunships at the end of the war. Well, as far as I know they were still functioning."

"But not your ship. That was scuttled, correct?"

Clement nodded, not really wanting to recall his most ignominious moment of the war. "Correct," he said. "Onto the surface of Argyle 4, a satellite of the main planet."

"Do you think this could be—"

"The purpose of scuttling a ship, Yan, is so that it can't be used in the future by your enemy."

"So then this could be another of the surrendered gunships. You said there were half a dozen."

"Yes, six." Clement went silent then as they made their way up the walkway and on to Deck 2, senior crew quarters. There was no doubt in Clement's mind now: they were on a Rim gunship.

"Looking familiar yet?" asked DeVore as she stopped one small flight of stairs short of what was undoubtedly the bridge.

"This is a Rim Confederation gunship, isn't it, Admiral? I can tell that this used to be part of the bridge area," Clement said.

DeVore smiled. "Indeed it is, or was. There have been so many changes, but the primary hull is a Rim gunship, yes. When we were proposing this mission the Admiralty wanted to risk as little 5 Suns Alliance materiel as possible because of the experimental nature of the missions, so I used a design that I was familiar with as a basis. Plus, the gunships had been in surplus for more than a decade. I also had a captain in mind for the mission, and I thought he might benefit from familiar surroundings," DeVore admitted. Clement just nodded and then went to the captain's cabin and opened the door. It was a wide and spacious stateroom inside, with a full bed, conference table for four, working area, and a private bath.

"This is nicer than my apartment on Argyle Station," commented Clement, "and a distinct upgrade over the original design."

"We went for a more spacious layout, seeing as we had free rein to refit her. The old gunships had crews of eighty, but this prototype can be run with a quarter of that, thanks to systems improvements and automation. There are five cabins here on Deck 2 plus a galley, and fourteen double berths below on Deck 5," DeVore said.

"That's why the cargo hold was so spacious. No need to cram sixty techs into the free space."

"Exactly." She looked at him expectantly as he stared up the last five steps of the gangway to the bridge.

"Lead on, Admiral," he said. She gestured for him to pass her by and Clement did so. He entered the bridge and looked around. The whole room was lit from below by blue glowing lights which gave off a steady luminosity about the bridge. The room was long and curved with a ceiling that inclined downward, and the station displays were lit with a mellow pink-maroon color. The front wall was a blank; there were no windows like in the original design, and besides the captain's couch there were just four other stations, likely for the helm, navigation, XO and engineer.

"Take a seat, Captain. Try her out," tempted DeVore. Clement looked at the captain's nest, an acceleration couch and console combination that fully dripped with the latest technology. Some of the systems were familiar, others not so much. He looked hard at the seat, something he'd sworn never to get into again.

"I'm not your captain yet, Admiral," he said.

DeVore waved off Wilcock and Yan, and they went a few feet away to check out the other stations and give DeVore and Clement some semblance of privacy.

For the first time in eleven years, DeVore reached out and touched Clement with genuine warmth. Her hand went to his shoulder and he turned to face her.

"I know what this represents to you, Clement. Betraying so many promises of things you swore you would never do again. But please look at the opportunity this represents. There's no one in the Rim or the 5 Suns Alliance that I want commanding this ship more than you. There's no one who deserves it more, and no one else I can trust with this mission. Please, Jared, take the seat."

He turned away from her, then stepped up and sat in the captain's chair. Damned if it didn't just feel *right* sitting in it.

DeVore smiled as Clement sat uncomfortably, wondering if he had just made a bargain with the Devil.

✣ 4 ✣

An hour later they were all back in the Admiral's office, sitting around the conference table.

"I have not officially said yes yet," insisted Clement as Captain Wilcock swept a series of papers in front of him, papers that would enlist him in the 5 Suns Alliance Navy again for the first time in over a decade.

DeVore sighed. "Just sign the goddamned paperwork, Jared. If you want out we'll tear it up later," she said.

"I have that option?" Clement asked. She nodded.

"Everyone enlisting in the 5 Suns Navy has three days to back out, the same as when you enlisted originally."

Clement looked at the first set of papers. It promised him the full rank of captain, serving at the pleasure of the Supreme Admiral of the 5 Suns Navy and his fleet-level designates (that meant DeVore); he would have to take the oath again, etc. He scribbled his signature at the bottom of the page, imprinted his thumb for authentication, then flipped over to the next. At the top of the page it had his full name, rank, and assignment. The salary was substantial, one hundred sixty-thousand 5 Suns crowns per year, nearly four times what he was making as an independent pilot. The commission was for five years, and officially designated as the 5 Suns Alliance Navy Exploratory Gunship *Beauregard*.

"Wait," he said, looking at DeVore. "You said this ship was one of the surrendered gunships—"

"I said it was a *Rim* gunship, not which one," said DeVore. Clement got up from the table and started pacing.

"We scuttled the *Beauregard*," he said plainly. "You were there."

DeVore stood with him. "Yes, we did. But what I needed for this mission was an intact hull. Not the engines, not the gun batteries or the missile complement, and I needed a very specific captain. So I ordered the *Beauregard* to be recovered, and when we got her, we found she could do the job more than adequately. The repairs and refit took two years. Now, do you want her back, or not?"

Clement looked to DeVore, then over to Yan, and back again.

"I need to sleep on it," he said.

"You have that option," DeVore replied.

"Then I will take my leave of you, Admiral. You'll have my decision at 0900 tomorrow." With that Clement started for the door and Yan started to follow. Clement stopped her with his outstretched hand and looked to DeVore. "I would prefer to have this time to myself, Admiral. Certainly Miss Yan here can find something to occupy her time besides me?"

DeVore nodded to Yan, who returned to her seat at the table.

"Until 0900 then," said DeVore.

"Until then." At that Clement was out the door of the Admiral's office, headed for The Battered Hull as fast as he could go.

The door chime buzzed incessantly for several minutes before Clement roused from his sleep. He'd been dreaming it was going off and remembered cursing it several times, though whether he did that in real life or just in the dream world he wasn't really sure of. He sat up and felt surprisingly good considering how much he'd drunk at The Battered Hull. He hit the privacy call button and said "Just a moment" in what sounded to his ears to be a very gravelly voice. He got no response but the buzzing stopped.

He checked his watch, just past midnight, and wondered who would be visiting him at such an hour. He supposed it was Yan, trying to influence him to take the mission command. He unzipped his uniform tunic, checked his breath, which was foul, and quickly went to freshen up in the bathroom. Two minutes later he was at the door and hit the privacy com.

"Who is it?" he asked pleasantly enough.

"Just open the goddamned door. I've been out here for twenty minutes," came a low, brusque voice. It *sounded* like Yan, but he couldn't be sure, so he opened the door. A woman brushed past him quickly, her face shrouded in a hooded cloak, then turned to face him as he closed the door behind him.

She pulled the hood off of her head. It was Elara DeVore.

The cloak was definitely not duty standard, and she unzipped it to reveal a black unibody suit underneath. She filled the suit, as always, with a firm and fit body. The sight startled him more than a bit.

"Admiral—"

"Cut the bullshit, Clement. We're not on duty and this is not happening."

He opened his mouth for a second, but couldn't think of anything to say until "I wasn't expecting you" came out.

"Obviously," she said. "I came here to give you something." He looked her up and down, the cloak draping off of her shoulders... "Not *that*," she said, frustrated with him.

He was confused now, a product of both his earlier drinking and the unexpected visit from the Admiral. "Then what?" he said.

She looked around and to his surprise she went to his bed and sat down at the foot of it. He went over and sat next to her, close, but not too close. She pulled a square, flat case out of a pocket in the cloak and handed it to him. It was padded, and he opened it from the top.

It was the commissioning plaque from the *Beauregard*. Not a new one from the 5 Suns Alliance Navy, but the original one from the Rim Confederation. He held it in his hands. It was battered and bruised, burnt from the obvious wear and tear it had endured: battles, fire damage, and finally the scuttling Clement had put it through when he thought he was destroying her forever. To Clement, it was a gift of unmeasurable kindness.

"I...I don't know what to say," he said, emotions welling up inside him.

"You don't have to say anything, Jared. And I'm not giving you this to try and influence your decision in any way. I just wanted you to have it, to keep it with you if you take the mission, or to take home to Argyle if you don't. You deserve to have it, and people deserve to know who you really are, not what they think you are now." Then she kissed him quickly on the cheek and got up, zipping up the cloak again and heading for the door.

He followed.

"Elara, wait," he said.

"No," she replied. "If I stay we both know what will happen, and I can't allow that. What was, was, and it can never happen again."

He hung his head. "Is there someone else in your life?" he asked.

She shook her head. "No, and there never has been, really. Bedmates, for sure, some short-term relationships that may have benefitted me in some way in my career, but no one like you, and there never will be again, I know that. Now I've got to *go*, Clement. What passed between us all those years ago is gone from my heart forever, and that's just the hard truth of it," she said with finality.

Clement watched her go, a mixture of emotions, gratefulness, and pain at her confession of their love and her gift to him roiling through his emotions. He set the plaque down on his coffee table and poured himself a drink from the bar, Argyle Scotch, the good stuff, and sat down to contemplate what had just happened.

More than a decade ago they had been intense lovers. She was a dominant woman, one that was hard to tame, in or out of bed. But Clement had never given in to her impulses to control things between them, until the last day they had been together. She had come over to his apartment, he thought to celebrate his new promotion to captain, but that wasn't the case. She had paced around the room, explaining her reasoning, telling him how she would always treasure what they had, etc. He hardly heard her words and just watched her prowl the room like a caged cat that wanted to run free. In that moment, he had truly regretted taking the captaincy of the *Beauregard* if it would cost him DeVore. Once she was finished, telling him of her decision to end their relationship, he had accepted what had to be, the only time he had ever given in to her. Once done, she had leapt on him like a hungry predator, and they'd made love for hours on end. Precisely at midnight, she had left his bed without another word. And then today, at midnight, she had returned.

On his second taste of the scotch the door chime buzzed again. He got up and went to the door, hesitated a second, then opened it.

DeVore came through again, pulling him in with one hand and shutting the door behind her with the other. With a quick motion she unzipped the cloak again and let it fall from her shoulders to the floor. She pulled him in close and then took his hands, running them over every curve of her body. She kissed him passionately, their tongues flicking in and out together. After a long kiss he pulled back.

"But I thought—" he started. She put a finger over his mouth, shaking her head.

"I lied," she said, "about everything," then she kissed him again, pulling him quickly over to the bed.

✴ 5 ✴

Clement was awake by 0600, but Elara was long gone. She'd left quietly in the night and he'd let her, pretending to be asleep. Their sex had been frantic, and everything he'd ever wanted from her she had given to him, but she was gone now, Elara was gone, and he was sure from here on out he would be dealing with her only as Fleet Admiral DeVore.

He got ready and dressed in his undecorated 5 Suns Navy captain's uniform, then made his way out to The Battered Hull for a leisurely early breakfast. He ordered the Sailor's Ale Special, which promised a quick hangover recovery from any antics the night before. He'd already had his pills, but if he was being truthful he'd admit they weren't as effective now as they used to be when he was younger. Or maybe it was just *him* that wasn't as effective. He sat back with a cup of mocha coffee from New Paris, which also claimed to have anti-hangover properties. It wasn't bad, not at all, and as he sat there nursing his cup, he was interrupted by a group of midshipmen, the same four middies he'd told old war stories to on his first night at the station.

"You're interrupting my breakfast, Middies," he said disdainfully, looking away, as if he was not giving them a second glance, or a second of his time.

"We apologize for that, sir," said the lead one, the sandy-haired leader of the quartet from their previous engagement. Clement didn't really want company, but he decided to humor them, if only for a moment.

"What are your names, Middies?" he asked.

The leader answered for them all. "I'm Caleb Daniel, from New Paris, Huang Tsu is from Shenghai, Kayla Adebayor is from Carribea, and the big quiet one is Frank Telco, from Columbia," he said.

Clement gave them nods of acknowledgement all around. "And what is it that you *middies* want?"

They all looked at Daniel eagerly.

"Sir, we've all just completed our final school exams, and we're due to get our commissions after another semester of post-grad service training," Daniel stated.

"And what's that to me?"

"Well, sir," Daniel said, then hesitated. "To be honest, the rumors are that you're about to get a command, sir. And being as straightforward as we can be, we'd like to volunteer for that mission. Each of us have to serve a three-month-minimum internship to get our graduation plaques, and we'd like to serve that time with you. Sir."

Clement looked from each one of the middies to the other. They were all very young, and obviously very eager. "Are you serious?" he asked. They all nodded yes. Clement laughed, then started in on them.

"First of all, I don't have a ship yet. In fact, I'm not even sure I want the mission I'm being offered. Second, this mission has a crew complement of only twenty, so you'll have to prove to me your worth taking over an experienced space tech at your position. So tell me what your specialties are and your class rank, one by one, and I'll decide if this goes forward," he said.

Daniel started. "Command track, sir. Top five in a class of fifty."

"Well I don't need a command officer, but I'm sure we can find something for you to do. Next."

Tsu stepped up. "Propulsion sciences, sir. Eighth out of fifty."

Clement rubbed at his chin in an affected manner. "Ever heard of a LEAP drive, Mr. Tsu?"

Tsu looked confused. "No, sir."

"Good. It's top secret. And you didn't hear that term from me." Clement looked to Kayla. "Miss Adebayor?"

"Star Navigation, sir. Third out of twenty."

"Hmm," said Clement. "Why only twenty in the class?"

"The other thirty dropped out, sir," she said. "Including Tsu." Tsu looked embarrassed at the revelation. Clement thought about that.

"Tell me why you only came third in your class, Middie," said Clement.

Adebayor looked at her friends. "Because I spent the first semester tutoring Middie Tsu, sir," she said. All the rest laughed except Tsu, who at least managed a smile.

"Very good, Navigator," he said, then he looked to Frank Telco. He was a big kid, even bigger than Tsu. "Mr. Telco?"

Telco stiffened as if at attention. "Weapons systems and security, sir," he said with confidence. "Top of my class, sir."

"I bet you could kill me with your dog tags," said Clement.

"Yes, sir!" replied Telco.

"Brains and brawn. You all make for a good mix of skills. I'll tell you what I'll do, I will put in a good word for you, but if you get on board my mission you'll have no rank status as middies. You'll do the least important tasks on board and you'll take orders from everyone, including the noncommissioned techs. I make no promises though, gentlemen. Is that good enough for you?"

They all smiled. "Good enough, sir!" said Daniel, the obvious leader.

"Great. Now make yourselves scarce. My breakfast is here." They all did as they were told, scattering out the door as the waitress laid out his breakfast plates.

"They seem like nice kids," said the waitress.

"They won't be nice when I'm done with them," said Clement, smiling. Then he dug into his food, suddenly finding himself very hungry.

Clement took the tram ride back to the Admiral's office, his belly full and his heart at peace for the first time in a long time. He knew what he was going to do.

On arrival he was quickly ushered into the meeting room with DeVore, Yan, and Wilcock. They all sat facing him on one side of the conference table while he sat alone on the other. Wilcock pushed the paperwork across the table to him again without a word. Clement found he didn't like Wilcock much. Too quiet and he looked like he'd never fired a weapon in his life.

It was Fleet Admiral DeVore who spoke first. "You've

seen our offer, Mr. Clement. I've done all I can to convince you how important this mission is. The question now is if you'll take the offer or not. Will you be captain of the *Beauregard* again, or will that honor fall to Commander Yan?"

Clement wasn't making eye contact with her, but he answered anyway. "All things considered, and I do mean *all* things, Admiral, I'd be lying if I didn't say I wanted this mission, and this command. But, given that, there are still certain conditions."

DeVore sighed, no doubt a bit annoyed at his "all things considered" comment, an obvious reference to their late-night tryst, which she much preferred to keep secret from her staff. "Of course you have conditions. Name them before I change my mind about offering you this job." To her surprise Clement reached in to the middle of the pile of paper and pulled out a single sheet.

"This clause limiting my right to consume alcohol has to go," he said.

"That clause is based on your behavior over the last decade. There have been several reported incidents while working, and we'd be negligent if we didn't indemnify ourselves against any 'unexpected' surprises," the Admiral said.

"Yet I never lost my flying license, and I think it's you, Admiral, not the 5 Suns Navy, who want some indemnification on this mission," Clement said. Devore stared at him, not giving a centimeter. Clement drew a big red X through the sheet and then turned it over and started writing (in blue) on the back. When he was done, he slid the sheet across the table to DeVore. She picked it up and began reading out loud.

"Six bottles of Argyle Scotch to be kept aboard at all times for the captain's personal use and pleasure, and to share with the crew at his discretion," she said aloud. Then she got out her pen, switching to red, and began marking up the paper herself, then slid it back to Clement to read.

"Three bottles of Argyle Scotch, to be kept in the possession of Commander Yan and distributed at her discretion," he read aloud. He was annoyed, but decided not to press the point. "Should I initial this?"

"Yes," DeVore said, and he did so.

"Item two, captain's choice of key bridge personnel and technicians. I have to be able to trust my command crew," he said.

"Understood. So who would you choose?" DeVore asked.

"Hassan Nobli for one, as my chief engineer. Mika Ori and Ivan Massif at helm and navigation, if you can find them and I can convince them," he said.

DeVore smiled. "Nobli signed on to the LEAP project two months ago. Mika and Ivan have been my guests here on Kemmerine Station for the last eight days, waiting for you. They'll join up as soon as you sign your papers and take the oath," she said.

Clement smiled at that. "Well played, Admiral," he said. She nodded as Clement signed off on the staff sheet.

"Anything else, Clement?"

"One more request. There are four middies that want to join this mission as part of their intern semester. I want to add them to the crew. We can bunk them in the cargo hold," he said.

DeVore shook her head strongly no. "This mission is top secret, Clement. It's no place for unseasoned middies. You've got the finest techs I could find for you. Why do you want four greenhorns in the way?"

"Because they asked, and that shows initiative and bravery, something I had once, and maybe, just a little bit, I've lost."

"So, they remind you of a younger you? That seems like slim reasoning to me."

"A chance to mold young minds, Admiral," he said. She crossed her arms and leaned back in her chair, shaking her head at his boldness.

"Yan, see to the bunks and extra rations. Captain Wilcock, run a background check on these four middies. If even one of them doesn't have a spotless record, none of them go. Clear, Clement?"

"Yes, Admiral. I'll forward the names to Captain Wilcock," he said, nodding toward the staff officer.

"And now I want something back from you," said DeVore. Clement nodded once to her, waiting to hear her conditions.

"Captain Wilcock here will go on the mission with you."

"What? Why would I need a staff officer?"

"Protocol."

"Protocol? You mean a spy. And besides, you've already got Yan for that," Clement said. Yan gave him a withering stare from across the table. Wilcock, for his part, said nothing.

"Take it or leave it," said DeVore. Clement looked

Wilcock over. Beady, shifty eyes. Clement was reminded that he'd had sweaty palms when they first shook. He didn't like him at all, but . . .

"Done, Admiral," Clement said.

"Good," said DeVore, slapping her palms on the table and then standing. "Finish your paperwork with Captain Wilcock here. We will get you proper rank adornments, and then you'll take the oath."

"How long until I can take her out for test runs?" asked Clement as he busily started signing papers.

"Oh, there's no test runs, Captain. The *Beauregard* leaves dock in slightly less than forty-eight hours. Now if you'll excuse me, I have a fleet to run." And with that she was off to her office desk, Clement staring after her.

"Can we just get the goddamn thing running?" The angry voice belonged to Captain Jared Clement of the *Beauregard*, less than twelve hours after he'd taken the 5 Suns Alliance Navy oath as her commander.

"This is precision work, Captain. One wrong move and we could disintegrate this ship in a microsecond. Antimatter is powerful stuff." The second voice belonged to Hassan Nobli, chief engineer of the *Beauregard*, and caretaker of the LEAP drive. Nobli was a disheveled-looking man with curly, unkempt hair and rounded wire-rim glasses, which Clement took for an affectation rather than a necessity. Nobli always seemed to be wearing a pair of coveralls soaked in grease of some kind, even when there wasn't any around, and this situation was no exception.

The two men were standing face to face in front of the

antimatter annihilation chamber. It was spherical, no bigger than a small steam boiler Clement had seen used on his home world of Ceta, and surprisingly simple in its design. The only sense of sophistication came from the eight exit pipes that would channel the antimatter material to the LEAP drive components on the ship's outer-perimeter drive ring.

"Look, Mika and Ivan haven't even so much as taken this thing for a drive around the block, let alone fire it up and take on the first faster-than-light interstellar mission in the history of mankind. Now how much longer will it be?" demanded Clement.

"The station scientists are monitoring the fluid outflow now, Captain. They say we should be ready to fire her up in about two hours, and I won't argue that point with them," said Nobli.

"Fine then," said Clement. "But I want you and your techs on this until we have the right mix. There won't be any second chances to get it right out in the wild."

"Understood, sir."

"In the meantime why don't you get that propulsion middie, Tsu, to warm up the conventional drives. I want Mika and Ivan to at least get a chance to handle the controls before we start surfing the universe."

"I'll get Middie Tsu on it right away," Nobli said. Secretly, he'd already had the conventional drives, ion plasma, and chemical thrusters fired up and ready to go, but giving the middie something to do would keep him out of Nobli's way, at least for a while. And it had the added effect of placating the annoyed captain of the *Beauregard*.

Clement pointed at Nobli. "I want hourly reports on this thing," he said.

"Of course, sir."

Clement started to walk away.

"Sir," Nobli called after him. Clement turned. "It's good to see you back, sir."

"It's good to be back. I think," said Clement. Then he was off to his next stop.

Down inside the cargo bay, Clement stopped to check in on his four middies. He had passed Tsu in the corridor on his way to assist Nobli, but Daniel, Adebayor, and Telco were all at their bunks. They stood and saluted as he came up. He saluted back.

"That's enough of that; we don't salute onboard. At ease, Middies," he said. They all relaxed, but just a bit. They were clearly nervous. "I hope you've settled in because we won't have much time to get you up to speed and I don't have time to babysit you, so you each have to find a sponsor and stick to them like glue, which means you do whatever they tell you to do, even if it's sweeping the floors.

"Now, Miss Adebayor, you'll be up first. I want you to meet with my navigator, Lieutenant Massif, at your first possible convenience. He's a top navigator and when you're plotting an interstellar mission, well, whatever he knows you should try to glom off of him. And also check in with the com and engineering techs. I may have a console for you on the bridge as Mr. Nobli likes running things from the bowels of the ship."

"Yes, sir," she said, with way too much enthusiasm.

"Daniel, there isn't much you'll be able to learn from me and I don't want you following me around like a puppy dog anyway. Commander Yan is an accomplished officer and on the command fast track so please communicate with her about your assignments. She probably won't like it but tell her that I insist. Oh, and stay away from Captain Wilcock. That's one career path you don't want to emulate, understood?"

"Aye, sir," said Daniel.

Clement turned to the last middie, Telco. "Mr. Telco, I have a special job for you. Inventory our weapons systems—missiles, torpedoes, energy weapons, and stashes of small arms. I want a complete accounting in two hours and I want you to familiarize yourself with all the ship's weapons systems. Understood?"

"Aye, Captain," said Telco, then added, "will do."

Clement eyed him, annoyed. "Cut out that last part, Middie. It will get annoying real fast."

Telco stiffened at that. "Yes, sir," he said.

"And one more thing I want you to do. Clear out some of these cargo boxes and set up a shooting range down here. God knows it's big enough with only a small crew. Once that's done I want you to find some of the techs when they're off rotation and make them shoot some rounds, once we're underway. I want as many as we can to get in shooting practice during the journey out."

Telco looked at his friends and they exchanged surprised looks.

Daniel, ever the leader, stepped in again. "Are you expecting that we may have to go into combat, sir?" he said.

"Gentlemen," Clement said, looking at the three of them, "we're heading to an unexplored star system aboard an experimental faster-than-light-speed prototype ship. I expect nothing, but I want us to be prepared for anything at all times, understood?"

"Yes, sir," came a chorus in reply.

Clement looked at his watch. "Then get to it. Admiral DeVore wants us gone inside thirty-six hours from now. Let's not disappoint her. Now off with you."

And with that they all scattered, and Clement made his way back toward his bridge.

✶ 6 ✶

Clement called together his first staff meeting in the tiny officer's galley on Deck 2 for 1930 hours. There were only six rooms on the deck: the captain's cabin on the port side, which was the most spacious, obviously; Commander Yan's across the hall starboard from him; then Mika Ori and Ivan Massif one door down from Yan; then the galley. On Clement's side of the aisle there was a cabin for Hassan Nobli that he hardly ever used, preferring to bunk with the crew closer to his engine room, and Captain Wilcock got the small room at the end of the hallway, which was really just a guest berth with no bathroom, and across from the officer's galley. Clement got some small satisfaction knowing that Wilcock would have to use the technician's shared bathroom two decks down every time he had to use the head.

They gathered quietly after a long day, most looking worn out but shunning coffee. It had been a full day and there was still work to do before their scheduled departure at 1200 hours tomorrow. They shuffled in, Yan sitting next to him, the gangly Massif and the tiny Ori sitting together, then Nobli and finally Wilcock filling out the table. Before he started, Clement flipped through a series of reports on his com pad and frowned. He looked up at Yan.

"This ship is severely under-armed," he said to her. "Midshipman Telco reports to me that we have only a half dozen cobra rifles on board, a smattering of handguns, and no grenades of any kind."

"There are only twenty crew," said Yan calmly. "Are you expecting to fight an army?"

"First of all, there are twenty-four crew with the middies, and no I'm not 'expecting' a fight, but this is a military vessel and as such we should be properly armed. I expect a full complement of rifles and pistols loaded aboard before we depart and plenty of extra ammo as well."

"How much 'ammo,' sir?" she replied sarcastically, with a smirk. This time Clement suspected he was being played with by Yan. He decided to double down.

"Two crates worth, of each," he said.

"But that would be—" started Yan.

"One hundred forty-four packs of each style," finished Wilcock.

"Thank you, Mr. Wilcock," said Clement. "And a crate of RPG rounds."

"Are you serious? That will take up half the cargo hold," protested Yan.

"Hardly. And may I remind you, Commander, this *is* a military mission, and I expect everyone to behave accordingly. This is not some show cruise and we are not explorers. So we follow the rules. We may not be expecting any trouble, but if my navy career is any indication, it often finds me," Clement noted before continuing. "And that reminds me again, this ship has literally no advanced armaments for protection. I want a full complement of missiles, conventional and atomic, brought on board."

This time it was Wilcock who spoke up. "I'm not sure the Admiral will authorize that," he said.

Clement looked up at him sharply. "This is a gunship, Captain. A gunship with no weapons is pretty useless. And may I remind you that you're on this ship as a favor to the Admiral, Mr. Wilcock. If I don't have a full missile room of sixty conventional missiles in my launch bays with at least a half dozen ten-kiloton nuke warheads on board by the time we head out, I'm leaving you on the loading dock."

"Is that *all*, sir?" said Wilcock, perturbed. "We don't even have a weapons tech on board." He had a soft, high voice, the kind that would annoy any crew, and it was annoying Clement already.

"We have Middie Telco. He'll have to do for now and I expect to have him properly trained on all types of missiles and warheads, by you."

"Do you think you'll need more missiles than just the nukes?" asked Yan, feigning surprise.

Clement looked at her, very seriously. "Commander Yan, the solution to almost any problem in space is more missiles," he deadpanned.

Yan sighed. "Boys and their toys," she said.

Clement ignored her and looked down the table. "Mr. Nobli, a report on the LEAP drive if you please," he said.

"Well," started Nobli, adjusting his glasses. He looked

for all the world like a misplaced university professor, not a spaceship engineer, as he scanned his hand-pad readouts. "I've got her humming pretty good, Captain. The nuclear accelerator seems to run as smoothly as promised, and I've no doubt once we release the hold on the two chambers of the LEAP reactor that everything will work smoothly and we can start annihilating antimatter universes."

Clement nodded. "That's . . . that's good, I guess?" he said. "What about the conventional drive?"

"Well, we've got a state of the art Xenon thruster system and an Ion plasma drive that will push us along at a clip we would have loved to have had during the war, but just like the LEAP system, they're both untested with humans on board," said Nobli.

"What about acceleration?"

"We can easily achieve six *g*s of acceleration inside two minutes. Enough speed to get us out of any pickle, I'd say."

"Thank you, Nobli. Fleet Admiral DeVore expects us to be half an AU from the station before we light up the LEAP reactor. Let's make sure we give the Ion plasma drive a good test on that run. It will be our primary means of travel inside the Trinity system," said Clement.

"Aye, sir."

Next Clement looked down the table to Mika Ori and Ivan Massif, his pilot and navigator. "I regret we won't be able to give you a chance to bust the seams on this baby before first flight, Mika," he said.

She nodded. "I understand the circumstances, sir. I'm looking forward to getting her under power." She'd been his pilot, and a damn good one, for three years on the original incarnation of the *Beauregard*.

"How's your station checking out?" asked Clement.

Ori shrugged. "It's state of the art, but I've spent most of the last decade on similar systems in the private sector, in fact, some of them I like better than this one. But I should be able to fly her, sir, if the Admiral ever lets us leave the dock."

"Oh, she will," smiled Clement. "Ivan?" he continued, pronouncing it the navigator's preferred way, *E-vaan*. Massif was a tall and lanky man, and a great navigator, but the LEAP drive would make him less relevant on this mission.

"I'm also familiar with this type of navigation system from our years running luxury yachts and the like. It's different though, in that it's really a 'point and shoot' system. Since we'll be traveling at FTL speeds in a quantum-fluid bubble the normal types of flight plans don't really come into the equation, as long as there aren't any uncharted rogue planets on our path that I don't know about," he said.

Clement smiled. "Sorry if you'll be bored, Ivan. We'll take the same path as the last LEAP probe, which should be clear of potential hazards. Once we're in the Trinity system though, we'll need you to be full up and ready to chart our path inwards toward the three habitable planets. I guess you'll just have to wait a couple of weeks to become important."

"Aye, sir, I'll be ready. I've already plotted us to follow the LEAP probe's course, sir. You just have to say the word."

"Good enough," said Clement, turning back to Yan.

"Do we have a medical officer aboard, Commander?" he asked. She scanned her own pad for personnel profiles.

"Lieutenant Pomeroy is the dedicated medic. She also doubles as a science tech," said Yan.

Clement nodded. "Good enough. Have her run you through the med bay equipment as a pre-req, and I want her to have a backup. Let's give Mr. Daniel a shot at that."

"Yes, sir," said Yan.

Clement looked around the room. "Anything else?" Everyone stayed silent. "Good. I want you all in bed by 2400 hours but I want my ordnance and equipment aboard and stored before 0800 tomorrow, so that duty falls to you, Mr. Wilcock."

"Understood, Captain."

"Then I'll leave you all to it," he said as the meeting broke up. Before they could all exit though, he added, "We're all clear for departure at 1200 hours tomorrow. I want us to be ready two hours prior to that." There were groans and acknowledgements as the command crew shuffled out. Clement reached out to Yan indicating she should stay.

"Do you think we'll be ready in time for the launch?" he asked when they were alone.

"I don't know, sir. You're a much different commander than this crew is used to, excepting your friends, of course. The 5 Suns Alliance Navy is a different kind of animal; they're more used to formality and protocol. They may fall in line with your style, or they may resist. It's up to you to find the right combination," she said.

"As long as I have your loyalty, Yan," he stated.

She looked at him, hesitating before answering. "You

do, Captain. For now," she said, and then went down the hall to her cabin.

Yan was surprised when she got a knock on her cabin door fifteen minutes later. She hit her visual monitor and found it was Captain Wilcock standing in the hallway. She could see over Wilcock's shoulder that Captain Clement's door was closed. She buzzed Wilcock in and he came in quickly and quietly. Yan looked at him. "What can I do for you, Mr. Wilcock?"

He quickly went over to her desk com system and started it up. "Message incoming from Fleet Admiral DeVore," he said.

"Shouldn't Clement—" Yan started.

"It's just for us, Commander," he replied as Admiral DeVore's image came up on the screen.

"Hello, Yan," she said.

"Hello, Admiral."

DeVore looked dead serious.

"Look, I want to make this quick and I want us all to be on the same page, is that clear?" Yan looked to Wilcock, who said nothing, and then back to the Admiral.

"Clear, Admiral."

"Good. I'm going to approve Clement's request for the conventional missiles and the small arms. The way I know him, he's looking to pick a fight and if I say no to his request he'll just sit on the dock until I give in. I want this mission off on time tomorrow—in fact, timing is critical for the *Beauregard* to reach Trinity."

This intrigued Yan, as to why timing was so critical, but she decided to say nothing for the moment.

DeVore continued. "But this request for atomic warheads, that's different. I can see no reason why he might need them, but I'm going to give him six warheads anyway, under certain conditions. The most important of these conditions, Yan, is that you and Wilcock have to be in agreement that use of the warheads is justified. To safeguard this condition, you're both going to have to wear security keys around your necks for the duration of the mission. You will both have to be in agreement to unlock the safe to access the warheads and you'll both have to agree the situation is dire enough to use them. The keys must be used simultaneously to both unlock the safe and release the missile controls for Clement to launch them. Do you understand, Yan?"

"I do, Admiral," she said. At that Wilcock handed her a small clear case with a nuclear key inside. Yan broke the seal and placed it around her neck, slipping it under her uniform tunic, then zipped back up. All command-level officers had taken atomic level protocol classes as a condition of their promotion, but this was the first time Yan had ever been issued one of the keys. When that was done DeVore looked to Wilcock.

"Your shipment of atomic warheads will arrive in a case at the loading dock in fifteen minutes. I expect you to be there and to secure the warheads personally. Understood, Captain Wilcock?"

"Understood, sir," he replied.

"Good. Then that's that. The rest of the conventional missiles and small arms will be aboard by 0600. Who's going to be in charge of loading them into the launch bays?"

"Middie Telco, ma'am," said Yan.

DeVore nodded. "Oversee his work, Yan. I don't want a middie blowing up my prototype in the dry dock."

"Aye, Admiral."

"Then off with the two of you," she said with a wave of her hand. "And good luck."

"Thank you, ma'am," said Yan as Wilcock mumbled some other reply. Yan found she didn't care much for his speaking voice, too soft and indistinguishable. She found she didn't trust him much either.

With that the com to DeVore's office severed and Wilcock made for the door. With his hand on the door control he stopped and looked back at her. "I appreciate your support on this, Yan," he said. She merely nodded in reply. A few seconds later and she watched him on her monitor as he went down the deck ladder and out of sight, heading toward the loading dock, there to presumably await the arrival of the atomic warheads. She waited a few moments more before heading across the hallway to Clement's cabin. She buzzed in. The door slid open silently.

Clement was at his office desk, rifling through various pads as he checked to see if his orders were being complied with and if the ship was ready for her manned maiden voyage.

"Can I help you, Yan?" he said, not looking up from his pile of pads and floating monitor displays.

"I just wanted you to know that your atomic warheads are coming on board presently, sir," she said.

"I assume that's what Captain Wilcock wanted from you in your quarters?" Clement replied.

It bothered Yan that her cabin was being monitored by him, but, "Yes, sir," she said without hesitation.

Clement continued to work, seeming to ignore her. "You realize not having the warheads already loaded onto a ship-to-ship missile will slow our response time, possibly to a very dangerous level?" he said.

"That's Captain Wilcock's purview, sir, not mine," she defended.

Now Clement looked up. "I don't trust Wilcock," he said.

"Neither do I, sir."

"Really? That's good to hear. But then I'm not entirely sure I trust you either, Yan."

She bristled inside at that, but she didn't back down from Clement's steel gaze on her. He had a way of making her feel like he could see right through her. "I hope I can change that opinion with time, sir," she said.

Clement leaned back from his displays. "Do you, Yan? I hope that's true," he said, then he got out of his chair and paced the cabin while Yan watched him. "Admiral DeVore—" he started. She cut him off before he could finish the thought.

"She's my primary report, sir. But you're my commanding officer on this mission," she offered, unsolicited. Clement took that in stride.

"Please understand, Yan, I have a long history with Mika, Ivan, and even Nobli. I don't have much history with you. I may make decisions you disagree with. I just need to know I won't find a cobra pistol round in my back if I do."

Now Yan got very serious. "Captain Clement, please don't question my loyalty to you or this mission."

"But you undoubtedly have private orders from Admiral DeVore, don't you?" he accused.

She nodded once. "I do, sir. But they are to protect the ship, protect the mission, and protect the crew. She wanted you for this command very badly, and I'll admit I don't know why. But beyond those general protocols, sir, you are my commanding officer, and I want you to know you can trust me," she said.

"Even with that atomic key hanging around your neck?"

Suddenly Yan became conscious of the cold metal between her breasts, set against her skin. Despite Clement pushing her to her limits, Yan didn't waver. "Yes, Captain, even with the key."

Now it was his turn to nod once, then he returned to his desk. "When will the missiles be loaded?" he asked.

"0600, sir."

"Make sure Middie Telco has a full set them packed and ready for the launch tubes well before we leave."

"I was just on my way to take care of that, sir."

"Good. And Yan, thank you."

"Aye, sir," she said, then turned on her heels and made her way out of his cabin. She went down toward the cargo hold, there to make sure the middie got his instructions as early as possible.

"Do you understand your orders, Middie?" said Yan to the strapping young middie Telco.

"Aye, ma'am," he said, bright-eyed and eager to please despite the ever-later hour.

"Good," she said. "Make sure you validate that the ordnance in those missiles is primed and ready to go. We don't want any surprises in the middle of a battle."

"Understood, ma'am."

"What about all the small arms?"

He stiffened. "As requested, ma'am. I've already tested the cobra rifles and pistols. The kinetic rounds work just fine, and the burner rounds have passed all the test marks. I haven't tested the RPGs for obvious reasons, but I have to say these are some of the finest guns I've ever seen. The workmanship is fantastic."

She smiled again at his youthful enthusiasm. "I imagine what you used in the academy weren't top-of-the-line materiel. The navy doesn't skimp on the real thing." Yan gestured to a bunk and Telco hopped up to the top of one of them. "Set your alarm early, Middie. The captain will want those missiles stored and ready to go as soon as they get here. In fact, I imagine he'll be checking in with you every few minutes after 0600. You shouldn't disappoint him. Now get some sleep, and when you see your friends tell them the same. Today has been a big day; tomorrow will be bigger," she said, then turned down the light in the middie's tiny berth, feeling all the world like a mother putting one of her children to bed. A very handsome young child at that.

"Do you think we'll see battle, ma'am?" said Telco with way too much enthusiasm.

Despite herself, Yan smiled at him. "I highly doubt it, Middie, but you never know," she said. "Now go lights out. We have a lot to do yet to get this bucket rolling."

He nodded. "Goodnight, ma'am," he said.

"Good night, Middie," she said, then shut the door behind her.

✳ 7 ✳

Clement was up and prowling the decks well before the missiles were scheduled to arrive at 0600. When he arrived at the loading dock Middie Telco was already there. He checked his watch. 0540. Not bad for a rookie.

After exchanging pleasantries, the two went silent, both anticipating the same thing. Ten minutes later at 0550 the missiles started arriving. Clement jumped right in with directions for the dock techs and Telco.

The ship-to-ship missiles were five meters long and came in crates of two, with the warheads stored separately. The cargo bay had an automated racking system which pulled the missiles from their crates and then shipped them via a gantry loader up two decks and forward to the missile room where they were re-racked, waiting for their warheads to be installed. Telco had arranged for Middie Daniel to take care of the warheads, and he had them all loaded onto an open lift for travel. In Clement's experience, it took about two hours to turn a load of crated missiles and a full complement of warheads into ready-racked missiles. Telco and Daniel had a lot of work ahead of them.

Once he was satisfied that the process was moving efficiently, Clement clicked the com to Daniel's channel and gave the middies final instructions. "It's 0615, Middies. My expectation is that you'll have these missiles racked and loaded in the forward missile center by 0830 hours. I hope you don't plan on disappointing me?"

"No, sir," they both said in unison. Clement turned to address Telco directly. "As of this moment, Middie, you are my missile-room tech. That's your station full time. Daniel, you will be his relief, covering the position while he eats, sleeps, and pisses. Am I clear?"

There was a round of "aye, sirs" from the two middies.

Clement looked at Telco one more time. "I'm holding you personally responsible for making sure those nuke warheads are stored within a hand's reach of the missiles at all times."

Telco looked concerned. "Sir, Captain Wilcock has insisted that the nuke warheads stay in the ordnance hold under lock and key. Sir," Telco said nervously.

"Unfortunately, Middie, Captain Wilcock is an idiot who has never had a ship command. You store them right where I said. If he wants to protest you come and get me. I'll be coming by before we shove off to check your work, you can count on that," Clement warned.

"Yes, sir. I'll see to it, sir."

"And one more thing. Make sure you rotate the rack so that six empty missiles are ready to be loaded with those nukes as soon as possible in an emergency situation. I don't want to wait for sixty missiles to roll by if I need a nuke," said the captain.

"Aye, sir," said Telco.

Clement nodded, then left him to his work.

Next Clement checked in with Nobli in the propulsion room.

"Are we ready to go interstellar surfing yet, Mr. Nobli?" said Clement, surprising his engineer, who turned quickly from his station at the antimatter annihilation chamber.

"You should never surprise a man who controls enough power to wipe out a star system," said Nobli, smiling. "Yes, sir, she's ready to go. Xenon drive thrusters and the Ion plasma impellers have been test-fired as well. I think she'll fly like a bumblebee, sir."

Clement frowned at the metaphor. "Uh, I don't know about where you're from, Nobli, but on Ceta bumblebees are kind of slow, lazy fliers," he said. Nobli was a native of Helios, like DeVore had been. The planet had no bees of any kind.

Nobli thought about that a minute. "Maybe I meant hummingbird," he said, shrugging.

Clement had never seen a hummingbird. Story was they hadn't been hardy enough to survive on the Rim worlds, but from what he knew, the analogy was a better match.

"I'll take that then," Clement said, and managed a wave to Middie Tsu, who was across a sea of pipes from the two men, adjusting a valve control as he waved back. Clement looked at his watch. "Just four and a half hours, Hassan, and we're back among the stars."

"Aye, sir. Never thought I'd see the day, but it's good to have you back in uniform. It's where you belong, sir."

Clement looked down at his uniform, not one he had

ever expected to wear again. "Don't get sentimental on me, Nobli. I'll have you running like a dog soon enough."

"I bet you will, sir."

Clement just nodded to his friend, then brought up another subject. "Have you done any research on other possible applications for the LEAP drive?"

Nobli looked at him sidelong. "Such as?"

Clement leaned in close to his engineer inside the noisy room. "Such as possible weapons applications? We are, after all, using a lot of energy in the drive."

"That we are, sir. There are some theoretical papers. I've skimmed them."

Clement stepped back. "Well, you'll have about seventeen days to look into it. I'd like you to give me an option before we arrive at Trinity. Something that works, Nobli."

Nobli nodded. "We do have the old forward plasma cannon array from the previous iteration of the *Beauregard*. Nobody uses those anymore. Last I saw it was still intact, but I don't know if the piping could hold that kind of energy output."

Clement nodded. "Well, check it out, and let me know in a couple of days, *after* you have everything LEAP-related running smoothly."

"Will do, sir," said Nobli, and then Clement was gone again.

Captain Clement sat and watched his crew from his command seat on the bridge. Ivan Massif was busy teaching young Middie Adebayor about some navigational principle or other. Mika Ori was at the helm, tinkering with the controls while reading a training manual on her hand pad. Yan's station was empty, as it had been for the last two hours, and Captain Wilcock was taking up the engineering console, watching everything like a curly-haired hawk. As a precaution, Clement had shut off the engineering controls, so mainly Wilcock had to stare at a blank panel, and that was fine with Clement.

Clement looked at his watch again. 1140 hours. Still twenty minutes to go and everything was green to go on his master console. They'd missed their two-hour early ready mark, but that had just given him the excuse to yell at everyone again. He'd just got back from one last sweep of the *Beauregard*'s stations, even stopping too take an inventory of medical supplies with Lieutenant Pomeroy. It had been his third such sweep of the morning.

Finally, he'd had enough.

"Commander Yan to the bridge, please," he said impatiently over the ship-wide com. A few seconds later and he heard her footsteps clanking on the open metal stairs to the bridge.

"I was just down in the galley having a last coffee," she said casually as she keyed in the code to unlock her station.

"I'm glad someone's relaxed," Clement said, then he keyed in the code through his com panel to the Admiralty, and Elara DeVore. "Middie Adebayor, do you have a communications badge?"

"I do, sir," she said after snapping around to him at attention.

"Then get on the engineering console and raise station traffic control."

"Aye, sir," she said, and started making her way to the console, which was occupied by Wilcock.

"Captain Wilcock," said Clement, "I'm afraid you'll have to sit this one out in your cabin."

"But, I have—"

"It's not my fault they made the bridge so small. You should register a complaint with the Admiral when you get back," Clement deadpanned. Wilcock scowled at Clement but reluctantly relinquished the station to Middie Adebayor. The sound of Wilcock's boots clinking down the short stairwell brought a smile to Clement's face.

A second later and Admiral DeVore popped up on the main bridge display.

"I was just about to call in and wish you all good luck," said the Admiral.

Clement smiled at her. "I'm actually just calling to ask for early clearance to depart. We've been ready for over an hour now . . . and frankly, I'm bored," he said, lying.

DeVore laughed. "I wouldn't expect anything else from you, Clement. Clearance is given. Good luck. We'll see you in about a month."

Clement stood. "Thank you, Admiral," he said, and snapped off a departure salute.

At that DeVore switched off the feed from her end.

Clement turned to his middie. "Do you have Kemmerine Station traffic control on the line, Middie Adebayor?"

"I do, Captain."

"Please inform them we are seeking early clearance from the dock. Fleet Admiral's priority," he said.

Adebayor repeated the same to traffic control and then got a positive beep in return.

"Stations, everyone. Prepare for departure," said Clement.

Yan got on the ship-wide com and repeated Clement's command. Within a minute all the boards showed fresh green lights again.

Clement turned to Mika Ori. "Lieutenant, you may shove off at your convenience," he said.

"Aye, sir," said Ori, then proceeded to turn to her station and cut the *Beauregard*'s moorings, using a tiny burst of the thrusters to move her away from the station. Once the ship was a hundred meters clear of the dock, Ori turned the ship expertly and began to accelerate using the thrusters, the station fading quickly behind her.

"Xenon thrusters making 0.0005 light, sir," said Ori.

Clement acknowledged and then sat back in his chair for the first time as in-service captain of the *Beauregard* in fifteen years.

"Light up the Ion drive, Lieutenant. Increase speed constant to 0.025 light. That should give us about three hours to the jump-off point for the Trinity system."

"Aye, sir," said Ori, quickly turning and making adjustments on her console board. They all felt a slight tug at the increase in speed as Ori activated the Ion plasma drive.

Clement turned to Ivan Massif. "What's our course, Navigator?" he asked.

"Generally on course for the Trinity system, sir," replied Massif.

Clement looked at the lanky Russian. "Generally on course?"

Massif shrugged. "It's not like navigating inside 5 Suns Alliance space, sir. Trinity is 11.5 light-years away. We can be off by quite a ways on our final target and still be well within the mission parameters, especially from this distance, sir. You don't want me to fly her right into the Trinity star, do you?"

Clement smiled. "No, Ivan, I don't. But if you don't mind me asking, what will be our dropout point in the system?"

"Based on what the last probe did, we'll be about ten AU out from the outermost planet, and that last planet is only about 0.06 AU from the Trinity star itself, sir," said Massif.

"Six *hundredths* of an AU? How many klicks is that?"

"Just under nine million kilometers, sir," chimed in Yan.

Clement mouthed a sardonic "thank you" without saying anything. "Those planets must be packed in tight," he then commented.

"The three habitable worlds are within 2.5 million kilometers of each other, sir," said Massif.

"Very close, then," said Clement.

"Short orbital years too, sir. Four, six, and nine days, sir," said Massif.

Clement whistled. "Just a fraction of 5 Suns Alliance space. This will be interesting flying, Mika. I hope you're ready," he said, turning to his pilot.

"Always ready, sir," she replied. "But for now it's just the milk run until we get that LEAP drive turned on. I could do it in my sleep, sir."

"I bet you could, Mika." Clement stood and took the short walk around his compact bridge. "Well, we're on our way. The next milestone should be in about three hours when we turn the LEAP engine on. Until then, I'll be in my cabin, monitoring. Call me if you need anything. And Commander Yan, call Captain Wilcock to the bridge to take the con. And tell him not to touch anything."

"Aye, sir," said Yan, smiling, as Clement departed the bridge.

Clement got a knock at his door, not an entry-request chime, mind you, but a real knock, about thirty minutes later. Clement pressed the OPEN button on his desk and the door slid aside. To his surprise it was Yan, bearing a bottle of Argyle whiskey and a pair of drinking glasses. He stood to greet her.

"Why, Commander, this is most unexpected of you. Cutting into my alcohol rations already, I see."

"I felt this was a moment worth celebrating," she said as she sat down in one of his desk chairs. Clement joined her at the table and after popping the bottle, he poured a healthy portion of whiskey into the glasses. She took her glass and raised her hand in a toast. "To Captain Jared Clement, and the crew of the 5SN *Beauregard*," she said.

"To the *Beauregard*." They clinked glasses and then drank, Clement savoring the taste. "Ah, god, that's good," he said, leaning back in his chair and then swiveling slowly back and forth. "I wish they'd outfitted this cabin with a recliner."

"For what? Watching tri-vee or your sports?"

"No, Yan. Just to have a drink in and read a good book."

"We have millions of books in the ship's library."

"True. But reading off a pad isn't as fun as holding a real book in your hands. Plus, there's the thrill of the hunt."

She frowned, looking perplexed. "Hunt? What do you mean?"

"Browsing through shops full of ancient leather-bound books. Finding just the right edition. I find it all very relaxing," he said.

"More relaxing than the whiskey?"

"Much," he said.

She put the cap back on the bottle. "Well, I think that's enough celebrating for one day," she said, then headed for the door. "Congratulations again, Captain," she added. "I'll see you on the bridge."

"On the bridge, Commander," he said, then finished his whiskey ration, savoring the taste.

Clement took over the bridge, relieving Wilcock, whom he exiled back to his quarters, with the *Beauregard* about twenty minutes from the agreed-upon jump coordinates. After running through reports from all his subordinates and doing his pad systems check, he called down to Hassan Nobli in the engine room.

"How's our new baby?" he asked.

"Purring like a kitten, sir, but ready to leap on a moment's notice."

Clement smiled. "Was that a pun, Mr. Nobli?"

"Do I really have to tell you that?"

"No," said Clement, smiling. "We'll be arriving at the

LEAP coordinates in about . . . " Clement trailed off as he checked his watch. "Eighteen minutes. Will you be ready?"

"Most definitely, sir. Will you be coming down to watch?"

"Honestly, I hadn't thought of that," admitted Clement.

"We'll give you a show, I promise. And if anything goes wrong, you'll be one of the first to die," joked Nobli.

Clement laughed. "Here's to hoping nothing goes wrong. I'll see you in a few minutes," he said.

"Aye, sir."

Clement slid out of the captain's couch and nodded to Middie Adebayor at the engineering console. "Raise the Admiral, please, Middie."

"Aye, sir," she said. About thirty seconds later she had DeVore on the line and put her image up on the main bridge display.

After a second or two delay, DeVore smiled. "All ready?" she asked.

"Ready, Admiral," Clement said. "Request permission to activate the LEAP drive and depart 5 Suns Alliance space."

There was that hanging delay again, then DeVore said, "Permission granted, Captain Clement. Good luck."

"Thank you, Admiral. We'll see you sooner than you think."

The local ansible network adjusted for the time delay at that moment and DeVore answered almost immediately. "Oh, I'm sure of that, Captain," she said.

With that Clement saluted and gave Adebayor the cutoff signal. DeVore faded from the screen and was replaced by a ship's system status view. Clement got on the all-ship com.

"Now hear this. All hands prepare for LEAP drive activation. Take all safety precautions. Captain Wilcock to the bridge," he said, then hung up the com. He turned to Yan. "You have the con, Yan."

"But sir, Captain Wilcock is the ranking—"

"Not on my ship, Yan. Now that we're about to leap out of the Admiral's jurisdiction, I make the rules. You have the con at all times in my absence, unless directed otherwise. Wilcock can take your station. I'll be in the engineering room watching Mr. Nobli light this baby up."

"Aye, sir."

And with that Clement was gone, Yan slipping comfortably into his chair.

Clement entered the engine room with three minutes to spare. He shook hands with Nobli and his technicians, who numbered three if you included Middie Tsu. The two senior men then entered Nobli's office, which had a full view of the engine apparatus and the console stations.

"You'll want to watch this monitor, sir," said Nobli, pointing to a display at the back of the room. Clement stepped up and examined it. It showed a diagram of the main LEAP drive components, the antimatter accelerator, the positive proton accelerator, the intermix reactor chamber, and the four drive infusers that would create the wave itself.

"I could monitor this from the bridge," complained Clement. "Plus, I have my back to the reactor."

Nobli shrugged. "Sorry about that, sir. But at least if

something goes wrong you'll have the knowledge that you'll be annihilated into subatomic particles before you have any chance to gripe about it." Then he turned to his techs. "Take your stations," he ordered. Clement watched as the three young crew members took their stations. One, a woman, was at the antimatter accelerator, the second at the proton accelerator, and Middie Tsu was at the intermix console facing the reactor.

"Isn't this just an automated process?" asked Clement.

Nobli shook his head. "I've been running this engine for six months, Captain. It can be temperamental. Each part of the process has to be carefully monitored and managed."

"Like what, for instance?"

"Like when we just let the software run the system, the engine start can be rocky. We even blew up one of the probes when they opened the intermix chamber too early. I've isolated those problems and we've now got it down to a fine art."

"Which is?"

Nobli never looked up from his board, nonplussed. "You have to let the protons warm up longer than the antimatter particles, by fractions of a second. If you release them too soon, sometimes things go boom. We give ourselves a safe margin, Captain. Don't you worry."

Clement turned to look at Middie Tsu at the intermix console. "Hassan, Tsu has only been on the ship for a day, and you've got him controlling the intermix chamber."

"I've run him through the process, sir; he's good at following orders." That didn't fill Clement with confidence.

Nobli looked at his watch. "Final reports," he called out with one minute on the clock. They all gave their assent to go. "Stand by for LEAP drive initiation on my mark."

Clement waited as Nobli counted down to ten seconds, then he took a deep breath and looked away from the crew and to his assigned monitor.

"Initiate proton accelerator," said Nobli from behind him. The left side of the monitor turned an icy blue. Seven seconds.

"Initiate antimatter accelerator." This time the right side lit up bright yellow. Five seconds.

The wait seemed like forever. Clement forced his attention to stay stuck to his monitor and let Nobli and his crew do their jobs. The last seconds clicked by . . .

"Now, Tsu! Open the reactor chamber!"

The entire board lit up a vibrant green as the energy filled the main chamber and then tracked outward along the four spines of the infusers, encompassing the drive carousel in an instant.

The carousel started spinning on the monitor.

"Confirm readouts," yelled Nobli as the LEAP drive hummed to life.

"Confirmed!" said the excited female tech from her station. "We have positive confirmation of a contained LEAP wave bubble."

"Are we moving yet?" asked Clement, turning away from his monitor.

"Just a second," said Nobli, holding up his hand. Then he smiled, relieved. "We're moving sir, .16 light and accelerating."

"How long—"

"Until we go superluminal? About two minutes at the recommended acceleration rate, sir," he said, not the least bit intimidated about interrupting his captain.

Now Nobli came to Clement's station. The two men watched in silence as the monitor showed steadily increasing levels of power, and steadily increasing speed. Almost dead on two minutes and the ship seemed to shift ever so slightly.

"That's it, sir, we're superluminal. 1.05 light speed!"

"Well done, Nobli," said Clement, shaking his chief engineer's hand, then repeating, "well done," to the three techs as he went and shook each of their hands. Clement started clapping and the rest of them all joined in. "Congratulations to you all. Well done," he said a third time as the com bell chimed.

Clement brought up the signal on his monitor. "Yes, Yan," he said.

"Captain," she replied. "You should come up here and see this. It's . . . spectacular."

"On my way, Yan," he said, then gave a last wave to the propulsion team and scrambled back across the cargo hold and up the gangway to the bridge.

Yan was right. Looking at the forward visual display was like looking at space through a fishbowl. Stars of all colors swept past them as they cruised by, the tiny dots representing passing stars, pulsars, globular clusters, nebula, and even distant galaxies. They all floated past the external camera and then twisted and distended as the *Beauregard* moved through the quantum fluid of distorted space, riding her wave of bent gravity at an ever increasing pace. Clement had to remember to breathe as he watched the sight go by on the bridge's three-dimensional monitor.

Spectacular indeed.

All one could really do was look at the passing starfield and marvel, but even that got repetitive. Mika Ori, for her part, called it "romantic," with a warm, knowing glance directed at her significant other. In a way he found himself envious of the two of them. They had something he had never had, and likely never would. Their obvious love for one another had never waned in the decade-plus he had known them.

Clement ordered the two of them to cross-train all the middies, just in case, and as a way of getting them to focus on something else besides each other.

Then he left the bridge, letting out a heavy sigh as he slowly navigated the hollow metal steps to his cabin, alone.

✼ 8 ✼

Three days later and the ship had settled into a routine. There wasn't much to do, and the crew, quite frankly, was getting bored, so Clement shortened duty shifts and let everyone cross-train in any area of service they were interested in, sort of as a hobby. That worked for a short time, but then Yan suggested he try something else to "spice things up."

"What do you mean by that?" he said, staring at his first officer from the opposite side of his office table.

"By 'spice things up' I mean lessening the rules against fraternization among the crew," she said.

"By fraternization, you mean sex?"

"Sexual intimacy, yes. When people get bored they will bend the rules, just for a break in the monotony. My experience has told me that it will happen anyway on long-duration space voyages, and a month or so is plenty of time for bored souls to get into trouble."

Clement leaned away from her. "I see. I confess to not having dealt with this problem before, so I will likely defer to your experience in the matter."

"Well, before it wasn't a problem because you always had Elara DeVore."

He sat back from the table, and spoke with an edge of anger at her implication. "Not in that way, Commander, not while I was captain. And that will not be happening for me on this mission."

She responded without any emotion or acknowledgement of his anger. "So you say, Captain. Nonetheless, you have my recommendation."

"I do, Commander. You're dismissed," he said curtly. He was beginning to wonder if having Yan on this mission was going to be a blessing or a curse—but, he did have to think of the welfare of his crew.

An hour later Clement issued a memo to the crew indicating he was suspending all rules against fraternization, on the condition that any crew "interactions" lead to "no drama" regarding daily work assignments. He tried with his wording of the memo to limit the "interactions" to those of similar rank to prevent any unease among the crew.

Soon it seemed everyone was enjoying their new freedoms, and taking every opportunity to exercise themselves in the bedroom. The new policy seemed to have the desired effect on the morale of the crew, and there were more than a few smiling faces around the ship. For Clement though, he had to console himself with the occasional drink from Yan's stash of whiskey.

The LEAP drive was humming along as usual, and Clement found himself astonished by the rhythmic ease with which the LEAP system performed, creating an antimatter singularity thousands of times per second, then annihilating it with a proton and capturing enough explosive power to bend the fabric of space. It all seemed so easy. *Probably make scientists from earlier centuries roll over in their graves*, he thought.

But this time his stop-in had another purpose, and he dragged Nobli into the small engineer's office in the Propulsion Center. "I think you know what I'm here to talk about," started Clement. "Have you come up with any ideas about converting some of the power the LEAP drive creates to a defensive weapon of some kind? Maybe a shield?"

Nobli smiled as he looked up at Clement from under his circular wire-rimmed glasses. "Oh, a bit of this and that," he said as he fiddled with his pad display, then handed it to Clement. The display showed fully drawn schematics, installation guides, and equipment specs for what Nobli was calling the "Matter Annihilation Device," or just MAD for short.

"What the hell," said Clement as he swept through the drawings. "Don't you have a hobby? Or at least a girlfriend?"

"No to both," said Nobli. "You give me an idea, I can't stop running with it, can't shut my mind down. It's one of my charms. I didn't sleep for three days until I had this all figured out."

"It's impressive," Clement conceded. "But how practical is it? Is this something we could really build?"

"Build? I've already prototyped it. It will work, that's for certain. But you can't fire it while we're using the LEAP drive reactor for propulsion, and we'd have to have a pretty clear line of sight to any ship to be sure of hitting anything."

"You're joking, right?"

Nobli shook his head. "Not in the least. The biggest problem was sheathing against the energy beam to keep it from annihilating *us* in the process of firing. I coated the old plasma-cannon piping with the same nanotube material as the reactor core is made of. Should be more than enough."

"But how would we aim such a weapon?" asked Clement.

"Line of sight? How did you aim the old plasma cannon?"

Clement thought for a second. "Through the helm station. There was a restrictor nozzle on the cannon port that the helmsman could use to aim. It wasn't very effective."

"And the nozzle will be burned off in the first microsecond if you ever light this thing up," said Nobli.

"So...you're telling me I have the most powerful weapon in the known universe but I can't aim it at anything?"

"True, but you did say this was only for emergencies. If that's the case, I recommend you personally take over firing control of the MAD, and you do the aiming yourself. And you'd better make sure you're damn close to your target when you fire on it."

Clement rubbed at his eyes. "What's the estimated range of this thing?" he asked.

Nobli looked at him with a very serious look on his face. "Somewhere between one klick and eternity," he said.

Clement took that as Nobli's usual sarcasm. "What about enemy shielding? Will it penetrate gravity shields?"

Nobli leaned back, a look of astonishment at his boneheaded commander on his face. "Captain, you're annihilating tens of thousands of micro-universes a second. I can't think of a goddamned thing in the universe that could stop that."

"How close?"

"What?"

Clement was frustrated. "How close is too close to fire this thing?"

"A thousand kilometers?"

"C'mon, Nobli, you said I had to get close. How close?"

Nobli looked down at the floor. "The destructive radius is probably close to one hundred klicks, maybe one hundred fifty. It's hard to say without test-firing it. You'll have to use your best judgment. And . . ."

"And what?"

"And . . . there's a chance that this weapon may not detonate in any traditional way, like ordinary or even nuclear ordnance. The beam could . . . just keep going."

Now Clement was confused. "Going? To where?"

Nobli just shrugged. "Anywhere. That's why I recommend you use your own best judgment before firing it."

"And that's what I don't want to do," Clement said, exasperated. "I want you to craft me a mechanism that tracks, aims, *and* fires. How soon until you can hook this thing up?"

Nobli scrambled around the floor of his office for a few seconds and then pulled out what looked like normal plumbing and pipes and held it out to Clement. "I told you I'd already prototyped it."

Clement held it in his hands, it was light to the touch, almost fragile. "You're sure this is—"

"Damn sure, Captain," said Nobli. "That long pipe hooks right into the plasma tube in the floor. The top vents into the reactor." Clement handed it back to his engineer. "But as I said, I suggest we don't try and install it until we arrive in the Trinity system and we're in normal space."

"Understood," said Clement. "Make it your first priority to hook this up when we shut down the reactor. And make me some kind of app control for firing it that I can use from my command console."

Nobli sighed. "Captain, I'm not a programmer," he protested.

"And that's why I want you to build the firing control for me. You'll keep it simple, and that's what I want."

"But, Captain—"

"Did that sound like a request, Engineer?"

Nobli sat on the edge of his swivel chair, staring at his commanding officer over the top of his wire frames. That was as close as he ever got to complaining. "Understood, sir," he said.

"Thanks, Hassan." With that Clement sauntered off to finish his rounds, unsure if his ship was safer or not.

With one more full day before arriving at the Trinity system, Clement and his team had one last round of entertainment planned. Middie Telco had set up a safe shooting range on the cargo deck as instructed by his captain, and there had been a shooting tournament almost every night since they'd gone under the LEAP drive.

Clement had won his share, but with only one more day to go everything was on the line.

The rules were simple: fire live rounds into targets, highest score wins. So far about 42 out of 50 had been the average to take a win, but this night felt different. Everyone was pumped up to win the final round.

Many of the crew had already tried their hands at the target; the high score on the board when Clement showed up was a 39 from Telco. Not bad, but not impossible to beat either.

The command crew was the last up, plus Lieutenant Pomeroy, the medic who had been doing some final prep for landfall at Trinity. Clement watched as Captain Wilcock took his rounds, scoring 32 out of 50. Wilcock always seemed to underperform somehow, no matter what the task. Nobli was staying out of the competition so next up was Ivan Massif. The lanky navigator was a good shot, but he was streaky. He hit his first seven shots but then missed three in a row. He ended up with a 37. Mika Ori came next and despite her diminutive figure she was a great shot and hit 43. Yan gave it her best but hand weapons were not her forte and she settled for 37 out of 50. Then it was down to two, himself and Pomeroy.

She was a tough-looking tech, probably Marine-trained from what Clement could tell, brown hair pulled back in a tight ponytail and she had that look of efficiency about her. Clement was sure he wasn't going to catch a break from her tonight. She came to him with a coin in her hand. "Flip you for it. Winner gets last shot." There was an "Ooo" of the challenge from the crowd of ten watching the contest.

"You're on," said Clement.

"Call it in the air." Pomeroy flipped the coin.

"Tails," called Clement. She caught the coin and flipped it over on to the back of her hand, then lifted her palm.

It was heads. The last shooter almost always had an advantage, knowing what score they had to beat. Clement went to the assortment of cobra pistols and tested each one for weight and balance, then loaded a ten clip of kinetic rounds and primed the first shot. He took to the stage inside the firing range. It was all black. The holographic targets would come up at random locations; you had to fire your rounds at the target and then reload four more times and get your shots off, all within sixty seconds.

The first target lit up. Clement raised his pistol and fired with expert precision. All ten shots lit up the target. After the reload he missed one each on the second and third rounds, and two on the fourth. The last round came up and he tracked the target, fully concentrating until he emptied his clip.

46 out of 50.

Pomeroy took that all in stride. She loaded up and entered the chamber before turning back to her captain.

"What does the winner get?" she challenged. Clement thought about that for a moment.

"Loser buys the first round at the first tiki bar we find on Trinity," he said. Everyone laughed at that, and Pomeroy smiled. "Loser buys a full round for the crew at The Battered Hull."

"Done," she said. As she turned back the first target lit

up and she started firing. She didn't miss any in the first two clips, one early in the third, then another in the fourth. Clement held his breath. He was nothing if not competitive, and he was, after all, the captain. A miss in the middle of the last clip gave him hope. Then the final bell sounded. Her minute was up.

47.

The crowd cheered as she came up and shook his hand. Clement couldn't help but smile.

"Well done," he said. "I owe you a drink."

"Yes you do, sir, and I'm going to hold you to it!" she said. "At Trinity?"

"At Trinity," he replied. "If we don't find that tiki bar, we'll build one ourselves."

Everyone was at their stations and prepped with twenty minutes to go to shut down of the LEAP drive. The bridge was quiet and everyone was ready, if not a bit tense. Clement ran through his command displays, noting the new icon for using the LEAP reactor as a weapon that Nobli had uploaded, then decided he wanted verbal reports from his people.

"Ivan, time for shut down of the LEAP drive?" he asked.

"Eighteen minutes now, sir," reported Massif.

"And what will happen when we exit quantum-fluid space?"

Massif turned to his captain. "The bubble will slowly dissipate. Of course, we'll lose speed rapidly when we hit normal space again, cruise for about an hour at near-superluminal speeds. Then the inertial dampeners will slowly take away our momentum during that time until we reach a manageable cruising speed. In fact, we've already been slowly decelerating for the last forty-eight hours; current speed is 1.12 light."

"And what if I want to slow us faster than that, to optimize our drift toward a planet, or maybe change direction toward an interesting object?"

Massif nodded to Mika Ori. She turned from her station then.

"We can use the thrust reversers," she said. "Of course, that will put *g*-force pressure on us, but nothing we shouldn't be able to handle. If there is an 'interesting object' in our path, we can use a variety of slingshot maneuvers to get where we're going, but the charts the unmanned probes made show nothing of significant mass in the area where we'll be dropping out of quantum space."

"And where is that, exactly?"

"There's nothing exact in all this, Captain, but the best guess is about 10.25 AU out from the primary star. That's approximately where the probes have come in."

Mika was always focused when on duty, and that's something Clement liked about her.

"Then what's the best guess time-wise to the first planet in the system?"

"About eight hours, sir. Our speed coming out of the fluid will be about 0.925 light, and it's hard to maneuver at that speed, but depending on how good the navigator is . . . " She trailed off, smirking at her husband.

"What will a 1.5 *g* break buy me?"

Ori did a quick calculation on her pad. "We can cut that

to about four hours, sir, give or take a quarter hour depending on our exact position, if we properly reorient the ship toward a particular destination," she said, directing the barb at her husband again. Ivan smiled this time but said nothing.

"And the length of the burn?"

"Twenty-two minutes by my calculations, sir," she said, without looking back to her pad. She had already figured it out in her head.

"Thank you, Mika. Let's plan for that."

"Aye, sir."

"Middie Adebayor," he said to his systems officer, "once we drop in on the Trinity system proper I want you to start a full-scan protocol on the planets, starting with Alphus, Bellus, and Camus," he ordered.

"Are you expecting communications, Captain?" asked Adebayor.

"No, but it is standard procedure for any ship entering a potential battlefield."

"Are you expecting a battle, sir?" asked Adebayor, again.

Yan cut in here. "You won't last long on this bridge if you question all of your captain's orders, Middie. That's my job. Yours is to do what your captain requests."

"Yes, ma'am," replied Adebayor. "But if I need clarification—"

"You don't in this case, Middie," said Yan, stepping out from behind her station. "Now I suggest you stick to your board and follow your orders."

"Yes, ma'am," said Adebayor again, and glued her eyes to her board, appropriately chastened. Yan came and stood beside Clement, who then called down to the propulsion room.

"Nobli here," came the reply. Clement looked up to the timer on the main screen display.

"Shut down the LEAP drive fourteen minutes from my mark, Mr. Nobli . . ." He looked down at his personal watch instead of the ship's clock, "Mark," Clement said.

"Aye, sir," acknowledged Nobli.

Clement shut off the com to propulsion and switched to Middie Telco in the weapons bay. Telco acknowledged.

"Store everything for the transition, Middie. We'll be running at 1.5 *g* deceleration for about four hours. After that, I want those missiles back up and ready, understood?"

"Completely sir. We'll be fully operational well before then, sir. 1.5 *g* isn't that much of a load."

"Spoken like a young man," replied Clement. "I'll hold you to that. And inform Captain Wilcock that he's to release the atomic warheads to you upon your request. I want us locked and loaded the whole way in, Middie."

"Aye, sir."

Clement turned to his first officer. "Commander Yan, call all hands to stations, prep for deceleration to exit LEAP space."

"Aye, sir," she replied, then she got on the ship-wide com and ordered everyone to take their deceleration stations.

The next few minutes rushed by as systems reports continued to come in. When the time mark finally came, Clement called down and gave Nobli the order to cut the LEAP drive at his discretion. The forward viewer showed the bending of space steadily decreasing until the flow of stars clarified and resumed a more normal appearance, or rather, as Clement thought, a much more mundane one. Nobli called up just as they all felt the tug of the *g*-force deceleration, in toward planet T-7, the outermost world in the Trinity system with a high-content methane-based atmosphere.

"As predicted, 0.925 light speed, sir," said Mika. "We're decelerating toward planet T-7, estimated time of arrival at target four hours, thirteen minutes, sir."

"Excellent work, everyone. What's our path inward from there?"

Ivan Massif had that calculation. "Based on our current trajectory and the alignment of the planets we can use T-7 to cut our speed through aero-braking, then swing in toward T-5, or Camus as they call it, break again, and that should put us at the fourth planet, Bellus, in about sixteen hours' time, sir. Our speed will be sufficiently low to be captured gravitationally by the planet, if the probe's reports on her mass is correct."

"Best get to reviewing all the reports from the probes and verifying the data against real measurables. I wouldn't want to skip past one of the new worlds and end up having to claw ourselves back using thrusters," said Clement.

"Aye, sir."

"Plot and execute," ordered Clement. Then he looked around his bridge, proud of his crew and excited for what the next part of the journey would entail.

❋ 9 ❋

Two hours into the *Beauregard*'s deceleration toward T-7, the first sign of trouble appeared when Middie Adebayor called Yan over to her station.

"Something wrong, Middie?" asked Yan.

"I'm not sure yet," said Adebayor. "I've been scanning for radio signals as the captain ordered, and so far I've just picked up the normal background signals from each of the bodies in the system. But I'm also picking up an anomalous signal that's *not* from the planets or the star, and it appears to be *behind* us, ma'am."

"You mean farther out?"

"Yes, ma'am. About six hundred AU, ma'am."

"That's quite a ways out, especially for a system as compact as this one. Is it moving?"

Adebayor looked at her instruments. "Yes, in our same general direction at about 0.15 light, ma'am, closely matching our own speed."

Yan thought for a moment about what to do next. "I'm going to take this up with the captain," she finally said and started to walk away.

"Do you want me to deploy the radio telescope array?" Adebayor asked as Yan moved off.

"Not yet," replied the second-in-command without turning around. "We'd just have to roll it back in for the aero-braking maneuver anyway."

Yan made her way down the five honeycombed metal steps to the command crew cabins and knocked on Clement's door. He responded with a positive chime and Yan made her way into his cabin.

"Business or pleasure?" said Clement, not looking up from his many technical systems pads.

"Business," replied Yan, taking his barb in stride. "Middie Adebayor has detected a radio-emitting signal about six hundred AU behind us."

This got Clement's attention. "Behind us? Is it moving?"

Yan nodded. "At about 0.15 light."

"That's pretty fast for a comet, and we can certainly rule out a planetoid or a spherical body with an atmosphere."

"I agree, sir."

Clement ran some calculations on one of his pads. "That puts the object about two weeks behind us, if it's making the same vector as we are," he said.

"Closer to thirteen days," Yan replied. Clement gave her an annoyed look. Yan sighed. "Sorry, I was brought up by a mathematician. The object's vector is roughly the same as ours."

Clement stood. "Do you think it's following us?"

Yan shook her head. "I could be wrong, but they would have had to know our arrival point and time in advance, and I doubt that's common knowledge, if it's a vessel," she said.

"Size?"

"Unable to tell at this distance. Middie Adebayor wants to pull out the radio array and get a better look at it."

Clement leaned on the edge of his desk. "It could be a natural object of some kind."

"Or it could be a ship."

"Noted, Commander. My advice is that we maintain our course and speed, continue through our aero-braking maneuvers, then deploy the array once we've established orbit over . . . what's the planet's name?"

"Bellus. Alphus, Bellus, Camus. A, B, C," she said.

Clement gave her a glare of annoyance. "We'll deploy the radio telescope array once we arrive at Bellus. We'll continue our planned survey from orbit while Middie Adebayor gets us some pictures. Further action will be determined at that time," he said. "Comments?"

Yan went to attention. "Your advice seems sound, Captain."

"Thank you, Commander." Clement looked at his watch. "The way I make it, officer's dinner is at 1700. Aero-braking at T-7 is at 1930 hours."

"I'll have the ship ready, Captain," said Yan. Then she turned and left the cabin without looking back.

Clement picked up one of his pads and switched the display to monitor Adebayor's station. The radio signal showed up as an amber blip on a red background. He put the pad back down, and started to worry.

Clement was on the bridge deck at 1900, a full thirty minutes ahead of the braking maneuver.

Yan hadn't rejoined the bridge crew yet, but Ivan Massif and Mika Ori were both at their stations, and

Middie Adebayor was handling the engineering console. Hassan Nobli was in the propulsion room and had refused to move away from his equipment. Captain Wilcock was at Yan's station but wasn't talking much, which suited Clement.

As he waited for Yan he patiently ran through ship's systems checks, checking off each one as he went. A shadow came over him then and surprisingly when he looked up, it wasn't Yan but Adebayor who stood over his station, blocking the light from the other consoles.

"Can I help you, Middie?" Clement said.

She cleared her throat before speaking. "Pardon for interrupting, sir," she started.

"Don't apologize for doing your duty, Middie. I assume this is something important?"

"Yes, sir. I believe so, sir." She hesitated as he looked at her expectantly. "Could you come to my station, sir?" Clement nodded and exited his command couch to take the few steps to port to the engineering console. Adebayor showed him her screen. "I've been tracking the anomaly, sir, and it's hard to track without the radio array, but it seems to me that the anomaly has changed course."

"Changed course?" said Clement, obviously disturbed by the news.

"Yes, sir. It appears to be on a vector now for the inner habitable world, Alphus, sir."

Clement looked at her projected course for the object. It was indeed on a course for Alphus.

"When did this course change happen?" demanded Clement.

"I first detected it about twenty minutes ago, sir."

"Twenty minutes? Why didn't you notify me immediately?"

She cleared her throat again. "You were unavailable in your cabin, sir. And I needed that time to verify that my observations were correct, sir," she said.

"Wait here," he said, then went back to his console and called Yan to the bridge. She arrived a few seconds later, swapping positions with Wilcock, who left the bridge.

"What's up?" she asked.

Clement led her to the engineering console and had Adebayor repeat her report to Yan.

"We have another ship then, and under intelligent control," Yan said.

"It seems so," replied Clement. He hesitated only a second before calling the entire command crew to the officer's galley.

Once inside the galley the command crew, all those on the bridge except Adebayor, were joined by Nobli and Wilcock. Clement cleared his throat before beginning. His explanation was to the point; there was another ship in the Trinity system.

"The question, gentlemen, is what we do about it. The thing is on a course for the inner planet, Alphus, while we are on a course for T-7 to pull off an aero-braking maneuver that will put us in orbit around Bellus. It seems to me that we have an obligation to investigate this object. Is it human? Is it one of ours—or perhaps it's even from Earth? Opinions," he said.

Ivan Massif spoke first. "It could be alien. And that would change everything." The fact was that in more than three hundred fifty years of sub-light interstellar space travel and colonization, no evidence of an alien civilization had ever been discovered, until possibly now. There were protocols for such things, but quite frankly Clement hadn't taken the time to review them, or even consider First Contact as a possibility. He realized now that he probably should have. This was, after all, the first superluminal human space mission in history.

"This is not an equipped First Contact mission," said Yan. "Our job is to survey the three habitable planets in this system and assess them for immediate habitation."

Nobli shrugged that off. "Equipped or not for First Contact, we are here, and so are they. I think we need to know who or what we're dealing with," he said.

Next Mika Ori piped up. "To proceed on to our target while they stay in orbit around Alphus would seem a waste. We should find out who and what they are, and find out now."

Clement turned to Wilcock for his opinion. "Captain?"

"I think we should complete our mission as scheduled, and report back to our superiors as ordered," he said in his whiny voice. It made Clement cringe involuntarily. It was also the exact answer Clement expected from a staff officer.

"In the three-plus centuries that humankind has been sending out ships into interstellar space, the 5 Suns are the only colonies that we know of that have ever been established. We don't know of any others, and we haven't had contact from Earth in almost three centuries. The possibility that this could be an alien probe is something we can't ignore. Further, the possibility that it could be an Earth-colony ship is also worth exploring." He looked around the table, and there was no dissent.

"Middie Adebayor wants to deploy the radio telescope to get a better look," said Clement.

"You can't do that while we're aero-braking, which by the way is only ten minutes away now," said Nobli.

"I'm aware of that. My thinking is that we need to find out what this thing is, as soon as possible?" Clement turned to Mika. "Can we adjust our aero-braking around Trinity-7 and use the effect to slingshot ourselves on to an intercept course with the anomaly?"

She slowly nodded her head. "We can, but you're asking me to calculate some pretty fine maneuvering in just a few minutes."

"Then you better get to it," said Clement, nodding toward the bridge. She left quickly.

"I'd better go plot that course," said Ivan, and followed her. Clement acknowledged silently with another nod, then turned to the rest of the crew.

"Stations for aero-braking, everyone. We're going to find out what this thing is, and what we might need to do about it," he said.

"So that's your final decision?" said Wilcock in a demanding tone.

Clement stood up, much taller than the diminutive captain. "It is, Captain Wilcock. Now since you're not needed on the bridge, I suggest you ride out the aero-braking in your cabin," he said, then walked away.

Yan gave Wilcock an annoyed look, then followed her commanding officer to the bridge.

"All stations report clear for aero-braking maneuver, sir," called Yan from her station.

Clement acknowledged and then looked down to his command board. All was green. His bridge crew was strapped in and ready.

"It's your call, Mika," he said out loud.

"Aye, sir, acknowledge I have the wheel. Aero-braking will commence in thirty seconds and should last about seven minutes in duration, pulling 5.5 gravities. Once clear of Trinity-7's atmosphere we will engage in a two-minute, thirty-second Ion plasma burst at three gs, which should allow us to intercept the unknown well before it reaches the inner planetary ring, if the navigator's course vectors are correct," she said, needling her lover's ego.

"They are," snapped back Massif. Clement gave a quick chuckle at that.

"My ship is yours, Pilot," he said to Ori.

On the mark Ori went on the ship-wide com and called out the beginning of the aero-braking cycle. It was rougher than Clement remembered from his old days in the Rim Confederation Navy, but as Ori had reminded them over the com, T-7 had a "bumpy" upper atmosphere. After seven full minutes of grinding and rattling the *Beauregard* was once again in open space and free floated for a few precious seconds, the crew weightless with the artificial gravity turned off. It was thirty seconds of bliss until Ori hit the thrusters, pushing the ship again on its new vector toward the unknown bogey.

After the two and a half minutes of thruster burn at three gs was up, Ori pronounced them on course for intercept of the mystery object. Clement ordered the artificial one g restored and everyone gave a sigh of relief as they were released from their acceleration couches.

Clement quickly ordered Adebayor to deploy the radio telescope array. "How long until we can get a good picture?" he asked of the middie.

"Ninety minutes for deployment and calibration, sir," she said.

"Then get to it." At that he ordered Yan back to his cabin for a conference.

"What do you think this thing is?" he asked her, almost before the door to his cabin had shut.

"It's hard to say, but my best guess is that it's an Ark ship," said Yan.

"Which means someone has previously surveyed this system and is so confident of its habitability that they sent a ship out a long time ago."

"Fifty years, at least. If it's a colony mission, yes, sir."

"But DeVore said this system was only explored a few months ago when they developed the LEAP drive. Whoever sent *that* ship, if it's in fact a colony vessel, sent it out decades ago. If it was the 5 Suns Alliance, they would have had to send it out a very long time ago, given the limits of faster-than-light travel. It's possible they could have observed this star system through some other means, and sent a covert colony ship back then."

"If that's the case then I would be curious as to the timing of our mission. The chances of us both arriving in-system at the same time by chance seems small," replied Yan.

"Agreed. It's quite possible that DeVore knew we'd find this ship when we arrived. It may even be the real reason for our mission," said Clement.

Yan nodded. "I have to admit with what I know of the Fleet Admiral that is at least a possibility. She's well known around the Alliance Navy for keeping information close at hand and she's got a reputation for springing surprises, especially ones that are to her advantage."

This time it was Clement's turn to nod agreement. "The question is why would she keep it from us? Even from her hand-chosen executive officer? I can see why she'd want me in command of this mission, *if* she believes this is a possibly hostile vessel."

Yan shook her head. "I don't follow you."

Clement crossed his arms, thinking out loud. "I'm disposable, Yan, and so is my crew. We're all rebels with no real value to the 5SA. This prototype is an old, reclaimed Rim Confederation gunship. Almost everything on this mission is expendable."

"Including me," said Yan. That realization hit her hard. "What about Captain Wilcock?"

"He could be working for her. We have to take precautions for that eventuality."

Now it was Yan's turn to be pensive. She paced back and forth in the cabin a couple of times, thinking. Finally, she said, "What's the point of all this, Clement? I mean, why lie to us?"

He shrugged. "To get us all on board for the mission. If we knew how potentially dangerous it was, would any of us have signed on? I don't think so. No, I think Fleet Admiral DeVore knew what this mission was really all about. She made up a romantic story about a prototype mission to test a revolutionary new technology and we all bought it. Our real mission was always to encounter and confront this Ark ship, which means it must have come from somewhere else."

"Earth?"

"That's most likely. The problem is we have no idea what Earth is like now, or rather, what it was like when this ship was launched. I suspect that the Admiral has her ideas about this Ark, and they're not good. If I can trust of what I know about Elara DeVore at all, I know her habits and work patterns, and I know she always has a backup plan. I highly doubt we are the only ship in the 5 Suns Navy that has the LEAP drive. And I'd bet my last whiskey that they're on their way here, right now. We're the bait, Yan. DeVore will find out all she needs to know about this colony ship from what happens to us."

"That's not the Fleet Admiral I thought I knew."

"And that's not the Elara DeVore that I know, or knew. She played me perfectly."

Both of them stood silently for a moment.

"What if this is, in fact, First Contact?" said Yan.

"I think it's unlikely this is an alien vessel. But then the question becomes, how did the Earthmen discover the Trinity system?"

Yan shrugged. "The same way we did, I suppose. Long-term probes, perhaps launched decades in the past. This system is a lot closer to Earth than the 5 Suns Alliance is."

"Or they have LEAP technology, or something similar."

"I'd bet dollars to doughnuts that ship is sub-light powered. We'd pick up some kind of radiant energy signature if it had FTL capabilities, I'm guessing," said Yan.

Clement nodded agreement. "That's a good guess, I think. But, what if it is aliens?"

Yan eyed him. "Then you were right to bring atomic weapons on board."

Clement shuffled uncomfortably in his seat again, then reached for his desk com.

"Captain Wilcock to my cabin, please," he said into the com, then cut it off before Wilcock could answer. The less interaction he had with the man the better he felt about things. Presently Wilcock buzzed at his door and Clement let him in. "Take a seat," said Clement. Wilcock sat down with the two mission commanders.

"Captain Wilcock," started in Clement, "as I'm sure you know I'm aware that you and Commander Yan have access to the keys and codes for the atomic warheads. I'd like you to load those warheads onto our missiles, please."

Wilcock frowned. "And as you know, Captain Clement, I need a command authorization or an imminent threat to do so. Since my commander is Fleet Admiral DeVore and she's weeks from here even at superluminal speeds, and as there is no imminent threat to the *Beauregard*, I must decline your . . . suggestion," said Wilcock.

Clement nodded but continued. "I understand your stance, Captain. But I do believe the *Beauregard* is under imminent threat. That unknown could be an alien ship, and we could be facing a showdown over the Trinity worlds. I'd much rather go into any contact scenario with my defenses fully prepared. For all we know that ship might attack us the minute we're in their range."

Wilcock shifted in his chair and looked toward Yan. She remained impassive.

"I'm not sure that this situation would require that level of preparedness—"

"Captain Wilcock, have you ever commanded a ship in battle?" interrupted Clement.

"No sir, but—"

"Then trust me on this. Every moment, every second, is crucial in a battle situation. If this *is* a hostile ship, and if it is aliens, they could have weapons so superior to ours that we might only last seconds against them. We need to be as prepared as we can be. Do you understand, Captain?"

Wilcock looked to Yan again, then swallowed hard. "Sir, I mean no disrespect, but—"

"I agree with the Captain," said Yan suddenly. Wilcock looked over at her, then back to the determined Clement. Seeing as he was now outvoted, Wilcock caved.

"Very well, sir. But I will be filing a protest over this in my log."

"That's your choice."

"It will take some time to prepare—"

"Middie Adebayor should be able to give us a look at this thing in an hour and a quarter. I expect you and Yan to have those warheads loaded by that time," said Clement.

"Aye, sir," said Wilcock, reluctantly.

Clement turned to Yan, who was already pulling out her activation key from around her neck.

"We'll report back within the hour," she said.

"Good," replied Clement, then watched them both leave his cabin, headed for the missile room.

Yan watched as Captain Wilcock opened the locker containing the atomic warheads by entering the release code. The doors to the locker opened automatically and he carefully pulled the first warhead, a stainless steel cylinder about thirty centimeters in length with three electronic leads and a small digital display panel, out of the locker and handed it to Middie Telco, who was in charge of loading it into the first missile. Telco did so with care, making sure the power leads to the device were secure. He checked again, as he had when they were first brought aboard, that the warhead had sufficient uranium density for use as a weapon. For the second time, Telco got an affirmative reply on his radiometry scanner. He nodded to Yan and Wilcock, and they began the process of arming the warhead by loading in their key codes from their random-number generators. Once both codes were locked into the arming panels, each of them in turn inserted their physical keys into the consoles and turned them to arm the warheads.

"First warhead armed," said Yan.

"First warhead armed," confirmed Wilcock. He then nodded to Telco, who activated the loader, and a second missile, sans warhead, slid into the loading catapult, pushing the first missile into firing position.

"Arming second warhead," said Wilcock.

When they had repeated the process six times and the missiles with the atomic warheads were loaded and locked down, Yan called to Clement to confirm.

"Get back up here stat," said Clement. "Middie Adebayor says she thinks she can get a signal in a few minutes."

"Aye, sir," said Yan, who then turned to Telco. "Keep this room locked down under guard, Middie. No one in or out of here unless it's your relief."

"Aye, sir," said Telco. Then Yan nodded and headed for the bridge. Wilcock, for his part, was already gone.

✻ ✻ ✻

They all squeezed into the cramped bridge, even Nobli and Captain Wilcock, to see the first images Adebayor was getting from the radio telescope array. Clement tried to be patient, his ship on a general intercept course with the unknown, but clearly artificial, object.

"I've got the first image Captain," said Adebayor. Clement merely nodded for her to put it up on the main screen display. A black background started to paint with a blotchy image of red, yellow, and green. What it showed was clear, a cylindrical-shaped object.

"I'd say artificiality is confirmed," said Yan.

"I agree," replied Clement.

"First Contact with an alien race?" said Yan.

Clement contemplated that possibility. "If it is, then we have to assume they have at least an equal technology to our own, if not likely superior."

"But from what we can tell, they don't have LEAP technology, or something similar."

"Then we need more answers. XO, please note the date and time of our first sighting of this vessel in the log. We could be living in a historic moment, and what we do next could affect more than one civilization. And please record all further interactions with this vessel. Perhaps it will be valuable to historians, some day."

"Aye, sir," said Yan, returning to her console to activate the log recorder.

Clement turned to the middie. "What telemetry can you give me on the object?"

"Coming in now, sir," said Adebayor. "Length, precisely six kilometers. Circumference, 0.05 kilometers. Speed continues to deplete to 0.012 light. Engine appears to be an electromagnetic particle drive geared for constant acceleration and deceleration. Vector unchanged toward the inner habitable planet, Alphus, sir."

"Are those hull measurements approximate?" asked Clement.

"Negative, sir," replied the middie. "Those measures are as exact as we can make them."

"Then it's one of ours. Human," stated Clement.

"How can you be sure?" questioned Yan, returning from her console.

"Six kilometers long by a 0.05 klick circumference? I'd bet my last dime on it. Kilometers are how humans measure things, Yan. And an Ion particle EM drive is exactly the kind of technology that was used to send ships out to the 5 Suns Alliance stars, four centuries ago."

"How do you know that?"

He smiled at her. "High school history, Commander," he said with a shrug. "The *Mayflower* was a one-hundred-foot English merchant sailing ship with three masts."

"What's a *Mayflower*?" said Yan, looking confused.

Clement smiled. "Later," he said, then turned to his navigator. "Mika, at our speed and theirs, can we intercept them?"

Lieutenant Ori looked at her display console. "Aye, sir, in about nine hours we should be able to match course and speed without too much trouble. Their deceleration is constant now."

"Then let's do it." Clement turned to Hassan Nobli. "Prep the shuttle, Nobli. We're going to be heading over there."

"Do you think that's wise?" replied the engineer.

Clement shook his head. "Wise? No. Necessary? Yes," said Clement, then he got up and headed for his cabin, the crew scrambling to their stations in his wake.

✵ 10 ✵

The unknown was close enough now for standard visual observation. It was a simple cylinder, but immensely long at six kilometers. If there were human colonists on board, there were a lot of them. The fact that it was constructed using a human measuring standard, however, almost certainly indicated a human origin. That was some small comfort, at least. The question at hand, though, was who had built it, and for what intent.

The Ark ship (as Clement was now convinced that it was, whether he was willing to share that with the crew or not) had a general silver-gray color with black caps at either end, with no discernable exterior features to distinguish it. It looked more like a great torpedo or missile than a colonization ship. Ark ships usually ran with large solar panels to power the interior environment for the passengers. Usually. It was possible this particular ship carried its crew in a deep sleep, however, powered by a nuclear fusion reactor, thus not requiring the typical level of active environmental systems.

"We'll be able to match her course and speed exactly, sir, if you give me another few minutes," said Mika Ori at the helm.

"Do it," replied Clement, then looked around the room before hitting the ship-wide com. "Attention, crew of the *Beauregard*," he said. "In a few minutes, we'll be in intercept position of the unknown. At that time, I will be taking over an expeditionary team in our only shuttle, leaving Commander Yan at the con. For this mission I will be needing a team of specialists to do an evaluation of whatever that ship is and what's on it. Therefore, I have selected the following crew to join me: Middie Daniel, Captain Wilcock, Middie Telco, and Medical Technician Pomeroy. Engineer Nobli will stay aboard with Commander Yan on the *Beauregard* to monitor our progress via visual com link. The rest of you are to be at your stations on high alert. We have to be ready to exit this area at high speed if necessary. So man your stations, do your jobs. I trust you. Clement out," he said as he shut down the com. Yan approached him then.

"Is it wise to go yourself?" she said.

"Always," replied Clement. "I never pass off what should be my responsibility. And I know you think you should lead the mission, but I want you here in case there's trouble."

She looked chagrined. "But why take Wilcock, and the two middies?"

Clement smiled. "Can you think of anyone on this ship more expendable than Wilcock? And Daniel hasn't had much to do. Telco and Pomeroy I trust with a cobra rifle. So that's that," he said.

Yan nodded, but she wasn't happy. "Understood, sir."

Twenty minutes later, after confirmation from Mika Ori of their match to the unknown for course and speed,

Clement was in the prep room with his team pulling on an EVA suit. Middie Telco came through, already suited but without his helmet on yet, and delivered weapons to each of the shuttle crew—standard cobra pistols for the suit side holsters and the key to one of the cobra rifles, preloaded—that were already on the shuttle. Clement watched with disdain as Wilcock attempted to holster his pistol. After the third try Wilcock's finger accidentally set off the safety and Clement rushed over and grabbed him hard by the wrist to stop him from burning off his leg.

"Didn't you get any goddamn basic training?" said Clement as he pulled the pistol from Wilcock's hand, reset the safety, and then put it in the holster himself.

"I did, sir," Wilcock protested. "I know how to use a weapon."

Clement just stared at him, then donned his helmet and sealed up his EVA suit.

"Everybody on board. When we get over there I want everyone to use their rifle as the main weapon of defense with the pistol as a secondary," he said.

"Are we expecting trouble, sir?" said the annoying Wilcock.

"Not necessarily, Captain, but we always prepare for it. Now all aboard."

With that the techs that had helped them prep vacated the cargo hold and the shuttle was positioned for launch. Once the room was cleared and the environment evacuated, Clement took to the pilot's seat with Pomeroy, who had a shuttle pilot's accreditation, next to him. The others gathered in the back and strapped in. Clement signaled up to Yan for launch clearance, which was given.

The cargo bay doors opened and Clement fired up the engine, hitting the gas hard as everyone slid back into their passenger seats. He leaned over to Pomeroy and joked, "Just making sure they're awake back there." She smiled.

The crossing was uneventful and Clement swung the shuttle into a close track to the unknown, heading down her length slowly. Clement tested his com link.

"Nobli, Yan, what do you make of that hull?" he asked. There was a pause, then Nobli came on the line.

"I'd say you're looking at reinforced regolith with a shiny coat of sealant on it, sir. The old Ark ships were designed this way, to keep things like meteors and other objects from destroying the ship in flight."

"What's regolith?" asked Pomeroy.

"It's solar system material from moons and asteroids, rocks and dirt, some metals. In advanced Ark design, they used a thick layer of it over an internal hull to protect the ships as they moved through the interstellar void. Common practice back in the Exodus days. Not surprised to see it here," said Nobli. At that Clement switched to the shuttle's com line to his crew.

"We're looking for anything that resembles a docking bay or external air lock," said Clement over the com. "Don't be afraid to go to the portside windows and have a look out." It was Middie Daniel who called in what looked to be an external air lock one third of the way down the length of the cylinder.

"Good eyes, Daniel," said Clement over the com.

"Thank you, sir," replied the middie, happy to be contributing.

"It sure doesn't look like a match for our docking mechanism," observed Pomeroy. Clement eyed the hatch. It was round. The shuttle's was rectangular, like the shape of a doorway, big enough for a human to pass through. Hopefully, the round shape of the Ark's door wasn't an indication of the crew's shape. That could indicate a nonhuman design.

"What do we do?" asked Pomeroy. Clement thought about that as he pulled the shuttle in close, matching course and speed with the unknown and the hatch.

"Middie Telco," Clement called over the com.

"Aye, sir," replied the eager young man.

"Vent the air lock to vacuum and prepare a tether, and four C-7 charges. We'll need to blow that hatch."

"Yes, sir!"

"And you'll be the one to set the charges," said Clement as he came down from the pilot's nest to the shuttle cabin.

"Aye, sir," Telco said, trying to stay calm, and quickly went about his business. Daniel helped him get tethered up and Wilcock handed him the four charges. Clement wanted someone else to handle the explosives, anyone, but he just bit his lip as Wilcock managed to get the job done correctly without destroying the shuttle.

"Could blowing the hatch be seen as an attack by us on them?" came Yan's voice over the com. Clement paused for a moment before responding.

"That is a consideration, Commander. But . . . looking down the full length of this ship I don't see any other such opening, so unless you're suggesting we knock on the door . . ."

"Understood, Captain," replied Yan, then cleared the channel.

A few seconds later and Telco entered the air lock, shutting the door behind him as he vented the chamber to space. Clement and the others watched as he used maneuvering jet bursts to cross the threshold of open space to the unknown's hatch, trailing the tether all the way. Telco set the charges expertly at twelve, three, six, and nine o'clock, then quickly jetted back to the shuttle. Once he was back inside and the air lock was sealed, Clement turned to Lieutenant Pomeroy.

"Take the controls and give us some distance, at least five hundred meters," he said. Pomeroy did as instructed. Then Clement turned to Telco. "Um, Telco, I almost forgot, did it look like there was any way in?"

"You know I was so busy setting the charges . . . "

"So, nobody looked for an air lock control?" asked Wilcock.

"Well, I guess our arrival will be a surprise, then," quipped Clement.

"Six hundred fifty meters, sir," called Pomeroy from her station. Clement acknowledged.

"Everyone lock down their EVA suits." There was a round of affirmatives.

"Vent the cabin pressure please, Pomeroy," ordered the Captain. They waited as the small shuttle quickly drained of environment. Then Clement turned to Telco.

"You have the controls, Middie," said Clement, giving the excited young man a chance to shine by handing him a remote detonator. "Detonate when ready."

Telco calmly counted down from five, then lit up the

explosives. After a flurry of cloudy gas escaping from the unknown, the area quickly cleared to reveal a fairly round gash in its side. Pomeroy maneuvered the shuttle in close again, then they loaded up their cobra rifles and proceeded over in an orderly manner, Telco taking the lead and acting as an anchor while the others made the tethered crossing.

They were in what appeared to be a long, twisting drain shaft of some kind which required them to crouch as they went. Telco took the lead, cobra rifle in hand, followed by Pomeroy, Clement, Daniel, and Wilcock, the least valuable member of the crew as Clement saw it, taking up the rear.

"What do you make of this shaft, Pomeroy?" asked Clement of the medic.

"Well, I'm no expert, but this appears to be a passageway designed to expel a specific cargo, something that fits the spherical shape of this tube. There are rails to speed up the process."

"Any guesses on what that cargo might be?"

"Not at the moment, sir."

They proceeded about thirty meters more until the passageway turned and came out at what appeared to be a maintenance room. The room had a doorway, with a locking mechanism. The door itself looked human-sized, if that meant anything. Clement fired up the com back to Nobli and Yan aboard the *Beauregard*.

"Hassan, can you see this?" said Clement. "We're in some kind of maintenance room. There's no gravity but there is a door lock."

"Can I see the door mechanism?" asked Nobli through the now scratchy com line. Clement moved up to the door and put his body camera close to a lit panel. There were red, amber, and green buttons on the left of the panel and a series of characters on the right, none of which Clement could read. The red light was lit.

"What do you make of it?" said Clement.

"Well, some of the characters look like Chinese," said Nobli. "But I can't read them."

"It's not Chinese," said Yan through the com. "It's Imperial Korean."

"And how do you know *that*?" asked Clement.

"I studied the history of the old Korean Empire on Earth, mid-twenty-first century. They took over almost everything in the Asia-Pacific region at that time. That looks like a more advanced form than I studied, probably mixed in with some traditional Chinese characters," said Yan.

"Can you read it?" asked Clement.

"I'll try . . ." They all waited impatiently as Yan stayed silent for at least thirty seconds. Finally, she said: "I think the red light is a warning indicator that the room is in vacuum. It's telling you . . . it's telling you that if you open the door decompression could occur. There's also another indicator . . . Do you see that blue bar just below the main console?"

"On the side here?"

"Yes, that's it. Press that bar."

Clement ordered everyone to get close to him before he pressed it, then hit the button on Yan's advice. A large bulkhead-type door slid down fast behind them, cutting off their exit through the tube as the room started normalizing atmosphere. The colors on the door panel lit up from red to amber to green.

"Pomeroy?"

"Atmosphere is breathable, sir. Outside temp is just over 14 C, sir. Not tropical but breathable," she said.

"Everyone keep their helmets on. We're not through this yet," warned Clement to his party. "Yan, in your opinion is it safe to go through this door?"

"Safe? That's relative, sir. You're there. You came for a reason, and that reason is to discover what's beyond that door, correct?"

"Correct. Um, how do you suggest we proceed?"

Yan laughed. "You might try pressing the green button," she said. Clement looked to Pomeroy, who nodded, then pressed the button.

The door opened to a dark and misty chamber, almost like a fog, and dimly lit. It was packed floor to ceiling with round capsules that were roughly man-sized, hanging from the ceiling. The capsules went on in multiple rows in both directions from where they stood, disappearing into the fog in the distance.

"So, this is eerie," cracked Pomeroy. Clement ignored her.

"Boots," said Clement, ordering everyone to activate their magnetic boots. There were bits of paper floating around the room, indicating a low- or zero-g environment. The team started slowly walking, Clement ordering them in farther. As they passed the individual capsules there were no windows discernible, no way to look in, and nothing moved on them except the occasional blinking monitor light.

"Opinions?" he asked as they looked around the room, taking their first exploratory steps.

"It's something you might expect on an Ark ship with

the crew in a deep freeze. There must be hundreds of these things," said Pomeroy. "Maybe more."

"Colonists, then?"

"Perhaps," came Nobli's voice over the com. "How big is that room?"

"Big enough we can't see the walls," said Clement. "Let's reconnoiter. Pomeroy with me. The rest of you take the far side of the room," he said, pointing to his right from the door. "And look for a way out of this room." There was a round of quiet "Aye, sir's" to that.

As they proceeded there were more and more rows of the capsules, and Clement was not prepared to crack one open and find out what was inside. He called to Telco with the other group. "Status?" he asked.

"No change, sir. Just lots and lots of these capsules. I'd say there are definitely people inside, human or otherwise, in stasis, sir," replied Telco.

"Agreed, Telco. Now if we just knew *who* they were." Clement checked his arm monitor. He set it for a counting procedure, and scanned up and down the rows with an amber light pulse. After a few seconds it came back with an estimate. "Monitor guesses there are more than four thousand of these capsules in here," he said.

"Brigade strength," piped in Daniel. That was smart.

"I wish you hadn't said that, Middie," said Clement. "All right, everyone proceed forward until we locate the far wall. Let's find a way out of here." As they walked slowly through the environmental mist Clement brought Yan in for a consultation over the private com.

"If each of these capsules has a single soldier in it . . ." He trailed off.

"Why are you assuming they're soldiers and not colonists?" replied Yan.

"Nothing about this ship indicates colonization, Yan. It seems strictly military in function, to me anyway."

"Assuming that's true, I'd say that those capsules are designed for use on a habitable world. That tunnel you blew your way into was probably for deploying the capsules to the surface."

"From space?" Clement said, a bit incredulous.

"They probably have thrusters for braking and landing on a lower-gravity world like Alphus. Remember, it's only about 0.66 g of Earth gravity."

"Okay . . ."

Yan continued. "The capsules likely contain everything they'd need, weapons, rations, equipment and the like. Just ready to be deployed."

"And the . . . passengers?"

"Likely not revived until the capsule was deposited on the target world."

This made Clement uncomfortable. "So you're leaning toward this being a military mission as well?"

Yan hesitated. "You've got to see the rest of the ship first before I could draw that conclusion."

"Thank you, Yan," he said, then cut the line. Now he was worried.

Middie Daniel found the outer door, complete with the same key that they had found in the maintenance room. Clement called over to Yan to get a reading of the commands, but it was just general information, no instructions. There was a key panel, though with Arabic numerals on it, the problem being that they didn't have the key code, or even a guess as to how to figure it out.

"Can't we just blast it?" said Telco.

"I see subtlety isn't your strong point, Middie. Other, more helpful suggestions?" Clement asked the expeditionary team.

"Your cobra pistol has an electromagnetic-pulse setting," said Nobli over the com from the *Beauregard* almost immediately.

"A what?" replied Clement.

"A small EM-pulse generator. It's a defensive setting, for when you might want to disable local enemy mobile communications and the like," replied Nobli.

"I had no idea," said Clement. Soon all five of the expeditionary team were playing with their cobra pistols to find the setting. Clement looked up and decided he had to put a stop to this fiddling or risk an accident. "Enough," he said, reaching out and putting his hand over Telco's pistol. They all stopped. "Someone volunteer."

"I'll do it," said Daniel, beating Telco to the punch to volunteer for once. Clement nodded.

"Gotta spread the love around, I guess. All right, Daniel, you get the assignment. Everyone else holster their pistols." Clement watched as they all did as ordered except Wilcock, who fumbled to get his pistol holstered again. Once that process was over without incident, Clement took Daniel's cobra pistol and, following Nobli's instructions, set the pistol for a short range EM pulse before handing it back to the middie.

"How far back do we have to be for this?" Clement asked Nobli.

"Three meters should do it. But Mr. Daniel should have the anti-pulse mode on his suit activated."

Clement let out an exasperated sigh. "And how do we do that?"

Nobli explained the process and Clement ordered everyone in the crew to do the same, then take their distance from Daniel. Once they were set, Clement gave the middie an order to proceed at his discretion.

Daniel stood half a meter from the door and pointed the pistol at the door lock, then counted down from five as Telco had done, then fired the pistol. There was a flash of blinding white light, and after his eyes cleared Clement could see the door mechanism had gone dark, as well as several monitor panels on the near wall. The rest of the room hummed on quietly, dim lights glowing in the near dark mist.

They all rushed up to the doorway to see the results of Daniel's handiwork. The locking mechanism was dead, and the door was slightly ajar. "It must have activated the door-opening sequence just before the circuits burned out," said Clement. Then he turned to his young crew members. "Well don't just stand there, Middies, get the damn thing open." He and Wilcock and Pomeroy stepped back while the two middies struggled with the door for a few minutes. At some point they must have hit a release mechanism as the door eventually slid open quickly.

Clement led his expeditionary team, cobra rifles drawn, into the dark. The hallway they were in was even dimmer than the capsule chamber, but minus the mist. That was a plus. They used their EVA suit lights to scan as they walked. The hallway was long and empty, with curved walls, and there were entry doors every few dozen meters on both the top and bottom of the hallway with no deference to gravity, or "up" and "down." Like being inside a can of peas.

"Split up again," ordered Clement. "Wilcock, you take the two middies that way"—he pointed back down the hallway they had just come up—"Pomeroy and I will go upstream. Report whatever you find." Then he looked down at his watch. "Rendezvous back here in thirty minutes. We don't want to overstay our welcome," he said.

Wilcock checked his watch and then led the two middies away while he and Pomeroy made their way to the nearest doorway, across the hall and up the wall from the capsule chamber. Clement called in a request to Nobli for a better way to enter and exit each room, which, surprisingly, Nobli provided. It turned out a negative EM pulse would clear the door codes without damaging the key. Pomeroy tried it on the near door, reset the key code randomly, and the door slid open. Before Clement let her go in he sent the procedure to Wilcock via the com for the second group to use. There was, however, increasing static interference in both their internal and external communications. That worried Clement.

He and Pomeroy stepped inside the chamber and found it nearly identical with the one they had entered originally. It was full of more capsules, and not much else. The same was repeated twice more before they entered the third chamber down from their original entry door.

The door opened into complete darkness. Even with both of their helmet lights on, the room had a deep, dark feeling and a coldness to it. Frankly, to Clement, it was downright creepy.

"I found a console," said Pomeroy. Clement went to her and looked at the panel, dimly lit from her suit light. "These look like environmental controls, and this should be power," she said, pointing to a glowing blue LED icon with an unreadable symbol on it. "Do we light it up?" she asked Clement.

"Hold on," he said, then tried to raise Wilcock and the middies. He couldn't connect with them. "Must be the walls in here," he said.

"They could be reinforced against unauthorized communications," posited Pomeroy.

"One question then, why would you do that if this were a civilian colony ship?"

Pomeroy shrugged. "There may be only one way to find that out," she said.

Clement looked at the panel with the power icon on it, and nodded.

Pomeroy pressed the button.

The panel started to light up slowly, activating systems in a seemingly pre-planned order. Eventually overhead lights came on from a single glowing light panel bolted to the ceiling.

A chamber below them started to light up. Clearly they were in a control room, high above what lay in the massive central chamber below. They went to the window and looked down.

There was a large collection of ships in what looked like an aircraft carrier bay. Some seemed sized for a small number of occupants, others were significantly larger.

"Attack ships," said Pomeroy, "Three-man light attack clippers, I'd bet."

"Dozens of them," replied Clement. "And those larger ships could be destroyers with ten to twenty in the crew." All of them were starting to receive power through the activation system they had just lit up.

Clement grabbed Pomeroy by the arm and quickly dragged her out of the room, not bothering to shut the door behind them. They "ran" as best they could in low gravity with their grav boots on, heading back the way they had come. Clement called to Wilcock on his com.

"Wilcock! Get back to the maintenance room. We're getting out of here," he said, a bit more frantically than he would have liked.

"Already on our way, sir," Wilcock replied through heavy static. "We found tons of military equipment in several chambers, and more capsules."

Clement stopped in his tracks. "What kind of equipment?"

"Armored vehicles. Mortars. Fixed gun emplacements and the like. Enough for a full division, or more."

"Shit!" said Clement, and started moving again. "Get to the maintenance room as fast as you can!"

"Aye, sir."

He and Pomeroy continued their "run" as best they could. Within a minute's time, Wilcock and the two middies were straight ahead of them at about two hundred meters, already at the door to the capsule chamber and maintenance room when the first shot was fired from behind Clement's shoulder. A bright red energy blast hit Middie Daniel in the gut and he fell. Clement whipped around and pulled his cobra rifle, quickly returning fire with kinetic tracer rounds.

"Unlock your boots! Go zero-g! Now!" he ordered.

Pomeroy did as ordered, pushing off the hallway wall and propelling herself toward Wilcock and the two middies. Telco was pulling Daniel inside the capsule chamber. Clement turned back and saw six soldiers in full EVA gear slowly coming at him, rifles drawn, in battle crouches. He unlocked his boots and then fired a volley of suppressing kinetic rounds at the soldiers, who scattered. The resultant force from his shots propelled Clement down the hallway at a fast clip. It was one way to hasten his departure, but a dangerous one. He kept shooting, and the soldiers kept scrambling, but he was going way too fast now . . .

The big arms of Middie Telco wrapped around him and both men hit the wall and then skidded down the hallway about ten meters before Telco's boot grips stopped them. Clement switched his magnetic boot controls back on and they both made for the capsule room door with Pomeroy and Wilcock supplying the suppressing fire for their retreat. Once at the door Telco pushed Clement through the threshold. On the ground was Middie Daniel's body, a hole burned clean through his abdomen.

"He's dead, sir," said Telco.

"He is, Middie. Let's get out of here." He ordered his remaining crew into full retreat, and they went back through the capsule chamber to the maintenance room, locking the door behind them. Telco had carried Middie Daniel's body over his shoulder. Clement opened the maintenance room door using the blue button again, then fired his cobra pistol in plasma mode to melt the control panel in place. He ordered his crew out of the deployment tube and they quickly tethered their way back to the shuttle. The crossing took longer than Clement wanted, Telco being slowed by carrying Daniel's body, and he worried about enemy soldiers shooting at them the whole time. Finally, they got back home and got the shuttle underway, moving away from the Ark ship and toward the *Beauregard* as fast as Clement could make the shuttle go.

Once they were clear and moving at an acceptable rate of speed, Clement turned the controls over to Pomeroy and went back to check on his crew. Daniel's body was laid out on the shuttle floor. Telco looked down on his friend.

"Those were soldiers, sir. And that ship. I didn't see anything that wasn't military grade," Telco said.

"We also saw a dedication plaque," said Wilcock. "If I read it right, the ship is called the *Li Shimen*, after a famous general of some kind."

Clement looked to Telco. "Middie Telco, when we get back aboard the *Beauregard*, get our missile tubes loaded with the nukes. We may need them all if we're going to escape this situation. And don't delay, you get me, Middie?" Clement turned to Wilcock. "You're with him."

"Understood," said Wilcock. "The warheads are already armed, sir."

"What about Daniel, sir?" Telco asked, looking at his dead friend's body. Clement shook his head.

"Leave it, son. There's no time."

"But—"

"The ship comes first, Middie. That's an order."

"Aye, sir."

Clement looked to Wilcock. "Give him whatever help he needs, Captain."

Wilcock nodded and exchanged a knowing glance with Clement. The middie needed to be kept busy.

Clement nodded back to Wilcock, hoping he could trust him, then went back to the shuttle pilot's nest.

"Time to the *Beauregard*?" he asked Pomeroy.

"Eight minutes, sir," she replied.

"Get me Yan on the com."

Pomeroy hooked up the com channel so he could raise his first officer on the link by switching to a private channel. "We have trouble coming, Yan. Prep the ship for battle, and fire up the Ion plasma drive," he said.

"What's happened? Our com link was cut off," said Yan.

Clement held his tongue for just a second, contemplating his next words.

"This is no colony ship, Yan. It's one hundred percent military, and unfortunately our presence there woke them up. They'll be coming. For us."

"Military? As in navy?"

"As in, invasion force. My guess is this is an Earth Ark, sent here to claim these planets before the 5 Suns Alliance can. And we're stuck right in the middle of that squabble," Clement said.

"She betrayed us?"

"She set us up, Yan, like we talked about in my cabin. It's going to be up to us to survive on our own now."

"I can't believe it, I can't believe—"

"Believe it, Yan. There's no time for tears over lost loves. We'll be on board in five minutes, Commander.

Have my ship ready to fight or run when I get there," finished Clement.

"Aye, sir, I will," said Yan.

And with that Clement shut off the com line.

❈ **11** ❈

They were still two minutes out from the *Beauregard*'s cargo deck when the first signs of trouble came. Light attack clippers, the three-man-style ships he and Pomeroy had seen activated in the ship's hold, came swarming out of the Ark. As near as Clement could tell they were in triangle formations, which was a standard tactic for LACs. The biggest problem, though, was that there were *a lot* of triangles.

"Estimate of the number of LACs, Pomeroy?" Clement said.

"At least sixty," she replied.

"We probably saw five times that number on the Ark."

"Then these are likely only the first group of teams to come out of hydro sleep."

Clement nodded agreement. "They have way too much firepower for this shuttle," he said, then called up Yan again. "Yan, I need my ship moving the moment we're down on the cargo deck."

"Understood, sir. Based on my observations so far those LACs warm up slow, especially after fifty years in hydro suspension. Likely the crews aren't very much 'with it' either. I know I'd be groggy after sleeping half a century," she said.

"We can't make any assumptions, Commander, just preparations. Get those nukes loaded and ready to fire, and set all of our conventional missiles to proximity detonation. There's too many LACs to ensure we can get them all with individual missiles."

"Understood, sir. See you in thirty seconds," replied Yan. Clement looked down at his watch, just to confirm.

"Take us in, Pomeroy," he said.

They landed hard and fast and Clement immediately made for the bridge, only pausing to let the air pressure between the cargo deck and the air lock equalize. He swept onto his bridge still in his EVA suit and took the center seat from Yan. She had immediately started the *Beauregard* on an escape path using the Ion plasma drive, but the old girl still took time to accelerate, and those LACs were closing to firing range. He got immediately on the com to Telco in the forward missile room.

"What's the status of my nukes, Middie?" he demanded.

"Locked and loaded in the tubes, sir," said Telco.

"Captain, we may want to wait on the nukes as a last resort, not a first option." This came from Yan.

Clement scanned his tactical screen, which identified the sixty incoming LACs, and it didn't look like they were coming to negotiate.

"Middie, load the main tubes with conventional missiles first, proximity warhead settings. Keep the nukes on standby, but I want them ready when I need them, Telco, or you'll be scrubbing the bathrooms all the way home," said Clement.

"Understood, Captain," replied Telco.

Clement looked to Yan. "You could have made that suggestion earlier," he said.

"I know, but—"

"No time, Yan," Clement said as he waved her off. He stood and started peeling off his EVA suit while giving orders at the same time. "Ivan, plot us a course that will take us toward Bellus. If that Ark wants to chase us they'll have to break off their original course to follow us. That could save us some time. What do you think, Mika?"

She turned from the pilot's seat, thinking for a second, then pulled up her plasma screen and made some calculations. "A day, maybe two if they parallel us. But they could also choose to use Alphus as a slingshot without a course change. If they do that, it might be less," she said.

"Why so little time?" asked Clement.

Ori canted her head a bit, looking at him. "This system is really packed. The planets are very close together compared to the 5 Suns, or even the Rim system, and thus easier to get to."

Clement nodded as he finished removing his EVA suit and tossed it aside, then sat back down at the captain's console. "We need another option," he said. He checked the tactical board, which showed the Earth Ark LACs were within eight minutes of firing range. He called down to Nobli. "Hassan, can we use the LEAP drive inside the system?"

"Well, yeah, you can use it anywhere. You just have to be aware it can cause collateral damage," replied Nobli.

"At this point that might be to our advantage. Can we *navigate* with it?"

"You mean use it as the main drive? I don't know. It was designed to get you from star system to star system, not planet to planet, which is a pinpoint target. Where did you want to go?"

"Bellus," he said.

"Jesus, Jared, that's a big ask. The calculations would take—"

"Five minutes, Hassan. I want your best guess to Ivan by that time. And make sure the drive is warm. We could need it at any time."

"Impossible to do, Captain. But of course if that's an order . . . "

"It is."

"Understood, sir."

Clement cut the line and then turned to Yan at the XO's console. "Battle status, XO."

"They're faster than us now, sir. They'll reach firing range on us in seven minutes, thirty seconds," said Yan.

"Engage the static field, and load up the first volley of missiles, Commander."

"Aye, sir," said Yan, scrambling over her board. The static field was designed to protect the ship from micrometeorites or small kinetic weapons like ball bearings, which could tear a ship to pieces if it was going the right speed.

"Prepare to fire on my mark."

Yan looked up at him. "Sir," she said, acknowledging her readiness.

The LACs were closing on the *Beauregard* and Clement had precious few seconds left to make his decisions. He called down to Nobli one last time.

"Do you have my calculation?" Clement demanded.

"I do, sir," replied Nobli. "It's rough, but a 0.085 second application of the LEAP drive should be enough to get us clear of the battlefield and propel us in the general direction of Bellus. I uploaded the calc to Ivan and he has the new control app."

"Very good, engineer. One more thing."

"There always is."

"The control app for the MAD weapon."

Nobli stayed silent for a moment, then said, "Already uploaded to your command console, sir."

Clement looked to his board and confirmed it was there.

"Do you intend to use it, sir?"

"Only in an emergency. Will it hinder our ability to use the LEAP drive for our escape?"

"Well, I don't recommend using them at the same time. That might rip a hole in *our* universe, or explode the whole damn thing. Just remember when you use the MAD it acts like a bypass valve. Once you activate it the power will flow out of the ship until you give the stop command, then the valve will turn off automatically. Like flipping a dead man switch."

"So I could use it as a weapon, then use the LEAP drive right after?" asked Clement.

"Theoretically, yes, sir."

"Thank you, Nobli." Clement looked down and activated the MAD control app. It lit up green on his console, then went to amber as he put it on standby.

"Yan, best guess to enemy firing range?"

She shrugged. "Any second now, Captain," Yan replied. Mika Ori turned quickly from her pilot's console.

"Incoming missiles, Captain," she reported.

"Sound the alarm. Evade and distract," Clement ordered. Claxons went off throughout the ship as Ori accelerated the *Beauregard* using the Xenon thrusters on top of the Ion plasma drive to evade the incoming missiles. She also activated her defensive countermeasures at the same time. Clement watched as the initial barrage of a dozen missiles were easily distracted by the *Beauregard's* defenses, exploding harmlessly in the jungle of chaff well away from her hull.

"Initial barrage ineffective, sir," reported Ori. "It appears their weapons use simple heat-seeking targeting. Good thing we warm up our countermeasures. Easily handled by our defenses, sir."

"So far, Mika. But I bet our friends learn quickly." He turned to Ivan Massif. "Ivan, program in our escape route to Bellus using a 0.085 second burst from the LEAP drive. I want to be ready to bug out as quickly as possible."

"Already done, sir," said Massif. It was the navigator who would control the LEAP burst from his navigation position.

"Shall we return fire, sir?" asked Yan in a rather urgent tone. "They're prepping another volley."

Clement shook his head. "Not yet, Yan. Let's see what our friends do next."

A few seconds later and the fleet of LACs answered with a second, and then a third barrage of twelve missiles each. Ori turned the *Beauregard* this way and that, swaying as the missiles approached. Clement didn't have to call for countermeasures this time. Mika knew her job.

The missile groups had been fired seconds apart, in a crisscrossing pattern to counter the *Beauregard's* defenses. The first batch fell prey to the countermeasures again, but the second was more effective, with three of the missiles acquiring a targeting ping on *Beauregard*.

"Defensive missiles, Yan," ordered Clement. Without a word Yan launched six conventional missiles to intercept the incoming enemy fire. All three enemy missiles were taken out at a range of five kilometers from the *Beauregard*.

"Reload conventional missiles," Yan called down to Telco in the missile room. Then she turned to Clement. "Five klicks isn't much of a safety margin," she said.

Clement nodded. "Agreed. Mika, how fast are they closing on us?"

Without turning she replied, "That five-kilometer cushion will be gone in two minutes, sir."

Clement hit his com. "Missile room, this is the captain. Belay that last missile command. Load two of the nuclear warhead missiles into the launchers. I repeat, load two nukes into launchers. Commander Yan will be down with her activation key."

"Aye, sir," said Telco, a bit of quaver apparent in his voice, even over the com.

Clement looked to Yan. "Go," he said with a nod. "Get Wilcock. I'll fire the missiles from here." She went.

Clement turned to Massif at the navigation station. "Ivan, prepare to activate the LEAP drive on the course Engineer Nobli gave you on my order."

"Sir," snapped Massif in acknowledgement.

Clement waited as the light attack clipper fleet closed again on the *Beauregard*. He got a green light confirming the nuclear missiles were locked and loaded. Yan came back to her station presently.

Then the LACs launched their next missile volley.

"Incoming! Thirty seconds!" declared Ori from her station. Clement didn't have to order the evasive countermeasures.

Five groups of twelve missiles launched in volleys one second apart, streaming in toward the *Beauregard* in a weave pattern that would be impossible to avoid. They were going to get their target, one way or another. Clement activated the MAD weapon and held his finger over the firing button, but he still had one more card to play.

"Commander Yan, are the nukes ready to fire?" he said over the com.

"Aye, sir," Yan replied.

"On my mark. Countdown please."

"Twenty seconds."

"Hold."

"Fifteen seconds."

"Hold."

"Ten—"

"Fire!"

The ship shook as the nukes rolled out of the launch tubes and accelerated at hyper-Mach speeds, far outpacing the incoming missiles. They all watched on the main tactical display as the nukes closed to proximity range of the enemy missiles in seconds, then detonated.

Nothing.

"Insufficient detonation, Captain!" exclaimed Yan over the com. "Nukes did not explode!"

Clement looked to the incoming countdown clock, which was at 0:03...

"Ivan—" he said.

Then the universe shifted around him.

✷ 12 ✷

Massif hadn't waited for Clement to give the order. He had engaged the LEAP drive and the *Beauregard* had slipped from normal space into its quantum-fluid bubble for a period of 0.086 seconds before automatically shutting down. In that time the *Beauregard* had traveled an indeterminate amount of distance and scrambled most of the crew's brains. Clement felt his mind returning to normal slowly, like pieces of a jigsaw puzzle coming together. He looked out on his dimly lit bridge as his crew struggled to regain their wits.

"Thank you, Ivan," he croaked out before clearing his throat and sitting up higher in his command chair. All the main systems on the bridge had blinked out and were rebooting.

"You're welcome, sir," said Massif.

"Mika . . ." He had to clear his throat again, then, "Where are we?"

"Uncertain, Captain," the pilot said from her station, her hand quivering on the controls and her voice weak. Clement could see she had been shaken by the LEAP transit. "My main tracking console is knocked out, but the underlying telemetry says we're still in the Trinity system."

"In the neighborhood, then?"

She turned, a wan smile on her face. "In the neighborhood, yes, sir." Then she ran her hands over her console more certainly as systems began to come back online. "I think I can get us a visual, if that would help, sir."

Clement nodded. "As good as anything, Lieutenant," he said. With that the main display screen lit up. It showed a blue-green mass in sunlight looming over them, but half the planet was eclipsed in darkness.

"Jesus Christ! Is that Bellus?" said Clement.

"I think so, sir. We were on a general heading for her, but I didn't think we'd be this close," said Massif.

Just then Yan returned to her station. "Systems coming back online, sir. We're just slightly less than eighteen thousand kilometers from Bellus, sir," she said.

Clement got on his com to Hassan Nobli. "That was quite a calculation, Engineer. Another tenth of a second and we'd have been in the mantle of the planet."

"You said you wanted my best guess, sir. You got what you asked for," replied Nobli.

"I did indeed. Thank you, Nobli."

"My pleasure, sir."

Clement shut off the com and then turned to Yan. "What happened with my nukes?" he asked in a demanding tone.

"I've already done a quick analysis, sir. The yield . . . the yield was insufficient for a fission explosion, sir," she said.

"Insufficient? You mean they were duds?"

Yan nodded. "Essentially, sir."

Clement slammed his fist on the arm of his command couch. "I thought we verified the nuclear yields back at Kemmerine Station?"

"We did, sir. My only conclusion is that the warheads had insufficient plutonium mass for detonation, and that some kind of masking agent was used to deceive us," she said.

Clement sat back in his command chair, his face flushing red with anger. "In other words, we were sabotaged by Admiral DeVore."

"It appears so, sir."

Clement leaned forward in his couch, clasping his hands together, speaking softly so that only she could hear. "We've been outsmarted by Elara DeVore for the last time, Yan," he said through tight lips. He felt like someone had just cut open his body and let his guts fall to the floor. "This betrayal . . . " he started, "this betrayal is absolute, Yan. And it's not the first time."

"What do you mean?"

"I mean I now know who betrayed me at the Battle of Argyle Station. Elara DeVore. That's how she was able to advance through the ranks of the 5 Suns Navy so fast. She sold us out, all of her crewmates and friends onboard the *Beauregard*, for her own advancement."

Yan hesitated. His words were filled with anger and resentment. She could almost feel his pain. But . . .

"That was a different war, Clement. It's over now. Now we have to focus on this ship, this crew, and how to save them," she said.

He finally exhaled and took in a deep breath. "I can't

deny that I want to crawl inside one of those whiskey bottles, Yan. Forever."

"You can't," she replied. "This ship needs you. Hell, *I* need you. The over-promoted rich girl from New Hong Kong. You're the only person who can make this work, Clement. We all need you."

Clement sat back, thinking. "If she was willing to go this far, she had to have an accomplice on board, someone to back her plan up."

Yan nodded. "Wilcock," she said.

Clement bolted from his seat. "Get your sidearm, Commander. Mika, get us into a higher, stable orbit over Bellus and maintain." He looked to Adebayor and Massif. "The two of you are to go to the armory and bring back one sidearm and one cobra rifle for each of you. When you return, seal the bridge and only open it on my personal orders. Understood?"

"Yes, sir," came the chorus reply.

"Mika, seal the bridge while they're gone, and only open it for them when they return."

"Will do, sir," she said.

Clement grabbed his cobra pistol from his discarded EVA suit and primed it, then looked to Yan. "Ready?" he asked.

"Ready, sir," she said with a nod, loaded pistol in her hand.

Then the two of them headed off the bridge and down the gangway, toward the forward missile room at a dead run.

"You know I could be working for Admiral DeVore

as well," said Yan as they ran to the forward missile room.

"You could be," admitted Clement. "But if you are then now would be a good time for you to put a cobra round in my back."

Yan reached out and stopped him. "You know that's not going to happen," she said. He looked at her, his face not giving away any emotion one way or another.

"I hope that's true, Yan. If I'm wrong about you then this whole mission is a suicide run, and every life on this ship is forfeit."

"It is true, sir," she said. "I'm loyal to you."

"Good," he said, again without commitment, then, with a nod of his head, "let's go get our traitor."

They picked up their pace, weapons drawn.

When they entered the missile room, two decks down and directly below the bridge, Captain Wilcock had his cobra pistol to the back of Middie Telco's head. Yan and Clement stood in the doorway, their sidearms laser-targeted on Wilcock's forehead.

"Traitor," said Clement, his aim not wavering. "What did you do to the warheads?"

Wilcock looked at him with disdain, but chose to answer. "Depleted uranium casings. Fooled all of you into thinking you had a fully functional nuke," said Wilcock as he shifted to put Telco's head between him and their targeting laser sights.

"That action could have killed us all. Those LACs had us dead to rights."

"I was ordered to sacrifice my life for this mission, if that was required," replied Wilcock, emotionless.

"Ordered by Fleet Admiral DeVore."

"Of course. Now enough of this. Let me through to the shuttle or Middie Telco here will get a softball-sized hole in his head."

Clement shook his head negative. "That's not happening," he stated flatly.

"This isn't a negotiation, *Captain*." He said the last word with open anger. "You've got five seconds to step out of the way."

Clement exchanged a glance with Yan. She took one step to the right.

"Keep moving," demanded Wilcock. Yan took another step, followed by Clement yielding the door opening. "More!" he said as he moved with Telco toward the yawning hatchway. Yan took two more steps, Clement one, and then Wilcock pushed Telco toward them and ran for the door, slamming the hatch behind him as the three of them tried to untangle themselves.

Yan ran to the door. "Sealed," she said. Clement waved her aside and raised his pistol at the door lock from barely a meter away.

"Jesus!" exclaimed Yan as she and Telco dove for cover. Clement fired at the lock mechanism, blowing the door clean off its hinges and into the hallway, then scrambled through the hatch and started running after Wilcock. He slid down the metal stairwell rails, barely touching the stairs with his feet as he ran. When he made it to the cargo hold Wilcock was ahead of him, running for the open shuttle door. He had one shot from almost 10 meters away with a close-range weapon.

He didn't hesitate. The kinetic cobra round hit Wilcock

in his outstretched left hand just as he was reaching for the shuttle stair railing, bits of metal and flesh splattering against the shuttle's hull. Wilcock fell in a sprawl off the shuttle steps and onto the deck. Instinctively he reached for his wounded hand with his free one and his pistol went skittering away. He howled in pain as Clement raced across the deck and then went into a slide, kicking Wilcock's discarded pistol under the shuttle. Seconds later Yan and Telco arrived, along with Pomeroy and a slew of the rest of the crew. Wilcock was still howling like a schoolgirl, holding his shattered left hand.

"Take charge of our prisoner, Mr. Telco," Clement said, then turned to Pomeroy, "Get him patched up, with as minimal medical supplies as possible, no pain meds, and then throw him in the brig."

"Uh, we don't have a brig, sir," said Telco.

Clement looked around the deck. "Well, we used to. Put him in the shuttle air lock then and attach him to a tether until we decide what to do with him."

"Aye, sir," said Telco as he and Pomeroy hauled the whining traitor off the deck.

Clement looked at Yan. "My cabin, five minutes," he said. She nodded as Clement stormed off.

Clement stopped at the bridge to give the all-clear and then ordered Massif, Ori, and Adebayor to begin a survey of the light side of the tidal-locked Bellus.

"What are we looking for?" asked Massif.

"Any place to set down. We may have to hide for a while. And get a bead on that Ark ship. I want to know where they're heading."

"Aye, sir," came the responses, and then Clement made for his cabin. When he opened the door, Yan was already inside.

"That was too goddamned close," she said as he entered.

"No kidding. That bastard Wilcock. Worthless piece of shit."

"You're forgetting Admiral DeVore."

Clement shook his head. "No, I'm not. But we can't deal with her out here. We can deal with Wilcock, though," he said. They both sat down, facing each other. Clement leaned forward.

"This is my fault, Yan. DeVore thought I would drink my way through this trip. She was counting on me *not* being the man I used to be. She expected I would be the lout I've been on Argyle Station for the last nine years since my war parole ended. She thought she knew what I would do. Well, I didn't disappoint her. I am that man. She played me easily enough. And to think I even slept with her on Kemmerine," he finished, shaking his head in disgrace.

Yan opened her mouth to talk but said nothing for a moment, then, "I disagree, Captain. You foiled her plans. We should all be dead by now, but you've saved us. You are not that man on Argyle Station. I know she's had you under observation for at least the last year, probably more than that. You were the perfect patsy, but you beat her. We're all still alive."

Now it was Clement's turn to stay quiet. After another minute he spoke again, changing the subject.

"I've no time to waste on Captain Wilcock right now. We have a military Earth Ark ship bearing down on us with a hundred times our firepower. We have no nukes to defend ourselves, and an Admiral back home who has deceived us and sacrificed us to the wolves for her own selfish reasons, and I'm just trying to figure out what to do next."

"About which part?"

Clement looked at her. "First things first. Wilcock, I guess. I'm having a hard time trying to avoid my first impulse," he said.

"Which is?"

"His actions warrant execution," he said. Yan went quiet and pensive at that. "You don't agree?" Clement prompted.

"I do agree."

Now it was Clement's turn to get quiet again as he thought about things. Finally, he stood up, his decision made, and Yan stood with him. "Call all ship's personnel to the loading dock in twenty minutes, save for Mika and Ivan."

"Yes, sir," said Yan. The two stood together as she looked at him, hoping for more, but he stayed resolved. With nothing more to say, she left the room to inform the crew. Once he was alone, Clement went to his cabinet and poured himself a glass of the Argyle whiskey. He drank it quickly, in one shot, to steel his resolve. He'd killed many enemies on the field of battle, but this was the first time he'd considered executing a man, even if he was a traitor.

Clement looked at the bottle again, and all it represented. He'd crawled in and out of a bottle like that a dozen times since the war, always wondering what had become of his friends, but never allowed to know what became of them by the rules of his war parole. Well, now he had found out. Elara DeVore was the one who betrayed them, no, *him*, at the Battle of Argyle Station. He wondered if delivering him to the 5 Suns Navy had been part of the deal she had obviously cut with them to betray the Rim. In any case, it had undoubtedly led to her decade-plus rise in the 5 Suns Navy, all the way to Fleet Admiral. Like he'd said to Yan, Elara DeVore always had a backup plan.

He looked at the bottle, longing for another hit, if nothing else just to numb the pain of his memories of DeVore, and of being her lover. He'd been through a lot in his life, but he had never felt betrayal like he felt it now. That's what DeVore had robbed him of: his ability to trust *anyone* from now on.

He turned away from the bottle, focusing on his tactical pad but not really looking at it. Captain Wilcock had no doubt been deceived by DeVore just as he had, but Wilcock had willingly put the entire crew in mortal danger, he'd committed treason, and mutiny. In Clement's mind, there was no real choice. Wilcock had to die. Regrettably, he was merely a pawn standing in for the person who was the true villain here, the one who should be standing for execution. In that moment, he silently vowed he would bring Elara DeVore to justice. Then he stood, and spoke out loud in his empty cabin.

"You'll be the first person I've ever executed, Captain Wilcock," he said quietly to himself, "but probably not the last." Then he put the bottle away and left his cabin, heading for the loading dock.

❖ ❖ ❖

Captain Wilcock was sealed in the shuttle air lock, facing the largest exterior door on the *Beauregard*. His injured hand was crudely wrapped and he winced in obvious pain, missing at least two fingers from his left hand. *It would be cruel to extend that pain*, thought Clement.

Most of the crew were now gathered around in a disorganized group, and Yan was the last to arrive with Lieutenant Pomeroy. Clement wasn't happy. He stood on the gantry landing, looking down on his crew.

"Commander Yan," he called out.

She snapped to attention and stepped forward, looking up at him from the deck. "Sir."

"Organize this rabble," he ordered. She did. Within a few seconds the crew had organized itself into three rows of five and two of four, by rank, with only Wilcock, Clement, Yan, the deceased middie Daniel, plus Ori and Massif (who were busy running the ship) missing from their ranks. Clement signaled to Telco to activate the com so that Wilcock could hear the conversation from inside the air lock, but not reply or be heard by the crew. Once that task was complete, Clement started in.

"We are here to enact punishment on a traitor, Captain Craig Wilcock, who deceived this ship and her crew by placing nonexplosive nuclear warheads into our defensive armament, thus endangering the entire crew aboard the *Beauregard* during the attack by the Earth Ark ship. I have debated those actions, along with his placing Middie Telco in peril by holding him hostage with a cobra pistol to the head, and his attempt to steal our only shuttle to escape justice. I believe Captain Wilcock was working with Fleet Admiral DeVore of the 5 Suns Alliance Navy, another traitor, to use this ship as a test to seek out the power of the Earth Ark ship we encountered. This ship and her crew were no doubt considered an acceptable expense by the 5 Suns Navy, or at least by Admiral DeVore herself. Neither I nor *any* of my crew were informed of this except for Captain Wilcock, who clearly had an escape plan in place if this ship was destroyed by a superior force. As captain of this ship I cannot condone, forgive, nor commute the penalties for Captain Wilcock's actions. I therefore sentence the traitor, Craig Wilcock, to capital punishment by evacuation into the vacuum of space, as prescribed in the 5 Suns Alliance Navy Code of Military Justice."

The crew was dead silent at this. Clement could hear Wilcock banging on the air lock door, a quiet thudding sound as he realized his final fate was at hand.

"This ship, her crew, and this mission have been betrayed by the Captain, the Admiral and the 5 Suns Navy. It is now up to each of you to decide where your loyalties lie. We are now a crew without a nation, a ship without a flag. We cannot trust the 5 Suns Navy, which commissioned this ship, nor the Fleet Admiral. Each of us, therefore, must decide our fate from this point forward. As my last order as the captain of this 5 Suns Alliance Navy vessel, I order the execution of Captain Wilcock and will carry it out myself. From that point onward your decisions to follow my orders will be completely voluntary. I leave that decision to each of you."

Clement stepped down from the gantry to the cargo deck and walked to the air lock door. Wilcock was in a

panic, beating the door with both his hands, leaving a
bloody stain on the window from his injury. The pain in
his face as he faced the terror of his own demise was
obvious, but Clement reminded himself of Wilcock's
cowardice, of his betrayal, of the people on the
Beauregard he could have killed. He knew it should be
Elara DeVore in that air lock, but she wasn't here, and
Wilcock had done enough to warrant this punishment on
his own. He wondered if he could do the same thing to
DeVore as he was doing to Wilcock. He decided at this
point, he could, to both of them.

He activated the outer door controls. The interior
alarms went off as Wilcock panicked even more, looking
for any way out. Clement pressed the release button.

The doors parted and Wilcock was quickly sucked out
by decompression, his body dangling about ten meters
outside the air lock, still tethered to the ship, spinning and
writhing in cold space. He flailed his limbs as he spun
around, out of control, with nothing to grasp on to but his
last breath. In seconds it was over, his body rigid and
lifeless. Mercifully Clement detached the tether, allowing
him to float away toward Bellus, where his body would burn
up in the atmosphere. Clement closed the outer doors and
activated the atmosphere controls, flooding the air lock
with environment again, then turned back to his crew.

"All hands, return to stations. Command crew will
meet in the officer's galley in thirty minutes to discuss our
next actions. Dismissed," he said, then walked straight
past Yan and back up the gangway, heading toward his
quarters.

※　※　※

Clement shut the officer's galley doors as the last of his command crew squeezed into the small space. Present were Yan, Nobli, Ori, Massif, and Lieutenant Pomeroy, who Clement had specifically invited. He'd left Adebayor to manage the ship now that Mika had put it in a stable orbit around Bellus, and they were only a few meters from the bridge at any rate.

"To business then," said Clement. "We're alone in an unknown star system, we've been betrayed by our commanders and are undoubtedly considered expendable by the 5 Suns Alliance Navy, and most especially Fleet Admiral DeVore. Are there any objections to my declaration that the *Beauregard* currently flies no flag, and that the decisions we make to survive are ours, and ours alone?" No one in the room said a word.

"Your silence is considered acceptance of our new standard. I will note in the log that we all took this stand of our own volition. From this point on, I propose that we adopt the 5 Suns Alliance military code as a temporary makeweight from which to conduct our onboard affairs. We are not pirates. Please state any objections now." Again, there were none. "Good. Now that that business is complete, I need reports on the condition of the ship, our tactical status, and a review of the data we have compiled on Bellus." He turned to his right. "Commander Yan?"

"The ship is running smoothly on all systems. We have forty-eight conventional warhead missiles remaining at our disposal, although it is uncertain how effective they would be against the Ark ship. On a tactical basis, the Ark ship remains in a deep-dive course inward toward Alphus.

From their current approach they could either do a burn to establish a stable orbit around the planet, or accelerate and use it as a slingshot to change their course back out toward Bellus, and us."

"We won't survive another encounter with that Ark ship, especially if we have to fight them with conventional weapons," said Clement.

"Is there another option? I mean, besides conventional weapons?" It was Mika Ori, the former fighter pilot, asking the question.

Clement exchanged a brief glance with Nobli. "No other options that I'm prepared to discuss at this time."

"But shouldn't—" started in Yan.

Clement cut her off. "Not at this time, *Commander*," he said firmly, then turned to Ivan Massif. "What have your surveys of Bellus turned up, Navigator?"

"We've made six orbits of the planet, sir. Our initial survey results have been . . . surprising."

"Such as?"

"We've identified abundant fresh water on the planet sir, above the ground. The planet is tidally locked to the Trinity star, with the same side facing the star constantly, and conditions are remarkably stable throughout the biosphere. There are high mountains in both the extreme north and south that receive regular snowfall and produce a near-constant melt that proceeds toward the equator of the planet through deep river valleys, where they collect in numerous freshwater lakes and seas. Surface temperatures throughout eighty percent of the planet average twenty-four degrees Celsius, with very rare variations. Vegetation is pervasive and there appears to be a lot of potential for animal life. There is also a large saltwater sea near the equator of the planet that could provide the seeds for ocean-based lifeforms."

Clement nodded. "Sounds like a paradise."

"There is one other issue, sir." This came from Pomeroy. Clement nodded for her to continue. "When I was conducting a survey for bioforms, I discovered signs of . . . more advanced life on the planet, sir."

"Advanced? Say what you mean, Lieutenant," demanded Clement.

"I would say, sir," she said hesitantly, "that these bioforms were organized in such a way as to be almost immediately recognizable as organized communities, sir."

"You mean some kind of, uh . . . intelligent communities?"

"Yes, sir. Things like simple artificial canals to serve the communities, potential crop fields, things of that nature. Sir."

"So there's some kind of potentially intelligent life on Bellus?"

"I would say so, sir," Pomeroy said.

Clement unconsciously rubbed at his chin. "Perhaps there've been missions to this system before. Could they be military bases left by previous Ark missions? Either from Earth or potentially from the 5 Suns?" he asked.

Pomeroy frowned slightly as she considered his question. "It seems unlikely that these are military settlements, sir. They aren't giving off any indications of advanced technology. They look more like primitive settlements, sir."

Clement leaned back in his chair. "So we have a

mystery. We'll have to take all of this into consideration should we go down to the surface. For now, let's continue our surveys and not jump to any conclusions."

"Aye, sir."

"One other thing, Lieutenant. As of right now I'm giving you a field promotion to Lieutenant Commander. This will become official once we decide whatever fleet we'll end up serving in." There was a chuckle at that around the room. He turned to Yan.

"I also want you to promote the middies to full ensigns. They've all earned it," he said.

"Understood, sir," Yan replied.

Clement turned to Nobli. "Status of the LEAP drive, Chief?"

"Ready to use at any time, sir," he said.

"So we can escape whenever we want; we just have nowhere to go."

"Exactly, sir."

Clement nodded. "Keep her ready, Chief. We may need to bug out of here at any time." He leaned forward then, addressing the entire room. "Continue with your surveys. As a precaution I want us to look for a safe place to set down, hopefully away from these communities, or whatever they might be. Mika, that will be your job. Ivan, I want you to let me know when and if that Earth Ark changes course or speed. If they use Alphus to slingshot toward us, we may have to find cover, and fast. Keep all the other systems at optimal. Be prepared for anything. Remember, we've been betrayed by the 5 Suns Alliance, and the Earthers are to be considered hostile until further notice. Dismissed," he said.

As the room emptied, Yan stayed behind for a private word.

"What about those 'communities' on the surface of Bellus?" she asked.

He considered her question for a moment. "Despite what Pomeroy says, I have to believe they're military. If they are, we may be stuck between a rock and a hard place. I'll need options, Yan. That's where you come in."

"That *is* my job, sir," she said.

He nodded. "Then I'll leave you to it."

She left without another word. After a few seconds Clement followed her to his bridge, and an unknown destiny.

✳ 13 ✳

Twelve hours later, after a full cycle of sleep and refreshment, Clement found himself back on the *Beauregard*'s bridge, staring intently at the input from the long-range radio telescope on the main wall display. All of the primary bridge crew were watching the image of the Earth Ark as it bore down on Alphus, the innermost habitable planet of the seven worlds that composed the Trinity system.

The tactical display showed the Ark as it decelerated into the gravity well of Alphus. If she was planning on making for Bellus to pursue the *Beauregard*, she would have to make her turn and accelerate by skipping off of Alphus' atmosphere and then firing her main engines in a five-gravity burst to change course. If, however, she intended to stay on her original course to orbit Alphus and deploy her forces there, she would have to make a much smoother turn and continue to decelerate until she had established a steady orbit over the planet.

The bridge was tense and quiet. "Distance of the Ark ship to Alphus, Navigator," Clement asked.

"One hundred fifty thousand kilometers and closing,

sir. At this pace she'll touch the atmosphere in twelve minutes, then she'll pass behind the planet and out of our line of sight. After about four minutes she should reappear on the other side of the planet, then either keep to an elliptical orbit and continue decelerating, or fire her mains and accelerate toward us," said Massif.

"How difficult a maneuver is this, Mika?" Clement asked of his pilot.

She shrugged. "I've never done it with anything remotely that size, sir, but my guess is they have a programmed autopilot carrying out the burn. They also have the gravity well of Alphus to help them, and although she's not as massive as Bellus or Camus, if I was betting on it, I'd say they can pull it off."

Clement nodded and turned to Yan. "Ship's status?"

"Ready for anything, sir. Locked down and prepared for any order you give."

"And if we have to go to ground?"

"We have a spot in the northern hemisphere at the convergence of three river valleys that we can set the *Beauregard* down on, about twelve klicks from the nearest of those settlements, sir."

"Thank you, Yan," he said, then turned his attention back to the display. The crew waited in silence, with Massif giving occasional updates. Finally, there was a glint of light as the Ark started her pass to the far side of Alphus.

"Atmospheric contact confirmed," said Massif. "They'll be out of viewing range for the next four minutes."

Clement fidgeted in his couch, which he was finding increasingly uncomfortable as time went by.

"Is it raise or call?" said Yan absently.

Clement looked at her, surprised by the poker reference, then turned back to the screen. They'd know soon enough.

There was another flash of light as the Ark ship came around the far edge of Alphus right on schedule, then the screen lit up with a bright flash of light that temporarily blinded the screen sensors. There could be little doubt now as to their intent. They'd fired their engines while they were still inside Alphus' atmosphere.

"How long until they get here, Ivan?" asked a disappointed Clement.

"Nine hours, twenty-seven minutes," said the *Beauregard*'s tall navigator.

Clement stood up and looked around his bridge. "Then we have half that long to get this ship down to a safe haven on Bellus," he said, then looked down at his watch. "Commencing now."

The next few hours Clement and Yan were a flurry of motion, validating landing procedures, surveying the landing site, prepping the ship for atmospheric travel. The *Beauregard* was never really made for operating in an atmosphere, but she always had the capability as a backup to staying space-borne. Clement had only ever landed her twice in her Rim Confederation Navy days, once on an asteroid to hide from 5 Suns Alliance hunter-killers that were pursuing her during the War of the 5 Suns, and once on a desperate resupply mission on Ceta near the end of the war. But this was a different *Beauregard* from the ship he had commanded, as Clement was well aware. Doing anything like a landing maneuver was going to be a completely new experience for everyone. He was with Mika Ori, looking at her proposed landing site.

"Will this area provide us enough cover?" said Clement.

"From what? Atomic missiles? Light attack drones? Pterodactyls?" she replied.

"Observation," he snapped back at her. "Can we find enough ground cover to hide the ship from military observation cameras, drone flybys, and the like?"

Her pretty face twisted a bit as she thought about the new problem her captain was presenting her. "We wanted to land here," she said, pointing to a peninsula between two of the rivers. "But there isn't any ground cover, at least not enough to cover a two-thousand-ton spacecraft. If we went inland another five klicks though, there is a river delta with a flat rocky sandbar closer to the mountains. If we come down there we'll have ready access to a large amount of vegetation that's taller than the ship herself. Knocking down some random trees could provide us with enough cover so we'd look like a natural formation from space. But if a drone got close, say within five hundred meters, we'd be dead meat."

"I'm more concerned with whether a sandbar could hold the weight of the ship. What about this clearing here?" said Clement, pointing to a smaller area another kilometer inland.

Mika pursed her lips as she was thinking. "It's a much tighter fit," she stated.

Clement looked up, catching her eyes as he smiled. "That's why I hired the best pilot in the fleet," he said.

She sighed and looked at the chart again. "This is what you want, isn't it? Make my job tougher."

"I just want the ship to be as safe as it can be, and I *know* you can fit us in there."

"Like thread through the eye of a needle, sir," she said.

He smiled wider. "I knew you wouldn't let me down."

With that he left Ori to calculate the braking maneuvers while he made his way down to see his chief engineer. Nobli looked up from behind his wire-rimmed glasses and crinkled his nose at Clement as he came in.

"I've got plenty to do here to get my LEAP drive secured for a planet-side landing, Captain, so I hope this isn't some kind of pep talk."

"It's not," said Clement, "rest assured."

The two men eyeballed each other, each waiting for the other to go first. Finally Clement spoke.

"Can we protect the LEAP drive components from damage as we touch down?" he asked his engineer.

Nobli shrugged, a noncommittal gesture. "Probably," Nobli said. "If we can keep her level, and the landing legs deploy properly, and about nine thousand other things don't happen."

"Because if they do we'll be stranded here with broken wheels and no way to drive home?"

"Close enough," said the engineer. "What you're doing isn't easy, Captain."

"I know that," snapped Clement, wiping sweat from his brow. It had been a stressful day, and it wasn't close to over. "If we shut down the LEAP drive, let it go completely cold, how long will it take to restart?"

Nobli leaned back, then scribbled some calculations on

a sheet of paper as Clement looked on, worried. Nobli looked up then.

"About 0.26 seconds," he said.

Clement let out a relieved sigh. "Remind me never to hire you again," he said.

Nobli laughed.

"You've forgotten about my sardonic sense of humor?"

"I never knew you had one." Nobli looked at his captain again. "Just don't let your hotshot pilot ruin my engine, and we'll get along fine," he said.

"I take it the thrusters can get us airborne in a hurry?"

"Absolutely. The mass of Bellus is slightly less than two-thirds of Earth, so escaping should be easy enough. Firing up the LEAP drive is no problem, *once* we're in space, and we have someplace to go."

Both men knew what the next question was.

"And the weapon?" asked Clement.

"Again, you'll have it when you need it, Captain. But we both know it's never been fired, and using it that way is only theoretical."

"Then let's pray we never have to use it," Clement said on his way back out the door.

With five hours to go until the Earth Ark had to make her initial fire to establish orbit around Bellus, Clement and his bridge crew were ready to descend to the surface. After verbally running an all-systems check with his crew and ordering all unnecessary (for the landing) personnel to their bunks to strap in, Clement turned his ship over to Mika Ori.

"Take her down, Pilot. And don't break her," he said.

"Aye, Captain," said Mika. Clement lay back deep in his safety couch while the pilot took over, activating the ship-wide com to address the full crew. "Course nominal on descent. Speed also nominal for this maneuver. Atmospheric insertion will occur in one minute, six seconds." Clement tried not to count off the seconds, leaving the calculating to the ship's timer. "We'll make one full orbit while we pass from the dark side of Bellus around to the light side a second time. By then our deceleration should be complete enough for me to fire the braking thrusters and take operational control of our flight."

"Will we be visible to the Earth Ark if we use the atmosphere to brake?" asked Clement.

Ori muted the com to reply to her captain. "The first twenty seconds we'll be visible, but it will be against the light side of Bellus. After that we'll pass behind the event horizon to the dark side and they won't be able to track us. When we come around again our speed should be sufficiently slowed so that we won't be visible to even their best cameras, if we've guessed at their level of technology correctly."

If, thought Clement. He hated that word. He said nothing more as Ori guided the *Beauregard* into the upper atmosphere of Bellus. Suddenly he wanted a drink of the Argyle whiskey badly. He suppressed the impulse, with difficulty.

When she hit the atmosphere bubble the external monitors started to flare to life, showing views of reentry plasma as the technical displays lit up with valuable data and telemetry.

"Let me know when we're out of sight of the Ark," said Clement. The next few seconds were hell for him, not knowing if the enemy could see his ship lighting up like a flare in the daylight.

Seconds later, Ori spoke to the entire crew again as the ship started to shake. "It's going to get a little rough for the next forty-five seconds or so, then it should calm down," she said reassuringly. Clement glanced to his right to look at Yan. Her eyes were closed and she had a death grip on the arms of her safety couch, holding on for dear life as the ship shook ever more violently. He looked down at his own hands then and realized he was in a similar posture, and he forced himself to relax.

The bridge crew of the *Beauregard* rode out the remaining seconds in agony, then savored the pause as the ship stopped shaking and resumed a more peaceful ride.

"You have a thirty-second respite," came Ori's voice over the com. "Then I'll fire the rockets again and we'll make the majority of our final descent on the dark side." Clement swallowed, wondering again why he hadn't taken a hard drink before they started this process, then switched on his monitor to a visual view of the dark side of Bellus.

Since the planet was tidal-locked to its nearby red dwarf star (only 4.25 million kilometers away), the light side was always facing the star, and the dark side always facing away. While the light side received nearly seventy percent of standard luminosity (measured by Earth standard, of course), the dark side, technically, would receive none. But as Clement could see, there was some light, no doubt a reflection of the luminosity of the third habitable world in the Trinity system, Camus, and perhaps even the sixth planet, a larger world with a greenish, clouded atmosphere only 0.017 AU distant. What could be made out was a rocky terrain, with mountains and floes of ice all bathed in a deep ruby glow. It was a place worth exploring someday, *but not just now*, Clement reminded himself.

Presently the *Beauregard* slid deeper into Bellus' atmosphere and Ori fired the thrusters, pushing the ship lower. This time the burn seemed to last interminable minutes, the g-forces tugging at the crew while they braked and decelerated. By the time they came around the event horizon again and into the light side, the burn had ended and the gravity relented. Clement looked up to see Ori piloting his ship from her console.

"Braking maneuvers complete," she said over the com. "The ship is under my active control. We're at five thousand meters and dropping quickly. Estimate nine minutes to landing site."

"Can they see us?" asked Clement.

"Doubtful," said Ori over the private com, "unless they have far better sensing equipment than they should have."

"Let's hope for that," replied Clement, then sat upright in his couch. The rest of the bridge crew followed suit with their captain. Clement glanced at Yan, whose eyes were red and watery, but she smiled wanly back at him without saying anything. He realized he was covered in sweat inside his navy fatigues, as likely was the rest of the crew.

Clement sat in silence as Ori guided the ship skillfully over a ridge of mountains and what looked to be green, junglelike vegetation, though Clement had only ever seen a jungle in education videos. Ceta, where he grew up, was a sparse and brown world, exactly the opposite of the Trinity worlds. Finally, as they broke through the cloud barrier, Clement could see their proposed landing site, a land of three rivers converging in dappled orange sunlight. One of the tributaries fed into the main river via a spectacular waterfall. It was beautiful. "Do you have our landing site, Mika?" said Clement.

"I do, sir. Setting her down won't be problem, sir, and there's plenty of cover. I could even put the *Beauregard* under that waterfall, if there's a big enough cave behind it."

"Not necessary, Pilot," he said, smiling. "Our original intended landing site will do just fine." And with that they all watched as Ori skillfully dropped the *Beauregard* from a hover mode, extending her landing legs and placing her right where her captain wanted her, in a clearing surrounded by trees. She landed and settled with a bump, Ori giving the final call of her narration.

"*Beauregard* is down. I repeat, *Beauregard* is down. Welcome to paradise, everyone."

At that Clement got up from his couch and started giving orders over the com. "Lieutenant Pomeroy, I want one last atmospheric check and virus scan. Middie Telco, correct that, Ensign Telco, organize a team and get some of those trees knocked down to provide us more cover, then deploy the shuttle, we might need her. Commander Yan"—he turned to his second-in-command—"prep an observation drone and get her ready to launch in one hour. I want to keep an eye on our friends up there," Clement said, pointing to the ceiling.

"Aye, sir," replied Yan, looking better every minute from the ordeal of landing. Then Clement looked around his bridge as it came to life with activity.

The *Beauregard* was down.

❋ 14 ❋

An hour later and the *Beauregard* had her air cover, a high atmosphere drone with an exceptional high-definition camera. The first pictures showed the Earth Ark making steady progress to its insertion point for orbit around Bellus. Clement got his team moving quickly, prepping the shuttle in case it was needed, and to his surprise, Ensign Telco was readying another vehicle.

"What is that?" he asked of Telco, pointing to a large structure the ensign was building out of what looked like empty missile casings.

"A pontoon boat," said Telco.

"A what?"

"It's a boat that sort of glides over the water. We have them all over on Metairie," he said.

"Where did you get it?"

Telco puffed out his chest a bit. "I made it, sir."

"You . . . made it. Out of what?"

"Everything was on board, sir. I remembered from reading the manifest before we arrived in-system. I used spare missile casings for pontoons, used weapons crates to build the carriage, and Mr. Nobli supplied me with a spare pylon motor from the LEAP drive stores for the engine. I thought it could come in handy in case we went planet-side," he finished.

"That it could," said Clement. "How long until you can have it in the water?"

"Any time, sir. She's ready now."

"Capacity?"

Telco looked at his creation. "I can configure her for six, sir, if you want to include weapons and provisions."

"I do, Ensign. Keep her undercover for now, at least until the Ark ship makes her first pass. We might have use for her to get upriver after that."

"Will do, sir. And sir, she'll have a much lower heat profile than the shuttle, sir. Almost negligible."

Clement smiled at the ensign's youthful enthusiasm. "Carry on, Ensign," he said as Yan came up to him. They started walking back to the *Beauregard* together.

"You're not thinking of actually using that thing, are you?" she asked.

"It's an option, Commander. I do want to get upriver and see those settlements."

"Before or after the Ark ship passes?"

"After," Clement said, looking up to the twilight sky. "How much time do we have?"

"Mika says about two and a half hours."

"Let's get her battened down, and call back our drone."

"Yes, sir," she replied.

A look of concern crossed his face then, and he did his best to hide it from Yan.

The crew waited in the cargo hold for the Ark ship to

pass. It was tense, and very quiet. Yan held up a finger to indicate the Ark would be right on top of them now. Every light, every system that could be shut down, was. Nobli had estimated that with the brush covering the *Beauregard* and the passing hours since she had gone cold that there was only a ten percent chance she'd be detected from space. But that surely wasn't the Ark ship's only means of detecting enemies, especially if she was a war ship.

Ten minutes after the Ark ship passed over their position, Clement ordered Telco to deploy his pontoon boat. Then he gathered with his command crew.

"We're going upriver to check out those settlements. It's about fifteen kilometers from here. How fast can your new boat go without creating a ruckus?" he said to Telco.

"At a safe speed of say, twenty klicks an hour, probably get there in about forty-five to fifty minutes," he said.

"Go fire her up," said Clement, nodding toward the boat. "We'll be there in five minutes."

Yan stepped up. "So who else gets to go on your little expedition?" she asked.

"Logically, you should stay behind and run the camp, but I know you want to go and frankly I could use your expertise. Mika and Ivan, I'll take you as well, since you both have some, uh, directional expertise."

"In other words, so we don't get lost," said Mika, teasing.

Clement smiled and nodded. "And lastly I want a field medic, so Lieutenant Pomeroy is in." He looked to his engineer.

"Oh, great," said Nobli sarcastically. "Just what I always wanted. My own command."

"Look, you're the best I have at organization. I want you to keep everybody busy setting up camp, establishing work shifts, and all of that. And keep the lights on minimum, just in case."

"Aye, sir," said Nobli, ever reluctant.

"Since this planet is tidal-locked to the star, it should never get either too light or too dark. Planets may pass between Bellus and the Trinity star from time to time. Remember this system has very tight orbits. Use that to your advantage, work at random times, keep energy expenditures to a minimum. Plan for that Ark to pass every . . ." he looked to Mika.

"Thirty-three minutes," she finished.

Clement nodded. "And no damn campfires," he said.

"Aye, sir," came Nobli's reply. Clement waved his crew toward the pontoon boat, then held back for a second.

"And Nobli, if they find you, if you've got incoming enemies, get the ship out of here. Even all the way back to Kemmerine if you have to. Understood?"

Nobli nodded reluctantly. "Understood, sir."

With that Clement made for the boat, where the crew had assembled and Ensign Telco had the engine rumbling quietly. He got on and helped push off into the gentle running waters of the river, the engine humming as they accelerated toward the settlement camp, and the unknown.

Thirty minutes in and five kilometers from the settlement Clement ordered Telco to slow the boat down. They'd seen precious little in the way of fauna, but Telco did spot some very terrestrial-looking river fish along the way. There was little in the way of insect life, with the banks of the river mostly inhabited by a mixture of tall grasses in green, purple and yellow. There were occasional breaks in the grass canopy but what glimpses they got of the river lowlands showed a mostly empty landscape of open meadows or stands of tropical-looking trees. Three klicks from the site of the settlement Clement ordered the boat to the shore and they started hiking inland. Mika peeled away her uniform jacket and tied it around her waist.

"God, fresh, humid, moist air again. I'd forgotten what a luxury it was," she said.

"It's beautiful here," agreed her husband as he walked up and put his arm around her.

"Let's stay focused," Clement said to the group. "Our objective is to observe these people and see what their function is, and identify if they're even human. We'll split up into pairs, spread ourselves out, and observe. Make for the settlement from three different directions, and stay in touch via your ear coms." Clement held his up so they could see it and then placed it in his ear.

Clement stayed the central course toward the settlement with Yan, while Mika and Ivan went to the right, with Telco and Pomeroy flanking left.

"It *is* beautiful here," Yan said as they made their way across the flat, grassy ground together in the dappled sunlight of Bellus. It was like pictures of the autumn season on the core planets that he had seen in school, only here, it had that golden-red glow all the time.

"Let's not get distracted," said Clement.

She responded by taking his hand as they walked. "Don't you ever enjoy a moment of peace and quiet?"

"Not when I'm exploring an unknown world filled with unknown people for the first time," he retorted, but he didn't pull his hand away. "For all we know they could think humans are delicious."

"Well, if you eat the right parts, I suppose that they are."

He shook his head in frustration at her. "You make my job very difficult, Yan," he said. She just smiled as they walked.

Presently they found themselves on softer ground. There were tall stalks of plant life ahead of them that had seemingly arranged themselves in a rough but orderly way. Clement stopped and kicked at the ground. It showed signs of having been recently turned.

"This is a crop field," he said, pushing his way through the plant stalks.

"How can you be sure?" asked Yan.

"I grew up on an agrarian planet, remember?"

He grabbed one of the stalks and pulled it toward him. It looked familiar. He ripped open a husk and it revealed the treasure inside. He showed it to Yan.

"This is corn," she said. "A hybrid I don't recognize, but undoubtedly corn."

Clement tapped his earpiece and got on his com. "We've found crops," he said. "Looks like an Earth-type corn. I'm afraid we have to assume that these camps were either from an earlier colonization, or from a military operation of some kind. Raise your awareness, and make sure your sidearms are loaded." The others all reported the same type of findings back, with crops like pumpkin, cabbage, and cauliflower. This definitely seemed like an Earth-seeded colony.

When Clement emerged from the cornfield, he made his way to Yan, who was staring at an amber glow of light a few hundred yards in the distance. "Yan, what are you—"

"Shhh—" she said, finger to her mouth. "Listen." She took him by the hand again.

In the distance, Clement could hear what amounted to the gentle splashing of water, and something else. The sound of what appeared to be a woman's voice.

She was singing.

They crawled to within about ten meters of what was clearly a water pond, hiding themselves in the tall grass. An amber glow came from the water, some form of bioluminescence it seemed, which lit up the pond around its edges. The singing was louder here, a lilting, content, and even evocative high sound. It was almost like the voice was in a state of harmony with the bioluminescent life-forms. They glowed brighter and warmer with each rising of her song.

Clement and Yan cleared some of the grass, to get a glimpse of what was making such a beautiful noise.

"There," Yan pointed. Across the small pond a creature was standing in the water, halfway immersed in the amber glow. It had long gray or white hair, a skin tone that matched the amber of the water, and it was playing as it sang, gently splashing the water. Then it turned to face them, looking around as if it had heard a noise.

It didn't take a genius to figure out they were staring at a woman, a humanoid woman. Two rounded and very feminine breasts danced buoyantly in the light as she resumed her playing and singing. Her rib cage was positioned exactly as a human woman's would be. She had two long arms, two legs, shoulders, and even a belly button. Her pubis was covered in the same fine white hair as was on her head. She frolicked in the water, diving in and then popping back up, swimming back and forth from side to side.

"Do you think—" started Clement, whispering, before Yan covered his mouth with her hand.

The creature stopped for a moment, looking in their direction as if it heard something again. They both hid, trying not to be detected. After a moment, the singing and splashing of the water resumed again. Clement looked to Yan and then leaned in to whisper in her ear, even quieter than before.

"That's a woman," he said. And she was, a beautiful, youthful, and very human-looking woman. Yan just nodded as he pulled back and they resumed observing her.

She played for a few more minutes and then decided to lie down on a sandy beach on the far side of the pond. They watched as she ran her hands through her long, wet hair, then she settled back on her elbows. After a few minutes of this, she lay down completely flat. They watched as a hand slid down her body, to her pubis, and she began a gentle rubbing of the area.

"No!" whispered Yan. This time Clement covered *her* mouth. They watched her together, the two of them moving closer together with each passing second, as the woman slowly pleasured herself, reaching her climax within a few short minutes.

As she lay basking in the afterglow, a new rustling came

from the tall grass. A male emerged, the same amber skin, the same white-colored hair. She rose and greeted him with a passionate kiss, wrapping her arms around his neck. After a moment of kissing and rising passion, they ran into the pond to play together, hand in hand. "Well," whispered Yan, "They do make them handsome here on this world."

"You mean they make them hung," he whispered back. Yan smiled playfully at Clement, then reached out to him.

"No need for embarrassment," she said. She slid closer to him, and he looked at her. She was beautiful, and what was going on in the pond was epically romantic. They continued to watch together as the couple engaged in flagrant and unabashed lovemaking, with her straddling him as he entered her, holding her just above the water line of the pond, her hands on his shoulders.

Several minutes passed as the couple engaged in a rousing session of sex play, including multiple positions and vigorous exertion on both their parts. When the moment of climax came they embraced each other, then slowly slid back into the water together. The amber glitter of the bioluminescence in the pool seemed drawn to them and they slowly rolled together in the afterglow.

"It's bliss," whispered Yan, holding Clement as close as he would let her. After a few more minutes of kissing, the couple left the pond together, hand in hand, chattering in a peculiar language as they walked off into the distance.

Clement looked to Yan and she leaned in and kissed him hard before he could stop her, and frankly, he didn't want to. He was aroused to the point of wanting to just let go with her, but he stopped himself.

"Not an option, Commander," he said. "You know that."

She blew out a hard breath of frustration and rolled onto her back, looking up at the stars. "Now I understand why you drink," she said. He was about to respond when they were both surprised by the flushed faces of Ivan Massif and Mika Ori looking down on them.

"Did you see that?" exclaimed Mika in a whispered voice. Both Clement and Yan scrambled to their feet. Mika and Ivan both had the warm glow of sex about them. They had clearly experienced the same inspiration as the couple and had acted on it. Who was he kidding? They always acted on it.

"We did," answered Clement, running his free hand through his hair. "Obviously."

"I see you two were inspired by the...display," commented Yan as she tidied up her tunic.

"How could you not be?" said Mika, smiling from ear to ear. "Weren't you?"

Clement shook his head. "Command protocol, and all that," he said.

"I can't believe you let that get in the way," teased Mika.

"As if you two need any excuse," said Clement, looking around, hoping to change the subject. "Where are Telco and Pomeroy?"

"Busy, if they were watching," joked Mika.

"I doubt that. Pomeroy prefers women," Clement said, then hit his com to call them. There was no answer for several minutes until Pomeroy came on, quite breathlessly.

"We'll be with you...in a few minutes," she said, then cut the line.

"Apparently she's had a change of heart," said Yan impishly. Clement just looked perplexed. When the two finally appeared they both looked as though they'd had a hot and heavy encounter. Clement ordered Telco to raise the ship and get a report, and he walked off to do so, while the rest of them interrogated Pomeroy.

"Um, that's not . . . like you, typically, is it?" started Clement.

"No, it's not," agreed Pomeroy. "I've played with Telco before, but with another woman present. I do have a theory though. That bioluminescent organism, it appeared to have an effect on our randy couple, and on me," she said. "I mean, I'm not normally attracted to men, but I couldn't keep my hands off Telco. Permission to take a sample, sir?"

"Of?" replied Clement, smirking.

Pomeroy sighed. "The bioluminescence, of course," she said.

"Granted," replied Clement. Pomeroy stormed off to the pond.

At Telco's return he reported back that everything was normal at the ship. This gave Clement free reign to explore further.

"So what do we do next?" asked Yan. Clement nodded as Pomeroy returned with her water samples.

"We go on," he said. "And follow our randy friends to their home."

"And then?" asked Yan. Clement shrugged his shoulders, looking around at his crew of intrepid explorers.

"We make contact."

❈ 15 ❈

Twenty minutes later and they were looking down on a large camp of rounded huts made of wood and dried straw. There was a path that led into the center of the camp where a bonfire burned in a pit with several people gathered around it. Men, women, and children dressed in simple clothing chattered around the fire in their language, eating, drinking, and socializing. The rounded huts went off into the distance, as did multiple pathways, and there were many other bonfires burning off in the distance.

Clement signaled his troupe to the ground with a silent hand gesture. He whispered to his team to keep their chances of being exposed to a minimum. "Observations," he said, looking from each one of his team to other. Pomeroy spoke first, quietly.

"This is clearly a simple culture. They don't seem to want for much in terms of food, fresh water, and the like. They obviously learned at some point how to cultivate crops, and the near-constant climate gives them no great challenges to overcome. The food is always plentiful, the water always flows . . . " She trailed off.

"In other words, no upward pressure on their society to move forward?" observed Clement.

Pomeroy nodded. "No need for innovation, no need to evolve, no new discoveries to kick them in the butt to move their culture upwards."

"Sounds like paradise," said Yan.

"If you're a type B personality," commented Clement.

"This lack of innovation may be bred into them over many generations," offered Pomeroy.

Clement turned to Telco, looking for a different perspective. "What do you see, Ensign?"

Telco looked around for a moment. "Looks like a stable society. No obvious predators. And the people seem happy," he said.

"Observe. Estimate the population," ordered Clement.

Telco took a few seconds to look around them. "I'd estimate around fifty of the huts. Seven to eight people per structure, so say population of this village would be around three hundred fifty."

Clement shook his head. "Look again." The closest bonfire had fifteen to twenty people around it with five huts nearby. There were several young couples going in and out of each hut, children running about from hut to hut, people moving around at a frequent pace. "I'd say more like ten to twelve people per hut, multiple families in each, or at least multiple sex partners. My best guess would be that we have a population of at least five hundred."

Telco nodded. "I see it now, sir," he acknowledged.

Anthropology lesson over, Clement turned to Ivan Massif. "Thoughts, Navigator?"

Massif pointed to the sky. "See that dark object?" They all looked skyward. There were affirmative grunts all around. "That's the next planet in, Alphus. My guess is it will partially obscure the Trinity star in about twenty hours. That will create a significant twilight at that time. The two inner planets also provide a nighttime obscurity on a regular, periodic schedule. I can calculate it when we get back."

"So it will get dark? Or darker," stated Yan.

"As close to dark as it gets here. Remember, all these planets are tidal-locked to the star, the same face toward the sun at all times. But with the planets so close together, I'm sure there are multiple occultations happening all the time. That would be an opportune time to return and observe, and perhaps introduce ourselves."

Clement agreed. "Let's come back at that time and evaluate what we have here," he said.

"But we're here now," said Yan.

"And we can come back," replied Clement. "I think this trip has been, uh, eventful as it is. Let's take what we have and get back to our ship. Agreed?"

They all nodded.

"Any chance of stopping by that pond one more time on the way back?" said Mika, impishly.

"You're insatiable," said Clement, shaking his head as he stood, then signaled his team to move out.

They were halfway back to the pontoon boat when Nobli called in his alert. They'd picked up a drone on the scanners, heading their way.

"Lock the ship down, we'll be back as soon as we can

get there," ordered Clement. Nobli acknowledged and Clement ordered his team to double-time back to the boat. Once aboard they shoved off quickly and headed downriver, but Clement ordered Telco to slow to half speed. Metal objects moving at speed could easily be picked up by a sophisticated drone, and Clement had to assume the Earth Ark builders had sophisticated military equipment.

The ride was tense as Nobli called in periodic updates. The drone ended up passing about thirty klicks south of their location, but if it were using an overlapping orbit to try and detect the *Beauregard*, it would move farther north in latitude on the next pass, and depending on the size of the overlap, it *could* detect the ship on the next pass.

"We have to take precautions," he said to Yan after he ordered Telco to push the boat to full speed.

"What about action against the drone? Can we take it out?" she asked.

"That could give away both our presence and our position."

"Could?" Clement shrugged.

"It would be a risk," Nobli said.

"What about using our own drone to take it out before it gets near the ship?"

Clement looked at her. "They probably have more than one, so we would just end up without a drone. It would put us at a disadvantage," he said in a dismissive tone. Clement was a man who had been in many battles. Yan clearly was not, and as much as he liked her, the gap in their combat experience was still vast. Yan gave him a sour look.

"I'm just trying to be helpful," she said.

"I understand," said Clement, then turned his attention back to the progress of the boat.

They arrived back at the *Beauregard* a few minutes later. Clement ordered his crew to prep for discovery by the drone on its next pass, which would be in thirty-two minutes.

"What are your orders, Captain?" said Nobli, thankfully relinquishing command back to his friend.

Clement took Nobli to the side. "If we shut down the *Beauregard*, went completely dark, what are the odds that drone would detect the ship?"

"I'd say less than fifty-fifty, but if we went completely cold it could take us up to three hours to refire the ship," the engineer said.

"Understood. But right now I'd take those odds over being discovered by that Earth Ark and her troops. And there's another complication. We discovered natives. They appear human, or at least humanoid," Clement said.

An astonished look crossed Nobli's face. "Natives? Human natives? You mean colonists, don't you?"

Clement shook his head. "I'm not so sure unless they were biologically modified for this planet in some way. We need to know more. I'm thinking that we should abandon the ship temporarily, and perhaps mix in with them, to study them some more. What do you think?"

"I think this mission has gone seriously off-kilter," said Nobli.

"Can't disagree with you there. Give me a number. How long to go cold?"

"If I shut down everything, maybe two hours before

the ship's radiation signatures would dissipate to background levels."

"That's close enough for me."

At that Clement brought the entire crew together in the clearing outside the ship. "The Earth Ark drone will pass over us in"—he looked down at his watch—"twenty-eight minutes. I'm ordering Engineer Nobli to shut down the *Beauregard* completely, to go cold, essentially. That will aid us in avoiding detection, but it's no guarantee. It will take approximately two hours for the ship to go completely cold, and we will require up to three hours to refire her and get her back into action once we return. So, there is a risk if we are attacked. My plan is for us to spread out into small groups of three to four individuals, and, using the natural wood and brush from the planet, light small fires to make it appear as though we are a small settlement of natives. Don't use any devices that would burn hotter than a natural fire. This should distract from any residual heat signatures the ship will be emitting and hopefully the drone will just pass us by. Once the drone has passed we'll begin the journey to the native encampment and try to contact the natives there. If they are friendly, we should be able to mix in with them and keep ourselves safe for a while."

"To what end?" questioned Yan. "I mean, what's our ultimate goal here?"

Clement looked to his first officer. "To keep the Earth Ark from detecting us and to determine what their mission in the Trinity system really is, then to try and counter it," he said.

"What about getting home?" asked Ensign Adebayor from the crowd.

"Getting home is our ultimate consideration," said Clement. "Survival is our immediate one. Since we are no longer under the protection of the flag of the 5 Suns Alliance Navy, we have to assume they will consider us as hostile as well. It seems likely that the navy, or rather, Fleet Admiral DeVore, never intended us to survive our first contact with the Earth Ark, which they surely knew we would encounter. So the question now is, what exactly is 'home' for us at this moment?"

"That's a question for another day," cut in Yan. Clement was thankful for her assistance in swaying the crew.

"Any further questions?" Clement stared down the crew, looking at each member, trying to detect dissent. He found none. "Then let's get started." He checked his watch again. "We now have twenty-five minutes. Form small groups, spread out and light fires, but be sure not to use anything that would give off an artificial heat signature. We want that drone to think of us just like the natives, not a sophisticated navy crew. Go!" he commanded, then raised his voice. "And be sure and take firearms, personal rations for three days, and any equipment that might come in handy in assessing the natives, as long as it carries a low energy signature." he said. And with that they all scattered.

With seven minutes to go Nobli sealed up the *Beauregard* and then was off with his group. Clement, Yan, Pomeroy, and Telco made a foursome and started away from the ship on the near bank of the river. Telco had covered the pontoon boat under shrubs and grasses. Clement observed small fires burning bright against the dimming sky as one of the two inner planets of the

Trinity system was partially obscuring the star, making for a brief twilight effect. He sat down around the campfire next to Yan.

Telco for his part was following Pomeroy around like a puppy dog, no doubt enamored by her after their brief solo affair at the pond. Pomeroy seemed indifferent to his presence as she was no doubt returning to her previous preferences for female companionship, now free of the aphrodisiac effects of the pond bioluminescence. But she kept the young ensign busy with small tasks like collecting wood for the fire while she set up some of her biological-testing equipment.

Yan sat silently next to Clement as he tried to track the Earth Ark drone with conventional field glasses. He had a pair with him that had been a memento of his father's time in the 5 Suns Alliance service and he'd grabbed them on his way out of the ship. Any powered glasses could have no doubt been detected by the passing drone.

"She should have passed over by now," he said, "but I didn't see her."

"Perhaps you're not as good with those as you thought," Yan said.

Clement dropped the glasses and looked at her. "I used to track communications satellites with these, home back on Ceta, when I was a kid. They're good enough. And any drone moving on a straight-line course should be detectable with the naked eye, let alone an assisted one," he said, then returned to his tracking. The "night" sky of Bellus was clear enough and dark enough that detection should have been possible, unless the drone was specifically designed for stealth, which a military one might be.

"There she is!" said Clement, pointing at the sky, picking up the drone and tracking her across the starfield. "She's moving fast and she's low, maybe fifteen hundred meters or léss. She may not detect us at all," he said. Presently he handed Yan the glasses and directed her where to look.

"I see her," said Yan. "Can she even detect us at that speed?"

"She can probably detect the fires, but I doubt she'd be able to take a count of our personnel. We'll probably just show up as a series of heat-signature blobs unless they really enhance the images. That could take hours of work, assuming they have similar technology to ours, and I doubt they'd bother if there's nothing anomalous on the scans. Her vector should take her well north of us on the next pass. We should be safe, for now."

Yan handed him back the glasses as he tracked the drone until she disappeared over the horizon. Clement got on the com system and declared the all-clear and for his team of twenty-two souls to re-form.

"Telco, Pomeroy, Yan, and I will head up the river to the settlement in the pontoon boat and make first contact with the natives. Ivan and Mika can direct the rest of you to the camp. That will give us about five hours to smooth things over with the natives before you arrive. Be aware of your surroundings at all times and don't take any chances. This planet seems like a paradise, with no large predators of any kind, but be on alert. Again, small groups would be best; spread out and then gather at the observation point above the settlement and wait for instructions from one of us. Good luck, and we'll see you at the camp," he said.

With that the four of them loaded the pontoon boat with the equipment Pomeroy had brought from the ship, started the motor and shoved off for the settlement. A few minutes in and the twilight sky was glowing amber.

"This is almost romantic," Yan said, leaning into him with her body. Clement nodded, but he didn't encourage her to come closer.

"Almost," he said, looking to the sky.

"Almost."

❊ **16** ❊

They stowed the boat and covered it near the same riverbank they had landed on the first time and made their way back toward the settlement camp. It was darker than before due to the occlusion of the inner planets, and walking was slower this time around. They arrived at the pond once again and Pomeroy stopped to take some additional samples of the water. The bioluminescence was even brighter than before and bathed them all in its amber glow. Clement detected a scent he hadn't before, sweet and aromatic, and it created a taste in his mouth, almost like vanilla. He noticed Yan lingering near him, touching his skin at every opportunity. He found himself aroused by her mere presence, but he fought off any baser thoughts and tried to focus on the mission at hand. It was difficult.

As they departed from the pond to head to the settlement he took Pomeroy aside.

"This bioluminescence, it has an airborne component, doesn't it?" he asked.

"Yes, I think so. I'll have to conduct some more tests, but I'm pretty sure it's got an aphrodisiac quality to it," she replied.

"No doubt about that. Plus, I smelled a vanilla scent, even tasted it in my mouth." She nodded.

"I did as well. And Ensign Telco's biceps were looking pretty tempting to me again," she joked.

"I wonder if that could be natural?"

"You mean my attraction to Telco? Unlikely."

Clement shook his head. "No, I meant the bioluminescent aphrodisiac," he deadpanned.

"Oh. I don't know," she admitted. "I'll need time to set up my equipment to come to any conclusions, but it certainly is a convenient coincidence if you wanted people to be fruitful and multiply."

"Well, I hope we can get you that time when we reach the settlement."

"Aye, sir," she said as they walked on.

A few minutes later they gathered on the outskirts of the settlement camp, looking down on the communal fire from a nearby hillside. Things had gone quiet coincident with the occultation of the Trinity star. It was noticeably darker, and it seemed many of the tribe must have been sleeping. Clement looked at his team.

"Yan and I will go in first and see how they greet us. You two will follow once I give the signal. Stay out in the open but out of the camp until I signal you in. We won't know how they will react to strangers until, well, until we know. If anything goes wrong . . . "

"Understood, sir," said Pomeroy, tapping her sidearm cobra pistol. Clement nodded and took Yan by the hand, trying to look as friendly as possible as they made their way toward the dwindling bonfire at the center of the first group of huts.

"Trying to start something, sir?" Yan teased.

Clement shook his head. "I think you know my stance on that by now, Commander. Just trying to look as friendly as possible to meet the natives."

As they approached the camp there were only three people in a rough circle around the fire, which was attended by an older woman with distinctly gray hair and a couple of young children, a boy and a girl, perhaps only five standard years old or so. The woman had loose-fitting clothing that appeared to be woven covering her body. When she saw Clement and Yan approaching she stood up and chattered something to the children, then raised her voice slightly. People began to stir in the huts at the sound of her voice. Clement and Yan came right up to the fire as she stared at them approaching her, still holding hands. They stood there, smiling, as adults and children of various ages started coming out of the huts. The looks on their faces were ones of astonishment and curiosity. They talked amongst themselves, looking and pointing fingers at the two strangers.

"Their language . . . " started Yan, "I can almost make out . . . it sounds similar to Old Imperial Korean, like the twenty-second-century language we found on the Ark."

"Can you talk to them?"

"I'll try," said Yan. She stepped forward, toward the bonfire, and said words Clement didn't understand to them. There were surprised looks, then a few laughs.

"What did you say?" asked Clement.

"I tried to say that we are friends, and asked if they would welcome us. Obviously, I got something wrong."

"Try again."

Yan turned to them again and spoke. This time there were nods and more smiles.

"I told them there were about twenty of us coming, and could they accommodate us," she said.

A young woman stepped forward and spoke to Yan in their language. "What did she say?" asked Clement.

"I think . . . she wants to know if we're the ones who were watching her at the pond," Yan said. "I guess we weren't as quiet as we thought."

"I guess not. Tell her it was you and I. Be honest," Clement said.

Yan spoke again, and the girl laughed, then turned to the gathering crowd and spoke to them, and then they all laughed. She turned back to Yan and said something else.

"She wants to know if we enjoyed watching them," said Yan, turning to Clement with a smirk on her face. Clement just shrugged; he couldn't keep himself from smiling, embarrassed they had been found out. Yan stated a positive response, and the crowd laughed again. Then the woman came forward and gave Yan a hug.

"Ask them if we are welcome. Tell them we are here to learn about their people," said Clement.

Yan, still in the girl's arms, asked her question. There were nods and welcome grunts all around. The girl pulled away from Yan, who was quickly surrounded by people touching her dark hair and coveralls, and came to Clement. She hugged him and then kissed him on the cheek, leading him by the hand back to the gathering crowd around the fire.

Fifteen minutes later they were sitting around the fire eating berries, some sort of baked cake, and fruits. Yan was conversing with the girl, whom Clement decided to call Mary. Clement had used his com to call in Pomeroy and Telco, and had relayed the friendliness of the natives to the rest of his approaching crew.

Communication was slow as Yan was the only one with the necessary language skills. Pomeroy had set up her equipment and was busy running tests, taking DNA swab samples from willing natives. Ensign Telco was very popular with the ladies, who seemed enamored with his dark hair and large, broad shoulders. He was taller than most of the males at six foot four. The men seemed to average about six one, the women were tall at five nine or five ten. There was a general uniformity of looks as well: the amber-toned skin, light hair, and they were almost all, both male and female, good-looking and well proportioned. Clement had his suspicions about these people and their origins, but he was willing to wait on Pomeroy's test results before expressing them. And one other oddity was that they had no proper names, at least not that Yan could figure out.

Within a few hours the rest of the crew arrived and Clement had them spread out among the settlement, to make friends and learn what they could. Mary, for her part, stayed with him and Yan almost exclusively, inviting others over when Yan had a question she could not answer.

After a few hours of questioning a picture of the settlers was beginning to form. They referred to themselves as the descendants of the "First Landers." It was unclear what this meant, and they had very little concept of numbers, but Clement and Yan suspected that the First Landers were the original group of colonists who had come to Bellus from "somewhere else," probably Earth, they surmised. It appeared as though the original colony had failed and the survivors had spread out until they occupied a large portion of the fruitful plain they lived on. They also were told of the "Hill Place," where the original colony had either been or had a base. Clement determined they would make a trek to the Hill Place in due time, if it could be found.

As one of the inner worlds occulted the Trinity star again and things began to get darker, the crowd quieted down and returned to their huts to sleep or conduct other activities, taking many of their new companions from the *Beauregard* with them. Mary, however, took Yan by the hand and started with her out of the camp, toward the pond.

"Going somewhere together?" asked Clement mischievously.

Yan turned back, smirking. "Oh," she said, "are you jealous?"

Clement looked at Mary and her barely-there clothing. "Very," he said. "These people seem to have a remarkably open sexuality."

"So I've noticed." Yan turned back and spoke to Mary, who chattered back at her, smiling. "She said you can come along, if you'd like," said Yan. Clement looked to Yan and the beautiful Mary.

"I don't want to be the third wheel—" he was interrupted by Mary's chattering again. Yan said something back to her, and the conversation went on like that, back and forth for a few moments.

"I think she feels sorry for you."

Clement hung his head. "I feel sorry for me too." He waved them on, then turned toward one of the beds in an empty hut. "Good night, Commander."

"I want you to know this is only for anthropological research," Yan said as he walked away.

"Of course it is," he said. Then Mary giggled, and the two women sauntered off together.

When Clement awoke he was still alone in the hut and it was "day," or what passed for daytime, outside. He rose and went to the communal food tray and ate. Eventually Yan turned up.

"You're awake," she said. "I guess you wouldn't have been much fun last night. You needed the rest, hmm?" He looked at his watch.

"I slept a standard eight hours," he said.

"Well, that's not standard for them. Mary was awake after three hours, as soon as it got lighter. I managed another two after that. I'm guessing this constant light-and-dark cycle plays hell with their circadian rhythms," she replied.

Clement gave her a quizzical look. "It doesn't seem to affect them. They seem to rest when they want to," he said.

"Yes." Yan looked up at the gentle salmon-colored sky. "Maybe this is Paradise," she said.

"Could be. Um, does Paradise have a latrine?" Yan smiled and pointed behind the row of huts.

"That way," she said.

Clement nodded. "When I get back I want to form a team and find this 'Hill Place.'"

"We'll be here, Captain," she said, smiling again.

After concluding his business, Clement called his team together and picked himself, Yan, Mary, Pomeroy, and Telco to go to the Hill Place. Mary assured them (through Yan) that she could find it. Pomeroy loaded up Telco with her technical equipment and Clement added a penetrating sonic radar–mapping kit. The young ensign took it all in stride.

On the way up, Pomeroy informed him of her initial test results.

"As you may have suspected, they are absolutely human in every way, but they seem to have been specifically adapted to this world, down to the melanin in their skin and the size of their eyes to adjust to the slightly darker sun," she said.

"Are they clones?" Clement asked.

Pomeroy shook her head no. "More likely . . . genetically engineered specifically for this world," she said.

"A eugenics program?" Pomeroy responded with a shrug.

"I'm no history expert, but it does seem to be in line with what Yan tells me about this ancient Korean empire on Earth."

Clement thought on that for a moment, then:

"What do you think the purpose was in putting them here? If we assume this planet, and perhaps the others, Alphus and Camus, were seeded with human life, what was the intended outcome?" he asked.

Pomeroy got a frown on her face. "I can only conclude they were put here as an advance population, a workforce of some kind."

Clement nodded. "Slaves?" he questioned. "But why such a long gap between the original seeding and the arrival of an overlord force? According to what Mary said last night they have been here for many generations."

"Could be lots of reasons. War back home, technological setback, a natural disaster on Earth. We just don't know. But it seems likely the people here were abandoned for at least a couple of centuries."

"Until now."

"Until now," she agreed.

"And now the masters have come back to claim their property, and the only thing that stands in their way, is us," said Clement, pointing at his chest.

"For the moment," replied Pomeroy. Clement thanked her and then caught up with Yan and Mary, who were busy chatting as they held hands, walking up the trail together.

"Can you ask her how much farther it is to the Hill Place?" said Clement. Yan chattered to Mary and Mary responded with a shrug.

"She said 'a bit more distance,' if that helps?"

Clement shook his head. "It does not."

By Clement's watch it took another thirty minutes of crisscrossing switchbacks before they reached a flat mountain plain. Another ten minutes after that and they finally reached the Hill Place.

What they found was an abandoned bunker of stone and concrete with a glass dome that had collapsed over years of decay. The bunker sat on a high rock ledge, looking out over the fertile valley below. Clement led the team to an overlook where he used his field glasses to survey the terrain below. It was low, flat land broken only by rivers and the occasional dot of light representing the odd settlement or two. Presently he handed the glasses to Telco. "What do you make of that plain, Ensign?"

Telco scanned the valley from left to right. "I'd say it's about one hundred fifty klicks across, sir. I count about a dozen settlements of various sizes, but there are probably more."

"Estimated population?" Telco put the glasses down and turned to his commander.

"Judging by the size of our camp, I'd estimate up to fifteen thousand, sir," he said.

Clement nodded approval at Telco's assessment and then proceeded inside the bunker with the rest of the team. The ruin was essentially empty, with very little in the way of equipment or any kind of recognizable technology. He ordered Yan and Pomeroy to spread out while he and Telco explored what seemed to be the main nerve center of the base. After thirty minutes of fruitless searching, he called them both back.

"Anything?" he asked.

"I found what appeared to be a space for a possible birthing center, a large refrigeration chamber, and the like. Beyond that . . . " She trailed off.

"Yan?"

"What looked like probable barracks for about thirty people. I suspect this was originally a camp for scientists. Probably where the original colony was set up. I'd speculate that as the population grew they were eventually sent down into the valley to live. This base was probably evacuated once it became clear that a follow-up mission wasn't forthcoming," she said.

"They couldn't survive up here—no place for growing crops and the like. Once they ran out of rations they had no choice but to join the populace on the valley floor. Eventually, the succeeding generations likely forgot what their original mission even was," speculated Clement.

"That does fit with what Mary has told me of their legends surrounding this place."

Clement looked at the three women, then turned to Telco. "Get me that sonic-mapping kit," he said to the young ensign. Telco responded quickly by unpacking the device and assembling it, then powered it up and handed it to Clement. Yan sent the ensign out to keep watch on the valley below while the adults continued their survey. Mary followed Telco back outside, apparently uninterested in what they were doing in the lab.

Clement turned the device around the room. It showed nothing but rock and concrete, except for one wall. "What do you make of this, Pomeroy?" he asked his science tech.

She came over and he handed her the bulky device. She scanned the wall at eye level, then took a few steps toward the wall. "I see a doorway, sir, covered up by the concrete." Then she pointed the device to the floor. "I can definitely make out a stairway leading down, sir, but the range of this device is only about ten meters."

"Down to where?" asked Yan.

Clement came up and confirmed Pomeroy's reading, then changed the mode of the device to deep-penetrating radar and handed it back to her.

"Try it now," he said.

Pomeroy looked down again, then let out a soft gasp of surprise. "Jesus, sir! There's all kinds of superstructure here, likely metal, beneath us, up the hill—Christ, it's all around us like latticework, sir!"

Clement nodded. It was what he had expected to find. He had Pomeroy give the device to Yan for a third view.

"This is an arcology," she confirmed. "An engineered structure."

"Pomeroy, how high is this 'hill'?" asked Clement.

"My measurements from the camp were twelve hundred meters, sir, almost precisely," she said.

"And this laboratory?"

"Three hundred fifty meters up, sir."

Clement nodded his head. "This entire hill, this mountain, is artificial."

"But to what purpose?" asked Yan.

"That's to be determined, Commander. One thing is sure, though: Earth did not have the technology to build this kind of structure back when the 5 Suns colonies were founded four centuries ago." He instructed Pomeroy to record the scans she was making and save all the telemetry for further analysis.

As Pomeroy was finishing her scans Clement was about to give further orders when he heard Telco calling them from the ledge. They scrambled out together.

"Something going on at the far side of the valley, sir," he said, handing Clement the field glasses. Clement looked to where Telco had pointed. There was a flashing of light and the distant crackle of ordnance, with smoke rising from the ground. Clement looked to the red-sunset sky. Streaks of yellow could be seen heading for the ground, descending through the thick, warm atmosphere.

"What is it?" asked Yan.

Clement scanned the sky. Dozens of ships were descending now. "Beachhead. They're landing," he said. "Ensign Telco, you and Lieutenant Pomeroy will stay here and man this observation post until relieved. I want details on the scale of this landing. Commander Yan and the native and I will return to the camp and began prepping the people for evacuation. Stay sharp, both of you, and be prepared to make for the ship at a moment's notice."

"Aye, sir," they both responded.

He handed the glasses back to Telco.

"Do you think they'll come here, sir?" asked Pomeroy.

"I hope not. But we have to be prepared. Do your duty. Keep track of the amount of force they're bringing to bear. I'll be in touch by com at the first opportunity after we assess the people's ability to evacuate."

Yan looked to Mary. "They may not even understand the concept of an attack. They've lived in peace and harmony for generations," she said.

"Then you'll have to help them understand," he replied, then took her by the arm as they moved out, Mary trailing a few steps behind them.

"How can I do that? They don't understand complex concepts like war, or even a ship from space," Yan said.

"We have to protect them any way we can, Yan. This is not merely a landing by the Earth Ark forces, it's an invasion," he said. Then he let her go, and they started swiftly back down the mountainside.

✦ 17 ✦

Telco called in and reported that landings had occurred near three of the larger native settlements in the valley, but he couldn't be sure what the size and scope of the invasion force was, or what the Earth Ark troops were doing with the people. Clement had his suspicions.

Once back in camp Clement ordered Yan to work with Mary to address the people and warn them of what would no doubt be an impending attack. Most of the natives in the camp just looked confused by what they were told. Explaining things the settlers had no concept of was proving difficult. After a few minutes of watching and observing and feeling useless, Clement took Nobli aside.

"Hassan, what's the possibility of getting our drone up to surveil the Earth Ark forces? Find out what they're up to?"

"Well, none at the moment, sir. We'll have to get back to the ship and fire her auxiliary power unit up before we can activate the drone. And even then I'd recommend a high-altitude surveillance. It would lessen the chances that the drone would be picked up by the enemy. If they're engaged in rounding these people up and putting them to work as slave labor, I doubt they'll be paying much attention to the sky."

"But they still know that we're in the system somewhere, and they'll be keeping an eye out for us. I want to get a technical team together ASAP and get back to the ship and warm her up. We may have to leave the planet at a moment's notice. Take Adebayor, Mika, and Ivan with you; they could come in handy if we have to leave in a hurry. I'll send the technical personnel back as well, and any natives that will heed our warning. Prepare some space for them in the cargo bay. We may have some passengers," said Clement.

"Aye, sir."

With that Clement went to find Yan and Mary. The conversations with the native people were difficult, as they simply had no understanding of what an attack from space was. They were a peaceful people, with no needs or wants, and the concept was just completely foreign to them. Telco's last report indicated that three camps had been assaulted but further incursions seemed to have stopped for the moment. The Earth Ark crew appeared to be consolidating their positions before advancing, but Clement had little doubt that they would. He ordered Telco and Pomeroy to come back down from the Hill Place and prep the pontoon boat for an evacuation.

Within two hours most of the crew was gone on their way back to the *Beauregard* and only Mary seemed willing to go with them from the natives, and that seemed to be mostly related to her attachment to Yan. He ordered the last of his people to the pontoon boat, but told Yan to tell Mary to stay behind with her people. The native girl seemed disappointed, but she gave Yan a very sensual kiss goodbye and then made off for her camp.

Telco and Pomeroy arrived presently and with that they made for the pontoon boat and loaded up. They headed back to the ship as fast as the boat would go. Clement, for his part, could only be concerned about the native people he had left behind. They were complete innocents, and they would be no match for the Earth Ark troops, when and if they came.

Once back in camp at the *Beauregard* Clement ordered the boat to be abandoned, except for the engine, in case they returned and wanted to use it again. Telco wasn't happy at leaving his innovation behind, but started working on removing the engine immediately.

Nobli got the APU working and refired the drone, sending it up to a high orbit, then set its course for a pass over the three settlements the Earth Ark forces had attacked. They waited for reconnaissance photos to be downloaded from the drone. Nobli handed him the first one and Clement placed it down on a light table. It was not promising.

The settlements had been completely destroyed, likely by Directed Energy Weapons from space by the pattern of the burn marks. There was a single fenced-in area that stood as a prison yard, and Clement estimated close to two thousand potential slave workers were inside the barriers.

"Preparing the prisoners for work camps," said Clement. Nobli nodded.

Yan sighed. "Is this their destiny now?"

"Not if I can help it," said Clement. "These areas here and here"—he pointed to a group of large equipment stacks—"they look like heavy-drilling equipment, possibly for oil and mining operations."

"We know where they're going to get their workforce," said Nobli, irritated. "How do we stop them?"

"First, we get this ship powered up. Then we get her back in the air, and take it from there," responded Clement. He looked to his engineer. "How long?"

Nobli checked his watch. "Forty-five minutes estimated to operational status, sir. But then I'd like to run readiness checks, especially on the, uh, weapons system," he said.

"No time," replied Clement. "Every second we're on the ground our heat signature gives us away as an artificial object, a potential target. Get her up and running, and you have my release to cut any corners you like. While we're on the ground here we're sitting ducks."

"Aye, sir," said Nobli.

Clement looked to Yan. "We may be in for a rough ride. I want the whole bridge crew ready in half an hour, Commander," he said, returning to the formal use of her rank to indicate his seriousness with the situation.

"Understood, Captain," she said, then hesitated. "Are you ever going to talk to me about the new weapon you have devised?"

Clement shook his head. "Not now, Commander," he said, then walked away from her.

Thirty-two minutes later and the bridge crew was assembled with Yan at her station, Mika and Ivan at helm and navigation, and Ensign Adebayor at the engineering station. Clement took his command couch and called down on the com to Ensign Telco in the missile room.

"Prep conventional ordnance, Ensign," he said. "But don't load the launch tubes. I don't want us going down with our belly full up with live warheads."

"Understood, sir," replied Telco. "Conventional missiles will be ready on your order, sir, but not until."

Satisfied, Clement called down to his engineer to check on the drive and his new weapon.

"All drives are humming, sir. I can give you Xenon thrusters, the main Ion plasma drive, or the LEAP drive at your discretion, Captain. We can really go at any time now," said Nobli.

"And the weapon?" said Clement, quietly.

"Same status as the engines, sir."

"Confirmed, Engineer," he said, then signed off. He hit the ship-wide com. "All stations, prepare for launch. I say again, prepare for launch. Be advised the ship may come under attack at any time. Be ready. That is all," he stated. He turned to Yan. "Final report, Exec."

"My board is green, Captain," said Yan. Clement turned to Mika Ori at the helm.

"Take us up, Pilot," he ordered.

"Aye, sir," she replied, then started the launch process. She took the ship nearly straight up using the thrusters, then activated the Ion plasma once they cleared the atmosphere. Seven minutes later they were in a high orbit, nearly twenty-five hundred kilometers, where hopefully they'd be looking down on their enemies.

"Ensign Adebayor, your task is to find and identify the Earth Ark location," Clement ordered. Adebayor acknowledged and began her scan. "Navigator, maintain high orbit over the planet. I want us to have the high ground in any conflict."

"Aye, sir," said Massif.

Mika Ori put the ship in motion, taking a longitudinal path that would put them over the slave encampments in sixteen minutes.

"Report, Ensign," he demanded of Adebayor after a few minutes of silence.

"No indication of the Earth Ark in orbit over Bellus, sir. No trace gasses, no propellant expended. I can't find anything, sir," she said.

Clement looked to Yan.

"Has she moved on?"

"Possible," Yan replied. "Leave just enough muscle here to do the job, then return to their initial objective."

"Which was Alphus if I recall. But why? Bellus has everything, resource-wise, that they could want. Slave labor, water, ample food stocks, minerals, energy sources . . . Alphus is a rougher environment, with only a strip of land at the edges of the habitable zone fit for colonization."

"Something else must have come up."

"Like what?" He turned to Adebayor again. "Expand your search away from Bellus, Ensign. Find me that Ark ship."

"Aye, sir," Adebayor said, and started manipulating her displays. "Permission to use the radio telescope?"

"Granted," he said. The ship moved on with silence among the bridge crew, all busy doing their duties. It was Yan who announced the first signs of trouble.

"Forward scans from the drone are picking up blips over the settlements, Captain. By displacement they look like the light attack clippers, and . . . " she hesitated, "three larger displacement vessels in stationary orbits, Captain."

"Let me see them," Clement ordered. The tactical screen lit up with a description and cross section of the three unidentified vessels. They were about three times the size of the *Beauregard*, and they were emitting alarming radiation signals.

"Light cruisers by displacement, and they have nukes," said Clement, a worried tone in his voice. "How many LACs, Yan?"

"Twenty clippers, sir. And three large transport ships."

"Those will be for the ground troops for the initial occupation. Have they seen us yet?"

"No change in their status, sir," reported Yan.

"Full stop, Mika. Recall the drone. What's our distance to the flotilla?"

"Seven minutes, sir," said Yan.

"Ensign Adebayor, anything on the Earth Ark?"

"Nothing yet, sir."

"All right, they don't know we're here and so we have the advantage, for now." He went to the com and called down to Nobli. "I need you in the galley, Engineer." Nobli acknowledged. He followed that with a call down to Telco to join them. "Yan, Mika, to the galley please. Ivan, you and Adebayor maintain status here. Let me know immediately if anything changes."

"You don't want me in the war conference?" asked Ivan in his Russian accent. He seemed offended.

Clement had no time for his feelings. "This concerns

the pilot, not the navigator, Ivan. I need you to stay on top of things here, and plot us an escape course, just in case things go wrong. I need my senior officers on one page," he said.

"Understood, sir," said Massif, reluctantly. Mika squeezed his arm as she slipped by, following Yan and Clement off the bridge and down the six steps to the galley deck.

Once they were all settled Clement started in immediately. "We're facing three light cruisers that have about three times our total conventional weapons displacement each and an additional twenty light attack clippers. Combined, their flotilla probably has anywhere from eight to ten times our ordnance to deliver, plus those cruisers have nukes and we don't. The transport ships probably have Directed Energy Weapons for ground support but I doubt they have missiles, so they're immaterial to a space battle. The Earth Ark appears to have bugged out for the moment. I need a strategy, one that will work for this confrontation. What's our conventional missile count, Ensign Telco?"

"We have forty-eight conventional missiles left, sir," said Telco. "I don't know if that's enough to take out this flotilla."

"It's not," said Clement flatly. He turned to his exec. "Opinion, Commander Yan?"

"It seems to me we have to deal with those cruisers first, then the LACs. The cruisers have tactical nukes, so getting them off the battlefield seems like our first priority."

"Agreed. Engineer Nobli? Any ideas on how we make that happen?"

"The MAD weapon," said Nobli. "It seems our only option."

"A weapon we've never fired, and that we don't even know if it will work?"

"You asked for my best option, Captain. I've just given it to you," Nobli said, then adjusted his wire-rimmed glasses and looked away.

"What is the MAD weapon?" asked Mika.

Clement became pensive, but he answered anyway. There was a time for everything to be revealed, and it seemed this was it. "Matter Annihilation Device, MAD. Essentially a sort of universal death ray. It will annihilate matter at a molecular level. We end up channeling the energy from the LEAP drive reactor into a particle beam. There's a shut-off valve that will end the stream, and we fire it through the old cobra cannon pipelines that have been treated with a carbon-nanotube coating. But essentially, it's a line-of-sight weapon, and not suitable for tactical targeting. Kind of like swatting a wasp with a sledgehammer. If you hit it, the target is done. If you miss . . . " He trailed off.

"Jesus Christ," said Mika. "Did DeVore give you this thing?"

Clement shook his head. "No. Engineer Nobli worked out the specs and built the piping for it on the outward leg. Essentially, it's a one-of-a-kind prototype, just like this ship."

"And let me guess, it's never been tested?" said Mika.

"Correct."

"So if it misfires, or blows up . . . "

"You can pretty much say goodbye to a large section of this solar system," said Clement. "But I see it as the only possibility for our success in this scenario, Pilot." He finished.

"Are you expecting me to target this weapon?" she asked.

Clement shook his head. "No Mika, I wouldn't lay that responsibility on you. I will target the weapon. I only need you to fly us into the enemy formation. My hope is we only have to fire it once and we can hopefully get all three cruisers before they target us. Understood?"

"Yes, sir. But they will see us coming. With that much time it will be difficult to get the ship into a prime firing position," she said.

"I understand that, Mika." Clement turned back to his engineer. "We need the element of surprise, Hassan. We can't get it using conventional means. That flotilla will cut us up before we get a chance to fire."

"So you're asking me if we can use 'unconventional' means?" Nobli asked.

Clement nodded. "Can we use the LEAP drive like we did before, to jump a short distance through normal space, and then appear right in front of our targets, convert the drive to the MAD weapon, and take out the three cruisers?"

"You're insane," said Nobli, dead serious. "It would be easier to find the Earth Ark and take it out than to do this to free a few thousand captives. The scale of the MAD weapon keeps us from close, tactical warfare. It's a weapon of mass destruction, like using a sledgehammer for swatting wasps, as you said. You're asking the impossible, Captain."

"I do, Engineer," replied Clement. "That's why I brought you along. I expect a plan presented to me on the bridge in thirty minutes, and I want you all to stay here until you have it." Then he stood and walked away, heading down to the technical labs.

He found Lieutenant Pomeroy in the sick bay.

"You didn't invite me to your little soiree," she said.

"It's a small room," he snapped back, deflecting her fake hurt feelings.

"I have something important to share with you," she said.

"Is it about the upcoming battle?"

"No . . ." She hesitated. "Not exactly."

He held up his hand. "Then it can wait. I know I've asked you for a lot of things that are out of your usual range of skills on this mission—"

"You have," she said, cutting in. He looked at her. She was plain-faced, rail-thin, and lean, with her dark hair pulled tightly back into a ponytail. She wasn't the kind of woman to be trifled with, he decided.

"What I need from you now is an estimate of how many of the natives might be killed if we take out that flotilla. There could be hundreds of troops on the ground already, based on the size of those transport ships. And if they decide they are vulnerable to attack from above . . ."

"Would they slaughter their captives? Unlikely, in my opinion. That's their workforce. But if they think we're going to attack them from the high ground, they could panic, depending on how well trained and disciplined they are," she said.

"From what I've seen I'm going to assume they are disciplined, experienced troops."

"Then I would say, don't threaten them. Take out the flotilla but leave them alone."

"Let them keep the captives?"

She nodded. "For now, yes, sir. The units on the ground we observed from the Hill Place looked fairly sophisticated, with equipment and armored vehicles. I say leave them alone, then make your way to deal with the Earth Ark, and whatever that problem may entail."

"And come back to free the natives later?"

She looked pensive. "If we survive the encounter with the Earth Ark, yes, sir."

Clement nodded. "I suppose it's irrelevant to ask how ill prepared we might be for a mass-casualty event?"

"Not irrelevant, sir, but the answer is clearly that we aren't. Anything much more than weapons burns or a skinned knee is going to be beyond our medical scope," she replied in a matter-of-fact tone.

"Understood. One more question. Those transport ships, they have no heavy armaments but they do have DEW weapons."

"'DEW' weapons, sir?" she asked, inquisitive.

"Directed Energy Weapons. To be used from space on a specific target. Do you think you and Ensign Telco could take the shuttle over and use that kind of weapon to free the settlers? Take down the fence lines and such? At least give them a chance to escape?" Clement asked.

"We can surely try sir, *if* those transports are empty."

"I'm willing to bet at least one of them is, Lieutenant. Draw up a contingency plan. We may need to use it, and read in Telco on the mission specs."

"Aye, sir."

Clement nodded again and started to walk away when Pomeroy grabbed him by the arm. He turned back to her.

"Lieutenant?"

"That 'something important' I mentioned before?"

Clement exhaled heavily but nodded for her to continue.

"I'm no biologist, and certainly not a DNA specialist of any kind, but I do have an abnormal finding about the settlers that I think you should know about, sir," Pomeroy said.

"The science can wait," he said, and started to turn away again.

She stopped him a second time. "Not this science, sir," she said. He gave her his full attention now. "I ran a DNA test on Mary while we were on the planet, sir. It was an exact match for a DNA sample I pulled from a settler burial mound, from a bone on one of the lowest layers. Just out of interest, I ran a carbon dating test on the ancient bone fragment, sir. The test was anomalous, so I ran it two more times."

"How anomalous?"

"Sir, the date came back the same on all three tests. The bone fragment was aged at over four hundred years."

Clement's brow furrowed. "I don't understand. Four hundred years is an impossible number. There were no colonization missions from Earth until a couple of centuries ago," he said.

"So we assumed. Sir, I'm no expert, but even I can see that these people were *designed* for this planet, by someone."

Clement did some quick math in his head. "So either someone on Earth had FTL technology far earlier than has been let on, or some unknown power back in the day had extensive knowledge of this system and sent pre-designed people here on a generation ship."

"Exactly."

"That's something we'll have to ponder on another day, Lieutenant. Right now I have bigger problems, like three nuclear-armed cruisers orbiting the planet," finished Clement, and then he was gone.

"Yes, sir," said Pomeroy to Clement's retreating back.

Clement was back on the bridge a minute later, waiting on the attack strategy from his team. He took in a deep breath, thinking about the information he had just received from Pomeroy, but it couldn't change his resolve. It was an issue for another day.

Presently the team returned to the bridge with their attack plan. They gathered at Yan's station. Clement motioned for Ivan Massif to join them. It was Nobli who started the presentation.

"Based on our previous short jump, by using a 0.000086 second microburst from the LEAP drive we can move the ship approximately twenty thousand kilometers from our current location to another position in space. The navigator, however, will have to keep us on the same plane of the ecliptic relative to the planet, or we could end up passing through the enemy vessels, which would be very bad for obvious reasons. We need clear space on a specific plane to make the maneuver. I will be able to program the LEAP drive burst to occur on your command, through the MAD application on your console. I'll need about five minutes to complete that update," Nobli stated.

Clement turned to his navigator. "Ivan, can you do this?"

Massif nodded. "Aye, sir. I can plot and lock our course so that we are clear of the enemy flotilla when we make our move." Clement acknowledged that with a nod in return and then Mika Ori took over the briefing.

"We'll need to move the ship within their range of vision so they can see us and start to make their move. If they come at us with the clippers first then our maneuver will place us behind the cruisers, which should give us clear shots at them. However, if they lead with the cruisers and then we pop up behind them, we'll have to fight our way through all the clippers, and that could take away our advantage of surprise and leave us exposed to their nukes. So no matter how it plays out, we'll have to be nimble, quick, and decisive," she said.

"Agreed. We only have one shot at this, people, let's make it work to our advantage. One more thing, I've ordered Lieutenant Pomeroy and Middie Telco on a separate mission with the shuttle, once the shooting stops, to take over one of their transports. They appear to have DEW weapons on board and I'm betting at least one of them is empty based on the number of troops we observed on the ground. I'm proposing that we take one of the transports and then use the DEW weapons to free the natives and at least give them a chance to escape captivity. Once we finish this operation we'll be off to hunt the Earth Ark, and the natives will be on their own," said Clement.

"Natives? You mean settlers?" quizzed Yan.

Clement gave her a brief glance of disapproval, indicating he didn't want to pursue this course of conversation. "I want to give them a fighting chance, Commander, until, or if, we can return," he said. She noted his change of tone on the subject. Clement called to the only other person on the bridge.

"Ensign Adebayor, please report on the Earth Ark," he ordered.

Adebayor turned to the group. "No physical sighting as of yet, sir. But I have picked up trace elements of their drive emissions. They appear to be heading outward from the inner system, on a course toward the third inhabitable world, Camus. I'd say they have half a day's head start on us, sir," she said.

"Thank you, Ensign, keep tracking until you find her." Adebayor acknowledged and returned to her scanning console. Clement turned his attention back to his tactical group.

"All the more reason we need to start moving this plan along. Can we be ready in fifteen minutes?"

"I can," said Nobli. The others nodded assent.

"Very well, so ordered." Clement looked up at the ship's clock and used the console controls to set the timer. "Fifteen minutes from my mark . . . mark." He turned to Ori. "Mika, I want you to take us toward the flotilla, but take us slowly. We want plenty of time for them to see us and then reveal their strategy, clear?"

"Clear, sir," she replied, then the group broke up to their stations.

The waiting was interminable for Clement. Yan left the bridge and then returned after coordinating the shuttle mission with Pomeroy and Telco. Nobli took almost the full fifteen minutes to program the LEAP drive jump app. Clement then changed his mind and had Nobli load it onto Massif's console.

"I'll just give the order, Ivan. I want you to carry it out," he said. It was a change of heart, but the local LEAP jumps were the navigator's job anyway. Firing the MAD weapon, however, was a larger moral choice and one he wanted to reserve for himself.

As the clock ran out on their prep Clement gave the order to Mika Ori to move the ship closer to the flotilla, following Massif's pre-designated course.

"Slow but sure, Mika," he said.

"Estimate three minutes until they spot us, sir," she replied.

"Keep a clear pathway for us to jump, Pilot," he reiterated.

"As you say, sir," she said with a wry smile, noting her captain's obvious nervousness at the situation.

The flotilla quickly picked up on their movements and started breaking into attack formations. The light attack clippers formed into three groups, each group protecting one of the cruisers. Two of the groups, containing seven clippers each, broke off and began accelerating toward the *Beauregard*, while a third group with six clippers held back near the transports, no doubt protecting the command cruiser of the flotilla.

"That's not what we planned for," said Clement. "Time to rethink our strategy."

"Instructions, sir?" asked Ori.

He pondered the situation for a moment, then came to a quick decision. "Pick the nearest subgroup that maintains our line of sight for the LEAP jump and make for them." He hit the com button to the missile room. "Ensign Telco, load all missile tubes."

"Missile tubes loading, aye, sir," came the response.

Clement waited while the tubes loaded up and his board went to green, one by one, then switched his attention to the tactical display as Mika maneuvered the ship closer to the nearest battle group.

"How long—" he started.

"Thirty seconds to firing range of our missiles," interrupted Ori, all business. The clippers were now placing themselves between the *Beauregard* and the first enemy cruiser. Clement decided to put the hammer down early. He looked down at his console again. All green on the missile tubes. He glanced over at Mika, who was watching her range clock countdown to under five seconds. When the clock hit zero Clement used his console to fire the missiles, then he turned to Ori.

"Accelerate us toward that cruiser, Mika. I want us inside the detonation range of their nukes so they can't use them without destroying themselves."

"That range would be about twenty kilometers, sir," said Mika, manipulating her controls at the captain's order. Clement felt the tug of gravity as the ship accelerated at a rapid rate toward the cruiser and its tiny flotilla. The clippers scattered as the *Beauregard*'s missiles homed in on them. The first missiles detonated and destroyed two of the clippers. Three more scattered and avoided direct hits but still took damage from the collective blasts. The last pair of clippers ran from the scene, circling back to protect their cruiser.

"Take us right at the cruiser, Mika," said Clement. "Accelerate to 1.5 gs." He hit the com to contact Telco again. "Have you got my missiles reloaded, Ensign?" he asked.

"Aye, sir," replied Telco. "You may fire at will."

Clement turned to Yan. "Target the cruiser with all six missiles, Commander," he ordered.

"Aye, sir," she acknowledged with a grave look on her face.

Clement turned quickly back to Mika Ori at the navigation console. "Distance to the cruiser," he demanded.

"Twelve hundred kilometers," she replied.

"How long—"

"Three minutes twenty seconds to optimal range," she replied.

"That's a lot of time to prep and fire a nuke," Yan commented.

Clement turned back to his executive officer. "Then let's give them something else to deal with," he said. "Firing all missiles."

Yan nodded in reply. "Missiles away, sir," she said.

Clement watched on his tactical screen as the six missiles left the *Beauregard*'s launch bay, heading directly for the cruiser. They would arrive at their target much sooner than the *Beauregard* could.

The *Beauregard* screamed past the five damaged and destroyed clippers, still accelerating and closing on the main cruiser. The second cruiser group was in turn closing on the *Beauregard* but was still out of their effective missile range. The two functional clippers from the first cruiser's flotilla desperately attempted to get between the *Beauregard*'s missiles and their cruiser. They fired Directed Energy Weapons and antimissile torpedoes into the path of the oncoming ordnance, but it was too little and too late. One of the clippers got caught in the detection path of one of the *Beauregard*'s oncoming missiles and it veered off, attracted by the clipper's engine heat signature. The resulting explosion was spectacular. This caused the Earth cruiser to change course away from the debris field of the clipper. She also had to decelerate, which only put her more and more into the *Beauregard*'s sights.

Two more of the *Beauregard*'s missiles veered off and struck the last undamaged clipper defending the Earth cruiser, totally destroying her. The cruiser was now hopelessly out of position, her midships exposed to the *Beauregard*'s final three conventional missiles. They hit her broadside and she went up in a sparkling explosion as her interior compartments were exposed to the vacuum of space, venting both oxygen and fuel, not to mention her personnel. She was at least crippled; at worst she was doomed and spinning now down toward the atmosphere of Bellus. But she still had an unfired nuclear missile and that made her a danger, especially to the settlers below.

"Bring us about, Pilot," said Clement. "Pursuit course."

"Sir?" asked Mika, questioning.

"She has an unfired nuke, Pilot, and we have to take her out before she hits the planet," he explained.

Mika acknowledged without a word and started the process of turning the ship toward the falling cruiser.

"Sir," warned Massif. "That will take us out of range for our LEAP jump."

Clement was nonplussed. "Then you'll have to recalculate from our expected intercept position for the cruiser, Ivan." Massif nodded, even though he was clearly unhappy. Clement knew his people and how well they did their jobs, even if they complained about it.

The ship and the crew strained against the new g-forces in play to intercept the falling cruiser. After two minutes Ori got the ship in line to fire and the acceleration rate reduced back to 1 g.

"In range to fire, Captain," said Ori. "But we're dangerously close to her detonation range."

Clement said nothing to that as his tactical screen showed him the same info. He called down to Ensign Telco. "Load one missile, Ensign. Once she's fired I want you to reload all the tubes, all six of them, understood?"

"Yes, sir," said Telco. "Your missile will be ready to fire in ten seconds."

Clement turned back to Yan again. "Target her remaining fuel, Commander, or what you think may be her missile bays. Prepare to fire on my command."

Yan acknowledged as Clement watched the tactical screen, waiting for the green light from Telco. Once he got it he didn't hesitate for a second, but took command.

"Firing!" he said. The missile was away, screaming toward the crippled cruiser.

"Get us out of here, Pilot!" ordered Clement.

The ship veered away at high acceleration again, pulling almost three gs, bearing loosely on the course that Navigator Massif had laid out for her. Clement switched the tactical screen to reverse angle as he watched the *Beauregard*'s missile close on the Earth cruiser. The resulting explosion totally destroyed the cruiser and a secondary explosion, a nuclear fireball, consumed everything within twenty kilometers around the cruiser, including one of the damaged clippers that was trying to rally back to its mother ship. The remaining two damaged clippers ran from the field of battle as quickly as they could. Once the *Beauregard* was back on Massif's preferred course Clement ordered Ori to decelerate the ship. The second incoming battle group was still a good ten thousand kilometers out, but closing. The command cruiser was still a quarter of the way around the circumference of Bellus, out of range for the moment, so they thought.

After demanding status from his crew and getting the reports, Clement moved on to the next phase of his plan. They gathered around Yan's console and he brought in Nobli and Telco through the com.

"We have eighteen minutes before that second battle group can engage us. Our goal, though, is to take out the command cruiser, and she's nineteen thousand klicks from us. This is where we have to use the LEAP drive to get us behind the Earth command cruiser battle group. If we have to fight that second battle group I don't think their commander will allow us to use the same tactics on them as we used on the first group. The element of surprise that the LEAP drive gives us is essential. If this doesn't work, I don't see any way we can fight off two Earth cruiser battle groups, especially with nukes, at the same time. Now, are we all convinced that this plan *can* work?" he said. Clement looked first to Massif.

"We have a pathway to a location behind the command cruiser group, sir, using the LEAP drive," he said, looking up to the ship's clock. "And by my mark we have about eight minutes to execute that maneuver."

"Can we be ready in eight minutes, Hassan?" said Clement through the com.

"We're ready now," replied Nobli. "Ensign Tsu has the drive warm and ready."

Clement nodded. "We'll bring the ship to full stop," Clement said to Ori. She nodded. "Ensign Telco," he said through the com, "I want my full complement of six missiles ready to fire on my command once we complete the LEAP jump."

"Ready now, sir, as you ordered," said Telco.

Finally, he turned to Yan. "You'll fire the missiles on my order, Commander. Make sure we target the command cruiser's critical systems."

"Aye, sir," said Yan.

Clement looked down to his watch. "We go in three minutes," he said, "and may the gods of the multiverse be with us."

Clement ordered everyone on the bridge crew to strap in for the leap. Lieutenant Ori brought the ship to full stop. Commander Yan dutifully reported on the closing speed of the second cruiser group. Clement glanced at his watch, ignoring the ship's clock out of habit, noting there was less than twenty seconds until the LEAP jump, so the second Earth cruiser group wouldn't be able to get within firing range of his ship. He noted the green lights on his board from both Ensign Telco and engineer Nobli. "You have command of my ship, Navigator," he said to Massif.

Massif went on the ship-wide com and counted down from ten. At zero, the universe shifted again.

The momentary disorientation followed, but Clement soon regained his bearings and demanded reports. Yan updated the tactical screen and it showed them just what they wanted to see. They were approximately seventy-five hundred kilometers behind the command cruiser tactical group, who were facing away from them, or rather, were facing toward where they *had* been only a few short seconds ago.

"Accelerate the ship, Pilot. I want that cruiser in range before they know where we are."

"Two minutes at 3.5 gs, Captain," Ori said.

"Acceptable," replied Clement, "but I want an escape course executed as soon as our missiles are away."

"Already plotted by the navigator and locked into my console," said Ori with a snarky smile to her captain as she hit the acceleration boost. Clement was pressed hard into his command couch. "One minute fifty-four seconds to firing range."

Clement's foot tapped the deck nervously as he watched their progress. "Do they see us yet?" he asked Yan at the 1:30 mark.

"Uncertain . . . wait. The six light attack clippers are starting to scramble. I'd say they've seen us, sir."

"Status of the command cruiser?" he asked.

"She's trying to accelerate away from us. But not very fast by our standards," said Yan.

"Mika—"

"Going to 3.75 g, sir," she said, interrupting him. Clement felt the press of weight on his chest, sinking him farther into his couch. He waited as long as his patience would let before asking for an update.

"Time to firing range, Pilot?"

"Forty-three seconds, sir, unless she's got some surprise we don't know about yet."

Clement leaned back deeper into his couch, praying there were no surprises.

Right on time (according to Ori's calculations) they reached missile-firing range. The command cruiser's evasive maneuvers had only gained them a few seconds as the *Beauregard* closed. The clippers, while more nimble than the cruiser, were still trying to turn and face the *Beauregard*. For all intents and purposes, it looked to Clement like he had them dead to rights. But he knew the battlefield could be a cruel mistress . . .

"Sir!" It was Yan, obviously alarmed.

"Commander?" demanded Clement.

"There's no nuke signature on that command cruiser, sir. She must have—"

"Offloaded the nuke to one of her clippers!" finished Clement. "Mika—"

"Moving us away from the battlefield, sir. Nuke detected on one of the clippers! She's closing!"

"How far?"

"Three thousand klicks and closing fast! Forty-eight seconds to contact!"

"Missiles?"

"Not at this range and speed, Captain," said Yan. "They're too close. Our missiles will never even start pinging."

Clement turned anxiously to his navigator. "Ivan, can we jump again?"

"Nothing calculated, sir. It would take at least three minutes for me to plot anything safe."

"What about unsafe?"

"At this range, we'd likely end up inside Bellus, sir."

"Time, Pilot?"

"Thirty-one seconds until we'll be in the destructive range of their nuke, Captain," said Ori.

Clement reached down to his com. "Nobli, prepare the MAD weapon," he said, not waiting for a reply. Then he flipped to another channel. "Ensign Telco, are my missile tubes loaded?"

"Aye, sir," came Telco's voice through the com line.

Clement cut the line and turned to his XO. "Commander Yan, target the command cruiser with a full volley of conventional missiles, and fire," he ordered.

She looked confused. "But sir, the nuke—"

"Follow my orders, Commander!" he roared.

She did. "Missiles away," Yan said.

"Time," demanded the captain.

"Eighteen seconds!" said Ori.

Clement looked down at the MAD weapon icon. It was all green and ready to fire. He looked up to his tactical screen, which showed the clippers coming straight at the *Beauregard* in a tight delta formation, almost like an arrowhead. *Suicide run*, he thought. He tracked and locked on them, and didn't hesitate.

He fired the MAD weapon.

Blinding white light seared out of the *Beauregard*, disintegrating the clipper formation in an instant. The beam kept going, out to a range where Ensign Adebayor could no longer track it, dissipating slightly as it left their tracking range. It would eventually be harmless, but for the purposes of space combat, its range was virtually unlimited.

They all watched in silence as the six conventional missiles the *Beauregard* had launched struck the command cruiser, exploding hard against its hull. The ship quickly nosedived into the atmosphere of Bellus, fatally crippled, and began burning up. The last cruiser and clipper flotilla was now retreating from the battlefield at close to three gravities.

Clement ordered Telco and Pomeroy to take the shuttle to one of the transports to carry out their mission. Then he left the bridge, heading for his cabin, and locking the door behind him.

❖ 18 ❖

It was thirty minutes before Clement emerged again. He had left a mostly empty bottle of Argyle Scotch on the table behind him. As he walked along the short metal grid and up the steps to his bridge he contemplated the situation. They'd narrowly averted destruction by the clipper's suicide run, and now he knew the fanatical nature of his enemies. He took his seat back on the bridge and looked to Yan.

"Status of the shuttle mission?" he demanded. Yan cleared her throat before reporting.

"Lieutenant Pomeroy reports that they have taken one of the troop carriers without incident and activated their Directed Energy Weapons. Awaiting your orders, sir," she said.

Clement nodded.

"Pipe me through," he said.

Yan hesitated as the rest of the bridge crew turned their heads to look in the general direction of their captain, but none had the bravery to make eye contact with him. Yan left her station and approached her commander. "Sir, I have a concern—"

"You mean 'we,' don't you, Commander?" said Clement, eyeing his bridge team one by one. He stood. "All eyes on me," he ordered.

Mika, Ivan, and Adebayor turned to face their commander.

"If you're wondering, yes, I've had a drink. In fact, more than one. Seeing the true nature of what human beings will do to other humans has shaken my faith in humanity, but it has not altered my resolve. I may be a man who has had too much alcohol in a single sitting in the past, but I am not at that point now. I am in full command of my capabilities, and clear in my decisions to resolve this conflict. The Earth Ark forces will do anything, sacrifice anything, and anyone, in order to fulfill their dreams of conquest. I will not stand idly by while those dreams crush innocent people, especially the innocents on the planet below us. I fought a war against the 5 Suns Navy for these same reasons, and no, I won't let go of these people and will do anything in my power to protect them, and us." He took in a deep breath. "Now pipe in the captured transport, Commander," he ordered, turning to Yan. Yan reached over to her console, pressed an icon, and nodded to Clement.

"Lieutenant Pomeroy," Clement said. All eyes on the bridge were still on him. "Report your status."

"The transport is ours, sir. All of them have been abandoned by the enemy, sir," came Pomeroy's scratchy voice through the com.

"That means all their troops and equipment are either on the surface of Bellus already or they have evacuated to one of the cruisers," replied Clement.

"That is our assumption, sir. We are in geostationary orbit over the work camp now, sir. Our estimate is approximately twelve hundred troops holding approximately three thousand prisoners. They appear to have a dozen armored vehicles on the surface, sir, and a lot of industrial equipment. I would expect mining operations to begin at any time," Pomeroy concluded.

"Ensign Telco," said Clement, "status of enemy weapons systems aboard the transport."

Telco came on the line. "Their Directed Energy Weapons are operational and can be precision-targeted, sir. They left the lights on for us. Only waiting on your orders, Captain."

Clement nodded. "Target their armored vehicles first, Ensign. Then take out the perimeter fencing and allow the prisoners to escape to any forest area closest to the fences."

"What if there are infantry units in those areas?" interjected Pomeroy. As ranking officer aboard the transport she was technically in command of the mission.

"Then eliminate any nearby infantry units," ordered Clement. There was a pause.

"Please clarify last order," came Pomeroy's voice over the com.

Clement didn't hesitate. "Use the weapons at your disposal to eliminate any infantry units that would be in a position to hinder the escape of, or bring harm to, the native prisoners," said Clement. "Is my order clear?"

Again there was a pause, then a quiet, "Yes, sir," from Pomeroy.

Clement continued. "From there, destroy the mining

tunnels and any heavy equipment in the camp. Scatter the remaining enemy forces. Once the mission is complete I want you back in the shuttle and back aboard the *Beauregard* ASAP. Are all of my orders understood?"

"Yes, sir," came Pomeroy's reply.

Then Clement gave the cutoff signal to Yan.

"Ensign Adebayor, bring up the camp location on the tactical board and throw it to the main display," he said. She did as ordered and a red-tinted tactical overview of the camp came up on the main board. Information bubbles quickly identified the prisoners, the electrified camp-border fencing, enemy armor, and troop units. They had to wait only a few seconds before the first flashes of DEW light from the transport struck the armored vehicles north of the prison yard. Every few seconds there followed another strike until the armored units encircling the camp were all burning. There was a long hesitation, nearly a minute, until the next burst of DEW fire hit two units on the northern perimeter. They could see individual troops scrambling for cover as the units were devastated by the attacks from their own weapons. The prisoners fled away from the onslaught as the transport's weapons turned to take out the perimeter fencing. It collapsed and burned like kindling. Realizing their chance, the native prisoners finally made a break for the open land, quickly emptying the prison yard as they fled north and into the forest.

The DEW bombardment was sporadic after that, taking out tactical units, five to six men at a time, if they chose to pursue the prisoners. Those who fled in other directions, away from the flood of escaping prisoners, were left untouched. The troops quickly got the message, and began flooding away from the prisoners. Regrettably, many of the troops fled to the mine shafts for cover, not knowing they had just made themselves targets of the next phase of the attack. Again, after what seemed to Clement to be a long hesitation, the DEW attacks turned to the mine shafts. They collapsed as the ground above was vaporized by six-thousand-degree Kelvin heat. Even reinforced metal or carbon-nanotube-coated materials would be vaporized. The mine shafts would become a crematorium. Once again, the attack abated, and then resumed, finally destroying the large stacks of mining equipment. Pomeroy had followed his orders to the letter.

There was no call of confirmation, just a readjustment of the transport's course toward the *Beauregard*. Soon the *Beauregard*'s shuttle emerged from the transport, heading home.

Clement shut down his station and turned to Yan. "Do we have missiles loaded?"

Yan looked to her board. "Negative, sir."

Clement called down to his engineer. "Mr. Nobli, send Ensign Tsu up to the missile room and have him load all six missile bays."

"Is he qualified for that?" replied Nobli.

"He is now," said Clement. "Tell him to get his ass up there."

"Yes, sir," replied Nobli, then shut off the line.

Clement turned to his pilot. "Once the shuttle is back on board secure the ship for acceleration. Best possible speed to that last cruiser group, Lieutenant Ori," he said.

"We're going to pursue?" she asked.

"No," replied Clement, shaking his head for emphasis. "We are going to intercept before they go to ground. Ensign Adebayor, reapply yourself to finding that Earth Ark. I want to know where the big game is hiding."

"Aye, sir," she replied.

Clement turned to Yan. "Destroy the empty transports, but leave the one Pomeroy and Telco occupied. We may need it again. And notify me five minutes before we accelerate. Up to five gs is authorized. I will be in my cabin. Orders understood, Commander?"

"Understood, sir," she said. Then Clement left the bridge, and everyone was silent behind him.

Yan tapped on his door twenty minutes later.

"Come in," he called.

She entered, noted the empty bottle on the table, and Clement, reclined in his club chair. She absently looked at her watch.

"Five minutes to acceleration. Mika says she might be able to get us to 5.5 gs. That would put us twenty-eight minutes away from the last cruiser battle group," she said.

"Thank you, Commander," he replied, staring at the ceiling.

Yan shuffled a bit, unsure what to say next.

Clement stepped in. "If you want to know my condition, Commander, it is as I stated on the bridge, fully capable of carrying out my duties. Regardless of what that empty bottle of scotch may imply," he said, then looked up to her. "Please sit down." She did, taking a seat at the conference table. Clement pulled his recliner up to a sitting position. "You want to know why I did what I did?" he asked.

She shook her head. "No, I understand your decisions. What I want to know is how *you* feel about them, and ask why we are pursuing a retreating enemy."

He hesitated, then: "After the last war I swore I would never take a life again unless it served some military purpose. But these Earth troops . . . " He trailed off. She waited. "They're much more than just military units. These people are conquerors. Slavers. Genocidal. Fanatics. They don't fight for a reason or a creed or a purpose, they only fight because they are ordered to. And we have to stop them. If we don't, who else will?"

"That's a question you know I don't have the answer to," she said. "So you want to pursue the last cruiser battle group, and then what?"

"That cruiser still has a nuke. We do not. It is a threat to every native settler on the planet and to this ship. And although I don't fancy myself as the defender of the meek, any chance those people have of peaceful self-determination cannot be left to an enemy that has a weapon that could wipe them out in a single flash of light. We will destroy that cruiser, and its weapon," he said.

Yan had a ready response. "There are some who said that you were indeed a crusader during the War of the Five Suns. A man who did everything he could to defend the meek and vulnerable. Are you sure that you're not re-fighting that war here?" Her words cut him hard, and he was thankful he'd drained the scotch, to numb his nerves, and his anger.

"That war was unwinnable from the beginning. Most of us knew that. But the Five Suns Congress left us no choice. The Rim planets were starving; that's why we fought. Here, the settlers have all they need to live, and much, much more. That should be protected for their benefit, as should their right to determine how their vast wealth is used. This is not a revolution, Commander. We're defending the innocent."

Yan nodded. "I understand," she said, then hesitated. "And I agree with you. I will follow your orders, Captain, and I will not question them again." Then she came across the room and kissed him on the cheek. "And now this ship needs its captain on the bridge." She extended her hand and he took it, then pulled himself up and walked past her, opening his cabin door and heading for the bridge.

The 5.5 g acceleration was uncomfortable, especially as the acceleration couches weren't really designed for battle speeds. They tracked the final cruiser group, which had been escaping at just under three gs and had obviously not expected such a hot pursuit by the *Beauregard*. They appeared to be building up speed slowly for an escape-velocity burn, possibly to the inner planet of Alphus, a habitable planet but much less hospitable than Bellus, and the original target of the Earth Ark before they had changed direction to come to Bellus.

"Time to intercept with that battle group?" Clement demanded from his couch, laying as he was in a reclined position. The tactical board glowed red, projected in the air above him.

"Twenty-four minutes at this speed, Captain," replied Mika Ori, with more than a bit of strain in her voice.

"How much longer . . ."

"Six more minutes, for the burn . . . Captain. They . . . are trying to accelerate . . . to reach an escape-velocity . . . burn . . . but . . . we will catch them . . . on the dark side of the planet . . . before they can burn . . . to Alphus."

Clement reminded himself how small Ori was, and how much the strain of high-gravity acceleration must be on her. It hurt him just to talk, let alone give orders.

He gritted out the final six minutes, until Ori's speed reduction to 2.5 gs felt like a vacation on a warm beach somewhere. The crew's couches all slowly resumed a more normal upright attitude as the g-forces steadily ablated back toward a normal one g. Clement decided that a twenty-six-minute burn at 5.5 gravities was about his limit. He knew he would be sore once his body fully absorbed the stress. They hit 1 g deceleration just eight minutes from the cruiser group.

The light attack clippers had formed a double formation, with three clippers in a triangle pointed toward the *Beauregard* and the other four spaced strategically in a flat line protecting their mother cruiser. It was apparent from this formation that it only mattered to their commanders if the cruiser escaped, not the clippers or their crews. Clement studied the formation. The three forward ships were clearly the sacrificial lambs, and he surmised they would make the first move, likely an aggressive one. The second group of four were much more likely to provide the counterattack to whatever move the *Beauregard* made. Though they were heavily outgunned, with just fighter-style conventional missiles and low-energy cobra weapons, they could provide enough stings, like a swarm of wasps, to damage the *Beauregard* and slow her

down. Her static shields would protect her from most of
the clipper's ordnance, but a lucky shot could prove
damaging to their effort, and any necessary repairs
would put them at a major disadvantage.

Clement decided to do what he did best and follow his
own battle philosophy: the best defense is a good offense.

"Time to the battlefield, Pilot," he demanded.

"Six minutes to the triangle formation, Captain. Eight
to the flat back four, and eleven to the cruiser," she said.

"How long until the cruiser can reach an escape vector
to Alphus, Navigator?"

"Twenty-two minutes until she can reach her minimum
burn vector, sir. After that we'll have precious little time
to intercept her," said Massif.

"So it's a very tight schedule." He looked to Yan. "Let's
act before they do. Prep three missiles for that triangle
group, Commander," he said. She looked a bit puzzled,
but complied, then looked at the clock.

"Remind the captain we are still three minutes from
firing range on that group, sir," she said.

"Noted, Commander," he replied. "Pilot, change
course to intercept those three clippers. Navigator, factor
in a thirty-degree variation in their course, toward us. As
soon as that maneuver is completed, put us back on the
course for the main group of four clippers. Calculate how
much time that will cost us."

"Already calculated," said Ori. She knew her captain.
"Three minutes adjustment time, sir."

Clement called down to the missile room. "Ensign
Telco, you and Ensign Tsu are responsible for the
loading of my missiles. Whatever we fire, I want

replaced immediately. Let me know when we get below ten in supply."

"Aye, sir," came Telco's prompt response.

At this Yan came up to him. "You're anticipating their attack?"

Clement smiled. "No, Commander, I'm guessing."

"A hunch?" she replied.

He shook his head. "I call it intuition."

"Let's hope yours is better than mine," she replied, and returned to her station.

Mika Ori turned around to give Yan a look of confidence and a nod. She knew Clement well, and how often his intuition had been proven right over the years.

"At your command, sir," said Ori.

Clement nodded. "Execute," he said.

Once again they were pushed back in their couches as the *Beauregard* changed course toward the group of three clippers, and away from the retreating cruiser battle group at 1.5 gs. Because of the distance between them the clippers could have changed course already, and the light of the maneuver simply hadn't caught up with their tactical screens yet. Clement had calculated when they would have had to make their move to make a curving strafing run, a time that had passed ninety seconds before. He guessed when their move would have to appear on his tactical screens for him to be right. Otherwise, he had just given up three minutes of pursuit time on the main Earth cruiser on a bad guess. He looked at his watch as the seconds ticked by.

By his count they made their break three seconds late, but it was within the acceptable limits of his calculation.

His missiles would pursue and detect, then pick up on the clipper's heat and electronic signatures. He looked to Yan.

"Missiles loaded?"

"Ready to fire, Captain," she said.

"At your will, Commander," he said confidently. She nodded and the tactical board showed three missiles away. "High in confidence, Commander?" he said to her. She smiled at him.

"No reason to waste ordnance, sir," she replied.

"Pilot?"

"Adjusting our course now, sir, back to the pursuit of the cruiser battle group," said Ori. "We'll pull 1.75 gs for two minutes, sir."

He sank back into the couch again, watching the three missiles closing in on the three-clipper group. They would have seen the launch by now, and perhaps tried an escape maneuver, but it was far too late already. He watched in satisfaction as the three missiles hunted down and destroyed each of their targets with a satisfying burst of light. Briefly, he thought of the nine men or women who had just died, but quickly pushed it out of his mind. In battle, there could only be allies and enemies, and he had no allies in the Trinity system.

"Back on our pursuit course for the cruiser battle group," reported Ori.

Clement called down to the missile room. "Ensign Telco, how many missiles do I have left?" he said.

"Twenty-seven, sir," came Telco's reply. "Six in the launch tubes and twenty-one in reserve."

"Not enough," he muttered, mostly to himself. Yan overheard him.

"So you're saying we need more missiles? Your solution to every problem?" she said, with a slight smirk.

"True," he replied. "Time to the cruiser group, pilot?" he asked Ori.

"Three minutes to firing range on the back four clippers, sir. Seven minutes until the cruiser is in range," she replied.

He looked at his tactical board. Those clippers knew they had to be sacrificial lambs for the cruiser, so their crews must know they were already given up for dead by the cruiser's commander. He simulated a strategy on his board, counted his missiles again, then called down to the missile room. This time he got Ensign Tsu.

"Ensign, de-rack two of my missiles," Clement ordered. There was a pause before the reply.

"Confirm, sir, you only want four missiles in the launch rack?" replied Tsu.

"Those are my orders, Ensign," he said, then cut the line. A few seconds later and the missile-room icon on his board went from amber to green. His missiles were loaded.

"Why only four, sir?" Yan asked.

Clement looked at her. "Intuition again, Commander. Target the Earth cruiser with our four missiles," he ordered. Yan looked puzzled. Mika Ori turned from her station.

"Sir, we're still a minute out from firing range on those clippers, and another five minutes before we're in range of the cruiser. Sir," she added the last with emphasis.

Clement looked to both women. "I'm fully capable of watching a clock. Now, target the Earth cruiser with our four missiles. That's an order," he said.

Ori turned back to her station while Yan programmed

in the coordinates of the cruiser. The conventional missiles would fall well short of their target.

"Ready, Captain," she finally said. "Cruiser is targeted."

"Time to the clippers, Pilot?" said Clement.

"Nineteen seconds," Ori replied. When they got within the last ten seconds she counted down to zero.

Clement turned to Yan. "Fire missiles," he ordered calmly.

They all watched on the tactical display as the missiles streaked out of their launch tubes and began arcing well away from the clippers, on a vector for the cruiser.

"They won't reach the cruiser," said Yan. As they watched in silence, suddenly the four clippers started moving, burning fuel in a high-acceleration maneuver. Within seconds, all four missiles impacted the remaining clippers, completely destroying them. The bridge was silent.

"How did you know?" said Yan. All eyes on the bridge looked to their captain for an answer.

"Those clippers were given up for dead by the cruiser commander. They knew facing us was suicide. I guessed they would follow their orders to the letter, and try and intercept any missiles targeting the main cruiser. I was right. It's what fanatics always do," he said.

"But our missiles were no danger to the cruiser. They don't have the range," said Yan.

Clement shrugged casually. "But they don't know that, Yan. I counted on their fanaticism overpowering their logic. If they'd calculated the burn rate of our missiles they would have seen that they were no threat. They'd still be alive, and I would be out four missiles," he said.

"Intuition, again?" Yan asked, giving him a look that indicated she was impressed.

"If you like, or experience. Now, how long until we reach actual firing range on that cruiser?"

"Three more minutes, Captain," said Ori.

Clement sat back in his couch and contemplated his next move.

The Earth cruiser had started evasive maneuvers at almost the same time as the last of its escort clippers had been destroyed. It was certain she would have multiple countermeasures available to her, including kinetic weapons (basically, small ball bearings or other material shot into a missile's path), chaff to distract, and possibly even drones that would simulate the cruiser's telltale signatures for heat and electronics. In Clement's experience, often hunting a single ship rather than attacking a battle group could be the more difficult proposition. With a single ship it was down to the particulars of a hull's design capabilities, and their captain's willingness to use those capabilities. Clement contemplated each factor as he formulated a strategy that would use minimal amounts of his remaining missiles. He had twenty-three left.

They entered firing range with the Earth cruiser still eleven minutes from her escape-burn vector for Alphus. Those would be very long minutes for the cruiser's captain. Clement decided he needed more information. He turned to his navigator.

"Mr. Massif," he started.

Massif turned to face his captain. "Aye, sir."

"Can you calculate the maximum course variability that cruiser can execute that will still allow them to reach their escape-burn point in the minimum amount of time?"

"If you give me a minute, sir," he replied.

"You have two," said Clement as the navigator pivoted back to his station to do the calculations. "Lieutenant Ori, no matter what course changes that cruiser makes I want us to stay within the maximum firing range of her at all times. That means stay on her tail, even if we lose some ground, as long as we maintain a firing lock on her."

"Yes, sir," said Ori. At this Yan approached his station.

"Why don't we fire now? We're in range," she said.

"We have twenty-three missiles left, Commander. I don't want to use all of them taking out this cruiser."

"You're planning on holding back, for going after the Earth Ark?"

"Do we have a choice?"

Yan contemplated him a minute, then said, "I suppose not," and quietly returned to her station.

Clement's thoughts turned back to his present battle tactics. "Mika, can that cruiser fire her nuke at us?" he asked.

Ori turned. "As far as I can tell, not from its current orientation. It seems to be a simple design, weapons in the front, propulsion in the back. Plus, I would bet her main focus right now is running her engines as hard as she can," she said.

"What's our time factor?"

"She's ten minutes from being able to make her escape burn, and we're seven minutes behind her. But she's pushing three gs now, which seems to be her max, and we're steadily losing momentum to Bellus' gravity and magnetic fields, and thus, time," Ori said.

Clement turned back to Ori's husband. "Do you have my calculations, Ivan?" he demanded.

"I do, sir." He threw his screen to the main tactical display. "She can only move within about a three-kilometer range and stay on her primary vector for the escape burn to Alphus," he stated. The screen showed the cruiser's maximum maneuvering range in relation to her escape-burn path.

"That's pretty wide for a conventional missile," commented Yan.

"I agree," Clement replied. "If only we had more information on her missile countermeasures." Yan smiled as Clement's face lit up with a slight smile. Then he stood.

"Course, Pilot?"

"Locked in on her, sir," said Ori.

"Time to burn range?"

"Nine minutes, sixteen seconds," replied Massif.

He turned to Yan. "Missile status?"

"All green on my board, Captain. Six missiles at your disposal," she replied.

"Prepare to fire one missile on my order," Clement said.

"Just one?" quizzed Yan.

"One," he repeated.

She complied. "Single missile ready, sir. Locked on target for the Earth cruiser."

"Fire," he said.

Yan launched the missile. It arced out toward the cruiser, accelerating at hypersonic speed. The cruiser probably had less than thirty seconds to respond before impact. Clement studied the enemy ship closely. She lurched starboard in a "Crazy Eddie" maneuver, trying to escape the incoming missile, releasing chaff and drones as well. The missile turned to follow the cruiser, and then impacted into a cloud of kinetic chaff which caused her to explode.

"Detonation half a kilometer from the cruiser, Captain. Enough to rough her up but not much else," reported Ori.

Clement stepped forward to Massif's station and started marking it up, laying plot lines across the screen with his digital pen. He turned to Massif.

"From what I saw, this is her maximum operational variance. Any more and she'll lose her track on her escape burn, which is her best chance of survival."

"She is starting to pull away from us, still burning her acceleration thrusters," interjected Ori.

"Yes, but we can still counter with another high-*g* burn and catch her. Her captain knows his best chance to escape is right now. We will eventually catch him," said Clement. "Do you agree with my assessment, Ivan?"

"Unless he has something else up his sleeve, I'd say you have it to about seventy-five percent, sir," he said.

Clement went back to his station and started typing in coordinates into his tactical screen, then threw them over to Yan's station.

"Three missiles, Commander. On my mark and on those vectors," he said.

"Ready," she said a few seconds later.

"Fire."

The three missiles streaked out of the *Beauregard*'s

missile tubes, two from the port launcher and one from starboard. They converged on the three courses. Clement waited as they closed on the cruiser, second by second. The cruiser captain tried the "Crazy Eddie" jump to the same side, starboard, as the first time, spewing out her chaff and counter measures.

One missile exploded into the kinetic chaff. The second picked up a decoy drone and exploded a kilometer from the cruiser. The third missile bored straight on, hitting the cruiser directly in her main propulsion unit. The resulting explosion was impressive, but not a kill shot. This ship, most likely the flotilla command ship, was built stronger than her predecessors. She tried desperately to use maneuvering thrusters to keep her from diving into the planet's atmosphere, but dive she did. Before they hit the upper atmosphere of Bellus, more than two dozen escape pods were birthed out of her as she dropped, a falling hulk, from the sky. They tracked the pods, twenty-six in all, as they fell to the surface on the dark side of the planet. Survival for very long in that environment seemed unlikely, and Clement pitied the survivors, but had no empathy for their plight. They would have destroyed his ship and his crew without a second thought.

They watched together in silence as the empty cruiser, save possibly her captain, entered Bellus' atmosphere and began burning. To their surprise much of the cruiser made it to the surface before it exploded in a nuclear fireball. Clement hoped the dark side was indeed an empty wasteland, as they had surmised.

He sat back in his command chair, called down to

Nobli and Telco and Tsu, thanking them for their work. Then he turned to Ensign Adebayor at the science station.

"Please tell me you have a course on the Earth Ark, Ensign?"

She smiled, her teeth bright white against her dark African face. "I do, sir. Estimate we can catch her in three days, if she stayed true to her original vector," Adebayor replied.

He nodded, then looked around the bridge at his crew. "Well done today, all of you. Mika, set us in a stable orbit around Bellus for the time being. Everyone take eight hours rest. Then we go to find out where that Earth Ark went, and that may be our biggest challenge yet," he said.

There was a chorus of "Aye, sir" and then Clement was off to his cabin, laying down, and finding sleep the moment his head hit the pillow.

✻ 19 ✻

Yan knocked on his stateroom door six hours later. It wasn't a perfect rest, but it was enough. He opened the door and let her in.

"I take it you want to chat," he said, making his way to his regular chair while she sat at the table again. He poured them both some water and they drank.

"I'll get right to the point," Yan said. "There is some questioning among the crew of our pursuit of the Earth Ark. Many think we have been through a harrowing time and fought battles we were never intended to fight. Remember, we had a small crew to begin with and we've lost two—"

"We didn't 'lose' Wilcock," he interrupted, "I executed him."

Yan paused before continuing. "Agreed, sir. But we are down on personnel and most of the crew is not military trained. They're techs and scientists and geo survey specialists. If you hadn't picked up those four middies—"

"Yes, but I did," he said, interrupting again. "because I knew we might need some military muscle. What's your point, Commander?"

"My point is this is not a gunship, regardless of what this hull used to do in the War of the 5 Suns. It is a prototype FTL ship sent on a science mission to test a revolutionary drive, survey three planets for possible colonization, and then return. Instead we have been involved in several military altercations and it appears you want to involve us in more. Many of the crew want to go home, to their husbands, wives, and families, not fight another battle against a far superior enemy," she said.

Clement contemplated her points. They were all well taken. He had a decision to make.

"And the fact that I will likely be arrested when I return to Kemmerine Station, and be tried as a traitor—do they think I'm delaying our return because of that?" he asked.

"Some do. Most just want us to go home. We're overdue as it is, so it's likely DeVore will send an unmanned probe to find out what happened to us soon, if not already."

"And the fact that many of them will likely be interrogated and possibly charged with treason for following my orders when we get back to Kemmerine Station?"

"I don't believe that's a strong consideration, sir. They're focused on getting home in one piece." Clement refilled their water glasses and drank again while he thought.

"And what about you, Commander? Where do you stand? Do we find out what that Earth Ark is up to? Or do we turn tail and run home?" he said.

"My heart says we should leave and come back with more force—"

"If we're not court-martialed. And *if* we can trust Admiral DeVore, which I don't believe we can," he replied.

Yan's frustration peaked and she stood up to face him. "If you'd let me finish . . ." she said. He nodded. "My heart says we should cut our losses, but my head knows by the time we get back Trinity may be in the hands of the Earth Ark forces, forever. And that's not the kind of future I want to leave for the natives, let alone the long-term consequences for the worlds of the 5 Suns. These natives are a good and sweet people, and we need to give them every chance to live their lives as they choose."

At that Clement stood. "One more thing I need to know, Commander. If I choose to continue pursuit of the Earth Ark, will you be with me and follow my orders?" he said.

She stared at him from across the room.

"I will, Captain. I will follow your orders whatever decision you make, whether I agree with that decision or not," she said.

He looked back at her, studying her eyes. Her gaze was steady and unwavering. In that moment he had never been more attracted to her. She was becoming a fine officer, but she was also an extraordinary woman.

"Tell the crew I will address them in the cargo bay in five minutes," he said. She nodded, and then left his cabin. Clement went to his sink and washed up, then wiped his face. His next choice would be decisive, and possibly seal the fate of the *Beauregard* and her crew. He was ready.

He left his cabin, heading for the cargo bay.

✿ ✿ ✿

The crew had gathered as he came down the gantry stairs, stopping on the metal landing about ten feet up, overlooking them. Yan stood next to him. The other bridge crew would listen in on the ship-wide com. He looked down at the assembled crew, looked at their faces, seeing them not as *his* crew, but as men and women who had been exemplary in their loyalty and performance under great duress and personal sacrifice.

He took a deep breath in before beginning.

"Loyal crew of the *Beauregard*. Commander Yan has done her duty and brought your concerns to my attention. I understand the desire to return home. It has been a long and difficult mission, and not one that you had expected this when you volunteered. I never intended this to become a military mission, but clearly Admiral DeVore did, as she sought out an experienced military captain to command it. I ask you to consider once more the fact that some of us, most likely me, will face charges when we return to 5 Suns Alliance space. I cannot tell you that has not crossed my mind. But I will say that it has not affected my decision-making. I believe we have made the right choices both for our own survival and for the natives we encountered on Bellus. I desire for them to live free, not as slaves to some heartless empire back on Earth that has most likely passed into history already."

He paused.

"My decision to pursue the Earth Ark is to determine her intent. She may be, for all we know, prepping to exit this system and return home. But the point is, we don't know. And I think it is vital that we find out why she left Bellus, and what her intent is, whether in this system, or some other. I have ordered a pursuit course to find out what her intentions are, whether we can do anything about it, or if retreat is our best option. I will not attack that ship without further provocation, and I do not want more battle. I had enough of that in the War of the 5 Suns.

"So each of you has a decision to make. Will you stay loyal to me and give me the two or three days I need to catch the Earth Ark and determine her intentions, or will you demand of me that we return home now, and leave this system and her people to an unknown fate? And one last point, although this is not a democracy, and I am not bound to your decision, I will follow what you decide, regardless of the personal cost to me."

He looked down over the faces of his crew. Seventeen people stared up at him, and besides Nobli, Pomeroy, Tsu, and Telco, he didn't really know any of them. He had left his fate to these people.

"Please let me know your desires by either leaving the deck if you wish to return to Kemmerine, or staying for thirty more seconds if you wish to see out the mission of locating the Earth Ark and determining her intentions." He held out his hands. "If you wish to return home, you may leave the deck now," he said.

Two techs quickly departed, and others moved around or shuffled their feet, but they all stayed focused on their captain. Yan watched the time on her watch and then dropped it to her side to indicate the thirty seconds was up. Clement looked to his crew and smiled.

"Thank you for putting your trust in me," he said, then went up the stairs to his bridge. Behind him, he heard Yan's voice call out:

"Ship's company, dismissed!"

He smiled.

Once on the bridge he took an informal poll of Mika, Ivan, and Adebayor. They were all with him. Yan followed him in and took her station.

"Orders, Captain?" she said.

Clement turned to Ensign Adebayor. "Ensign . . . I have to confess I've forgotten your first name?" he said.

"It's Kayla, sir," she replied with a smile.

"Kayla, what do you have for me on the Earth Ark?"

"Nothing visual, I'm afraid, sir. She's out of range of our telescope and scanners. But I do have a track for her based on her Ion plasma propulsion emissions. She made first for Camus—the third habitable world and fifth in the system—made multiple orbits there, then left a track as she accelerated away toward a course that would take her between the two gas planets in the outer part of the system."

"Could that track put her on a vector to escape the system? Do we know if she left any forces on Camus?" Clement asked.

"She is not on an escape vector as far as my analysis shows," cut in Ivan Massif. "From what I can tell she is heading for a Lagrange point between the two gas planets. The two planets are very close together, the outer one being 0.015 AU from the larger, inner planet," said Massif.

"And how far is the inner gas planet from Camus?" asked Clement.

"0.008 AU, Captain."

"And how far are we here at Bellus from Camus?"

"0.09 AU, sir."

Clement crossed his arms, thinking. "Add it up for me, Ivan. How much time to each destination?"

"Given the relative positions of the planets—and they do orbit at differing speeds despite their close proximity—I make it sixteen hours to Camus with a 1.25 g burn, sir," said Massif.

"What if we made it a 1.5 g burn?" he asked.

Mika Ori chimed in here. "I was thinking of the comfort of the crew, sir, but at 1.5 g we could cut that to twelve hours."

Clement didn't hesitate. "Let's do it at 1.5 g. How long will the burn have to be to get to Camus in twelve hours?"

"I'd like to make one more full orbit after this one, sir, to pick up some momentum. The navigator and I will set the vector to Camus, but I'd like to go closer to Bellus to take advantage of her gravity to slingshot us, sir. I make it twenty-eight minutes until our burn, then another nineteen minutes for the 1.5 g burn, sir," Ori said.

"And then at least two orbits of Camus once we arrive to verify whether the Earth Ark left any forces there," said Clement, rubbing his chin as he thought.

"Thirty-nine minutes to make an orbit of Camus, sir," said Ori without Clement even asking.

The captain looked up to Massif.

"Once we establish a vector to the Lagrange point, another twelve-minute burn at 1.5 g to get us out there to 0.045 AU, sir. Nine hours estimated travel time," finished Massif.

"That's assuming she's still out there," Clement said. It all added up to about twenty-six hours of maneuvering.

He turned back to Adebayor. "Good work, Ensign Kayla. I'll be needing long-range scans of Camus well before our arrival to see if they left us any surprises," Clement said.

"Yes, sir," she replied enthusiastically.

He turned to Yan. "Inform the crew of our schedule, Commander. Everyone can ride the burn out in their couches if they like. It looks like the best time to get some rest will be during the twelve-hour flight time to Camus. I want to make sure we have at least two of you on the bridge at all times. Oh, and Mika and Ivan, I know how much you like, uh, spending your time off together, but I'll need one of you on the bridge at all times, for safety's sake."

The *Beauregard*'s pilot gave him a mock pout and then turned back to her station.

Massif just shrugged his shoulders. "Of course, sir," he said.

"Ensign Kayla," Clement said to Adebayor, "you're relived for the next six hours unless called."

"Aye, sir," she said.

He turned to Ori. "Mika, once the burns are completed I want you in your quarters as well for six hours. You can relieve your husband at that point. Same for you, Yan, six hours down time, beginning immediately," Clement ordered.

"And what about you, Captain?" Yan asked.

"You can relieve me at the end of your rest period. I can't promise I'll sleep during that time, but I'll try," replied Clement. "In the meantime I'll stay on my bridge. I like it here," he said. Yan and Adebayor started to exit the bridge, Adebayor yawning as she departed.

Yan lingered for a second, then whispered to Clement, "I'll have Pomeroy issue you a five-hour-timed sleep pill," she said.

"You know I hate those things," he whispered back.

"As your exec, I'm not giving you a choice, Captain," she finished, then left for her quarters.

Two hours after the burn and acceleration and well into the rest shifts, Clement took a break, leaving Massif alone on the bridge to relieve himself for a few minutes. As he went down the six metal steps to the command cabins, he saw motion at the end of the hall. He had given Lieutenant Pomeroy Captain Wilcock's old stateroom, and he was surprised to see the back end of Ensign Telco departing her cabin. He watched as they kissed goodbye at the doorway, and Telco left without noticing him in the hall, heading back down the gantry steps to the missile room. Pomeroy, for her part, did see him, and came up to him as if to give an explanation. Clement attempted to wave her off with both hands.

"No explanation needed, Lieutenant," he said in a low, almost whispered, voice.

She kept coming anyway.

"You deserve to know what's happening on your ship, sir," she said in an equally low voice. Clement put his hands behind his back, attentive, but saying nothing.

"Since the sex pond incident on Bellus, sir, Ensign Telco has developed a sort of youthful attachment to me," she said.

"Anyone can see *that*, Lieutenant," replied Clement with a slight smile.

"I have tried repeatedly to discourage him, as you know where my preferences lie in regards to...intimate relations," she said.

"Of course."

"Well the fact is this crew is mostly men and the other women frankly either don't share my interests or they just don't fancy me. So I finally gave in to Ensign Telco's affections. He's a very likeable kid, sir. And I'm sure he's learning a lot," she said.

Clement smiled broader. "And that's all to his benefit," he said. Pomeroy looked at him, then looked away. "Just don't let him get too attached," Clement warned.

She nodded. "Duly noted. I just wanted you to know, sir," she said.

"Thank you, Lieutenant. Carry on." She smiled and nodded again, then headed back to her cabin.

Clement returned to the bridge. "Ivan," he said to his navigator, "I think it's time you had a brief break. Everything is on automatic pilot and I can certainly handle any emergencies from here for a few minutes."

"That's very kind of you, sir," said Massif.

Clement looked down at his console before he spoke again. "I was thinking fifteen minutes, perhaps even twenty, if you think that would be...enough time?"

"I do, sir. Twenty minutes should be more than enough. Sir," Massif said, smiling broadly at his captain's generosity. He quickly transferred full control to Clement's console and then rushed down the stairs to his cabin.

Clement shook his head and smiled.

✿   ✿   ✿

Yan did indeed force him to take the five-hour sleeping pill, and he happily slept, waking on time to clean up and get back to his bridge, which was once again fully manned. He sat down in his seat and pulled his console closer to him. He checked his status board and saw all green on the ship's systems. He pushed the console aside. "Reports," he said loudly. His staff turned to face him. He wanted to hear it from them directly, not read it on some com board. "Our position, Lieutenant Ori?"

She turned from her console. Her face was flushed and her hair was slightly mussed from her encounter with her husband, but Clement could tell she was in good spirits. "Decelerating toward the planet Camus, sir. Our vector will put us in an orbit of four hundred sixty-two kilometers above the planet's surface," she said. "The navigator did an excellent job," she said, smiling.

Now Massif turned from his station, also smiling. "Really, sir, the credit goes to the pilot. She executed my instructions and followed my direction perfectly," he said.

"Well, congratulations to you both for an excellent . . . planetary insertion. Carry on," Clement said. Yan giggled audibly at that. Clement stood and quickly changed the subject from orbital mechanics.

"Ensign Adebayor, can you report on the course and speed of the Earth Ark?"

Adebayor stood up from her station to address her captain. "Tracing the propulsion track of the Earth Ark I can now say with more certainty that they were here approximately forty-eight hours ago. They made three orbits, then used the planet's gravity to accelerate on to the next location, the Lagrange point between the two gas planets," she said.

"Well done, Ensign," the captain said, then addressed the full bridge crew. "We'll make three orbits, as they did, then use the planet's gravity to accelerate away to the Lagrange point. Somewhere in there, we'll hopefully get a line of sight of them in open space. That will be up to you, Ensign," he said, nodding to Adebayor. "Your radio telescope will have to find them."

"Understood, sir," she said.

Clement addressed Ori again. "Take us into orbit, Pilot," he said.

"Aye, sir."

"Commander Yan, conduct a survey of the habitable side of Camus, see if it matches up with the unmanned probe's observations. And please look for signs of natives," he said.

"Aye, sir," replied Yan.

It took another forty minutes for the *Beauregard* to achieve a stable orbit over Camus, initially on her permanent dark side. The ship came around quickly to the sun-facing side of the tidal-locked planet. Clement examined the 5 Suns Alliance probe's records on the planet. Camus was approximately fifteen percent larger than her inner neighbor, Bellus, but just as pleasant according to the probe's records. Her mass was 0.68 of standard, but very close to the 0.62 of Bellus. The principal difference in the worlds was that the main land mass of Camus was in a ring around a large central saltwater ocean, which made it look like an eyeball planet.

Several islands, some that almost qualified as minor continents, dotted the ocean. The planet was warm and inviting, and seemed just as bright a prospect for colonization as her two sister worlds.

By the time they made their way to the light side of Camus her large central ocean was a gleaming blue, even in the dim red light of her tiny Trinity sun. Yan's scans showed Camus had a high oxygen content, higher even than Bellus, with an average planetary temperature of 20.5 Celsius from nearly pole to pole. Not quite as warm as Bellus, but still quite comfortable, and a positively blissful twenty-four Celsius at the equator, where a convenient string of nine large islands/small continents dotted the ocean. The band of central warmth that ran diagonally across the planet was nearly thirty-seven hundred kilometers wide, and the large islands were all comfortably ensconced in that region, both north and south of her equatorial line.

"Good design," muttered Clement as he read Yan's report. She heard him, and came to his station.

"There is something else," she said, with some trepidation.

"Something you didn't put it in your report? Why not?"

"Because I'm not sure of the scans. Each of those islands showed . . . anomalies."

Clement shifted in his chair. "Define 'anomalies,' Commander."

"I can't be certain, but each of those islands had mountains that were . . . highly regular in shape and height. Geometrically regular. Like . . ." She trailed off and looked away, almost as if she were unable to say it.

"Say it, Commander."

"Like ... pyramids, sir."

"Pyramids? As in ... constructed objects? Why wouldn't the previous probes have picked them up?"

"The automated probes were only designed for basic evaluation and survey, not for detailed exploration, sir. Also, the pyramids are offset in such a way as to appear to be a bit more natural. They could have easily escaped the probe's analysis. Sir, these pyramids, their scale is off the charts. Kilometers high. If they are constructs, no technology known to humanity could have built them," Yan said.

"What would their purpose be?"

"That I certainly can't say. But it is a mystery, one worth exploring further, in my opinion."

Clement thought about that. It was quite possible that DeVore had learned about these pyramids from the previous probe's telemetry, and he surmised that could be another reason why she wanted control of this system so badly. Possible alien technology ...

"Lieutenant Ori," he said. "Can we adjust our orbit on the next pass to fly over the equatorial islands and not disrupt our escape vector?"

"Let me check," she replied, looking down on her handheld tablet and running quick calculations. "We can do it, yes, sir. It will take a sixty-second thruster burn on our next dark-side pass"—she looked up at the ship's clock—"in thirteen minutes."

"Do it," Clement said. Then he went to Adebayor's station, trailed by Yan.

"Ensign, we're going to need full observational scans

on each of the equatorial islands. There are some mountains there that Commander Yan wants to take a closer look at. She'll pass on the coordinates."

"Aye, sir. What type of scans, Commander?" said Adebayor to Yan.

"Infrared. X-ray. Ground-penetrating radar, if you've got it, and high-resolution color photographs. Can we do all that?" asked Yan.

Adebayor nodded. "We can, sir. However, at our current orbital speed it will be difficult to get all nine islands. How many do you need?"

"A minimum of three, but five would be preferable," replied Yan.

"I can do five, sir. I'll set up an algorithm to optimize the procedure."

"Can you have it ready by our next light-side pass?" the captain asked, looking at his watch. "That's in thirty-six minutes."

"Can do, sir."

"Thank you, Ensign."

Mika Ori executed the thruster maneuver without incident, and they were soon on the light side of Camus again. Adebayor began taking her pictures as Yan monitored them in real-time from her station. Clement watched as a worrying frown came across his first officer's face. He put it down to her concentrating on the data, rather than her displeasure with what she was seeing. It took about fifteen minutes for Adebayor to complete her scans of the five islands Yan needed to make her assessment, and another twenty for Yan to analyze the results before she looked up at her captain.

"I'd like to consult with you in your cabin, Captain," she said in a noncommittal tone.

"Of course," he replied to her, then addressed Ori. "Time to our escape burn, Pilot?"

"From our current position to the initial burn point on the dark side, thirty-eight minutes, Captain," she said, then added: "It will be a 1.50 g burn, for seven minutes, sir."

"Set the ship's clock to count down to that point, Pilot. Navigator, are we still on vector for an escape burn that will take us to the Lagrange point between planets six and seven?"

"We are, sir," replied Massif.

"Prep the crew for the escape burn. Inform them safety couches are not required but they can be used at their discretion," said Clement.

"Aye, sir," said Massif with a nod.

"The commander and I will be in my cabin for the next . . . ten minutes or so?" he said, turning to Yan for confirmation. She nodded. He caught Mika Ori's eye as Yan passed him to go down the steps to his cabin, and she winked at him. He shook his head and mouthed "no," letting Ori know this was ship's business, not playtime.

He entered his cabin and shut the door behind him, joining Yan at his conference table. "You have something to report, Commander?"

"Yes, sir. Sir, those mountains . . . even from the scans that I received, which are not definitive, they are not mountains, sir. They measure almost identical in height, dimensions, square kilometers of their bases, all close enough to identical to make their differences meaningless." She pulled out her tablet and slid it across the table to Clement. "Scroll through the next five photos," she said.

Clement looked at the first one, a high-definition shot of the first island. The "mountain" was covered in greenery, the base surrounded by rich vegetation. Out of the top there was a plume of white vapor emerging. He slid to the next photo, which was at a different angle but showed essentially the same thing, without the plume. The next three photos were also similar, with some minor variations. Two of those photos showed the plumes.

"What am I looking at here, Commander?" he said.

She sat back in her chair as he slid the tablet back to her. "Essentially, Captain, these are *not* natural formations. They are architectural constructs, placed on Camus by some unknown intelligent entities."

"Human?" he asked.

She shook her head. "Unlikely. From what we've seen of Earth technology from the Ark ship they don't seem to have the scale for it. If we assume Earth technology is approximately equal with the level of the 5 Suns Alliance, then this is beyond them. It's certainly beyond us."

"Could this be technology from another Earth colony? One that was established after the 5 Suns Alliance?" he asked. She leaned forward again.

"It's been four centuries since the 5 Suns Alliance colonies were established. Another colony certainly *could* have been established somewhere in another star system, but no one who immigrated from the Sol system ever mentioned it. As far as we know, the 5 Suns Alliance are the only colonies Earth ever established. And my guess would be that if another colony *was* founded, they'd have had a very difficult time reaching this level of technology so quickly."

"You keep referring to it as 'technology,' but all I see are very large hills. Artificial, yes, but what are they for?" asked Clement.

"Terraforming," said Yan. "Those plumes you see are a combination of oxygen, nitrogen, carbon dioxide, and trace organic materials. Whoever made these pyramids is clearly engaged in terraforming, and it appears to be an ongoing process. My studies show the ocean depth between the islands to be somewhere between ten and twenty meters. It is my belief that these 'islands' were once part of a single land mass. The ocean levels have risen over time and much of the land mass is now below the waterline."

"How long would a process like that take?"

"My best guess is about five centuries, but I'm no geologist, though we do have one on board. Should I put that question to him?"

"No," said Clement. He looked at the tablet pictures again. "What about—"

"Inhabitants? I have found some indication that they are down there, though obviously in a primitive social state, much like Mary and our friends on Bellus," Yan said.

"Now I can see why Admiral DeVore wants this system so badly. It's a treasure trove of natural resources and advanced technology, whether that technology is human or . . . otherwise. Let's keep this between you and me for now, Yan. We won't be going down to Camus on this trip, that much is certain. I suggest we go back to our bridge and concentrate on our escape burn to the Lagrange point."

"Yes, sir," said Yan, taking back her tablet. Right at that moment Clement's com chimed in. It was Ivan Massif from the bridge.

"Captain, we may have a situation up here," he said, speaking with urgency in his voice.

"We'll be right there."

With that Clement and Yan were up and out of his cabin and heading to the bridge.

"The bogey has been shadowing us for seven minutes now, sir," said Mika Ori.

Clement looked at his tactical display and found a small black dot tracking their every move. "Where did it come from?"

"After using our telemetry to retrace its track, we picked it up on the last pass over the dark side of Camus. My guess is it was on the surface just waiting for us to pass by overhead," replied Massif.

"Yes, but was it left here by the Earth Ark or by... someone else?" Clement asked.

"Someone else? Who could that be?" asked Ori.

Clement deflected that question with another. "Can we get a shot of it from one of our scanners or cameras, Ensign Adebayor?"

"Trying now, sir," she replied.

Clement turned back to Ori. "What's her speed?"

"Matching ours exactly, sir," replied Ori.

"Distance?"

"Ten thousand kilometers and holding, sir."

Clement looked up at the ship's clock; still seventeen minutes to the *Beauregard*'s escape burn. He called down to Nobli in the reactor room. "Hassan, how much time would you need to prep the LEAP engine for another in-system jump?" he asked.

"To where?" replied Nobli.

"To the Lagrange point between the two outer gas giants."

Nobli hesitated. "I can warm her now, sir, but I don't recommend we keep making these short jumps as a matter of course. Is it absolutely necessary?"

"I don't know that yet, Engineer," Clement replied.

"Sir," said Nobli over the com, "these short jumps put an awful lot of stress on the reactor casings. You're releasing a tremendous amount of energy in a very short time frame. The reactor was designed to run constantly for long durations, like a thirty-four-day journey. It wasn't designed to be used for microsecond jumps inside star systems, or as a weapon, for that matter."

"I hear you, Engineer," said Clement. "Can I trust you to hold her together two or three more times?"

"I can't guarantee that, sir, in all honesty."

Clement thought about the situation. Nobli's honesty gave him pause. They had a little over fifteen minutes to the escape burn, which would almost certainly place them in a hostile environment. The likelihood he would need the weapon again seemed high, but he couldn't use it on their mysterious pursuer, nor could he use missiles. He'd have to turn the ship for that, and if the bogey attacked, they could get caught in the middle of their turn maneuver.

"Warm the LEAP reactor, Engineer. Coordinate with the navigator on our destination point. We may have to use the LEAP engine to escape the situation we find ourselves in. Prompt me at my command console when she's ready. If we have to make the jump to the Lagrange point, I'll need you to keep the reactor up and running in case we have to use the weapon. Understood?"

"Understood, sir. But if she cracks . . . we could lose the ship. Hell, half the solar system. And there's still the issue of the return trip home."

"Acknowledged, Nobli. Proceed as ordered," Clement said, then signed off. "Ensign Adebayor, do we have an analysis of the bogey yet?"

"Just coming up now, sir," she replied.

"Show me."

The tactical display lit up with a basic outline of a flat-headed cylinder with a protruding end cap. A simple design, with a high-yield atomic thrust cluster in the back. "Radiation scan?"

"Just coming in now, sir," said Yan from her station. "Indications of a two-kiloton warhead attached, sir."

Clement stepped down from his station and looked at the design as it spun on the tactical display in a 3D graphics presentation. "This is a hunter-killer," he said. "An automated weapon designed to be used to hunt targets stealthily until it unleashes its full power on the target. My guess is she can accelerate to overtake us any time she wants. In such a situation, we'd only have seconds to respond. These kinds of weapons were outlawed in the War of the 5 Suns because the use of AI was considered immoral. But our enemies seem to have no such moral compunction against using them." He hurried back to his station. The LEAP engine icon was green, indicating the reactor was warm enough to be put into use, albeit in an increasingly dangerous maneuver.

"Pilot, increase speed to 1.25 g," he called. That was the minimum required for their escape burn.

"1.25 g, aye, sir."

Clement turned to Yan. "Inform the crew we may be experiencing higher than expected g-force acceleration. Tell them to prep for a possible LEAP jump. Everyone not required to run the reactor to acceleration couches."

"Aye, sir," said Yan, then repeated Clement's instructions on the ship-wide com.

"Report, pilot."

"Bogey has increased speed to 1.25 g. Now 1.3 gs. Now 1.5. Continuing to accelerate, sir."

"Thrusters to three gs, pilot," said Clement, raising his voice.

"Sir, not all the crew has signaled ready," chimed in Yan.

"No time. They'll have to rough it out," Clement responded as Ori hit the thrusters and the weight of three-g acceleration pushed him back in his couch. He watched the tactical display.

"Bogey has increased speed. 3.5 gs and range is closing. Estimate intercept in one hundred forty-one seconds, sir. Bogey speed now 5.25 gs and continuing to accelerate. Should I activate the main burn thruster, sir?" said Ori.

"Negative. Navigator?"

"Vector established for LEAP jump, but not as precise

as I'd like," said Massif, struggling against gravity to get the words out.

"Bogey at six *g*s, sir," grunted out Ori. "Seven-teeeeeen . . . seconds . . . to . . . inter . . . cept . . ."

There was no choice now. With difficulty, he pulled his console close with just seconds to spare . . .

Clement woke up on the floor below his station. He'd neglected to strap in before the LEAP engine was activated. He wanted to vomit, and retched for a few seconds before his head stopped spinning and he stabilized. Mika Ori ran past him, holding her hand to her mouth as she ran for her cabin. He lifted a heavy hand to grip his couch and dragged himself up to his station. The tactical telemetry showed him his ship was decelerating at a steady rate, 2.5 *g*s, 2.4, and so on. He looked to Yan. She was pale and drawn-looking but at least she'd had the sense to strap in. Mika returned to the bridge in about a minute. Massif gave her a comforting hug.

"Status report," Clement said, his voice cracking. Ori chimed in first.

"Decelerating to one *g*, Captain. We should be there in about three minutes," she said. Clement sat more upright in his couch.

"What's our position, Navigator?"

"We overshot the Lagrange point by 0.000086 AU, sir, about thirteen thousand kilometers. I told you we couldn't be precise."

"Acknowledged. Ensign Adebayor, what's the status of the Earth Ark? Is she at the Lagrange point? Can you find her?"

"Negative, sir. It looks like she pushed on toward the

outer gas planet at some point, but her trail is still fresh. Estimate we're less than eight hours behind her," said Adebayor. Clement turned his attention back to Ori.

"Set speed at 1.5 g for the duration, Pilot, pursuit course." Ori hesitated a second before replying, as if reluctant to follow her orders. Finally, she gave an "Aye, sir" and complied. A second later Nobli was chiming in on Clement's com.

"Report, Engineer."

"We have a broken reactor, sir," said Nobli with just a trace of resignation in his voice. "I warned you this could happen. Microfractures in the reactor casing, sir. One or a million of those mini anti-matter universes we annihilate every second could have escaped through the cracks. We got lucky, sir."

"Better lucky than dead, Engineer. How long until the reactor can be repaired?" said Clement.

"I'm not sure it can be repaired. It will have to be scrapped and replaced when we get back to Kemmerine, sir."

"We can't get back to Kemmerine in our lifetimes if it can't be repaired. Unacceptable, Engineer. Give me an alternative."

"Oh, I can patch the micro-fissures, if I can find them all, with carbon-fiber nanotubes and the like, but she's forever fractured, and I can't guarantee she won't implode on us if we try to jump like that again. Once she's patched we can likely run her in a steady-state condition for the trip home, but that's about all I can promise you."

"And the weapon?"

"Untenable at this time, Captain," snapped Nobli with

a touch of anger in his voice that the captain would even ask such a thing. Clement thought about that, but not for long. He needed his MAD capability.

"Get to work with Ensign Tsu and borrow any techs you need to patch the casing."

"That will take many hours, Captain."

"Understood, Nobli. You have about eight, maybe less. But . . . I may need that reactor to hold on long enough to use the weapon again."

"I don't recommend that," said Nobli flatly.

"Note your protest in the engineer's log. My orders stand. Prep her for use as a weapon, and make sure she has enough left over to get us home," snapped Clement, then he cut the line. Like it or not, this had to work. It *had* to.

Thirty minutes later and Clement was in his cabin, monitoring all the ship's functions. The hunter-killer had vainly tried to catch the *Beauregard* and stayed on her intercept course even after the gunship had made her LEAP jump. Telemetry showed it eventually burned through its fuel supply and would now drift through the Trinity system on the same trajectory for eons, no longer a threat to anyone. He noted its location. They could intercept it on a future mission or destroy it outright. But not now. For now it was just flying in a straight line with no more fuel, drifting alone in space.

Scans along the path of the Earth Ark indicated they were closing in on her, but precisely what she was doing out here at the edge of the Trinity system near two uninhabitable planets was uncertain. It was something he wanted to figure out before they made the LEAP home, rather than leave the system undefended. And, if he was honest, he still wanted to disable or destroy the thing, if possible. It was a risk worth taking, in his eyes.

The knock on his door came from Yan, as expected. What she presented to him, though, was not.

"Most of the crew want to go home, now," she said as she sat across from him at his worktable, her hands clasped together. She was all business. "Rumors have gotten around that the LEAP drive is compromised, but that you still may want to use her as a weapon—"

"Nobli . . ." started Clement, shaking his head, angry at his engineer. Yan continued talking over her captain.

"It was Ensign Tsu that alerted me, Captain, not Nobli. To continue, most of the crew are now against further conflict. They think you're risking the ship to get revenge."

"Revenge? On whom or what would I be taking this revenge?" Clement demanded. He did not like the tone or direction this conversation was taking.

"The Earthers, for killing Daniel. DeVore. The entire 5 Suns Alliance. There are plenty of conspiracy theories going around." Clement sat back, rocking in his chair briskly as he contemplated her, and the implications of this situation.

"We already *had* a vote, Commander. They agreed to pursue the Earth Ark until its location and purpose could be determined. We are still on that mission. My hope is that the MAD weapon never has to be used again, but we need it for our own protection, just in case we get into a tactically untenable situation. I still intend to take this ship home, but perhaps not on the crew's schedule." He looked at his watch, synchronized with the ship's clock on the bridge. "In less than six hours we should be able to observe the Earth Ark. She has slowed her speed consistent with decelerating to a destination. What the destination is, I don't know. But I intend to find out," he said.

"So you refuse to take us home at this time?"

He nodded. "That's my decision, and I thought it was the crew's as well."

At that Yan got up and went to his cabin door, opening it from the inside. Several crew members, led by Lieutenant Pomeroy, came into the room, some standing outside the doorway, filling the hall. He recognized Telco and Tsu among them, but none of the bridge crew. Pomeroy, Telco, and Tsu were armed with cobra pistols.

"So it's to be a mutiny, Yan?" Clement said, standing but staying as cool as he could under the circumstances. "After you swore your allegiance to me more than once? And now it's come to this? I overestimated you, Commander, and your honesty."

"I have family in the 5 Suns Alliance, Jared, you know that," she said.

"All of us do," added Pomeroy. Yan looked to the deck, then back up at Clement.

"Captain Jared Clement, in the name of the 5 Suns Alliance Navy I am hereby"—she paused here and took a deep breath—"*relieving* you of command of the 5SN gunship *Beauregard* under Article Three, Section 5.1a of the Navy Code of Justice. You will remain in this cabin under confinement to quarters until further notice. When we return to Kemmerine Station you will be turned over to the Naval Military Service for your court-martial to be adjudicated. Do you understand this order?" she said, implying her rank was now higher than his.

"I do," replied Clement. "But may I remind all of you that you swore an oath to follow me, not the 5 Suns Alliance Navy Command, just a few hours ago. All of you will likely stand trial for that action, and whatever justice I receive I'm sure you are likely to receive something similar from the 5SN. So, if you wish to go through with this, just be reminded that the penalty for mutiny under both the 5 Suns Alliance and the old Rim Confederation Code of Justice is death by hanging. If that's what you wish to risk, I can't stop you. But the fact is, that I am far more likely to be lenient with you than Admiral DeVore will be. May I remind you she sabotaged this mission by giving us fake nuclear missiles. She gave this ship, and all of your lives, up as a sacrifice just so she could see what kind of threat this Earth Ark presented. If that is the person you wish to follow now, I won't resist you. But think on this: We have the means and ability to finish off this threat from the Earth Ark, and guarantee this system is free of outside threats to its native peoples. This will give the 5 Suns, and each of your families, a fighting chance to survive for the next hundred years, and beyond. But if we lose this system, we could lose everything, our entire civilization, in our lifetimes. If you wish to follow your current course, then so be it. There's nothing more I can do." At this Clement sat down, resigned to his fate.

A second later, things changed. Ensign Telco pointed his pistol at Tsu and then disarmed him, tossing the weapon to Clement, who caught it and trained it on

Pomeroy. The ship's medic also handed her weapon to Telco, who backed up to Clement's side of the room, and the mutineers began slowly raising their hands.

"There will be no mutiny on my watch," said Telco. "The captain's right. I swore loyalty to him and to this mission. And we can't trust Admiral DeVore, that much is for sure."

"Thank you, Mr. Telco," said Clement. "We can't have this on board the *Beauregard*. A mutiny, failed or not, cannot stand. We have to trust each other for this to work." He powered down his cobra pistol and walked over, handing it to Yan. Telco followed his lead, giving his guns back to Tsu and Lieutenant Pomeroy. None of the guns were raised now. Clement hit the com button.

"Engineer Nobli, there are some very concerned people in my cabin who think we should return home to Kemmerine Station immediately. Is that possible?" he said.

"Another few hours of patching the reactor and we could do it, sir," replied Nobli.

"Fine. Another question, Hassan. Since you're the only one on board who can operate the reactor, would you activate it if someone besides me was giving you the order to go back home to Kemmerine?"

"Kemmerine was never my home, sir. Argyle is; you know that. And I will follow no one's orders but yours, sir. You saved my life a dozen times in the Rim Confederation Navy."

"Thank you, Hassan," Clement said, then cut the line and turned back to the would-be mutineers. "I think you would find similar sentiments among the pilot, navigator, and obviously your missile-room tech," he said with a nod toward Telco.

"You stacked the key positions with people loyal to you," said Pomeroy, angry.

"That's what every captain does, Lieutenant," replied Clement. He looked around the room at the faces of his crew. Few of them would meet his gaze. "I understand all of your concerns, believe me. My parents still live on Ceta and the decisions I make here could adversely affect them if I'm wrong. I know you're worried. So am I. But my suggestion is that we all let his situation play itself out, allow me to go forward with our surveillance of the Earth Ark, which will only be for a few hours more. I will allow Commander Yan and Lieutenant Pomeroy to act as advisors to represent the rest of the crew, if they think I am putting the ship in *unnecessary* danger, I will give them the power of the veto over my orders. Are these terms acceptable?"

There were mutters of agreement and some negative grumbling, but ultimately no one spoke up in opposition to the proposal. When things settled down again, he said, "Then let's get back to work, and quite bluntly, forget this incident ever happened."

At this the crowd started to break up. Pomeroy looked to Yan, who could only hang her head in shame. Telco collected the cobra pistols and they all shuffled back to their assignments, leaving him and Yan alone. Yan looked up to face her commander.

"Captain, I wish to . . . take some time to reflect on my recent actions, in my cabin, sir," she said.

"Take all the time you need, Commander," replied

Clement. "But don't be too hard on yourself. This mission has been difficult for all of us, and I still need you functioning as my effective XO."

Yan nodded without another word and departed his cabin.

Once Yan was gone Clement thanked Telco and ordered him back to the missile room, and to be sure to lock the weapons lockers. With that Clement went back to his bridge and found Massif, Ori, and Adebayor waiting for him. Both Massif and Ori wore holstered sidearms.

"We were never giving command of this ship to mutineers, Captain. We wanted you to know that," said Massif. Clement nodded.

"Thank you, Ivan." He turned on the ship-wide com and spoke into it in a calm voice.

"All hands return to your stations and resume your assignments. All is well," he said. Then he sat down heavily in his command couch and sighed.

❋ 20 ❋

The next five hours were tense. Yan did not return to the bridge until a few minutes before the radio-telescope scans were projected to sight the Earth Ark. She asked for Clement's permission to take her station, and he granted it, but not without making her linger at the threshold for more than a few seconds. He wasn't happy with her involvement in the mutiny, and he reserved the right to be pissed off about it. Until that point he had thought they had developed an excellent commander/first officer rapport, but now he felt that trust was broken and he admitted to himself that his feelings were hurt, and that was something he had to be conscious of going forward.

He watched as Yan took her station and activated her dark console. Just then Mika Ori unstrapped her holster and pulled her sidearm slightly out, fingering the safety by clicking it off and on several times before returning the weapon to the holster. She never looked at Yan, but the message was clear, and he was sure Yan picked up on the unspoken signal. There would be a price to pay if she undermined her captain again. Unfortunately, Yan decided to speak up about it.

"Are sidearms now standard issue on the bridge, Captain?" she said.

Clement took a deep breath before responding.

"Lieutenant Ori and Lieutenant Commander Massif have my permission to wear a sidearm at all times, as does Ensign Telco. I would prefer the rest of the crew remains unarmed," he said in as calm and even a voice as he could muster. Ori glared at Yan with an angry look on her face, and Clement did nothing to discourage her, sitting with his hands folded across his console. After a tense moment Yan looked down at her board and Ori returned her attention to her console.

"Do we have a bead on the Earth Ark yet, Ensign?" Clement asked Adebayor.

"Long-range scanners should pick up the Ark in another thirty-three minutes, sir," she said.

"Thank you, Ensign. Navigator, range to the intercept point of the Earth Ark?"

"Seven hundred fifty thousand kilometers, sir. Suggest we begin deceleration to slow our approach to any potential battlefield, sir," Massif said. Ori turned and Clement nodded.

"As suggested, Pilot," he said. She turned and began the deceleration process.

"Are we planning on entering a battlefield?" This came from Yan, and was seen as an unwelcome comment from the rest of the bridge crew, including Clement, who swiveled to face her, speaking slowly.

"I have no intent of taking this ship into battle again, Commander. But I do intend to get close enough to that Earth Ark to determine what she's doing out here, and what her future intent is in the Trinity system and toward the natives. When that is done, other courses of action will be considered, including retreating to Kemmerine, but not until. Is that clear?" he said. His anger was apparent to all the bridge crew, including Yan.

"It is clear, sir," was all she managed in reply.

"Good," he said, swiveling back to the main screen. "Feel free to share the same with your colleagues, Commander," he said, meaning of course her fellow failed mutineers.

Clement called down to Adebayor again. "Does the deceleration change your calculation to visual observation of the Earth Ark, Ensign?" he said.

"No, sir," she said, flashing her stunning smile. "I calculated a standard deceleration into my equations, sir."

"And what if I chose a nonstandard deceleration plan, Ensign?" said Ori, challenging the young officer.

The smile faded from Adebayor's face. "Then obviously, ma'am, I would have to recalculate," said Adebayor.

"Hmm . . ." said Ori, then: "Deceleration rate is standard. Carry on, Ensign."

"Yes, ma'am." Clement smiled to himself at the exchange. This crew needed more of that, experienced spacers pushing the young officers to improve. He regretted it would probably not happen on this ill-fated mission.

Thirty-two minutes later they got their first ping.

"Detecting multiple large objects, about where we would expect them to be," reported Adebayor.

"Multiple objects? Are you sure, Ensign?"

Adebayor threw her console display to the main screen. It showed a long cylinder, obviously the Earth Ark, but two more large blobs flanking her.

"Is that the best visual we can do?" Clement said.

"We're still eighty thousand klicks from the Ark, sir, and moving, as are they," said Massif, helping out the young Ensign with an explanation of the poor visual quality.

"I should be able to get higher-definition photography with the radio telescope as we get closer," stated Adebayor.

"Keep it on the main screen, Ensign, and put up a tactical window as well."

"Aye, sir."

Clement watched as the main screen painted a new view about every ten seconds. With each pass, the picture became clearer. Clement went to the ship-wide com.

"All hands, this is the captain. We are now in visual range of the Earth Ark. She is moving slowly; her direction is pointing away from us, but her actions at this time are yet to be determined. As we get closer and the visual definition of the situation becomes more clear, I will update you on our status. Clement out."

The bridge crew watched in silence as the picture continually repainted for several minutes. The tactical display gave no indication of any further identification of the two blobs on the Earth Ark's flanks. Things stayed tense and quiet until the *Beauregard* reached the ten-thousand-kilometer mark. The two flanking clouds now had some definition, and Clement ordered Adebayor to enhance her scans on the closest visual blob of data near the Earth Ark.

The scan repainted a few more times before Clement ordered a hold. He pointed at the screen. "That's a flotilla formation," he said. "I'd stake my reputation on it. I can make out individual ships. That one there looks like one of the Earth Ark cruisers. Do you agree, Ivan?"

"I do, sir," he said.

"I can make out the clippers as well," said Mika Ori.

"There's another class of ship—let me see if I can make it out," piped in Yan, trying to contribute.

"Don't bother. Those tubelike objects are hunter-killers," said Clement. A few seconds later and the tactical system alerts went off like wildfire. The numbers came across the screen in rapid succession. Twenty-four of the cruisers. Over sixty light attack clippers and thirty hunter-killers. No doubt the other flanking formation was made up of similar numbers. "By volume and displacement, I'm willing to bet she's deployed her entire battle force in those two formations. Do you agree, Mika?"

The *Beauregard*'s pilot nodded. "I do, sir. The other formation is now coming in with similar numbers. Assuming the rest of her mass area is reserved for ground soldiers and transports, I'd say she's maxed out her space-borne battle capabilities."

"Sir, those two battle groups are accelerating, pulling away from the Ark," said Adebayor, a nervous tone in her voice.

"But pulling away toward what?" said Clement out loud. He sat back down in his couch and studied both the tactical and visual live streams of data.

"I would say this, sir." The voice belonged to Ivan Massif, and he threw his navigational tracker to the main screen.

It showed a distant group of objects with glowing thrusters, their engines burning bright, hurtling toward the Earth Ark's position at high speed. The Ark's attack flotillas were accelerating to meet them.

"We've stumbled onto that battlefield," said Clement.

"But who are they fighting?" asked Yan, looking to Clement. "The terraformers?"

Mika Ori's head snapped around at that comment, but she said nothing.

Clement looked to his first officer, then back to the screen. He stepped forward and spoke loudly enough so that everyone on the bridge could hear him. "No, not terraformers," he said, shaking his head. "But I'm willing to bet my entire bonus that the fleet coming at us is commanded by Admiral Elara DeVore."

The bridge was dead silent at his proclamation, and no one challenged it. Within a few minutes they had confirmation of the same. The 5 Suns Alliance Navy fleet consisted of three battlecruisers, half of what was based at Kemmerine Station when they had left; and twelve heavy cruisers, sixteen destroyers, and five gunships, which Clement guessed were the remaining hulls from the Rim Confederation fleet, converted to use by the Admiral just as the *Beauregard* had been. They were in a spread wing formation, or "Eagle" as they termed it, much like he had faced many times in the War of the 5 Suns. The flanking pair of battlecruisers were surrounded by formations of four heavy cruisers and five destroyers each, with the central group having the extra sixth destroyer protecting the capital ship. The command battlecruiser, no doubt

Admiral DeVore's flagship, was positioned the furthest back in the formation. The five gunships were at the front of the whole fleet, essentially missile-launching platforms spread out evenly in the formation. The battlecruiser groups were designed to move independently if need be, or to be used as a blunt-force hammer if they stayed together.

The Earth forces were aligned in a seemingly haphazard way, with the light cruisers at different, random positions, the hunter-killers moving to the front of the formation, and the clippers mixing in at random throughout the formation. Both fleets were closing fast on each other now.

"I thought we were the only 5 Suns Navy ship that had the LEAP drive. Weren't we supposed to be a prototype?" said Yan.

Clement shook his head. "No, Commander. We were just the bait. Admiral DeVore must have made this plan from the moment one of her automated probes detected the Earth Ark approaching the Trinity system," he responded. "Estimation of the time until the two forces engage on the battlefield," commanded Clement, not caring who answered the question.

It was Mika Ori. "Seven minutes until the 5 Suns Alliance ships reach missile range, sir, but at the rate everyone's moving, they'll crash into each other first and then it will be a free-for-all," she said.

"I wouldn't expect that from Admiral DeVore," Clement replied, relying on his experiences with her in the War of the 5 Suns. "She's usually quite calculated in how she approaches these things." *And many others*, he thought to himself.

"What do we do?" It was Yan asking the question.

"We lay back and watch, then deal with the winner," said Clement. "Bring us to full stop, Pilot."

"Full stop, aye, sir," said Ori.

"What about the Earth Ark itself? She's just laying back," said Yan.

"Keep an eye on her, Commander. And let me know if she starts to move." Yan just nodded, upset at being relegated to side duty, but Clement didn't care. She had made her own bed, now she had to lie in it.

They all watched as the two fleets closed on each other at incredible speeds. Ori had been right. It would be like a jousting match, both "horsemen" taking their best shots, then breaking off the attack and reforming for another run. It was the kind of battle that could only be conducted with large forces, but Clement found it wasteful. Many lives would be lost in the first few minutes, snuffed out in an instant, men and women disintegrated by atomic missiles or torn apart to die in space by kinetic weapons. And then it would get dirty. Ship-to-ship warfare, probably at too close of quarters for atomic weapons. It would devolve to Directed Energy Weapons or short-range conventional missiles, cutting each fleet to pieces, and possibly even boarding parties, invading and slaughtering each other. Clement had seen enough of it in the War of the 5 Suns, and had hoped never to see it again. In that moment, he regretted ever taking this command.

As he expected, Admiral DeVore made the first move. The starboard battlecruiser group broke from the Eagle formation and made a slashing, high-speed run at the corresponding Earth Ark battle group. The central and port 5 Suns battlecruiser groups, the central one being led by DeVore, both broke to the port side of the Earth Ark formation. They quickly regrouped into an attacking cylinder formation, with the battlecruisers enveloped by their heavy cruisers and destroyers. To his surprise, the five converted Rim Confederation gunships went to the front of the larger attacking group and accelerated, dropping some kind of kinetic charges ahead of the attacking fleet.

"What are those? Scatter mines?" asked Ori.

"Looks like it," said Clement. "We don't have any scatter mines on board and we're not even designed to deploy them. Those gunships were probably retrofitted to carry them."

They watched the portside battle formations as the Earth Ark's hunter-killers took the initiative, fifteen of them accelerating at high-g speeds the manned ships couldn't match. They were trying to get under the curtain of descending scatter mines that the gunships had laid down, but it would be a closely run thing. Very close. If the HuKs could get under the mines, they could attack the underbelly of Admiral DeVore's portside battle group.

The scatter mines had a limited mobility programmed into them, and they burned their thrusters trying to reach the hunter-killers. The HuKs kept varying their approaches, trying to create different angles of attack.

The HuKs slammed into the minefield, several of them exploding in nuclear fireballs on contact. The mines were reacting by trying to track the HuKs and get close enough to detonate, but in the end six of the fifteen Earth weapons got through the initial Five Suns fleet line of defense.

Next, DeVore sent her heavy cruisers and destroyers into the fray against the Earth Ark's light cruisers and clippers. Almost immediately two of the HuKs homed in on one of the 5 Suns cruisers and hit it almost simultaneously, with the heavy cruiser going up in a fireball of nuclear fission. DeVore's destroyers and gunships then barraged the remaining HuKs with a copious amount of missiles, conventional ones, designed to create a literal web of explosive power in their paths. This was a tactic Clement had seen before in battles with the 5 Suns Alliance Navy many times. It was a sheer numbers game and the 5SN had the advantage, and whenever they had the advantage, they used it.

The four remaining HuKs weren't smart enough to change course to avoid the web of incoming ordnance. They slammed into the missile barrage, exploding on contact with missiles or disintegrating into shredded metal as their speed itself tore them apart. At this, DeVore's fleet started the long curve back to intercept the remainder of the Earth Ark's forces. There were scattered skirmishes between the Earth light cruisers and DeVore's destroyers, and the Earth ships had the firepower advantage there. But it would take any two Earth cruisers to take on one of the 5 Suns Alliance heavy cruisers, and DeVore had seven of those left in her formation. The clippers, for their part, simply picked out individual targets and hit them with missiles or DEW beams, trying to cut pieces into the larger 5 Suns Alliance ships. A group of the clippers broke away from the main group and pursued the gunships.

Privately, Clement hoped the gunships survived, more out of nostalgia for his old Rim Confederation Navy days than anything else, but he showed none of that emotion to his crew.

He switched his attention back to the starboard battle group. They had engaged at a much slower pace than DeVore's main battle group. The Earth hunter-killers had taken a toll on the 5 Suns heavy cruisers and destroyers. There was no doubt that this 5 Suns battle group had a reliable commander, but he or she hadn't had the advantage of the scatter-mine web that had been dropped by the gunships. The commander had endured the heavy punishment of the hunter-killers, taking three of the Earth weapons out with missiles before they could reach their targets. The destroyers and heavy cruisers had taken on the hard task of clearing the field of the remaining HuKs, and one of each of those class of ships had been taken out by the Earth weapons. The group commander had moved his battlecruiser up into the fray, unlike DeVore and her battle group, which had held the two capital ships back. The battlecruiser took hits from two of the surviving HuKs, but seemed none the worse for wear. She had ragged-edged tears in her port side and had no doubt lost crew, but she was actively engaging the Earth force's light cruisers and clippers with her DEW weapons and a flurry of low-yield, high-speed conventional missiles. With the two groups so closely aligned, the use of nuclear weapons would have assured mutual destruction, so for the moment, they weren't being used. Clement wondered if the Earth cruiser commanders had orders to self-destruct in the event of a potential loss. It certainly fit their previous mode of operation, and that made him worry.

He turned his attention back to the gunships that were attempting to get behind DeVore's destroyer line while being pursued by the large flotilla of Earth clippers. One of the fleeing gunships had suffered propulsion damage of some kind, and at least a dozen of the clippers swarmed over her, attacking with their DEW weapons and short-range missiles. She was damaged and listing, and looked to be in serious trouble. The lead gunship commander, however, decelerated and then turned their ship toward the swarms of clippers, engaging in a rear-guard action to allow his fellow gunships to escape beyond DeVore's destroyer line, while also attempting to rescue his wounded sister ship. He fired a barrage of six high-yield missiles, followed ten seconds later by a second volley. The missiles did the trick, taking out almost all of the clippers. The gunship commander pursued the remaining few enemy clippers and took them out with heavy Directed Energy Weapons fire. They were too late to save their sister ship, though. The mortally wounded gunship drifted, spinning rapidly and burning as it vented oxygen, fire, and probably crew into space. The gunship group commander watched from a safe distance as the critically damaged gunship exploded. There was a brief respite as the group commander waded in on the wreckage of its lost sister ship, no doubt searching for escape pods. Clement had been in one of those before and it was no safe haven in the midst of a battle. The command gunship completed a quick search, and finding no survivors, turned and made its way back to DeVore's battle group, which was engaged in a maneuver to put it back onto the main battlefield. Clement wondered what the gunship's captain must have been thinking. He'd been faced with the same situation many times, and it had always hurt to lose comrades.

While the portside battle group commander was simply holding the line against the arrayed Earth forces, Admiral DeVore's starboard group was once again fully engaged in maneuvers against her foes. She hadn't committed either of her battlecruisers yet, but he expected her to play that trump card soon, and she didn't disappoint. The secondary battlecruiser jumped into the fray with DEW and high-yield conventional missiles, just a notch below a nuke in their total expended-energy levels. The use of the capital ship looked like it was going to be a decisive one.

The Earth forces responded the only way they could: by committing their ships to ramming their superior opponents. One of the Earth cruisers collided with a 5 Suns Alliance heavy cruiser and then did the unthinkable.

She detonated a nuke, destroying both ships.

"Oh my god," said Mika Ori, her hand going to cover her mouth in horror. Clement was brought back to reality by the shock of seeing the Earth cruiser commit suicide, but he wasn't surprised.

"We can't be moved by what we see," he said to his bridge crew, trying to reassure everyone. "The Earth forces play a different set of rules than we do. We've seen that already." A second suicide explosion occurred and then a third happened, and the 5 Suns Alliance forces smartly began to pull back from the Earth ships.

For their part, the clippers had taken to ramming the 5 Suns Alliance destroyers, something they were clearly designed to do, then attacking them with boarding parties. Clement saw one of the 5 Suns destroyers go up in flames, most likely from a nonatomic detonation. He doubted the 5 Suns Alliance crew would do such a thing, so it seemed likely that one of the clipper boarding parties had taken the destroyer's missile room and detonated a warhead inside the ship, the resulting chain reaction leading to the fatal explosion. Another 5 Suns Alliance destroyer had six clippers dangling off of it as it listed through the battlefield. He watched as the destroyer turned on a nearby heavy cruiser, both ships flying the 5 Suns flag, and started firing missiles at it. Clearly the Earth forces boarding party had taken control of the destroyer's bridge. A second 5 Suns heavy cruiser broke off from its engagement with two Earth cruisers and swept toward the rogue destroyer, firing missiles and DEW beams as it came. The destroyer, already damaged by the clippers and no doubt taken over by their Earth crews, didn't last long under that barrage, exploding as her engine drives were taken out.

Finally, DeVore got the rest of her capital ships into the fray. Both battlecruisers slashed at the Earth force formation from different sides, DEW cannons firing but holding back on missiles. It was a crowded battlefield, and using even conventional missiles at these kinds of ranges could create serious battle damage to friendly forces. Clement wondered if the battlecruisers had something else up their sleeves, and it didn't take long to detect a new development. Streaks of kinetic weapons, like long metal poles, started hitting the remaining Earth forces dead on.

"What are those things?" asked Ori.

"Some kind of nonexplosive kinetic rounds, likely fired by a rail gun of some kind. They look pretty long," he said.

"I make them at almost twenty meters," said Adebayor, surprise in her voice.

"About the height of your average telephone pole," said Clement.

"What's a 'telephone pole'?" asked Yan.

Clement shook his head at Yan's ignorance, but it was to be expected based on her privileged upbringing on Shenghai. "A telephone pole is a wooden pole stuck into the ground that carries elevated power, telecommunications, and information lines to rural houses, farms, and the like," he said.

"I've never heard of such a thing," said Yan, still surprised.

Clement turned to her, speaking without a hint of sympathy in his voice. "If you'd grown up on a Rim planet, like Ceta, or Argyle, or Helios, you'd know what they are. Coming from a privileged colony like Shenghai, I'm not surprised you've never seen one. Only poor colonies have to use them," he said, then turned away from her.

"They're made of some kind of metal alloy," piped in Adebayor. "My scans show that much."

"Most likely titanium and depleted uranium. They've been used in kinetic weapons for literally hundreds of years. Accelerated by a rail gun, their destructive power comes mostly from kinetic energy. You could cut a ship to pieces using one, especially with the penetrating properties of depleted uranium, and they're a lot cheaper than missiles," Clement said.

"It's like a lance from Hell," commented Ori.

"I like that," said Clement, "Hell Lances."

They watched as the two battlecruisers continued to bombard the Earth cruisers and clippers with the Hell Lances, cutting them to pieces with dozens of them with each pass through the battlefield. The destroyers and heavy cruisers swarmed the wounded Earth forces, finishing them off.

On the portside battlefield, things were more even, but the 5 Suns Alliance battlecruiser, obviously freed to use their own Hell Lances, was starting to cut up the Earth light cruisers and clippers. It wasn't a fair fight to begin with, and now Elara DeVore turned her own formation toward the second battlefield.

It would be a slaughter.

They watched for a few minutes more as the Earth ships fought to the bitter end, but DeVore's combined fleet finished them off to the last man, which is probably the way the Earth forces wanted it.

The total 5 Suns Alliance attack fleet reformed around the capital battlecruisers, and Clement did a recount of Admiral DeVore's remaining ships. The three battlecruisers were mostly untouched. There were nine heavy cruisers still left and thirteen destroyers, although ships of both of those groups had taken some serious battle damage, but were still operational. Those plus the four gunships left Devore with twenty-nine operational ships.

"What now?" asked Ori.

"Now, I would assume they will take out the Earth Ark itself," said Clement.

"How?"

"If it was me, I'd just fire long-range nukes and be done with her. But Admiral DeVore may have other plans. Captured technology is valuable technology."

They watched as DeVore sent in the gunships to launch missiles at the Earth Ark. To his surprise the Ark didn't respond to this provocation, and the conventional missiles did only minimal damage to the Ark's reinforced hull. Next, she sent in a formation of three destroyers. They were clearly among the most damaged ships in her fleet, indicating she was not willing to risk her best. That was telling as to her regard for the people that served under her.

Two of the destroyers closed on the Ark. The third destroyer seemed to be having propulsion problems and ended up dropping back several klicks from the other two. In the next few seconds, it would be her saving grace.

The first two destroyers began a bombardment of the Earth Ark with higher-yield missiles and DEW fire. The missiles had more of an effect than the ones launched by the gunships, but it was still fairly insignificant damage against the massive Ark. The directed-energy fire was a difference-maker though. The two destroyers began cutting into the sides of the Ark, exposing ragged gashes of her inner superstructure. In one case, there seemed to be a hit on a troop-containment area, and several bodies began pouring out of a jagged hole into space. Whether they were dead before or after the chamber they were in was exposed to space, Clement couldn't answer.

It was then that the Earth Ark finally responded. A ring of energy formed around the Arks' midsection, and then suddenly a beam of dark orange directed energy lanced out and cut the two destroyers to pieces in a single strike. At this the trailing destroyer turned as quickly as she could and retreated back to the main fleet. The Ark wound up a second DEW beam from her forward section, directing it toward the retreating destroyer, but missed as she maneuvered away at her best possible speed. At that point she was safe and out of range.

"Ivan, how far is the 5 Suns Alliance fleet from the Ark?" asked Clement.

"I make it three hundred kilometers, more or less, sir," he responded. "Right now, except for that retreating destroyer, the whole fleet is at station-keeping."

"So what's her game? Does she attack in an all-out attempt to take the Ark intact? Or does she just nuke it from her safe location?" It was Yan asking the question. Mika Ori answered.

"The Elara DeVore that I knew would plan a strategy, but she would never hold back on anything once she committed to that plan. Once she started, it was all attack, all the time," said Ori.

"But this is a very different Elara DeVore, Mika. She's not the same woman we knew fifteen years ago," said Clement. That created a feeling of regret in his gut; she surely wasn't the woman he had once loved. He had to actively push that thought out of his mind. He turned slightly toward Yan, but not all the way, before asking his next question. "Yan, can you detect any communications between the Ark and the 5 Suns fleet?"

Yan checked her board for a few seconds. "No, sir, nothing. No attempts being made by either side," she said, then added, "It looks like we have a stalemate."

"Perhaps," said Clement. Then: "That Earth Ark has got to be made of hardened regolith. If she is, then she can withstand conventional attack for days," he posited.

"What's regolith?" asked Yan.

Clement responded. "Surface material from a moon or asteroid, likely poured over an inner superstructure then compressed and hardened. Very helpful for avoiding collisions, say with meteors or other foreign objects, in deep space on long-duration space voyages. I'm not surprised they made their Ark out of it. A fifty-year journey leaves a lot of possibility for unwanted collisions."

"If that hull is made of regolith, it will be very hard to penetrate," interjected Ori, "or especially to land a boarding party."

"I suspect that's what the Admiral is thinking about right now," said Clement, then said to Adebayor, "Any sign that either party has noticed us, Ensign?"

The young Ensign shook her head before saying, "Negative, sir. I've detected no incoming scans or attempts at communication, and none of the ships in the 5 Suns Alliance fleet has pinged our IFF beacon."

"We're five thousand klicks from the Earth Ark in this position, so unless they're actively looking for a ship in this area, their odds of finding us without a deep-space scan are minimal," said Massif.

"I suspect they both have all eyes on each other," commented Clement. "So what's the next move?"

"Sir." It was Yan again.

He turned to her, fully this time. "Commander?" said Clement, not hiding his annoyance at her continued interruptions.

She stiffened, facing his glare. "Might I suggest that we have now completed our mission? In fact, I would say we have even surpassed it, knowing that the Earth Ark fleet has been destroyed, she poses no threat to this system. Perhaps, sir, it is time for us to go home," she said.

Clement then pressed an icon on his console before answering.

"Our 5 Suns Alliance mission is complete, I agree with you on that," he started. "But we still have additional interests in this star system, and that would be the natives. And, to be honest with you, I'm not sure leaving this system in the hands of Admiral Elara DeVore and the 5 Suns Alliance fleet is any better than leaving it to the Earth Ark forces."

"So you're refusing my demand that we vacate the battlefield and return home? That *was* part of our agreement to stand down from mutiny."

"I understand that, Commander. What I'm saying is that this ship has a weapon powerful enough to decide the outcome of this battle, and the terms and conditions under which we leave this system. Trading one set of slavers for another is not an option I'm willing to accept."

"You know goddamn well using the MAD weapon again could crack the reactor permanently, stranding us here," snapped Yan.

"Yes, but under those conditions we could go back to Bellus and live among the natives, then hitch a ride home on a 5 Suns Alliance ship when they took over the system. A ride that, I might add, would surely find me enjoying the trip in the brig. No, Commander, I'm not willing to head home to an unknown fate, not when this entire crew could end up facing court-martial. I'm of a mind to stay, and perhaps even help determine the outcome," he said.

"So you're breaking our agreement?" said Yan, demanding an answer.

"I never negotiate with mutineers," he said, turning away from her.

"So you lied?"

Instead of answering, Clement hit the com on his console. "Ensign Telco, is the reactor room secure?"

"Aye, sir," came Telco's reply over the com speakers. "As soon as I got your ping I locked up the missile room and came down to Engineering, just like we talked about," he said. "The room is now locked and I'm armed, sir."

"Good work, Ensign," said Clement. He stood. "Lieutenant Ori, please escort Commander Yan to her quarters and lock her inside."

When Yan turned, Ori already had her cobra pistol trained on her. She surrendered without a fight and Ori took her down the six metal steps to the cabin area. Clement hit the com again.

"Telco, you still there?"

"Sir," replied Telco.

"Put Mr. Nobli on."

After a second of shuffling Nobli's gruff voice came over the com. "What do you demand of me now, tyrant?" he said.

Clement smiled, just a little, at that. "Condition of the LEAP reactor?"

"The cracks have been sealed, but she's still fragile."

"Can we use her as a weapon without destroying the ship?"

Nobli paused before answering. "It's a risk, sir. As I said before, opening up a contained system like this for just fractions of a second to make a short jump or fire the weapon would put a great strain on her. She could fracture again, enough so that we couldn't repair her, then we couldn't get home. Or worse, she could break wide open, in which case we'd likely be consumed by an implosion, along with anything within an astronomical unit, give or take."

"That would be the entire solar system, including the star," said Clement. "Any other alternatives?"

"All I can say, sir, is if you're going to use this thing as a weapon, use it for a sustained period; don't turn it on and off quickly. That would allow us to back the thing down slowly, and create much less stress on the reactor casing," Nobli said.

"I hear you," said Clement. "Thank you, Nobli." He shut down the com as Mika Ori returned to the bridge.

"The commander is safely ensconced in her cabin, sir. I even gave her a chance to get some food and tea from the galley, so we don't have to worry about her for quite a while," she said. "The access hatch from the cargo bay is also secure and the rest of the crew have no access to the cabin area, bridge, or critical systems."

"Well done, Ori. The missile room is secure and Telco just locked down the LEAP reactor room. You all did your jobs well," Clement said, then he turned to Adebayor.

"Ensign, these people have been part of my crew for long time. We are loyal to each other in every way. But I want you to know that I do not and would not require you to serve against your will. The actions we take next could be considered capital offenses by the 5 Suns Navy, or they could result in a positive outcome for both us onboard the *Beauregard* and the settlers in this system. If you have any doubts, then you are free to go to the spare cabin and sit this one out," he said.

Adebayor turned to face him directly. "I understand, sir. I've come this far, and I'm committed to the outcome of this mission, so I will give my commitment to you for the duration of this action, however it might come out," she said.

Clement nodded. "You're a very brave young woman, Kayla Adebayor," he said to her. "Also, know that I'm going to wipe the mission tapes from this little adventure before we get home, so when we do get back, you will be under no obligation to me. Your record will be clean."

"Understood, sir. Thank you, sir."

"Carry on," he said, which was the highest compliment he could give her.

"So what do we do next?" asked Massif.

Clement looked back and forth to his small crew. "Pilot, fire the engines and accelerate us toward the Earth Ark at 1.5 gs," he said. "Navigator, make sure that our flight path will keep us aligned with the 5 Suns Navy fleet as well."

"Aligned in what way?" Massif asked.

Clement clasped his hands behind his back. "Aligned so that we can fire the weapon at them both, the Ark and the fleet," stated Clement flatly. "We're going to end this battle."

✷ 21 ✷

About fifteen minutes into their acceleration burn, they started getting the attention of the 5 Suns Alliance fleet, and presumably, Admiral DeVore. She sent her four converted gunships to intercept the *Beauregard*, essentially outgunning her four to one, in conventional weaponry anyway. Clement ordered no response to the gunships, as they would have to do quite a bit of chasing to catch his ship before she inserted herself into the battlefield at the speed the *Beauregard* was traveling. Clement had a plan, but he wasn't willing to share it with his crew just yet.

When it became obvious the chasing 5 Suns Alliance gunships couldn't complete their intercept of the *Beauregard* before she reached the battle zone, they received an Identification Friend or Foe ping from the main-fleet battlecruiser, and Admiral DeVore. Clement wondered what she must be thinking about his ship still being operational, let alone entering an active battlefield. No doubt she would have expected his ship to have been destroyed by the Earth Ark forces by now.

"Receiving an IFF ping from the 5 Suns Alliance flagship, sir. How do we respond?" asked Adebayor.

"We wait," replied Clement, watching on his tactical screen as his ship drew ever closer to both the Earth Ark and the 5 Suns Alliance ships. The bridge stayed tense and quiet for what seemed like an eternity before the flagship repeated her ping.

"Sir?" asked Adebayor.

"I haven't made up my mind yet, Ensign."

At this both Ori and Massif turned to him.

"Whose side are we on?" asked Ori.

"Our own, Mika. Admiral DeVore has betrayed us and gave us up for dead to the Earth forces. The Earth Ark is here to destroy any enemy and enslave the people in this system. I am opposed to both sides of this conflict," Clement said. "Are the rest of you of the same mind?" He looked around the room.

"We're behind you, whatever decisions you make, sir," said Massif.

"Thank you, Ivan."

Thirty seconds later the third ping came. All eyes were on their captain. Finally, Clement was being forced to make a decision.

"Ignore the ping, Ensign. Admiral DeVore knows damn well who we are. Mika, increase speed to 1.75 g and take us to within three hundred kilometers from the Earth Ark, but keep her between us and the 5 Suns Alliance fleet."

"Aye, sir," said Ori, and began her acceleration burn. DeVore's gunships fell farther behind the *Beauregard*, and were now essentially out of the fray for the moment. Clement calculated the decisive moment in this battle would come well before the sister 5 Suns gunships could get within firing range of the *Beauregard*. DeVore seemed to realize this as well, as the gunships abruptly changed course, retreating toward the 5 Suns Alliance fleet while keeping a safe distance from the Earth Ark.

"And now there are three of us on the chessboard," said Clement.

"But they have no idea we have the MAD weapon, sir. Could the 5 Suns Alliance fleet have developed it as well, or something similar?" asked Ori.

"It's possible," admitted Clement, "but not probable. The MAD is a Hassan Nobli special for the moment, and that is our only advantage. How long to our destination, Navigator?"

"I make it seven minutes, including the deceleration," replied Massif.

Those would be seven *very* long minutes.

"We've arrived at the designated position, Captain," reported Ori, "three hundred kilometers from the Earth Ark."

"Indeed we have. Thrusters to full stop," he said, once more scanning his tactical display. "The question is, now what? Who makes the next move?"

They didn't have to wait long for the answer.

The fleet com line lit up for the first time in the entire mission.

"Incoming com from the 5 Suns Alliance flagship, sir— voice only," said Adebayor.

Clement sat forward in his couch. "Bring it up, Ensign." She did as instructed, and a gravelly male voice came over the bridge com line.

"This is the 5 Suns Alliance Navy battlecruiser *Wellington* calling unknown ship. Identify yourself and return our IFF ping or you will be considered an enemy combatant and be subject to attack," it said.

Clement held up his hand to Adebayor, watching the clock tick for a full minute before responding.

"5SN Battlecruiser *Wellington*, you know damn well who we are," he said, then gave Adebayor the cut sign. A full two minutes went by before the *Wellington* responded again with the same message from the same source. This time Clement signaled Adebayor to respond immediately, and she patched him in.

"If you want to know who we are, *Wellington*, ask your flag officer, Admiral DeVore," he said. Mika Ori snickered at this response.

It took almost three minutes for the *Wellington* to respond this time, and when it did, it was a very different voice speaking.

"This is Admiral Elara DeVore of the 5 Suns Alliance Navy battlecruiser *Wellington*. To whom am I speaking? Is that you, Clement?" she said.

"This is Captain Jared Clement of the . . ." He trailed off and looked around the room for suggestions as to what navy they represented, but got no help, so he made a name up on the spot. "Trinity Republic Navy gunship *Beauregard*," he said.

For a few seconds, well beyond the normal broadcast delay, they heard nothing, then:

"We do not recognize the navy you have identified, or the Trinity Republic. With what authority do you speak for this alleged entity?" came DeVore's voice.

"You know damn well who we are, Elara. Quit the bullshit," said Clement. Again there was a long pause before she continued.

"We're pleased to find you alive and well, Captain Clement," said DeVore. "We recognize a 5 Suns Alliance Navy ship with the name *Beauregard*, but not one in the Trinity Navy, or whatever you just called it," she said. "And how many ships do you have in this 'navy' of yours?"

Clement smiled, then spoke into the com. "We are a fleet of one, Admiral." There was a dramatic pause again when the only sounds were the crack and pop of the com line.

"You appear to be outgunned, Captain," she finally said, quietly and with determination in her voice.

"That's what the Earth Ark forces thought too, Admiral," replied Clement. "But we're still here, much to your unpleasant surprise, I'm sure."

Her tone went angry now. "I have no time to dawdle with you, Clement. You're in violation of the 5 Suns Alliance Navy military code. You have disobeyed orders and declared yourself flying the flag of an unknown enemy. You are a traitor. Surrender your vessel now, and stand aside. Otherwise you, and your crew, will be considered as enemy combatants."

"I regret I can do neither of those things, Admiral," said Clement. "In fact, I suggest that you withdraw your fleet from this system, and let us deal with the invading Earth forces." He knew that would stick in her craw. She came back on the line, with a laugh.

"You have *one* ship, Clement! A gunship at that, of which I have four left. You have no nukes aboard because

I denied them to you. You were a great ship captain in your day, Jared, but that day is long gone. You will all be considered as enemies and your ship will be destroyed," she said.

"Does that death sentence include your adjutant, Commander Yan?" Clement asked, knowing she would be monitoring communications from her cabin. "She was loyal to you." Again, there was a pause.

"Yan signed up for the risks. Every naval officer does," replied DeVore. "Now stand aside, and we will deal with you later."

"Well, since I don't fly your flag anymore, you won't mind if I watch your next move from right here, do you?" Clement said. This time, she didn't respond, and the com line went silent.

It took a few minutes, but her next move smacked of a bit of desperation as she sent in her two sister battlecruisers toward the Earth Ark. They volleyed missile after missile at her, but the Earth Ark stayed resilient, taking the explosions of conventional weapons as scrapes on her hardened regolith hull. They would have to use nukes to have any chance of penetrating the Ark; but it was clear now that DeVore wanted the Ark intact, to strip her of any valuable tech. Clement intended to deny her that prize.

The battlecruisers accelerated their approach then and started firing Hell Lances at the Ark, dozens of them. These had more impact on the hull, but not enough to be decisive. The Ark fired back with her orange DEW beams, but to little effect. No doubt the battlecruisers had hardened hulls against such weapons, unlike the destroyers, and quite possibly energized defensive fields too. A strong enough energy field could deflect a like type of energy. A gravity-based defensive system could even disperse the incoming wave.

What was now obvious was that DeVore would have to commit most of her fleet to take the Earth vessel. Clement was indecisive about whether he should simply allow her to do that and watch her fleet take severe casualties or get involved himself, and end the battle before it started. DeVore made the final decision for him.

A small flotilla of two heavy cruisers and three destroyers, all superior in firepower to the *Beauregard*, broke away from the main fleet and began making for his position. It was obvious their orders were to destroy the *Beauregard*. Clement couldn't have that. He called down on the com to Nobli.

"Hassan, what's the current status of the LEAP reactor?"

"She's warm and ready, sir, but I'd be much happier if we were tuning her up to head home than to use the MAD weapon," he said honestly. Clement nodded even though Nobli couldn't see him.

"I understand. You said it would be better for the reactor, increase our chances of it staying stable and not cracking again, if instead of a quick microburst of energy we used the weapon wide open, in a constant flow for a lengthier period of time," stated Clement.

"I said something to that effect," said Nobli. "But let's face it, any use of the weapon will be experimental and highly problematic. It's a great risk, Captain."

"Acknowledged. How long?"

"What?" said Nobli.

"How long should I keep the weapon open and firing?" There was a long silence before Nobli answered.

"Uncertain."

"Can you estimate the weapon's range of effectiveness?"

"Again, uncertain, sir. It could be anywhere from one kilometer to the end of the universe. We just don't know."

"So, what your saying is, I won't know how well it works until I fire it, and if I do, I should keep it firing for an unknown period of time?"

"Five seconds at a minimum sir. After that, take whatever time you need. I'll be able to gradually back off the reactor power once you shut down the weapon from your console, sir."

"Keep this channel open, Engineer, and prepare to fire the MAD weapon," finished Clement.

"Aye, sir."

Clement turned to his bridge crew. "How long until DeVore's flotilla gets within range to destroy us?" he asked.

Massif answered. "They're two hundred fifty klicks out, sir, and closing fast. I'd say we have two minutes until we're in range of their nukes, sir."

Clement turned to Ori. "Options, Lieutenant?"

"I'd say none, sir. From what we saw of the Ark's DEW range, it's at least one hundred kilometers. If we go toward her, she'll fry us. At the speed the 5 Suns Alliance ships are closing, we have little to no chance to escape, even if we did a max engine burn. And even at that, the best odds I can give you on escape is fifty-fifty, maybe less," Ori said.

"So it appears we only have one option," stated Clement. "Use the MAD weapon on 5 Suns Alliance Navy ships." He looked to his two compatriots. Mika Ori had always been his conscience on decisions like this, providing her thoughts and advice during the War of the 5 Suns. She and Elara DeVore had often butted heads on what was legitimate strategy and what wasn't.

"I don't see any other viable choice, Captain," she said. He looked to Massif.

"You know I have no love for the 5 Suns Alliance, sir. I say do what we have to do to stay alive," he said.

Clement looked up at the ship's clock, then over to the young Ensign Adebayor. "Ensign?"

"I want to live, sir," was all she had to say. Clement sighed and sat back in his command chair.

"Nobli, arm the MAD weapon," he said into the com.

"Armed," was Nobli's only reply.

Clement called up the tactical screen on the main display. The 5 Suns flotilla was closing. He only had one minute and twenty seconds before they could fire nukes at him and destroy the *Beauregard*. He looked down at the MAD weapon icon on his console. It was green and ready to fire. He aimed the weapon as best he could, sighting the lead heavy cruiser in the middle of the 5 Suns Alliance formation. He took in one last, deep, breath.

And fired.

The white energy of the Matter Annihilation Device surged out of the *Beauregard*'s forward cannon port. It took microseconds to cross the space between his ship and the 5 Suns Alliance flotilla. The lead heavy cruiser simply ceased to exist. The flanking ships on either side were swept up by the beam as Clement moved it back and forth from side to side, manually aiming at the enemy fleet with his fingers on the targeting control. He went past the five-second safety margin and let the beam go on for a ten count before he shut it down. The ships of the 5 Suns Navy flotilla were gone from the universe.

The bridge stayed dead quiet.

"Nobli, report," Clement demanded.

"Weapon successfully fired, sir. System gradually backed down to within safety limits," reported Nobli.

"Can I use it again?"

"I would say yes, Captain. The reactor didn't even flinch at the firing. I think she was glad to expend some energy, finally."

Clement smiled at that. "Have I ever told you that you need a girlfriend, Nobli?"

"Many times, sir," he replied.

Clement turned to his navigator. "Ivan, could you track the range of the weapon?"

"I lost it after ten thousand kilometers, sir. It was simply moving too fast," said Massif.

"Let's hope it dissipates," replied Clement. He looked to Ori. "Pilot, take us toward the Earth Ark, thrusters only," he ordered.

"Aye, sir."

"We didn't start this war, but it's within our power to end it," he said, then he leaned back in his couch to watch his ship close in on its next target.

The 5 Suns Alliance Navy battlecruisers were engaged in a death dance with the Earth Ark. Though the Ark was mostly stationary, it was using maneuvering thrusters to get different angles for its DEW beam weapons, trained now on the two attacking battlecruisers. The battlecruisers for their part were moving in a sweeping spiral motion, attacking from various angles, then adjusting their courses and making another run. The toll they were inflicting was heavy, but they failed to penetrate the regolith layers protecting the hull of the Ark. It was a constant flow of Directed Energy Weapons, missiles (from the battlecruisers—the Ark didn't appear to have any), Hell Lances, and smaller kinetic weapons. No nukes. DeVore wanted the Ark intact, but she didn't know her enemy were fanatics, and they would never let that happen. Clement momentarily mused over the possibility of just sitting back and watching the two forces destroy themselves, but then discarded the idea. He was a man of action.

Ultimately, the 5 Suns Navy barrage was ineffective. Admiral DeVore had to make another move, and Clement knew she knew that. She had undoubtedly seen her flotilla destroyed by the MAD weapon, and she made no more attempts to intercept the *Beauregard*, who for its part was now within one hundred twenty klicks of the Ark and the battlecruiser group, and perilously close to the Ark's DEW weapon range.

Clement ordered full stop and watched as DeVore committed another group of her ships, heavy cruisers and destroyers, to the battlefield.

"Those ships are going to get eaten up by the Ark," said Mika Ori. "They don't have the gravity shields against enemy weapons that the battlecruisers do."

"It's possible that the heavy cruisers have gravity shields," commented Clement. "They're big enough to carry the generators."

"They didn't have them during the War of the 5 Suns," said Massif.

"That was fifteen years ago, Ivan. I don't think Admiral DeVore has been sitting around in regards to military improvements for her fleet," said Clement. Clement had seen designs for energy shielding during the war, but the Rim Confederation simply didn't have the resources, or the ships, to carry such a defensive upgrade because of the size of the field generators. It was possible the 5 Suns Alliance Navy had solved that problem.

Clement watched the tactical screen as the second 5 Suns Navy flotilla committed to the battle. DeVore herself hung back on her battlecruiser with a small defensive group of five destroyers, three heavy cruisers, and the four remaining gunships. Everything else was now committed to the battlefield.

He watched as the battlecruisers cut off their attacks and reformed with the approaching 5 Suns Alliance battle group. The destroyers, the most vulnerable ships, went first, followed by the heavy cruisers and then the battlecruisers. Again, the weakest ships out front, as cannon fodder. It showed ultimately that their commanding officer didn't care if they lived or died.

The destroyers for their part stayed well out of range of the Ark's DEW weapons, then lobbed a single missile from each ship.

"Those have to be nukes," said Mika Ori.

"Confirmed," said Adebayor from her station. "I'm

guessing one-kiloton warheads from their energy signatures."

"Trying to blow a hole in her sides, but not destroy her. They want her tech," said Clement. The Ark lit up its DEW defenses and took out some of the missiles as they came in range, but three got through. They impacted on the hull of the Ark, one forward, one near the middle, and another at the Ark's stern, closest to the *Beauregard*.

"Looks like they're trying to take out her DEW defenses," said Ori.

Clement made no comment. There was a flurry of angry communications between the *Wellington* and the destroyer commanders. It seemed someone was unhappy they hadn't gone closer to the Ark to launch their missiles.

They watched as the heavy cruisers moved up and launched another volley of missiles.

"Ensign?" asked Clement of Adebayor.

"These are carrying a heavier load, Captain. Scans say somewhere between three and five kilotons each."

Clement watched as several of the missiles were taken out by the forward and midships DEW arrays; the rear one near the stern, and closest to the *Beauregard*, appeared to have been knocked out. Still, one missile got through. It was enough. The missile struck home near the midship DEW array. It blew a sizeable hole in the side of the Ark, more than big enough for a boarding party to invade her. She was helpless now, and it was only a matter of time before her crew was annihilated by 5 Suns Alliance Marines, offloaded from the battlecruisers.

They were closing now—no fear of the Earth Ark's defenses. They took out the remaining DEW array with a pinpoint nuclear strike from a destroyer, and she was defenseless. In a matter of minutes the boarding would commence, the slaughter would start, and the battle would be over.

"Do we destroy the Ark before DeVore can get her hands on it?" asked Ori.

"The Ark crew is doomed anyway," said Clement. "If we use the MAD weapon we may be doing them a favor compared to what the 5 Suns Alliance Marines might do to them."

Clement called down to Nobli to warm the MAD weapon again, and a few seconds later he had the green light on his console.

"How close to boarding are those 5 Suns Alliance ships?" Clement asked.

"Estimate three minutes until the heavy cruisers and destroyers reach the hole in the hull and begin boarding her," replied Massif. "The battlecruisers are hanging back."

"In case she chooses to destroy herself," said Clement. The scene was an ugly one, with no good choices. Clement was resigned to his decision. He would have to destroy the Ark to keep it out of DeVore's hands.

"Captain!" the warning came from Adebayor. "I have movement from the rest of the attack fleet."

"Throw it to the screen, Ensign."

The main tactical display was replaced by a scan of the remaining 5 Suns Alliance ships, the destroyers and heavy cruisers that had hung back with the *Wellington*. It didn't take a genius to see what they were doing. The ships had regrouped, and they were making straight for the *Beauregard*.

"Ivan?"

"Seven minutes until they are within missile range of us, Captain."

Clement did not take that well.

"It appears they learned nothing from their first attack," said Ori.

Clement nodded, thinking of the lives already lost; the lives on board the Earth Ark and the 5 Suns Alliance Navy ships; the lives of the natives back on Bellus; and the fact that Elara DeVore, a woman he once loved, was trying to kill everyone left in his life that he cared about. He made his decision.

"Pilot, turn the ship"—he looked down at his tactical board—"nineteen degrees port."

"Nineteen degrees port, aye, sir," Ori replied. He waited until she had completed her maneuver, then threw the tactical screen back up for all to see. He trained the sight for the MAD weapon on the Earth Ark. From the angle he had he could likely envelop most of the Ark in the first few seconds.

"Engineer, is the MAD weapon ready?"

"You have a green light on your board, Captain," said Nobli in a noncommittal tone.

"Acknowledged. Count me down from five, Pilot," Clement said.

Ori did, and as she reached one, Clement hesitated, only for a moment, and then fired. The Ark disintegrated first, enveloped by the weapon's blinding white energy beam. Clement swept the aiming control across his board, from port to starboard, hitting and disintegrating the two attacking 5 Suns battlecruisers next. The final sweep encompassed the attack group heading for the *Beauregard*, and they were swept from existence, all hands lost in a matter of seconds. The beam carried on into space, and coincidentally took out one of Admiral DeVore's remaining defensive destroyers, quite by accident.

Clement shut down the weapon, then put his head in his hands, rubbed his face, and gave a deep sigh. "Pilot," he said in a quiet voice, "thrusters ahead, full max, close on the remaining 5 Suns Alliance fleet."

"Aye, Captain," replied Ori quietly. She knew what a heavy burden her captain carried with him now.

"Ensign Adebayor," said Clement.

"Sir," she replied.

"Send a text communiqué, to the 5SN *Wellington*, and Admiral DeVore by name. Tell them we are demanding their immediate surrender. No terms offered; no conditions will be considered. Tell them they have five minutes to reply with their unconditional surrender. Tag it with my name and rank, as Captain of the . . . Trinity Republic Navy ship *Beauregard*," he said.

"Aye, sir," she replied, and began crafting the communiqué.

"Will she surrender?" asked Ori. Clement gave a tired, tight smile.

"I hope so," he said. "I've had enough killing for one day."

22

It was a long five minutes, but eventually Admiral DeVore and the *Wellington* did surrender. In the wake of the overwhelming power of the MAD weapon, it wasn't surprising. Still, he had to plan for all contingencies, seeing as the remaining fleet was still led by DeVore, and he didn't trust her. At all.

Clement ordered all the remaining 5 Suns Alliance Navy ships to disgorge themselves of their weapons, dumping them in a specific area of space, which they did, as far as the *Beauregard* could determine. It was a lot of weaponry, conventional missiles, nukes, warheads, Hell Lances, scatter mines. They all were set adrift in space. Then Clement ordered the 5 Suns Navy ships to move off to a safe distance. He had Telco fire two conventional missiles into the floating pile of ordnance. The resulting series of explosions was both spectacular and rewarding. Clement had disarmed the enemy.

He ordered the 5 Suns fleet to make a course for the innermost habitable planet in the Trinity system, Alphus. Admiral DeVore never made direct contact with them during any of the negotiations.

The trek was a slow one, on thrusters only, with the

Beauregard trailing the rest of the 5 Suns Navy fleet all the way. Nobli had privately informed Clement that the MAD weapon could likely never be fired again if they were to complete their trip home, and that suited Clement, who swore Nobli to absolute secrecy on the subject. No one needed to know the greatest weapon in the history of humankind couldn't be fired again. Intimidation was the key factor; the weapon's power had already been demonstrated.

At one point, one of DeVore's remaining destroyers started to drift from the preapproved flight path. It was one that had taken a good deal of damage in the battle against the Earth Ark. Nonetheless, Clement, giving no quarter, ordered a double missile launch, the conventional weapons exploding near enough to the struggling destroyer for her captain to get the message. The ship chugged along, getting back into formation, but under great duress. Clement called on the fleet channel and ordered her to either be towed or abandoned by the 5 Suns Alliance fleet. Presently a heavy cruiser swept into position and put a tow line on her little sister, and further discipline was avoided.

Early on the second day of the voyage inward, Clement ordered Yan released from her cabin, and given free run of the ship again, except for the bridge. For his part he stayed in his cabin, out of the way of the crew, but assuring them at every turn that the fighting was over and they'd be heading home soon.

He was surprised when he heard the knock at his door, his monitor showing Yan standing outside. "Yes, Yan?" he said through the com.

She pressed the com panel outside his cabin to reply. "Permission to enter, Captain?" she said.

He hesitated for a second, then said, "You don't have a weapon, do you?" It was supposed to be a joke, but even Clement wasn't sure if that's how he meant it.

"No, sir."

At that Clement slid open the cabin door and stood to face his former first officer. It was the first time she had been in his cabin since the mutiny. He motioned for her to take a seat at the table across from him.

"Please," he said. She declined with a shake of the head. Clement sat back down.

"What then, Commander?" he said expectantly.

"I don't think I hold that rank anymore, Captain," she said. Vaguely, he felt sorry for her, but he wasn't going to let that affect his decision-making processes.

"I'm not sure it's at all clear who holds what rank in what navy right now, Yan," he said, trying to be comforting in some way, if he could. "You wear the rank of commander in the 5 Suns Alliance Navy, so that is how I will address you. Now, I assume you have something to say to me?"

She straightened and looked straight ahead, but not directly at Clement. "Sir, I came to apologize. The mutiny action was ill-advised, and I expect to be dealt with as any mutineer would."

Clement held up his hand to stop her. "It was a mistake," he said. "If I put everyone who had a mutinous thought or action on this mission up to the bar of military justice there would be no one left to fly this bird."

"Sir, I—"

"Wait," he interrupted her. "This mission put you and all the others under the strain of choosing between your homeland, your families, and the mission. You didn't choose that. Admiral DeVore made that choice for you when she set us up for destruction at the hands of the Earth Ark. No one on this ship will be referred for judgment by me, in any navy, when we get home. You all did your jobs as best you could and quite frankly, I'm proud of all of you. You're forgiven."

"Sir, if you'll let me finish . . ."

Clement looked at her. Her eyes were red, she had obviously been crying very recently, and she looked disheveled, like she hadn't slept well for several days.

Clement nodded for her to continue.

"I came here to apologize to you as your first officer, sir, but it's more than that . . ." She trailed off again, and now Clement was confused.

"Yan?" he said in a tone that indicated he was trying to reassure her. Now she looked directly at him.

"Sir . . . I'm trying to apologize to you as a woman. I betrayed you, betrayed the relationship and trust we had developed. That meant something to me, and I think to you too. I think I know how you must have felt being betrayed by Elara DeVore, and in many ways, I did the same thing to you. I wouldn't blame you if you hated me. That's what I came here to apologize for. Sir," she finished, and lowered her gaze, head down in submission.

Clement hesitated for a second, then he got up and went to her, put his arms around her as she leaned into his chest, crying softly. He kissed her on the forehead.

"You're forgiven for that as well, Yan," he said. She

continued to cry. They stood there for a long time before she composed herself. She nodded at him and then turned to leave.

She got to the door before she turned back and said, "Thank you, Jared." He smiled at her, and she left.

Then he sat down in his chair, and sighed.

After a trip of three days the fleet arrived and made orbit over Alphus, and the cleanup began in earnest. Clement sat on his bridge with his command crew, sans Yan, and watched as the 5 Suns Navy fleet followed his orders.

The crews were evacuating from their ships and heading for the surface of Alphus, one ship at a time. Clement had allowed them enough equipment to set up individual camps up and down the habitable strip of the innermost Earthlike planet of the Trinity system. Alphus was unique in that its sun-facing side was mostly too hot for life to thrive, except for a two-hundred-fifty-kilometer-wide strip of green which encircled the otherwise dry, desert planet just at the edge of its light side. There was a range of high mountains that defined the break between the dark and light sides of the tidal-locked world. These mountains received enough snow to create a constant runoff of fresh water down into the valleys below. The habitable zone of the planet ran the circumference of the planet, north to south, and it created a comfortable ring of life that could be colonized, or in this case, used to exile a crew of undesirables. Clement had no time to investigate the planet, to see if it had the signs of terraforming that her sisters Bellus and Camus had, but he suspected they would find that evidence eventually, along with the

possibility of native settlers, as on the other two worlds.
The ring of mountains that separated the light side of the
planet from the dark side seemed very regular. It could
have been the result of thousands of years of consistent
tidal-lock pressure from the Trinity star, or something
more...artificial...in nature.

Clement made the evacuated crews spread out along
the ring, so that they couldn't form communities easily.
He wanted them to struggle on their own as much as
possible, and certainly not work together with Admiral
DeVore. If they were focused on survival, they would be
far less likely to cause future trouble.

Once each ship was emptied and the crews relocated
to the surface of Alphus, Clement ordered the ships of the
5 Suns Alliance fleet to be scuttled on the dark side. They
did so one by one, the only exceptions being the former
Rim Confederation Navy gunships. Clement wanted
those for himself, eventually, so he had Ivan Massif
program them for an automated burn to orbit around
Bellus, out of range of any remote control the 5 Suns
Alliance fleet survivors may have. After five days of this
process and relocating the crews to camps dotted
throughout the habitable ring, it was time to deal with
Admiral Elara DeVore and the battlecruiser *Wellington*.

Clement went to the surface in the *Beauregard*'s
shuttle, with ensigns Telco and Tsu aboard for muscle,
along with Tanitha Yan. She had a decision to make. After
looking over the large camp made by the *Wellington*'s nine
hundred fifty crew and verifying for himself that they had
proper supplies, access to water, and no weaponry, he
went to a high ridge, looking down over the wastelands of

Alphus' sprawling desert. He sent orders for Admiral DeVore to join him there. Telco and Tsu stood watch for him, armed, as they waited for the Admiral to arrive. Yan stood off to one side, looking very unsure of herself.

To his surprise, DeVore came alone, without an escort of any kind. Clement waved off the young ensigns to a safe distance, and Yan stepped away so the two commanders could speak alone.

"Admiral," Clement said, with only a slight nod of respect as she came up. They stood side by side on the ridge, not looking at each other, but rather looking out over Alphus' searing wasteland instead.

"Mr. Clement," she replied, not willing to acknowledge his rank in any way.

"Your surrender saved many lives, Admiral," he said, trying to be a bit the gentleman.

"Your betrayal of the 5 Suns Alliance Navy caused many unnecessary deaths, all of them at your hands," she snapped back. That set him off.

"You know damn well it was *you* who betrayed *us*. You never intended for my ship or my crew to survive. You planted a saboteur, deceived us by not giving us real nukes, and never told us we would be facing an incoming enemy force from Earth. Those who were killed died on the field of battle, honorably, with the exception of Captain Wilcock, who was executed by expulsion to vacuum for his treason. You sent flotillas to try and destroy my ship two separate times, but we had a weapon quite superior to anything in your arsenal," he said, pausing before delivering the coup de grace: "Which is why you are my prisoner, and not the other way around."

"We'll figure out how to match your weapon, Clement. And when we do, there will be hell to pay for you and your worlds," DeVore said.

Clement snapped around to face her. "Have you forgotten you come from one of those worlds, Admiral? Have you forgotten why we fought the War of the 5 Suns? Have you forgotten the people of Helios?"

"That's ancient history, Clement. My plans for this star system are far more important than the inevitable death of three Rim planets which have no hope of surviving on their own."

"These plans of yours, they're more important than the rest of the 5 Suns Alliance? I've figured out your plan, Elara. You intended to come here and set up your own little despotic rule, free of the 5 Suns Alliance and any responsibility, all built on the backs of slaves left here hundreds of years ago by forces unknown. You planned to seize and reverse engineer alien technology, or whatever it was that left the terraforming tech on those planets. It's why you were building such a large fleet at Kemmerine, to break away from the 5 Suns Alliance, and claim these worlds as your own," he said.

"Perhaps," she said, then looked away from him.

He eyed her. There was nothing left of his feelings for her. She was an arrogant despot, nothing like the woman he had been in love with so many years ago. He pressed his point to her. "Did you ever think that the terraforming technology on these planets could be used to improve life on the Rim worlds, or was it only to build your personal empire here?"

"It never crossed my mind, Captain. Not even for a

second. Those worlds, that war, it's all in the distant past for me. Trinity is the future, and regardless of this situation, my vision for this star system will prevail."

"Your . . . vision?" He was getting angrier now. She still wouldn't look at him.

"Perhaps my original intent was to prevent a cascading failure event from driving the 5 Suns Alliance into barbarism. That doesn't matter now, anyway. The remainder of the fleet at Kemmerine will eventually come looking for us, and we'll be rescued, and then we will take this system."

"Delusional," he said. "Your ships have been most helpful in replenishing the *Beauregard* for our trip back to 5 Suns space, Admiral. And when we get to Kemmerine, with our new weapon, *your* command base will become *our* command base, and the people there will have to decide to join *us*, or leave forever."

"And just who is 'us,' Captain?"

"The Trinity Republic Navy, Admiral. Thanks to you I'll have almost thirty ships waiting for me when I get to Kemmerine, plus science labs, transports, and battleships that can all be equipped with the LEAP drive. We'll move the population willing to immigrate from the poorest planets in the 5 Suns Alliance to the richest ever discovered, where we will live in harmony with ourselves and our native brothers and sisters," he finished.

She turned back to him. "Pie in the sky, Captain."

He took a step toward her. "It's clear you need a demonstration, Admiral. You may want these," Clement said, handing her a pair of light-blocking goggles. She took them reluctantly and put them on. Clement signaled to

Telco, who went to his com and communicated an order as they looked out over the empty plain of Alphus' desert.

Slowly, from the sky, a dark shape began to descend, picking up speed and burning brighter with every second as it pierced the atmosphere. It was the *Wellington*, being scuttled in full view of her commanding officer. The ship descended with a haunting slowness of speed, seemingly dragging out its own death for its audience. As the flaming hulk hit the surface there was a blinding flash of the nuclear warhead Clement had ordered left aboard her, lighting up the sky in Alphus' full red-yellow daylight. They all looked away from the brightness; even with the benefit of their protective goggles, it was a strain on the eyes. The light soon faded and Clement removed his glasses. In the desert, many kilometers away, the sight of a mushroom cloud grew in the sky like a fierce storm.

"I will see you hang for this, Clement," DeVore said, dropping her goggles to the ground as if they were useless.

"That's a discussion we can have if you ever get off this rock, Admiral. You and your crew are prisoners of the Trinity Republic Navy, the full force of which I have just invoked on you, your crew, and your ship. You will remain here, surviving if you can on your own resources and what you can find from nature. When I return to this system, I will deal with each of you appropriately."

"Will you execute me, your former lover?" said DeVore, taunting him.

His head snapped around to her, his hand going to his cobra pistol in its holster. "I'd like to do that right now, Admiral. But I've decided that I like the idea of trial and execution by lawful forces better than a swift end for you.

Captain Wilcock got lucky. He died in seconds. I want you to ponder your own demise, which is why I'm stranding you on this rock. For now."

"I thought you would have learned your lesson about fighting powers bigger than you in the War of the 5 Suns," DeVore said.

"Clearly not, Admiral, and neither have you, apparently. You're the one who unwittingly gave me the most powerful weapon in the known universe. You're the one who mounted it on a Rim Confederation Navy gunship, and you're the one who put a rebel captain in command of it. Whatever you've reaped from this situation, it's you that's sown it." He started to walk away from her.

"Our scientists on Kemmerine Station will soon develop your weapon too," she said. "It's undoubtedly based on the LEAP drive reactor."

He looked back at her. "Thirty-four days from now those scientists will be *our* scientists, Admiral. I intend to take Kemmerine and make it our base of operations for the migration from the Rim planets to Trinity. And I think the 5 Suns Alliance government will find your little adventure out here to be very illuminating. Do they even know about LEAP technology? I doubt it. Hell, they might even join us against you when they find out the level of your betrayal. Now goodbye, Admiral, and good riddance." Once again he turned to walk away.

"I'm still Elara DeVore, Jared. And whether you believe it or not, I still love you," she said.

He turned back to her for the last time, shaking his head. "The Elara DeVore I loved died a long time ago. You're nothing like the woman I fell in love with, Admiral.

I've moved on. I suggest you do too. And by the way, I know you were the one who betrayed the *Beauregard* to the 5 Suns Navy, back in the war. I once swore I'd put a knife in the traitor if I ever found out who it was, and now that I have, I think somehow that being stranded here, your fleet and your dreams of power destroyed, is a much better punishment. You'll have plenty of time to think on your past sins."

At that, he started to walk away, the two ensigns going with him.

"What about me?" called Yan from behind him. Clement stopped to look at her.

"I assumed you'd want to stay with your commanding officer," he said with a nod to DeVore.

Yan shook her head at him. "No, sir, not anymore. Not after what I've seen and heard." She turned to DeVore. "Admiral DeVore, I hereby resign my commission in the 5 Suns Alliance Navy, effective immediately."

"Think about what you're doing, Yan," said DeVore, a clear warning in her tone.

"I have thought about it, Admiral, and my decision is easy. After seeing your true nature I'd prefer to take my chances in an untried fleet with only one ship than to serve another minute under you, and those of your kind. I'll gladly join the Trinity Republic Navy, if Captain Clement here will have me," Yan said.

"I will," Clement said quickly. "But I won't tell you it will be simple, or as easy as leaving the 5 Suns Alliance fleet."

"I'm well aware of that," she said, then ran to catch up with him and the two ensigns.

"I would never have given you command of a ship, Yan. I suspected you were too self-serving, a spoiled rich girl. Then you proved the point for me. And I can now see that my judgment on that was correct," said DeVore, turning away from her.

"Well, at least I have the satisfaction of knowing that my captain will never send me on a one-way mission to die, Admiral. That's more than I can say about most of the poor souls that served under you." And with that Clement and the rest were gone, leaving Fleet Admiral Elara DeVore to stare out at the glowing remnants of her once powerful fleet.

✵23✵

The return trip to Kemmerine station was a bit of a celebration, at least at first. The crew had managed to strip the 5 Suns Alliance ships of the best rations and alcohol they had, including wines, exotic cheeses and meats, brandy, cognac, and many more luxuries. Clement, though, stayed away from the alcohol. He wanted a clear head for the challenges that waited at home. Everyone was imbibing and having fun, relaxed for the first time on their entire voyage.

When they arrived home to 5 Suns Alliance space once again there was renewed hope among the crew, hope that things would now start to get better, for all of the worlds of the 5 Suns Alliance. Their arrival at Kemmerine station was greeted with a full battle alert by the station, but thankfully no ships were scrambled to intercept the *Beauregard*.

Clement hailed them by com and told the command staff of officers running the station of the events in the Trinity system, its riches and bounty, and of his intention to take control of the station in the name of the new Trinity Republic. He also told them of his plan to help the poorest of the people of the 5 Suns Alliance to begin migration there. The officers at Kemmerine were skeptical, until Clement showed them the outcome of the battle for the Trinity worlds and the *Beauregard*'s new weapon via a visual com link. Behind the scenes, Nobli was begging him not to use the MAD weapon again in a demonstration of power. Clement didn't want to, but if the Kemmerine officers resisted...

In the end, they didn't. The com evidence and the accompanying telemetry seemed to be enough for the Kemmerine Station managers, in the absence of their commanding officer and the entire expeditionary fleet she had left with. They quickly negotiated terms of armistice with Clement and his mythical Trinity Republic Navy, and allowed for the *Beauregard*'s return. Clement in turn ordered all the ships at the station to stand down and for their crews to depart their ships before he would bring the *Beauregard* in.

A few hours later, Clement docked the *Beauregard* at the station in the same port she had left from, Dock 19, and the first of the crew scrambled off the ship to book trips home to their families as quickly as they could. In the end, all except for the core group of Massif, Ori, Nobli, Yan, and the three surviving ensigns, Telco, Adebayor, and Tsu, stayed aboard with Clement. Pomeroy came to Clement before she left and pledged her future support, if he would allow her a quick trip home to New Paris to see her family, which he accepted.

Eventually they all went aboard the station themselves, locking the ship down and then warning the ranking station officers that the *Beauregard* was set to use the weapon on every ship in the dock if her hull was breached without the proper entry codes and DNA match. It was a bluff, but one the officers were unwilling to call.

Clement dismissed his crew to find quarters before he was escorted, with Yan, to the Admiral's office. He noticed DeVore's name was nowhere to be found on the large oak doors or anywhere else in the office. He swore the station's officers in as temporary attachés to his command, and they readily agreed. It appeared that Admiral DeVore had run a very tight command, with her chosen officers on the inside and any others she disapproved of, regardless of their skills or experience, on the outside.

He and Yan began the long work of inventorying the station's remaining ships, personnel, and supplies. He also ordered the station to full military alert and all nonmilitary personnel off the station immediately. This caused a scramble as civilians had to book passage home, but it was done in a modicum of order, led by the able Commander Yan.

The ship inventory was sparse. DeVore had left the station with twenty-six ships: twelve destroyers, all older models than the ones she had taken to Trinity; ten light cruisers, which were at least twenty years old and likely relics from the War of the 5 Suns; three transports, which could move about three thousand people at a time; and one unfinished modern battlecruiser. All had been retrofitted, or were in the process of being retrofitted, with LEAP reactors, and the battlecruiser had two. Clement ordered the retrofitting work to continue, but he placed priority on getting the large, unnamed battlecruiser ready. They had to order the gravity-shield generators from Shenghai for all ships that were big enough to carry them, those being the older generation light cruisers. It would be weeks before they could be delivered.

Having set things in motion to his desired purpose, Clement agreed to meet with a council of five senior station commanders. All of them had ties to the Kemmerine sector, and none were from the core systems of Colonus A and B, or for that matter even Virginis. Both Kemmerine, with two inhabited planets, and the three Rim worlds were far distant from the central systems and often had different agendas from the main body of the 5 Suns Alliance. They were also poorer planets than the core systems.

Yan sat to Clement's right as his adjutant as he addressed the command council.

"Gentlemen, what we have here is an opportunity unique in human history, a chance to start anew on planets that are rich and bountiful. It is my belief that the people of both the Rim worlds and the Kemmerine sector could benefit greatly from migration to these new worlds. If you read the classified report that I sent you last night, you are aware of Admiral DeVore's plans for populating these new worlds with settlers from both the Rim and Kemmerine sector. Kemmerine is rich enough to survive on its own, especially with trade from the new Trinity planets, but the Rim planets are all failing, and the populations there face starvation if we don't intervene. Hell, it's the reason we fought the War of the 5 Suns in the first place. This migration solves the cascading societal-collapse scenario that Admiral DeVore outlined and that the 5 Suns

Alliance government will face within a decade. The development of the LEAP drive opens up new possibilities for trade with the Trinity worlds, so all of the original colonies can begin to flourish again."

The command council seemed convinced by his arguments, if not totally sold on the idea of breaking away from the 5 Suns Alliance central government. An older man named Colonel Gwyneth spoke for the station commanders.

"You may not be aware of this, Captain, but since the war the penalties for treason have been enhanced," he said.

"What can be worse than hanging?" asked Clement, confused.

"They take your assets, and immediate family members can be arrested and held for long periods—years, in fact. So you can see our reluctance to break with the 5 Suns Alliance completely."

"I do see *your* problem, Colonel, but this is not a revolution, it is a migration, an opportunity to save all the 5 Suns Alliance from collapse."

"Yes," said Gwyneth, "but you are declaring your ship as part of the 'Trinity Republic Navy,' which we both know does not exist. I propose a more . . . diffident approach to the 5 Suns government."

Clement sat back, intrigued by this proposal. "I'm listening," he said.

Gwyneth cleared his throat before starting again. "We here on this council, we are old men and women, not youthful like you are."

"I'm forty-four," cut in Clement.

"Yes, but still, a man very much in his prime. We here"—at this his hand swept the room—"are not of a mind to change allegiances at this time in our lives, to upset the apple cart, if you will."

"I'm waiting for you to get to the point."

Gwyneth faced his palms to Clement in a soothing gesture. "We think, sir, that a project of this size, an undertaking of this sort—millions being moved from our star systems to other, unknown, worlds—this is a job for a younger man, one with the vigor and ambition that we, in some ways, lack. We think you would find a receptive audience for your proposals in the Core Alliance Command, if you contacted them."

At that, a gray-haired woman spoke up. "Sir, my name is Commander Gracel. What we are trying to offer you is our support of your mission in the Trinity system, and since the 5 Suns Core Command knew nothing of Admiral DeVore's plans, we believe, with our backing, that you have a very good opportunity to be placed in command of this station, not as a potential adversary, but as its legitimate commander, if you are willing to perform your duties under the 5 Suns Navy flag."

"Are you willing to accept that, Captain?" said Gwyneth. "Come back to the 5 Suns Navy, and share the proposal you have with the Core Command?"

Clement looked to Yan, who stayed stoic, and then smiled. "That I am, Colonel. That I am. But there is one thing I haven't mentioned about Trinity, and that is the presence of natives," said Clement. There were surprised looks around the conference table.

"Natives?" said Gwyneth. At this Yan cut in.

"A few hundred thousand, combined, likely on all three worlds. We don't know who placed them there, or why, but they are completely human in every way," she said. At this Clement jumped back in to the conversation.

"It is our intention to set aside reserved areas for their society to flourish, to live naturally, as they have for many decades. We believe it should be up to this command, Kemmerine Station, to ensure their peaceful survival."

After another hour of this, going over high-level plans and a proposed schedule, Clement left it to the station commanders to make their decisions. The next morning they told him they would present his proposals to the 5 Suns Alliance Core Command, along with the evidence against Admiral DeVore. Clement decided that was good enough.

It would have to be.

✲ 24 ✲

It took a few more weeks for everything to be figured out, but eventually the 5 Suns Alliance government agreed to terms for the migration and placed Clement in charge of the entire Kemmerine and Rim sectors, as a 5 Suns Navy Admiral. Clement had to re-swear his oath, and this time he was frankly glad to take it, for the first time in his life.

In all honesty the 5 Suns government seemed glad to be rid of the problems with the Rim planets, and they voluntarily ceded responsibility for oversight of them to Clement. For his part, Clement agreed to full, free trade with the alliance in exchange for a revenue-sharing agreement of seventeen percent to his station. That would be enough to modernize his fleet and keep the Core Command out of his hair for a very long time.

About a quarter of the station workers and navy personnel opted to leave Kemmerine for home or the Core worlds, but they were quickly replaced by new recruits from the Rim, and others from the two Kemmerine worlds, New Paris and Shenghai. It would be a difficult transition for a new administration at the station, but Clement was confident that would work itself out with time.

The transition was already well underway when the crew of the *Beauregard* gathered at The Battered Hull a month later for a reunion of sorts. Clement and Yan were joined by Massif, Ori, Pomeroy, the three ensigns—whom Clement had promoted again to full lieutenants—and even the mostly socially inept Nobli came by. Yan was at his side in a fresh uniform denoting her new rank of captain.

Admiral Clement led a toast for Lieutenant Daniel, lost on the excursion to the Earth Ark. He made sure all the lieutenants got their new ranks made official, with Daniel's awarded posthumously. He even sent a letter to Daniel's parents personally on 5 Suns Alliance Navy letterhead.

As the party wound down, a rather drunk Yan came up to him and put one arm over his shoulder.

"Would you like to go . . . " Then she seemed to lose her train of thought.

"Go where?"

"I don't know. New Hong Kong. See the sites, take a vacation for once."

It had been a very long time since he'd had a vacation, but: "I'm making plans for the next week or so. You'll have to survive without me for a while."

"What? What could be more important than me?" she slurred, clomping her beer glass down on the heavy wood table, some of the contents sloshing out. Then she got distracted trying to wipe up the table. Clement signaled a bar girl who came over with a wet rag and cleaned up Yan's mess quickly. Yan turned to him again.

"Where?" she said.

"Where what?"

"Where are you going?"

Clement finished his glass of sailor's ⌐before answering. "I'm going home," he said.

She looked confused. "To Argyle?"

He shook his head. "No, to Ceta. I'm going to try to convince my parents to emigrate to the Trinity system."

"Never been to Ceta," she mumbled. "But why go now? It will be at least six months before the first colonists go out ... there," she said, pointing to nowhere in particular. She drank again from her glass before Clement pulled it away from her. He grabbed her around the waist and spun her close so that they were facing each other on their bar stools.

"Why can't I come?" she asked.

"Well, for one thing, you're drunk," he replied.

She mock slapped him on the shoulder. "Am not."

"Are."

"Not."

He let that hang in the air between them for a moment. "But, well, if you've never seen Ceta ..." He trailed off.

"Can I go? Can I? Can I go with you?"

"There's not much to see. No monorails like on Shenghai, just railroads. No big, beautiful oceans or mountains, just salty lakes and a few brown rolling hills. It's a very dull planet."

He was playing with her and she knew it.

"I want to go."

"Why?"

"To be with you, Jared. You're ... my only real friend," she said, turning away and taking another, much smaller, drink from her ale. He reached up and pushed a hanging bang away from her face.

"Well, having a traveling companion does sound like fun."

"It's settled then. What time are we leaving?"

"The shuttle to Argyle is at 5:00 A.M." She looked down at her watch, which read ten past midnight.

"Better take hangover repressors," she said.

"Good idea. But not just yet. I kinda like you when you're drunk," he said.

"You have a one-track mind," she replied, pointing an accusing finger at him.

"I don't."

"Hmm," she said, wrapping her arms around his neck. "It's time to go, Admiral, sir. We have a busy day tomorrow."

"Yes, we do." Clement looked around the room. The three newly minted lieutenants were sitting together, chattering up a storm. Mika Ori and Massif and Pomeroy were engaged in a deep and meaningful conversation, about what he wasn't sure, but with those three, you never knew.

He took Yan by the hand and led her out of The Battered Hull, but stopped at the door and turned back one last time, looking at his crew. They had all done a hell of a job. And then he noticed something he'd never seen before. Hassan Nobli was waving his hands back and forth, no doubt explaining some complex engineering concept to the bar girl, who sat enraptured at his every word and gesture, laughing and smiling. Then Clement smiled too.

Hell, maybe Nobli would finally get that girlfriend after all.

The glass walls and ceilings had begun to shake and the sound of rotors thundered overhead.

Bolan drew his Beretta and rose. His team followed suit. He scanned the skies, searching for the chopper. "We're about to get hit." Looking around the open, gold and glass penthouse, he knew it would be easier than shooting fish in an aquarium. "Kill the lights, and we need bigger guns."

De Jong jerked his head at one of his gigantic guards. "Turn off the lights! Go into my bedroom and get the—"

Glass shattered overhead and shards fell like miniature guillotines. A Bell 204 helicopter took a tight orbit and a man in chicken straps hung halfway out the door behind an M-60 machine gun. Bolan ignored the piece of glass that cut his arm and began squeezing off three-round bursts from his Beretta. The three remaining bodyguards sprayed their weapons skyward. Sparks ricocheted off the fuselage and the helicopter banked away into the glow of the skyline.

Bolan spun around as a second chopper roared overhead. It was a much smaller OH-6. A man leaned out each door firing rifles on full auto. Bolan printed a three-round burst into the starboard assassin who fell out of the chopper and crashed through the glass roof of De Jong's master bathroom. Something clattered to the glass-strewn hardwood floor. Bolan hurled himself over a couch and roared, "Grenade!"

MACK BOLAN ®

The Executioner

#352 Killing Trade

#353 Black Death Reprise

#354 Ambush Force

#355 Outback Assault

#356 Defense Breach

#357 Extreme Justice

#358 Blood Toll

#359 Desperate Passage

#360 Mission to Burma

#361 Final Resort

#362 Patriot Acts

#363 Face of Terror

#364 Hostile Odds

#365 Collision Course

#366 Pele's Fire

#367 Loose Cannon

#368 Crisis Nation

#369 Dangerous Tides

#370 Dark Alliance

#371 Fire Zone

#372 Lethal Compound

#373 Code of Honor

#374 System Corruption

#375 Salvador Strike

#376 Frontier Fury

#377 Desperate Cargo

#378 Death Run

#379 Deep Recon

#380 Silent Threat

#381 Killing Ground

#382 Threat Factor

#383 Raw Fury

#384 Cartel Clash

#385 Recovery Force

#386 Crucial Intercept

#387 Powder Burn

#388 Final Coup

#389 Deadly Command

#390 Toxic Terrain

#391 Enemy Agents

#392 Shadow Hunt

#393 Stand Down

#394 Trial by Fire

#395 Hazard Zone

#396 Fatal Combat

#397 Damage Radius

#398 Battle Cry

#399 Nuclear Storm

#400 Blind Justice

#401 Jungle Hunt

#402 Rebel Trade

#403 Line of Honor

#404 Final Judgment

#405 Lethal Diversion

#406 Survival Mission

#407 Throw Down

#408 Border Offensive

#409 Blood Vendetta

#410 Hostile Force

#411 Cold Fusion

#412 Night's Reckoning

#413 Double Cross

#414 Prison Code

#415 Ivory Wave

#416 Extraction

#417 Rogue Assault

#418 Viral Siege

#419 Sleeping Dragons

#420 Rebel Blast

#421 Hard Targets

#422 Nigeria Meltdown

#423 Breakout

#424 Amazon Impunity

#425 Patriot Strike

#426 Pirate Offensive

#427 Pacific Creed

The Executioner®
Don Pendleton's
PACIFIC CREED

A GOLD EAGLE BOOK FROM
W⊕RLDWIDE®

TORONTO • NEW YORK • LONDON
AMSTERDAM • PARIS • SYDNEY • HAMBURG
STOCKHOLM • ATHENS • TOKYO • MILAN
MADRID • WARSAW • BUDAPEST • AUCKLAND

Recycling programs
for this product may
not exist in your area.

First edition June 2014

ISBN-13: 978-0-373-64427-8

Special thanks and acknowledgment to
Charles Rogers for his contribution to this work.

PACIFIC CREED

Printed in U.S.A.

Whoever fights monsters should see to it that in the process he does not become a monster. And if you gaze long enough into an abyss, the abyss will gaze back into you.
—Friedrich Nietzsche

The true monster is the man who does nothing, allowing evil to flourish. I will never stop hunting down the monsters who prey on innocent citizens, and I won't rest until I've brought them to justice.
—Mack Bolan

THE
MACK BOLAN
LEGEND

Nothing less than a war could have fashioned the destiny of the man called Mack Bolan. Bolan earned the Executioner title in the jungle hell of Vietnam.

But this soldier also wore another name—Sergeant Mercy. He was so tagged because of the compassion he showed to wounded comrades-in-arms and Vietnamese civilians.

Mack Bolan's second tour of duty ended prematurely when he was given emergency leave to return home and bury his family, victims of the Mob. Then he declared a one-man war against the Mafia.

He confronted the Families head-on from coast to coast, and soon a hope of victory began to appear. But Bolan had broken society's every rule. That same society started gunning for this elusive warrior—to no avail.

So Bolan was offered amnesty to work within the system against terrorism. This time, as an employee of Uncle Sam, Bolan became Colonel John Phoenix. With a command center at Stony Man Farm in Virginia, he and his new allies—Able Team and Phoenix Force—waged relentless war on a new adversary: the KGB.

But when his one true love, April Rose, died at the hands of the Soviet terror machine, Bolan severed all ties with Establishment authority.

Now, after a lengthy lone-wolf struggle and much soul-searching, the Executioner has agreed to enter an "arm's-length" alliance with his government once more, reserving the right to pursue personal missions in his Everlasting War.

Chinatown, Honolulu

The soldier staggered down the wrong street in Honolulu's red-light district. He'd deliberately left behind the walled courtyards that had been converted into malls and the fading green clapboard storefronts of the merchants dealing in traditional herbs, teas and imported goods from China. Those establishments had all closed their doors hours ago. The soldier immersed himself in the narrow alleys that lead down toward the Nuuanu stream. These streets were crowded with pool halls, massage parlors and heavy-duty bars where people drank to get drunk and prostitutes and pushers plied their wares. He was far from the only military man indulging himself, but he was on a mission, and his mission had taken him to the bad part of town. The soldier was looking for a real party.

He found it.

It was unseasonably hot in Honolulu and it hadn't rained in two days. Nonetheless when he stepped into the alley, his foot splashed in a puddle of mystery moisture. He pulled his foot out of the liquid and shook it. "Eew!"

A mountain of a man stepped out of the shadows. He was of Hawaiian or Samoan extraction. A ferret-faced individual whose aloha T-shirt was the most Hawaiian thing about him came into formation with the giant. "Hey, *haole*," the man-mountain rumbled. "You lost?"

"I was lost." The soldier smiled and spread his arms wide. "But now I'm found!"

The man-mountain guffawed against his will. "You know? They say the gods favor the dumb, and this *haole?* He's so dumb I almost like him."

Ferret-face glared daggers. "I don't like him at all."

"Bro, you don't even know me." The soldier belched. "That's messed up."

"You!" Ferret-face went livid. "You don't ever call anyone on this island *bro!*"

The soldier registered two individuals stepping into the alley behind him to block his escape. "Bruddah?" he tried.

"You're dead, white-boy."

"That's white-man to you, *poi*-boy," the soldier corrected.

Ferret-face's flinty eyes went cold. "This one we put in the ground. Bundle him." In a pinwheel of sharpened steel, he snick-snick-snacked open a butterfly knife. "Get his dog tags."

The soldier blinked. "Bundled?"

"Sorry, *bruddah.*" The man-mountain kicked off his sandals and came on with deceptive grace for his bulk. "This gonna hurt."

The soldier shot out a one-knuckle jab for the big man's throat. Man-mountain's right hand intercepted the blow like a magic trick. Massive fingers enfolded the soldier's fist like a catcher's mitt and squeezed. White fire shot down the soldier's forearm as giant fingers burrowed into the nerve points in the top of his hand like cold chisels. The soldier threw a haymaker with his right hand for all he was worth.

The giant flicked his other hand up as though he was catching flies. "Ah, bruddah, you— God!" The man-mountain groaned in shock as the slapjack—which the soldier had palmed during the exchange—broke three metacarpal bones. The giant's grip weakened and the soldier ripped his throbbing hand free. The soldier stepped to his left, keeping the giant between him and Ferret-face's knife. The giant's broken left hand shot forward and he gasped in shock as the soldier flicked the sap into his injured hand again and broke a few phalanges. The man-mountain couldn't help but retract his hand. The soldier lunged and snapped the sap like a towel just behind the giant's ear.

Man-mountain collapsed like an avalanche.

Ferret-face moved in like a fencer. The soldier recognized an accomplished killer was coming to carve him up. However that was the knife-fighter's Achilles' heel. Most schools of blade fighting taught that your first target was the enemy's knife hand. Ferret-face had seen what the soldier had done to the giant. The soldier feinted with his slapjack toward the butterfly knife. Ferret-face's hand turned and ghosted away from the blow with the grace of a hula dancer.

The soldier stepped in and snapped the concealed steel toe of his dress shoe into the knife-fighter's lead shin.

Ferret-face gasped as his tibia fractured. He tottered and pulled his injured leg back, waving his knife to ward the soldier off. The soldier took the opportunity to give the assassin a second snap kick under the kneecap of his good leg. Ferret-face fell like a house of cards.

The soldier spun.

One of the two men hung back, but the second charged toward him, shouting some kind of Hawaiian war cry and wielding a short, paddle-shaped wooden club. The soldier flung his sap into the man's face. The war cry faltered as the man took the equivalent of a deep-sea fishing sinker between the eyes. His club sagged like a reed. The soldier's fist followed the sap about six inches lower to the point of the jaw.

The soldier's assailant dropped as if he'd been shot.

The soldier regarded the fourth man at the entrance to the alley and cracked his knuckles. The man broke and ran for the lights and people of the main drag. The soldier stood over Ferret-face. "Bundled?"

"Fuck you!" Ferret-face screamed. He was in the fetal position clutching his right shin and his left knee. "We will hunt you down, *haole!* We will bundle you and—" The rant ended abruptly as the soldier flicked a steel-capped shoe into Ferretface's jaw and unhinged it. The man sagged unconscious.

The soldier reached under his shirt and took out a syringe that looked more suitable for horses than people. He took a knee beside the unconscious man-mountain and examined the broken bunch of bananas he called a left hand. It was swelling as though he was holding a purple golf ball. The soldier sank the needle between the broken second and third metacarpals and had to press hard to express the contents. The syringe didn't contain drugs but a Radio Frequency Identification Device. The antenna, battery and transmitter were linked in a line like boxcars in a flexible glass sheath about as thick around as a grain of rice and twice as long. Any X-ray of the big man's hand would clearly show a foreign object, but the soldier was betting the giant wouldn't go to a hospital with his injury, and among the pain, swelling and broken bones he wouldn't notice the invader. All the soldier needed was a couple of days of tracking.

Mack Bolan, aka the Executioner, took out his cell. He touched an app and typed in his security code. "Bear, this is Striker. I've had contact. Very high target probability. I have an RFID embedded. Target is unconscious. Activate tracking."

Aaron "the Bear" Kurtzman was Stony Man Farm's resident computer wizard and head of the cyber team.

"Acknowledged, Striker," Kurtzman said from the clandestine base in Virginia. "Broadcasting activation signal now." His voice warmed with success. "We have a positive RFID activation and eyes on the target. Transmitting feed."

A window appeared in Bolan's phone and he saw a glowing pinprick blinking beneath an overlaid satellite grid of Chinatown. "Affirmative. I have eyes on."

"Battery is at full charge. Unless the target literally goes underground we should have a good ninety-six hours of telemetry, and I have Pentagon confirmation on continuous satellite windows for all four days. Tracking of target is go."

"Good work, Bear. Be advised I have three hostiles down." Bolan swiftly went through the three men's pockets. None was carrying ID. Bolan took pictures of his three unconscious assailants. "I don't think it's likely, but monitor local hospitals and clinics for descriptions of target A with broken left hand and concussion; target B with fractured tibia, broken knee and dislocated jaw; and target C with broken nose and possible concussion respectively. Run facial recognition software with local law-enforcement databases."

"On it."

Bolan rose. It was time to vacate the scene. "Oh. And, Bear?"

"Yes, Striker?"

"Look up 'bundling.'"

Kurtzman paused. "What? You mean like cable, internet and phone service?"

"No. As a cultural practice."

Kurtzman considered this weird and wonderful question. Strange requests were part and parcel of working with Mack Bolan. The soldier was at war with the worst evil that humanity could produce, and his adversaries ran the gamut from street-level thugs to those intent on changing the balance of world power and everything in between. Processing information streams and solving problems for Mack was one of the best parts of Aaron Kurtzman's job, and he was proud of it. Some of the most confounding joys were questions from Mack that came straight out of left field. Others, such as this one, arrived like visitors from Mars.

Kurtzman summoned up an answer from his own memory. "Last I heard 'bundling' was something Pennsylvania Dutch did when two adolescents were courting. They would be allowed to sleep in the same bed but were professionally straitjacketed in separate bedding, often with a bundling board between them. They could kiss, and if they worked at it hands could roam, but it curtailed any serious hanky-panky."

"Well, that's fascinating, Bear, but I'm looking at bundling from a Hawaiian cultural perspective. One of the perps used the word twice, directed at me, and I don't think he wanted to suck face over sleeping bags on the lanai. I don't know if it's slang, but I'm thinking it's something you don't want to be on the wrong end of."

"Right, bad Hawaiian bundling. On it."

"Do I have Koa?"

Luke Koa was Stony Man Farm's current and only resident Hawaiian blacksuit. He had been a Military Police officer in West Germany before the Wall had fallen, and at the frantic end of the Cold War, as the U.S.S.R. fell, he'd specialized in what could best be described as "extracurricular scouting activities" for Uncle Sam on both sides of the border. Being Hawaiian, he couldn't blend in with the native population, so Luke Koa had highly developed sneaking, peeking and, if it was called for, taking down skills. In essence he'd been a Special Forces border patrolman, and he had an unparalleled nose for trouble and things that did not belong.

When the current Hawaiian mission had come up, Koa had been an obvious choice as an asset. Bolan had brought up the mission parameters and Koa had volunteered. Kurtzman had kicked it up the chain.

Kurtzman liked and respected Koa. Everyone at the Farm did, but the man was by training a soldier, a policeman and a scout, not an undercover operative, and all signs indicated he would be operating against his own people. A very violent and dangerous splinter group, but they were still his own. Nonetheless Koa was an ace card they could not afford to hold back. He'd volunteered for the job, and the powers that be had agreed. "We have permission."

"Then tell Koa I've had a serious contact in Chinatown.

Send him everything I've sent you to review. Tell him he's active, and I need him."

"He activated himself. When I told him you had gone undercover in Chinatown he took the initiative and got on a plane. He'll hit Honolulu International tomorrow at 10:15 a.m. Pickup not required. He'll arrive at the safehouse in a green Jeep."

"Copy that. Will rendezvous at safehouse. Tell him I'm going by Matt Cooper. Striker out." Bolan emerged like Orpheus out of Chinatown's darkest alleys. He shook his head at the physical carnage he'd left behind him and the questions it had raised. "Bundling..." Bolan mused.

Honolulu Safehouse

"Bundling sucks, Matt. You don't want any part of it." Luke Koa feigned a crouch. Bolan fell for it and jumped. The soldier hit his apogee as Koa grinned. Gravity pulled Bolan down and Koa made a jump shot. His three-pointer floated inches past Bolan's fingertips and caught nothing but net. Hawaii was Koa's turf, and the safehouse driveway and its basketball net were swiftly becoming his yard. "I thought you *haoles* were supposed to be the masters of the three-pointer." Koa was smiling. "You've been eating mine all morning."

There was no getting around the fact that Koa was taking Bolan to town. "Haven't seen you dunk yet."

"You keep your six-footer shit to yourself, and now it's nine." The Hawaiian soldier didn't smile often. He was built like a middleweight who spent a lot of time under a bench press. Koa shot Bolan a grin. "But we can go to twenty-one if you want."

The Hawaiian surged forward and pulled a Harlem-Globetrotter-worthy up-and-under. His layup was gorgeous to behold. He sighed at Bolan with immense false sympathy. "Eleven."

Bolan retrieved the ball and passed it back. "What do you know about *Lua?*"

Koa shot for fun and sank a basket from the curb cut that served as the top of the key. "You mean *Kapu Ku'ialua?*"

Bolan caught the ball and passed it back. "Yeah."

Koa dribbled to the corner of the driveway. "What do you know about it, Matt?"

"*Lua* means 'bone breaking.' It's the traditional martial art of the Islands."

"Well," Koa acknowledged, "that's the Wikipedia version."

"So?"

"So it's *kapu*." Koa sank another basket.

The *Hawaiian for Dummies* definition of *kapu* was "taboo," but if you looked deeper into the language and culture the word was an intricate blend of "sacred," "consecrated," "restricted" or perhaps even "marked off." He shot the ball back. "There are three *Lua* schools within walking distance, Koa. I can sign up today."

"Where are you from again?"

"East coast."

"Okay, *haole*. You go down to your local strip mall. You pay your three hundred dollars, buy your American-flag harem pants and get your black belt in Rex Kwon Do in twelve easy lessons. Do you learn anything?"

"I take your point, but I think I met a *Lua* master last night and the only thing that saved me was the slapjack I'd palmed. I broke his hands while he was in midmonologue."

Koa shook his head sadly and sank his shot. "We were warriors once. Nothing's what it used to be."

"Yeah, and now there's a nativistic murder spree going on. Will you tell me about bundling?"

"Well, they say that back in the day, a *Koa*—a Hawaiian warrior of the royal class—studied *Lua*. A true master could defeat an opponent, dislocate every joint in his body, and then reset them again. Though sometimes the victim died from shock."

"That's bundling?"

"No. According to legend, there's another side to *Lua*. A

Koa might defeat an opponent in single combat, dislocate all his joints and then fold him up like a cricket."

"Bundling him."

"Yeah."

"Then what?"

"Then he'd be roasted and eaten. At least, that's the story." Koa sank another basket. "Why do you ask?"

"Last night a man told his three buddies to bundle me."

"That's messed up. You sure they weren't Amish or something?"

Bolan laughed. "They were not plain."

"Sounds like we have a problem. What's the plan? I infiltrate?"

"We both infiltrate. You're my ticket in."

Koa looked Bolan up and down. "Good luck, Your Caucasianess."

"I'm getting some help with that."

"Should be interesting."

Bolan lifted his chin at a red Jeep coming down the street. "You'll get to see it now."

CIA groomer Pegarella Hu barely cracked five feet. She literally jumped out of the Jeep with what looked like a massive fishing tackle box tucked under her arm. In South Pacific intelligence circles she was famous for her smile, her designer cupcakes and her ability to facilitate field operation role camouflage. Her cereal-box-worthy grin faded slightly as she looked at Bolan from head to toe. "You're the one I'm supposed to Island up?"

"Yup."

"This should be interesting."

Koa nodded. "Yeah, that's what I said."

"You ready for your big reveal?" Hu asked.

"Can't wait, Peg," Bolan replied. His skin and scalp were alternately burning and tingling. The soldier stood, turned and looked at himself in the mirror.

"Well, fuck me running with a pitchfork," Koa said.

Wearing only a pair of boxers, Bolan stared at himself. He had to admit it was an impressive sight. Hu had taken her CIA grooming skills and gone to town. She had depilated Bolan from his upper lip to his insteps. Hu had thickened, coarsened and extended Bolan's naturally black hair into a shag. She had thinned his eyebrows and created a few other minor miracles with the help of cosmetics, but it was Bolan's skin that was most impressive.

The soldier had spent more time than was wise under desert, jungle and equatorial suns. He tanned, and when he did it turned him ruddy and coppery. Agent Hu had stained his skin with a Da Vinci–like grasp of color. She had artificially tanned him but now his skin had a subtle but unmistakable golden base. Bolan and Koa looked nothing alike—and Hu had made Bolan's skin several shades darker—but she'd given Bolan the same complexion as Koa.

Hu had also chemically tightened Bolan's pores to give him the porcelain skin look. There wasn't much to be done about his nose, cheekbones or chin, but Bolan looked like a product of the cultural crossroads the Hawaiian Islands had become. The *haole* was there in his bone structure for everyone to see, but by dint of Agent Hu's artistry, if Bolan claimed to have a Hawaiian father or said he was half Portuguese and half Samoan, no Islander would dispute him at first glance. The lines and cicatrices of his numerous battle scars would only cement the deal. "You're amazing."

Hu shot him a smile. "I know. Listen, a lot of the work won't last much more than the week. With three-quarters of your pores closed you need to worry about overheating if you overexert." She gazed at Bolan in open appreciation. "And your beard and chest hair will start reasserting themselves ASAP."

"What about the hairdo and the skin?"

Hu laughed. "It'll take a chemical peel or a month to undo

what I did to your skin, and if you want your hair back to normal you'll have to let it grow out or come and see me."

"What if I don't want to come back? What if I asked you to stick around for a while?"

Hu perked an eyebrow. "What exactly are you saying, sunshine?"

"I like your style. I'm forming a posse. You want to be deputized?"

"Love it," Hu responded. "But I'm not a field agent."

"I know, but I'm thinking I need a girl on the ground who can blend in, run interference and run errands Koa and I can't."

Hu wrinkled her nose delightfully. "I don't know how I would clear that with my superiors."

"My people will clear it with your bosses. Can you shoot?"

"I've got an AK hidden in the Jeep." Hu spread her hands and feet wide in invitation. "And if you want to see where I keep my PPK? We'll just need to have ourselves a game of Treasure Island."

Koa nodded. "I like her."

Bolan met his own cobalt-blue gaze in the mirror. "What about the eyes?"

"I have three pairs of extended-wear browns for you, but since we're already working you as a pleasing example of hybrid vigor, I'd stay with your oh-so-arctic blues. It's downright striking, and you only have one chance to make a first impression. I say we throw off the opposition with your disturbing power."

Bolan nodded at his reflection. "Koa?"

Koa let out a long breath as he took in Bolan's transformation. "What Peg said. Given what the girl has done? You'll have the power to seriously freak out some locals."

Koa took a notebook out of his back pocket that looked as if it had seen heavy use in the past forty-eight hours. "Here're some notes I made for you. It's too late to teach you any slang much less the language—you'll just screw it up.

The good news is when my parents moved to the mainland some of our family was already there. I had a half cousin I barely knew. He dropped out of high school, moved to the east coast with some girl and just disappeared. You're him."

"What's my name?"

"Makaha," Koa said.

Bolan admired the randomness of it. "So we're cousins?"

"That's right. That gives me all rights to introduce you around and defend your ignorant, mainland-corrupted ways."

"Nice."

"I thought so."

"So what's the plan?"

"You're looking for murder, mayhem and a native uprising?" Koa asked.

"That's the current theory."

"Then we go to my old stomping grounds. The most violent place in the Islands."

"Where's that?"

Koa nodded knowingly. "Happy Valley."

Happy Valley, Maui

"You want to turn back?" Koa lifted his chin at the sliding-glass doors of the Takamiya Market as he drove. "This is where we U-turn."

Bolan had spent the island-hopper flight and the drive studying Koa's rather extensive notes on Hawaiian crime, culture and Bolan's alias. He lowered the minor tome and gazed out the window of the ancient Toyota Land Cruiser the CIA had provided. Outwardly, the 1970s vintage 4 x 4 looked as if it was held together by rust and primer. Underneath the chassis, the engine and the suspension were tip-top. Bolan ran his eyes over the seemingly sleepy island borough. Happy Valley didn't look like a ghetto, much less a slum. The heartachingly blue skies, lush hillsides and palm trees did a lot to dispel that, but there was obviously trouble in paradise.

The ironically named Happy Valley was a hotbed of drug dealing, prostitution and gang-related crime. At the end of the day, criminals who wanted to make a mark on the island had to come here and pay respect to the locals or try to carve it out of them. The local vibe was very strong, and the code of silence was even stronger. "This is where you did your damage?" Bolan asked.

"Back in the day, Matt." Koa nodded.

"Then keep your eyes on the road."

"Hell with that," Koa countered. He took a right off the main drive. "I want a beer."

"It's not even noon!" Hu said.

"You want to meet the local royalty?" Koa asked. "Now is the time."

"Is this like having cannelloni on a Tuesday with the dons in Jersey?"

"Yeah, except these dons don't need help to break every bone in your body. Oh, and do me a favor, Matt."

"What's that?"

"Don't piss off the Samoans."

Hu sighed. "That's good advice."

"Don't piss off the Samoans," Bolan repeated. "Got it."

"Good, make that your mantra. I don't want to die today." Koa pulled up next to a wall that was blank save for a door and bracket where a sign had been torn off. Bolan noted three bullet strikes in the stucco. "Where are we?"

"Melika's. It's named after the woman who used to own it. I made a call, and her daughter owns it now."

"What's her name?"

"Melika."

Bolan's phone rang. It looked like an old, battered, first-generation 'droid, but it was actually state-of-the-art Farm technology. Bolan answered. "Bear."

"You've stopped."

"Yeah, Koa wants a beer."

A picture appeared on Bolan's phone. It was a satellite image of Happy Valley.

"You want to see something interesting?" Kurtzman inquired.

"Always."

The satellite image zoomed in. Bolan made out the Land Cruiser. A superimposed green dot blinked on Melika's. "Really."

"The tracker you placed on your assailant in Chinatown is in that bar."

"Well, that's convenient. If I don't contact you in half an hour, get worried."

"I'm worried now."

Bolan clicked off and nodded at Koa. "Let's do it."

Koa took point and they entered Melika's.

After the brilliant sunshine the bar's interior felt like a photographic darkroom. Hawaiian slack key guitar lilted over the sound system. A trio of withered old men sat at the bar drinking their social security checks. A giant Samoan man with an Afro held down bouncer and security duties. He gave Bolan and Koa a hard stare. He leered at Hu. The woman behind the bar was tall, Polynesian, and had a smile that lit up the dingy surroundings. Bolan sat at the counter. "You must be Melika."

"That's me. What can I get you before you get your asses killed?"

"Primos. The lady will have an appletini."

Melika shrugged. "Coming right up."

Bolan locked his eyes with the Hawaiian crime patriarchs holding court at the booth in the far corner. One was built like an aging Olympic shot-putter. The other man filled half the booth like a retired sumo wrestler. Shot-put wore a red-and-blue aloha shirt and his iron-gray hair was cut in a shag. Sumo was a monstrosity in a men's XXXL pink-and-black bowling shirt and had his hair pulled back into a short ponytail. Bolan kept his face stony as alarm bells rang up and down his spine.

Also seated in the booth was Man-mountain with his hand in a cast and a dressing behind his left ear.

The Samoan moved around the bar and loomed over Bolan. He gave Koa a disgusted look. "You seem a little lost, *kolohe*." The Samoan leaned in and mad-dogged Bolan. "And I don't know who this *lolo haole* is, but I don't give a shit."

Bolan's cram sessions told him that he'd just been called an idiot white man and Koa had been called a trouble-maker. The stone face of the morbidly obese man in the booth cracked as he squinted at Koa in recognition. "Luke?"

Koa nodded. "Uncle Aikane."

Melika clapped her hands. "Luke!"

The dangerous men in the booth suddenly smiled.

Bolan knew "uncle" or "aunt" was a term of respect in Hawaiian for any elder or better. "Aikane" was the Hawaiian word for friend, and it was a much stronger word than the English version. "Uncle Friendly" the crime lord had just recognized Koa. Bolan was starting to get the impression that Koa had earned himself a reputation way back when.

The Samoan bouncer's eyes widened disbelievingly. "Koa?"

Koa stared at the Samoan without an ounce of warmth. "Remember you, Tino. From back in the day, and that's my cousin you're talking to."

Tino's eyes flared. "Hey, brah, I—"

Bolan spun up from his bar stool and hurled a right-hand lead with every ounce of strength he had. The Samoan's nose was already flat as a squid and took up nearly half his face. Bolan felt the cartilage crunch beneath his knuckles and saw the tear ducts squirt. Tino pawed for the bar and failed to find purchase. He fell backward and landed hard on the ancient linoleum.

Bolan sat on his bar stool and regarded the Primo beer

Melika had set in front of him with grave consideration. "Guess I need a new mantra…"

Uncle Aikane held up a huge hand in friendship and as a sign for the violence to end. "Who is your cousin, Luke?"

In Hawaiian, "cousin" could mean any number of relationships both inside and out of kinship. The other side of the coin was that the Islands were small, and a great deal of mixing had been going on. There was a joke that when local singles met they had to compare family trees to make sure they weren't breaking any laws of man or nature.

Koa stared at Uncle Aikane with great seriousness. "Makaha is my half cousin, Uncle."

Wheels turned behind Uncle Aikane's eyes. The massive killer suddenly smiled happily. "Little Luana! Married that sailor boy! Years ago! Moved to the mainland!" He nodded at Bolan. "You Luana's boy?"

Bolan nodded. "Yes, Uncle."

The leaner, older man clapped his hands. "You are Makaha!"

"Yes, Uncle."

"Makaha!" Uncle Aikane laughed. "Your uncle Nui only pretends he knows you!"

"I remember Makaha well!" Nui protested. "He was even whiter in his crib!"

"How is your mother, Makaha?" Aikane asked.

"Many years in the grave, Uncle."

"Mmm." Uncle Aikane, Nui and the *Lua* master all nodded gravely. "Your father?"

Bolan put a terrible look on his face. "I don't remember him."

U.S. soldiers and sailors marrying local girls, having children and then disappearing was not exactly an unknown story in the Hawaiian Islands. The elders received this information with equal gravity. Dignity required the subject not be pursued. Aikane returned his attention to Koa.

"You are back, Luke."

"I heard my cousin was in a bad place. I went east and

got him out of it. And then? We decided there was nothing on the mainland for us. We came home."

The elders nodded. After World War II there had been a significant diaspora, and among the Hawaiian expatriates even onto the second and third generation there was a powerful desire to return. Uncle Aikane nodded very slowly. "Aloha, Koa. Aloha, Makaha."

Koa nodded in return. "Aloha" was another Hawaiian word with a lot of meanings. It could mean hello, goodbye, welcome or even I love you. In this setting Bolan perceived at the very least it meant "Welcome, returned ones." Bolan and Koa were in, and their covers were hanging by threads.

They both responded in unison. "Aloha."

3

The Annex, Stony Man Farm

"They're in," Kurtzman confirmed. Barbara Price, Stony Man Farm's mission controller, gave the computer expert a look, and he sighed. He felt the same way she did. Bolan had been on some very deep-cover missions before, but the Hawaiian job was pushing the limits.

"You really think they can pull this off?" Price asked.

"You saw the picture of Mack after Agent Hu got through with him. Are you going to walk up to him in a bar in Waikiki and tell him he's not Hawaiian enough?"

"No, but the locals have a very strong vibe."

"I know. That's why Koa came up with the story about a prodigal son lost to the mainland and returning to his heritage. It will explain lapses, and Bolan has Koa to smooth things over for him. Plus if it looks like he's desperate to prove himself, the bad guys may accelerate him into the inner circle of evil."

"Yes, and just who are the bad guys again?" That was the million-dollar question. The mission was troublingly vague. Price looked at the converging data streams. "We have young female tourists disappearing—that implies white slavery—and two intercepted gun shipments."

"Girls for guns." Kurtzman scowled. He found the sex-slavery trade particularly abhorrent. "It's not as if it hasn't been done before."

"In the United States? In Hawaii?"

"If it's true, it's bad," Kurtzman agreed.

"I'm still trying to figure out the spike in violence against tourists and military personnel."

"Hawaii has had locals-only trouble before," Kurtzman countered.

"Yeah, and this is swiftly reaching the levels of the bad old days in the '70s."

Kurtzman nodded. Hawaiians were now a minority in their own islands, and they also made up the poorest segment of the Aloha State's extremely cosmopolitan society. Their native discontent had sporadically manifested itself in violence, mostly against tourists, despite the fact that tourists and the U.S. military presence were two of the major pillars of the Hawaiian economy. Now the violence was spiking precipitously, and no one was talking. In fact, locally, a lot of people seemed scared. "We've heard 'drive out the colonizers and invaders' before. The Hawaiian Sovereignty Movement and its rivals and affiliates mostly send papers and delegations to the U.S. Congress and the United Nations demanding reparations. We definitely have something new going on here."

"I know." There was nothing about this mission that Price liked. The chatter was that something very big was going on in Hawaii, and something related was happening in the Pacific. She tapped a very thin file on her tablet. "This is the most troubling. The hints of a massive strike against the invaders. We've never heard that before." Price brought up a sore point. "And so far all we have is a hula master who likes to beat up G.I.s."

"That's a *Lua* master," Kurtzman corrected. "And we have a tracking device in his hand. Mack is working his way up the food chain."

"I prefer it when Mack swoops in by surprise, mops the floor with the bad guys and then buys me dinner in D.C."

Kurtzman smiled. "Yeah, that works for me, too."

"He's operating on U.S. soil and he's almost never been this thin on assets."

"We have full war loads in strategic locations."

"But unless he breaks cover right now all he has is his phone and his fists."

"And Koa."

Price nodded. She liked the Hawaiian and she'd been infinitely relieved that he had volunteered to be on Mack's six. "So they're acquiring equipment locally?"

"We went 'round and 'round on that. Fact is Mack may not get a chance. As you mentioned, this cover is about as deep as it gets and as thin as it's ever been. Until Mack proves himself, he and Koa might be ambushed or hit with a drive-by."

"Tell me they're armed."

"Armed and waiting," Kurtzman confirmed. "And now the ball is in the bad guys' court."

Wailuku Town: "Pakuz"

"I TOLD YOU not to piss off the Samoans," Koa muttered.

Bolan sat in the tiny den and cleaned his CIA-provided pistol. The old GI .45 came from Hawaiian National Guard storage. The soldier suspected it had been WWII issue. It showed a great deal of holster wear but as a National Guard weapon not a lot of use. The bore was clean and with a little oiling the action was slick. "I didn't piss off the Samoans. I punched Tino in the face. Then I bought him a beer. Now he loves me. He's calling me cuz. What's not to like?"

"That did go better than expected," Koa admitted. The Hawaiian had a similar pistol and was scrupulously checking the quality of the magazines they'd been issued.

"So what's the *Lua* guy's name? I didn't catch it."

"Me, either, and he scares the shit out of me. I think you got real lucky the other night, and even luckier he didn't recognize you." Koa grunted in amusement. "Though I think he liked it when you broke Tino's nose."

"I think the entire Island of Oahu liked it when I broke Tino's nose."

"There is that."

Agent Hu gave Bolan a knowing look. "Melika sure liked it."

Bolan began wrapping beige rubber bands around the .45's grip. If he was going to pose as a low-level Hawaiian hoodlum who was willing to turn terrorist, a carry rig was out of the question. His options were front-of-the-waist or small-of-the-back, and he needed some friction to hold the big steel piece in place. He nodded at Koa. "Everything went better than expected, cuz, admit it."

Koa's brow bunched as though he was getting a headache. "Don't call me that."

"It's our cover. Get used to it."

"I don't want to get used to it."

"You want the grease gun or the kidney-buster?"

Koa nodded at the old Ithaca 12-gauge riot gun. "I'll take the shotgun. I qualified expert on those. Not that model, but how much different can it be?" Koa warily eyed the ancient piece of ordnance on the coffee table next to the 12 gauge. "Those? Man, back when I was in this man's army, the only people who were issued those were tankers or truckers, because they never expected to use them."

Bolan put down his pistol and took up the antique M-3 submachine gun, which did bear a striking resemblance to a mechanic's grease gun. It was also inaccurate, unwieldy and notoriously unreliable under field conditions. It wouldn't have been in Bolan's top five hundred choices for armament, but if you had to defend a Hawaiian bungalow on the wrong side of town, the men who kicked down the door were in for a very nasty surprise.

"Pakuz," as the locals called it, was a suburb of Wailuku Town. It had a straight shot to Main Street but the foreclosed bungalow the CIA had acquired abutted the foothills. It was just slightly off the beaten track and left several escape routes open. Pakuz was right next to and half the size of Happy Valley and, like the aforementioned and ironically named area, was a hotbed of crime and violence. If Hawaii really was spawning terrorist cells then any economically depressed areas could be hothouses where the revolution's foot soldiers would be nurtured and grown.

"What did you do with the revolvers?" Bolan asked.

Bolan had requested some backup weapons in case they got arrested or had to hand over their weapons. The CIA had come up with four 4-inch Smith & Wesson Military and Police .38s of dubious vintage.

Koa slid shells into the Ithaca. "Put one in a waterproof bag in the toilet tank. Buried two in the backyard next to the banana tree." He nodded at Hu. "The fourth one I gave to her."

"Pegarella Hu, CIA agent, groomer…" Hu grinned. "Gun moll."

Someone banged on the door as if he was about to knock it off its hinges. "Koa!" Tino roared. "Makaha!"

Bolan rose and tucked his pistol into the back of his waistband. Koa took up his shotgun and stepped to one side to give himself a lane of fire down the tiny hallway. Bolan opened the door and found himself staring down the two men he had delivered beat-downs to in the past twenty-four hours. Both Tino and the man-mountain whose name Bolan didn't know stood in front of him on the landing. A third man—a thin-as-a-whip Polynesian—stood scowling by the driver's door of a red VW van. Tino grinned past the bandaged bridge of his nose. "Aloha!"

"Aloha, Tino," Bolan said. "You wanna come in? We got beer and chicken."

"No, brah." Tino shook his head. "Bring your grind. You and Koa are coming with us. You got people you need to meet. People who want to meet you."

The *Lua* master nodded. It had been dark on the streets of Chinatown, and Bolan had been blond, with a totally different voice, demeanor and complexion and wearing a uniform. If this was the big fat kill, the Hawaiian and the Samoan were hiding it with the skill of trained intelligence agents. "Hey, Koa!" Bolan called. "Tino says we gotta go!"

"I wanna come with!" Hu called out.

The thin man by the van spoke for the first time. "The bitch stays."

Hu stopped short of hissing like a cat. Bolan muttered a low "Hey, Tino?"

"Yeah?"

"Who's Prince Charming?"

Tino made an amused noise and answered softly. "Best you don't ask a lot of questions, Makaha. Not yet, anyway."

"Got it."

Koa came to the door sans shotgun and holding a six-pack and a bucket of chicken. He called back over his shoulder to Hu, "Don't know when we'll be back!"

The temperature in the bungalow dropped precipitously. "Whatever…"

THE VAN BUCKED and bumped through the darkened back roads. Bolan hadn't known there was such a thing as angry Hawaiian rap music, but Tino blared it loud enough to wake the dead. They had driven out of Happy Valley and entered state forestland. Bolan knew they were no longer traveling on state-maintained roads. Leaves and branches scraped the sides of the van. The forest formed a thick, sheltering canopy above when it wasn't so low it scratched the roof. This was a smugglers road, most likely barely maintained by the local marijuana growers. Tino appeared to know the route like the back of his hand.

He killed the lights and spent the next ten minutes driving through the pitch black seemingly led by sense of smell. The white-knuckle ride ended as the van broke into a clearing and Tino brought the VW van to a halt beneath the stars. "We're here."

The *Lua* master turned around in the shotgun seat and held out his good hand. "The guns, bruddahs."

Bolan smiled in the moonlight coming through the windows. "You can tell?"

"I don't see everything, Makaha—" the *Lua* master smiled back "—but you'd be surprised what I do notice."

Bolan withdrew his .45. He gave it 50/50 they'd been compromised the minute the *Lua* master had seen him in Melika's bar. The soldier rolled the dice and gave himself to fate as he handed over the pistol. "Man, I thought I was all slick and shit."

"You're not bad." The *Lua* man shrugged his mighty shoulders. "But I'm better. The knife, too."

Bolan shook his head ruefully and handed over his knife. Koa gave up his gun. "You're not going to put sacks over our heads and walk us into the volcano, are you?"

The thin man spoke. He sat in the backseat by himself, and Bolan had felt his eyes and his gun pointing at his back the entire ride. "We wouldn't drop you in the volcano. But would you jump in if you were told?"

Koa met the thin man's stare. "You know? I had just about enough of being told when I was in the army."

The *Lua* man spoke quietly. "Would you jump in if you were asked, Koa?"

Bolan matched the man's tone. "I would, if the right man asked me. For the right reason."

Tino and the *Lua* master both nodded at the sagacity of Bolan's words.

"What he said," Koa agreed.

The *Lua* man got out and slid open the VW's cabin door. "Then come out."

Bolan stepped into the Hawaiian night. He still had his phone and his bare hands, which was far more armament than most would suspect. But they wouldn't save him from a bullet in the back.

The *Lua* master nodded. "Follow me."

Bolan and Koa followed as Tino and the thin man took their six. They walked out of the clearing into the darkness. The *Lua* man was barely discernible but he moved unerringly down a clearly cut and maintained path. Soon Bolan both smelled and heard the Pacific. They came to a clearing about the size of a large recreational vehicle. Overhead military camouflage netting stretched to form a canopy thickly interwoven with the boughs of overhanging trees. A pair of red military emergency lights lit the forest encampment. Solar panels stacked to one side told Bolan the camp was powered by batteries. It would give off little or no recognizable heat signatures to imaging satellites and there wouldn't be any light leakage visible to passing aircraft. Nor would the red lights ruin the night vision of anyone in camp if they suddenly went lights off.

It was a very professional setup.

Three sawhorse and plank tables were piled with very suspicious-looking, four-foot-long military crates. The *Lua* master, Tino and the thin man waited. Bolan and Koa stepped forward. Bolan unboxed a rifle. It appeared to be a 1980s or '90s vintage M-16 A2. He held up the weapon as if he were admiring it. Bolan had fought with this type of rifle many times. If it hadn't been parkerized black, the rifle would have glittered with newness. The M-203 grenade launcher mounted beneath the barrel was new, as well. There were no serial markings, which told the soldier it was most likely a Chinese or Philippine knock-off.

"Sweet," Bolan proclaimed.

Koa racked the action on a rifle and peered through the sights. "Same model I learned on in basic."

The *Lua* man nodded. "We need a lot more of them."

Koa set the rifle on his shoulder. "I know a little something about smuggling. AKs would be a lot cheaper. Shit, they're disappearing from Iraqi and Afghani inventory by the day, and for that matter the Russians and Chinese sell to anybody."

Bolan knew the answer but kept his mouth shut. The weapons mimicked U.S. National Guard issue. A real insurgent force wanted the same weapons as their oppressor, so they could steal compatible parts, ammo and magazines. On a secondary note, until one of the weapons was taken from a captured or killed Hawaiian secessionist, the sight of them would send U.S. law enforcement scrambling to find out what military depot in the Islands was hemorrhaging storage guns. That would give the smugglers a few more moments of cover.

A few more moments might be all they needed. All evidence and Bolan's hard-won instincts reaffirmed that something very bad was going to happen soon.

Bolan kept the frown off his face. If they added a few stolen military uniforms to the mix, the secessionists would be able to drive up to a Hawaiian military base as if they belonged and engage in some serious slaughter. "A lot more are going to cost a lot of money." Bolan gazed meaningfully at the inland pot grower's paradise. "Mary Jane going to pay for that?"

The *Lua* master went Island-style stone face. "How bad you want to know?"

Koa put down the weapon. "I trust you, and Uncle Aikane. Whatever it is, I'm down with it. All the way. Makaha?"

Bolan nodded slowly. "You got me out of Pennsylvania, back to my island and back to my *ohana*." Everyone nodded at the all-encompassing Hawaiian word for family. *Ohana* meant family by blood or otherwise, friendship, as well as race. "If I don't have your six by now, then you should have left me. You decide to jump in the volcano? I'll jump in right next to you."

"Good." The *Lua* man nodded. "Good. Then follow me a little farther." Bolan and Koa walked into the nearly pitch black once more. The ocean breeze began to blow stiffly in their faces. They broke out into starlight and found themselves on a cliff. The *Lua* man spoke over his shoulder as he vanished through a cleft in the rock. "Careful."

Bolan climbed down ancient steps cut into the lava rock. The Pacific thundered and crashed against the cliffs below. Happy Valley and Wailuku were close to the beach, but their shores were not tourist destinations. The locals were not particularly friendly, and the rip tides and undertows made surfing and swimming a suicidal proposition. The rest of the coastline was a series of jagged lava cliffs carved by eons of tidal surges.

Bolan knew from experience that lava eruptions and the action of the ocean often meant caves.

The steps were so steep they almost became a ladder, and then the ladder turned into a lava chimney. The *Lua* master's voice spoke from below. "Six more feet, brah." Bolan clambered down into the blackness. His bottom foot found empty air and a huge hand caught his ankle. "Just drop."

Bolan dropped and bent his knees as he hit soft sand. He found himself in a cave lit by a red emergency light, with the roar of the surf outside. The soldier grinned at the *Lua* man guilelessly. "You did that climb one-handed?"

The man made a pleased grunt. "Been doing it since I was six, bruddah."

Bolan knew he was on Hawaiian Holy Ground. The muted sound of feminine fear and misery coming from the gloom told him Hawaiian Holy Ground had been violated.

Koa dropped down, followed by Tino and the thin man. Bolan kept an exhilarated look on his face as Ferret-face came hobbling out of the dark on crutches with his hatchet jaw set in an orthodontic brace. If the big kill was going to come, it was going to come now, and his bundled body would be consigned to the surf outside.

Tino spoke happily to Ferret-face. "They're in! All the way!"

The thin man spoke. "We're gonna see."

Ferret-face turned and crutched awkwardly through the sand back the way he'd come. The thin man took up an electric lantern and turned it on. Bolan saw a pair of small boats parked in the sand and more sawhorse tables laden with boxes and crates. Beside solar panels stacked for the night the cave was equipped with a pair of small gas-powered generators and fuel drums. A threesome of small shipping containers that had been dragged in with obvious effort dominated the back of the cave. Two of them had been converted into living quarters.

The group stopped beside a little side cave formed by a pocket of superheated gas eons ago.

Bolan kept his thoughts off his face as he gazed upon the battered, terrified women weeping and squinting blindly into the LED glare of the lantern. Bolan counted seven women. Most of them were blonde and in their teens and they cringed and clutched each other with their bound hands. One woman might have been in her forties, with somewhat obvious surgical enhancements to her face and body. She glared at Bolan and company in open defiance despite a black eye. Tino's huge meat hook slammed onto Bolan's shoulder and gave it a meaningful squeeze. "This is a pass-fail situation, brah."

The soldier knew what was expected of him. He pointed at the older one. "Her."

"Nice choice!" Tino laughed. "No one misses a slice from a cut loaf!"

The men in the cave laughed as though this was the height of humor.

Bolan let some ugliness come into his voice. "I just want to wipe that look off her face."

More laughs followed. The woman continued to glare but tears spilled down her face. She yipped as Bolan seized her by the neck and propelled her across the sand toward one of the containers to the cheers of the other men.

4

Mack Bolan slung his chosen woman into the container and slammed the door shut behind them. Tino whooped. A part of Bolan had been trying to build some kind of empathy for the Samoan street criminal. Tino's cavalier attitude toward sexual slavery had just soured the relationship. The woman cringed as Bolan took out his phone and hit the Farm-built electronic surveillance app. She was still defiant. "Screw you, asshole!"

Bolan grinned and hit the camera app. His phone flashed as he walked around the woman and took pictures of her. At the same time, the camera application was firing off infrared lasers looking for camera lenses and the electronic countermeasures probed for bugs. Bolan's phone flashed an extra time. That told him the phone had detected nothing. He suspected that if he was being watched, the cavalry would have hit the container hard and told him no flash photography of the fun was allowed. Bolan sent the woman's picture to the Farm and left the audio on for Kurtzman. "What's your name?"

"Screw you."

"And what do your friends call you?"

She sobbed. "Becca."

"Rebecca?"

"Why do you care?"

Bolan laughed loud and spoke low. "Because I'm going to get you out of here."

Becca stared at Bolan with something as dangerous as hope. "You mean that?"

"You have two ways out of here. Neither of them is good."

Becca's collagen-enhanced lips twisted. Bolan suspected Becca might be or had been a pro. She had seen bad times and bad things. A slave-cave below the water line in Hawaii with a one-way ticket to hell was pushing her limits. A terrible, fragile smile of defiance crossed Becca's face. "Lay it on me, Island boy."

"I'm not from the Islands." Bolan forked his fingers at his arctic-blue orbs. "Look in these eyes."

Becca stared back in surprise. "You're no choir boy." A short, broken laugh forced itself out of Becca. "But you're a Boy Scout, aren't you?"

Bolan considered his past. "What if I told you I would have gone for Eagle Scout but a war got in the way?"

Becca smiled. "What're my two choices again?"

"A and B. A is you saying 'get me out of here now,' so we walk out of this container and I try to kill our way out against all resistance."

Becca's smile died. "And what's Option B?"

"They sell you and the other girls for guns, intel and who knows what else. They put you on a boat and sail you west to God knows where. But I can put a tracking device on you and try to rescue you before you hit slave market central. Option A? Frankly I give me and my friend about a ten percent chance of overpowering everybody with our bare hands and finding our way out of the forest with you and the rest of the girls alive. Option B? You and the girls are most likely going to get loaded into a boat. I track you and rescue you." Bolan didn't sugarcoat it. "And you endure whatever happens until then."

"And which one are you recommending?"

"Would you believe B?"

"God, you're an asshole!"

"Yeah, I get that a lot," Bolan conceded. "The problem

is we're outnumbered, I don't have a gun, and it's a fight to the finish. No way they'll let us get out of here alive. B gives me a chance to gear up, and it also gives me a lead on where you're being taken, which means I can crush the slave trade at both ends."

"And you're going to put a tracking device on me how?"

Bolan took out his phone, opened the battery compartment and slid out the RFID the Farm was tracking him with. It was far more powerful and sophisticated than the one he had injected into the *Lua* man's hand. It was the size and shape of a quarter and about as thick as a PC's processing chip. "You can't swallow it—it won't stand up to digestive juices."

Becca gave the tracking device a very dry look. "I've dealt with worse."

Bolan handed Becca the device. She blinked as he stripped off his shirt and flopped on a futon. "Would you give me a back rub? I need to stay awhile."

Becca straddled Bolan's hips and dug her thumbs into his trapezius with skill and alacrity.

BOLAN LEFT THE container. Becca whimpered and cried in a convincing show of shame and degradation.

"You're my hero, brah!" Tino's voice boomed. "Man, I gotta get me a piece of that—"

"She's mine, until she's gone," Bolan said.

"Well, shit, brah, you don't have to—"

The *Lua* master spoke gravely. "This isn't a party, Tino. This is a grave necessity. We all know Koa's reputation, but Makaha had to prove that he's all in. We're going to hurt the *haoles*. We're going to hurt them in every way possible. Makaha had to prove that he's willing to do what has to be done."

Bolan gave Koa a defiant look. "Don't tell Melika."

Koa gave Bolan a faux "saddened that you would even ask" look. "That's not going to happen."

"It's like killing people, Makaha!" Tino just kept digging his own grave as he leered. "It gets easier with practice, except it's not as much fun."

"Done that." Bolan stared into the middle distance in memory. "It never got easier. I just got better at it."

The *Lua* master, Ferret-face and the thin man reappraised Bolan. The *Lua* man took out two thick, rubber-banded rolls of twenties. "Take this."

"You want to pay me?" Bolan put pure disdain on his face as he jerked his head at the container. "For that?"

The man looked genuinely hurt. "No, Makaha. This is walking-around money. From your uncle Aikane. You telling me you're flush?"

Bolan looked away as though he was ashamed. "Nah, I spent my last bills on chicken and beer today. Koa spent all he had on plane tickets."

The thin man's voice went from sneering to a neutral tone that almost had a tinge of respect. "Tino will take you home. Take a day off. Take two. Forget chicken and beer. Get some real grind. Koa, get reacquainted with your home." The thin man came dangerously close to being friendly as he wrinkled his nose at Bolan. "And show this lost home-slice what he's been missing."

Even Ferret-face beamed a little.

Honolulu safehouse

"I GOTTA GO." Bolan shoved a few personals into a bag. They hadn't gotten out of the forest and back in Wailuku Valley until after sunrise. He suspected the girls had been taken out to a ship and were already on their way to a short life of sex slavery, heroin addiction and an unceremonious death, dismemberment and dumping.

"You sure you don't want me along?" Koa asked.

"I need you to take Peg, like now, and get Melika. Kidnap her if you have to, but then disappear as though we four went on a romantic couples' weekend."

Koa raised his hands in warning. "If Peg and I show up and say, 'Hey, let's go meet Makaha,' she'll come, but if you aren't there? She won't take kidnapping too kindly, man. Back in the '70s, Mama Melika was like a genuine Island-style Ma Barker, and she taught her daughter well. There's a reason we found all the uncles hanging out at her place yesterday."

Agent Hu tossed her hair. "I'm not afraid of her."

"I am," Koa countered. "And you should be."

"I need Melika on our side." Bolan gave Koa a hard look. "And I need her sat on until I get back and can turn her."

"Matt, we got Uncle Aikane trusting us. We can work with that."

"I think Melika might be my key to getting in all the way."

Koa clearly didn't like it. "I know it was my idea, but we took a big chance going into her bar and—"

"And I'm doubling down. Koa, I'm getting the feeling this is starting to step on your loyalties, and I get it, but I need you to get her. Get her now, or punch out of this mission."

Koa went pure Island-style stone face. Bolan realized Koa had deeper misgivings about this mission than he'd let on. Koa lifted his chin. "And if me and Peg sit on Melika and your charms fail, what are you going to do with the home girl?"

"Let her go."

Koa's eyebrows rose in surprise. "You're just going to let her go, and let her compromise us and burn the entire mission down."

"No, I'll hold her for forty-eight hours first, and me, you and Hu go in hard, guns blazing on the camp, the cave, Uncle Aikane and the targets we know. We try to break it open the ugly way. Melika comes to no harm from my end."

"Well, shit," Koa opined.

"Yeah, it's a bad deal all the way around."

"I don't like it."

"You don't have to like it, and you can hate me after. Question is, will you do it?"

"You know I volunteered for this one."

"I know, and thanks."

Koa nodded at Hu. "Pack for a picnic and a kidnapping."

Hu shot a killer grin. "I can take her."

Koa shook his head sadly. "No, you can't."

Bolan tapped an app on his phone. "Bear."

Kurtzman came on instantly. "Striker."

"Tell me we have tracking."

"Tracking confirmed, Striker." Kurtzman added, "But we don't have tracking on you, and your tracer is no longer connected to your phone's battery. Our tracking window is getting narrow."

"Where are they headed?"

"West, as you can imagine. But when it comes to slavery there are a host of final destinations along the way."

"Best estimate?"

"The tracker is currently on board a small freighter, the *Pukulan Anggun*. She has Dutch registration, but she's currently flying Indonesian colors."

Bolan saw the scenario. "Heading southwest for the North Equatorial Current. Straight shot for the Jakarta or Manila flesh markets."

"That's the way I'm seeing it, Striker."

"Bear, it's going to be a solo airborne mid-ocean interdiction. I need a plane and a jump rig."

"Way ahead of you. I have a bird lined up at Coast Guard Maui station. I think we can get you in the air within twenty-four."

Bolan breathed a sigh of relief. The U.S. Coast Guard had a very strong presence in Hawaii and often got some of the latest ships and aircraft. "I need a war load, stat."

"The commander of Coast Guard North Pacific Sector has been informed that he'll have a guest to whom, if he felt so inclined, he might show every courtesy. You'll have your pick of their armory and stores, but it's going to be Coast Guard armory and stores. Their rigs are mostly rescue jumpers rather than military stealth, but that is your fastest option, and you have a green light as of five minutes ago."

Bolan quoted the United States Coast Guard motto. *"'Semper Paratus.'"* *Always Ready.*

Kurtzman made an amused noise. "I will see to it that the USCG is loved and thanked for their cooperation."

"Thanks, Bear. Koa and Hu are going to kidnap a U.S. citizen and go dark."

Kurtzman paused for a second. "How is that again?"

"I'll let Koa explain it to you."

Koa folded his arms and shook his head. "You're a dick."

Bolan nodded and scooped up his bug-out bag. "Bear, I'm in a Jeep and inbound for the Oahu Coast Guard station."

5

North Pacific, 6,000 feet

A maelstrom of violent air roared into the hold of the HC-144A Ocean Sentry search and rescue plane as the loading ramp lowered. The interior lights blinked off and the emergency red lights lit. The bewildered and amused U.S. Coast Guard jumpmaster shouted over the wind. "Two minutes to target!"

Bolan rose. "Thank you, Sergeant!"

The six-man United States Coast Guard Port Security unit that had been scrambled out of Honolulu cradled their Colt carbines and Remington shotguns and observed Bolan with keen interest.

Bolan was dripping in Coast Guard issue. The jump rig was big, bulky and far from stealthy, but it was designed for operations at sea. The Mk11 Mod 0 rifle he carried resembled an M-16 on steroids. At nearly four feet long and weighing more than ten pounds, it wasn't the ideal weapon to jump out of a plane with. However this was the only weapon in the Coast Guard armory that had a sound suppressor attached. Bolan hoped the sight of the big, silent, semiautomatic sniper rifle would put the fear of God into sailor and slaver alike. With luck they would never see it at all, much less hear it. He had also picked up a pair of .40 caliber SIG pistols and a Mark 3 Navy knife along with his jump rig and night-vision goggles. Spare magazines, flash stun grenades and flares made up the rest of his kit.

Sergeant Goldstein of the Security Unit gave Bolan a sympathetic look. "You sure you don't want someone to come with you? I got three men who are jump qualified, including me!"

"Nothing I would like more, Sergeant. But not this time."

"Are you expendable and deniable 'n' stuff?" the sergeant inquired.

Bolan nodded. "'N' stuff."

"Awesome!"

"One minute!" the jumpmaster shouted. "We have an FLIR on target. The rain shouldn't start for another ten minutes. The sea is pretty heavy and she's only doing eight knots. You have a good glide path and a good window. Within thirty it's going to start getting rough."

Bolan nodded. The Ocean Sentry's Forward Looking Infrared RADAR had eyes on the target and that meant so did he. He pulled his night-vision goggles over his eyes and powered them up. The world turned into a grainy screen of greens, blacks and grays.

The freighter's manifest indicated it had taken on coffee and automotive parts on the main island. According to an NSA satellite Kurtzman had access to, the *Anggun* was also carrying the RFID Bolan had given Becca. Bolan was hoping it meant she was still alive.

The red lights blinked. The jumpmaster got excited. "You are over the target! Go! Go! Go!"

Bolan nodded and gave the jumpmaster a thumbs-up.

The soldier stepped into space and arched hard. The dark bulk of the blacked-out Ocean Sentry was silhouetted by the stars for a few fleeting moments and then it droned away to leave him with nothing but the bejeweled sky above and the water below. Bolan pulled his ripcord and felt his straps cinch as the canopy filled with air and the sudden drag yanked against his weight.

The *Anggun* wasn't hard to find. She was a small tramp freighter in a great big ocean but she was the only light source for hundreds of miles. Bolan pulled on his steering toggles and began his approach. Details of the ship swiftly resolved in Bolan's goggles as he descended. He spotted a dark area—out of sight behind the wheelhouse—crowded with the lifeboat and nautical objects he couldn't yet identify. Bolan nodded to himself.

That was his LZ.

Bolan began a slow spiral, constantly compensating for the forward motion of the ship. A tailwind was pushing him in faster than he liked. If the soldier missed his LZ he'd be swimming. Bolan flared his chute and pulled his knees into his chest to clear the stern rail. He avoided a capstan and the chain curled around it and hit the deck in a textbook landing. The wet deck countered by shifting beneath his feet in the swell, sending him skidding. The soldier hit the orange steel side of an inverted lifeboat. His NVGs skewed on his head and Bolan fell back.

His chute filled with wind and began dragging him backward. Bolan's straps cinched as his canopy dipped beneath the level of the rail and began to wildly billow and gyrate in the chop. Bolan tried to grab the slick hull of the lifeboat, but his fingers slid off, wet with his own blood. He was dragged inexorably backward and he lurched as his chute dipped into the sea. The canopy became an instant sea anchor and the soldier was violently pulled toward the rail.

Bolan's Navy diving knife cleared its sheath with a rasp. He twisted and slashed at his lines. If the canopy managed to tangle in the propeller there was an excellent chance he'd be reeled in like a fish to a watery meat-grinding grave. Bolan hacked through his portside shrouding. The strain eased as the canopy went from a water scoop to a long soggy ribbon in the bow wake. He hooked an arm and a leg into the railing and cut his remaining lines. Bolan sagged to the deck and spat blood. He gave his septum an experimental and mildly agonizing wiggle.

His nose wasn't broken but blood poured down his chin. Bolan reset his NVGs on his face and made double sure his rifle's optics and suppressor were still in alignment. He gazed up at the wheelhouse but he had no visual on whoever might be inside. No one had gone to the rear window to see what had happened. The sea was rough, a storm was on the way and ships were noisy. Bolan doubted his landing, inglorious as it was, had registered over the sound of the engines and the swell. The soldier secured his phone to his left forearm and hit an app. Becca's tracer was blinking away belowdecks.

Bolan rose and moved to the rear hatchway.

The hatch was open. All the lights were on and everybody was home. Bolan pushed up his NVGs and moved down the stairs that led below. The smell of tamarind, hot chilies, peanut sauce and rice frying told him he was indeed on an Indonesian ship.

Bolan moved along the corridor and took the second set of suicide steps down into the main cargo hold. Cigarette smoke and the sound of harsh laughter rose to meet him. Containers were stacked two high with narrow corridors between them. The center of the hold formed a small open area. Becca hung by her wrists from the starboard fork of a forklift at maximum height. Most of her clothes lay on the floor in sliced condition. A shirtless Indonesian man with a traditional parang sneered endearments in Malay as he laid the heavily curved machete blade between the shuddering woman's collarbones. Five more men sat smoking, drinking beer and shoving fried rice down their maws as they watched. Bolan had the terrible feeling that Becca was considered a little too long in the tooth for the slave market and was being sacrificed to the crew's appetites. Becca's bra popped away beneath the blade.

Bolan sent three heavy, subsonic .30 calibers between machete man's shoulder blades.

The rape crew watched for a stunned moment as the first in line fell and his blade hit the deck with a clang. They heard the clinking of Bolan's spent brass a half second later and leaped to their feet clawing for pistols and blades. Bolan gave each man two rounds through the face in as many heartbeats. The slavers dropped dead like dominos in a neat semicircle. The soldier stepped out of the shadows, and Becca sagged in her restraints at the sight of him.

"You're late."

Bolan took out his knife and cut Becca free. "I know, and I am sorry." He scooped up the machete man's cast-off T-shirt and tossed it to her. "Can you find it in your heart to forgive me?"

Becca pulled the stained V-neck over her head. "Just get me and the girls out of here."

"On it. Can you shoot?"

"My last boyfriend was a cop. He let me shoot his Glock."

Bolan scooped up two of the slaver's pistols. "These are Browning Hi-Powers." He cocked them and left them unlocked. "Just pull the trigger. You have thirteen shots in each one. Where are the rest of the girls?"

Becca took the pistols and seemed to visibly gain strength from them. "They're in the two blue containers down to the right. They want them delivered unbruised so someone else can damage them."

Bolan knew the vicissitudes of the modern slave trade all too well. "Still just you girls from the cave?"

"No, there are twenty of us now. There were some girls already on the boat when we were loaded. A couple of Canadian girls and three Mexicans—they've been on board for a while."

"I hate to say it but I can't let them out just yet."

"They're safest where they are." Becca nodded. "Got it. How do we play it?"

"I'm going to take the ship."

Becca stared at the pistols in her hands then back at Bolan. "Awesome. I want in."

"It's a small freighter, and it has a small crew. I just took out five. I gather none of these assholes is the captain?"

"No."

"Then I'm figuring he's in his cabin or on the bridge with at least one other crewman. Is there any other crew you would recognize?"

"The cook. He was decent to us. He actually seemed sad, but not enough to do anything about it. There're at least three guys I've seen besides the ones you just took care of."

"Any Hawaiians?"

"No, but one is just about the creepiest Euro-trash ass-hole you ever met."

"Dunno. I've met some pretty creepy ones."

"I bet you have. Did you kill them?"

"The ones who were actively in the slave trade? Yeah, mostly."

"Good." Becca's pistols began shaking in her hands. "Hey, can I ask you a favor?"

"You're about to freak out."

"Yeah."

"But we need to kick some ass and get this shit done."

"You know?" Becca managed a tremulous smile. "I finally find a sensitive man and every time we meet, it's in a rape cave or a slave ship."

"We get out of here alive? And it's a mani-pedi and dinner at the restaurant of your choice on Maui," Bolan said.

"And why do I believe you again?"

"Because I've never lied to any woman I've rescued from a slave ship."

"You do this often?" Becca challenged.

"Often is too strong a word." Bolan furrowed his brow. "What do you say to Sarento's On The Beach after the day spa?"

"Let's do this."

"We're heading for the bridge. Keep an eye on our six and try not to shoot me in the back."

"Can do."

Bolan moved out slowly to let the beaten, barefoot and admirably belligerent member of his two-man fire team stay in covering position. He circled back for the starboard set of steps that led to the main deck. The hull gently throbbed with the vibration of the engine. Bolan stopped by the galley door. "You said the cook was kind to you?"

"I got the impression he never signed up for this."

Bolan nodded and took a small bundle of para cord from his web gear. The kitchen door had no lock and opened inward so the soldier simply tied off the handle, stretched the cord to a pipe in the ceiling and tied it off taut.

Bolan went up the stairs to the main deck. He emerged at the base of the superstructure below the wheelhouse. Rain was just starting to patter on the deck. Becca shivered in the wind of the coming storm. "So, are the Navy SEALs or the United States Marine Corps coming or something?"

Bolan gazed up at the yellow light spilling out of the bridge windows. "No."

"No?"

"Becca, we're taking the ship. Me and you."

Becca looked to be about a millimeter away from tears. "Okay…"

Bolan went up the gangway. Bare feet pattered on the steel steps in the rain behind him. The soldier hit the landing and saw three men on the bridge. Bolan kicked open the door. He immediately made the Indonesian captain drinking coffee and one of his mates at the helm. The Euro-trash slave trader was easily identifiable by his six feet and blue eyes. His beard, mustache and hair were all shaved to the same stubble.

Becca snarled like a she-cougar. "Screw you!" Both of her pistols detonated like dynamite in the confines of the tiny bridge. Euro-slaver fell to the deck clutching the twin holes his belly.

"I told you to watch my six."

Becca stood with smoking pistols in both hands. Hatred radiated from her in waves. "He was in charge of inspections."

The slaver moaned. The captain and his mate stared in horror at Bolan and the heavily armed woman. Bolan dropped to his heels beside the wounded man and removed a Glock from his waistband. "What's your name?"

The man grimaced in credible manliness.

Bolan shook his head, "Tell me your name or I am going to step on your stomach and keep stepping on it."

"Pashke!"

"Pashke, you're in a lot of trouble. You've got two bullets in your belly, but you've also got three choices. You talk to me, and you get medical attention and live. You can clam up, in which case I end your suffering and put you over the side for the sharks. Three, you say something really stupid and insulting and I take the Skipper and Gilligan downstairs and give Becca ten minutes alone with you to fulfill her revenge fantasies. Which is it?"

Pashke shuddered through the pain of his ruptured viscera. "I will talk!"

"Keep that in mind, focus on it and suffer for a little bit." Bolan rose and pointed his rifle at the captain. "Name."

The man hissed through clenched teeth. "Narang."

"Your crewman?"

"First Mate, Sadarso."

"Excellent." Bolan tapped the Nautical GPS tracking app on his phone and checked his position. "You've made excellent time, Captain. Take a heading three degrees south by southwest."

Captain Narang gave Bolan a surly look and nodded at First Mate Sadarso. "Make it so."

Sadarso complied.

Becca kept her pistol trained on the first mate. "Shouldn't we, like, do a 180 and turn these guys over to Five-O?"

Bolan shrugged and considered the worsening weather outside. "I don't have the authority to turn them over to Five-O. These are international waters, and technically I've committed an act of piracy. It would complicate their prosecution by U.S. authorities immensely."

The first mate shot Bolan a triumphant look.

Bolan aimed his rifle at the first mate's forehead. "Keep your eyes on the road, Mr. Sadarso."

Captain Narang nearly jumped out of his shoes as he looked at his chart, his new course, and did the math in sudden horror. "There are no landing facilities!"

Bolan shook his head. "Nope."

"We will run aground!"

Bolan nodded as he spotted the dark mass of land dead ahead. "Yup."

The first mate fired off a stream of Indonesian at his captain.

"Becca?" Bolan asked.

"Yeah?"

"If Sadarso says one more word in a language you don't understand? Shoot him in the stomach."

"You got it." The former kidnapping victim shot the first mate a look of sheer bloodlust. "Go ahead, matey. Make my day."

Bolan was beginning to think Becca might make a decent pirate queen herself. He flipped the switch on the intercom and spoke to the captive women in the hold. "Ladies, you are currently being rescued. We're about to make landfall, and it's going to be rough. Grab hold of something solid and hang on tight."

Narang exploded. "We will crash!"

"Hold your course," Bolan advised.

Thunder rolled behind the freighter. Storm clouds gathered above and the rain hit harder. Ahead, scraps of starlight were enough to establish the difference between the roiling Pacific and the motionless darkened mass of what appeared to be an island.

"Becca. Grab on to something."

Becca shoved one Hi-Power into her shorts and hugged a bulkhead. Bolan slung his rifle and withdrew a SIG. He waved the pistol at the deck. "Hit the floor." The captain and first mate dropped to the deck. Bolan stepped behind the chart table, which was bolted down. "Here we go."

The *Anggun* screamed as her belly scraped across coral. Alarms began sounding and lights blinked red across the control consoles. The bridge tilted violently but the forward momentum of the ship took her over the fringing reef and straight for the beach. Everything went flying as the *Anggun* hit water too shallow for her draft and the sand grabbed her. Becca yelped and nearly lost her purchase on the bulkhead. The captain, the first mate and Pashke the slaver tumbled across the bridge like flotsam and jetsam in a rip curl. Bolan was braced against the chart table but he still slammed against it hard enough to set his nose to bleeding again. He spat to the side and concentrated on holding on while the *Anggun* took its shrieking sleigh ride onto the shore.

The ship ground to a halt with her bow on the beach and her stern sand-vised in the lagoon. The deck tilted at a 20-degree angle. Becca let go, yelped and promptly slid across the deck into Bolan's arms. "You all right?"

The woman managed an impish grin. "Let's do it again."

"Keep your guns on the boys."

Becca turned her pistol on the pile of slavers lying in a heap against the portside wall of the bridge.

Bolan texted the Farm.

We're here, target secure.

Kurtzman replied.

Copy that.

The starlight disappeared as the storm overtook the island. The HC-144A Ocean Sentry turned on all of its lights to reveal a rough runway that took up most of the island's length. A six-man team deployed across the coral atoll on the double. A rope ladder hooked over the gunwale and armed men came aboard the *Anggun*.

The door to the bridge flew open and a very large man announced loudly, "I am Sergeant Cassius Goldstein of the United States Coast Guard! You seem to have run aground. Are you in need of assistance?"

Captain Narang rose hissing like a cat. "This man has attacked my ship in an act of piracy!"

Sergeant Goldstein blinked twice at the area Bolan occupied on the bridge. "What man?"

Captain Narang stopped short of hopping up and down as he pointed. "That man!"

Sergeant Goldstein blinked again and shook his head. "I don't follow."

"Him!" Narang shrieked.

"Captain! Have you sustained a head injury?" Sergeant Goldstein asked. "I don't see anyone on the bridge save you and your mate."

Bolan grinned and gave Becca an arm. A second plane came out of the storm and began its approach toward the landing strip. "Let's go."

6

Honolulu safehouse

Bolan sat at the breakfast table and read the *Waikiki News* story on his tablet.

Ship of Horror! Slavery Ring Exposed!

Last night the United States Coast Guard rescued more than a dozen women who'd been locked in the hold of a freighter. Names have not been released but it is believed several of the victims were reported missing in the Hawaiian Islands this week. The Coast Guard unit also discovered signs of a bloody gun battle on board with multiple casualties. The captain and first mate as well as an unidentified wounded man have been turned over to FBI custody. The ship *Pukulan Anggun,* flying under Indonesian colors, ran aground on Johnston Atoll, an unincorporated territory of the United States....

Koa read the print version. "Nice work, Matt."

Hu came over with a fresh pot of coffee. "Very nice."

"Thanks." Bolan finished his coffee and sighed. Taking over a ship at sea single-handedly and breaking a slavery ring had been relatively easy. This morning's mission was going to be rough. He eyed Hu's black eye and the bandage over Koa's nose. "So, let me guess. She ain't happy?"

"No, she is not," Koa confirmed.

"Well, I guess I should go have a talk with the girl."

"Good luck with that."

Hu's hand unconsciously went to her face. "Watch out for her fists."

"Watch out for her feet," Koa recommended.

Bolan rose and took his tablet and a fresh cup of coffee to the basement door. He knocked politely. "Melika, it's Makaha."

A majestic stream of profanity greeted the announcement.

"You want coffee?" Bolan offered.

Melika told Bolan in no uncertain terms what he could do with his coffee.

"I'm coming down." Bolan went down the steps. Melika appeared to be a "hell hath no fury like a woman kidnapped" kind of girl. Her cot was overturned. The TV was smashed. Despite being handcuffed by one wrist to a pipe, she had somehow managed to overturn the clothes dryer. Both last night's dinner and this morning's breakfast currently formed a work of abstract art on the opposite wall. Despite being a trained military policeman it had cost Koa a bloody nose and some significant bruising to establish a dead zone around Melika. There was nothing else within her reach. The woman sat against the wall and gave Bolan a look. Bolan raised the steaming mug. "So, coffee?"

Melika smiled angelically. "I'd love some." Bolan held out the mug just within range of Melika's fingers. She took the coffee and sighed as she closed her eyes and sipped. "Mmm...that's good."

"Glad you like it. Peg is—" Bolan ducked as the mug flew toward his face and avoided most of the coffee comet tail trailing behind it.

"You're fast," Melika admitted. "Maybe faster than Koa, and he used to be a local legend."

"Thank you."

"So what do you sickos want?"

"I want you to be my girlfriend."

Melika smiled like a she-wolf baring her teeth. "Well, why don't you come a little closer and let's do this."

"Actually, I want you to pretend to be my girlfriend for the next forty-eight hours, possibly a week."

The Hawaiian spitfire pondered this unexpected development. "Pretend? Like you're going to untie me and we're going to have dates and go grind?"

"Something like that."

"And if I say no?"

"I untie you and buy you some grind?"

"What the hell is wrong with you people?"

Bolan held forth his tablet. "This is a very expensive piece of equipment. A friend made it for me custom, so there are only a few like it in the world. Please don't throw it." Bolan tapped an app and brought back the *Waikiki News'* lead story. He held it up for a moment so Melika saw the headline then consigned Kurtzman's pride and joy to its fate. Melika took the tablet. Her brow furrowed as she read.

Bolan nodded. "I was on that ship last night. The night before I was in a cave with Tino, the big man with the broken hand, and some really unpleasant guy I hadn't seen before. So were those girls."

Melika flinched.

"Some really bad stuff is going down. I think you already have an inkling of it. It's running the gamut from slavery to murder, and I have a feeling something far worse is lurking at the end of it."

"And who are you, again?"

"The guy who's going to stop it. Hopefully with your help."

"What? You want me to go undercover?"

"I want you to help keep my cover firmly established, but I also know that your mother drove the bar into the ground and you had to borrow money from Uncle Aikane to buy it back. You're close to him, and I bet you hear things."

Melika flinched as though she'd been punched.

Bolan hadn't known it was Uncle Aikane, but it was an easy guess.

"I won't betray my people."

"I'm asking you to help me save lives on these islands. A whole hell of a lot of those lives are going to be your people's." Bolan took the handcuff key out of his pocket and stepped into the danger zone. Melika watched as he uncuffed her and rubbed the bruises on her wrist. "So what do you say? You wanna go steady?"

Melika stared.

Bolan shrugged. "Buy you a cup of coffee while you think about it?"

"I'd prefer a margarita."

"Well, it's happy hour somewhere," Bolan said.

Naval Health Clinic
Pearl Harbor, Hawaii

BOLAN JUMPED OUT of the U.S. Coast Guard chopper onto the clinic's rooftop helipad. A tall blond man in an almost stereotypical tropical-weight blue suit and mirrored shades stood by the roof access door. He stuck out his hand and shouted over the rotor noise. "I'm Agent Rind. You must be Cooper."

"Glad to meet you."

Agent Rind looked at Koa. "Who's your friend?"

"A friend."

"Right." Rind stuck out his hand again. "Glad to meet you, friend."

"Likewise," Koa said.

Agent Rind ushered them down to the top floor of the clinic.

"You get anything out of our suspect?" Bolan asked.

"Only two 9 millimeters."

Bolan snorted as they walked past two armed Marines guarding the doorway and entered the intensive care unit. The suspect lay awake in bed and was clearly horrified to see Bolan. "So, Pashke. That's Albanian, isn't it?"

What little color Pashke had drained out of his face. He cringed into his pillows as Bolan took a seat on the bed. "You don't mind if I sit, do you? Good. Listen, how about a last name?"

The Albanian slaver clenched his teeth.

"Oh, c'mon," Bolan cajoled. "We have your fingerprints. It's only a matter of time before you turn up in one of our databases."

Pashke resolutely stared at his vital signs monitor.

"You know who might have something on an Albanian sex slaver, Pashke? Serbian intelligence."

Pashke's eyes flew wide in alarm.

"Rind, what's our boy's immigration status?"

"He never got his passport stamped in Honolulu. Technically he's an illegal alien who is a suspect in multiple kidnappings of U.S., Canadian and Mexican citizens."

"Deport him immediately to Belgrade. I know a guy in BIA who owes me a favor."

Pashke went from pale to green as Bolan mentioned the Serbian Security Information Agency. The Balkans could be a rough place, and the Serbian BIA currently held the crown of "that which goes bump in the night" in the Balkan Peninsula. Pashke spat out a word. "Xhindi."

"Pashke Xhindi. Now that's a fine Albanian name. Rind, would you run that?"

Rind was grinning and texting. "Oh, I'm already on it!"

"So, Pashke, I want you to tell me everything."

"Everything?"

"From start to finish. Where you came from. Whom you dealt with in Hawaii. Where you were going. Whom you were selling the girls to, and everything you know about them."

"What if I want lawyer?"

Bolan shrugged. "I guess I might have to let you go."

Pashke Xhindi blinked. "You let me go?"

Bolan snapped his fingers. "Like that, amigo."

Xhindi searched for the rub.

Bolan gave it to him.

"You see, it would probably cause Agent Rind and the State Department a great deal of grief to declare you a terrorist and send you to Belgrade. But I can pull some strings, and as soon as the finest medical treatment the U.S. Navy can provide sets you to rights, I can send you home on a one-way ticket to Tirana."

Bolan drew the Beretta 93-R machine pistol he had taken with him from the CIA safehouse and pushed the selector to three-round burst mode with a click-clack. The Executioner's cobalt-blue eyes burned into the Albanian's flinching browns. "But I will be waiting for you, and I will shoot you twenty-one times in the stomach for the flesh-peddling scum you are." Bolan leaned in until they were nearly nose-to-nose and smelled the Albanian's fear. "I've killed people I liked a lot more for a lot less."

Xhindi swallowed hard. "And if I am cooperating?"

"Then you get medical treatment and a one-way ticket to Tirana, except I'm not waiting."

Xhindi managed to relax slightly.

"I am going to run you through every database I know of, and I am going to call my good friend in BIA who owes me his life, and should you ever return to your scumbag ways, you will wake up in a sub-basement in Belgrade from which you will never leave."

Xhindi shuddered. "I am cooperating."

"God, I love this guy!" Agent Rind said. "How do I get a job on Team Cooper?"

Bolan regarded the FBI special agent seriously. "You know, I might have a job for you."

Agent Rind stopped just short of dancing like Snoopy. "Do I get a machine pistol?"

"That can be arranged."

The Sulu Sea, 40,000 feet

THREE EA-18G GROWLER jets streaked across the Pacific. The two-seat, electronic warfare aircraft, which were versions of the Navy F/A-18 Hornet fighter, cruised at just over the speed of sound. The Pacific was vast, and time and distance were Bolan's implacable foes in an undercover mission, so the Farm had arranged some supersonic transportation out of Pearl Harbor. Koa and Agent Rind were absolutely delighted to be sitting in a fighter plane for the first time. The pilot spoke over his shoulder. "Striker, we have an ETA of five minutes on the *Gipper*."

"Thank you, Lieutenant." After a rendezvous with the aircraft carrier USS *Ronald Reagan,* they'd deploy into Indonesia. Bolan reexamined the bullet points from the Pashke Xhindi file on his tablet.

It made for interesting reading.

Xhindi had delivered sterile M-16 rifle clones from the Philippines to Indonesia in exchange for women and drugs. He had apparently broadened his reach to Hawaii.

For their target in Indonesia, Pashke Xhindi was only a name and a bank account. Bolan had persuaded the Albanian to text the enemy on his private phone, saying that he'd escaped the massacre and grounding of the *Anggun* and was looking to come in with some money in hand.

"Beginning approach," the pilot advised.

Bolan saw the landing lights on the steel island below. The jet fighter seemed to drop like a rock toward the narrow and all too short landing strip on the Nimitz-class supercarrier.

The Growler hit the deck and Bolan slammed against his harness as the jet fighter dropped its arrestor hook and grabbed cable then violently decelerated. "We are down, Striker!"

"Thank you, Lieutenant!"

The EA-18G came to a halt and powered down. The canopy rose and *Gipper*'s flight-deck crew ran up to perform their post-flight roles. Bolan looked over as the second Growler came to a halt and the canopy lifted. Agent Rind shot his hands into the Pacific sky in victory. "Breaking the sound barrier? Scratch that off the bucket list!" The *Gipper*'s deck crew seemed amused.

Agent Rind seemed to be the closest thing to a loose cannon the FBI had these days. Bolan was starting to get a good feeling about the mission. He climbed down the ladder and high-fived Agent Rind once he'd clambered down. The deck crew waved at them to get the hell off the flight deck amid the roar of engine noise. The soldier and the FBI agent watched Koa's EA-18G make its steep approach.

"This is awesome!" Rind enthused.

"You ready to be an Albanian slaver's bodyguard?"

"Did I mention I double majored in law and film with a minor in theater?"

"No."

The third fighter came to a halt and Koa shot them the thumbs-up.

Rind returned the gesture. "This is going to be epic."

Bolan refrained from rolling his eyes. He generally approved of FBI agents, and he liked Rind's can-do attitude. "It's going to be something…."

7

Manila, Republic of the Philippines

Mack Bolan slid into the rented Land Rover. His shopping
mission at the United States' consulate had been successful.
Koa eyed the bulging gear bag. "We cool?"

"Cool as we're going to get at 2:00 a.m. in Manila."

The captain of the USS *Ronald Reagan* had loaned Bolan
and his tiny team one of the *Gipper*'s motor launches. Koa
was a proficient seaman and the ride from the Nimitz-class
carrier to the main island had been a relatively speedy two-
hour run on seas that were becalmed after the storm. The
Farm had already made arrangements for weapons, vehicles and gear.

"So what's the plan?" Agent Rind asked.

Bolan drew a Glock 18 select-fire pistol from his gear
bag. "Here's your machine pistol."

Agent Rind grabbed the gun giddily. "Awesome!"

"Have you ever fired a machine pistol?"

"Dude, I qualified on Glocks. It's what I carry."

"Have you ever fired a machine pistol?" Bolan reiterated.

"No…" Agent Rind admitted.

"Then keep the selector lever on semiauto unless you
need to shoot down a helicopter or light up a speeding car."

"I will."

Bolan handed out a second one. "Here's your spare."

"Sweet!"

Koa, sitting in the driver's seat of their 4 x 4, was studying the file Kurtzman had put together. He was scowling at the contact name Xhindi had provided. "This De Jong guy is a total jag-off. I don't like him."

Bolan agreed. Jagon De Jong was indeed a total jag-off, but he was also the equivalent of Filipino crime royalty. His father had been a two-time Olympic bantamweight boxing champion; a national hero who had gone into politics and gleefully hurled himself into utter corruption. His mother had been a much beloved singer and soap opera star in her youth, and every male member of her family was a pirate or a smuggler. She currently hosted Filipino reality and talent shows. De Jong had grown up a celebrity bad boy who had gotten involved in very bad business. Manila was a significant transshipment point for all sorts of smuggling in the Pacific. De Jong was a connected middleman who had to be given his piece of the action on a respectable swathe of the capital city's smuggling. By all accounts, unless De Jong was caught with a flamethrower burning down an orphanage, he was untouchable.

Bolan intended to reach out and touch Jagon De Jong tonight…with a clenched fist. "Xhindi said he's spoken with De Jong twice. We're going to try to talk our way in."

Rind, riding shotgun, turned and gave Bolan a grim look. "You think you can?"

"He talked his way into the Maui underworld," Koa admitted, setting the file aside and starting the engine. "I've stopped questioning the man."

Bolan cleared his throat, got into character and channeled his inner Xhindi as he quoted the Albanian gangster verbatim. "'What if I want lawyer? And if I am cooperating? I am cooperating.'"

Rind stared at Bolan in awe. "It's uncanny."

Koa took the 4 x 4 into the Ermita District, one of Manila's cultural and entertainment centers. Museums, casinos and theaters all fought for space among the gleaming skyscrapers. Koa pulled up to the curb in front of a shiny new high-rise and a valet dressed in an organ grinder's monkey suit materialized. "Gentlemen, may I—"

Koa pulled the Hawaiian stone face. "We have business with *Señor* Jagon."

Rind looked at the hapless valet as if the man were an insect.

Bolan sat in the back wearing a black duster and smoking French cigarettes as if he owned all of Manila. There had been no time to chemically peel the South Seas patina Hu had given him, so Bolan had been forced to resort to makeup, and it wouldn't last long. Rind looked like total Euro-trash and Koa just looked dangerous. The valet did an admirable job of shuddering while standing his ground. "*Señors,* I must—"

Agent Rind glared. "Tell Mr. Jagon that Mr. Xhindi regrets the time of night, but nonetheless wishes to pay his respects."

Bolan nodded. Rind put his hand under his jacket and waited. The valet weighed what might be hidden there. "One moment, *señors,* I will—"

Rind held up a respectable wad of Filipino pesos.

The valet took the cash and wrung his hands obsequiously as he backed away and made a phone call. "Señor De Jong will see you."

Koa slid out and tossed the valet the keys. Rind took position on Bolan's six. The valet gave the keys to one of his flunkies in a less ornate monkey suit and led Bolan's team to the private elevator. They stepped within the exotic hardwood-paneled interior and the valet hit the button for the penthouse. It was a respectably long ride to the top but the elevator didn't pause at any of the intervening seventy-five floors. The door pinged open and Jagon De Jong threw out his arms. De Jong was built like a welterweight and stood in front of them in a red smoking jacket and green-and-gold Thai kickboxing trunks. In one hand he held a bottle of champagne. "Pashke! Baby!"

Bolan regarded the Filipino gangster blandly. "Didn't I tell you to never call me that?"

De Jong searched his eyebrows for several moments. "No?"

"I'm telling you now."

De Jong spread his arms again in supplication. "Don't be that guy."

Bolan read his unwary and somewhat drunken opponent and knew how to play him. "You are a charming gangster. I'll give you that."

De Jong beamed. "Come in! Come in!"

The team entered a penthouse that could only be described as palatial. De Jong had a fetish for gold plating that the most jaded Russian mafia don would admire, and the number of ivory religious carvings occupying nearly every gold-plated surface warranted a U.N. investigation. Many of the walls and ceilings were glass.

De Jong led them to the center of his web of gold and glass. Three individuals draped themselves on a four-sided box of golden couches. One was a slinky-looking Thai woman. The second was a fey Vietnamese young man, and the third was a six-foot, Nordic-looking blonde whose exact gender was in doubt. Her stunning curves and even more stunning face were clearly the product of science. She caressed a pair of black-and-white French bulldogs. All of them wore black satin robes with a JDJ monogram in gold. The young man and woman regarded Bolan with bored looks. The transsexual looked upon Bolan with genuine interest. The Frenchies wagged their stubby tails.

De Jong grinned happily. "You see? If Apollo and Zeus like you, I know you're good people!" The gangster leered. "And if Belle-Belen likes you? You're in for the night of your life! Belle! More champagne for our guests. Please, Pashke! Have a seat!"

Belle rose and disappeared behind a glittering glass-brick façade. Bolan and his team sat. "We have a problem." Bolan's tone grated.

De Jong pointed at the champagne bottle. "You know? I heard all about it. Heard the ship ran aground, half the crew wiped out, all the girls back at home in their beds." De Jong leaned back into his golden silk sofa and put a hand to his head as though he had a headache. The young man and woman instantly began massaging his shoulders. "But that is your problem, Señor Xhindi. I fulfilled my part to the letter."

Belle came out with champagne flutes and two open bottles of Dom Pérignon on a golden tray. Bolan took a glass. "I am out the guns you sold me and out the girls I bought. I have men dead, I am on the run and I'm out every last dollar I invested. I ask you, how did my operation get compromised?"

"I have no idea."

Bolan put some controlled fury into his voice. "It was an inside job."

De Jong took his fingers from his brow and snapped them.

Four of the biggest Filipinos Bolan had ever seen emerged from opposite doorways in matching white track suits armed with gold-plated Sterling submachine guns with gold-plated bayonets. They put Bolan's team in their crosshairs.

De Jong pulled a gold-plated Walther PPK from his smoking jacket and the laser sight printed a red dot on Bolan's chest where the red hole was about to be. Belle produced a Browning Hi-Power pistol that was cold blue steel and looked to have seen some use. De Jong sighed. "We seem to be having some sort of misunderstanding, Mr. Xhindi."

"You misunderstand me completely, Mr. De Jong," Bolan agreed.

De Jong almost looked hopeful. "Oh?"

"I trust you completely."

"I am very glad to hear that."

Bolan read his target and chose his words carefully. "You

know they call you a playboy, a dilettante, a criminal rock star."

De Jong smiled. "Now that is some serious sunshine you are pumping up my ass, Xhindi, not that I don't like it, but—"

"But like you said," Bolan continued. "You fulfilled your part of the deal to the letter. That is how you survive in this business, except no one survives in this business. That's how men like you and I last, until we decide to go legit."

"True." De Jong frowned in his semi-drunkenness. "So what are you saying?"

"If I didn't give me up, and you didn't give me up, who did?"

The gangster's jaw dropped. "That's messed up." He frowned again. "What's his profit?"

"None," Bolan replied. "So the question is, what would be his motivation?"

De Jong surged to his feet. "Stinking rat!"

Bolan sighed. "I'm just an Albanian boy trying to make his way in the world, ten thousand kilometers from Tirana and home. I'm easy to give up, but if your associate has been gotten to, and if he's giving people up? You are part of the chain, De Jong, and once a rat starts squealing, they just squeal louder, and louder and louder."

De Jong purpled. The concubines cringed. Belle-Belen's eyes positively gleamed. Her pistol never wavered.

Bolan lit a cigarette. "May I ask you a terrible question?"

"Yeah!" De Jong slopped champagne as he angrily re-filled his glass. "You go right ahead!"

"Who is he?"

De Jong stared at Bolan long and hard.

"This cannot go unanswered." Bolan locked eyes. "Rats require extermination. I think I must kill this man. Best if I do it with your permission, Mr. De Jong. Better still if we are together in this. I have never been to Indonesia."

De Jong slammed back his flute of champagne. "Well, I

have! You want this bastard? I'll…" De Jong trailed off as Bolan's attention was drawn to the glass ceiling. "What?"

"You expecting company?"

"I wasn't expecting you."

The glass walls and ceilings began to shake and the sound of rotors thundered overhead. Bolan drew his Beretta and rose. His team and Belle-Belen followed suit. Bolan scanned the skies, searching for the chopper. "We're about to get hit." Looking around the open, gold-and-glass penthouse, he knew it would be easier than shooting fish in an aquarium. "Kill the lights, and we need bigger guns."

De Jong jerked his head at one of his gigantic guards. "Pepe! Turn off the lights! Go into my bedroom and get the—"

Glass shattered overhead as a machine gun stitched Pepe from crotch to collar. Shards fell like miniature guillotines and the fey young man screamed as he was slashed from above. A Bell 204 helicopter took a tight orbit overhead and a man in chicken straps hung halfway out the door behind an M-60 machine gun.

Bolan ignored the piece of glass that cut his arm and began squeezing off three round bursts from his Beretta. Rind burned a magazine from his machine pistol into the chopper and Koa fired his .45 as fast as he could pull the trigger. Belle very coolly aimed and fired each shot as though she was at a target range while the three remaining bodyguards sprayed their weapons skyward. Sparks ricocheted off the fuselage and the helicopter banked away into the glow of the skyline.

Bolan spun around as a second chopper thundered overhead. It was a much smaller OH-6. A man leaned out each door firing rifles on full auto. Bolan printed a three-round burst into the starboard assassin, who fell out of the chopper and crashed through the glass roof of De Jong's master bathroom. Something clattered to the glass-strewed floor. Bolan hurled himself over a couch and roared. "Grenade!"

The golden silk inches above Bolan's face pulsed as shrapnel tore through it like an invisible scythe. People screamed but Bolan couldn't tell who. The soldier rolled to one knee and fired his 93-R into the tail boom of the helicopter until it was empty. He took three steps and slid as if to beat the ball to first base as a line of machine gun fire crossed the room. Bolan came to a stop beside Pepe's ruptured corpse and relieved him of his gold-plated submachine gun. The soldier rose. He knew he was standing in a pool of light by a huge golden lamp. The pilot of the OH-6 saw him leveling his gleaming weapon and made the mistake of trying to bank rather than power forward at full speed.

Bolan burned all thirty rounds into the little helicopter's cockpit.

Several firearms in the penthouse joined the chorus.

The little egg-shaped helicopter did a 360 spin and came to a violent landing in De Jong's penthouse swimming pool, the rotors snapping on the cement.

A feminine voice dropped an octave as it screamed in victorious Swedish.

Bolan found a spare magazine on Pepe's corpse and reloaded. "Koa!" Bolan shouted.

"Yo!"

"Rind!"

"Yeah!"

"Belle!"

"Oh, yeah, baby!"

"De Jong!"

Jagon De Jong came running out of his bedroom with a gold-plated Minimi light machine gun. "Bastards!"

"Your people?"

One giant waddled after his master.

"I got one!"

Bolan intercepted the gangster and ripped the gun out of his hands. "Gimme that."

De Jong seemed somewhat relieved to give up his weapon. "Okay…"

Bolan noticed the push button on the grip. "You have a gold-plated, laser-sighted light machine gun?"

De Jong shrugged and took up Bolan's abandoned submachine gun. "Well, yeah."

Bolan snapped out the left bipod strut for a forward grip and took a knee to turn himself into a human anti-aircraft gun. "Nice."

"Thanks!"

Bolan checked his new team. Koa had acquired a gleaming submachine gun. So had Belle-Belen. Rind held a Glock machine pistol in either hand and scanned the skies. Having read the agent's file, Bolan knew that while Rind had used his service pistol before, this was his first genuine battle. "How you doing, Rind?"

Rind grinned and waggled his Glocks at the smoking, bubbling aircraft in the swimming pool. "You said I could put them on full auto if I needed to shoot down a helicopter!"

"That I did." Bolan lifted his chin at rotor noise. "Three o'clock! Here he comes!"

The helicopter's lights blinked as it banked in.

Agent Rind's Glocks began spewing fire. Tracers streamed, seeking out the FBI agent's life. Everyone else began firing. Bolan waited to see the whites of his enemy's eyes. The helicopter ignored the incoming fire and swooped in a hard arc with three men firing out the side doors. A fourth man pushed the tube of a rocket launcher between his compatriots.

Bolan ignored rifles and rockets as he painted the engine cowling just below the rotor shaft with the laser sight and burned his one-hundred-round belt of ammo into the chopper's heart. The helicopter lurched. The assassin's rocket hissed off-target from its tube and sent a geyser up from De Jong's pool. Two men tumbled out of the doors, missed the pool as well as the roof entirely, and fell screaming to the late-night streets of Ermita below.

Bolan grimaced as he lowered his smoking, empty, golden weapon and watched the chopper boomerang across the sky. Dropping a chopper in one of the most densely populated cities in the world would be a collateral damage disaster. He was infinitely relieved as it scythed into the adjoining skyscraper's rooftop and broke apart rather than exploded.

Bolan rose and scanned the skies. No more helicopters were coming. Police, fire and the Filipino military would be. De Jong stopped short of pointing his submachine gun at Bolan.

"You seem very military for an Albanian slaver man."

Bolan looked the Filipino gangster straight in the eye and spoke the truth. "I have fought in Serbia and Croatia. Bosnia was the worst."

"Jesus…"

Bolan patted the blinged-out, modified and smoking light machine gun he held. "I'm keeping this."

De Jong nodded. "It looks good on you."

8

On approach to
Soekarno-Hatta International Airport

Bolan's team flew into Jakarta, Indonesia, in the De Jong family private jet. It wasn't gold-plated, but the Phenom 300 executive jet was a plush ride and Bolan absolutely approved of the stewardess's skill with a pistol. Belle sat in the server's seat and smiled at Bolan in open speculation while she caressed her Frenchies. Koa leaned over. The Hawaiian warrior held up his watch and spoke low. "Time is getting thin, Cooper."

Bolan knew it. His West Pacific team was on a highly successful rolling war but the home team was in Hawaii, and if the boys weren't back soon the girls might have hell to pay. "I know."

"We are out on a limb, and we're putting good people out on a limb."

"I know." Bolan sighed. "You're one of them."

"Yeah, I know you know, but what the hell? How did they find out we were in Manila?"

"They didn't. When I took the *Anggun* someone decided to take matters into their own hands and clean up any loose ends."

"You think there's another cleaning squad heading for Hawaii?"

"Probably already there," Bolan admitted. "Listen, I need

you for twenty-four hours in Indonesia, Koa. After that? You go ahead and break for your people and your Islands. I'll understand and catch up when and if I can."

Koa absorbed what that statement meant. "You're an asshole."

"Got you gold-plated guns."

"Yeah." Koa considered the Sterling in his lap. "You're still an asshole."

"I get that a lot."

"You say that a lot, and I believe you. So what?"

"Tell me you have my six for twenty-four in Jakarta."

Koa gave Bolan the Hawaiian stone stare. "You fascinate me."

Rind leaned his head in between the seats. "I'm excited about this plan, and I'm thankful to be a part of it. Let's do it!"

"I'll take that as a yes from both of you." Bolan looked up the tiny aisle. De Jong was snoring away in his seat. His remaining track-suited security walrus, Marwin, sawed logs next to him. Belle eyed the Bolan trio steadily. Bolan winked at her and Belle's smile lit up the cabin. Bolan grinned. "Where'd you learn to shoot?"

Belle's voice was a smoky alto that had almost no discernible accent. "Every good Swedish boy does his year of compulsory service in the military. I was in the military police, and I rated expert with pistol and submachine gun." She caressed her golden Sterling. "It's not a Carl Gustav, but I like it."

"You're a bodyguard?"

"I make adult films. I date very rich men and do bodyguard work. Sometimes I can combine two if not all three. As a bodyguard, I am the last thing a kidnapper expects. Me with a gun? That is the last thing they see."

Rind grinned. "I like her!"

"Most do," Belle agreed.

"What do you know about our Indonesian gangster?" Bolan asked.

"Not much." Belle gave Bolan the glad eye. "What I do know is you're not an Albanian slaver."

Bolan eyed the snoring Filipino gangsters in the front of the cabin. Belle hadn't seemed to have bothered to pass this knowledge on to De Jong, so he didn't bother denying it.

"How do you know?"

"I've dated Albanian gangsters."

"Oh?"

"Yes, but I was living in Germany then. I was a redhead, and my name was Louise."

Bolan smiled.

De Jong snorted awake, peered back blearily, grinned, and then rested his head on Marwin's massive shoulder and went back to whistling and wheezing.

Bolan smiled at the scientifically constructed feminine pulchritude in front of him. "You're a sweet girl."

Belle smirked. "Sweet, hell."

"You want out?"

"Out? Of this mission?"

"No." Bolan lifted his chin at De Jong. "I mean out."

Belle's eyes went to slits. "What do you mean?"

"You know how to keep a beautiful girl in line?"

Belle's face hardened. Bolan knew he had once again read his target well. "You rent her a beautiful apartment. Buy her beautiful clothes. Take her out to the best restaurants. Fly her around the world. Give her the keys to your most expensive cars. Take her to the casinos and cover her bets. Hell, give her gold-plated guns." Bolan let out a long breath. "And give her all the drugs she wants."

Belle flinched.

"But you never give her money of her own, and you keep her in debt. Every cent she makes on her own doesn't even keep up with interest."

Belle stared at Bolan like a cat. "You speak from experience."

"No, but I've known plenty of men who treat women like that."

"Oh?"

"Killed my fair share of them."

Belle stared.

Bolan made his decision. "You want out?"

"You have no idea how much debt I'm carrying, much less—" a terrible look passed across the surgically sculpted face "—what kind of favors I owe."

"I can cover it."

"You can't—"

"And if I can't cover all your debts?" Bolan's burning blue stare spoke far more than words. "Believe me, I can make your creditors see reason."

Belle shook. "What do I have to do?"

"Choose."

"Choose what?"

"Team Cooper for the next seventy-two hours. Say yes."

"And if you get your head blown off?"

Koa nodded his head at Bolan. "It's likely, but if you like Hawaii? I have friends."

Rind lowered his voice. "You've heard of FBI witness relocation?"

Belle nodded slowly.

"Well, you're not a witness. You're a teammate, and a member of my fire team. I will pull strings."

Tears spilled down Belle's Nordic cheekbones. "Count me in."

Jakarta

"WE'RE HERE." Koa parked the rental Land Rover in front of a warehouse.

Bolan glanced up from his tablet. Belle had changed into

black cargo pants, black designer combat boots and a black tank top. She had dyed her hair black in the jet's bathroom and pulled it back into a ponytail. Marwin's tracksuit was reversible and he had suddenly gone sumo-ninja with a black do-rag. Despite the sweltering heat De Jong had changed into black leather pants and a black leather jacket straight out of Elvis's comeback special.

The soldier thought the gold-plated guns negated the blackout camouflage but there was nothing to be done about it; he was carrying one himself. The battle in Manila had been successful against all odds, but none of the assassins had survived. They had very little on their adversary save redacted files and rumors.

Bolan took a final glance at his tablet. Tonight's quarry was Ramad "the Handyman" Handi. A picture of the criminal showed a middle-aged Indonesian man in a blue guayabera with a horrific, nearly hand-shaped comb-over spreading its lank grip across his sweaty skull. He looked like the last man you would ever buy a used car from, but if you needed a crate of assault rifles, a kilo of coke or a human kidney, the Handyman was your man. Jagon De Jong was a criminal dilettante, but he had a few loveably loathsome re-deeming qualities. The Handyman was a straight-up scum-bag—the exact breed of evil Bolan had first declared his War Everlasting against years ago. The Handyman was rumored to be an international concern whose fingers stretched across the Pacific into some very dark and interesting corners.

Bolan took in the Handyman's lair.

De Jong had lived in the penthouse of a gleaming spire until Bolan had dropped a helicopter into it. The Handyman lived in a converted warehouse in a very bad part of town. "You ready?" Bolan asked.

De Jong produced a butterfly knife and a small plastic bag filled with some sort of blue flake product. He dipped his knife into the bag and took a hefty snort up each nos-tril. "Oh, yeah!"

De Jong handed the knife and the plastic bag to Belle. Belle winced in shame and took a snort anyway. "Can I ask you a question?" De Jong asked.

"Go ahead."

"You're not Pashke Xhindi, are you?"

Bolan saw no reason to lie and dropped his accent. "No."

De Jong looked genuinely hurt. "You tricked me."

"Yeah."

"But you didn't know Handi had sent a hit squad to kill me?"

"I didn't know his name until you told me. But I think he has an agenda bigger than just your guns and girls deal, and he needs to clean up loose ends. You're one of them."

"So, who are you?

"The guy who decided not to kill you when I knocked on your door."

De Jong sniffed and wiped at his nose. "Okay."

"You ready?"

The Philippine gangster prodigy brightened. "Oh, yeah!"

"Go."

De Jong literally fell out of the Land Rover and staggered to the warehouse security door. He sounded close to tears as he pounded on the steel. "Handi! Handi! Answer the door!"

Bolan watched through the tinted windows as the security camera above the door regarded De Jong coldly. A voice spoke over an intercom. "Jagon?"

"For God's sake!" De Jong bawled. "You have to let me in!"

Bolan knew Handi was shocked that De Jong was still alive much less whimpering on his doorstep. The intercom crackled. "Jagon, what are you doing here?"

"The Albanian! He lost his boat, his money, his girls and his guns! I think he ordered a hit on me tonight!"

Koa shook his head grudgingly. "He's not bad."

"Man deserves an award," Rind opined.

There was no answer from the warehouse as Handi pondered this turn of events.

"Sweet Jesus! Google my name!" De Jong sobbed. Handi had to know his hit team was gone. The Philippine online news organizations were on fire with stories of gun battles in downtown Manila, helicopters falling out of the sky and the mysterious disappearance of gangster playboy Jagon De Jong. De Jong shrieked. "The son of a bitch is killing everyone!"

Handi made his decision. "Are you alone?"

"I'm with Marwin and Belle! Goddamn Xhindi burned up my penthouse and killed everyone else!"

A note of cupidity entered Handi's voice over the intercom. "Belle? The *waria?*"

Bolan knew *waria* was the Indonesian word for a transgendered individual.

"Yes!" De Jong howled.

The door buzzed. "Come in."

"Belle, Marwin." Bolan lifted his chin at the converted warehouse. "You're on."

Marwin and Belle rolled out of the Land Rover. The intercom crackled. "Leave the guns."

De Jong nodded at his minions. Marwin and Belle tossed their gold-plated guns back into the vehicle as Bolan and his team stayed low. Team Jagon entered the warehouse and the door closed behind them. Bolan checked his weapon a final time. "Handi is going to want some answers out of Jag-off. It sounds as though he wants a lot more out of Belle. Wait for my signal and then drive around back and blow through the loading ramp door."

Koa nodded. "Got it."

Rind took a stick of dynamite and a roll of duct tape out of the communal gear bag. De Jong hadn't been able to get any heavy weapons but his family had multiple mining concerns in the Philippine Islands and a box of suspiciously sweaty dynamite had been in the Phenom jet's stores at takeoff.

Bolan slung his golden light machine gun and sub over his shoulders. He knew the inside team had only seconds before horrible things started happening. He stepped out of the Land Rover bold as brass and taped the stick of dynamite to the warehouse door. The Land Rover's tires shrieked as Koa and Rind pulled away for the safety of the side street. Bolan lit the dynamite with a lighter he had bought at the Jakarta International gift shop. He ran across the street and hurled himself over a low wall as the fuse sparked and sputtered.

The street turned orange as the stick of dynamite went off.

Bolan rose in the smoking afterglow. He shoved his shining light machine gun into the hip-assault position and charged for the torn black hole that was now the warehouse frontage.

Handguns began popping inside the building. Bolan had instructed his team to hit the dirt when the blast struck. As he entered the breach, the soldier went hunting for muzzle-flashes in the smoke with bursts from the Minimi. The red laser made a pleasing line through the smoke and Bolan's five-round bursts tracked along the line and silenced the opposition. By the same token the line let everyone know exactly where he was if his muzzle-flashes hadn't and several returning shots came uncomfortably close.

An engine roared. Lights flared and the tires of an SUV parked within the building screamed against the cement floor. Bolan spun, took a knee and burned what remained of his hundred-round belt between the headlights. The engine cut and so did the lights. Bolan dropped the spent light machine gun and pulled his sub. He affixed the gold-plated bayonet for the hell of it and moved through the smoke. The soldier crouched after he nearly tripped over Marwin. The big man appeared to have been clubbed behind the ear. He was breathing but his eyelids were fluttering.

"Cooper!" De Jong was screaming in the smoke and darkness somewhere to Bolan's left. "Cooper!"

"Shut up!" Bolan roared. "Stay down!"

Bullets sought them both. A second vehicle roared into life and began to roll for the massive breach in the side of the warehouse. Bolan put several bursts into it and automatic rifles fired back.

The former door of the warehouse's loading dock shattered as Koa brought the Land Rover ramming through. The Hawaiian fishtailed for one second then caught sight of the other vehicle, corrected and T-boned it broadside. Rind ripped his way past the air bags and emerged with his machine pistols rolling in each hand as he peppered the vehicle with bursts.

Most of the overhead lighting had been shattered by the blast. Sparks flew as the generator kicked in and the two remaining overhead fixtures blinked on. At the same time the fire sprinklers belatedly hissed into life.

The Handyman snarled. "Enough!" Bolan turned to find Handi holding Belle in a one-armed chokehold. The front of her black shirt glistened with blood and he held a pistol under her jaw. Handi screwed the muzzle underneath Belle's soft palate.

De Jong rose and dropped his pistol in a panic. "No! Don't do it!"

Handi scanned the room at Rind, Koa and Bolan. "I'll blow the bitch's brains out!"

Bolan kept his Sterling leveled but nodded in disgust at the FBI agent. "Rind! Drop them!"

"Oh, for—"

"Do it!"

Rind dropped his Glocks. Bolan duly noted Handi's eyes had flicked to the FBI man as he dropped his weapons.

Handi put the gun into Belle's temple. "All of you!"

"Koa!" Bolan called.

"Hell with that!"

"Do it! We're done here! He lets her go? We walk away!"

Koa's weapon stood rock steady. "You think he's going to let her go? You think any of us walk out?"

Bolan hoped to hell the Hawaiian would understand his impromptu code. "You don't think I can make him see reason?"

Koa didn't blink. He simply dropped his weapon. Handi watched it fall. Belle was looking at Bolan in desperation. Bolan hoped she got his code, as well, as he looked at her feet and jerked his head both ways and up.

Belle jumped, her feet apart a meter, and shoved her hands up against the butt of the Hi-Power pistol screwed against her skull. She screamed as the gun went off. Bolan lowered his aim between Belle's legs and held the trigger of his Sterling down.

Most of the Handyman's right tibia shattered and collapsed under the onslaught. Handi toppled backward, screaming. Belle staggered forward two steps, clutching her right ear, and fell to her knees. Koa vaulted a couch and landed with a knee in Handi's chest. He took the Indonesian gangster's gun and choked him unconscious.

"Rind! De Jong! Clear the building!"

Rind scooped up his pistols, hauled De Jong to his feet and shoved a weapon into the gangster's hand as he began a professional sweep. Bolan went to Belle. Blood trickled beneath the hand covering her ear. "Can you hear me?"

Belle tilted her head as though she had the worst migraine on earth. "On the left side."

"I think your eardrum is perforated."

Rind called out. "Clear!"

"See to Marwin! Koa?"

Koa had finished applying a tourniquet to Handi's leg. "He'll live."

"Run a sweep for any laptops or tablets. Get their phones. We're out of here. De Jong! I need a medic!"

De Jong grinned. "I happen to know a guy in town!"

9

Glodok, Jakarta

"You do know who that is?" Dr. Dewa asked, looking none too happy.

Bolan glanced down at the Handyman. Whatever drugs De Jong had shared with him on the trip to Chinatown clearly weren't doing enough to take the edge off the gangster's pain. He shook and sweated and moaned on the gurney. Bolan nodded at his prey. "Oh, yeah."

"Do you want me to try to save the leg?" Dr. Dewa looked dubiously at the mess Bolan's burst had made of the Handyman's lower leg. Dewa was a very serious-looking young doctor—a member of the long and less-than-distinguished line of medical professionals who through addiction to drugs or gambling—in his case both—had been forced to relaunch his medical career catering exclusively to criminals. He had made the severe mistake of getting himself indebted to Jakarta's Chinese organized crime element.

"Can you?" Bolan inquired.

"It would take multiple operations. I would have to call in some people to help. He needs—"

"He needs to speak with me immediately."

Dewa tsked thoughtfully. "I see."

Bolan was pretty sure this wasn't the first time one of Dewa's patients had been assessed this way.

Koa gazed down upon Handi in grim amusement. "I think One Foot Wonder suits him better than Handyman, anyway."

Marwin held an icepack against the purple lump on the back of his head. "Screw him."

"De Jong?"

"Do you even have to ask?"

"Rind," Bolan called, "you got any love for this man?"

Rind didn't bother looking up from his rampaging through the laptops and tablets they had taken from the warehouse. "None whatsoever, Coop. The Handyman? Total scumbag."

Handi sweated through his clothes. Bolan shook his head. "Vote's going against you, you know."

The gangster's comb-over had flopped to one side on his pillow, giving him a remarkable kraken/cranium effect. He remained defiant. "If you wanted me dead I'd be dead."

"That's right!" Bolan brightened. "So I'll make you a deal. Morphine, your leg and your life, in that order."

"And in return you want what?"

Bolan sighed. "Is that the foot you want to put forward?"

"As it stands you only have one," Koa cautioned. "I'd make it your best one."

"Morphine," Handi countered. "And have the doctor prep me for surgery."

"Dose him," Bolan agreed.

Dr. Dewa pressed an auto-injector against Handi's thigh. The gangster sighed and blissfully sagged back into his rolling bed. "Ah."

"So tell me."

"Tell you what?"

"You sent the hit squads to kill De Jong in Manila."

"Of course."

"Bastard!" De Jong snarled.

Bolan held up a placating hand. They knew that already, but getting a suspect's first willing admission was key to any interrogation. "You want a cigarette?"

"Of course."

The cloying sweet mixture of tobacco, cloves and cocoa wrapped in corn husk filled the infirmary as Bolan lit Handi one of his Kretek cigarettes from the pack he'd been carrying when he was captured. Handi sighed with pleasure. Bolan perked an eyebrow. Handi was sweating bullets from the bodily stress of pain, but the Indonesian gangster did not stink of fear. Something was wrong. "Marwin, watch him."

Bolan pulled his team into the foyer. The soldier spoke low. "He's not afraid."

"Give me five minutes with him." Belle cracked her man-size knuckles. "I'll teach him fear."

"I'm sure you could teach a man all sorts of things about himself." Bolan smiled. "But hold that thought."

Belle smirked.

"Sociopath?" Rind suggested.

Bolan had met a number of sociopaths and ended most of them. "No, your first assessment was correct. Handi's a straight-up scumbag. A professional criminal from a long line of professional criminals, with an organization around him. Now he's in unknown hands, possibly crippled, with his career in ruins, and he's calm, cool and collected."

"He was salty even before Dewa hit him with the morphine," Koa noted.

Bolan nodded. "And so?"

The Hawaiian warrior saw it. "And so I think someone got inside Handi's head."

"You and me both, brother."

Koa gazed heavenward for strength. "You know? Strangely enough, I like it better when you call me brother rather than cuz."

Bolan turned to the FBI agent. "Rind?"

"You're thinking he's undergone some sort of conversion?"

"It would explain a lot. It might even explain how a bunch of admittedly misguided sons of the Aloha State are stockpiling weapons and recruiting for some kind of doomsday Island repatriation act."

"Do I detect sarcasm?" Koa questioned.

Rind frowned. "I see where you're going, except for the fact that according to our files Handi was at least ostensibly raised Muslim."

"And?"

"And the majority of Hawaiians are Christian."

"Yeah." Bolan nodded. "But it seems to me our boys back in the Islands are starting to go nativistic."

"Which makes no sense," Rind scoffed.

Koa went from stone face to genuinely dour. "It makes every bit of sense."

"I don't get it."

Koa folded his arms across his chest. "Syncretism."

Rind looked to Bolan for a lifeline. Bolan tossed it to him. "The fusion of differing systems of belief."

"Yeah." Rind saw it. "At the academy we took classes about the pan-Jihadist threat. They talked about how historically Islam had been incredibly successful in piggy-backing onto animist religions. It's how it penetrated so deeply and so swiftly into Africa, Asia and the Pacific archipelagos. It makes a crazy kind of sense."

Koa nodded at the agent. "Our tax dollars at work."

"The boy's got a future," Bolan agreed.

Rind ignored the comments. "You're not trying to tell me Handi and Uncle Friendly are on the same page?"

Bolan shook his head. "If we're right—and that's a big if—I don't think the grand syncretism has happened yet. In the meantime, I think something is being set up. Something big enough to qualify as a human-initiated disaster in Hawaii, and from Indonesia to the Philippines to Hawaii someone is linking Pacific Islands like a necklace."

Koa took up his golden gun and snapped out the folding stock. "So we're about to get our asses hammered again?"

"I'd say it's a good bet." The soldier limbered up his light machine gun. "Everyone gear up."

Belle scowled at her weapon. "We're low on ammo."

Bolan racked a round and wished he had a spare belt of ammunition. "Short bursts, if it comes to it." His team fanned out to cover the windows and entrances. The soldier strode back into the infirmary. "So who's coming?"

Handi's smile was sickening. "Thank you for the cigarette, and the morphine."

Bolan tapped his phone. "Bear, do we have satellite on my location?"

"Our next satellite window on Jakarta is thirty-five minutes out."

"Cooper!" De Jong's voice rose a very distressed octave. "They're coming! And they have a tank!"

Koa shook his head as he peered out of his firing position. "That's an IFV."

De Jong was not consoled. "A what?"

"Infantry Fighting Vehicle. It has six wheels. Tanks have tracks."

De Jong gazed upon the wheeled, armored beast in sheer terror. "Well, that makes it all better then, doesn't it!"

Bolan looked out over De Jong's shoulder and frowned. Technically it wasn't a tank or an IFV. It was an armored car, possibly forty years old. He watched the olive-drab, ex-Indonesian army, Saladin-armored car rumble down the street. The impending priority would be the turret-mounted 76 mm cannon and two general-purpose machine guns aiming at the infirmary over the armored car's squat hull. His team had nothing that would breach the vehicle's rolled-steel armor. A reinforced squad of gunmen trotted behind it. "Koa, I need a diversion."

Koa considered the request. "Oh, you want me to attract an IFV's attention?"

"While I assault it." Bolan sighed fatalistically. "Unless you want to switch jobs."

"Oh, no, you go right ahead."

"I thought you'd say that. De Jong! Tell me we have some dynamite left."

"Ooh!" De Jong suddenly got happy as he yanked open the satchel. "Six sticks!"

Bolan peered down into the alligator-skin satchel. The sticks of dynamite lay sweating in sawdust, but with none of the sweaty confidence of the Handyman. It was a blow-at-any-second sort of sweating. Bolan could smell the nitro.

"Koa, I need you to throw two lit sticks out onto the street."

"And you're charging the armor with the other four?"

"Yeah, and everyone is giving me covering fire."

For the first time during the mission Rind showed reluctance. "There's no covering fire against cannons."

"You ever see a stick of dynamite go off?"

"Actually I just directed a short film where we used explosives."

"And?"

Rind saw it. "Smoke and fire!"

"That's right. You pour in fire to keep them buttoned up and Koa throws the TNT to give me a smoke screen."

Belle sighed. "While you go dynamite torch runner on their armored asses."

Bolan grinned. "You're hot."

"You are mad, bad and dangerous to know."

The coaxial gun opened up and began raking the side of the infirmary. A man jumped up out of the top hatch and grabbed the grips of the anti-aircraft gun and began hammering the siding. Gunmen deployed on either side and discharged assault rifles. Bolan's team dropped as bullets streaked through the thin aluminum walls.

Koa took up a sweating stick of dynamite.

"Now!" Bolan shouted.

Belle appeared at Koa's elbow and chinked open her lighter.

Koa shook his head as he regarded the unstable explosive. "Now or not at all!" Bolan roared.

Koa gave himself to fate and held out the stick. Belle lit it. The Hawaiian hurled the dynamite out into the night. "And the chances of the blast wave detonating the rest of them are—"

The dynamite went off like a Hollywood special effect. The walls shuddered. Bolan took up two sticks and felt the glycerin-slick explosives squirm greasily in his fingers. "Again!"

Koa held out the TNT and Belle lit it. Acrid smoke filled the street. Koa sent the dynamite revolving out into the street. The gunmen crouched behind the armored car and the blast wave shook the avenue. Black smoke roiled. Bolan pulled his lighter, leaped out of the window and charged through the fog of war.

The armored car's machine guns shrieked bullets through the smoke. Bolan's team cut loose with covering shots. The Saladin's cannon belched fire in response and blew a huge hole through the wall of the infirmary. Bolan had no time for it. He breathed brimstone and smoke and lit a stick of TNT. The soldier tossed it over the armored car and into the milling mass of men taking cover behind. Gunmen screamed as they saw the spitting and sparking explosive among them. Bolan lit his second stick and skimmed it beneath the armored vehicle. The only safe place was up top. Bolan charged forward and ran up the sloped prow of the vehicle. The top gunner perceived Bolan through the smoke and yanked his machine gun around on its pintle mount.

Bolan swung his machine gun on its sling and put a burst through the enemy gunner's chest. The soldier dropped on top of the steel glacis.

The first stick of dynamite detonated behind the armored car.

The gunmen's screams were lost as the second stick of dynamite beneath the Saladin went off and the armored car rose like a fire-fueled elevator beneath Bolan. He clung to the external cargo cleats as the vehicle dropped and failed to bounce on its shattered axles. Bolan jumped up and emptied his light machine gun into the smoke behind the Saladin. He dropped the gold-plated weapon and yanked the ventilated top gunner out of the hatch. The top half of the dead man came up, his lower half stayed in the car. The riven corpse tumbled down the sloped armor as Bolan dropped down the hatch.

Smoke filled the cramped interior. The dynamite had cracked the thin underarmor of the Saladin like an egg and the driver and gunner were mostly spread around the interior like farmer-style lasagna. Bolan pushed a very loosely held together sack of humanity out of the gunner's seat and climbed behind the controls. He was pleased that despite the damage, the turret traversed as he worked the joystick.

Bolan leaned into the aged rubber mask of the optical sight and took note of men running for three black Daihatsu panel vans that hadn't been on the street five minutes earlier. The chamber indicator on the 76 mm L-5A1 gun indicated the gunner had kindly reloaded before Bolan had flung his dynamite. Bolan lined up his sighting gradient with the van in the middle. The soldier fired. The Saladin rocked on its shattered axles with the recoil and nearly tipped over before it crunched back semi-upright like a beached boat. Bolan scanned through his sight. The middle van had blown sky-high and its two flanking Daihatsu brethren were burning out of control. The street was empty save for fiery vehicles and blasted bodies. Bolan hit the traverse, but the turret motor whined and died. He sat for a moment in smoke-blackened, wall-to-wall, blood-spattered safety before getting out and taking a closer look at the smoking hole the cannon had torn through the infirmary. "Koa, how we doing?"

"Marwin may have a second concussion. Other than that, the team is tip-top. I'm sorry to report that the 76 mm they fired did the Handyman no favors. I mean none whatsoever. You wouldn't believe what's left of him."

"I think I was sitting in something similar."

"I bet you were."

"How's Dewa?"

"Freaking out."

"Bag the Handyman. Load up the team. We are out of here."

10

CIA safehouse, Jakarta

"I found it…" Dr. Dewa was drenched in gore up to his elbows. Koa had unbagged what was left of the Handyman into the safehouse claw-foot bathtub and Bolan had directed the good doctor to go on a treasure hunt for foreign objects. Dewa raised his forceps, which held a bloody little piece of something. Bolan recognized a Radio Frequency Identification Device. He had suspected as much and had told Dewa the usual places these chips were imbedded in human subjects. The doctor had sweated through his shirt from exhaustion, fear and the heat. Bolan sighed. "De Jong?"

"Yup!"

Bolan wrapped the RFID in a tea towel from the kitchen and handed it over along with the car keys. "This is a tracking device. Take it for a ride. A fun one. I want it followed but not to here. If you get into trouble, dump it down a sewer. I'll call you when we're ready to bolt."

De Jong was giddy. "I love this James Bond stuff! Marwin! *Ándele!*"

Marwin raised his mighty concussed bulk with a grunt.

Bolan went back to the main room and sank into a sofa that was still covered with a sheet. The safehouse was a Dutch Colonial. It hadn't been used in a while and smelled of tropical mildew and stale air. In its favor, the safehouse was squat and Dutch built and included an outer curtain wall and an iron gate. Sirens wailed in the distance. Jakarta was a violent town by anyone's standards but they were not used to gun battles involving dynamite and armored vehicles twice in the same night. Roadblocks were everywhere. The good news was the authorities knew well of the Handyman and Dr. Dewa's activities. For them it was a "round up the usual suspects" situation and raids against known crime lords and gangs were taking place all over the city. Bolan and his team were still completely off the radar.

Nevertheless getting out of town was going to be interesting.

The electric mixer ground into life in the kitchen as Belle worked with the groceries she had bought down the street. Rind was hacking away at his laptop and his grin might well have to be surgically removed.

"How we doing, Agent?"

"I got machine pistols. I'm in Jakarta. I got in a fight with a tank. This is epic. This is going to be a movie. Your buddy the Bear is nothing short of genius."

Bolan nodded knowingly.

Belle came in and offered Bolan a pint glass of what appeared to be agricultural runoff on the rocks. Bolan peered at it. "And?"

"It's a jackfruit, young coconut, ginseng, cardamom and *ishin nha* crushed-ice smoothie. Best I could do with what the market down the street had on hand."

Bolan rummaged through his mental index of the intriguing and unlikely things he'd ingested during his travels. "What's *ishin nha?*"

"You don't want to know, but it invigorates the testicles and makes your sperm powerful."

Bolan took the glass. "I'll take every advantage I can get."

Belle watched approvingly as Bolan poured half the concoction down his throat. It was slightly spicy, sweet and smooth, save for a few suspicious lumps. Koa flopped onto the opposite couch. "Man, I want one!"

"Coming right up, sex machine." Belle put a wiggle in her walk and headed back into the kitchen.

"She called me sex machine."

Bolan sipped his smoothie. "I won't tell Peg."

"So what's the plan?"

Bolan looked at Rind. "And?"

Rind grinned. "Recently the Handyman has been quiet. Too quiet. Operations of his that Interpol, the DEA and Indonesian law enforcement have been monitoring have literally dried up. He's been flying under the radar, having himself implanted with radio tracking devices and God only knows what else."

Koa stretched and sighed. "We were talking religion and syncretism. You got anything along that line?"

"A few newspaper articles, but they're mostly hearsay. Last year there was an imam in town who stirred up some controversy."

Bolan's instincts spoke to him. "Controversy how?"

"Oh, he was calling down the usual fire and brimstone, but he pissed off the local imams."

"He wasn't local?" Bolan asked.

"No, they denounced him for being an upstart American who had never been to Mecca."

"But he said that he wasn't an American."

"He said he was Hawaiian," Koa concluded. "And that was different."

"On the nose," Rind confirmed. He shook his head at the hacked Indonesian police report Kurtzman had translated and provided. "And two of the imams who denounced him were found dead in an indescribable condition."

Bolan and Koa spoke in unison. "Bundled."

"Yeah. The report I'm reading doesn't actually describe it, but you can tell they were appalled—and this is the Jakarta authorities. It takes a lot to appall them."

"Do we have a name on the Hawaiian imam?"

"The handle we have is Musa Jalaluddin."

Bolan wasn't surprised. It was almost certainly a name the man had chosen for himself upon conversion or it was given to him by his religious instructor. Musa was Arabic for "Moses" and Moses had delivered his children from the pharaoh.

It stank real hard of a hardcore liberation theology.

"We have a picture of this guy?"

Rind handed over his tablet.

The photo wasn't good. It was a grainy black-and-white taken from a local Indonesian newspaper, but it was enough to put a frown on Bolan's face.

Musa Jalaluddin looked to be in his mid-fifties. He wore a traditional Muslim tunic with a shawl. His mighty frame stretched the fabric in ring-ready, or more likely, bundling-ready hypertrophy. He had a Ten Commandments' worthy beard that curled down past his clavicles and hair that rioted down across his shoulders in unruly locks. Jalaluddin glared into the camera and pointed his finger in condemnation. His eyes radiated God's fury at the unbeliever, or more than likely, his own rage that he adorned with God's name.

Musa Jalaluddin looked as though he could walk into Melika's bar and take out Uncle Aikane, Nui and the *Lua* master with his bare hands and then work Tino like an after-dinner mint. When it came to disassembling people with his bare hands, Bolan had a very intriguing candy store of useful flavors, but he was not a martial artist; and he had a very bad feeling that if they fought hand-to-hand, Musa the radicalized Hawaiian prophet wasn't going to fall for any of them. "Have we got a given Hawaiian name and a social security number on this guy?"

Rind rolled his eyes. "We got nothing. He's a mystery. My best guess is he was born up in the hills or back streets of the Hawaiian Islands and took some real dark turns a long time ago."

Bolan sent the files to his phone. "We have the Handyman's tracking device, and I suspect he's a major part of whatever is going on. We need to get back to Hawaii and take care of our people."

Belle came out of the kitchen with smoothies for Rind and Koa. The Hawaiian warrior took a healthy slug. "And the bad guys looming on every Pacific Island from Catalina to Kamchatka?"

"They don't know Handi is dead. We take the RFID with us and see who comes calling."

"You don't think that could screw up what we have going on undercover in Oahu?"

"It could screw it up huge. You got a better idea?"

Koa poured back his smoothie. "No, unfortunately I don't."

"Rind?"

"This is epic!"

"Rind is with us," Bolan concluded. "Belle?"

Belle gave Bolan a smoky-eyed look. "I am in this for the duration."

"That's my girl."

Belle smirked.

Koa shook his head. "I can't wait to see you explain your new girl to Melika."

Honolulu safehouse

"WHAT IN THE blue hell, Makaha!" Melika looked ready to beat the tar out of just about everybody. "You brought some Norwegian porn star back from your sex tour in Subic Bay?"

Belle lit herself a Kretek cigarette and regarded the Hawaiian spitfire coolly. "Swedish."

"Whatever!" Melika suddenly stabbed out her finger. "And no smoking!"

Belle erotically blew a smoke ring, a second and a third, and then blew a perfect stream of blue smoke through the concentric circles. Melika cracked her knuckles. "And what about this gangsta trash you dragged in with her?"

De Jong looked hurt. Marwin sighed the sigh of big men in female situations where size didn't matter.

Bolan spoke quietly. "Melika, we're very tired. It's been a long seventy-two hours. We've been fighting and flying nonstop. Some of us are messed up. Please, help my friends."

Melika's eyes narrowed but she automatically went into Hawaiian hostess mode. "We'll discuss what you owe me later. I'll go cook."

"Thank you."

The team took seats around the dining table. Peg had been quiet, and she waited as Melika left the room. "It's getting spooky around here. We have strangers in the neighborhood."

"What kinds of strangers?" Bolan asked.

"Dunno, big guys. Showing up at the bar, buying drinks. Going into stores. Holding down tables in the local restaurants."

"They asking questions?"

"No, that's the creepy thing. They just show up, observe and disappear. Of course Melika and I are supposed to be off on a romantic weekend with you and Koa, so we were lying low and couldn't do any serious digging for intel, but the locals are nervous, uptight and scared."

Koa echoed Bolan's thoughts. "Whatever is going down is going down soon."

"No one has any clue who I am," Rind ventured. "I could go out and—"

"You would be bundled in seconds," Koa suggested.

"I could," Marwin announced. The entire team looked at the massive Filipino. He'd changed into a blue 3XL Primo beer tank top, a pair of cargo shorts that could have doubled as khaki theater curtains and sandals. Marwin threw a Hawaiian-worthy shrug. "I could just be a big fat guy looking for my cousins who called me." He looked at Bolan and Koa. "I could be looking for you, because you called me, and then they bring me in. That would give us a lot of the lower-level players if we pull our stakeout right."

De Jong pumped his fists. "My man Marwin!"

Marwin did genuinely look as though he belonged in Happy Valley. Bolan turned to Koa. "Koa?"

The Hawaiian soldier shrugged. "It's not bad. It could work. The bigger and fatter you are around here the more respect you get."

Marwin looked hurt. "I have a glandular condition."

Bolan decided. "We're going to insert you as if you just got off a plane. Go to Melika's bar and start asking around."

Marwin smiled for the first time since Bolan had known him. "I'm in."

De Jong took the RFID out of his pocket. "What about the tracking device?"

Bolan nodded at it. "When I checked it on the plane it was still active." The soldier pointed his phone at the blood-caked device and hit an app. "And it still is."

"So they know we're here."

"They know the device and possibly the Handyman are at this location. As for 'we,' they have no clue."

Rind grinned. "So we are going to see who comes calling. We going to track the trackers or lay an ambush?"

"Maybe a little of both. The problem is Koa and our dates have to get back to Happy Valley stat. I'm surprised the phone hasn't rung already. So I think the first thing to do is to establish whether we're being tracked in Hawaii and then run the trackers around for a little while. You think you can manage that, Special Agent?"

"I've been on both ends of a wild-goose chase, Cooper."

"Good, take De Jong with you for backup."

De Jong clapped his hands happily. "Cool! I can't— Wait a minute!" The gangster suddenly got suspicious. "What about Belle?"

"Yes." Belle stubbed out her cigarette. "What about me?"

"Well, it's like you say, no one ever expects you. We're bringing you in but just short of Happy Valley."

"So I'm your secret weapon?"

"I prefer to say unexpected bombshell."

"You say the sweetest things…"

Happy Valley

BOLAN ROLLED THE Land Cruiser to a stop outside Melika's Place and his undercover team unloaded. It was late, and the soldier didn't have to feign exhaustion from an exciting weekend but he did put a smile on his face and fired off a belly laugh as he jumped out of the 4 x 4. Melika spooned against him as though she had been doing it all her life. Koa and Hu went into happy couple mode. Bolan slung his duffel bag and the team entered the bar.

Court was in session.

Uncle Aikane and Uncle Nui sat in state one booth forward from the corner. Bolan made it a baker's dozen of Hawaiian hardcases at the bar and at tables. Tino stood behind the bar.

The corner booth caught Bolan's attention. Melika's Place wasn't exactly well lit, but the light over the corner booth was out. It formed a pool of blackness in the back of the bar. Enfolded in that darkness, Bolan could barely make out the shape of a very large man. The thin man stood in a pool of light beside him like an adjutant. Uncle Aikane spoke quietly. "Koa, Makaha, Melika." He gave Hu a nod. "Little One." He turned his attention back to his fellow Hawaiian. "How was your weekend, Koa?"

"Sun, surf, some beer, some grind. What's not to like?"

Uncle Aikane eyed Bolan shrewdly. "You look tired, Makaha."

Bolan gave Melika a squeeze. "What's not to like?"

Melika managed a giggle and blushed. This elicited some grunts of amusement from around the bar.

"The time for partying is over, Koa," Uncle Aikane intoned. "Now is the time to walk the path."

Koa disengaged himself from Hu and regarded Aikane

with utmost seriousness. "I'm ready, and if I'm not, you will teach me what I need to know, Uncle."

Grunts of approval rounded the bar.

Aikane turned his attention on Bolan. "And you, Makaha?"

"I have my cousin's back, and my *ohana*. To the end."

Very dangerous men nodded as the die was cast.

"Very well, Koa, you will come with me. Makaha? You will go with Rasul."

The thin man nodded. Bolan kept his poker face. "Rasul" sure as hell wasn't a traditional Hawaiian name. Bolan and Koa both nodded. "Yes, Uncle."

Three men detached themselves from the bar. One was short compared to the roomful of big men but he made up for it by having the T-shirt-stretching physique of a national class bodybuilder. Between his muscle-bound short neck, short arms and short torso he looked like a human fire hydrant. The other two men were lanky and could have almost passed for twins. All three looked to be in their twenties and they all wore T-shirts, cargo shorts and all-terrain sandals. The men looked as though they were about to go hiking save that it was close to two o'clock in the morning. The fire hydrant confirmed Bolan's suspicions by grabbing a knapsack.

Bolan turned to Koa and gave him the Hawaiian handshake the warrior had taught him. Koa was a past master of the stone face but his eyes conveyed he knew something was terribly wrong. Bolan grinned. "Catch you on the flip side, cuz." He turned to Melika. Despite having been a bartender for most of her adult life her poker face was breaking. She looked as if only iron determination was keeping her from crying. Bolan gave her a big wet one right on the lips. He stood in front of the assembled Hawaiians and shrugged. "Let's kick this pig."

Fire Hydrant and the two brothers filed down the narrow

bar toward the back exit. Tino dropped his bar towel and followed them. Rasul held out his hand to Bolan and beckoned. "Come, Makaha."

11

The forest, dawn

The van ground to a halt. Once again Tino was driving. Rasul smiled from the front passenger seat without an ounce of warmth. "We're here."

Fire Hydrant pulled open the sliding door. "Out."

Bolan hopped out and stretched. He'd been in three fire fights in three days, crossed half the Pacific and back and spent precious little of it sleeping. His tank was on E and he was running on fumes. Rasul and the other two men got out of the van. Tino stayed behind the wheel. The two brothers unlashed a long, tarp-wrapped package from the luggage rack and laid it down reverently.

"This is an initiation?" Bolan asked.

Rasul eyed Bolan steadily. "Yes, Makaha."

Bolan started to get a very bad feeling. They had taken his phone and his knife and he was ripe for an execution. The brothers unlashed the package at both ends and laid the tarp open. It contained five spears. Rasul scooped up a spear and tossed it to Bolan.

Bolan's eyes widened slightly at its weight—it felt like polished stone. It was six and a half feet long and made of koa wood. The heavy shaft was topped with sixteen inches of swordfish bill, most likely Blue Marlin. The bill was wide and flat like a sword blade and wickedly pointed. Red rooster feathers formed a fringe around the socket. Bolan hefted the weapon and considered plunging it into Rasul's chest. He had a further bad feeling that Rasul was ready for that. "For hunting."

"Yes, Makaha."

"Boar?"

"Yes."

Bolan raised an eyebrow at Rasul. "This isn't my initiation."

"No, Makaha." Rasul nodded at Fire Hydrant. "It is Ahmed's."

Koa's Muslim/Hawaiian syncretism theory had just bloomed into full fruition. Ahmed stripped off his shirt to reveal his gym-forged physique. He took up a spear and began mad-dogging Bolan in earnest. Ahmed bugged his eyes and shifted from foot to foot as he flexed his massive muscles and shook his spear. The rooster feathers rustled. Bolan ignored the attempted intimidation and watched the spear. "And I'm the hunt."

"Yes, Makaha."

"Why don't you just shoot me?"

"You are the boar, Makaha. Ahmed needs to make his first kill, and partake of the sacrament." A cold wind blew through Bolan at the word "sacrament." Rasul shook his head derisively at the two brothers as they took up their spears. "And Osama and Salman need more practice at bundling."

"Where's Koa?" Bolan asked. "You hunting him on the other side of the mountain?"

"Koa is true *ohana*. He is a soldier. He has many skills we need. He will be brought into the inner circle."

Bolan hefted the spear in his hand. "I just don't think Koa's going to approve of any of this, brah."

"Koa, like you, expressed his willingness to step into the volcano if asked. You will serve your purpose this day, Makaha, and Koa will be told, truthfully, that you failed to survive the initiation. Then he will be forced to make a decision. That will be his test."

Bolan searched his eyebrows for a moment as if he was doing math. "Yeah, but what if I survive?"

Rasul actually laughed. So did Ahmed, Osama and Salman. None of their spears wavered. "Well," Rasul mused, "should you succeed in killing all four of us? There is a man who will want to talk with you. Though what happens to you after that? Allah knows, but I do not." Ahmed, Osama and Salman roared at this new height of Hawaiian-Muslim-Jihadist-syncretism humor.

Bolan knew if he wanted Rasul to monologue any further he was going to have to force it. Failing that, he needed his opponents to make a mistake if he was going to have any hope of surviving. "You're cowards."

The laughter stopped.

Bolan spit in Rasul's face.

Ahmed and his initiation buddies roared and stepped forward. Rasul held up a restraining hand. The killer actually regarded Bolan with a grain of respect. "You have no idea what kind of courage it takes to walk our path, much less to face the destiny at the end of it. You never will. Nevertheless, you are of the *ohana,* Makaha. Tainted as your blood is by the white *haole* and degraded as you are in spirit by mainland ways and filth, you are going to be given an honorable death, one that will serve your people. Your courage in the face of death has been noted, and the *ohana* will know it." Rasul wiped the spittle from his face.

Bolan considered the foursome. Despite being vertically challenged, Ahmed looked as though he could bench press a baby elephant, but Bolan doubted the younger man's lungs would last during a long chase. Osama and Salman appeared to be in pretty good shape, probably from some hardcore training in their ancestral arts. Rasul was clearly Bolan's elder by at least a decade, but his whiplike frame indicated a martial artist at the peak of his powers. Bolan gazed through the windshield at Tino. The Samoan shook his head sadly and looked away. "Do I get a thirty-second head start?" Bolan asked.

Rasul nodded. "Of course. Or you may stand and fight. If you do, I give you my word we will engage you one at a time."

All ego aside, Bolan knew he was an excellent bayonet fighter; but traditional Hawaiian spear fighting with six-and-a-half-foot weapons was out of his purview—he wasn't going to win four individual spear duels this morning. Bolan spun and bolted into the forest. Laughter and catcalls chased him. Rasul broke into genuinely happy laughter. "Run, Makaha!"

Ahmed shouted out, "Run as fast as you can!"

Osama and Salman joined the chorus.

They had taken him to this place at night, and through the twisting and turning of the forest paths Bolan had lost his compass points. The canopy was too thick for him to find a mountain and he had no other points of reference. He was sure Rasul knew this forest like the back of his hand. Bolan also suspected the initiates had been well prepped for this morning's hunt. They had bottled water and snacks and Bolan was all out of luck in that department. He stopped behind a tree and listened. There was no discernible sound of pursuit. It seemed they really were giving him a head start.

Bolan eyed his spear. It wasn't going to do him much good in this configuration. He stuck the point into the soft loam and rammed his heel into the socket. Being a traditional Hawaiian weapon, it was bound and glued rather than riveted in place, so the swordfish bill snapped off. Bolan knelt and unwound the olona fiber. He now had a dagger, a staff and slightly more than six feet of cord. Bolan ripped off his left shirtsleeve and tore a shoulder-to-wrist strip from it. He wound the strip around the base of the swordfish bill to protect his hand and tucked his new shank under his belt. He pocketed the rest of the cloth and the cord, took up his staff and began an easy lope through the forest. The soldier made no attempt to cover his tracks as he plunged through the underbrush and picked up a game trail. Game trails often lead to water. Rasul would be expecting him to search for water and blunder down easy trails.

"I know where you are, Makaha!" Ahmed called out. "I know where you're going!"

Bolan loped ahead and found his spot. The game trail suddenly turned into a three-foot ledge that dropped into a stream. The soldier yanked out the olona cord and tied it around the base of a sapling just off the trail.

"Makaha!" Ahmed called. "Makaha!"

Bolan dug a trench with his finger across the forest path and buried the cord an inch deep and a foot from the drop-off. The length of cord ended conveniently behind a clump of rocks.

Bolan took up his staff and jogged back up the winding trail a few dozen meters, put his hands on his knees and bent over as if exhausted. He suspected his opponents were better martial artists than he was. His opponents suspected he was probably a tough guy, but a punk criminal from the mainland. What they did not know was that Mack Bolan was quite possibly Planet Earth's most lethal living jungle fighter.

"Makaha!" Ahmed caught sight of his prey and charged through the trees with his spear leveled.

Bolan broke into a run. While his stamina held, he was faster than Ahmed and he managed to break line of sight for a moment. He hit the creek and jumped into it with a splash loud enough for Ahmed to hear. Bolan rolled behind the rocks and wound the end of the cord around his fist.

Ahmed whooped as he spied the creek. "Coming for you, Makaha! Coming for y—"

Bolan yanked the cord up to shin height and tight against the rocks. Ahmed hit the trip cord and went airborne into a Looney-Tunes-worthy pratfall. He nose-dived and ate the creek face-first. Bolan dropped the cord and drew his sailfish short sword. Ahmed came up sputtering and the soldier's boot to the face knocked the initiate onto his back. Ahmed gasped and let out a scream as Bolan lunged.

His enemies intended to spear him, bundle him and barbecue him. There was no room for mercy in the Hawaiian forest this morning.

The soldier spiked the swordfish bill through the thick plate of Ahmed's left pec then drove the weapon through his heart. Ahmed's eyes rolled and his corpse subsided bonelessly into the stream. Bolan left the swordbill in Ahmed's chest and relieved him of his bottle of water, energy bar, phone and wallet. He retrieved his cord and staff and took up Ahmed's spear.

"Ahmed!" The initiate's scream had been heard and the rest of the dead man's team called out frantically as they charged through the trees. "Ahmed!"

Bolan faded into the forest.

"Bismillah!" Rasul stared at Ahmed's corpse where it lay heart-spiked and gently undulating with the creek's current.

Salman howled.

"Dead!" Osama screamed to the heavens and shook his spear in rage. "Do you hear me, Makaha! You're dead! I'm going to—"

Six and a half feet of polished, weapon-grade koa wood flew like a thunderbolt out of the trees and struck Osama between the eyes. The heavy wood shaft made a terrible thump as it collided with the Hawaiian's skull and then fell to the stream with a splash. Osama's eyes crossed and his eyelids fluttered. His mouth worked several times and he collapsed into the water beside Ahmed. Rasul and Salman crouched in fighting stances with their spears poised. Rasul just caught sight of the quarry through the trees and then the man he knew as Makaha disappeared.

Rasul nodded at Osama where he lay fallen. "Salman, see to your brother."

Salman knelt beside his brother and howled as he checked his pulse. "He's dead!"

Rasul took out his phone and tapped in a number. It was a call he dreaded. The man on the other end answered on the first ring. "It is done?"

"No."

"Makaha lives?"

"Yes, and Ahmed and Osama are fallen."

"Makaha has done this?"

Rasul sighed grimly. "It seems Makaha is a warrior, after all."

"That is a shame."

"Yes, perhaps he would have served us well."

"I believe it is too late for that. I fear he will not forgive us. Can you take him?"

Rasul had absolute faith that once he closed with Makaha, the *haole* was finished. "I have looked into his eyes. He is weary. He spent three days drinking and fornicating and Allah knows what else. He cannot hide his trail from me. I will run him down. I will put my spear through his stomach, bundle him, and bring him still alive to the *imu* pit for roasting."

"Try to avoid his bowels," the voice advised. "It ruins the taste of the meat."

BOLAN WAS EXHAUSTED. Too many battles. Too many explosions. Too many fist fights, and far too many midnight rides in ships, planes and automobiles. He had spent the past four hours at a good, ground-eating lope but he wouldn't be able to keep it up much longer, and he was leaving a trail a child could follow. The terrain had risen—he was in the hills—and it was sapping his strength. The enemy had made no attempt to overtake him. Bolan knew he was probably heading exactly where they wanted him to be.

It was time to take the battle to the enemy again.

He stopped and polished off his water bottle and considered his resources. He'd eaten the energy bar hours ago. Bolan took out Ahmed's phone. It had dried off a bit but still wasn't functioning. The phone was a very valuable intel asset, but he would have to live long enough to get it to the Farm for data extraction. He had a spear. Once again he broke off his spearhead and pocketed the cord. He wrapped more sleeve around the base to make a handle, and then began awkwardly climbing up the worst part of the hillside while juggling a staff heavy enough to be made out of stone.

Bolan found his spot at the hill's summit. It wasn't a vertical climb but it was steep. Anyone following his trail would have to walk on a patch of earth shaped like a step. Using the swordfish bill, Bolan swiftly dug a hole the size of a shoe box and three times as deep. He worked about a foot of the swordfish bill down into floor of the hole and packed the earth tight around it with his fist.

Bolan removed his shirt and tore it in two.

He took one half and stretched it out over the hole. He pinned the four corners with twigs and pushed them down level. Bolan scooped dirt out from under a tree root and put about two centimeters of soil over the fabric. He reached up and grabbed a liana vine to support himself and very lightly pushed his heel down over the trap. The fabric held and went taut again. Bolan leaned back and admired his handiwork. What he saw was a scuffed step in the hillside with a boot print on it. With luck whoever followed him would instinctively follow his steps up the steep terrain.

Bolan gave it 50/50 whether Rasul would fall for his punji stick pit. On the other hand he would be willing to bet good money that Rasul was running Salman slightly ahead of him to try to tempt Bolan into attacking. The soldier clambered up to the top of the hill. He found himself in a little flat-topped glade girded by trees almost like a cathedral. The sun came down through the hole in the canopy. He leaned on his staff, let his breathing return to normal and waited.

Bolan didn't wait long.

Rasul's voice spoke quietly at the bottom of the hill. "Be careful, he may be waiting at the top."

"He will get one spear cast, Uncle," Salman declared. "And then he will die. If he is stupid enough not to cast his spear and fight me? Then he will die badly."

"Be wary. I am right behind you."

Bolan took his staff in both hands and stepped into view, on the crown of the little hill. "I am going to kill you, Salman."

The two Hawaiians looked up from the base of the hill. Rasul gave Bolan a shrewd look. "He has broken off his spearhead again. He carries it behind his back. Watch for it."

Salman hit the steep hillside like a mountain goat. He never broke eye contact with Bolan. "Go ahead! Cast your staff, Makaha! Coward! I dare you!"

Bolan watched his would-be assassin with grim finality. "I will not kill you until you are within my reach. I give you my word."

"Fuck you, Makaha!"

Salman took the hill like a staircase. "You die, Makaha! For what you did to Ahmed! For what you did to my brother!"

Bolan stood waiting. "Bring it."

"We will feast on you as the warriors of old!" Salman grabbed the liana vine hanging from the trees above and did a Tarzan-worthy leap to the prepared step. "You will die in my fire! You—"

Salman's sandaled foot plunged through the dirt and cotton covering the pit. The Hawaiian's scream told Bolan the swordfish sword had done its work.

"Salman!" Rasul began tearing his way up the hill. "Salman!"

Salman keened like a rabbit being killed.

Bolan slid three feet down the hill. He raised the six and a half feet of koa wood like a splitting ax and Salman's screaming ended as Bolan brought it down with a crunch through his skull. Bolan grabbed Salman's spear before it could slide down the hill and scrambled back to the top. He now had a stave and a spear. Bolan sprinted across the clearing and back into the trees.

He wished he'd had time to take Salman's water and food.

12

Bolan staggered.

He was done. He would have thrown up again but he didn't have the water in his body to do so. Agent Hu hadn't lied. With three quarters of his pores closed, he was red-lining into heat exhaustion. The daily downpour had briefly cooled him off but his internal temperature was climbing. It was about noon and he figured a thermometer would register ninety-five something. He was moving downhill, from the hills to foothills, but twice when Bolan had crested a rise he caught sight of Rasul on his trail, and he knew Rasul had seen him. Both times Rasul had been ever closer. Bolan staggered to a stop.

The forest had ceased and he found himself confronted by a ten-foot-tall hedge.

It was shaggy on the forest side but immaculately trimmed at the top. Bolan noted several golf balls lying in the forest duff. The Executioner sighed, hefted his spear so that his forearms guarded his face and hit the plant wall at a run. Branches and stems tore at the flesh of Bolan's bare torso. Vegetation snapped and Bolan just barely kept his feet as he plunged through.

Four middle-aged Japanese men in checked golf pants, polo shirts and sun visors screamed in unison. Bolan considered the golf course spreading out ahead of him, the tee party in front of him and the enemy behind him. Bolan stood on one leg, bare-chested and bleeding, and roared as he brandished his spear.

"Huaaaaaah!"

The foursome screamed again and dropped their clubs. They bolted for their golf cart and tore away as their speedometer pegged out at twelve miles per hour. Bolan stepped away from the hole he had torn in the hedge. He stabbed his staff into the lawn for quick retrieval, hefted his spear and waited.

The hedgerow twitched and shuddered as someone pushed through it.

Bolan hurled his spear with all of his might and instantly yanked up his staff.

Rasul seemed to ooze out of the hedgerow. Blood poured down his jaw from Bolan's spear cast. It had cut his cheek to the bone. Rasul smiled through his mutilation as he set foot on the golf course green. "Close, Makaha. Very close."

Bolan took a step forward and sent his staff scything at shin level.

Rasul easily hopped over the awkward attempt. He tossed his immensely heavy spear lightly in his hand. "Now, Makaha. What do you intend to do?"

Bolan retreated.

Rasul raised his spear like a javelin. "You think you can make the clubhouse before I put this through your kidneys?"

Bolan slowly knelt and pulled a gold-colored driver from a fallen golf bag. It was a fifteen-hundred-dollar club. "Brave." Rasul grunted. The Hawaiian raised his spear overhead in a wide two-handed hold. "But foolish."

Bolan raised his new driver overhead like a samurai sword.

Rasul advanced with a sneer. "Pathetic."

Bolan stepped forward to meet him and swung as if he intended to split Rasul's skull. In Bolan's experience the greatest flaw of most martial artists was that they nearly always practiced against members of their own art. Rasul snapped his spear in a horizontal high block as if Bolan had lashed at him with one of the many Koa wood weapons Rasul had defended against in decades of practice.

But the lightweight graphite shaft of the driver was designed for flexibility. It bent around the Koa wood spear haft rather than rebounding or breaking and the forged titanium face collided with the fontanel of Rasul's skull.

Bone crunched.

Rasul dropped as though he'd been shot.

Bolan tossed the ruined driver away. He put his hands on his knees for real and took long, deep breaths. There were no sirens to be heard yet, but screaming and consternation were spreading from hole to hole. Bolan relieved Rasul of his phone, wolfed down his energy bar and drank greedily from what remained of his water bottle. He snapped off the tip of Rasul's spear and grimaced as branches tore at him once more as he went back through the hedge.

One reason Bolan had made no attempt to conceal his tracks was that he knew if he lived he would have to retrace them. He stared up at the sun and vainly wished for the rest he just wasn't going to get. He judged it was between two and two-thirty. He needed to retrace his steps and surprise Tino before it got dark. Bolan took the last slug of water from Rasul's bottle and tossed it away. If he moved fast whatever food and water Salman had left was waiting for him. After that Ahmed and Osama were lying in a creek that ran cool and clear. Bolan broke into one more very weary run.

He wanted to hit Melika's bar before closing time.

Melika's Place

BOLAN SHOVED TINO inside. The bar was packed, but no one was minding the door because no one in Happy Valley was stupid enough to come in unannounced tonight. Bolan had come upon Tino right around sunset. He was still sitting in the van, eating cold fried macaroni and cheese while involved in a very important Angry Birds battle on his phone. It had required rebreaking Tino's nose, knocking him half unconscious, and putting a swordfish bill to his throat, but in the end the Samoan had agreed to drive Bolan back to civilization.

Bolan had given Tino an elbow shot to the right kidney to make him pliable as they approached the door and then flung him spread-eagled to the peanut-shell-strewn floor of Melika's in dramatic fashion. The back booth was still dark but Bolan could make out a big man sitting there. Koa sat with Uncle Aikane and Nui. He shot Bolan a wink and the soldier knew their covers weren't quite blown yet. Bolan stood in the doorway and let his rage manifest itself.

"The hell with you!"

He stepped on Tino's spine as he made his way into the bar. Tino groaned as Bolan stepped off him and strode toward Uncle Aikane and Nui's booth.

"Screw you all's!"

Guns came out all around the bar. Bolan ignored them and tossed four swordfish bills, two of them caked with blood, onto the table in front of Uncle Aikane. Aikane stared long and hard at the assembled spearheads. "Listen, Makaha—"

Bolan let his rage boil over, but he stepped back and threw up his hands. "I wish I had a gun! I'd kill all of you! Let's go out back! I'll fight any of you! I'll fight all of you!"

Aikane's face was terrible; like a man who knew he had betrayed a child. "Nephew…"

Bolan stabbed forth a terrible, judging finger at the big Hawaiian. "You're not my uncle!"

Guns twitched in the shocked silence.

Koa broke it. "Makaha."

Bolan flung his arms skyward in outrage. "They hunt me? They gonna bundle me and barbecue me! Do it! Do it now! Any asshole who wants to try!"

Koa turned to Aikane. "Uncle, tell me my cousin has passed."

Aikane nodded. "Beyond all expectations."

"Cousin." Koa's eyes were soft but iron. "Stand down."

"Screw you!"

"Stand down!" Koa roared.

Bolan clenched his fists, spun and slammed himself into a seat at the bar. Melika brought him a Koko Brown ale without being asked.

Koa stood. He shouted for everyone to hear but he faced the darkened booth in the back. "No one messes with my cousin!"

The darkness met this with silence.

Bolan took a huge risk. He stood and walked toward the booth. Guns came out all around again. Bolan reached into his pockets and he heard several safeties come off. It was a terrible intel loss, but Bolan tossed Ahmed, Osama, Salman and Rasul's cell phones on the table. He gave the shadow a terrible grimace. "I figured no one should find these."

A massive mocha-colored hand reached out of the pool of darkness and pulled the phones in. A very deep voice spoke. "Makaha, how can this be made up to you?"

"I'm done. Just let me walk. Let me out."

"You will not walk out of this bar alive."

"Then let me in." Bolan balled his fist and made another terrible face. "All the way."

"You will not walk out of that alive, either."

Bolan spoke without turning from the darkness. "Koa?"

"I'm still in."

"After what they did to me?"

"I am, and I'm begging you, cuz. I need you on my six. For what has to be done."

Bolan shoved every ounce of will out of his eyes at the shape in the darkness. "Tell me I die going forward instead of with a spear in my back."

"Makaha?" The voice was surprisingly lighthearted. "You're going all the way."

Honolulu safehouse

MELIKA HAD POWERFUL thumbs.

Bolan groaned as she ground the knots out of his extremely weary shoulders. "You killed all four of them?"

"Yeah."

"Makaha, they—"

"They were going to bundle me and cook me like a pig."

"Eew!" Melika shuddered. "I'm still having a hard time with that. What the hell are they into?"

"Have you gotten a look at the guy holding down your corner booth?"

"No, no one does unless they're summoned. And everyone who sits at the table goes off on some mission and never comes back. That's mostly hearsay because just about every time I try to tend my bar I get sent away and Tino takes over... I don't like Tino."

Bolan winced as Melika's elbow bored into his flesh. "I don't think anybody does, and I tried."

He gritted his teeth as Melika poured on a little more *kukui* nut oil and went meat tenderizer on his right buttock. The soldier realized she was going over just about every muscle in his body. Bolan smiled in the dark as Melika practiced her ancestral arts down through his calves and toes. He spoke very quietly. "You want out?"

"I just want you to stop whatever they're doing and stop it quick. I have a terrible feeling. Finish this. I'll do whatever I can."

"Thank you."

"Roll over." Bolan rolled. Melika began to work the plates of Bolan's chest.

When she'd finished, Bolan sighed contentedly and closed his eyes.

THE SOLDIER SMELLED Kona coffee brewing. Melika made a noise as he left the tiny twin bed. Sunlight spilled through the curtains. Bolan pulled on a pair of shorts and walked out to find Koa reading the paper with his shotgun close to hand. A coffee urn sat on the bungalow's hotplate.

"Any relevant local news?" Bolan asked.

"There was a particularly brutal murder at the golf course yesterday afternoon. Five-O is completely stumped."

"Awful."

Koa nodded. "So now you're tapping Melika?"

"She decided she'd rather torture me." Bolan rolled his shoulders. The Hawaiian warrior massage had done him a world of good.

"Yeah, I can smell the *kukui* oil on you. Rumor is Melika still knows the old ways. You're a lucky man." Koa's face turned gravely serious. "So. They hunted you? With spears?"

"Yeah."

"I didn't believe it, until Uncle Nui showed me the *imu* pit. They were heating the stones. I'm pretty sure I was going to have to eat some of you over rice."

Bolan poured himself a cup of joe and topped off his teammate. "So what's on the agenda for today?"

"Don't know. I'm thinking it may be the big Jihadist/ Syncretism meet and greet. I'd bet we're going to get in- vited to a luau."

"How do you figure that?"

"Because they prepared an *imu* pit."

"I thought I wasn't for dinner tonight."

"Yeah." Koa smiled knowingly. "But it's an awful lot of work to dig the pit and then heat the stones. I'll bet they threw in a pig."

Bolan considered his own narrow escape. "Or something."

A huge fist pounded on the door. "Koa! Makaha! Come on!" Tino bellowed. "We gonna have grind today like you haven't had in years!"

13

It was just about the best pig Bolan had ever eaten. The secret cannibal sacrament had turned into a genuine party since Mack was off the menu. At least a hundred people filled Uncle Aikane's palatial backyard. A group of men sat playing guitars and ukuleles while people sang along to traditional Hawaiian songs intermixed with pop and country-and-western favorites. Some people were dancing. Children and dogs ran underfoot. Folding tables groaned beneath the weight of rice, long rice, lumpia, chicken wings and several dozen more luau favorites born of Hawaii's melting pot. The pig held the place of pride. A traditional Hawaiian benediction of thanks had accompanied its unearthing. People formed a long line as women shredded the meat off the bones and forked it over rice. Ribs and other choice pieces were given out to guests of prominence. Bolan gave his platter of ribs a silent "Better you than me, brother" thanksgiving and tucked in.

The soldier was nearly strangled as Tino's massive meat hook swatted him between the shoulder blades. "Better pork on your plate than you on mine! Right, brah?"

A part of Bolan found it interesting that just twenty-four hours ago Tino had driven him to a rendezvous with impalement, torture and slow roasting, and now the Samoan was joking about it. Bolan grinned back. "You wouldn't like it. I got too much *haole* in me."

Tino leered in an all too familiar fashion. "Oh, *haoles* are soft and sweet, Makaha!" He punched Bolan in the shoulder as if they were childhood pals. "You'd be too tough because your blood runs true, bruddah!"

Bolan raised his beer. "*Ohana, cuz.*"

Tino stopped short of blushing and clanked bottles happily. "*Ohana, cuz!*" The Samoan suddenly remembered his business. "Hey, man, polish off your grind and head up to the house. Uncle Aikane wants to see you."

Bolan kept his regret off his face as he handed Tino his loaded plate. "Don't let it get cold, brah."

"Ooh! Yeah!"

Bolan wiped his hands and walked up to the house. The slobbering sounds behind him told the soldier he had already been forgotten. Bolan caught sight of Koa coming toward the house from the opposite side of the yard and knew the Hawaiian had received a similar summons. The two warriors fell into formation. "Man," Koa sighed. "I was just settling in to some serious eating."

"Tino's polishing off my plate."

"And that's a damned shame."

"You're telling me."

Bolan and Koa stopped at the lanai steps. They were confronted by half a dozen of Uncle Aikane's security. They came in assorted sizes ranging from larger than the average bear to gigantic, and all bore a family resemblance to the Hawaiian crime lord/newly minted separatist/terrorist. A particularly titanic specimen in a 3XL aloha shirt and sarong who was clearly packing heat gave Koa and Bolan the fish-eye.

"You boys packin'?"

"That you, Bolo?" Koa asked.

Bolo smiled in recognition. "Know you, Koa." The fish-eye returned. "Don't know Makaha, except that he killed a couple of people I know."

Bolan glanced at the army of trees girding Uncle Aikane's estate. "We can take two spears and walk into the forest if you want, Bolo."

"No!" Bolo burst into laughter. "Oh, hell no! You two come right on in."

Bolan and Koa were ushered downstairs into a plushly appointed man-cave. Uncle Aikane, Uncle Nui and the *Lua* master sat at a round, green-felted card table playing some kind of arcane Hawaiian Hold'em. Bolan noted they were all drinking small glasses of what looked like weakly mixed Ovaltine. The odd smell, with hints of black pepper, informed Bolan the men were drinking kava. Ferret-face stood behind the wet bar leaning on his crutches and scowling as usual.

Uncle Aikane looked up from his cards. "Koa, Makaha! You've met your uncle Lau Lau?"

The *Lua* master waved his cast.

Bolan and Koa nodded. "Uncle."

"Sit down, take your ease."

Ferret-face poured two glasses of kava for the guests. He gave Bolan a very long look that Bolan didn't care for. The killer clearly hadn't realized it was Bolan who'd put him in crutches, but it was also clear that he was doing a lot of math in his head. Bolan hid in plain sight and sat at the bar. Koa took his glass and sat on the couch facing the giant screen TV set to the golf channel. Bolan sipped his kava. It was strong, and Bolan's lips tingled and started going numb. The soldier vainly wished for one of Belle's concoctions, or better yet a beer. He was aware of the effects of kava. It relaxed people both mentally and physically and made them talkative. A few glasses of kava wouldn't be a bad opening salvo for a friendly interrogation.

Bolan slurped his kava down and shoved the glass across the bar. "What's your name again?"

Ferret-face poured another and spoke through clenched teeth. "Ezekiel."

"Thanks, Zeke." Bolan took up his glass and toasted the assembled Hawaiian crime elders. The big men gravely toasted back and drank. Bolan polished off his glass and slammed it down. Uncle Aikane shook his head in regret. "Makaha, there is no apology I can make that—"

"So don't bother," Bolan said.

The elders were sorry about what had happened, but their furrowed brows at the disrespect indicated there was still a good chance an *imu* pit up in the hills had Bolan's name on it. Uncle Nui spoke in a stern, fatherly tone. "Makaha…"

"There's no need for an apology, Uncle." Bolan lifted his chin at Koa. "He's the one you wanted."

The big men shifted in their seats.

Bolan put bitterness into his voice. "Koa the soldier. Koa the warrior. The son of your *ohana,* come home. Not me." Bolan gave his reflection in the mirror behind the bar the thousand-yard stare. "Say it, Uncle Nui!"

Nui let out a long breath. "Yes, Makaha."

Bolan shoved his glass at Ezekiel for more kava. He could barely feel his tongue so he let it run. "You saw me, and you saw a *haole* mutt, trash, begging at the door like a stray dog. A junkie. A mainland punk. You saw a liability to the *ohana* and an anchor dragging Koa down."

Uncle Aikane rumbled a low, "Yes, Makaha."

Bolan poured back another round and slowly revolved his bar stool to face the terrorist, criminal crime lords. "Tell me you were wrong. Or give me a spear and test me again."

Uncle Lau Lau grunted in approval at Bolan's courage and shot a hard glance at Nui and Aikane.

Aikane nodded slowly. "We misjudged you, Makaha."

"Yes," Nui affirmed. "We misjudged you. Badly. We will not do so again."

Bolan rose. "Well, then, Tino's eating my ribs, I haven't had any grind in two days, and Melika's probably wondering about me."

Uncle Nui laughed. "Well, then, Makaha! Why don't you stay here in the air conditioning with your uncles for a little bit? Out on the side lanai we got Kobe beef about to go on the grill."

Koa went stone-faced at the mention of Kobe beef. "We're staying."

IT WAS DARK by the time Bolan and Koa came staggering and bloated out of the main house. They were stuffed full of grilled Kobe, Lomi Lomi salmon, octopus in cooked ti leaves and half a dozen other ancient Hawaiian specialties. He'd gathered no hard intel, but the private party had served its purpose. The kava flowed. The old men told stories from back in the day, some of them about highly illegal activities ranging from the hilarious to the harrowing. Bolan and Koa had listened in awe like newbs. Nothing that was said hinted about what was to come, and Bolan and Koa hadn't asked, but the fact was, they were in.

Koa let out a long belch and the security on the lanai sighed with mild jealousy. Out in the yard a bonfire had been lit and a number of couples were dancing. The two warriors descended the steps. Koa let out another belch. "My left arm is tingling. That was some serious grind."

Bolan pushed his fingers against his lips and cheeks experimentally. "I can't feel my face."

"Yeah, you hit the kava hard. I'm surprised you didn't give them the address to the Farm and say the next luau was on you."

Bolan grinned. "Would you believe that I've been subjected to far harsher chemical interrogations?"

"I'm still betting the *lau lau* almost broke you," Koa said, referring to the butterfish and pork wrapped and steamed in ti leaves.

"Almost," Bolan agreed. He held up the plastic bag that contained his leftovers in Tupperware. "And still maybe."

Melika materialized in front of them, fists on hips. "And where have you been?"

"Falling in love with *lau lau*."

Melika wrinkled her nose. "You've fallen in love with Uncle Lau Lau?"

"No." Bolan held up his goody bag. *"Lau lau."*

Jealousy twisted across Melika's beautiful face. "You got *lau lau?*"

Bolan shook the bag. "Brought you some."

"Oh! Gimme!" Melika snatched it out of Bolan's hand.

"What's the story out here?" Bolan asked.

"Some very dangerous members of the community are missing, and rumor is you killed them, Makaha. Then you got invited to the main house for some private grind." Melika rummaged through the goody bag. "Rumor confirmed."

"And?"

"And you just walked out, apparently forgiven. You've got some pretty huge machismo right now. Some people don't like it, but everyone knows something big is going down soon and now you're part of it. Add that to the fact that you and Koa are running buddies? You're achieving godlike status."

Bolan turned to Koa. "Just what did you do back in the day?"

Koa shrugged. "Someday I'll confide in you."

The soldier glanced around. "Where's Hu?"

"She's getting hit on by every man at the party. Koa, you better go rescue her."

Koa frowned. "All the bruddahs are trying to steal my girl? What the hell, Melika?"

Melika's voice dropped low. "That's the other rumor. Apparently, you and Makaha aren't going to live through whatever is going down. You're going to be martyrs to the cause. Some people thought you might not even come out of the house tonight." Melika looked back toward the beer keg and Hu. Huge Hawaiian admirers ringed the diminutive agent. "And the widow-humpers are lining up and taking numbers."

Bolan raised an eyebrow. "And you're not defending her because...?"

"She said she was going to gather intel. I think she's in over her head."

Koa cracked his knuckles. "Let's just put a stop to this, shall we?" The Hawaiian warrior strode toward the party surrounding Hu.

Melika stared incredulously. "You're not going to help him?"

"He doesn't need my help."

"Probably not," Melika agreed. "So what do we do?"

"What do you want to do?"

Melika's teeth flashed in the dark as she shook the goody bag. "Grind!"

"Didn't you get enough to eat already?"

"There's always room for *lau lau*. Besides, what do you want to do?"

Bolan lifted his chin at the bonfire and the couples dancing to old-school slow jams.

Melika's smile lit up the lawn. "Show me your moves, *haole!*"

Bolan slid his arm around Melika's waist and squired her toward the light, the heat and the rhythm of music and swaying bodies.

Honolulu safehouse

BOLAN AWOKE. Something was wrong. The soldier's internal clock told him it was a little after 4:00 a.m. Melika lay next to him naked, warm and smiling in her sleep. Bolan heard the bungalow's side gate creak. He put on a pair of cargo shorts, reached down between the headboard and the wall and took up his locked and loaded grease gun. He slung a Korean War vintage six magazine pouch over his shoulder and stepped into the bungalow's tiny foyer.

Koa came out of the side bedroom dressed in boxer shorts with his shotgun and a bandolier of twelve-gauge shells.

Bolan snapped out his submachine gun's folding wire stock. "We're about to get hit."

Hu appeared behind Koa with the .38 Bolan had given her. "You think?"

Bolan heard a branch snap outside by the bathroom window. "Koa, I thought we were cool."

Koa took a knee and leveled his kidney buster at the front door. "You killed some people the other day, Makaha. Their people may be showing up for some payback, no matter what Uncle Aikane says. Blood calls for blood."

"Hawaiian hillbilly vengeance?"

"Something like that."

Melika appeared in the darkened hallway and took a knee. "Gimme a gun."

Bolan nodded toward the bathroom. "There's a revolver in the toilet tank with a dozen spare rounds. Stay there and stay low."

"You don't have to tell me twice." Melika scampered for the bathroom.

A voice Bolan recognized shouted out, "Hear you moving around in there!"

Bolan sighed. "Bolo."

Koa shouted out. "That you, Bolo?"

"Yeah! Send out Makaha! We want him!"

"You want my cousin?"

"We want the *haole!* He's done damage to the *ohana*. We got cousins dead, Koa! And Makaha's gotta pay!"

Bolan heard the unmistakable "klatch" of Kalashnikov automatic rifle safety levers going off. "Everyone down." The team hugged ancient linoleum as multiple assault weapons began tearing through the bungalow. The fusillade suddenly ceased and the click and clack of automatic rifles being reloaded broke the silence.

Koa roared, "We got women inside, asshole!"

"So send out Makaha! Or you all die!"

Koa looked at Bolan. "Are we in 'hit 'em all and let God sort them out' mode yet?"

"Thirty seconds ago," Bolan confirmed.

Koa shouted his defiance into the night. "Kill you all, Bolo!"

Bolo yelled back. "You don't even have a gun, Koa! You got nothing! Don't make us come in there!"

Koa smiled over his shotgun in the dark. "Got a ball-peen hammer with your name on it, Bolo! Come in and get it!"

Melika stuck her head out of the bathroom and whispered, "You got two or more in the backyard."

Bolo bellowed. "Send out Makaha!"

"Eat shit!"

The rifles ripped through the house again and stopped when magazines ran empty. Hu's hands shook as she pointed her .38 at the side door across the kitchen.

"Wait for it," Bolan ordered. "Wait until you can see your target."

"Jesus! I do hair and makeup! I—"

"Here they come." Bolan heard the slap of sandaled feet out on the street. The front door smashed off its hinges and a man who could have been Bolo's twin literally filled the doorframe. The grease gun thundered in Bolan's hands as he filled the big man full of lead. The giant dropped his AK and sagged backward.

Ezekiel tried to manage his crutches, an automatic rifle and a four-hundred-plus-pound corpse at the same time and failed. His crutches slid out from underneath him and he screamed as he fell to the ground and the big man landed on top of him. A third man fired his entire magazine into the darkened house interior. Koa put a pattern of buckshot into his chest and smashed the would-be assassin to the lawn.

The bathroom window broke.

Melika snarled an obscenity and her .38 pop-pop-popped. A man outside screamed in response. Out front someone shouted frantically, "Willie! Bolo! What's happening?"

Bolan moved to the door. "Koa, hold down the house. I'm going to sweep."

"Copy that."

Bolan stepped into the cool night air. Dogs were barking and women were screaming up and down the dead-end street. He kicked Ezekiel's AK out of reach as the man feebly pawed for it from under a mountain of flesh. The shouting man stood next to an old Ford Bronco. He stopped shouting at the sight of Bolan in the dim street light. Bolan put a burst into his chest. The man's AK clattered to the street and he joined it a heartbeat later. The soldier slapped in a fresh magazine and moved to the open side gate. He heard the back door of the house crash open. Koa's shotgun boomed and the girls' revolvers popped. AKs tore into life. Bolan walked past the garbage cans and rounded on the backyard. Bolo and another man were taking turns blindly shoving their rifles around the doorjamb and emptying them into the interior. Another man lay facedown and unmoving in the grass.

Bolo whipped his reloaded weapon around the doorjamb. Bolan burned him down before he got a shot off. His partner screamed at the sight of Bolan and lunged for the dubious safety of the house. Koa's shotgun roared and the assassin staggered outside again. A pair of pistol shots coincided with Koa's second blast and the man made a decent effort to fly apart and then fell. "Clear!" Bolan called.

"Clear!" Koa called back.

"Continuing sweep!"

"Copy that! Holding position!"

"Copy!"

Bolan went around to the other side of the house. A man sat against the fence with a pair of leaking holes in his face you could put your finger through. Bolan avoided the broken bathroom window glass and emerged out front. "Coming in the front door!"

"Clear!" Koa called.

Bolan stepped inside. "We got three dead on the lawn.

Three dead out back including Bolo and one down outside the bathroom."

Koa was rapidly tapping on the tablet the Farm had issued him. "And we have police responding. ETA five minutes."

"We gotta go, and we're going to split up. Peg, you're with Koa. Grab your things and take our car. Koa, get hold of Rind and De Jong. Have Rind set up a safe place for us to link back up. Melika, you're with me. Grab our stuff. We're taking Bolo's Bronco and grabbing Belle on the way out of town." Bolan stepped back outside. He gave Ezekiel a very severe look. "You are going to talk to me."

Ezekiel moaned.

Melika came out of the house dressed in one of Bolan's T-shirts and bearing their sparse luggage. She tossed him an aloha shirt and grinned as the soldier caught it. "What?" Bolan asked.

"You look smoking hot half naked with a machine gun in your hand."

Bolan nodded at the wisdom of the statement. "I get that a lot."

"I just bet you do." Melika ran to the Bronco. "Keys are in it!"

Koa and Hu appeared, bug-out bags ready. Bolan returned his attention to Ezekiel pinned beneath four hundred pounds of flesh. "Koa, give me a hand with this piece of shit. He's taking a ride with me." Ezekiel started blubbering.

Bolan considered that a good start to the interrogation.

14

FBI safehouse

"Swanky," Bolan said. Technically, like the Pakuz dwelling they had deserted, it was a bungalow, but it was a bungalow that hung off a forested mountainside as though defying gravity, and it was appointed with millionaire tourists in mind. "From the east deck you can see the ocean and the sun rise. Oh, and check this, you'll love it." Rind nodded at the French doors leading to the front deck. "From the lanai you can see the golf course. You know, I believe you beat a man to death with a putter on the fourteenth hole."

"It was a driver," Bolan corrected.

Belle sat smoking in the breakfast nook with Ezekiel. She was now a redhead. Ezekiel was tied to his chair and Belle sat with the muzzle of her Hi-Power shoved in his crotch. "I miss all the fun."

"You should have seen him half naked, going Rambo on Ezekiel and his boys." Melika sighed at the memory. "It was breathtaking."

Belle jabbed Ezekiel in his nethers with her pistol. "I bet you got to see it. Did it take your breath away? Did it?" Ezekiel winced and shifted uncomfortably in his bonds. Pain meds for his fractures lay on the kitchen table with a glass of water but with his hands bound he couldn't reach them. It was very clear Ezekiel had finally realized that Bolan was the man who had put him in crutches in Honolulu just a few nights ago.

Koa checked his phone as it buzzed. "Uncle Aikane is calling again."

"Let him stew a little more." Bolan sank into a butter-soft leather chair. "Thanks for the crash pad, Rind."

"Courtesy of the FBI. This is one of the ones they keep for VIP security in Hawaii, and tonight that's you, big guy."

The soldier smiled tiredly. "What happened on your end?"

"Yesterday late afternoon we definitely picked up a tail. So I drove De Jong around while your buddy the Bear got a satellite tracking him. Bear gave me the word and I lost him downtown."

"You should see Rind drive, man!" De Jong enthused. "Like Steve McQueen!"

Rind smiled tolerantly. "Anyway, we lost him in traffic and the Bear did something with his satellite to jam the RFID signal. He's doing it intermittently, as if the device is dying."

"Did the bad guys get a look at you?"

"Nah, all they saw was a rental with tinted windows."

"Total super spy!" De Jong seemed positively giddy.

Bolan rolled his eyes. "And how did our boy Jagon behave?"

"Super fly!" Rind grinned. "Best stakeout partner I ever had. Best stakeout takeout I ever had, for that matter. I've never had lobster sushi before, much less fatty tuna belly and caviar. Jagon spared no expense."

De Jong actually blushed. "It was the least I could do."

Bolan thought De Jong's gratitude might be misplaced. After all, the soldier had dropped in on De Jong, dropped a helicopter through his roof and destroyed one of his operations. On the other hand, De Jong appeared to be living out his ultimate James Bond Meets *Hawaii Five-0* fantasy.

"Now—" Rind held up a finger "—the coolest part? De Jong happens to know of some real asshole variety local criminals. Once Bear established satellite tracking on our tail we drove by some of their residences and parked for a few minutes. Made it look like the Handyman was on the run and calling in favors or begging for asylum." Rind shot De Jong a grudging look of respect. "That was his idea by the way."

De Jong looked like a little kid who was earning his Junior G-Man badge. "I like to help!"

"Where is the RFID now?"

Rind tapped his pocket. "Right here. It's currently being jammed. The question is how do you want to play it now?"

"By now Uncle Aikane is well aware Bolo and company tried to take us out last night. He knows they failed and we've beaten it for the hills, and he thinks we are seriously outraged but don't know where to go or what to do about it. I'm going to let him sweat for another day before reestablishing contact. Meantime we focus on your guys. If they flew to Hawaii from God knows where tracking an RFID signal, they must be pretty high up the food chain."

Bolan opened his laptop and established a link with the Farm. Kurtzman's face appeared and it frowned at Bolan. "You look tired."

"I've had a long week. What are Rind's pals up to?"

"There are four of them. But the imaging couldn't establish much else. They've gone to ground, squatting in an unfinished housing development in the suburbs. I'm betting whoever owns it is involved, and their car hasn't moved."

Agent Rind had laid his machine pistols on the table on either side of his laptop. He placed his hands across them in loving meaning. "Tell me we're going to mess with these guys tonight."

Bolan smiled. "We're going to mess with them today, approximately a shower and shave away from now."

De Jong pumped his fists. "Yeah!"

Koa was flipping through the laminated bungalow menu. "'Traditional Hawaiian delights as well as Pan-Asian cuisine are available in the clubhouse as well as delivered to your door twenty-four hours a day.'"

De Jong stabbed his finger at Bolan delightedly. "You deserve a snack!"

Bolan nodded. He did. "De Jong, I leave it to your educated palate. Bear, I need access, egress and ownership on that housing development." Bolan reclined his chair. "Rind, I know I'm pushing FBI courtesy but I need some guns, and I need at least one that's silenced."

Rind chewed his lip. "Requisitioning guns is going to be hard, and it'll probably take some time."

De Jong's hand shot up like a little kid in school who has the answer. "I can get you guns! I can! I know a guy! Right in town!"

Rind sighed and stood. "I'm going to have to leave the room now."

De Jong threw up his hands as his new man-crush went out onto the patio. "What's his problem? I gave him guns. Gold-plated guns! You gave him machine pistols!"

"Rind is an agent of the Federal Bureau of Investigation, this is U.S. soil, and you're about to go acquire illegal weapons."

"Oh, yeah. Sorry."

"Koa, you mind going with him?"

Koa rose. "Let's roll."

"Order the food first." Bolan reclined the chair and spoke to the room at large. "I'm going to close my eyes. Wake me when the food shows up. Order a shitload of coffee."

Kelani Gated Community Development

BOLAN DIDN'T LIKE IT. The bad guys were hiding out in the construction site of a gated community. Half-built condos, the skeleton frames of buildings, loaded pallets and construction vehicles made for a maze of hiding places and ambush points. The good news was that De Jong had come through yet again. The Filipino gangster had some serious connections, and now Bolan held a Daewoo K-7 suppressed submachine gun. Bolan approved of Korean kit. The weapon's built-in suppressor was one of the better ones, drastically suppressing the sound of the gun firing and distorting the sound, too. The short notice of the acquisition meant no tactical lights, lasers or optics but the shortness of the timetable meant this was a daylight operation anyway. Bolan crouched on the hillside just above the development. His fire teams consisted of Koa and Belle, Rind and De Jong.

When De Jong had racked his weapon and shouted, "Whoo! You and me, baby! Like Bonnie and Clyde!" at Belle, Bolan had broken up that fire-and-maneuver team right there. The good news was De Jong hadn't seemed to mind so much. The Filipino gangster was still so excited about his *Hawaii Five-0* weekend with Rind that there was a good chance he might actually do what the special agent told him to in a firefight. Belle was a drug-addicted sex worker, but in her favor, if she wasn't jonesing for a fix she was cold as ice in a firefight. Hu and Melika had the RFID and one of the rentals and were back in the city streets.

Whoever the bad guys were, they hadn't taken the bait and gone to any of the places Rind and De Jong had laid out. That showed a level of professionalism Bolan didn't care for. They were waiting to acquire direct contact. Bolan intended to give it to them. He spoke into his phone. "Peg, Melika, you ready?"

"Copy that," Hu responded.

Bolan's biggest concern was that the enemy had sent in more teams. Hu and Melika had covered themselves with glory in their first firefight in Pakuz, but neither was a soldier nor a field agent. A car chase and a gun battle in the streets of Honolulu could end very badly for them. But both women had volunteered, and the opportunity to grab some of the enemy's RFID tracking heavy-hitters was too good to pass up.

Bolan's phone was on conference and his teams were getting every word. His two fire-and-maneuver teams were in the trees at the bottom of the hill, in position to put the access road in a cross fire once the enemy rolled through the chain-link gate. The plan was for the bad guys to come rolling out in their vehicle—following the RFID signal—and for the team to stop them cold and take prisoners. It was possible that when they had gone to ground at the development, they'd brought in reinforcements, and when the fight started they would boil out of the incomplete condo complex like ants. Bolan took a long breath and let it out. He was 99 percent sure it would come down to a firefight, but he'd done everything he could to give his team every advantage. There was nothing left he could do except fight the fight.

"Team One?"

"Team One ready," Koa responded.

"Team Two?"

"Locked and loaded," Rind replied.

"Unless you are fired upon, wait on me."

Bolan's two fire units responded in the affirmative.

It was go time. "Bear," Bolan ordered, "cease jamming."

Kurtzman's voice came back from Virginia. "Copy that. Radio jamming terminated. Confirm, RFID is still active. Repeat, RFID is still active."

"Copy that." Bolan commenced waiting. He knew somewhere in the jungle of construction below some very intense conversations were going on both in person and over lines of communication Bolan didn't have access to.

Yet.

"Bear?"

"Scanning. Nothing coming out over any radio frequencies. Trying to track cell phones is pretty much useless without an inside line. We're scanning the local carriers, but we are trying to crunch data on tens of thousands of signals in the middle of the day, and if these guys are talking on sat phones we have nothing."

"I know, keep trying."

Bolan waited. Twice Rind had to tell De Jong to shut up. Koa and Belle were silent and frosty.

Kurtzman spoke. "Movement. One vehicle."

A granite-gray Chrysler 300 with tinted windows rolled into view from the maze of half-finished housing. "Copy that," Bolan confirmed. "Eyes on. Teams One and Two, wait for my signal. Here we go."

Bolan's units came back in the affirmative.

The Chrysler rolled up to the gate and stopped. A man in a suit and sunglasses got out of the rear passenger-side door and unlocked the padlock on the gate. He was tall but had brassy skin behind his shades. Bolan could tell the man was wearing something in a shoulder holster.

"All units. Hold fire, hold positions," Bolan ordered. "I want that gate locked behind them. The only way they rabbit is straight through us with reinforcements hindered."

"Copy that."

The Chrysler pulled through and paused as the man closed and relocked the gate behind them. He jumped back into the 300 and the tires spit gravel as the driver stepped on it as though he had an RFID to catch. Bolan strolled onto the unfinished road. The driver slammed on his brakes at the sight of the soldier. "Now!" Bolan ordered.

The men in the Chrysler had their tinted windows rolled up. They heard no suppressed gunshots, nor would they have seen any muzzle-flashes even if they were looking for them. All they saw was a man with a weapon stepping out of the trees into the road fifty meters in front of them. Even more anomalously, all four of their tires magically burst at the same time and the Chrysler's rims sank into gravel as the driver stood on his brakes. The driver gunned his V-8 and managed to shred his deflated rubber and dig himself through the thin layer of gravel and deep into the dirt.

The 300 was going nowhere.

"Now!" Bolan ordered.

Bolan's team stepped out of the shrubbery, each with an automatic weapon pointed at their assigned passenger window.

Bolan advanced. He aimed his muzzle at where he guessed the driver's headrest would be and jerked his head in an unmistakable "out" motion. The 300 lay in the gravel like a ship run aground. The engine kept running. Bolan could discern no movement through the darkened windows. "Belle?"

Belle ripped a warning burst into the trunk.

At the same time Bolan continued advancing and walked ten rounds of subsonic hollowpoints across the hood. He popped a wiper blade out of its socket and stopped just short of putting one through the windshield. Bolan once again raised his weapon to the unseen driver's head level and gave him a last jerk of the head to get out.

Nothing moved.

"They know we want them alive," Rind advised.

Bolan was a step ahead. "Copy that. Reinforcements are inbound. Plan B!" The soldier stepped forward and raised his weapon. If the son of a bitch behind the wheel was too dumb to duck, it was on him. Bolan put ten rounds high through the windshield. The glass spider-webbed like an ice sheet. Bolan strode toward the beer-can-size hole he had punched in the glass. He ripped the pin out of one of the four tear gas grenades De Jong had procured and shoved it through the jagged hole.

All four doors flew open at the same time. Clouds of tear gas and weeping, choking assassins boiled out of the vehicle in all directions.

Koa and Rind strode up, gave their two men the wire struts of their K-7 butt stocks to the side of the neck and dropped the suspects. They grabbed them by the hair and dragged them free. Belle was a little more vicious and broke a jaw. De Jong kicked his own half-blind opponent in the testicles and stayed in the expanding gas cloud to stomp him. "Oh, yeah! How do you like it? How do you like it?" De Jong started hacking and choking. "Look what you're making me do!"

"De Jong!" Bolan ordered. "Extract your target!"

De Jong wheezed and wept. "Right!" The gangster grabbed his fetal opponent by his jacket collar and dragged him out of the gas.

Koa had his man zip-tied and dropped him next to Rind's prisoner at the extraction point. The Hawaiian ran back to help Belle. Bolan jerked his head at Rind. "Extraction! Go!"

Rind ran for the rental Lincoln back up the road in the trees. De Jong coughed and streamed tears as he dragged his man to the prisoner pile. "You all right?" Bolan asked.

"Whoo-oo-oo!" De Jong wheezed.

Kurtzman's voice came urgently across everyone's phone. "Movement in the development! I have another vehicle! Big one!"

A Humvee rolled into view. Half a dozen men with automatic rifles trotted at the double alongside the vehicle. Of most concern was the man standing in the roof weapon station. Bolan saw the six barrels of a minigun behind an armored plate traversing in his direction. "Scatter! Scatter! Scatter!" Bolan bellowed at his team.

The Humvee crashed the locked gate as if it didn't exist. Bolan's team bolted for the trees on either side of the road and dropped into the drainage ditches. The minigun spun into life and the little valley echoed with the ripping sound of 7.62 mm NATO rounds. The gunner walked his fire into the pile of prisoners and they stopped short of bursting like blood-filled balloons as they were stitched.

"That was cold!" Belle observed.

"That Humvee is U.S. military issue!" Koa shouted. "I make it Hawaiian National Guard!"

Bolan's team hugged ditch as the enemy minigun drew laser lines of tracers along the gravel top over their heads.

"Infantry is coming in under the covering fire!" Koa shouted. "You got a plan?"

"I'm in the car!" Rind shouted across the phone link. "I can ram them!"

"You'd lose," Bolan stated. He unzipped the ditty bag over his shoulder and reached for the last of the De Jong dynamite. By the time they'd gotten to Hawaii the three sticks of TNT were sweating candlesticks of horror that the soldier had worried a rough landing would detonate. They'd been sitting in rice for the past two days and looked deceivingly refreshed. "Belle! De Jong! Covering fire!"

The pair popped up and each fired off a burst. De Jong missed one of the trotting gunmen. Belle walked a burst up the minigunner's armored shield. They succeeded in attracting attention. The killers had some very expensive equipment but it was apparent they were not trained soldiers. They swung their weapons at De Jong and Belle.

Bolan rose and flung a stick of dynamite at the Humvee as it came within range. He didn't bother to light it. The soldier just sent it revolving at the grille of the Humvee like a tomahawk. The sweating dynamite needed no fusing as it slammed into steel. The daylight detonation was impressive. The front of the Humvee shredded away, the front axle broke and three of the men trotting alongside it went flying.

Koa popped up and trip-hammered three bursts into the chests of the remaining three footmen. Bolan flung his second stick of dynamite. It hit the gunner's shield and the gunner and his weapon station exploded and streamed away into shreds and twists of not much.

The echoes of the detonations bounced off the hills. Bolan scanned the battle zone and shook his head at the dearth of living prisoners.

Koa spoke low. "There might be someone alive in the back of the Humvee."

"De Jong, you're with me. Belle, Koa, covering fire."

De Jong popped up. "Oh, yeah!"

Bolan rose. "Finger off the trigger. You take the passenger side." The soldier and his entirely too eager wingman advanced on the smoking Humvee. Bolan figured it was better than getting shot in the back by his too eager covering fire. "Rind, bring up the car. Open the sunroof and all the windows. Point her out of this valley and rejoin the team. You and Belle covering. When Rind is in place, Koa, start advancing."

The team copied.

Bolan and De Jong approached the vehicle. The soldier spoke into his phone. "Bear?"

"No movement inside the development."

Bolan leaned into a shattered window, leading with the muzzle of his K-7. The outside of the Humvee looked like a crushed beer can. The inside looked like stepped-on spaghetti. Dynamite was unforgiving of human flesh. De Jong wrinkled his nose at the smell of burned human insides. "So, should we get a DNA sample or something?"

Bolan smiled against his will. "Thinking all the time, De Jong."

"Been hanging out with Agent Rind," De Jong said proudly. "So, we…?"

Bolan's instincts spoke to him. There were still bad guys in the development. "We assault, and if you whoo-hoo one more time, I will shoot you."

"Man, I thought I was proving myself and stuff."

"And stuff," Bolan agreed. He glanced up the road and saw the black Lincoln pull a bootlegger turn and position itself for a quick getaway. Agent Rind jumped out and re-acquired De Jong. Koa shook his head as he linked back up with Belle. "Our targets are toast."

Bolan was starting to get a real bad feeling about this. "Bear, what do you see?"

"No movement. The Humvee and the men came out of the center building. Looks like the clubhouse." A satellite photo blipped onto Bolan's screen and he saw a mostly finished two-story with an unfinished Olympic-size swimming pool behind it. "Seems to have a garage for shuttle buses and golf carts."

"We have blueprints?"

"Working on it."

"Advancing. Teams One and Two, cover me." Bolan moved at a low run through the broken gate. No bullets sought him out and he took cover behind the reassuringly solid bulk of a Bobcat. "Teams, advance."

Bolan's fire teams moved along the ditches flanking the access road. Rind and De Jong broke left and found cover behind a steamroller. Koa and Belle took a pyramid of dry concrete bags to the right. The clubhouse frontage was in a decent cross fire. Bolan broke cover and the clubhouse doors flew open. Two men with rifles opened up. Bolan dove behind a pickup as his teams returned fire and one of the men fell. The second man kicked the doors shut.

"Bear, is the garage entrance in the back or on the side?"

"Northern side, right across from the pool. Be advised, satellite has heat signatures in the garage."

Bolan doubted golf carts would generate enough heat for a satellite to pick up. "Team One, to my position! Team Two, cover!"

Koa and Belle broke from behind the concrete bags and charged to Bolan's position. "Koa, take command on the frontage. I want you to have lanes of fire on the front of the clubhouse and the side road to the garage."

"You and Belle are flanking?"

"I think the bad guys are about to make a break for it. They have vehicles in the garage and the only way out is the way we came in. Watch for the diversion from the front."

Koa slapped in a fresh magazine. "Got it."

"Belle, you're with me. Koa, Team Two, covering fire." Bolan flanked the clubhouse with Belle on his six. Kurtzman spoke through the phone. "Shooter on the roof! Moving toward northern edge!"

"Copy that!" Bolan raised his K-7. "Belle! Hit the pool!"

Belle ran and jumped into the unfinished pool across the road from the garage. The gunman appeared at the eaves of the garage roof. Bolan's suppressed weapon chuffed and clicked and sent seven subsonic rounds through the shooter's chest. The man's knees collapsed from underneath him and he pulled a very ugly belly flop onto the freshly paved road, his old-style M-16 A1 rifle falling beside him. Bolan's boots hit concrete as he leaped into the pool beside Belle.

"I can hear the engine," Belle reported. "Sounds like a diesel."

One of the garage bays opened. Two men with rifles charged out and Bolan and Belle cut them down simultaneously. An M-35 military truck rolled forward. The passenger-side glass had been removed and a man fired a machine gun out of it. The driver's glass had been replaced by a piece of steel "hillbilly" armor with an observation slit. A man hung out the door, blasting away with a rifle. Another rifleman lay on top of the cab and bullets sparked and chipped off the lip of the pool. Belle fired her weapon dry and dropped down. "Shit!"

Bolan silently concurred. Shit was right. Even without the after-market armor, subsonic pistol bullets weren't going to take out a truck weighing a deuce and a half. The soldier emptied his weapon into the truck's grille and dropped down. Rice spilled as he pulled the last stick of dynamite from his goody bag. Bolan rose and threw the stick at the front of the truck as it emerged from the garage.

The sweaty, unstable stick of TNT slammed into the truck's grille, bounced off the steel bumper and fell inertly to the ground. Bolan refrained from rolling his eyes as the truck advanced.

There was no time to reload.

Bolan snapped up his DP-52 in both hands and squeezed the grip. The laser sight blinked into life and painted a bright red dot on the dynamite as the truck's chassis conveniently threw the stick into shadow.

Bolan fired and the dynamite detonated. The soldier threw himself back as heat and blast washed over the top of the unfinished pool in a wave. The secondary explosion sent an orange tsunami sheeting across the sky and threatened to suck Bolan's lungs out of his body. He managed to clap his hands over his face—covering his eyes and mouth—and shoved his thumbs in his ears. He hugged wall as a tertiary explosion shook the pool foundation. Bolan opened his eyes and watched a minor mushroom cloud plume skyward.

He yawned at the ringing in his ears, reloaded his pistol and called out to his team over his phone. "Sound off!"

Every team member came back in the affirmative.

"So that would have been a truck bomb?" Belle suggested.

Bolan took in the unique smell of burning fertilizer. Bits of debris both large and small began raining down. He stayed close to the pool wall as a smoldering propane tank valve clanked to the concrete beside him. "To the deuce." The soldier raised his head over the lip of the pool. The truck were gone. The garage and the vast majority of the clubhouse was rubble. The bits of structure still left were on fire.

"Whooo-hoooo!" De Jong howled like a frat boy at a kegger. "Cooper! Walking Tall! With the biggest stick there is! Stick-of-dynamite, assholes!"

Bolan refrained from shooting the giddy gangster. "Maintain your position, De Jong."

"Oops! Sorry!"

Kurtzman spoke across the phone link. "That was pretty spectacular from our vantage, Striker. I counted three detonations. First one was yours?"

"Affirmative." Bolan grimaced as he surveyed the destruction. "Rind, bring up the car. We are extracting now."

"Copy that!"

Belle gave Bolan a coquettish smile. "Oh, cheer up. Jagon's right. We kicked their bitch asses."

"I doubt we have a single living suspect, and I just blew up a massive amount of evidence. We can't afford to stick around. This was a goat screw."

"So what do we do?"

Rind brought the Lincoln to a gravel-spitting halt in front

of the sundered gate. "We're going to have to pray that Rind's buddies at the Federal Bureau of Investigation can pull something of use out of the wreckage, and hope they can do it in time. Meantime, we resurface in Happy Valley and see if our uncles still love us."

15

FBI safehouse

Agent Rind sat at the minibar with his back turned and winced as someone with a very high pay grade somewhere in Washington, D.C., went to town on him over the battle at Kelani Gated Community Development. Rind's entire end of the conversation consisted of ever-increasingly meek, "Yes, Directors." He set his phone down, stared at himself in the minibar mirror and saw a man who'd soon have a desk job in some lightless, low bowel of the J. Edgar Hoover building. Bolan nodded in sympathy.

"How's it hanging, Special Agent?"

"How do you think it's hanging?"

"You got ninety-eight problems and owning a pair of machine pistols ain't any of them?"

Rind laughed against his will. "I have that."

"Keep a stiff upper lip. There's a chance you can still come out of this golden."

"That would be epic."

Bolan passed by the coffee table. Koa had pulled up several YouTube videos about the care of Korean small arms on his tablet and was busy cleaning guns. He handed Bolan the DP-52. "The laser was off by a hair, not that that stopped you, Captain Dynamite."

Bolan brought the pistol up and squeezed the grip. The red dot printed perfectly in line with the small and simple sights. "Thanks." He tucked the pistol away along with a triplet of spare magazines. Melika and Hu were down the mountain at the golf club's restaurant picking up takeout. The RFID had died and the trail it had lead to was now a smoking hole a mountain and a half away, undoubtedly lit up in a lunar glare of floodlights and crawling with federal agents.

De Jong was in the bathroom and not making much of an effort to conceal the fact that he was snorting something. Belle stood out on the liana. She hugged herself, smoking and gazing down at the small constellation of lights in the darkened valley. Bolan frowned as she compulsively scratched her arms. He stepped out and admired the evening view.

"Belle?"

"Yes?"

"Now's not the time to kick."

Belle trembled and took a shaky drag from her cigarette. "I feel sick."

"I know."

"No, I feel sick every time you see me do it, or when I know you know I'm sneaking off to do it."

Bolan sighed and nodded. "Well, I am known to have a positive moral influence on people."

Belle giggled. "Screw you."

"Though I admit a transgendered, potty-mouthed mercenary is new even for me."

"I'm not a mercenary," Belle said seriously.

"Transgendered glamour girl with a gun?" Bolan tried.

"He learns fast, and he's good-looking, too." Belle gave Bolan a demure look. "I don't suppose there's any chance at all that..."

"Well, if I was the last boy on earth, and you were the last..." Belle smirked.

"Transgendered glamour girl with a gun?"

"Yeah."

"Yeah?"

"We'd play a lot of chess."

Belle wrinkled her surgically enhanced nose. "I'm Swedish, you'd lose."

Bolan nodded. "It's possible."

"You know? I always fall in love with the wrong men." Belle tossed her newly hennaed hair.

Bolan's laptop very conveniently gave the "Bear on the line" signal. "I gotta take that."

"I have to go powder my nose."

Bolan took the armchair by the coffee table. Koa watched Belle walk to the bathroom. "What was that all about?"

"Belle thinks I'm hot."

"I got no prepared response to that."

Bolan clicked a key on his laptop. "What do we have, Bear?"

"Well, you made a mess."

"I know."

Kurtzman made a bemused noise. "We have no living suspects and most of the corpses are in really bad shape. The FBI is on scene checking fingerprints and dental records. We'll have whatever they come up with ASAP."

"Rind's in trouble."

Rind called out from the bar. "Copy that!"

"I'm making calls. Straight to the top."

"Thanks, Bear. Do we have anything?"

"Something, and it isn't good."

"What's that?" Bolan asked.

"Residual radioactivity."

Bolan's blood went cold. "The truck bombs were dirty?"

"We're not sure."

"Do I need to be worried about my team?"

Koa racked a fresh round into a K-7. "Shit…"

"Does Koa need to worry about having two-headed kids?"

Koa took up a fresh weapon. "I already have kids. I have grandkids. And I also have a magnificent head of hair. I ain't looking forward to coughing up blood and going bald."

"Bear?" Bolan asked. "What about the Hawaiian bro fro?"

"As I said, according to the FBI, it's residual. More like the bad guys were storing radioactive material there, long enough and stored badly enough to leave a footprint. I'm checking the local hospitals and clinics for anyone displaying symptoms of radiation sickness."

"So we're good?"

"No! We ain't good!" Koa's face twisted. "We got what looks like a planned pair of dirty deuce-and-a-half truck bombs! On my Island heritage! We ain't good at all!"

Bolan nodded. "Bear, we ain't good."

"I'm on it. I have everyone on it."

"I'm going to need some radiation detectors."

"I've appropriated four from Pearl. They should be at the safehouse within the hour."

"Thanks."

"I wish I had more."

"You'll get more. I know you. Out." Bolan rose and poured himself a club soda from the bar. De Jong and Belle came out of the bathroom. The Filipino gangster was positively jovial. Belle couldn't meet Bolan's eyes.

Koa's phone rang. The Hawaiian frowned at the screen. "It's Marwin."

De Jong threw his hands up. "Why the hell is Marwin calling you?"

Bolan leaned in close enough to make De Jong flinch backward. "Because he's posing as my and Koa's cousin."

"Oh shit! I forgot!"

Bolan jerked his head at Koa. "Answer it. De Jong? Not a word."

De Jong pantomimed zipping his lips shut.

Koa answered. "Yeah?" He listened for long moments. "Marwin's at Melika's bar. Says he's in trouble and was ordered to call us. He wants us to come. Our uncles want us to come. We going?"

"Yeah." Bolan nodded. "We're going."

"We're coming, cuz." Koa killed the connection.

Melika's Place

THE BAR WAS packed, and not with patrons. Bolan and Koa walked in bold as brass with Melika and Hu in tow. Rind was in charge of the silenced submachine gun team, waiting a block away and ready to storm the place if it went bad. Of course that would be too late.

Marwin sat at the bar with a sea of beer bottles around him. He was bracketed by two men even larger than him and didn't look happy. Tino was behind the bar. The uncles held down their usual booth, and the VIP booth was once again drenched in darkness, but Bolan could detect more than one man holding court. Bolan could just see a huge hand in a cast resting on the table, barely illuminated in the dim glow of a beer sign. A lot of very hard-looking men were holding down the bar and most of the tables.

Uncle Aikane waved. "Koa! Makaha! Come! Sit with your uncles."

Bolan and Koa took a seat at the booth of royalty with Aikane and Nui. Melika went behind her bar and started harshly whispering at Tino. Hu sat at a lone table and once again became the subject of leers and speculation. Bolan let Koa take lead as Uncle Nui poured two mugs of Koko Brown ale and pushed them at Bolan and Koa. Uncle Nui grunted and shook his head. "We missed you. We worried about you."

"We worried about us, too, brah." Nui flinched. Koa's voice went cold. "When Bolo, Ezekiel and their friends came at us we had women in the house. Melika was in the house. She's *ohana*. Turned the place into last dance with Butch and Sundance."

Bolan admired the poetry. He also noted that Koa had called Nui "brah" rather than uncle. Koa was working the *ohana* outrage angle to the hilt, and no one was scolding him.

Aikane spoke. "You brought Makaha here."

"And you sent him to die! Sent people to kill me and my girl!"

"I didn't send Bolo and Ezekiel. You know that. It was personal and I would have stopped it had I known."

Koa scowled into his brown ale.

"Koa, where is Ezekiel?"

Koa ad-libbed. "You don't want to know what Makaha did to him."

Aikane went stone-faced. "And? Makaha?"

"I know for a fact you did not send Bolo or Ezekiel, Uncle. Ezekiel told me, and I made him tell me until I believed him."

Aikane and Nui regarded Bolan with a new and leery respect.

Koa shook his head and drank. "It was screwed up."

"It's all screwed up." Bolan nodded and poured back half his beer. "Tell me, Uncle. Me and Koa messed up beyond repair?"

"What if I say yes?"

Bolan finished his beer and rolled his shoulders. "Koa and I are strapped."

"We know. So is every man in this bar. What does that have to do with anything?"

"It means you tell me Melika keeps her bar and Hu goes back to California where she belongs. You promise me."

Aikane grunted and sipped beer. "And if I do?"

"I'll hand you my gun and go wherever you want with whoever you want. Back to the golf course if you say so."

Aikane's grunt had a tinge of amusement. "And if I don't?"

"It goes down. Here. Now. Blaze of glory."

Aikane looked at Nui. Nui looked at Bolan and nodded toward Marwin. "You know that fat piece of shit?"

Bolan glared at Marwin. Marwin flinched. Bolan shook his head. "Never seen him in my life."

Marwin looked genuinely hurt but he stayed in character. Nui looked at Koa. "You know him?"

"Uncle?" Koa looked amazed. "That's cousin Marwin."

Aikane and Nui blinked as they once again did very complicated Hawaiian family-tree math.

"Uncle." Koa looked incredulous. "You know I got a Filipino streak in me."

Nui nodded. "We know."

Koa grinned and pointed his finger at the mass of Filipino flesh at the bar. "That is the house that lumpia built." Laughs broke out around the bar as Koa described both Marwin and Philippine cuisine egg rolls. "I was two years in Subic Bay. My mother told me to look up some of her people. You wouldn't believe the shit Marwin and I got into back in the day. Uncle, I'm begging you, throw the fat bastard a bone."

More laughs broke out. Nui gestured. "Marwin, bring your glass. Join us."

Marwin ambled over, sweating with relief. "Shit, I'm the biggest thing I've ever seen in the Philippines, then I come here, and it's like I'm a hobbit…"

Laughs broke out again. Nui actually clapped him on the shoulder good-naturedly. Bolan poured Marwin a beer. De Jong's personal thug took the mug in three swallows. "Man, it was starting to get unneighborly in here."

"Why are you here, Marwin?" Aikane asked.

"Told you, my cuz Koa called me and said he was in some serious shit. Said he needed someone on his six. I got my ass on a plane."

"Do you still want that job?" Nui prodded.

"It's not a job. It's like an obligation and stuff."

Aikane tilted his head slightly. "No matter what?"

Marwin nodded with schoolboy earnestness. "No matter what."

Aikane smiled. "What about Makaha?"

"He scares the shit out of me—" Marwin glanced nervously around the room "—but you all scare the shit out of me."

Very tough men around the bar made amused noises. Bolan kept the smile off his face. Marwin was making a serious stab at this year's best actor in a supporting role. Aikane nodded thoughtfully. "Koa, are you still with us?"

"Bolo's problem was his problem. I solved it for him. Makaha took care of Ezekiel's bullshit. This is about the *ohana*. This is about our Islands. It's bigger than personal problems and bullshit."

Nui looked at Bolan. "And you, Makaha?"

"I'm like Marwin. I have Koa's back no matter what."

Marwin nodded vigorously. "Yeah, I'm like what he said."

Aikane made his decision. "You can't go back to Pakuz. Stay at Melika's tonight. Tomorrow you have to leave the girls behind. Tomorrow you leave everything behind. The day after that I can promise you nothing, except that you will be remembered for all time."

Bolan and Koa nodded grimly. Marwin gaped as if he had just fallen off a pineapple truck.

Aikane looked to the bar. "Tino! Before sunrise take Koa, Makaha and Marwin to my retreat. We trust them, but take the forest route anyway."

Tino grinned. "Yes, Uncle!"

Aikane spoke low. "We have had setbacks, but things will start happening very fast now."

16

Bolan lay awake as the dawn turned from purple to pink to orange through the blinds. His every instinct told him the next forty-eight hours were going to decide everything. Melika made a noise as Bolan rose and began to prepare himself. His grease gun, his K-7 and the CIA-supplied weapons were all with Rind and the assault team. Bolan had the Korean .22 De Jong had acquired for him and Koa had his .45. Marwin had nothing. Still, Bolan had taken precautions.

When Melika and Hu had finished their "running the RFID" duties, Bolan had asked the ladies to do a little shopping for the undercover team. Melika had bought him a folding Buck knife. In fact Bolan had asked her to buy two, and he'd given both a shaving-sharp edge. There was still a good chance their guns would be taken. He'd also had Melika pick up a straight razor. The handle was faux tortoiseshell and the blade a brittle three inches long. But the little razor weighed only two ounces and was less than a quarter of an inch thick. It would ride easily in a boot top or slide into the side of a loosely tied shoe, and would require a very professional pat-down to detect.

Koa walked into the room as Bolan tucked the razor in his shoe. "That is some old-school shit. You really know how to fight with one of those things?"

Bolan gave Koa a look.

Koa shook his head. "Right, dumb question."

Bolan finished dressing and tucked his pistol, knives and spare magazines away. "You ready?"

"As I'll ever be," Koa said.

The two warriors walked into the living room to find themselves serenaded by the sound of Marwin blissfully sawing logs on the couch. "Marwin," Bolan called. "Up and at 'em."

Marwin blinked, snuffled, wheezed and licked his chops like a Great Dane as he rolled his bulk into a sitting position. "What's for breakfast?"

Melika padded out of the bedroom. "Loco Moco, you want hamburger or SPAM?"

Marwin rubbed his stomach. "SPAM!"

"Koa?" Melika asked.

"SPAM."

"Coop?"

Bolan kept his expression neutral in the face of the Pacific Island love of Minnesota's processed pork product. "Hamburger."

Melika went into the kitchen and began rattling pans in preparation of one-bowl meals of rice topped with meat, topped with fried eggs and topped with gravy. Agent Hu came out of the tiny guest room wearing one of Koa's shirts and carrying a .38 in each hand. She held out both to Marwin. "Here, you may need these, and I have more."

Marwin looked as though he might cry. "Thanks, Peg!"

Hu reached into a shirt pocket and produced a handful of spare shells. She jumped as Tino's fist slammed against the door. "Koa!" His voice sounded a little ragged as he called out. "Makaha! Marwin!"

Marwin went into bodyguard mode. He made his weapons disappear and answered the door. Tino filled it from top to bottom. "Hey, big man!"

Tino scowled and pushed his way inside. "Hey, fatty."

Bolan eyed the big Samoan. He looked exhausted. Dark circles bruised the skin beneath his eyes and a peaked pallor beneath his normally bronze skin made it look ashy. His massive eyebrows seemed permanently bunched, almost as though he was in pain. "You all ready?"

Koa frowned. "About to have our morning grind, brah. Melika's Loco Moco."

"Tino!" Melika called out from the kitchen. "I know you like bacon on yours!"

Tino grimaced and went a little greener. "Nah, nothin' for me, Meli." Shocked silence reigned in the kitchen at this anomalous development. The Samoan shook his head in agitation. "We got no time for this. We gotta go, and we gotta go now. Saddle up."

"But…" Marwin looked genuinely heartbroken. "Loco Moco…"

"Missing a meal won't hurt your fat, Flip ass one bit," Tino snarled. "Make yourself a sandwich and take it on the road, bitch!"

Marwin looked ready to do something about it, and he struggled to stay in character. Tino seemed too distracted to notice the danger he was in. He waved his hands in disgust at the room in general. "All you assholes get your shit together! The hos stay here! I'll be in the van! The bus is leaving in five! Doom on you if you ain't on it! And give me your phones!"

Bolan kept his expression neutral. Tino didn't look good at all. Bolan, Koa and Marwin handed over their phones. The Samoan slammed the door behind him and his stomping echoed on the steps. Marwin turned to Bolan and jerked his thumb at the door. "Is he hungover or something?"

"He looks like shit," Koa agreed.

"Did he just call me a ho?" Hu said.

Bolan was starting to get a very bad feeling. "Mel?"

"Yeah?" Melika came out of the kitchen as Bolan opened the package Kurtzman had delivered. He took out a white plastic device that bore a startling resemblance to a household wall thermostat. He ran the test mode. The device peeped all was in order, and Bolan disabled the alarm and audio sound prompts. He set the preferences and handed it to Melika "You got Alka-Seltzer?"

Melika took the device and gave Bolan a dry look. "I own and operate a bar."

"Put on a robe, tuck this between your breasts but keep it covered. Take the Alka-Seltzer and a glass of water down to Tino. Chat him up for about thirty seconds. Lean in the window and make soothing noises. Then come back."

"Okay…" Melika disappeared.

Marwin looked back and forth between Bolan and Koa. "What's going on?"

Koa went all stone face. "Was that what I think it is?"

Bolan nodded. "Yeah."

Melika reappeared in a tantalizingly short kimono that she'd pulled demurely tight across her collarbones. She carried a glass of water and a packet of extra-strength Alka-Seltzer. She gave Bolan a questioning look in passing and went downstairs.

Marwin folded his huge arms across his equally huge and sagging chest. "So?"

"Like Tino said—get your shit together. And he might be right. Make yourself a sandwich. Make three if you would."

"I can do that." Marwin shucked into his sandals, filled his pockets and went into the kitchen.

Koa muttered low, "So I'm thinking this is bad."

"Keep your fingers crossed that I'm wrong," Bolan advised. "Praying might be appropriate."

Bolan and Koa gathered their few belongings that would pass scrutiny. Marwin came out of the kitchen with a serving tray laden with white-bread sandwiches consisting of SPAM, peanut butter and mayonnaise, with sodas on the side. The saving grace was that Marwin had cut off the crusts and sliced them diagonally. Bolan silently muttered the soldier in the field's mantra "fuel…" and took a sandwich and an orange soda. "Thanks, Marwin."

Marwin beamed. "You're welcome!"

Koa tucked in as though there was nothing wrong with any of this. Melika came back in with an empty glass. She opened her kimono and produced the device. "He drank it. He burped. He seemed pathetically grateful."

Bolan took the device. He looked at the readout and his blood went cold. He had felt a little bad about what the extra-strength aspirin in the Alka-Seltzer might do to Tino's possibly bleeding insides, but that was now the least of the giant Samoan's problems.

Melika clearly didn't like the look on Bolan's face. "So what is that thing?"

"Digital radiation monitor."

Melika's eyes went wide. Marwin's jaw dropped. Koa let out a long breath as his worst fears were confirmed. "And?"

The DRM's readout was a numeric obituary. The soldier steeled himself for what was to come. The readout might very well be Bolan's own obit before this mission was finished. "Tino's going to be dead within the next twenty-four to forty-eight," he answered. "And if we don't find out what he's been into, I'm thinking thousands of people in Hawaii are going to be the same."

The forest

TINO DROVE THE van unerringly through barely perceptible jungle paths. Once again, despite a hard-earned sense of direction Bolan did not know which way they were going. Bolan and his team still had their weapons. Tino had their phones but Bolan had removed the GPS tracker so even if Kurtzman and his team couldn't see him or talk to him, they knew where he was. The tracker did have one communication function Rind and Kurtzman were monitoring. If he pressed the button it meant "FUBAR—converge on my signal." Bolan's misgivings grew. Tino was constantly coughing into a blood-stained bandanna. "How's it hanging, big man?"

"Screw you," Tino muttered.

"Maybe we should be driving to a hospital," Bolan suggested.

"Screw you."

"Brah, you don't look good."

Tino stood on the brakes. The Samoan turned red-rimmed, broken-vesseled eyes on Bolan. "Make me say it a third time, Makaha! Make me say it again and watch what happens! You sucker-punched me at Melika's! You think you can do it again? Any of you assholes think you can?"

Koa and Marwin were silent. Bolan shook his head grimly at the dying Samoan. "No, brah. Next time we tangle? I only want your best."

Tino turned and rammed the van back in gear. "My best is behind me, brah…" He broke off into another fit of coughing. Koa shot Bolan a look. Marwin looked as though he might start crying. For a morbidly obese Filipino enforcer, Marwin was surprisingly sensitive.

Bolan watched the terrain. It was getting darker and more crowded beneath the trees. They were definitely headed downhill. They'd repeatedly splashed through streams on their journey, and Bolan deduced they were probably in a valley that led to the sea.

Bolan smelled the ocean before he heard it and the first thing he heard was the pop and crack of rifle fire in the distance. The forest ended like a knife cut and the van came to a stop on a yellow sand beach. Half a dozen Hawaiian men of various ages were practicing with M-16 A2s. Uncle Nui seemed to be overseeing the proceedings. Sawhorse tables had been set up beneath the trees and weapons were racked. The firing line was literally a line drawn in the sand under the palm trees. The targets were two-liter pop bottles set up beneath a cliff. Uncle Aikane waved and walked over. He gave Tino a very grim once-over. "How are you, Tino?"

"Right as rain," the Samoan rasped. Bolan and his team piled out of the van. Aikane gestured. "Come over here."

The huge Hawaiian led them to one of the tables. He pointed at a faithful copy of an M-16. "You remember these, Koa?"

"Like an old friend." Koa hefted a rifle. "Just like what I carried in Germany."

"And you, Marwin?"

Marwin sighed at the unfamiliar weapon. There just weren't any gold-plated British submachine guns on the beach today. Aikane nodded. "Koa, you will teach him today. We don't have much time."

"I'll whip him into shape."

Aikane eyed the trio. "Do any of you know how to use a scope?"

"Makaha told me he did some hunting back east," Koa ad-libbed.

Bolan took the ball and ran with it. "I had a stepfather who taught me. He belonged to a deer camp. I got a buck every season. Took a black bear once, before I moved on."

"Good." Aikane nodded. "Very good." The crime lord went to the table and unzipped a battered leather rifle bag. Bolan beheld an old Remington 600 Magnum. "Nice." He took up the 1960s antique. Despite its name the little rifle had a very short eighteen-and-a-half-inch barrel and used a short action. The laminate stock showed a great deal of wear from years of use. Bolan worked the bolt. It was glass-slick from obvious heavy use and care. He brought the rifle to his shoulder and traversed the shore, scanning the breakers through the old Leupold 4X mountaineer scope. Bolan squeezed the trigger and it broke cleanly with a sharp click and almost no creep. He dismounted the rifle and glanced at the three old cardboard boxes of squat, soft-pointed bullets. The .350 Remington Magnum cartridges would make the little carbine kick like a mule. "It'll do," Bolan stated.

"Good. It should be sighted in, but you can take one box of ammo and get familiar with it. Save the rest."

"Thanks."

"Your shooting is going to be very important. A hundred meters is a short distance in the scheme of things, but you're going to have to be fast, and you cannot afford to miss. Not once."

Bolan examined what this might mean. "I will practice."

"I want you to show us now."

Bolan took up a box of ammo. The cardboard was weathered and falling apart. He shook out five fat shells and began loading the rifle. Bolan shot Aikane a sly grin as he clicked the safety.

"Nui! Clear the line!"

"Tell them to set five."

"Set five, Nui!" Aikane called out. He grunted at Bolan in approval as Nui put out five fresh bottles and the shooters moved back into the trees. "Show me."

Bolan began walking. Aikane and Koa followed and Marwin hustled his bulk to catch up. "Hey! Wait for me!"

Bolan paced out along the tree line until his sniper's eye told him he was at three hundred. He suddenly swung around and fired. The soft-point bullet caught plastic and the bottle flew upward as though an invisible angler had suddenly yanked it up. Bolan flicked the bolt and fired again. The next bottle shredded as if struck by a sword. Bolan fired again. The third bottle kicked over and spun away as if he was bowling and had picked up a spare.

The men in the trees cheered.

Bolan flicked the bolt and deliberately let the fourth shot kick up sand a few feet in front of his target. "Damn!"

A groan of disappointment came from the trainees.

Koa took the hand-off. "You're out of practice. Steady down."

"You can do it, Makaha!" Marwin enthused.

Bolan took several long moments and fired his fifth shot and the fourth bottle did a back flip. The men in the trees whooped. Bolan flicked open the action and let smoke curl out. Aikane looked at Bolan with admiration. "Very good, Makaha."

"Pop bottles at three hundred meters with a scope, Uncle. If you were taught right—" Bolan closed the action "—it's not hard."

Koa spoke iron wisdom. "Pop bottles don't fire back, Makaha."

Bolan nodded. "That's why we got you, Koa."

Aikane smiled with pleasure at the exchange. "It is good to have real warriors back in the *ohana*. We have lost too many, and many of the new generation are weak and foolish."

"The *ohana* calls to its own," Koa intoned. "The Islands call to their own."

"It is no accident that we are here now," Bolan finished. "I can feel it."

Aikane was clearly moved. "Koa, I want you to watch the men shoot."

"I will, Uncle."

"Makaha, practice a little more. Your uncle Nui went diving this morning and speared good fish and octopus. We will eat together and then take our ease in the hammocks beneath the trees. This afternoon, there is something I want to show you."

17

The training camp

Mack Bolan found himself in the shadow of Musa Jalaluddin. The Hawaiian had shaved off his "mad prophet of the desert" wild locks and beard, and from his anvil jaw to the top of his massive skull his head gleamed like forged bronze. His eyes still bore the unmistakable flash of the crazy holy warrior. Jalaluddin wore nothing but a sarong. His arms and legs were sleeved in tattoos of entwined native Hawaiian, Christian and Muslim symbols. Bolan rated him an ongoing concern at around six foot four and a chiseled two hundred and fifty pounds. Jalaluddin perked a bemused eyebrow at Bolan as he lay in his hammock. "At last, Makaha. We meet."

Bolan decided on boldness and met the Hawaiian's powerful gaze with his own. "Who the hell are you?"

Jalaluddin threw back his head and laughed. "For a half *haole,* you have balls."

"You know, I get really tired of hearing about that."

"This is Hawaii, Makaha. We can teach the Italians something about breaking each other's balls, but looking at you I bet you didn't get much of it on the mainland."

For a sociopathic, possibly cannibalistic, religious terrorist, Jalaluddin was remarkably charming. Bolan smiled back ruefully. "No, I didn't, but I've been getting my balls broken nonstop since the second I set foot in Happy Valley."

The man laughed again. "I hear you've done most of the

ball breaking, most of the bone breaking, as well as breaking most everything that isn't nailed down. You know? I like you, Makaha."

"You're kind of scaring the shit out of me, brah."

Jalaluddin shrugged. "You want some grind? Nui's slicing up poke as fresh as it gets."

"Definitely." Bolan rolled out of the hammock and followed Jalaluddin over to two long tables pushed together and surrounded by the men of the camp. He was greeted heartily and clapped on the back by anyone within reach. Koa and Marwin were already there. A young man not out of his teens stared at Bolan as if he was star-struck. "I have heard all about you!"

Koa made a noise and the other men laughed.

The young man was undeterred. "I am Keolakupaianaha!"

Bolan shook his head. "Just going to call you Keo."

Keo beamed. "Everyone does!"

"And everyone calls me Makaha."

"Makaha!"

Bolan settled in for some grind. Nui presided over a huge wooden bowl filled with well over a dozen pounds of freshly caught fish and octopus. Bolan could smell the *kukui* nuts Nui had roasted and chopped in. Red seaweed was the main garnish and Bolan saw the traditional Hawaiian black salt made of sea salt mixed with charcoal. There were no Pan-Pacific flourishes. It was about as simple as poke got. Bolan tucked in. It was the best poke he'd ever had.

The men laughed and ate and talked about the morning's training. Jalaluddin was mostly silent as he ate except to make a pointed remark about one warrior or another's abilities or lack thereof. Bolan laughed with the men. The man was funny as hell, and Bolan knew it was another one of the reasons the warriors loved him. Keo and the younger warriors hung on his every word. Jalaluddin was a born leader of men.

Jalaluddin looked proudly at the dozen men around the

table. "People thought the Hawaiian spirit was extinct. They thought *koas* were extinct, that there were no more warriors in the Islands. We are living proof that people are wrong, and we are going to teach them their error."

Warriors whooped and cheered. Nui watched the young warriors eating his grind with pleasure. Aikane was beaming. Bolan could smell the kava that was brewing somewhere in camp and he was pretty sure some of the older men had dipped in early. "It is a shame, Koa," Aikane sighed, "that you came too late for the *Lua* training."

Koa nodded soberly. "I have two regrets. I spent far too many years on the mainland and away from my people."

"The other?" Nui prompted.

"The American government taught me to be a soldier. The warrior skills I know are Japanese." Koa met Jalaluddin's piercing stare. "I regret that I will never get to train with the kahuna."

Bolan knew that "kahuna" had multiple meanings. In ancient days it could often mean shaman or sorcerer, but it was always a term of tremendous respect, and in any context it meant the man was at the pinnacle of ability and power. The men around the table muttered in low tones of approval and nodded. Koa had acknowledged Musa Jalaluddin as a kahuna. He had also acknowledged this was a suicide mission, and that he knew he was going to die.

Jalaluddin nodded very slowly. "Koa, our people will know our names forever. Our people's enemies will know our names, and all will speak them in the same sentence."

The assembled suicide warriors pounded the table boards and roared.

Bolan shook his head. "What am I? Chopped liver?"

Laughter and mostly good-natured insults flew from all corners of the table. Koa turned to Aikane. "Uncle, what's the Hawaiian name for good with a golf club?"

More roars met this. Bolan was getting the feeling that Rasul hadn't been particularly popular with the troops. The

men laughed and talked but terrible purpose lurked behind
the levity. By mutual agreement it wasn't spoken of. Koa
was accorded demigod status. Marwin was taking a lot of
ribbing but fitting right in. Bolan caught Jalaluddin's eye.
The giant nodded and the two of them rose and moved back
into the trees.

"What troubles you, Makaha?"

Bolan spoke the truth. "You know I am not afraid to die."

"I know."

"Tino looks like shit."

Jalaluddin grunted and nodded.

"And where is my uncle Lau Lau? I heard a whisper he
was going to train us in *Lua*. Now no one has seen him."

Jalaluddin locked eyes with Bolan. "Your uncle Lau Lau
looks like shit, too."

Bolan's worst suspicions were confirmed. Radioactive
horror was on the way. "So it's one way, all the way."

"The results will be beyond expectation. Survival will
be slim. I promise you nothing save that the glory will be
forever."

Bolan met the man's gaze. The Hawaiian mystic's personality was nearly as powerful as his own. Jalaluddin suddenly
quirked his eyebrow. "Do you know how to drive a truck?"

Bolan scratched his head. "Jeez, it's been years. I had a
city job for a while back east, working for the corp yard. I
drove the cherry picker and the hauler. Nothing bigger than
a deuce and a half."

"Good, very good."

Bolan put a little disappointment in his voice. "You want
me to drive a truck? I thought you wanted me shooting."

"Well, Makaha—" Jalaluddin gave Bolan a smirk "—you
did kill one of our drivers."

The soldier grimaced as if he was being dressed down.

Jalaluddin laughed. "Not that I blame you, but you have
left a few gaps in our ranks."

"Well, shit." Bolan squared his shoulders. "You want me

on the trigger? I'm on it. You want me behind the wheel? I'm your wheelman."

"That is good." Jalaluddin turned back toward the feast and paused. "Do not worry, Makaha. Once you park the truck—if you are still alive—your shooting will be very important."

BOLAN SHOT THE RIFLE. It might have been the kava talking but he was becoming rather fond of the little 600. The muzzle blast from the magnum round was Fourth-of-July worthy, and Bolan hoped he wouldn't have to fire at night. One shot would flash blind him and announce his presence to the entire planet.

Koa sat in the shade sipping kava and enjoying the show. "I hear you're driving tomorrow."

Bolan loaded five more shells. "That is the rumor."

"They got some huts back in the woods. Rumor is Tino and Uncle Lau Lau are lying in hammocks. Rumor is they're never going to get out of them."

"I believe it." Bolan aimed at one of the white fuel drums beneath the ledge three hundred meters away. After the feast, Koa had spent the early afternoon teaching fundamentals. The terrorists weren't up to Farm standard but they were a lot more accurate than they had been an hour ago—most of the fuel drums now looked like Swiss cheese. Bolan squeezed the trigger. The 600 slammed back into his shoulder. The ragged hole his bullet tore in the drum was pleasingly larger than the ones the M-16s had printed.

"So we're hauling something radioactive?"

"It looks that way. The radiation meter wondered why Tino wasn't glowing this morning. He's taken an LD 100."

"What's that?"

"LD is lethal dose. One hundred stands for one hundred percent fatal. I'm thinking Tino got exposed to at least a thousand rads. Whatever Musa has—" Bolan shook his head "—it is not properly contained."

"Great! So we die bleeding out our eyes and crapping out our insides! Why don't you seem all that worried about it?"

"Actually I'm very worried." Bolan fired again and punched another hole in his vertical line.

"You don't look it!"

"Musa said I shot one of his drivers. That implies there are more than one. He's had you training up the boys and me practicing my marksmanship. He's keeping us away from it. He doesn't want his killers showing up at the target site coughing up blood. I'd bet there are two trucks. One will be hauling the merchandise and one hauling the shooters. We're shooters. We won't be exposed until it's time to make the magic happen, whatever that may be. Our job is to stop it before it happens, and with luck no one else gets exposed at all."

"Oh, well, I feel all better now."

"I live to serve." Bolan fired another shot. "This string could be lined up with a ruler."

"Well—" Koa sighed fatalistically "—watching you shoot actually does make me feel a little hopeful."

Bolan fired a final practice shot. He had deliberately raised his aim slightly and dotted the "i." "Talk like that will get you a date to prom."

Koa laughed. "Oh, Keo is your date. That kid worships you."

"I know." Bolan picked up his spent brass. Keo was like Ahmed—young, dumb and full of fervor, except without any of the young bodybuilder's malignance. He'd bet Keo was a decent kid, and probably had it very rough growing up. Then he'd met Musa Jalaluddin. He'd been starstruck and heard the Good Word. Jalaluddin had given Keo a community and a purpose. Now Keo was a true believer. Like all young people he thought he was immortal, and by the same token he was ready to die for glory and the cause.

Koa had spent the day shaping these mostly young warriors into soldiers. Bolan and Koa had broken bread with these men and accepted their adulation.

Tomorrow it was very likely they would have to kill them all or die trying.

Koa read Bolan's mind and sighed. "Yeah, I know."

Bolan had five more practice rounds. He rolled them between his fingers and slid them into his pocket.

Aikane came through the trees and held up his hands. "Cease fire!" Bolan opened the action on his rifle and leaned it against a tree. Aikane was nearly always friendly and quietly smiling but he looked positively grim as he approached. "Koa, Makaha."

Bolan and Koa nodded. "Uncle."

"Your uncle Lau Lau would like to see you." Aikane looked at Bolan. "Tino asked for you specifically, Makaha."

BOLAN GAZED DOWN upon the living dead. Most people had never seen an LD 100 case. Tino looked like an Auschwitz victim with Ebola.

It was a sight Bolan had seen far too many times, and given the current situation, there was a very good chance the radiation-ravaged thing that had once been a man was Bolan's future.

Koa was making a mighty attempt not to throw up.

Bolan spoke. "Tino."

Tino slowly opened his crusted and scabbed eyelids. He turned bleeding eyes up at Bolan. It took him a moment for recognition to glint through the broken blood vessels. "Makaha..."

"Yeah."

"You still think you can take me?"

"I told you, I only want your best."

"Told you, brah, my best is behind me."

"And thank God for that," Bolan muttered. "Damn gigantic son of a bitch. Nearly broke both my hands on your thick skull."

Tino's throat rattled and he winced as blood leaked from

the corners of his mouth. "Aw, brah, don't make me laugh... it hurts."

"You need anything?"

"Nah. Glad you came."

"No problem."

Tino's eyes were already closed again. Aikane gestured and Bolan and Koa followed him to another hut. A middle-aged woman Bolan hadn't met tended Uncle Lau Lau. He looked as though the zombie apocalypse had happened and he'd been turned about a week ago. Bolan wondered if the radiation had fried the RFID in his hand. Lau Lau was awake. He was clearly blind, and yet there was still a spark of vitality in the *Lua* master. "Koa...Makaha...that you?"

Koa took the ball. "Yes, Uncle."

"Promise me, Koa..."

"What, Uncle?"

"Do what you must do."

Koa stared at the dying man and spoke solemnly. "I will do what I have to do. I swear it."

Lau Lau nodded and groaned. "Makaha..."

"Yes, Uncle. I am here."

"You are new to the *ohana,* but defend it, fight for it."

Bolan considered the Hawaiians he had known in his life, the people he'd met at the luau, Melika, Koa, the inhabitants of the fiftieth state of the United States of America. He thought about the two men in their hammocks and what the word *ohana* really meant. "I will defend the *ohana* to the death."

18

Honolulu International Airport

The suicide squad disembarked. Bolan ran his hand over his head and felt where Hu's hair extensions and his own black locks used to be. It had been some time since he'd sported a military high-and-tight. The squad wore Army combat uniforms, and their flashes and badges showed they were the 299th Cavalry Regiment of the Hawaiian Army National Guard. Bolan had risked a great deal smuggling the razor in his boot but TSA had ushered them right through from their puddle jumper flight from the other side of the island with hardly a glance at their papers. They were soldiers on active duty, and everyone in the airport was happy to see them.

People waiting behind the gates for friends and loved ones actually cheered. A group of vets, some in wheelchairs and wearing the caps and even the uniforms of their service, saluted. Bolan knew these men, like other vets around the country, came once a week, some every day, to greet returning service men and women. Bolan and Koa saluted back and the rest of the squad followed suit. A little girl wearing a Girl Scout uniform charged the gate and pressed a tiny teddy bear into Bolan's hand. "Thank you for your service!"

Bolan's throat tightened just a little. "What's his name?"

"She's a girl, silly!"

"What's your name?"

"Yukiko!"

Bolan nodded very seriously at the little brown bear in his palm. "Her name is Kiko-Bear, and I will keep her forever."

Yukiko's smile lit up the terminal. "Yay!"

"Thank you very much, Yukiko."

"Daddy says you fight to keep us safe!"

"I try." Bolan nodded. "And I always will."

"Okay 'bye!" The little scout ran giggling back to her friends and chaperones.

Koa stage whispered, "Makaha, you're so handsome and strong. You're my hero…"

The squad laughed. Bolan tucked Kiko-Bear into one of his cargo pockets. "Screw you, Koa. I got a bear. You didn't get shit."

The squad marched out to the parking lot. A shuttle bus was waiting for them with Uncle Nui in the driver's seat. Rifle bags occupied most of the seats. Bolan found his 600 near the front and sat. Nui and their weapons had taken a different route into Honolulu. Jalaluddin and Aikane were nowhere to be seen. Bolan wondered at the risk of sending the squad through the terminal. The only explanation was that Jalaluddin and his people wanted the squad seen, and once whatever horror they intended to perpetrate was enacted, he wanted everyone to know who had done it. Nui drove them through town and toward the hills. The squad was quiet. They still had no idea what their mission was but they knew this was it.

The shuttle stopped at a light. Bolan glanced around Honolulu and his gaze locked on the newsstand at the corner. The situation went to worst-case scenario as Bolan read the full-page headline on the *Waikiki News:* President's Surprise Visit! Bolan elbowed Koa and jerked his head. Koa's eyes went wide. Bolan just caught a sub-header about the President dining with the troops as the shuttle pulled away. The squad had been kept incommunicado for the past forty-eight hours and now Bolan knew why. Koa shot Bolan a "Now what?" look.

Bolan was very tempted to hit the emergency beacon on his tracking device, but he still had no idea where Jalaluddin or the radioactive material might be.

Nui took the shuttle through the suburbs and out of town. They headed into the hills. More of Bolan's suspicions were confirmed when they pulled up to a fire road entrance. Two military trucks sat parked in the shade. Jalaluddin and Uncle Aikane stood under the trees and both were in uniform. "Everybody arm up and move out," Nui ordered.

Bolan hit his emergency beacon. The jungle camp had been in the middle of the forest hours from Happy Valley. Bolan was hoping Agent Rind had moved the team to Honolulu so he could marshal his resources and move in any direction when Bolan emerged. The bad part was that the strike team would be coming in blind, but there was nothing to be done about that. The squad unzipped their rifle bags and strapped into their web gear. Bolan checked the loads in his rifle. The five practice rounds he had stolen were still secreted in the rifle bag's padding. He stowed his ammunition and tucked his knives away.

Marwin squeezed his bulk past Bolan and the soldier felt a pistol press against his back. "Take this, bro. I got a bad feeling."

Bolan took one of Hu's .38s and tucked it into the small of his back. "How'd you manage that?"

"No one expects the fat guy to be smart, and no one expects him to be light-fingered."

"You're a good man, Marwin." They climbed down and joined the squad.

Jalaluddin inspected them. "Good, very good. Koa, you will ride in the lead truck with me and Makaha. Everyone else in the back. Your uncle Aikane will drive the second truck. Go!"

Bolan clambered up into the cab and got the old girl in gear. Koa and Jalaluddin climbed in and the big Hawaiian handed him a map with a route highlighted in red. "Follow this."

Bolan nodded. Their destination did not seem very far away. They dipped into a little valley and drove up to a chainlink fence. The fence surrounded a facility consisting of a small blockhouse with some very large pipes and vales coming in and out of the ground. It all looked very new.

Bolan read the sign on the fence: Honolulu Water District Pearl Pumping Station.

According to the sign, the new station proudly served the service men and women at Pearl Harbor. A potbellied man in a guard uniform came up to the gate. His nametag read Mahoe. He grinned up at Jalaluddin. "What's happening, fellas?"

"Security."

Mahoe blinked. "But I'm security."

Jalaluddin grinned conspiratorially and nodded at Pearl Harbor below. "Do you know who's down there today?"

Mahoe grinned back. "The Prez!"

"You're supposed to officially start pumping in…what? Two hours?"

"An hour," Mahoe corrected.

"Well, some reporters and dignitaries are going to show up and take pictures. The big kahunas at Pearl want a few of the guardsmen standing around and looking sharp for the cameras. Me and mine will stay out of your way, unless you need something, and don't be afraid to ask."

"Thanks."

"Oh, and I hear they're sending up a catering truck. Make sure you grab some grind."

"Thanks!" Mahoe happily opened the gate. Bolan and Aikane drove in and parked in the tiny parking lot by the blockhouse. A dozen workers in orange vests and safety helmets were standing around but they weren't working. They mostly smoked and drank sodas and appeared to be waiting. Other than flipping the switches, they were here for the cameras, as well.

"Everybody out!" Jalaluddin ordered. "No killing. Not yet. Follow my lead."

The squad jumped out, rifles in hand. Some of the workers looked askance at the armed squad. Mahoe walked over from the gate. "Jeez, brah. You going to give the pump a twenty-one-gun salute or something?"

Jalaluddin cracked his rifle butt across Mahoe's jaw and dropped him, then ripped a full auto burst into the air. "Down! Down! Down! Everyone down!" Workers shouted and screamed but nearly all dropped. All they saw were Hawaiian soldiers. The squad gleefully clubbed the few who didn't drop until they were on the ground. "Get their phones! Koa, take Keo and two men. Clear the blockhouse! Makaha, stick with me. Everyone else, start tying them up!"

Nui produced rope and the squad started immobilizing prisoners.

Koa swept the blockhouse like a pro. "No one inside! They got a yellow ribbon that ain't cut yet!"

"Good! Watch the perimeter!" Jalaluddin smiled at Bolan. "Would you like to see something?"

"Well, since it's my last day on earth, sure."

"Follow me." The big Hawaiian walked back to the second truck. Uncle Aikane stood by it. Aikane wasn't looking very well. Bolan's skin prickled at the rads he imagined were coming off the truck. Jalaluddin walked to the rear of the truck bed and threw back the canvas curtain.

The two-and-a-half-ton truck was being used as a tanker.

The military used the same type of truck to haul fuel, and woodland fire services used the same rig as a portable water source. Bolan figured he was looking at twelve thousand gallons of radioactive horror. "What's in it?"

"Water."

Bolan raised an eyebrow. "We brought water to the water station?"

"This is water from Fukushima. Do you know what that is?"

Bolan kept the revulsion off his face. "That Japanese power plant. That got hit by the tsunami."

"Correct."

"You're going to poison the water?"

"How do they enslave us?" Jalaluddin asked in return.

Bolan looked out toward the gleaming waters of Pearl Harbor. "The military."

"Correct. Our islands can no longer live without the money they bring. We service the service men of our oppressors. It is a sickness, and a dependency. One we are going to wean ourselves off, today."

Bolan examined the tank. "Is that going to be enough?"

"The initial poisoning will be quite brutal, but of course the radioactive water will quickly disperse through the system and dilute. There will be a purge of the system, and a massive cleanup effort. But thousands of people will sicken and die for years to come. The revulsion of the Hawaiian people will ensure that the base is never reopened, nor will they allow such massive military bases to ever be built in Hawaii again. For those who wish to see Hawaii free and sovereign? Radioactive horror at U.S. military bases is a good place to start."

"How did you get it?"

"To this day things are quite confused at Fukushima. There are thousands of foreign workers and specialists. Some water is treated and deemed releasable in the atmosphere. Some goes into the sea. Much is transported away and placed in storage sites. Such as this water, which has crawled in the belly of a broken reactor. Where there is the will, and the money, there is a way, Makaha. And there are others who wish to see the United States' power in the Pacific greatly diminished.

Bolan sighed. "It makes me sad."

Jalaluddin's brow clouded dangerously. "Why?"

"Pearl is ours. It is a shame to poison it."

The big Hawaiian regained his smile. "Makaha, Pearl Harbor is a cancer on our Islands. This is the radiation treatment."

Bolan grunted and smiled as if he got it.

"Would you care to live?"

"I'm not afraid to die."

"I know that, and that is why I ask. You and Koa are extremely valuable to our cause, and that is why I have kept you away from the tanker and what it contains. You will most likely die, but this is only one of many battles to come."

"What do you want me to do?"

"For the moment, consider yourself my bodyguard. Aikane will direct the men in transferring the water into the mains." Jalaluddin turned and started walking back toward the blockhouse. The Executioner raised his rifle and pulled the trigger. The hammer fell with a dull click on a dud round. He flicked the bolt and pulled the trigger again. The dead click of the hammer was his death sentence. Bolan found himself staring down the barrel of a U.S. Military Beretta in Jalaluddin's hand.

"You disappoint me, Makaha."

Bolan's eyes slid to Koa in time to see Aikane buckle him with a blow to the kidneys. The big man threw Koa to the ground and pinned him. The squad looked around in consternation. Jalaluddin twitched the muzzle of his pistol. "Drop it."

Bolan dropped his rifle.

"You are going to survive today, Makaha, but you'll wish you hadn't."

Bolan relaxed and prepared to draw down on a man who already had the drop on him. Some of the squad shouted in alarm and rifles began firing. A black Lincoln Town Car rammed the gate.

Bolan slapped leather.

Bolan drew down. Bits of unburned smokeless powder peppered his cheek, and he heard the zip of a 9 mm pass by his
left ear as Jalaluddin's shot missed. Bolan dug the revolver
out of his belt and shoved it forward. The big Hawaiian dived
for the truck and rolled beneath as Bolan's bullet tore turf.
Bolan dropped prone. Jalaluddin cleared the chassis and was
starting to roll up to his feet. Bolan fired and Jalaluddin
jerked but then he disappeared behind the driver's wheel. The
soldier popped up and spun on Aikane and Koa. Aikane bellowed like a bull. "I'll kill him! I'll snap his neck like a—"

Bolan shot Aikane in the face.

Koa grunted as the dead bulk of the Hawaiian fell on top
of him. The pumping station descended into chaos. Rind
had spun the Town Car broadside to form cover. His team
had spilled out the opposite side and he, De Jong and Belle
were unleashing hell with Korean K-7s. The shackled civilians lying in the dirt screamed and screamed. Bullets ripped
across the Lincoln as the suicide squad addressed the invaders. Marwin took the opportunity to double tap three
of them in the back with his revolver. Then his bulk jiggled
grotesquely as he charged and tackled a fourth and began
pistol whipping him.

Koa had emerged from beneath Uncle Aikane's dead-
weight. "Koa!" Bolan shouted. "Get—"

Keo came around the front of the truck and shot Koa. Koa
dropped. Keo lowered his aim. "Traitor!"

Bolan fired. Keo's burst went wild and tore turf. He tried to bring his muzzle around on Bolan. Bolan pulled the trigger four more times in rapid succession, shattering the young man's chest and taking whatever future he might have had. The soldier scooped up the 600 and racked out the three remaining dummy rounds. He replaced them with the five he had retained from his practice session. Bolan ran to Koa. The Hawaiian had risen and found an M-16. He had a bad wound low on his right side but it would take some time to kill him. "Musa and Nui!"

"They're already over the fence!" Koa snarled. "Go!"

"FBI!" Rind roared. "On your knees!"

The three remaining suicide soldiers dropped their rifles and fell to their knees. Bolan ran around the truck and caught sight of Jalaluddin's size-fourteen boot prints in the dirt. He also saw De Jong lying beneath the bumper of the Lincoln with a head wound.

Belle aimed her submachine gun one-handed as the other lay bloody along her side.

"Rind!" Bolan bellowed. "We don't know if they have backup. The truck is loaded with radioactive material. Defend it!"

Agent Rind tossed away his spent K-7 and drew his machine Glocks. "Go!"

Marwin shouted from behind. "I'm with you, bro!"

"Stay with Rind!" Bolan hit the fence and was over it and into the trees. Jalaluddin might have been a master of Hawaiian martial arts and prophet of the apocalypse, but he was not a woodsman. The trail he left was easy to follow. Nui was running in Jalaluddin's footsteps and Bolan could tell by the spoor Uncle Nui was starting to lag. Bolan could hear Marwin crashing through the underbrush behind him but there was no way to stop him save shooting him, and the morbidly obese Filipino was already falling far behind.

Bolan fell into a hunter's lope that allowed him to examine the trail ahead of him. Nui was an immensely powerful man but he was old. Jalaluddin was carrying the physique of a professional wrestling champion at the physical peak of perfection, but there was a good chance that he was not a distance runner. Neither were professional soldiers. Bolan was betting one or both would weary and start making the mistakes of the exhausted. Despite a spate of bad fights and brutal excursions, Bolan was one of the most fighting fit humans on earth, and he currently had a good night's sleep and breakfast under his belt. And he knew something about running the bad guys down.

Bolan took another hillside. He could see where Nui had grabbed and torn trees and roots to pull himself up. The soldier dropped short of the crest. A hump of rocks blocked the left. Bolan took a hanging trail of roots and erosion and pulled a Spider-Man to his right. He could hear Nui wheezing.

Bolan took a chance and put the 600's sling between his teeth. He grabbed two saplings hanging off the hill and kip-upped to the plateau. Nui's jaw dropped in horror as Bolan appeared like a magic trick. Nui leveled his M-16 and his burst ripped through the trees as Bolan ducked. Bolan fired from the hip and the .350 Magnum ripped through Nui's side and turned him. The soldier flicked his bolt and fired as Nui ripped off another burst. Nui took the hit through the guts and screamed as he kept coming forward firing. Bolan and Nui exchanged fire from nearly spitting distance, except Bolan's big-game bullets kept smashing the Hawaiian off his aim. Nui's assault rifle clacked open on empty. He dropped the weapon and charged at Bolan screaming Hawaiian imprecations with his massive hands curled into claws.

Bolan took a heartbeat to raise his aim and blew Nui's brains out.

Nui toppled to the sward.

Bolan flicked the bolt. The 600 was empty, but he traversed the hilltop as if he still held thunder. "Surrender, Musa! And I'll—"

Jalaluddin exploded out of the underbrush right next to Bolan. The massive Hawaiian psychopath might not have been an experienced gunfighter or woodsman but he had skills. Bolan wasn't used to being surprised. He had spent a great deal of time and effort training to make that impossible.

Jalaluddin's huge hand wrapped around the hot barrel of Bolan's rifle. Bolan's arm was still in the sling and his limb was nearly torn out of its socket as the weapon was ripped out of his grasp. The big Hawaiian flipped the rifle around like a toy and caught it by the grip. He slid his finger into the trigger guard and effortlessly pointed the rifle at Bolan one-handed as if it was a giant pistol. Bolan ignored the Hawaiian and rolled his arm in its socket. His shoulder felt as though it was on fire but everything was still connected. "Rifle's empty."

"Makaha, I—" Bolan produced his Buck knife, snapped it open by the blade and threw it in nearly one motion. Jalaluddin didn't flinch or dodge. He simply tilted his head to one side and let the knife flash past his face. It stuck into the trunk of a tree behind him. His head stayed tilted and the mocking eyebrow rose once more. It rose a millimeter higher as Bolan took out his second knife and snapped it open by the handle.

Bolan considered his options. They weren't good. Jalaluddin was larger than him, stronger than him, faster than him as well as far more skilled at hand-to-hand. Jalaluddin quite clearly, and smugly, was aware of Bolan's dilemma, as well. He made a sympathetic noise. "Despite having only half a Hawaiian heart, I had fostered hopes for you in mine, Makaha."

Bolan let his tongue drip scorn. "I'm about as much Hawaiian as you're Zulu, idiot."

Jalaluddin's brows drew down.

He clearly wasn't used to disrespect and Bolan worked it. "One coating of Man-tan, some hair extensions, a can of SPAM and you and your whole *ohana* were fooled. Oh, and you think I'm working alone? You Hawaiian hillbillies! I swear, you're like children."

Psychosis flashed for a hideous second in the big Hawaiian's eyes, and then he smiled. He flipped the rifle again so that the barrel landed in his palm and he backhanded the weapon against a koa tree. Springs flew like shrapnel and the stock broke in two different directions. Bolan thought that was a waste of a mighty fine little rifle. On the other hand shattering a laminated stock one-handed was one hell of an intimidation maneuver. It was also extremely troublesome that Jalaluddin hadn't pulled the trigger when Bolan had thrown the knife. The Hawaiian hadn't even bothered to see if Bolan was lying about the weapon being loaded before smashing it. He didn't seem much concerned about the knife in the tree behind him, much less the knife in Bolan's hand.

Jalaluddin spoke to Bolan as though he was a small child in the wrong. "You are not working alone. You are working with Koa. I see no gunships or Navy SEALs. I do not yet know who you are or what you represent, but you are alone. You're going to die alone and—"

Bolan attacked.

He took a stutter step and dragged the toe of his boot along the ground. Bolan kicked it up and sent a decent clod of dirt and debris at Jalaluddin's face. Bolan came in low with his knife edge-up to zipper-cut the big Hawaiian from his bladder to his sternum.

The soldier barely saw the hand that chopped into his wrist and sent the knife spinning away. Jalaluddin's backhand nearly unhinged Bolan's jaw. The soldier staggered back seeing stars. Bolan's head stopped just short of exploding as Jalaluddin gave Bolan the hand again, forehand, upside the skull at full strength. The soldier went sprawling in the dirt.

The man was bitch-slapping him to death. Bolan rolled badly but sheer instinct allowed him to roll up with a knee under him. He was off balance but lurched upward raising his hands in a palsied, all too stunned defense.

Jalaluddin was upon him.

The huge Hawaiian knocked aside Bolan's hands and seized him. Jalaluddin bodily pressed the soldier over his head and hurled him against the koa. Bolan's body curled sideways around the trunk with bone-shattering force and he slid off the towering hardwood to the forest floor like a cracked egg. He barely had time for one ragged gasp as Jalaluddin picked him up like a sack of potatoes, inverted him, and charged the tree as if it was a football blocking sled. Jalaluddin was the hammer. The massive tree was the anvil. Bolan was the sack of meat between a rock and a hard place as they collided. His vision went dark as he ate tree upside down and his every internal organ violently compressed. He didn't feel himself hit the ground. Despite the fact that Bolan was now limp he presented no trouble to Jalaluddin as the Hawaiian picked him up once more and hurled him at nothing in particular, as though he was a human caber. The soldier flew through the air and met the ground without even a pretense of trying to slap out or roll.

Bolan lay facedown in the grass. It seemed like a very nice place and he never wanted to leave it. Physically he had red lights blinking across the board, but his battle instincts were still semi-consciously running assessments. He didn't feel the telltale nausea of broken bones. He took a ragged breath and air filled his lungs without burning agony. Bolan deliberately blinked twice and his vision slewed back into the binocular. His mental tactical center was also firing urgent messages.

Jalaluddin hadn't snapped his spine or crushed his skull. The big Hawaiian was playing with him, and the psycho wasn't finished. Jalaluddin's voice sounded as though it came from underwater or very far away as he spoke. "Get up, Makaha." Bolan yawned and spit blood. The second "Get up" was much clearer. The soldier got to his elbows and knees. He kept his right side away from Jalaluddin. He got one foot under him and groaned as he faked toppling to his right. The groaning and the toppling didn't take much faking.

"Try harder, Makaha."

Bolan pushed himself back up. He slid his fingers inside his boot as he did and palmed his concealed razor. Bolan fell back to his hands and knees and pitched a coughing fit as he pinched the blade loose and low between his thumb and forefinger. His little finger flicked the handle open along his inner forearm and held it in place. He left his two middle fingers open. To conceal the razor, Bolan let his arm hang against his side as if it was hurt as he rose. He didn't need to fake reeling as his vision skewed again. The soldier took long breaths and let his vision clear. He bared his bloody teeth at his foe in a dead man's smile. "Screw…you…"

"Good!" Jalaluddin nodded. "Do you know what I am going to do now?"

"I don't know." Bolan spat more blood and was surprised no teeth came out with it. "Bundle me?"

"Yes, Makaha. I am going to bundle you, alive. I will spend a day doing it, and during this time you will tell me absolutely everything about who you are and who you work for. Then I am going to bury you, up to your neck, bundled, in the forest, in a small pit that will accommodate your new size. I will keep you alive, feeding you like a *poi* dog. After you have rotted and tenderized for a week, and the ants have eaten your eyes, I will disinter you, and I will barbecue you, alive. You will die screaming in my fire." Jalaluddin smiled beatifically as he ran the movie in his mind. "Then I, and the *ohana*, will feast upon your flesh and eat your soul."

Bolan was fairly certain this wasn't Jalaluddin's first trip to the syncretism rodeo. "You know?" Bolan let blood and spit pool under his tongue. "You are one sick bastard."

"Is that the best you can do, Makaha? The gods are watching."

"Okay." Bolan considered a proper response. "We should

have let the Japanese take these islands, so they could have taught you and your inbred, poi-eating, screw-faced *ohana* fear, respect and personal hygiene."

Jalaluddin grinned delightedly. "I am going to knock you unconscious now, and take you to the place of woe."

Bolan spit blood at the psycho's face and despite his condition threw a right-hand lead with surprising snap and alacrity. Jalaluddin's huge hand enclosed Bolan's fist as he caught the punch like a softball. He grinned through the blood and spittle spackling his face. "Oh, Makaha, you—" The big Hawaiian hissed and his eyes flared as Bolan twisted his fist in Jalaluddin's grip and yanked. The man reflexively released Bolan as the razor sliced his palm to the bone. Bolan threw another right but rather than a punch it was more like the paw-swipe of a bear. Jalaluddin tucked his head as he recoiled and rather than cutting the Hawaiian from carotid to Adam's apple, Bolan laid open his jaw from his ear to his chin. Blood flew in a spectacular fashion and Jalaluddin's face fell open.

Bolan dropped to one knee and swung a razor-loaded uppercut at the man's crotch. Jalaluddin was still fast, far too fast, and Bolan was in bad shape. His right hand struck like a snake and seized Bolan's wrist in a bone-crusher as Bolan knew he would. The soldier allowed it and simply dropped the razor into his left hand.

Bolan snapped the razor edge-up against Jalaluddin's wrist. He found the groove beneath the heel of the Hawaiian's hand as though he was deboning a chicken and carved. Bolan opened Jalaluddin's wrist from radius to ulna.

The soldier barely managed to cross his arms in an X-block as the Hawaiian's knee hurtled toward his head like a battering ram. Bolan's arm bones ached like tetanus with the effort of stopping the blow and he lost the razor. Blood showered over the soldier as the big Hawaiian raised his hands and sent a second knee strike and then a third through Bolan's crumbling defenses. The third knee clipped Bolan's chin and sent him toppling backward. He managed to pull a decent back roll and stood shakily with his back against the koa. Bolan reached up. His hand closed around the knife he had thrown and he pulled it free from the bark. Jalaluddin came forward, bleeding a river out of his arms, but his feet were shifting like a capoeira expert.

Bolan flung his Buck knife a second time at Jalaluddin's face. The Hawaiian brought up his mangled appendages in defense and the knife stuck in his already mutilated left palm like stigmata. Jalaluddin stared in disbelief. He tried to pull the knife out but his right hand was nonfunctional. The flashing, all-knowing eyes now registered doubt. Bolan took that moment of his crisis to take three big steps backward. He bent and picked up his broken 600. The scope was gone and the rest of the rifle's shattered stock fell away as he hefted it. Bolan held an eighteen-and-a-half-inch Remington cold-forged barrel with an action, bolt and a bit of shattered trigger assembly hanging off the end. He took a deep breath and projected far more strength than he had left as he tapped the action into his palm. "Last chance, Musa. Surrender or this gets rough."

Jalaluddin's pupils narrowed to pinholes of insanity. His left hand twitched and jerked from severed tendons and nerves misfiring. His right hand hung by threads and the only reason he hadn't bled to death yet was that the veins had collapsed. Nonetheless he was bleeding rivers.

"Last chance for romance," Bolan advised. He gauged the insanity of the bleeding-out Hawaiian and, based on his own condition, decided it was now or never. "I won't bundle you or barbecue you, but I will tenderize you for transport. Hit the dirt and I won't ask you to raise your hands."

Jalaluddin screamed. He charged forward, dirt flying from beneath his feet and blood ribboning out of his arms. The big Hawaiian leaped into the air and butterfly kicked at Bolan's head. Bolan dodged. Jalaluddin twisted in midair and sent a reverse kick with his back leg. It was just about the most athletic martial arts move Bolan had ever had directed at him. He didn't meet the attack or try to block it. It wasn't very dignified, but he sat down beneath the flurry of feet and rolled to one side. Jalaluddin literally landed sideways on the koa and kicked off. His right foot scythed for Bolan's head. If he hadn't seen it with his own eyes, Bolan would have sworn it was a Hollywood special effect and Jalaluddin was fighting suspended by wires.

Unfortunately for Jalaluddin, he wasn't.

Gravity still constrained the huge Hawaiian, and jumping, spinning and kicking off a tree left him with almost no momentum or force behind his last blow. It also left him with no ability to alter his course. Bolan stood. Jalaluddin landed and as he did Bolan snapped the barreled action of the Remington into the Hawaiian's nearly severed right hand. The big man screamed. Bolan drew back and swung the steel like a forehand shot in tennis. Jalaluddin took the bolt assembly to the face. Teeth flew. The cheekbone gave and the bolt assembly burst apart. Bolan summoned what remained of his flagging strength and laid on. He ducked behind Jalaluddin and slammed the action into the man's left knee. Jalaluddin buckled. Bolan spun and kneecapped the cannibal-prophet-killer's right leg and dropped him. The man flopped to the ground screaming and screaming. Bolan broke one elbow and then the other as the big Hawaiian flailed his arms in defense. "Kill you!" Jalaluddin howled. "Kill you!"

Bolan took the barreled action in both hands and began letting it rise and fall as if it was a pickax and he was trying to dig a hole through Jalaluddin until he saw China. He laid it on until the Hawaiian was reduced to bubbling and twitching.

Bolan fell back against the koa and sat.

Jalaluddin bubbled and twitched, but he kept on breathing as Bolan had intended.

Bolan laid the blood-crusted rifle barrel across his knees. He took halting, hacking breaths as he struggled to fill his lungs. Slowly the soldier's breathing returned to normal. He lifted the rifle barrel as he caught sound in the trees. Marwin staggered out of the shrubbery with an M-16 with the bayonet fixed. He had sweated through his uniform and his shirtfront was covered with his breakfast from where he had puked during his uphill, manatee-run through the Hawaiian hillsides. Marwin tottered forward gasping and wiped his chin. "Makaha!"

Bolan nodded. It was just about the last physical action he was capable of. "Marwin."

Marwin looked around as he bent over and laid his rifle across his knees. "Did I miss it?"

"Yeah."

Marwin looked as though he might start crying or throw up again. "I'm sorry, bro. I'm so sorry. I just couldn't keep up."

"Don't worry about it, buddy. Could have used you, but be glad you missed it. It wasn't pretty."

"You okay?" Marwin straightened. "You don't look so good."

"I've been better," Bolan admitted. "How's De Jong?"

Marwin stopped short of whimpering. "My man's dead…"

"I'm sorry." Bolan was starting to believe Marwin had serious man-crush issues with his boss. "He really came through. The Philippines lost a warrior today."

Marwin snuffled. "You know? He really liked you, and Koa. He loved rolling with Rind. He died like a gangsta. I know he's glad. He's up there, upstairs, and proud." Marwin wept openly. "I'm Filipino." He slammed his fist against his chest. "Original Gangsta, for life. Jagon De Jong? He will live in the hearts of all OGs, in our Islands, in these Islands, for life."

Bolan coughed and felt it around his floating ribs. "I'll always remember him."

Marwin blinked and gave Bolan a lip-quivering smile. "That's very kind of you."

"You don't got any water, do you?"

"No, sorry, bro."

"That's all right. Thanks for coming on my six. It means a lot."

Marwin stared disbelievingly at the bubbling side of beef that had once been Musa Jalaluddin. "You took him? Hand-to-hand?"

No snappy comeback came to Bolan. The soldier just concentrated on breathing. "He just had to be stopped."

Marwin looked at Bolan with man-crush eyes. "Dude, can I roll with you?"

"Dude, you and me been rolling for days."

Marwin blushed.

"Do me a favor?"

Marwin nodded eagerly. "Anything!"

"Take care of Belle. I'll deal with her creditors, but don't let her get into any more messed-up shit meantime."

"You know?" Marwin wiped his nose with his giant wrist. "That was pretty much my job already, until you showed up."

Bolan and Marwin looked upward as military helicopters thundered overhead.

"You want me to get you some water or something?"

"Do you know CPR?"

Marwin started crying again. "You're not going to die, are you?"

"No, but you could sit with me for a while until Rind gets here." It took all of Bolan's remaining strength to turn his head and look at Jalaluddin. "And don't let that bastard croak. I want to have words with him."

20

Tripler Army Medical Center

Bolan and Koa sat in wheelchairs and took in the sun. Bolan didn't feel as though he needed one; he had no specific life-threatening injuries. The general prognosis was combat fatigue and having been beaten to a pulp. He wasn't going to argue as Melika rubbed his shoulders. Hu was rubbing Koa's. The Hawaiian was going to be off active duty for the Farm security detail for a while. Tripler was the headquarters of the Pacific Regional Medical Command and it was one of the most gorgeous hospitals on earth. Hawaii was a good place to be injured or wounded. Bolan glanced up as Rind and Belle entered the solarium. Belle's arm was in a sling.

Bolan lifted his chin at her injury. "How's the arm?"

Belle made a face. "It's going to take time."

"Kick the drugs, get back in shape, and someday I may call upon you again."

Belle smirked. "You're cute."

"I'm serious."

"I know."

"Where's Marwin?"

Belle's face fell. "He took Jagon home. To his family. To see him buried. I couldn't go. It's…complicated."

Bolan let that lie. "Is he okay?"

"Oh, the De Jong family loves him. He'll be fine." Belle's lips quirked. "He was practically in love with Jagon."

"I caught that vibe."

"He has a serious crush on you."

Bolan shrugged.

"So do I."

Melika's fingers dug a little harder into Bolan's shoulders.

Belle gave Bolan her best smirk. "A three-hundred-pound Filipino leg-breaker and a transgendered gun moll both have crushes on you. How does that make you feel?"

Bolan considered. "Awesome?"

Koa shook his head. "You know? No shit. You really are my hero."

Agent Rind grinned and joined Koa in the head-shaking department. "Dude, you are awesome, but do you know the trouble I'm in right now with the Bureau?"

"I can guess, and I'm sorry, but whatever happens? You can keep the machine pistols."

"Epic!"

"Plus I'll have my people talk to yours."

Koa raised his hand. "Can I ask a question?"

"Shoot."

"What now?"

Bolan stared out into the lush hillsides surrounding Tripler. Hawaii was one of the most beautiful places on earth, a genuine Island paradise, and someone had taken a gigantic stab at destabilizing it. The President of the United States had avoided drinking a radioactive cocktail, and Pearl Harbor had dodged becoming a twenty-first-century version of *On the Beach*.

But Bolan had to give the enemy their due. Their attack had been nearly flawless. Only his and Koa's interference as outsider wildcards had turned the tide.

They had met some good people, and some good bad people who had helped. Far too much luck had been involved. The Fukushima water had been contained. Multinational investigations were looking into all levels of the breach, but Bolan had a terrible feeling there was more out there. Musa

Jalaluddin was done. The syncretism *ohana* movement in Happy Valley had been crushed. The fact remained that there was a new player in the centuries-old power struggle in the Pacific. Or it was an old player with a new plan, and Bolan had no idea who it was. Making Jalaluddin talk would be problematic.

"We need to get healthy, Koa. Back in fighting shape. This isn't over."

* * * * *

My name is Callum Ormond.
I am sixteen
and I am a hunted fugitive . . .

CONSPIRACY 365

BOOK TWELVE: DECEMBER

To James

Scholastic Canada Ltd.
604 King Street West, Toronto, Ontario M5V 1E1, Canada

Scholastic Inc.
557 Broadway, New York, NY 10012, USA

Scholastic Australia Pty Limited
PO Box 579, Gosford, NSW 2250, Australia

Scholastic New Zealand Limited
Private Bag 94407, Botany, Manukau 2163, New Zealand

Scholastic Children's Books
Euston House, 24 Eversholt Street, London NW1 1DB, UK

Library and Archives Canada Cataloguing in Publication
Lord, Gabrielle
        December / Gabrielle Lord.
(Conspiracy 365)
ISBN 978-1-4431-0479-1
        I. Title. II. Series: Lord, Gabrielle. Conspiracy 365
(Toronto, Ont.).

PZ7.L869De 2010   j823'.914   C2010-901823-0

First published by Scholastic Australia in 2010.
This edition published in Canada by Scholastic Canada Ltd. in 2010.
Text copyright © Gabrielle Lord, 2010.
Illustrations copyright © Scholastic Australia, 2010.
Illustrations by Rebecca Young.
Graphics by Nicole Leary.
Cover copyright © Scholastic Australia, 2010.
Cover design by Natalie Winter.
Cover photography: boy's face by Wendell Levi Teodoro (www.zeduce.org)
© Scholastic Australia 2010; close-up of boy's face by Michael Bagnall © Scholastic
Australia 2010; man jumping © Chengas/Corbis; person running © Monkey Business
Images/Shutterstock; fire © Rui Ferreira/Shutterstock; man running © Radoslaw
Korga/Shutterstock; cloister © Grischa Georgiew/Shutterstock; stone wall © Stephen
Aaron Rees/Shutterstock; smoke © Gershberg Yuri/Shutterstock; castle © Gabrielle
Lord. Internal photography: paper on pages 193, 192 and 168 © istockphoto.com/
Tomasz Pietryszek; aged paper on page 024 © istockphoto.com/Mike Bentley.
All rights reserved.

6 5 4 3 2 1   Printed in Canada 116   10 11 12 13

CONSPIRACY 365

BOOK TWELVE: DECEMBER

GABRIELLE LORD

Scholastic Canada Ltd.
Toronto New York London Auckland Sydney
Mexico City New Delhi Hong Kong Buenos Aires

PREVIOUSLY...

1 NOVEMBER

The Special FX canister finally explodes, giving me enough cover to escape the ring of cops and the chopper. My hunters soon lock onto my position again, but my double—Ryan Spencer—comes to my rescue. We swap clothes and he acts as a decoy, fooling the cops and luring them away from me.

2 NOVEMBER

The Caesar shift hasn't revealed anything hidden within the Ormond Riddle, and we wonder if it only applies to the missing two lines. Somehow, we must travel to Ireland, visit the Keeper of Rare Books, and investigate further.

Anxiety is high as Boges, Winter and I talk about the DMO. Just after we realise someone's hacked my blog, repeating "November 11" all over the page, we're interrupted by the arrival of cops—Winter's building is surrounded!

I make a terrifying leap from one rooftop to another, and urge Winter and Boges to flee as well. On my run from Lesley Street, I stop by Ryan Spencer's apartment. It turns out his birthday is November 11—the mysterious date from my blog!

6 NOVEMBER
Nelson Sharkey thinks he can arrange a fake passport for my trip to Ireland. I hope that the remainder of my gold stash will cover the cost.

9 NOVEMBER
We need more money, so Winter decides she'll steal some from the cash-lined cigar boxes in Sligo's "scram bag," hidden inside his wardrobe.

11 NOVEMBER
The day my blog hacker warned me about has arrived. I'm too nervous to go anywhere, so I keep low in the treehouse that has become my latest refuge.

13 NOVEMBER
Boges and I wait outside Sligo's house as Winter attempts to steal his money, while pretending to be over for a swim.

Winter arrives back at the beach rendezvous

point with good news—she snuck out ten thousand dollars for us!

14 NOVEMBER

Back at the treehouse, Winter tells me more about the day of her parents' fatal car crash. She wants to move on, but believes she can only do so after she's seen the wreck and confirmed whether the crash really was an accident or whether something more sinister was involved.

17 NOVEMBER

On my way to meet Eric Blair, I am captured by two burly thugs who take me to see Murray "Toecutter" Durham. Toecutter is deathly ill, and wants to make a confession. He reveals that he was involved in the abduction of twin babies, years ago, and failed to dispose of them. After a scare with the police, the babies were separated. One was left behind and later returned to his family—me—while the other was kept by Toecutter until adopted out, illegally. This baby was Samuel—my twin—now known as Ryan Spencer.

Back at the treehouse, I call Mum to tell her Samuel is alive.

18 NOVEMBER

At the library I find another article about the

twin baby abduction. In it, Rafe was interviewed, showing a side of his relationship with Dad I had never seen. They used to be very close.

Finally I meet Eric Blair. I realise that he is the crazy guy from New Year's Eve who warned me I had 365 days to survive! Blair says he suffered an unknown viral infection and doesn't remember the incident!

20 NOVEMBER
While investigating Rathbone's list of nicknames, we discover that he will be soon heading to Dublin. He could beat us to the Ormond Singularity!

24 NOVEMBER
Eric Blair poses the question—what if the illness that killed my dad, and caused his own illness, was not a virus, but something deliberate?

29 NOVEMBER
The cops have taken Boges for questioning, Winter is scared, and Sligo is becoming increasingly suspicious. I receive a message from Winter, but before I can call her, I am crash-tackled by police! Just as they are dragging me to the car, Sharkey appears and presents my fake passport, saving me with my new identity.

I now have a few missed messages from Winter,

but am spotted by Capsicum Cop and chased into a sports stadium with wild crowds of fans. Somehow I end up running onto the field with the players, and a massive close-up of my face appears on the big-screen. The crowd is chanting my name as I'm pursued. I run down to the underground quarters and am forced to find a hiding place in a locker room. I jump inside an empty koala mascot costume—successfully hiding in plain sight when the cops search the place.

30 NOVEMBER

Rafe admits he believes I saved him at the chapel and that he's been trying to protect me from the dangers of the Ormond Singularity.

While I'm waiting for Winter at the beach, Griff Kirby shows up, telling me that he saw her being tossed into a black Subaru. Sligo has her! We race to the scene of the kidnapping, then to Sligo's car yard. There we see Zombie Two locking up a shipping container—Winter might be trapped inside. Zombie Two and Bruno are alerted to our presence and they attack. Before we know it, we're tied up and shoved into the container ourselves.

Griff makes a horrifying discovery—Winter's body, cold and lifeless. Her voicemail messages reveal that she'd found out Sligo killed her parents by cutting the brake lines of their car. She confronted him, alone, because I didn't call her back. I wasn't there for her.

Now it's too late.

1 DECEMBER

31 days to go . . .

Car yard

12:00 am

I couldn't move, couldn't speak, almost couldn't breathe. Winter's final words echoed through the black, suffocating space we were locked in, like a haunting message from the grave.

I held her slumped body next to mine. Her wild hair fell over my knees and onto the floor of the container. I tried to say her name, but all that came out was a croaking sound.

She'd saved my life so many times, and I had completely failed her. The one time she'd needed *me* I had ignored her calls until it was too late. She was gone. The beautiful raven-haired stranger who'd saved me from drowning in an oil tank was now dead.

If I'd been there for her—calmed her down and talked sense into her—she would never have confronted Sligo. She would have waited until it was safe. If I had answered just one of her calls, she wouldn't be lying cold and silent in my arms. She would still be alive.

A numbing sensation took over me as I rocked back and forth with her body in my arms.

"Cal!"

Griff was elbowing me in the ribs—his hands were still bound behind his back.

"Cal, let go of her!"

I shook him off. He was the last person I wanted to talk to right now, but he kept persisting.

"Let her go!" he shouted, shoving me with his shoulder.

I swung my arm out and pushed him away. "I don't want to let her go!" I shouted back at him, tears now stinging my eyes. "I won't let her go!"

"You have to, Cal."

"I don't have to do anything! Winter was my friend! She was—"

"She's breathing, Cal," Griff spoke over me as he steadied himself. "I swear. That's all I'm trying to tell you. Listen."

I ignored him. I didn't want to hear his voice right now.

"Winter's *breathing*," he said, urgently kneeling closer to her. "Listen to me! Here, help me sit her up."

His words finally penetrated the blackness of my thoughts.

"She's breathing?" I repeated. As I spoke, I felt Winter stir.

I loosened my hold on her and a second later her body convulsed into life. She started struggling, groaning, trying to pull away from me.

"Winter!" I gripped her shoulders, crazy with relief. "Winter? Are you OK?" I asked, trying hopelessly to keep my voice steady. "It's me! Cal!" I added, half laughing, half crying.

"Let me go!" she screeched, squirming with panic. "Get your hands off me!"

"It's me!" I said again. "You're OK, you're with me!"

"Huh?" she said, sounding dazed, as I helped her sit up. "What's happened? Where am I? Cal, is that you?"

"Yes, I'm here!" I squeezed both of her hands, and tried to move her towards some light that was seeping in through a rusty crack in the container.

"Where have you been?" she murmured.

"I'm *so* sorry I didn't call you back," I said, my guilt gushing out. "I'm sorry I wasn't there for you when you phoned. I just—" I stopped, not knowing how to explain myself. "I can't believe this; I thought you were dead a second ago!"

"Give her some air, Cal," suggested Griff. He was awkwardly trying to rub Winter's arm to help warm her up. "She doesn't need to hear your apologies right now."

"Who's that?" asked Winter, squinting into the darkness of the container.

"You're in here with me and Griff Kirby," I explained.

"You and *Griff*?" she said slowly, bewildered and fearful. "What are you talking about? *Why*? Where are we?"

"We're all in the same boat," said Griff. "Or should I say *container*?"

"Container? Cal, what is he talking about?"

Winter tried to get up, but toppled right over.

"They must have drugged you," said Griff, helping her straighten up, "and you're still feeling the effects of it. I saw them dragging you into the black Subaru. You yelled out to me, remember?" he reminded her, as I worked on unwrapping the tape around his wrists. "You told me to go and get Cal."

"Yeah," she murmured. "From the beach."

"That's right," I said. "You told Griff he'd find me at the beach."

"And I did find him," added Griff, "but by the time we got back to the spot where you'd been shoved into the Subaru, all that was left behind were your things, scattered all over the road."

Winter began groping around in the darkness.

"We're in the car yard," I explained. "Griff and I came looking for you, but Zombie Two and Bruno caught us. Next thing we knew, they'd locked us in this container. You were already in here."

"We're in a *shipping* container?"

"Yep," said Griff. "On the back of a truck."

"Are they going to take us somewhere? How will we get out?"

They were questions we couldn't answer. Winter continued fumbling her way around the walls. She was nothing but a faint, wobbly silhouette in the darkness.

Next, she started banging, like she was testing the walls for a weak spot or a potential opening. Before long, Griff—whose hands were finally free—joined her.

"Help!" Griff shouted as he thumped on the walls. "Let us out!"

The metal shuddered, sending reverberations around us.

"Help!" they both called out, repeatedly, each cry more desperate than the last. "Help!"

It was getting louder and louder—Griff and Winter weren't letting up. Now they were both throwing themselves at the walls, like they were desperately trying to crack the container open. The noise was throbbing like a giant gong in my head.

I covered my ears—I couldn't take it any longer.

"Stop!" I screeched over the top of them. "Stop it! Banging on the walls isn't going to get us out of here! Would you both just calm down and think about this? There's nobody out there, and anybody that *could* be out there wants us to stay trapped in here! You're wasting your time!"

Winter and Griff slumped onto the metal floor. Silence returned to the container.

I stared into the blackness, hopelessly wondering how we were going to get out.

1:05 am

Finally, Winter broke the silence. "Cal, when I didn't hear back from you I just lost it. I wanted to talk to you so bad. I had the biggest news, ever, and no one to share it with."

My stomach twisted with guilt.

"It was like everything inside me was boiling over," she continued, sounding increasingly agitated, "and I couldn't cool down. At first I was so relieved to have found the truth, but then fury took over! I always *knew* he killed my parents! I always knew it wasn't just an accident, and finally I'd found the proof. That lying murderer!" she screamed, kicking her boot into the wall.

"Hey," I said softly, trying to calm her down again.

"My head was telling me the time wasn't right—it was telling me it would be stupid to confront him. But my heart couldn't wait. I knew he'd forged my dad's signature on the will, and I had the evidence to prove it. I'd also found our car in his car yard—more proof of foul play."

I shuddered at the thought of her facing up to Sligo. "And you found a drawing or something?" I asked, trying to recall what she'd said in her voicemail messages earlier.

"Remember when we first went searching together, I told you I was looking for a little something extra on the upholstery in the back?"

"Yeah," I said, "you mean the drawing of a bird or something?"

"A swallow. When I was about nine, I got into a tonne of trouble after a long drive up the coast . . . I was bored and drew a small bird on the back seat of the car. As soon as I spotted our gold BMW in the yard, I crawled into the wreck and located the drawing, scrawled onto the seat fabric, just where I'd left it. It was faded, but it was there. That was our car, all right."

A sliver of moonlight fell through a crack and across Winter's face as she held her wrist up to look at her bird tattoo. No wonder it meant so much to her.

Her hand abruptly fell back to her lap with

a slapping sound. "So next I checked the brake lines," she said. "Those brake lines weren't worn down like the police reported—they'd been cut. Clean cuts—the sort made by sharp pliers. That car crash was no accident. It had nothing to do with the weather. It was—"

"—*murder*," I whispered.

"Somehow, after the crash, he must have swapped vehicles, replacing my parents' car with another one of the same make and model that *did* have worn brakes. So the police accident report didn't lie—it just described some other wreck."

"He must have broken into the secure police car yard to do that," I said. "Or paid someone to do it for him."

"Sligo has his tentacles everywhere," she said. "He's proven he's capable of anything. Like I was saying, I charged over to his house and into his study, in a fit of fury. He was sitting behind his desk, drinking from some fancy, gold-rimmed, glass tumbler. I started yelling at him, accusing him of forgery and sabotage. He denied it, of course. He brushed me off and told me to get out and stop being a drama queen."

"You should have gone straight to the police," I said.

"I realise that now. It's probably the dumbest

thing I've ever done. He wasn't taking me seriously, so I showed him the proof I had—photos I'd taken on my mobile phone—" Winter stopped talking abruptly. "*My phone!*" she screeched. "Do you have it?"

"Battery's dead," Griff answered quickly. "I just checked it a second ago . . . I can't believe I don't have *my* phone on me."

"*My* phone!" I shouted, practically throwing my bag off my back and fumbling over the ground for it.

As soon as I picked it up I tried to switch it on, but it too was dead. I'd forgotten to hang it up after hearing Winter's voicemail messages, so the battery had completely drained.

"No good?" asked Winter, hopefully.

"Nope."

Griff swore.

Frustrated, I shoved everything back into my bag.

"So how did Sligo react to the photos?" I asked Winter.

"He looked at them, just to humour me at first, but once he realised what I had found, his pompous grin disappeared. He puffed up like a great big toad, purple with rage. He crushed the glass tumbler he was clutching, with his *bare fist*. I was so scared, I thought I was dead. He came at me with his eyes bulging and fists throbbing and I snatched my phone away from him and backed off, thinking he was about to grab me and wring my neck!"

Winter paused and let out an exhausted breath.

"Then he changed," she continued. "As quickly as he'd blown up, he calmed down. He started laughing like he suddenly thought it was hilarious. He said I was as smart as he was—maybe even smarter—and that I should channel my talent and become a partner in his business. He promised to give me the money owing to me as long as I kept my mouth shut, and as long as I sat beside him at his New Year's Eve ball like a perfect princess. He also said he was on the verge of making a whole lot more money."

"A whole lot more?" I asked, instantly panicking about him unravelling the DMO before us.

"He said he 'had to' reach the Ormond Singularity before the end of December," she explained, confirming my fears. "By that time I'd realised how much danger I was in, but I was all alone. No-one knew where I was. I didn't have backup."

Her words hit me hard.

"I decided to play along, pretending that I was seriously considering his offer. I walked around as if I was deep in thought while he threw the shards of broken glass from his desk in the bin and poured himself another drink. He offered me a juice, and I nervously sipped on it as I paced the room."

"Did he say anything else about the Ormond Singularity?"

"The Ormond Singularity?" Griff was muttering to himself, clearly confused.

"Sligo kept raving on about how he needed to crack it so that he could display the Ormond Jewel around my neck at the ball and make his name as a great medievalist and antiquarian. I could be his 'equal partner.' He said the entire world would be at *our* feet. I was pretending to be impressed but the whole time I was planning how to get out. I excused myself to go to the bathroom, then I bolted. I was on my way to the police station when I started to feel really weird—all weak and floppy. Every sound around me was fading and my vision was going blurry. I sat down on some steps, thinking it must have been the heat. Then I remembered the fruit juice—Sligo had put something in it! Next thing I know, Bruno's dragging me off the street into the car. I kicked as hard as I could, but I couldn't stop him!"

"That's when I saw you," said Griff.

"Sligo made a final phone call to your mobile," I said. "He didn't realise I'd picked it up from the road. He said enough for me to guess you'd been taken to the car yard. When we got here and I saw the container, I was pretty sure you'd be in it. Then Bruno and Zombie Two sprung us—"

"And locked us in here with you," Griff finished for me, feeling around the container again. "We're all up to speed now, so how about we focus on getting out of here?"

Griff's suggestion was met with stifling silence. Clearly, none of us had any good ideas.

Outside the container and beyond the deserted car yard, the sounds of distant traffic hummed almost inaudibly.

Griff spoke again. "We're better off trying to escape now, while we at least know where we are. If this truck moves us, we could end up stacked like bricks in concrete on a container ship in the middle of the ocean. We'd die there, for sure."

"I'm scared," whispered Winter.

1:29 am

I stood up and started pacing the length of the dark space of the container. If only there was something I could do. If only I could find some way to connect with the outside world. With Boges or—

"The distress beacon!" I shouted.

"The what?" said Griff.

"The micro distress beacon Boges gave you!"

Winter shouted, excitedly. She jumped to her feet and awkwardly hugged me.

"I have a distress beacon stowed in my shoe," I explained to Griff. "My buddy Boges gave it to me, for use in an emergency!"

"And you've only just thought of it now?" he said in frustrated disbelief.

"I'd almost forgotten all about it, but *who cares*?! It means we're getting out of here!"

I sat back down and wrenched my shoe off. "Once he realises we're missing, he'll check the tracking program to see if we've activated the beacon. Then he can follow the signal to this container."

"But what about the police?" asked Winter. "They're watching him. What if they follow him here?"

"Boges will be vigilant. He knows how important our freedom is. But let's not worry about that right now, I have to get this beacon activated."

With shaking fingers, I pulled up the inner sole from my sneaker and started to rip away the tape. I located the beacon and pressed the tiny switch.

It didn't make a sound, but I had to believe it was working.

If Boges didn't activate his tracking system

before this container was picked up and shipped out, I didn't like to think what might happen to us. Griff was right—we needed to get out before they moved us.

Now we had to play the waiting game.

9:01 am

"Who's that?" hissed Winter, grabbing my arm suddenly.

I froze and listened carefully. I could hear footsteps and the murmur of a voice approaching.

"Do you think it's Boges?" Griff whispered.

"Shh," I said, straining to hear whether the voice outside was familiar or not.

As it became louder, I recognised who it was.

It wasn't Boges.

It was Zombie Two.

"In the container," he said, loud enough for the three of us to hear. "We both come back tomorrow morning to remove."

We all shuddered as his voice moved away again. Eventually we heard a car driving off and hoped that meant Zombie Two had left again.

"Your friend had better get here before *they* do," warned Griff.

8:15 pm

The day blended into the night as the three of us

huddled for hours and hours, anxiously waiting in the darkness of the container. All of us would jump at the slightest sound, hoping it was Boges, coming to our rescue, while fearing it was Bruno, Zombie Two or Sligo, back again to *remove* us.

But no one had come.

Eventually, Winter and Griff fell silent and I could hear Winter's steady breathing beside me. The air inside the container was getting thicker and thicker.

I couldn't fall asleep—I was tormented with horrible thoughts. What if Boges didn't think to check up on his tracking program? What if the three of us were left here to die—from thirst and starvation—without anyone but the people who put us here ever knowing? What did Sligo plan on doing with us tomorrow morning? I didn't want to stick around and find out.

The way I'd felt when I'd held Winter in my arms earlier, thinking she was dead, wouldn't leave my mind either. I needed the chance to make a lot up to her. She'd been through so much and she'd been so brave. And now, just when she had the evidence she needed to get Sligo right out of her life forever and claim what was rightfully hers, she was trapped.

Guilty. I felt so guilty.

Because of me, Boges had been picked up and

questioned by the police. For all I knew, they could have arrested him by now. Because of me, his future was uncertain. On top of that, I'd only just realised that I'd forgotten his birthday.

2 DECEMBER

30 days to go . . .

8:26 am

"Hey," said Griff, shaking me. I must have finally dozed off to sleep. "There's someone outside! They're here! That big guy's come back like he said he would!"

I sat up, alert. He was right—I could hear footsteps.

"Can't you hear it? Winter, wake up!" Griff shouted. "They're here!"

"Shh!" I hissed. "If it *is* Sligo we don't want him knowing we're all still alive!"

That quietened him. He crouched down silently.

"Someone's here?" Winter asked in a low voice, only just waking up.

"Sounds like it," I whispered. "Zombie Two said they'd be back in the morning, so if it's them, then the minute the doors are opened we all need to charge out as fast and as hard as we can. It's our only hope. If we all charge together, one of us might make it past them and be able to get help. OK?"

"OK," agreed Winter and Griff.

"Ready?"

"Ready!"

We braced ourselves, ready to spring, as we heard the clanging and creaking of the heavy container doors opening.

As fresh air gushed towards us and daylight shone in, I squinted and flew at the two silhouettes before us.

I took down the first guy, knocking him hard to the ground. Bodies thudded and struggled beside me, too.

"Hey! Easy, dude, it's me!" Boges shoved me off him.

"Boges!" I said. "Man, I am so sorry!"

"Get off me!" I heard a familiar voice grunt beside me. It was Nelson Sharkey. Griff and Winter had both tackled him and pinned him to the ground.

"We didn't know whether the distress beacon would work!" exclaimed Winter, helping Sharkey to his feet, before running over to hug Boges. "We're so glad to see you!"

"You should never have doubted my craftsmanship," scoffed Boges, dusting off his notebook and straightening his shirt.

My eyes were slowly adjusting to the light as

I scoped the car yard. Sharkey's car was parked just outside the entry gates. I couldn't see any sign of Sligo or his goons, but I knew they could turn up at any moment.

"Let's get out of here," I said, hauling up my backpack.

8:37 am

We crawled, one after another, through the opening in the fence that Sharkey had made with bolt cutters, then piled into his car and took off, skidding and screeching.

"As soon as I realised you were both MIA," said Boges, "I immediately opened the program for the distress beacon. The second I saw your signal I called Nelson. He picked me up and helped me trace you. It didn't take us too long to track you down to the vicinity of Sligo's car yard."

Sharkey pulled the car over to drop Griff off, not too far from his aunty's hotel near the docks. We'd driven past a huge Christmas tree decorated with tinsel and golden boxes tied up with gleaming ribbons that had been set up in the park nearby. I could hardly believe it was almost Christmas. That meant the end of the year was way too close for comfort.

"I'll call you," said Griff, as he climbed out of the car. "But not too soon, OK?"

I understood—Griff and I were both guilty of bringing trouble to each other, but without him I never would have found Winter.

"Thanks!" I shouted out as he ran away into a crowd of shoppers.

"OK," said Sharkey, from the driver's seat. "Where to next?"

Winter looked at me apprehensively from the front passenger seat. She opened her mouth to say something and then stopped.

"Your place?" Sharkey asked her. "I think I remember where that is."

Winter shook her head and it hit me. Now she was like me. She couldn't go back home. She didn't have a home any more. Neither of us did.

"Let's go to Lovett's?" Boges suggested, like he was reading my mind.

I nodded.

He gave Sharkey directions while I wondered if I could ever pay my friends back.

"Boges," I said quietly. "Sorry I forgot your birthday. Next year will be different, I swear."

Treehouse

10:20 am

Sharkey dropped the three of us off on the road that led to Luke Lovett's place. Before he drove away, I asked him, "Nelson, when you were working on a tough case in the police force and you ran up against a brick wall, what did you do?"

Nelson leaned his elbow on the window ledge. "I began again, Cal. Went back to the start. The PLS."

"The PLS?" I asked, aware of Boges and Winter listening attentively beside me.

"The Point Last Seen. If it's a missing person, you go back over the investigation. You go back to the place where they disappeared. You re-interview people, you ask for other witnesses to come forward. You hope to find fresh clues that maybe you'd overlooked before. Walk-throughs are really helpful because memory is state dependent."

"Meaning?" Winter asked.

"You know when you're in the house and you're walking to a room to get something and by the time you get there you forget what you were looking for?" Sharkey continued.

"Yep," we all answered.

"Then you retrace your steps to where you were standing or sitting when you first got the idea, and then suddenly it pops back into your head again—it's like doing that," said Sharkey. "Now are you guys right? I have to keep moving. I'll look into flights for us all and get back to you, OK?"

"Cool. Thanks again," I said as he drove off, leaving just the three of us, dishevelled and relieved.

"Winter, you'd better hang with me until you've organised another place Sligo doesn't know about," I said as we all crept towards the back of Luke's place.

I saw the strain and exhaustion in her face. The happiness that had shone in her eyes as we were freed from the container was long gone. I'd been living rough for almost a year now, but she'd been living on a razor's edge, keeping her secrets and suspicions from Sligo, for the last six years. All while practically living in the dragon's den.

"It's OK, Winter," I began, reaching for her shoulder.

"It's not OK," she said, shaking my hand off. "All my stuff is back at the apartment and I can't go back and get it. I'm used to being alone, but now I have nothing. Nothing! My bag was smashed on the road when I was hijacked, I don't have a phone and we have to get to Ireland and it'll be freezing there. I have no clothes and I'm filthy!"

"I have your phone," I said, digging it out of my backpack. "It just needs charging."

She took it and we continued walking.

"Cal and I will break into your apartment," said

Boges, bravely. "We can try and pick up your stuff for you."

We pushed through the bushes that formed the back boundary of Luke's family property and hurried over to the massive tree at the back of Luke's place, huddling together under its wide canopy. I reached up and yanked the rope down from where it had been thrown up out of the way over a low-lying bough.

Winter sighed as she climbed the rope. "Here I go again. Gorilla girl and the monkey boys. So where's the bathroom?" she asked, once at the top.

I pointed to a tap near the back fence.

"You're joking."

I shrugged.

Boges hauled himself up into the treehouse. "Peaceful hideaway, leafy aspect. Open plan for easy living. Carpeted throughout. Bright and airy. Loads of character."

"Exactly," I said. "Not so bad."

"*Character* is a word real estate agents use when a place needs to meet a wrecking ball more than a new tenant." She sat down cross-legged on the bench and tied her hair back with an elastic from her wrist. "I have to go back to my place. I have to get my passport, at least, otherwise going with you guys to Ireland and cracking the Ormond Singularity will be nothing but a dream for me."

"Like Boges said, we'll watch your apartment and if it's safe," I said, "we'll retrieve your things for you."

The colour suddenly drained from Winter's face. "The money! I don't have the money!"

"Where is it?" Boges asked, alarmed.

"Back at the apartment! What if Sligo's already found where I've hidden it?"

"Where'd you hide it?" I asked, hoping it wasn't just in a drawer or something.

"Inside the sofa. It's not the best hiding spot, but maybe he won't look in there unless he's realised the cash from his scram bag is missing . . ."

"We'll find out soon enough," said Boges. "We're gonna have to go there tonight."

12 Lesley Street

9:45 pm

Boges and I squatted in the darkness across the road from Winter's building. We checked out every parked car to make sure they were empty. Once we'd confirmed there was no one watching the building from the outside, and that there was no sign of Sligo, Bruno or Zombie Two, we snuck over to the fire escape stairs and silently made our way up.

The key to Winter's door wasn't working.

"Let me have a go," said Boges. But he couldn't turn it either.

"Sligo's changed the locks already," I hissed, glancing around us nervously. "We'll have to break in."

Above us, the stars, dull because of the pollution from the city, twinkled faint and distant. An aeroplane coming in to land over the sea soared overhead.

"Watch out," I said to Boges as I picked up one of the potted plants Winter had growing at the front of her tiny apartment. Taking advantage of the roaring of the aeroplane, I smashed the plant through the window.

The shattering glass still sounded deafening and we froze, nervous someone had heard it and would come to investigate the noise on the roof.

Nothing happened. No one came.

I carefully knocked out the remaining glass fragments and climbed inside, then unlocked the door for Boges.

Using flashlights, we found our way to the sofa, digging our arms in under the cushions, searching for the hole Winter had told us was there. I pushed my hands around, grazing my fingers on rough, iron springs.

"Anything?" Boges asked anxiously.

I shook my head.

My grasping fingertips finally felt something—wads of folded notes, held by rubber bands.

"Got it!" I said, pulling them out one by one.

"Hurry, dude," said Boges, who was now up and standing guard at the smashed window, looking out into the night. "I don't want us to be here one second longer than we need to be."

I didn't need any urging. I shoved the wads of money into my backpack, on top of my fake passport, and then started looking for the things Winter had asked us to collect. I grabbed her mobile charger and scooped up some clothes from her drawer, while Boges grabbed her sleeping bag and things from her bathroom.

Boges pointed his flashlight to a spot on the ground. Lit up were the two photos of Winter's parents, both lying crookedly in their frames under shattered glass.

"Sligo must have trampled them in a rage," said Boges.

I saw a copy of *The Little Prince* lying nearby and impulsively picked it up and shoved it in my backpack.

"I can't find her notes," whispered Boges, shining the light over the desk where Winter had said she had left them. "Where could they be?"

Our eyes met over the empty table.

"Sligo," we said, our voices overlapping.

Treehouse

10:31 pm

"So Sligo has all our information on the Ormond Singularity?" Winter cried.

I nodded. It was just the two of us in the tree-house. Boges had gone home after the Lesley Street raid, leaving me to make the trek to the treehouse alone.

"But Cal," she argued, "Sligo could join Rathbone in Ireland and the two of them could go straight for it! Forget about the Jewel and the Riddle! They can do everything *we* planned on doing—using the photos and other clues to find the location!"

"We can't give up now. Nobody has the last two lines of the Riddle."

"*Yet*," said Winter. "And we don't have them either." She unrolled her sleeping bag and laid it out. It took up almost a third of the floor space.

A wave of anxiety unsettled my guts. "At least we have the money, right?"

"We do have that. Thanks for getting my other stuff too," she said, reaching into the box in the corner for a couple of muesli bars Boges had left behind. "Did you see the photos of my mum and dad?"

I pictured them, trampled on the floor. "I'm sorry, I forgot to grab them," I lied. "I'm going back to the PLS," I said, changing the subject and tearing the wrapper off the bar she'd tossed me.

"The point last seen of your original backpack? The bag containing the Jewel and the Riddle?"

"Right," I said.

"Which means a second visit to Rathbone's? The undertakers'?"

"Right again. I've been thinking about what Sharkey said about memory being state dependent. If I re-enact my last visit there, I just might remember what that familiar smell was. Plus we need to search the place. Crims often hide stuff with their families. Maybe Sheldrake Rathbone has stored something there that will give us a clue as to where my bag went, or something that might help us uncover the identities of Deep Water, Double Trouble and the Little Prince," I added, as she leafed through the white book I'd brought back for her. "Until Sharkey books our flights, there's not much else we can do."

11:11 pm

Winter curled up and went to sleep, while I worried about Sligo and Rathbone getting together in Ireland and beating us to the truth. We *couldn't* let that happen. Things Rafe had revealed to me in our phone conversation last month repeated in my head, too.

"I've got it!" yelled Winter, abruptly kicking her sleeping bag off and sitting up. "Cal," she whispered now, remembering to keep her voice down. "How could we have been so *stupid*?"

I jumped up and almost banged my head on the low ceiling. "What are you talking about?"

"I know who the Little Prince is! I can't believe it's taken us so long to work it out!"

"Who is it? Tell me!"

"Just think about it," she said, reaching for the nearby book. "It has a boy all alone, a crashed aeroplane, drawings, a rose, adults who can't be trusted . . . The boy is a prince from a faraway place. A prince is someone who inherits a title, riches, someone who is an heir. Who does that remind you of?"

"Me," I whispered. "I'm the Little Prince on Rathbone's list." I looked at her, dumbfounded. "Rathbone must think it's possible I have the Riddle and the Jewel."

"And *we* know you don't," Winter continued. "So that only leaves Deep Water and Double Trouble."

3 DECEMBER

29 days to go . . .

Temperance Lane

9:37 pm

We were across the road from Rathbone, Greaves and Diggory—the funeral parlour. Inside the shop a soft light was glowing, suggesting someone was still in there. The rest of the street was dark and empty apart from a few parked cars. Nothing stirred, not even a cat.

"By the way," said Boges, quietly, "I visited Gabbi today and she convinced me to give her your phone number. She's promised not to give it to anyone else and promised me she wouldn't use it unless it's an emergency. I hope that's OK."

"Sure," I said, hoping it wouldn't get either of us into any trouble.

We shrank down as the lights in the storefront went out, then scrambled around the back of the premises, through the gate and huddled behind a dumpster, carefully waiting to see who was leaving.

Eventually, the back door opened and a thin, weedy guy stepped outside, turned back and locked up.

I'd never seen him before. He walked away from us, in the direction of a car. Within minutes, he'd driven off.

"Come on," said Winter, creeping out of the shadows and running over to the door. She waved her hands, gesturing to us to follow her. "Hmm, this lock is not going to be easy."

"Maybe this isn't such a good idea," said Boges, looking over his shoulder to the street. "I don't like the thought of all those stiffs lying in there. Plus I don't want to *become* one of them if we're caught!"

Winter pulled a metal nail file out from under her sleeve and started poking it around the lock.

"Hurry, please," urged Boges. "Let's get this over and done with."

"Must be a *dead*bolt," joked Winter, as she struggled to get the door open.

Boges's face was serious.

"Not funny," he said.

"Whatever it is, I can't do it," she said, finally. "This is a serious lock. My nail file can't compete with it."

The sound of a car made us bolt from the door and across to the cover of the bin again. It was the weedy guy. He must have forgotten something. We watched him get out of his car, approach the back door, unlock it and disappear inside once more.

"He's left the door open a crack," I whispered. "Now's our chance. He probably won't be in there for long. Come on, Boges. The three of us could take on that little guy if we had to."

Winter tugged Boges's arm as we snuck over to the door. I peered in and could see a light on in the office area.

"Quick, follow me," I hissed to my friends, before stealthily leading them inside the dark, short hallway and towards the showroom. I remembered the layout from my last visit, shivering from the memory.

We crept into the main showroom, walking directly past the office where the weedy guy was. I could hear him shuffling papers in there. The light from the office discreetly touched on the rows of coffins and caskets on display.

The three of us ducked down in the furthest corner, behind a long counter draped with lacy fabric, presenting an open coffin on its surface.

"What's that funny smell?" Winter asked.

"Probably embalming fluid," shuddered Boges.

"Gross," Winter whispered beside me.

"Shh," I hissed at them as the light in the office went out and footsteps clicked across the floor.

We waited until the door was locked from the outside and the car drove away before we emerged from our hiding place.

"I'm going to search the office," I said.

"I'll help," said Boges. "I'll start on the cupboards."

"I'll do the desk," Winter offered.

10:03 pm

"Nothing," said Boges, after he'd finished with the cupboards.

"Nothing here, either," said Winter, straightening up from the desk. "Just catalogues of coffins, caskets and artificial wreaths. What's that?" she asked, alerted by a sound from the back of the building. "Don't tell me that scrawny guy's forgotten something else!"

"It's nothing, just someone getting into their car," I said. "Boges, what if this place has a back-to-base alarm?"

"Then we're in big trouble," he said. "Let's get a move on. Let's see if that painted coffin is still here—that was about the last thing you saw before you blacked out, right?"

"That's where my bag was thrown."

"Wait—what if someone's," Boges paused to clear his throat, "living in there?"

"*Living*'s not the right verb," Winter corrected

him. "Besides, these are just display coffins," she said. "Just samples. People look at them and then order the one they like. They're empty." She began giggling and flapping her arms like a chicken, until Boges gave her a shove.

We moved back into the display area and I waved the beam of light from my flashlight around the showroom until it landed on the familiar white coffin with its Sistine Chapel skies and angels inside it.

"That's the one," I said. "I walked up to what I thought was a counter, here, like this," I explained, re-enacting the steps I had taken on that July night. "The envelope I had come for was sitting on top of it, so I picked it up and then bam!"

I jumped back, illustrating the force of the impact that had knocked me off my feet.

"The counter was actually a coffin. Somebody flew out of it, and before I could do anything I was overpowered and jabbed in the neck with some sort of drug. I started trying to get up, but was too groggy. All I saw was my backpack being chucked into that coffin over there."

I stood still, closed my eyes and took a deep breath. Then something amazing happened.

I spun around to my friends. "The smell! I almost had it! Sharkey was right! By retracing my steps and standing here just like I did last time, and *feeling* the way I did last time, it almost came back to me. Damn!" I said. "It's like a sneeze that won't burst out! It's so frustrating! It's on the tip of my—"

"Nose?" Winter suggested.

Boges looked like he wanted to shake the answer out of me.

"I almost had it, I swear."

I walked away from the coffin and then turned, retracing my footsteps once more. Maybe one more approach would trigger the deep unconscious memory that lurked somewhere in the back of my mind.

It was no use. That initial powerful surge towards remembering didn't happen again. Instead, it faded on me.

A howling shriek from Boges instantly snapped my attention his way. Winter and I shone our lights on him—he was flat up against the wall, as white as a ghost.

"I thought you said there weren't any bodies in here!"

"There shouldn't be," Winter said, peering into the open coffin Boges was backing away from. I looked over her shoulder. A bloodied corpse?

The sound of a vehicle being driven up and parked out the back made us freeze again. We ran to the rear door and flattened ourselves on either side of it.

I peered out the window and spotted a van.

Boges's eyes were even wider with fear.

"I think someone's about to come inside," I hissed, hearing the van door open and close just metres away. I pressed against the wall, shaking with tension. "Stay quiet, wait till they've stepped all the way through the door, then the three of us bolt out and turn left down Temperance Lane. OK?"

My friends nervously nodded.

The sound of something being unloaded outside was quickly followed by the approach of footsteps, the jangle of keys and the twisting of the rear-door handle. We watched the handle turn, then the door opened slowly.

In the soft glow of the streetlight I spotted the gleam of the front end of a chrome-plated collapsible trolley. It was wheeled awkwardly through the doorway, followed by a stooped figure pushing it.

As soon as the guy and the trolley were in, I gave the signal to my friends.

He let out a terrified scream as the three of us sprang out of the darkness, shoved past him and ran out the door.

We pelted down the laneway and down the street.

"Poor guy," said Winter as we raced away,

"must have thought some of the deceased had escaped! I hope he doesn't die of heart failure!"

10:34 pm

"What was that body doing in there?" asked Boges, as we all caught our breath in a deserted churchyard. "Were they bullet wounds?"

Before I could answer, I felt my phone vibrating in my pocket.

My friends nodded to me, urging me to answer it.

"Yes?" I said, firmly.

"Cal!"

"Gabbi?" I said, instantly alarmed. "What is it? What's wrong?"

"You've got to come!"

"Calm down and tell me what's going on."

"The voices woke me up!"

"Whose voices?"

"Mum and Uncle Rafe—they were yelling at each other. Mum was going nuts and screaming about something and Rafe was trying to calm her down. Cal, I think she's really lost it. Uncle Rafe must have come home late—he wasn't home when I went to bed. I don't know how it all started, but when I got up I saw Mum all red in the face, angry and upset. She was chucking things around!"

"It's OK, Gab, everyone has fights. Really big

ones sometimes. They'll calm down and forget all about it."

"I don't think so. This is big, Cal. Mum ran right out of the house. I thought she'd left me behind!"

"Mum would never do that," I said, unconvincingly.

"Rafe raced out after her, begging her to relax and come back. He wanted her to take her medication. She just told him to get away from her, then she ran back into the house and grabbed me from where I was on the stairs. I was really scared. She dragged me out the back, then we climbed into the car and drove off. Rafe was yelling out the front that she shouldn't be driving in that state. It was horrible!"

"Where are you now?" I asked.

"Marjorie's place. Marjorie helped calm her down. They're out the back talking now. Mum's still crying, I think. I tried to hear what they're saying . . . but—"

"Where's Rafe?"

"I don't know, we just left him standing in the dark, outside the house. Cal, I don't know what to do—Mum's not the same as she used to be. She's never lost it before like she did tonight. Can you please come and see me?" my sister cried.

I didn't know what to do.

"Please, Cal!" she begged, in between sobbing and sniffling.

"I'll come around as soon as I can," I decided, impulsively. I hated hearing her sound so upset. "You'll have to sneak out front to meet me. Nobody can know about this. You'll have to be very careful, OK?"

"OK."

I hung up the phone and turned to the others.

"We're coming with you," they said together.

"I'll be quicker alone," I said, "and more discreet. I'll meet up with you both at the cenotaph in two, maybe three, hours?"

"Cool," said Boges. "Hey, look, a taxi's coming. It'd be a lot quicker than walking from here to Richmond . . ."

"I'm grabbing it," I said, making a rash decision and rushing out to the road.

"Are you sure?" asked Winter. "It'll be faster, but it might not be safe."

I nodded, flagging down the taxi. I needed to get to Gabbi as fast as possible. "Let's hope it's a good omen."

Flood Street, Richmond

10:43 pm

I hung my head low and paid the driver. Luckily

he'd been completely focused on a phone call to another driver that he was taking on speaker. I climbed out and he drove away, leaving me at the end of my old street.

I tried not to look at our house as I passed it, now inhabited by strangers. It sat there surrounded by bushes and trees that were so much taller than I remembered.

Gabbi was waiting for me behind Mum's car, parked outside Marjorie's house. She threw herself at me and hugged me so tight it felt like I was being smothered by a small bear.

"Hey, hey, steady, Gab," I gasped as she squeezed me. "It's OK. I'm here now." I eased her off me and ducked down with her behind the car again.

"But I don't want to stay here," she said, her eyes bloodshot from crying. "I want to go back to Mum and Uncle Rafe's place. I feel weird here."

I took her hands in mine. "Gab, you might have to stay here at Marjorie's until Mum sorts out whatever problem she's having. You can go back home later."

Gabbi's eyes shone with tears as she swung round and pointed over to our old house. "*That's* my home! That's where I want to go! I want it to be back to when we were all together again, living there in our proper house, just like it used to be before Dad died. Before all those bad things happened to you . . . and before Mum changed . . . and went crazy."

I put my arms around her. "We'd all love that, Gab," I said helplessly as she snuggled into me.

Then she leaned back to look me in the face. "Please come home soon, Cal. I hate not having you around. It's so quiet. I miss my brother."

"I promise it won't be like this for much longer. But for now, both of us have to stay strong. I know it's not easy, living with Mum the way she is right now, but having Rafe helps, doesn't it?"

"It does," she nodded. "He's all right. I never liked him much before, but he's different now. *Better* different. He's been getting along so well with Mum—he still wants to marry her, you know—but you should have heard her yelling at him tonight."

"What was it about? What set her off?"

"I don't know, she wouldn't tell me anything. Rafe phoned Marjorie a few minutes ago and said he was going to come by as soon as he'd picked up Mum's prescription. He said he was on his way to a twenty-four-hour drugstore in the city."

That trip would take him at least an hour, I figured. It gave me an idea.

"Gab, I have to go now. Look, you and Mum will be OK." I thought about the 365-day countdown and looming deadline. No matter what happened to me, this mess was going to be over soon, one way or another. "Go back inside. We'll see each other again soon."

"OK," she said, her voice muffled by tears once more. "But where are you going to go now?"

"I have something I need to check out," I said, not wanting to give too much away, "and then I'm going to meet Winter and Boges at Memorial Park."

Gabbi hugged me and touched the Celtic ring on my finger before sneaking back into the house. She glanced over at me one last time as she quietly closed the door.

I started sprinting towards Dolphin Point. There was something I really wanted to check out there, and time was going to be tight.

Rafe's House
Surfside Street, Dolphin Point

11:40 pm

There was no sign of Rafe's car outside his house, but there was a light on inside. I was hoping that in the craziness of Mum and Gab's exit, Rafe had simply forgotten to turn off the lights and, more importantly, forgotten to set the security system.

I raced around the back to the patio and my eyes darted to the glass doors. They *were* open!

I held my breath as I eased the doors wider and stepped through.

Silence. The alarm was *not* on.

The living room looked a mess. Mum's favourite purple mug lay on the floor in pieces, the remainder of her herbal tea forming a small, wet, brown puddle in the middle of them. Books and papers were scattered all over the place, as if someone had been impatiently looking for something, sending everything flying without care. Or was this just the proof of Mum's irrational outburst, when she'd gone crazy like Gabbi had said, throwing things around?

Mum sure had changed over the last year. She'd never been the sort of person to lose her temper and throw things. She used to have everything under control. She used to be calm. She used to be reasonable.

Mum *used to* be a lot of things.

Rafe's old photo albums were stored on a low bookcase next to his vinyl records. I'd noticed them when searching through his house before, but had never actually stopped to look at any of the pictures inside.

In the last few weeks, so many things had happened that made me curious about Rafe. It was almost like he'd lived two completely different lives. The "Twin Tragedy" article I'd read, for instance, where he'd sadly spoken of my missing twin, and lovingly of his own twin, my dad, had made me look at him differently. Even Eric Blair had said that in college Rafe was always by my dad's side. Everything pointed to him living a completely different life before the abduction—before Samuel was taken, and before I was returned.

But was it true?

Rafe had admitted knowing I had come to his "rescue" at Chapel-by-the-Sea, and he also knew so much more about the DMO than I ever realised.

I cleared the space on the floor beside the shelf, kicking some loose papers out of the way. I knelt down and pulled out a couple of the fattest albums and began turning their pages, all the while listening carefully for the sound of a returning car.

The first album was filled with photos from Uncle Rafe's wedding. There were mostly pictures of him with Aunty Klara, posing together. Rafe was smiling in the pictures, but I could almost see something like sadness in his eyes.

I didn't know Aunty Klara that well before she died. From what I remembered, she was pretty quiet and kept to herself, even though she seemed nice enough. I never really thought about how lonely Rafe must have been after he lost her.

I slotted the wedding album back into place on the shelf.

The next album I opened was older and dustier. Straightaway I recognised Rafe and Dad together when they were young, probably about my age. I frowned, looking at them more closely.

In almost every photo, Dad had his arm over Rafe's shoulder, or the other way around. They both wore wide grins. They looked identical. They looked happy.

I pulled the album closer and flicked through it, eager to see more. Photo after photo showed the pair together; pulling silly faces and poses, blowing out candles on shared birthday cakes, dressed up in matching powder-blue suits at friends' parties, proudly holding their surfboards. There must have been hundreds of photos of the pair.

Rafe's words returned to me: "a special bond," he'd said, about being a twin. I sat back on my heels.

I frowned over pages of baby photos I recognised were of me, hauling myself up by a chair leg and standing up. My dad and Rafe stood side-by-side in the background. I wondered for a second about the discoloured squares in the album, where pictures had been removed . . . before realising that Rafe must have taken out all the shots of Samuel.

There wasn't much more to see after that. There were a few random shots of plants and buildings, but it seemed like Rafe had lost interest in tracking his life.

As I placed the last of the albums back on the shelf, an unopened envelope fell out from one of the film negative pockets.

Curious, I read who it was addressed to.

Tom Ormond.

On the back was Rafe's name and old address. Why had it been returned? Why had Dad never read it?

Carefully, I prised it open.

Tom,

You must stop blaming yourself for
what happened to the boys. It wasn't
your fault. It wasn't anyone's fault.
Callum will stop pining for his little
brother soon. I know it's tough to
hear it, but he's lucky enough to
forget he ever had a twin.

Losing little Sam's been hard on me, too.
I know he's not my son, but you know how
much I love those boys. I love them
like they're my own.

I understand if seeing me at the moment
is too much for you — if it brings up too
many difficult thoughts of your lost son
and the fact that Callum may never have
what you and I have. Soon, when time
has helped heal the wounds a little, I hope

you'll be able to let me back into your life again. Like old times. Shutting me out is not going to make things easier for you, Tom.

I know the timing is terrible, but Klara and I have decided to go ahead with our wedding. I'd still love for you to stand by me and be my best man, but if you can't I will accept your decision.

Hoping you'll say yes.

Your brother,

Rafe

4 DECEMBER

28 days to go . . .

12:01 am

My hands were shaking as I held Rafe's rejected letter. *Dad* was the one who'd walked away from his relationship with Rafe? I couldn't believe it. I always thought Dad was the one who was being shut out, not the other way around.

I'd looked through Rafe's wedding photos pretty closely and Dad had not been in any of them—he definitely wasn't standing by his twin as the best man. He must have ended up letting his brother down. Maybe that was why Rafe didn't look as happy as he should have . . . Dad must have found it too painful to be around his twin, after the loss of one of his twin sons. It didn't make complete sense to me, but I knew from my experience that grief can do weird things to people. It can change them.

Like what was happening to Mum.

I refolded the letter and put it back in its envelope.

I thought again of all the things Rafe had done for us since Dad died. He'd given Mum a home when she was losing her own. He'd provided Gabbi with the best medical attention possible when she was in a coma, even changing the structure of his house for her. He'd taken Gabbi and Mum under his wing at a time when they needed protection most.

Maybe this was how involved in our family he'd wanted to be all along.

12:13 am

The coast was still clear outside, but I needed to get going. I figured Rafe would have made it to Marjorie's by now, and would be back here any second.

I had a quick final glance around the room and noticed Mum's red leather handbag on the floor near the dining table, half spilling out. She must have been really upset to have left that behind—it was usually glued to her.

Her bag seemed much heavier than it should have been. Inside was a bulging padded envelope. Curious, I pulled it out.

I couldn't believe what I was seeing printed on the top left-hand corner of the large envelope. "Rathbone and Associates."

What?

My head was spinning. What was Mum doing with a thick, bulky envelope from Sheldrake Rathbone?

There had to be an innocent explanation. *Right?*

The sound of a car in the street snapped me into action. I pocketed Dad's unread letter, shoved the heavy envelope from Mum's bag into my backpack and bolted out the back door.

Sure enough, Rafe had returned. He'd just pulled up on the driveway and already I could hear Gabbi's voice as she climbed out of the car, alongside Mum.

While they shuffled into the house, I ran out onto the road.

As my feet pounded the ground, on my way to Memorial Park, my thoughts whirled like a tornado; *Dad* had been responsible for the split from Rafe, not the other way around, and now it seemed as if Mum had been dealing with Rathbone. What was going on? Everything I thought I knew had been turned upside down.

Cenotaph
Memorial Park

1:12 am

Boges and Winter emerged from the shadows as

I ran up the steps and into the circular enclosure, where dead leaves skittered over the mosaic floor.

The moon was shining brilliantly through the stained glass window above and the Ormond Angel seemed to look sternly down on us.

"What is it?" Winter asked. "You're so pale."

"It's just the moonlight," I replied. "Let's sit down," I suggested as the pair scrutinised my face.

After I'd filled them in on my trip to Dolphin Point, I handed them Dad's unread letter from Rafe. They both skimmed over it, eagerly.

"Rafe was telling the truth," said Boges. "He and your dad *were* really close until . . ."

". . . until the kidnapping," Winter whispered.

"Didn't see that coming," added Boges.

"Me neither," I said, pulling the padded envelope out of my backpack. "This is what I found in my mum's bag."

Winter eyed it closely.

"Well go on," she said. "Open it!"

I did so, reluctantly, afraid of what I was about to find. Boges and Winter jostled around me to see.

I tipped the contents out.

None of us could speak at first.

It wasn't a fat wad of documents. There, gleaming in the moonlight, beneath the radiant Angel above us, glowed the Ormond Jewel on top of the Ormond Riddle.

Winter took the Jewel in her hand. "*Amor et suevre tosjors celer,*" she whispered eerily, reciting the inscription inside, as her forefinger traced the almost invisible letters. "A love whose works must always be kept secret." She looked up at me and asked the question that was in all of our minds. "Why would *your mum* have these?"

I could see my own shocked expression mirrored on the faces of Boges and Winter. We should have felt fantastic. We should have felt like leaping over the cenotaph in a single bound. Instead, dark questions had taken over.

"Your mum?" Boges asked slowly. "Your mum is Deep Water or Double Trouble?"

"It can't be right." I shook my head, refusing to accept it. "There must be an explanation."

"That scent that you almost identified back there at the undertakers' . . . Maybe you're repressing the memory," Boges continued, hinting at my reaction to the scent of Mum's perfume the last time we snuck into Rafe's house. "Maybe you know exactly who it belongs to but can't bear to face the truth, and that's why you can't bring yourself to recall it. It's your heart stopping you." Boges shook his head and ran his hands through his hair. "I can't believe your mum is *in* on this . . . Mrs O," he said in disbelief.

"Hang on a minute," I said defensively. "You don't know that's true. She could—"

"Oh wow! What is that?" a voice interrupted us.

I swung round.

"What are you doing here, Gabbi?"

"You said you were coming here, so as soon as Uncle Rafe and Mum went to bed, I snuck out. Don't worry, they don't have a clue I'm gone!"

My little sister didn't look the least bit sorry about breaking the rules. In fact, she looked pretty proud of herself for wandering out alone to find me.

She'd been *kidnapped* before, but I didn't have the heart to tell her off, especially not right now when I was sick with suspicions about Mum.

She ran over to hug Boges and Winter.

"That's the Ormond Jewel," I said, finally answering Gabbi's question, "and that is the Ormond Riddle. These are the two things everyone's been after."

"Where did you find them?" she asked.

Winter looked down, avoiding the question, and fiddled with the laces on her sneakers, while Boges remained stunned, the two frown lines on his forehead forging together in a deep trough.

"Is that a real emerald?" she said, coming closer.

"You bet," said Boges, finally speaking up for all of us. "It's the real thing. 'Big as a pigeon's egg,'" he quoted.

While Gabbi and Boges talked, Winter pulled me aside against the dark, curving wall of the cenotaph.

"Your *mum* had these? From Rathbone? In her bag?" she whispered, her worried eyes searching mine.

I nodded.

"*Mum* had them?" asked Gabbi, swinging around from Boges. "How come Mum had these things if everyone's been after them? I thought you said she didn't know anything about this."

I was lost for words. As I shrugged my shoulders, things seemed to slowly come into place. My mum must have always known more than she'd let on. After all, she'd seen the transparency and the empty jewel box, and she'd heard Rafe questioning me about the Ormond Riddle—she'd been there all along. I recalled her staring at Dad's drawing of the Angel up on my wall before this mess began . . .

The cenotaph started to spin around me like I was trapped inside one of those anti-gravity carnival rides. *Mum?* Could Mum have been the person who—I tried to stop my brain from going there, but it was determined. My mum had been acting like a stranger to me almost all year. If she was capable of turning her back on her son, could she also have been capable of . . . attacking me? Locking me in a coffin and leaving me to die underground?

"Somebody say something!" cried Gabbi, walking over to me and tugging on my jacket. She slipped her hands into my pockets and I brushed her away.

"My hands are cold," she whined. "What's wrong with you guys?"

"There has to be an explanation," I said.

"*Hello*?" said Gabbi. "Am I invisible? Why are you ignoring me?"

"Sorry Gabs," said Boges. "We're just a little distracted right now with some new . . . umm . . . developments. Look, Cal," he said. "Let's just focus on the fact that we have them back. That's *good* news. Let's worry about the other things later, huh?"

"Boges is right," said Winter, with an arm around Gabbi. "There could be a perfectly reasonable explanation."

She hugged my sister, who was turning the Jewel over in her hands.

"We'd better get you back home," said Boges, tugging on one of Gabbi's plaits.

My sister groaned and brushed Boges away. "I

can *help* you guys," she said. "I'm not a kid any more. Why can't you see that?"

"We know," said Winter, "but it's just too dangerous right now. You need to stay home . . . and keep an eye on your mum and Rafe. We need someone to make sure they're OK. OK?"

"Let's go," said Boges to Gab. "I'll walk you home."

Treehouse

3:00 am

Back at the treehouse I charged up my phone and realised I had a couple of missed calls from Sharkey. Winter and I listened carefully to his voicemail message, hopeful for news on our trip.

"Cal, it's Nelson," he'd said. "I have the tickets. The four of us are booked to fly out on the twenty-third. Do yourselves a favour and stay out of trouble until then."

"Wow, it's all happening!" said Winter, excitedly. "Can you believe we finally have a date, plus the Jewel and the Riddle in our possession?"

"Crazy stuff," I said, relieved, but unable to shake off the bad feelings I had about Mum.

A tiny spider crawled up Winter's arm. She yawned and shook it off gently.

"Until we fly out, I'm going to have to find better

accommodation, Cal. A girl like me can only live up a tree for so long. I might give Sharkey a buzz back and see if he can hook me up with a place to stay. Somewhere Sligo will never find me."

9 DECEMBER

23 days to go . . .

Fit for Life

4:40 pm

Boges, Winter and I sat on upturned crates out the back of the gym. We were meeting up with Sharkey to go over our travel plans, and were waiting for him to return from the showers.

I'd missed Winter's company in the last few days. Sharkey had set her up in a motel that was run by a retired cop he knew. She'd tried to convince me to join her there, but I felt safer up the tree on Luke Lovett's property. I also didn't want to risk bringing any attention to her. We couldn't let Sligo find her.

"I have something for you," said Boges proudly. He passed me some sort of diving watch. "It works like a regular watch but it's also a radio beacon."

"Another distress beacon?"

"Yep. Consider it an early Christmas present.

I've adapted the winder so that if you press it like so," Boges leaned over and depressed the tiny button, which lit the watch-face up with a strange, blue pulsing light, "you'll activate the emergency radio signal. I have the receiver here," he said, holding out a similar watch on his wrist. "This watch picks up the signal and gives me the GPS coordinates of where you are."

I tightened the watch around my wrist, while Winter shuffled forward to get a closer look at it.

"Awesome, Boges," she said. "Hopefully he won't need to use it like last time."

"Better safe than sorry," he said. "I was hoping it would soften some other news I have," Boges began.

I groaned. "Spit it out."

"I read a report online this morning that the authorities believe you're a flight risk."

"A flight risk? How do they know?"

"I'm not sure, but they're upping security at all the major airports until you're detained."

"They'll have to catch you first," said Winter.

"OK," said Nelson, stepping out of the back door with a clap of his hands. He pulled a crate over to us and sat down on it. His dark hair was wet and slicked back. "I figured it would be a good idea to make a basic plan and start getting used to our stories ahead of time. So here's the deal. We're travelling as a school group, OK? I'm your teacher."

"Cool," said Boges. "Our history teacher? You kinda look like you could be a history teacher."

"Suits me," said Nelson. "I suggest we all drive together to the airport. I'm happy to leave my car in one of the parking stations. You'll be safer, Cal, as part of a group. Have you heard about the airport alerts?"

"Boges just told me."

"The authorities will be on the alert for an individual, not a group."

"We might be travelling as a group," I said, "but everyone still has to go through security as an individual . . . I hope I make it through OK."

"Yeah, I'm not so sure I'll be OK either," said Boges. "I'm known to the police, as they say. I could be on their radar. Do you think they'll pull *me* up?" he asked Sharkey. "Do you think my name's on some sort of watch list?"

"Won't be a problem," said Sharkey, patting Boges on the shoulder.

"How can you be so sure?" Boges replied, puzzled.

Sharkey dug into his gym bag and pulled out a brown paper bag. He tossed it to Boges.

"What's this?" asked Boges as he pulled out a dark blue passport.

"Open it."

Boges leafed through the pages. "Hey, that's my picture! *Joshua Stern*?" he read.

"That's your new name, buddy," said Sharkey.

Boges started shaking his head. "Nelson," he said, with a worried look, "this would be great, but it was hard enough us getting the money together for Cal's passport and our tickets. We don't have enough left over for this one."

"Don't worry about the money," said Nelson. "I bargained with the forger and convinced him to do another two for me."

"Two?" I asked.

Sharkey promptly produced another brown bag and tossed it to Winter.

Winter caught it with the excitement of a kid at Christmas.

"Grace Lee?" she read.

"That's right," said Sharkey. "With Vulkan Sligo's connections, we don't want your name alerting the authorities to our presence at the airport either."

I reached out to shake Sharkey's hand. "Thanks so much," I told him. "You must have done some sweet talking to get three passports for us. Ireland would be nothing but a pipe dream if we didn't have you to help us out."

"Forget about it. The thing you guys really

need to do now," he said, "is to practise your new names until you respond to them just like you do to your real names. Like you, Matt Marlow," he added, eyeballing me.

"Yes, sir," I said. "Maybe you could all call me Matt from now on?"

"Sure thing, Matty," said Winter.

"Thanks, Grace. You, too, Josh," I added.

"No problem, Matt," Boges replied.

"Good," said Sharkey. "Our departure date's going to come around fast. In the meantime, get to know the details on your passports and start packing. I'll hold onto the tickets for now and I'll call you to organise another meeting soon."

"Sharkey," said Boges, "is it OK if I give my mum your number to call—she's a bit concerned about this 'study trip' occurring over Christmas. Can you just tell her it's legit?"

Sharkey looked at Boges sternly and pursed his lips. "I don't like lying, but I'll do it."

13 DECEMBER

19 days to go . . .

Outside Ryan Spencer's Flat

8:10 am

Ryan had been on my mind for days, and this morning I was drawn to his place like a magnet, as though I had to see him and start making up for lost time. I think it was all the photos of Dad and Rafe I'd been mulling over that made me want to speak to *my* twin.

Even though I hardly knew him, he was the only family member I felt safe seeking out, and he deserved to know everything *I* now knew about our history.

I had no way of getting in touch with him, so I had no choice but to linger outside his apartment building, hoping he'd show up sooner or later. I leaned against the fence, reading a copy of yesterday's newspaper that I'd found in a nearby recycling bin.

It was a hot December morning, and if it

hadn't been for the questions squirming around in my mind concerning my mum, I would have felt great about getting closer and closer to our goal in Ireland.

"Good morning, Ryan," said an old lady, passing by the letterboxes.

I looked up, startled, realising she'd mistaken me for my brother.

"Hi," I answered, flustered, hoping she'd be happy with that and move on.

"How's your dear mother?" she continued.

"She's good, thanks," I replied, as plainly as I could, silently begging her to leave me alone.

"Be a pet and tell her I said hello," she added, before finally shuffling along to the building next door.

I breathed a huge sigh of relief, just as a familiar figure appeared at the door to the building.

"Ryan!" I called out.

I hurried across to him and his face lit up when he saw me.

"Hey!" he said. "I wanted to get in touch with you but didn't know how. Quick, come upstairs."

"I don't want to freak your mum out again," I said, cautiously, thinking about how last time I'd been here, I'd left him behind with his mum— the woman who'd adopted him—lying unconscious on the floor.

"She's not here—already left for work. The place is empty."

"So you don't have to be somewhere?"

"Nowhere that can't wait."

8:42 am

Ryan hunched opposite me, listening intently over the coffee table in his living room. I tried to tell him everything I possibly could about us, and tried to answer all of his questions about *his* mum, and whether she knew who he really was.

"We were abducted?" Ryan asked, his eyes searching my face.

"Yes."

"And my mum—I mean, my *adoptive* mum—had no idea of who I really was? That I was the missing baby, Samuel?"

"That's right."

After I'd passed on everything I knew, Ryan was silent for a long time. I wondered what was going through his mind—was he angry? Upset? He stood up and went to the window, looking out across the rooftop where I'd once chased him.

Finally, he turned to me and said, "This explains something I've thought about for as long as I can remember—that something wasn't quite right with me, not right with my family. I've never really fit in. I don't look like my mum, and we're both really different people. I've always had this nagging feeling that something . . ."

"Something was missing?" I finished for him.

He nodded. "I've always had this dream, too," he began, "which is finally starting to make sense. I'm in this cold, dark place, crying, then all of a sudden I'm somewhere else, but wanting to go back . . . It must have been about you," he said. "You were left behind in that building."

Goosebumps crawled across the skin on my forearms. The incident had haunted his dreams, too.

"But why did Murray Durham want to do away with us?" asked Ryan. "I don't get it."

I shook my head. "He was just carrying out orders."

"From who?"

"I don't know. Durham didn't know either."

"Cal, I want to ask a favour."

"Go on."

"I really want to speak to your mum. I mean *our* mum." He pulled out his mobile. "I just want to talk to her. Tell her I'm OK. Will you call her for me?"

I thought about it for a second. There were so many reasons why I should have said no. Including my suspicions about her involvement in the

DMO. But this was her missing child. Maybe she'd listen to him.

"Here, use my phone," said Ryan, handing his mobile to me. He looked so hopeful, nervous, brave.

"That's OK," I said, turning down his phone. "I'll use mine." I stopped thinking about it, pulled out my phone and just dialled her number.

"It's ringing," I said, already starting to have second thoughts. Could I make things worse and put Ryan in danger? But he wasn't the heir— *I* was the first-born son. *I'd* beaten him into the world. I hoped that meant he was safe.

Before I could decide, she answered.

"Hello?"

I took a deep breath. "Mum," I said. "It's me. Don't hang up. Just hear me out. I have Ryan Spencer with me. My twin brother. *Samuel*, Mum."

I waited for her to say something, but she didn't.

"He's here and he'd really like to talk to you," I added.

"Cal, please leave Samuel's memory alone. He's dead and gone—" her voice choked on a sob. "Why are you torturing me like this?"

"But Mum, he's just here! I promise I'm not lying! Please at least talk to him?"

"I can't, Cal. I just can't. I have to go."

The line went dead. I felt a mixture of pain and fury spin through me. She didn't want to listen.

I looked over at Ryan. "No good, huh?" he asked.

I shook my head.

He looked pretty disappointed, but quickly shrugged it off. "She'll come around sooner or later," he said with conviction. "Especially when we meet, face-to-face."

I couldn't imagine that happening, with Mum acting the way she was, but I kept my mouth shut.

"I'd better go," I said. "I have lots to do before I—" I hesitated, unsure about whether I should mention my Ireland plans.

"Before you what?" he asked, curiously. "You can trust me, you know. I am your brother, after all. We have at least fifteen years' worth of helping each other out of trouble to catch up on. You can count on me."

In this new world of not being able to trust anyone, even those closest to me, I was surprised I believed him.

"I'm flying out," I explained. "Going to Ireland—leaving in the afternoon of the twenty-third."

"How come? Won't that be dangerous? Aren't you worried you'll be caught, going to an airport? Isn't that a bit—"

"Stupid?" I interrupted. "Possibly, but I just have to risk it. If I can make it to Ireland, there's a chance I can clear my name. I have to take that chance. I have a fake passport and I'm hoping that's enough. I have no alternative and time's running out."

"No alternative, eh?" he said, giving me a long, hard look. "I guess I should say good luck."

"Thanks," I said.

We exchanged phone numbers, said goodbye and I headed back to the treehouse.

18 DECEMBER

14 days to go . . .

Treehouse

4:36 pm

Our plane to Ireland was leaving in less than a week, so Boges, Winter and I were poring over everything we had so far on the DMO, in preparation.

I spread everything out on the floor as best I could, while Winter wrote up a quick list.

"The first thing we need to do when we get there," announced Winter as she handed me her list, "is set up a meeting with the Keeper of Rare Books at Trinity College in Dublin. We play it low-key—we don't want to reveal everything we know—we just want to find out what he can offer us. If he can help us find the missing two lines from the Riddle, we'll be way ahead of the game."

Boges and I must have looked unconvinced.

DRAWINGS

Angel — Ormond Angel, Piers Ormond

Butler with blackjack — Black Tom Butler, the tenth Earl of
Ormond and Queen Elizabeth's agent in Ireland. Given the OJ
by QE1.

Things that can be worn — the Ormond Jewel

Collared monkey with ball — painting of Queen Elizabeth?

Sphinx and Roman bust — Ormond Riddle . . . and Caesar shift?

Boy with rose — Ormond Singularity heir? Tudor rose?

Door with number '5' — link to photos from memory stick?

Kilfane & G'managh transparency — a map?

ORMOND JEWEL & ORMOND RIDDLE —
double-key code link to Ormond Singularity.

PHOTOS FROM MEMORY STICK

Castle ruins

Gate with number '5' in it — link to cupboard/door drawing?

Carved wardrobe — same as above

"I don't care what contacts and resources Rathbone or even Sligo have," Winter scoffed. "That doesn't mean they'll beat us." She flicked her hair back from her face before speaking again. "Then, depending on how our meeting with the Keeper goes, I think we should head to the place your dad was staying in—the Clonmel Way Guest House in Carrick-on-Suir. Boges, I mean, *Josh*, did you bring the map of Ireland you printed out?"

"Sure did, *Grace*," he said, unfolding a huge map and spreading it out over the top of the papers on the floor. The three of us peered over it, examining it closely.

"Carrick-on-Suir is some way from Dublin," said Winter, "but not so far by bus or train."

"As soon as we reach the guesthouse we should start searching the area. Maybe a local will recognise this." I pulled out a photo of the castle ruins.

"And remember," said Boges, "we'll be travelling in an Irish winter. It could be snowing so pack plenty of warm gear." With that he pulled out a blue and white striped beanie and tugged it on his head. It entirely covered his curly hair, which was slowly growing back after Winter had shaved it.

I looked up from the transparency. "There's so much we still don't know. That black dot could be pointing out nothing but a good place to grab lunch."

"That would be good, too, but not exactly what we were hoping for." Boges laughed and started packing up his gear. "I'm off to meet Nelson now, just to go over the final details. Wow, you guys," he said, a broad smile stretching across his face, "can you believe this is all really happening? We're actually going to Ireland!"

"It *is* pretty awesome," agreed Winter, a smile growing across her lips too. "I'm excited. It's going to be one huge adventure, no matter what happens."

"You're right, guys," I said, starting to feel the enthusiasm building. "I guess I'll see you both next week—ready and raring to go!"

6:10 pm

As soon as I was alone again, my nerves resurfaced. Every time thoughts of my mum crept into my mind, I tried to push them away and focus on going to Ireland. Whenever thoughts of being captured at the airport before even setting foot on the plane snuck in, I'd wipe them out by imagining the exhilaration I knew I would feel as soon as I was finally on my way.

23 DECEMBER

9 days to go . . .

11:00 am

Outside the treehouse window, the sun was shining. The birds in a tree nearby were squawking so loudly that I could hardly hear Winter's voice on the phone.

"Speak up," I asked her.

"I'm all ready," she said, louder, her voice trembling with excitement. "Nelson's picking up *Josh* first, then me, then we're coming over to collect you. He'll be here at the motel any minute . . . I hate to say it, but I'm feeling pretty nervous. What if something goes wrong?"

"We can't let it," I said, even though I was feeling just as freaked out by what we were about to do.

11:21 am

As I waited, I checked and re-checked my backpack, anxiously making sure I had everything I needed. We were supposed to be at the airport by one o'clock, for our flight at three. I combed my hands through my hair, styling it forward so that it hung across my face, almost covering my eyes.

The contacts! I'd almost forgotten all about the dark contacts Winter had given me. I quickly dug them out of my bag and blinked madly as I put them in.

11:29 am

When I heard Sharkey's car pulling up in the lane behind the back fence, I checked the coast was clear, then clambered down the treehouse rope, and snuck out of the Lovetts' yard for the last time.

"Good morning, sir," I joked, as I climbed into Sharkey's car.

Sharkey laughed awkwardly, making me feel even more nervous than I already was. I looked around the car at my friends—everyone looked really uneasy.

"What's wrong?" I asked. "I mean, apart from the obvious—the fact that you're a phoney school group helping the notorious Psycho Kid escape the country."

"Sharkey just told us some bad news," replied Boges.

"There's a huge security convention happening over the next four days," explained Sharkey, as we headed for the airport. "Counter-terrorism squads from all over the world have descended on the city. They'll be practising manoeuvres—raiding buildings, securing roads and bridges, locking down the airport, that sort of thing."

"Locking down the airport?" I asked, recalling what Eric Blair had told me about Strike Force Predator.

"The airports were already on high alert, but now security has tripled," Sharkey continued. "Random stop-and-search exercises of cars and public transport will be carried out, I heard."

Boges shook his head. "It gets worse. The police commissioner has said that instead of this exercise being a sterile operation, they're giving the program real focus by having your capture as part of the agenda. Apparently the authorities are even going to be doing a bit of random fingerprinting at Departures."

"What do we do?"

"Nothing we *can* do," replied Sharkey. "We've just gotta do everything we planned and hope we slip through somehow."

I exhaled loudly and stared through the window at the fast-moving world outside.

"Come on," Winter comforted me, patting my knee like my mum used to. "Somehow we'll get through. I can feel it."

I turned to her and forced a smile. She was wearing an emerald-green beret and her dark hair tumbled down over her shoulders. I hoped her feeling was right.

"Do you all have your stories straight?" Sharkey asked.

"Absolutely," I replied, happy to have something to distract me from the somersaults in my stomach. "I'm Matt Marlow, travelling to Ireland with my friends Joshua Stern and Grace Lee, and our history teacher Mr Nelson Sharkey."

Sharkey nodded, but I could see that even he was nervous. He was used to being the law-abiding good guy, and now he was aiding and abetting a wanted fugitive.

The number of police cars on the street, and helicopters in the sky, grew thicker the closer we came to the airport. Luckily the lane leading to Departures that the police had taken over for random checking was full as we cruised past.

12:25 pm

Sharkey parked and we all began the nail-biting trek inside. I stopped myself from looking around, but couldn't control the sweat that had broken out on my forehead. I knew the guys on passport control were trained to look for suspicious characters, and if I didn't control my anxious, darting glances, and do something about the sweating, I'd be discovered.

With Christmas so near, the whole airport was buzzing. I guessed most travellers were going on holidays, maybe joining their families overseas, like Sharkey. They were fussing over luggage labels, chasing kids around, wheeling suitcases that were probably weighed down with presents. I felt like our sombre group was sticking out like a sore thumb.

For me this was the first part of the final obstacle in this year-long quest. I could almost taste victory. I shifted the weight of my backpack. Inside I had warm clothes Boges had lent me for the Irish winter, and beneath them was a smaller zip-lock bag containing the Riddle, the Jewel and our notes. I wasn't checking my backpack in—nothing was going to separate me from everything I had inside.

"Just relax, Matt," said Winter, who had obviously noticed the state I was in.

"I'm trying, *Grace*," I said through gritted teeth.

"OK," Nelson interrupted. "We have our stories straight, so let's check in. Any questions, just refer to me."

I looked up and noticed that Sharkey had beads of sweat on his brow. He seemed really nervous for me; his eyes were scanning the international check-in area.

We just had to make it onto the plane.

1:21 pm

The four of us had made it through check-in—our fake passports had held up so far—and we were following Sharkey, walking over to the queue for passport control. None of us had said anything to each other since checking in—we were all too tense.

Suddenly Sharkey slowed up, forcing us to stop abruptly behind him. He casually turned around to us, but the look on his face was more than unsettling.

I quickly peered past him and a feeling of horror took over as I realised we were walking towards the security convention's fingerprinting station.

"What do we do?" Winter whispered.

Sharkey looked stumped for a second.

"Just walk on by as confidently as you can," he eventually instructed, while pretending to look for something in his wallet. "There's no turning back for us now. We're just a school group, remember? Hopefully they won't pick us out and call us over. If they *do* call us over, then I guess we'd all better start praying for a miracle."

My heart was beating out of my chest as Sharkey turned around and continued walking. My two friends and I had no choice but to follow.

"Excuse me, sir," a voice called out from the security station. "Would you and your group please step over here for a random fingerprint test?"

Those words winded me like a punch in the gut. The kind of punch that sends you crashing to the ground. The kind of punch that you don't recover from.

I panicked, looking at Boges and Winter frantically. They looked as petrified as me.

Sharkey turned to us once more and I felt sick. "Come along, kids," he said to us, but I could see in his saddened eyes that he knew our quest was over. We were about to have our fingerprints taken, and that meant the police had won. They were about to capture their target.

We'd failed. Solving the DMO just wasn't meant to happen.

I closed my eyes and thought of the life I wanted to have—the normal life with Mum, Gabbi, Rafe and my twin. The life I imagined was about to be irrevocably lost.

A rapid change in the energy of the crowds suddenly washed over us. The line-up of police and security guards at the fingerprinting station ahead abruptly dismantled. Officers stood up from their posts and rushed over to a TV screen. Others nearby reached for their walkie-talkies.

What was happening?

My heart was thumping in my throat as my eyes darted around again, trying to make sense of the commotion. Had they locked onto me through the surveillance cameras? Was a riot squad about to tackle me down?

Where could I hide? Where could I go? I was trapped!

I spun around. The whole airport erupted into chaos. Travellers were dropping their bags and rushing to catch a glimpse of the airport TV screens, talking and gesturing excitedly to each other.

What was happening?

"Look!" cried Winter, pointing to a smaller screen in the quarantine area.

The four of us squinted up at the screen. It was a news report. A breaking news banner ran beneath the announcer.

"'Teen fugitive, Callum Ormond,'" I read, "'leads police on wild chase. Police Commissioner calls for calm.'"

Winter grabbed my arm.

"We interrupt this broadcast for breaking news," the announcer declared. I strained my ears to hear her words over the hubbub around me. "We're going live to our on-the-scene reporter. Tell us, Anton, we've had reports that Callum Ormond has been located and is leading police on a *car* chase? Where is he and what is happening as we speak?"

"It's a baffling scene here, Julia. It appears that shortly after two o'clock this afternoon, wanted fugitive, Callum Ormond, rammed a car into the doors of the city police headquarters. He then jumped out and fled *on foot*, and was captured just moments ago outside Town Hall. The entire incident was caught on closed-circuit TV and police have confirmed that they have arrested Ormond and that he has been taken into custody."

What?

Boges, Winter and Sharkey stood rooted beside me, staring at the screen.

"What on earth is going on?" hissed Boges. "They've arrested Callum Ormond? But—"

"*Ryan!*" I softly cried, with unspeakable relief. "Ryan must be behind this! He knew I was flying out today! He's done this to make sure I get out of the country!"

Overhead, we could hear the helicopters that were hovering near the airport move away, towards the city.

The officer who had called us over earlier

waved us on hurriedly. "We'd better make our move right now," said Sharkey, confidence returning to his eyes.

He beamed as he led us towards the distracted customs counter. He knew we were safe. No one would be looking for me now.

2:32 pm

We'd made it. The four of us slumped into the stiff chairs of the boarding lounge, exhausted, drained, relieved. We'd be on the plane within minutes.

I pulled out my phone, preparing to switch it off, when I noticed an unread message sitting in my inbox from about an hour or so ago.

📱 cal, it's ryan. i'm about to do something pretty crazy . . . i really hope it helps u make it through the airport & onto that plane. who knows, it may even force our mother into seeing me. hopefully the cops believe me when i tell them it's just an innocent driving lesson gone wrong! safe trip, bro! see u when u get back!

24 DECEMBER

8 days to go . . .

Temple Inn
Dublin

7:26 pm

The freezing-cold air of Christmas Eve was a shock even though we'd anticipated it. We hailed a taxi to take us to our small hotel in Temple Bar, in the south-west of Dublin. Christmas lights lined the riverside quays and the driver commented on several points of interest, including the Liffey River, the Abbey Theatre and the blue lights of the Garda—the police station. We were too exhausted to take much notice, although it was good to know that the Garda wouldn't be looking out for Psycho Kid.

At the hotel, we all checked in under our fake names. Boges and I were sharing a room, while Winter had a tiny attic room above us. She could barely turn around in there, but was more than happy with it. Nelson Sharkey's room was just across the corridor from us. Other Sharkeys from all over the world had also arrived in Ireland for their huge Christmas reunion. Their celebrations were starting tomorrow, at a place called Roscommon, so Sharkey was only staying one night. In the morning he would be heading off then meeting up with us again after a few days.

9:00 pm

After we'd settled in, Boges and I called Dr Theophilus Brinsley, the Keeper of Rare Books, to let him know we'd arrived.

"Tomorrow's Christmas Day," he said. "How about we meet on Boxing Day? The library will be quiet, because of the holiday. Meet me outside on the stairs at ten o'clock."

"Perfect. See you soon. Oh, and merry Christmas," I added before hanging up.

I looked over to Boges. He'd already collapsed back into his bed, softly snoring. I wanted to do exactly that too—sleep. On a bed. A *bed*. With sheets and a pillow and a clean pillowcase. For the first time in almost a year, I felt safe enough to sleep soundly.

Before I drifted off, I pictured my dad. I shoved all of my recent suspicions and uncertainties out of my mind and visualised him as I remembered him on the day he left for Ireland. Being here, I was feeling closer to him than ever. Soon I would go to Clonmel Way Guest House and retrace his last known steps.

25 DECEMBER

7 days to go . . .

10:15 am

The breakfast room was festooned with coloured lights, and two wooden reindeer stood by the entrance—their antlers decorated with shiny baubles hanging on golden threads. We were the only people in there.

Sharkey had shared a quick cup of coffee with us before leaving to go and meet his relatives for lunch. He'd looked a bit unsettled, and I guessed it was because he was missing his kids. Boges, too, was looking a bit down. He'd called his mum and gran earlier, but had never been happy about leaving them alone at Christmas.

"As soon as we get back home, we'll have to have our own Christmas lunch together. With lots of presents and a big roast with lots of potatoes," I said, wishfully.

"Can't wait," said Winter.

"Me neither," said Boges, "especially for the feed."

Past Christmases with Mum and Dad had always made me and Gab think about how lucky we were. I knew Gabbi would be missing me today, but I wondered how my mum felt and whether she'd met Ryan—her lost son—yet. Then I looked at this amazing girl across from me now, Winter, who'd lost so much and yet had such fierce determination to recover what was rightfully hers, while also helping me recover what was rightfully mine. I then turned to Boges, my loyal mate and ally. He was as solid as a rock.

"What's this?" asked Winter, picking up a small white envelope from the table, left where Sharkey had been sitting.

For Cal, Boges and Winter,
Merry Christmas!
Nelson.

"Open it," I urged.

Winter carefully eased it open and out slipped a small plastic sleeve, the size of a credit card. Inside was a flat-pressed four-leaf clover.

"How sweet," exclaimed Winter, holding it up for us to see. "He must have been too shy to just give it to us, so he left it behind. I hope it really is lucky!"

"That's cool," said Boges, examining it closely.

I looked down at the clover Sharkey had left behind. He was doing for us what I was sure he wished he could do for his own kids. Maybe I could somehow help him reunite with them, once we were back home.

11:45 am

We'd decided to check out the location of tomorrow's meeting with the Keeper of Rare Books, so we bundled up and headed out into a bleak Christmas morning. We strolled along the cobbled streets, past pubs and convenience stores, following the map the hotel owner had given us for Trinity College.

Winter walked briskly beside me, wearing a long white coat and a red woollen scarf tied around her neck. The green beret sat crookedly on her head and she tugged on it to straighten it. Boges and I were both wearing long black woollen trench coats and caps.

Being in Ireland, so far away from home, had definitely made me relax more than usual, but I was still very aware that Sheldrake Rathbone could be anywhere.

Trinity College
Dublin

12:00 pm

Church bells chimed as we walked through the quiet streets and through the huge Trinity College gateway. On the other side was an almost deserted quadrangle dominated by a bell tower in the middle of the large open square, surrounded by grand buildings. Only a few people, heads buried in their collars against the cold air, crossed the pathways through the perfect lawns. We paused at the bell tower and then followed the sign pointing towards the old library.

Standing on the steps outside, shivering in the cold, we smiled at each other. It was finally happening after all these months. We'd made it to Ireland and we were almost ready to take the prize. By tomorrow afternoon we could have the last two lines of the Ormond Riddle, and maybe we'd even know the location of the ruins in the photos Dad had taken. We could be way ahead of Rathbone in just twenty-four hours.

26 DECEMBER

6 days to go . . .

Trinity College
Dublin

9:55 am

Dr Brinsley was a tall man with wispy white hair, a deeply furrowed brow and unusual, half-moon glasses perched on his nose. He inspected the three of us over the top of his glasses with sharp, glittering eyes. We shook hands and his glance fell on the Celtic ring I wore.

"Ah, it's nice to see an old classic. The Carrick bend," he said, with a light Irish accent, pointing to the angular Celtic pattern woven in the silver band. "Sometimes also called the Carrick knot. It's a popular design in the south-east of the country. So," he continued, "you're the infamous young man who's finally obtained the Ormond Riddle?"

I nodded, not sure how to respond.

"I must say, as much as I was hoping to meet you, I don't think I ever really expected to see

you here. It must have been exceptionally difficult to make it out of your country."

"Yes," I admitted.

"So you have the Riddle, but not the last two
lines, eh?"

"You said you could help me with those," I
reminded him as we followed him through some
large double doors. I was really hoping I could
trust this guy.

"Yes, yes," he said, turning and closing the
double doors behind us. "Follow me, please."

He led us to the back offices of the library,
crowded with shelves that stood far too close to
each other, leaving only narrow passages between
them. It reminded me of Repro's old place. Once
through this maze we came to another door
which he unlocked and ushered us through.

We were standing on a small landing with
a railing around it, similar to the dress circle
of a theatre, overlooking the main body of the
library below. The gallery stretched away for
hundreds of metres, completely crammed with
brown, leather-clad books, sectioned into alcoves
soaring up to the cathedral-like ceiling.

"Wow," said Winter. "What a library! I've never
seen anything like it, except in the movies."

"Coolest library ever," exclaimed Boges,
leaning over the railing beside me. "Look at all

those ancient books! There must be millions in here!"

"Not quite," said Dr Brinsley. "We house over two hundred thousand antiquarian volumes, and the Book of Kells is just over there, in the Treasury building."

I didn't know what the "Book of Kells" was, but it must have been important.

"You have a treasure of your own," continued Brinsley, "which I am most anxious to see. Let's take a look at it, shall we?"

His eager eyes shone with greedy anticipation as he cleared some space on a nearby desk, piled high with ancient books and papers. The Keeper of Rare Books removed some boxes from a bench and an armchair and gestured to us to sit down, before sitting behind the desk himself.

What if Brinsley had been waiting for this moment—a moment to seize our "treasure"? Any moment now he could draw a weapon and turn on us.

Or would Rathbone suddenly jump out from an alcove, demanding someone ring the Garda and waving extradition papers that would have me on the next flight back home to face arrest?

I couldn't tell if I was just being paranoid or cautious. With the stakes getting higher now the end was so near, I didn't want to stuff up now.

My friends and I sat down and I carefully drew out the Ormond Riddle. I placed it on the Keeper's desk, just in front of me, my fingers firmly holding it in place as he leaned over it, fervently.

"Ah! Here it is at last! The Ormond Riddle," he breathed. "We all thought it had been lost forever. Can it be true?" He snatched up a magnifying glass from a drawer and started scanning the medieval script.

Finally he straightened up and his face was shining. His eyes even looked watery with elation.

"All my life, ever since I was a little boy and first heard about the Ormond Singularity, I've always wished that I could find the truth. My grandfather first told me about it. He'd heard about the legend from *his* grandfather. He'd grown up in Kilkenny, where it was rumoured that the huge secret concerning the Ormond family was hidden in one of Black Tom's castles."

"Kilkenny?" I interrupted, thinking of Great-uncle Bartholomew's property in Mount Helicon. "Kilkenny" must have been an important place for him to name his home after it. I dug out one of Dad's ruin photos. "Is this a castle in Kilkenny? One of Black Tom's castles?"

Boges and Winter, who'd been keeping pretty quiet, both shot me wary glares.

Dr Brinsley took the photo from me, looked at it and shook his head. "That's certainly not the famous Kilkenny Castle. Kilkenny Castle was saved from ruin, and is open to the public—you should visit it. But this," he said, examining the photo, "is unfamiliar to me. These sorts of ruins are all over Ireland. It could be anywhere."

Kilkenny Castle definitely sounded like something we should check out, but my shoulders slumped—finding the location in the photos was going to be much harder than we'd anticipated. I wondered how we could find out whether it was one of Black Tom's castles—one of the castles that could be hiding the secret of the Ormond Singularity.

He peered closer at the picture, picking up the magnifying glass again. "What's that figure there? Carved in the stones? That's very unusual for the times."

I stared hard and tried to make it out. I could almost see a figure cut into the stones of an upper turret, but I couldn't make out the detail. The angle of the photo made it almost impossible.

Dr Brinsley straightened up, and handed the photo back to me. "My grandfather also said that the Ormond Singularity gives passage to unimaginable treasure and wealth," he said, as though he were recalling an ancient myth. "As to the treasure trove," he continued, "you know how these stories grow over the centuries. Who knows what it really means?"

Unimaginable treasure and wealth. The phrase, so similar to my dad's, repeated itself in my mind. No wonder everyone was after it. Was that the secret that was hidden?

"Treasure?" asked Boges. "Do you believe there's some sort of buried treasure at one of Black Tom's castles?"

Dr Brinsley shrugged. "Possibly. But the Ormond Singularity runs out in a matter of days. On 31 December, at midnight, to be exact. I happen to know that because I've been working on old titles and legal documents awaiting repeal. We have to find places here to house them all."

I looked around at the already over-stuffed shelves, desks and floor, and understood his problem.

"If something valuable—the treasure, so to speak—is found after that time," continued Dr Brinsley, "it will all revert to the Crown. Which, of course, is where it is rumoured to have originated."

"Let me get this straight," I said. "You're saying that the Ormond Singularity began with the Crown? With Queen Elizabeth the First and the

Ormond family?" I asked him, careful not to let on how much we knew already.

"It was something Queen Elizabeth granted to the Ormond family. Black Tom—the tenth Earl of Ormond—was her vice-regent here, protecting her interests against his Irish countrymen. He was the first Irishman to be given the Order of the Garter and he wore it to bed every night."

"He wore it *to bed*?"

"That is so."

Winter nudged me. "Sounds like a serious crush to me," she whispered.

"But the Ormond Singularity is something much bigger than some decoration from the Queen," I said, thinking of the Ormond Jewel, "if you're talking about something like hidden treasure, here in Ireland."

My brain started turning around at those words. *Treasure . . . in Ireland.* Suddenly something made sense.

I turned to my friends. "Jennifer Smith said my dad had hurled a copy of Robert Louis Stevenson's *Treasure Island* across the room, frustrated that no one could understand what he was trying to say. He didn't want to *read* the book, he was trying to tell us about treasure *in* Ireland!"

"Your father knew something about this treasure trove?" Brinsley asked, frowning. "What else did he tell you?"

Immediately, I realised I'd said too much. "I don't know," I said, trying to brush it off. "He was so sick at the time, he was probably just hallucinating."

"That's right," Boges added, shaking his head. "Cal's dad died from an unknown virus that really messed with his head. He didn't know what he was saying."

I could see that Dr Brinsley suspected we knew a great deal more than we were letting on. He turned his attention back to the Riddle on his desk.

"Sacrilege," he said, examining the clean cut across the bottom, "cutting off the last two lines."

"Yes," I agreed. "So you said you have information about the last two lines, and where they could be?"

"First things first," he replied. "Do you also have the Ormond Jewel?"

I felt Boges kick my ankle, hard.

"It's in a safe," said Winter quickly. "Maybe we could organise for you to have a look at it."

"May I ask how you came by it? My grandfather told me that there was once such a Jewel but that it had been lost generations ago. There had always been some connection between the Ormond

Riddle and the Jewel, he believed. Although what it might have been, exactly, he did not know."

"It was recently acquired by my family," I said, reluctant to say that Dad had bought it while he was over here.

Dr Brinsley squinted at me, as though willing me to hand over more information. "The Ormond Jewel—perhaps you could tell me what it looks like?"

Boges tentatively pulled out some photos of the Jewel, and looked to me for approval to hand them over. I nodded to him.

"Here," he said, placing them in Brinsley's eager hands. There were four photos of the Jewel; one showing it closed, one showing it opened—revealing the portrait of Elizabeth the First inside, one showing the back with the rose and rosebud, while the last was a magnified depiction of the Middle French inscription.

After studying the photos for some time, Dr Brinsley sat back and fanned himself with a wad of papers. "I must say," he said, "this is incredible. The usual explanation for this sort of precious, antiquarian item reappearing in modern day is that it has been held by a family for hundreds of years, so long that its origin and importance has been forgotten or lost, then the piece is sold when a family finds itself in financial difficulties. I'd say it came on the market fairly recently, was bought up by a dealer who also didn't know its history, and then was sold for its face value—a jewelled miniature of Queen Elizabeth the First by an unknown artist. It would bring a high price just as it is, but certainly not the price it is actually worth."

The Keeper's face was filled with enthusiasm. "I think I'm starting to get some idea of what the Ormond Singularity might be. Mind you, it's only a guess—an educated guess—but there's something I have at home that I think you should see."

He pulled out a handkerchief and blew his nose, then leaned over to his desk and unlocked a drawer.

"In the meantime, I have this," he said, taking out a small document. It seemed to be written in Latin, but I could understand the date—1575. "It's a record of a marriage. The marriage of one of Black Tom's illegitimate sons, Piers Duiske Ormond—a secret marriage contracted at Duiske Abbey, Graignamanagh."

"G'managh? That's one of the names on the transparency," I said, swinging round to Boges. "Piers must have been a common name."

"This shows that Piers Duiske Ormond married a young lady called Anne Desmond," said the Keeper, "before he married the woman who is known to history as his wife, and with whom he had his son Edward."

I was confused. Too many names were being thrown around.

"Never mind all that," Dr Brinsley said, as if reading my mind. "What *is* important is the record of this secret marriage. Especially since I suppose you already know that Black Tom out-lived his legitimate heirs?"

"What's all this got to do with the Riddle and the Jewel, Dr Brinsley?" I asked.

"It will make sense in good time, young man." He paused to take a sip of water from a mug on his desk. "Someone had hidden it in one of the ancient books that we bought from the Black Abbey some years ago."

Piers Ormond of the stained glass window had been at the Black Abbey. Had he hidden the original record of the secret wedding after copy-ing it for his collection of papers? Had he been meaning to return and collect it when he had more information, before the war prevented his plan?

"Here," said the Keeper, "is the name of Piers Duiske Ormond's father, the tenth Earl of Ormond, Black Tom Butler. And here, where his mother's name *should* be, there's only this—" The Keeper adjusted his half-moon glasses and cleared his throat. "*Magna domina incognita*," he intoned in Latin.

"A great lady. Unnamed, unknown," Boges translated.

"Well done, young man. I see you know your Latin."

"But I still don't see what this has to do with anything," I said.

"It has *everything* to do with it. I've been studying the Singularity for years now. I don't have the whole picture by any means, but I have some information about it. Just now, seeing the photos of the Jewel, the text of the inscribed motto and what it implies . . . I can't help playing around with certain possibilities." He looked around suddenly, as if wary of his surroundings. "This place is too public for this sort of discussion. This may be even more dangerous than I first anticipated."

"Oh, it's a dangerous business," I assured him, considering the countless times in the last year I had come close to death. "No doubt about that."

Dr Brinsley gestured towards us, urging us to lean in closer to hear what he had to say. "Please come to my house tomorrow evening," he whispered. "There's a sketch my grandfather did that I want to show you. After seeing the Jewel with its inscription, my instincts tell me that the sketch is of great importance. Perhaps you might be able to help? Especially when I tell you some thoughts I'm starting to entertain as a possibility, wild as they might be."

I'd come to Dublin to get answers, not a whole bunch of new questions. I directed the conversation back to basics.

"You told us you had information about the missing last two lines of the Ormond Riddle," I said again.

"Ah, yes," he said. "I *can* help you with that. Somewhat."

"Please tell us what you know," said Winter, her face eager. "That's what we're here for, after all."

"Those last two lines are believed to have been written by Black Tom himself." He looked at us as if waiting for a response. I didn't care who'd written them, I just wanted to *see* them, read them, apply the Caesar shift to them. Every instinct told me that the last two lines would deliver the secret of the Ormond Singularity to us.

"So do you have the last two lines or not?" urged Winter, clearly becoming as impatient as I was feeling.

"Not exactly, but I can tell you where I believe they are. In a copy of an antique book. Sir James Butler's *Lives of the Saints*."

"Is it here?" asked Boges, glancing over the

thousands of books shelved from floor to ceiling all the way along both sides of the immense expanse of the long gallery.

"I'm afraid it's not quite as simple as that," Brinsley replied. He raised his eyebrows before continuing. "As I told your friend who phoned last night—"

"*My friend who phoned last night*?" I repeated, frowning, looking around at the others. I was met with shocked silence. "None of us phoned last night," I said firmly. A cold chill ran through my bloodstream.

"No," said Boges. "None of us phoned you. Who do you mean? Who did you speak to about this?"

"You must be mistaken," said Dr Brinsley, peering at me. "He knew all about *you*. Introduced himself to me and informed me of how he was here in Ireland helping you search for the meaning of the Ormond Singularity. He had an unusual first name, although his second name is common in Ireland—as a place name too."

I tensed up at the threat to us that this revelation implied. "There's a place in Ireland called 'Rathbone'?"

"'Rathbone'?" Dr Brinsley repeated. "What does Rathbone have to do with it? No, the chap's name was Sligo. Vulkan Sligo. *County* Sligo's in the west-coast province of Connacht."

Winter stiffened with fear beside me.

Vulkan Sligo was in Ireland!

"What did you tell him?" I demanded, jumping out of my chair, and joining Boges and Winter who were already on their feet, ready to run.

Dr Brinsley looked confused and concerned. "Just that I hoped I'd be seeing you today."

"You told him we'd be here?" shrieked Winter. "What else did you tell him?"

"That you had the text of the Ormond Riddle," replied Brinsley, flustered. "He sounded a perfect gentleman."

"He's a notorious criminal!" shouted Winter. "He's tried to kill us! He wants Cal dead! Cal, we have to get out of here, now! He could be in here somewhere!" Her eyes darted around—she was petrified. Boges, too, was wide eyed and panicking, leaning over the railing, scanning the library for any sign of Sligo or one of his thugs.

"All right, let's go," I said to my friends. I stopped for a second to warn Brinsley. "Dr Brinsley," I said, "I don't want to scare you, but you could be in great danger too. You must believe me. Vulkan Sligo has been trying get me out of the way—"

"—*kill* you," Winter interrupted, her face pale. "He's been trying to *kill* you, Cal." She turned to Dr Brinsley. "He wants him out of the way so he can beat him to the Ormond Singularity."

The Keeper of Rare Books gave me a hard look that I couldn't interpret. Maybe he just didn't *want* to believe this.

"I said I would help you with the last two lines of the Ormond Riddle and that offer still stands." Brinsley grabbed a pen and started scrawling an address on the back of an envelope. "Tomorrow I should be finished up here by eight. Come to my place at nine. Come through the back door. Here's my address," he added, handing me the envelope.

"Cal, we have to get out of here," Winter pleaded.

"I know, I know," I said. "Please, Dr Brinsley," I begged him. "If you hear from Sligo again, please don't tell him you saw us here today. Don't tell him anything. Our lives depend on it."

He picked up the Ormond Riddle, after I'd let go of it in a panic. I could see something in his face that looked like rabid hunger. Everyone who'd heard of this business seemed to want a piece of the action.

"I'd like that back now, please," I said, trying to sound casual and cool.

Dr Brinsley flashed me a glinting smile. "You could always leave it with me until tomorrow evening . . ."

Boges stepped forward. "Not negotiable," he said, swiftly snatching up the Riddle.

With that, we ran back the way we'd come— swiftly weaving through the towers of books and mazes of shelving, before quickly disappearing into the cold quadrangle outside.

12:13 pm

Hands shoved deep in pockets, and wishing I'd worn a scarf like Winter, I walked nervously with the others around St Stephen's Green. Bare trees raised their dark limbs to the white sky, and even the ducks on the half-frozen ponds looked chilly.

We were all frustrated and angry. The vague feeling of ease we'd experienced on arrival had been short-lived. I was just as on edge as I'd been back at home. In fact, I was worse. Time was ticking by and now I was being hunted down in a foreign country.

My breath steamed in the air ahead of us as I spoke. "Dr Brinsley just doesn't realise the danger surrounding the Ormond Singularity. He wasn't taking our warnings seriously enough." Something else was troubling me too. "What if Sligo's already swayed him?" I asked the others. "What if tomorrow night's meeting is a trap? We may have dodged Sligo today, but what if he's at Brinsley's place, waiting for us, at nine o'clock tomorrow?"

"It's a possibility that we have to be prepared for, dude," Boges replied. "It's a risk we have to take."

"What if Brinsley intends on stealing the Ormond Riddle for himself?" asked Winter. "Did you see the look on his face when he was examining it? He didn't want to hand it back once you let go, Cal."

"He sure didn't," said Boges. "It was like he realised something as we were sitting there. Like he saw something, understood something, that he wasn't quite ready to share just yet. Tomorrow night's going to be interesting."

4:05 pm

We spent the rest of the day trying to see as much of Dublin as we could, although we were pretty uneasy knowing that Sligo was in town. Winter fell in love with the wrought-iron seahorses on the lamp posts—cool horses with arched necks, their raised front legs ending in layered fins, and muscular upper bodies tapering down into scaly mermaid-like tails.

We were jumping at the sound of every passing car and we constantly used counter-surveillance, taking sudden turns and doubling back on ourselves until we were hopelessly lost and had to pull out the map that we'd taken from the hotel.

It was impossible to relax. Eventually we decided it would be best to go back to the hotel. The thought of somewhere private and warm was too tempting.

Winter was really worried about Sligo tracking her down, but she hadn't checked in under her real name, so we hoped that would keep her safe, for now.

27 DECEMBER

5 days to go . . .

Parnell Square

8:35 pm

We found the address Brinsley had given us in Parnell Square, north of the Liffey River. His place was a stone terrace house with a few steps leading up to the red front door. The brass door knocker, decorated with a green and red holly wreath, gleamed in the streetlight.

I took one last look around as we returned from checking out the lane that ran along the back of the terrace houses. There was no one around. Except for us, Parnell Square was deserted.

I made a quick call to Nelson Sharkey. I'd told him about the meeting over the phone last night.

"Nelson speaking," he said, and I could hear the sounds of people talking and laughing in the background.

"We're about to go inside," I said. "If anything goes wrong, you have his address."

"OK, got that. But I'm a few hours away, remember. Be very careful. You can't trust anyone. Are you sure you haven't been followed?"

"Pretty sure," I answered.

"Have you checked the rear of the property? Checked no one's watching the place?"

"Yep, we're cool."

"No sign of Sligo?"

"Nope. Anyway, it sounds like the party needs you. Call you later." I hung up and looked at my shivering friends. "Let's do it."

We walked back round to the lane at the rear of the house, went through the gate and knocked on the back door.

"Dr Brinsley?" I called out after a minute or two.

The door wasn't locked and, with the slightest push, it swung open. The three of us wandered inside and looked around. Several closed wood-panelled doors led off from the black-and-white marble-floored square we'd walked into, and I could see a staircase leading to the upper floor.

"Dr Brinsley?" I called again, as our shoes tapped against the floor.

"I don't like this," said Boges. "Something feels wrong."

I felt Winter shivering beside me. "I feel it, too," she said, stepping a little further into the house. "He's expecting us. He should have been listening for us. Hello?" she called, louder than I had. "Dr Brinsley?"

We stood in the cold room, waiting.

"Why isn't he answering us?" whispered Winter.

A huge empty fireplace to my left had several fire tools hanging from a bar. I picked up the heavy poker. Winter and Boges followed suit, also picking up potential weapons. If Sligo was in here somewhere, we'd need to protect ourselves.

Soundlessly, we crept towards a light at the end of a small hallway behind the staircase, iron tools raised.

Soft music came from behind the door to the room with the light on. Maybe Dr Brinsley was listening to music and was lost in it. Maybe I was just paranoid. I lowered the poker.

I knocked gently. "It's Cal. I'm here with my friends. We let ourselves in. You asked us to come over at nine, right?"

No answer.

"You two wait here," I whispered. "I'm going in."

I pushed the door open with my shoulder.

The room felt empty although a fire crackled in a fireplace in the corner. I quickly scanned the scene. Books and papers were scattered around in wild and torn jumbles. The glass doors of a tall bookcase were hanging open, half off their hinges. A desk in the corner had been violently cleared—pens and paper clips were all over the floor.

Someone had been here. Someone madly searching for something.

I started to fear for Dr Brinsley.

"This is crazy!" said Boges who'd come in behind me, along with Winter. "Someone has trashed the place!"

Winter gasped. I turned to her—her face was ghostly. Her lips were trembling. She pointed to the ground.

Then I noticed what she was pointing to. Lying half buried under a series of old, leather-bound volumes.

An outflung arm.

Brinsley's half-moon spectacles lay on the hearth rug, the golden rims and arms bent out of shape.

I was fixed to the spot. A dark red stain was spreading over the rug near his body. Even without checking, I knew he was dead.

Winter fell to her knees and started pulling the books and debris off him, turning him over.

"He's dead!" she cried. "Dead! Sligo's been here and he's done this! He's murdered poor Dr Brinsley!"

Boges bent down to Winter and pulled her

away from the body. "Don't touch anything," he said. "We've gotta get out of here."

"What about the police?" she asked, getting back to her feet.

"We'll call the cops later—Sligo could still be here," he said. "We'd better run."

I turned around, preparing to walk carefully out of the room the same way I had come in, but as I was about to put my right foot down near Dr Brinsley's outstretched hand, I paused mid-step. A piece of paper under the desk caught my eye. Familiar words jumped out at me . . . *TOSJORS CELER.*

Cautiously, I bent over and picked it up. The words were part of an old pencil sketch of a ruin, smeared and yellowing with age. The sketch showed crumbling stone walls, collapsed fireplaces, vines growing in through unglazed windows and piles of fallen masonry. This was what he'd wanted to show us.

"Dude, we've gotta get out and call the Garda," Boges said. "Come on, try not to touch anything."

I grabbed Boges's cap off his head and wrapped my hand in it, turning the door handle and rubbing my prints off it. A sudden gust of wind rushed through from the hall, causing several of the books on the floor to flutter their pages.

From one of them lifted some sort of pamphlet,

rising and diving like a paper plane, almost landing at my feet as if it was trying its best to get my attention.

It was a catalogue of books to be sold at an upcoming second-hand book sale. I squinted at the long list of titles printed on it, and there, between John Ferdinand Bottomley's *Roman Epigrams in Irish Poetry* and Alferic Buxtehude's *Romance and Reality: The Celtic Twilight* I read "Sir James Butler's *Lives of the Saints*."

"Check this out," I said, picking it up. "Look, the book Dr Brinsley was talking about. He knew it was going to be in this sale."

"Whatever, Cal," said Boges, practically dragging me out of the room. "Tell us about it when we're not in the room with a dead guy."

I pocketed the catalogue and we hurried out of Brinsley's house, shaken up and shocked.

We half-walked, half-ran from Parnell Square, heading south down the street, stopping only at a public phone in the foyer of a noisy restaurant.

"Here," said Winter, snatching the phone from me, "I'll do it. Away with ye," she continued in a thick Irish accent, before speaking into the receiver. "A man has been murdered in Parnell Square," she said, disguising her own accent perfectly. She gave the address to the constable who'd answered, then hung up.

We headed off again, hurrying back to a café close to our hotel. We huddled in an empty corner and all tried to gather our shocked wits. Winter was trembling and it wasn't just the cold. Boges was shaking too.

"That poor man," murmured Winter. "We were only just talking with him. I can't believe it. He was innocent. Just caught up in this mess for no good reason."

She was right. I felt nauseous. I'd been responsible for another innocent person's death.

"Take a look at this," I said, pulling out the sketch, trying to focus our attention onto something else.

"Man," exclaimed Boges. "This has been taken from a crime scene. Could make you an accessory after the fact. I can see the headlines now: 'Psycho Kid strikes in Ireland.'"

Winter glared at the drawing with glassy eyes.

"Look," I pointed. "The motto inscribed in the Jewel is here in this picture."

Although the drawing was faded, and the interior that it depicted was crumbled and decaying, the words that had mesmerised me, drawn my eyes to the sketch—"AMOR ET SUEVRE TOSJORS CELER"—could just be seen in the stucco. They were barely legible in places, letters missing or eroded away, but still enough of them were left for us to be able to recognise the words of the motto inscribed inside the Jewel.

"So it is," said Winter, sounding a little less shaken up than a moment ago.

"That's why Dr Brinsley got so excited when he saw the photo of the Jewel, and that enlargement of the inscription," I said. "He recognised the motto from the sketch. He made a connection between the Jewel and this building—whatever it is, wherever it is. We don't know where this sketch fits in," I said, "but whoever killed Dr Brinsley and trashed the place missed this."

"It must have been Sligo," said Winter. "He must have been after that book—the one Dr Brinsley told us about. *Lives of the Saints.*"

"Probably," I agreed, pulling out the catalogue of books. "It looks like it's going to be here at this sale," I said, pointing at the listing. "It's on in a couple of days, in Kilkenny. At the Black Abbey. We'll have to go there and buy it before someone else does. The Clonmel Way Guest House will just have to wait."

"Dude, it's some kind of antique. It'll cost loads."

"Might have to steal it," suggested Winter.

"Maybe we won't have to do either of those things," I said. "If the last two lines of the Riddle are in there, like Brinsley said, then we just need to take them out. We can leave the book behind."

"I don't get it," said Winter, slowly. "If the last two lines of the Ormond Riddle have just been tucked in to this book, wouldn't someone have found them already?"

"I hope not," I said. "It's the only lead we have."

28 DECEMBER

4 days to go . . .

8:00 am

During the darkness of a winter dawn, we all got up and left the hotel behind. We had to move on. Time was ticking down and we were keen to leave Sligo and the bad memories of our encounters with Brinsley behind. At the bus station we bought tickets to Kilkenny.

We were stinging for Sharkey to return from his reunion so he could join us, but he was going to have to follow us to Kilkenny later.

The Waterford Bed and Breakfast Kilkenny

11:18 am

"We'd love to see the Black Abbey," Winter said to the landlady, Mrs O'Leary, as we were checking in. "We've heard there's a big book sale happening there shortly."

"Yes, yes, they have it every year," Mrs O'Leary

cheerfully comfirmed. "Fond of books, are you? Well, you might find something very old and very rare for a good price."

She gave us directions to Kilkenny Castle, too, and we bundled up and headed for the old attraction.

KilKenny Castle

2:01 pm

As we walked the paths under the dripping trees, we tried to imagine how the castle would look in summer with the huge oak trees full of leaves and the roses blooming.

But after some aimless wandering, I stopped walking and sat down on a low brick wall.

"What is it?" Winter asked, sitting down beside me.

"I feel like we're wasting time. I don't think there are any answers for us here. How about we go back to the Waterford and get our flashlights—we can go check out the Black Abbey tonight, see if we can find more information about the book sale tomorrow. Don't want anyone getting their hands on *Lives of the Saints* before we do."

"Sounds like a good idea to me," she responded.

"Let's move," said Boges, giving his cap a tug.

Black Abbey

8:14 pm

I couldn't help thinking, as we hurried through the dark, sleety night, up the hill towards the Black Abbey, that this could all add up to a big fat zero. All we had was the word of one man—now dead—who thought the last two lines of the Ormond Riddle were in this mysterious book.

I wondered, too, why Sligo had murdered Dr Theophilus Brinsley. Was it out of frustration when he realised that Brinsley didn't have the missing two lines? Or was it because Dr Brinsley wouldn't tell him where they were?

But what if he *had* told him where they were? That would mean Sligo could already be in Kilkenny. Instinctively, I looked around us, even though it was almost impossible to see anything in the darkness.

The bulk of the Black Abbey loomed ahead. It was a low building with a short, square tower, its turrets barely discernible against the night sky. As we approached the stone wall that surrounded it, I grabbed the others, stopping them in their tracks.

"There's somebody there, look. See that van parked over there?"

"Dude, let's check out who it is. I've been

wondering whether Sligo would be here already," said Boges.

"Me too," I admitted.

"Me three," added Winter, gripping my arm tightly.

We pressed on, cautiously, trying to keep out of sight of anyone near the van.

The van had its headlights on, illuminating the door to a stone building adjacent to the Black Abbey, that I had mistakenly thought was part of the abbey itself.

"What are they doing?" whispered Winter.

"Looks like they're unloading something," said Boges, close behind me, as we watched two people vanish through the doorway.

"They're unloading books," I said. "Setting up for tomorrow."

I put my hand in my pocket and grabbed my light. This was a piece of unexpected good luck. Maybe we could sneak in and get a preview.

The three of us hurried through the drizzle and over to the deserted van. Inside, it was empty. They must have only just unloaded the last of the boxes.

Silently, we sneaked inside the building, following the same path the people from the van had taken. The sound of footsteps and voices echoed from the other end of the corridor.

"Quick! They're coming back!" I hissed.

I opened the nearest door and the three of us scrambled inside, closing the door again behind us. I pressed my ear up against it, listening for movement. I heard the movers pass by outside in the corridor, then they left, slamming the door behind them.

A few moments later, the van started up and drove away.

"OK," I breathed, slowly turning the handle of the door and checking the corridor outside. "We're alone now. Let's see what we can find."

The lights had been switched off but we used our flashlights to guide us. We hurried to the end of the dark corridor where a door on my left and a flight of stairs on my right formed a T-junction. Passing my flashlight to Boges, I tried the door. It wasn't locked. I opened it and walked inside.

Ahead of us were three long trestle tables, each one covered with tablecloths and piled high with books for tomorrow's sale.

My heart was beating like a drum as excitement mounted in me. Winter and Boges rushed to the books and started looking through them and I quickly followed. Somewhere in this collection, I hoped, was the book containing the missing last two lines of the Riddle. The answer to the mystery of the Ormond Singularity was at our fingertips.

"OK dude," said Boges, "I'll take this table, Winter's on that one," he said, pointing to the furthest one. "You take the middle."

The smell of musty old books in the freezing air filled my nostrils as I ran the light from my flashlight over the spines and covers of the ancient books. Some were in Latin with old-fashioned marbled endpapers. Some were in Gaelic with faded gold lettering on their covers.

After about half an hour, I'd been through every book on my table.

"I think I'm done, guys. Either of you have any luck?"

"No," they both answered, their disappointment obvious in their tones.

I swore. It wasn't here. What were we going to do now? What if Sligo already had it?

"Quick, hide!" I ordered the others, as unknown voices interrupted the air.

We scrambled under the trestle table furthest from the door, huddling in the darkness, shielded, I hoped, by the tablecloth and other book-covered trestle tables. Someone was in the building with us.

Footsteps approached. The door handle squeaked as it was opened and someone came into the cluttered space. I didn't dare move to see who it was.

Foreign light started darting around the room, wavering across the floor and over the tables. We squashed ourselves as hard as we could against the wall, hoping the light wouldn't pick us up. I bumped my body into a box that had been shoved under the table.

I peered into the box and focused on a thin book sitting on top. The lettering was barely visible in the dark, but the shape of the title had grabbed me.

My eyes widened with stunned surprise. My head started spinning and it wasn't because of the imminent threat of being discovered—I was staring straight at the book we were after! I couldn't believe it! I bit my tongue and tried to keep still.

Once satisfied that everything was in order, the security guard or whoever it was stepped back out into the corridor, closing the door behind them.

I exhaled and grabbed the book out of the box. I turned to my friends and shone my flashlight on it so they could both see what I had found.

"You found it!" said Boges, trying not to shout.

"Amazing!" Winter smiled, shuffling in closer, and wiping dust from its cover. "No point sticking around any longer. Hold onto it for dear life and follow me out of here!"

Winter crawled out from under the table, then

stealthily led us over to the door, down the corridor, outside and away from the Black Abbey.

We ran, without stopping, all the way back to the Waterford.

The Waterford Bed and Breakfast Kilkenny

10:01 pm

Breathlessly, I opened Butler's *Lives of the Saints*, as Winter and Boges practically bounced with excitement on the bed beside me. My hands were shaking as I flicked through the heavy paper with its dense printing, checking page after page.

Pretty quickly my excitement vanished.

"There's nothing in it. Nothing!" I yelled, throwing the book down on the floor. "Just page after page of rubbish about ancient old saints!"

"Don't give up so quickly," said Winter, hopping off the bed and picking the book back up. "Maybe the lines have been written *in* somewhere—along an inside margin or something. Let me have a careful look."

She plopped down on the bed again and slowly, methodically, started turning every page, running her finger down the central margins of each one before turning to the next page. She used her flashlight to throw extra light on the yellowing pages.

"I just don't know how we're going to beat the deadline," I said. "I was so sure we were on the right track, but we still don't really even know what we're doing, where we should be going. We don't even know what we're looking for."

Winter turned her smoky eyes on me. "Cal," she said, "I have a feeling that everything's going to fall into place for us. Everything will come together. You'll see."

Outside, the wind had picked up and heavy rain was driving against the window, rattling the wooden frames. I went over to pull the heavy curtains shut but before I did, I peered out into the darkness. I had a horrible feeling that someone was out there. I dragged the curtains across quickly and sat back down.

"No good," admitted Winter, closing the book after her closer examination.

"Still thinking everything's going to work out?" I asked her.

She replied with an unimpressed look.

"My turn," said Boges, before he too went through it. He ran a magnifying glass carefully over every page and margin, and peered down the cracking spine of the old-fashioned book.

But there was nothing in there that we wanted.

We sat in a triangle, staring blankly at each

other. None of us had any energy or will left to bother saying anything. Eventually we just picked ourselves up and called it a night, crawling into bed, hoping tomorrow would deliver us a break.

29 DECEMBER

3 days to go . . .

10:16 am

"I just have a couple more family meals to survive here," Sharkey joked over the phone, "before I can come to you guys. I've had enough of the Sharkey family, to be honest. They just want to talk, talk, talk. The murder of Dr Brinsley has been massive news," he said. "Everyone knows about it. At this stage the Garda don't have any leads."

"At least *I'm* not on their radar," I said. That was one good thing. We'd avoided talking about it, but the death of Dr Brinsley was hanging over us like a black cloud, reminding us of the huge danger that accompanied our quest.

"So you've checked the book thoroughly?" he asked. "Been over the margins?"

"Nelson, we've gone over it with a fine-tooth comb. If the last two lines of the Ormond Riddle were ever in that book, they sure aren't now."

Sharkey groaned. "What a waste of time," he

said. "Look, I have to go again, but you three be very careful," he warned. "I'll join you soon as I can. Don't go anywhere you don't need to go, OK?"

"We're leaving Kilkenny and going to Carrick-on-Suir today," I said. "Off to the Clonmel Way Guest House, where my dad stayed last year."

"Good idea. Stay safe and I'll see you soon."

2:21 pm

A bus took us all the way down to Carrick-on-Suir. We stepped out into another cold, grey day, and as I walked down the cobbled streets with my two friends, I felt a confused mix of emotions: sad that this was where my dad first became so sick, but almost excited to be walking where he'd walked.

The drawings that I still carried with me had started me off on this huge journey. Time was running out. I only had three days left. It wasn't just about survival any more.

"Oh look!" cried Winter, pointing to a decaying tower sticking up like a rotten tooth over some long grey walls in the distance. "Do you think that's one of Black Tom's castles?"

I checked the small map I'd picked up at the bus station. "It sure is," I said, "Ormond Castle. We should check that out, but first we've got to find the guest house. It should be just up here," I said, indicating the end of a narrowing road, lined with houses.

Clonmel Way Guest House was the last building in a row of homes that backed onto the broad quay along the river. I could see the sign, cut in the shape of a salmon, swinging in the wind.

Clonmel Way Guest House
Carrick-on-Suir

3:20 pm

The narrow, two-storeyed property was painted blue and white, and had a small winter garden.

I went to open the gate and stopped abruptly. Winter gasped behind me. Boges swore under his breath.

There in the rusty wrought iron of the gate, in an enamelled oval, was the *number five*, just like in my dad's drawing!

"See?" cried Winter. "I told you things were going to come together!"

The drawing suddenly became clear—Dad had been trying to point out this place! I felt a surge of new energy powering through me, easing my disappointment about not finding the last two lines of the Riddle. We'd just have to find another way to get to the right destination.

I opened the gate and walked up the short path, knocking on the bright red door. A brass plaque above the doorway read: Clonmel Way Guest House; Imelda Fitzgerald, Proprietor.

A fair woman with rosy cheeks opened the door. She smiled broadly and welcomed us inside.

"I have plenty of rooms this time of year," she said. "You look like you could do with some good Irish scones and a cup of tea. Come in out of the cold."

We happily followed her into the cosy interior—a small foyer where plump crimson lounges and armchairs were grouped around a blazing fire. Old sepia photos above the fireplace captured horses towing barges along the riverside.

I introduced myself as Matt Marlow, along with my friends Grace and Josh.

"Like I say," said Mrs Fitzgerald, "it's not the best time of year. Doesn't do the place justice. Still, there's plenty to do, even in winter, and we have a couple of cots down on the river for the use of our guests."

"Cots?" asked Boges, a funny look on his face.

Mrs Fitzgerald laughed. "That's the name of the famous Carrick fishing boats. The Carrick cots. That's if you like messing about in boats."

Mrs Fitzgerald chatted on. She knew all about Black Tom's Ormond Castle, built at the end of the town. It was a feature of the township and a reason why visitors came to Carrick.

"It's the best example of an Elizabethan manor house in the land," she gloated. "I heard that the ruins of one of Black Tom's other old castles is being shipped back to the USA, block by block, to be rebuilt in Kentucky. Those Americans," she said with a smile. "Do you know they have a London Bridge in Arizona?"

Mrs Fitzgerald drew the curtains aside and we looked out the window to the rear of the property. There was a short yard, surrounded by a low fence, and beyond that was a broad pathway along the river, wide enough for horses.

The tide was out and several small canoes lay half on their sides in the muddy sand, awaiting the surge that would lift them up and float them again. In a paddock across the river, a couple of horses leaned over a fence, just visible in the cold misty air.

Mrs Fitzgerald noticed the direction of my gaze. "You like horses?" she asked. "They belong to the Travellers—the gypsies. You could probably hire a couple if you like riding."

"I'd love to, but I'm not actually here for a holiday," I said turning back from the window. I wanted information, so I needed to tell her who I was. Kind of.

"My *uncle*," I lied, "Tom Ormond, stayed here last year. Until he became sick."

Mrs Fitzgerald's face lost its smile. "God rest his soul. You're Tom Ormond's nephew?"

"I am," I said, hoping she wasn't going to think too much about it and ask me any difficult questions. "These are my friends, *Grace* and *Josh*," I repeated nervously.

"I was so sorry to hear about his illness . . . and then his death," she said, solemnly. "It was a terrible job I had, packing up his clothing and things. He was such a lovely fellow. You've come to see where he stayed before he was sick?"

"I'd like to see his room," I said, nodding. "We were very close. I miss him very much."

"Of course you do," she said, picking a key up from the hall table. "Nothing's changed in here. It's exactly as it was when he was staying. We haven't had many guests this year," she admitted with a hint of embarrassment. "Come with me."

We followed her down the hallway to where she opened a door at the end and stepped back, allowing us to walk inside ahead of her. It was a small room, painted white, and in an alcove on the right was a bay window with a vase of yellow paper roses. A sink and tap with a hot plate and an electric jug formed the kitchen area.

"Your uncle cooked on that," Mrs Fitzgerald said, noticing me looking at the hot plate.

"Uncle Tom? Cooking?" I asked, surprised. "That's weird. My *aunty* never let him cook at home—he was a shocker! Aunty Win used to—" I stopped speaking as memories of my home life with Mum and Dad surfaced. I felt Winter's light touch on the back of my hand. "He was always burning things. Even at family barbecues. I guess being here alone forced him to give it another go."

"I'm sorry to tell you he hadn't improved," confessed Mrs Fitzgerald with a chuckle. "One night I caught him trying to cook this sloppy soup." She wrinkled up her nose in distaste. "Some sort of vegetable and herb soup. He must have let it boil for so long that it all just turned to mush."

I smiled, picturing Dad trying his best.

"I called in to drop off some clean laundry," continued Mrs Fitzgerald, "and I could see past his shoulder and into the kitchen sink. He'd made such a mess! There was a pile of veggie skins, herbs and even something that looked like ferns on the bench." She shook her head. "He hadn't told me he'd be in for dinner that night, but really, I could have arranged something else for him. Parsley, coriander and basil I understand, but ferns? I think I might have offended him with my offer of a slice of shepherd's pie, to have instead."

I wandered further into the room. Beyond the kitchen, a bed, a table and chair, a fireplace set with pine cones and a big, carved wardrobe completed the furnishings.

A wardrobe!

A *carved* wardrobe!

I stopped, rooted to the spot. Boges and Winter crashed into me.

"Move along there, dude," said Boges. Until he saw the reason for my shock. "A wardrobe!"

"A wardrobe!" Winter cried, jigging up and down. "I told you! I told you! We're on the right track. The carved doors!"

"Er, yes," said Mrs Fitzgerald, clearly confused about our excitement over a basic piece of furniture. She must have thought we'd never seen a wardrobe before! "Tis rather a grand cupboard, I suppose," she continued. "Big and roomy."

The telephone rang from down the hall and she excused herself before hurriedly shuffling away.

The fancy carving and the big metal ring at the front of the wardrobe were distinct—this was definitely the door from my dad's drawing! I darted across the room and opened it. It creaked as I peered inside.

It had an odd, woody smell, a tall space for hanging clothes, and an open shelf on the right on top of three drawers. Quickly, I opened them all, one after the other, but they were empty.

I squatted down to check the dark space underneath the drawers.

"There's nothing in here," I said, straightening up, disappointment rearing its ugly head again. I felt my fists clench. "We've come all this way—for what? We haven't found the last lines of the Riddle, and now there's nothing in this stupid cupboard!"

"Cal," said Winter, "don't panic. All your dad's drawings mean something. We've been able to work them out. We can do it with this one, too."

"But maybe what he wanted us to see isn't here any more," I said. "Which means the drawing was pointless. A dead end."

"Let's just all take a breath and wait a moment," continued Winter, staring inside the wardrobe. "Something could suddenly make sense."

I turned my head, about to whack the cupboard in hopelessness, when Winter shoved herself in between me and the door.

"What's this?" she said, running a finger over the paper lining on the inside of the door. "This isn't lining, it's a map!"

She moved over so I could have a closer look.

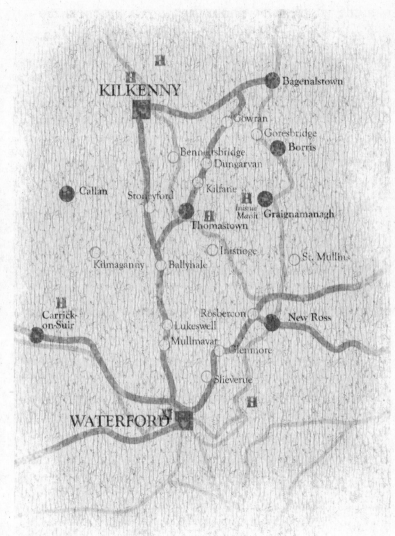

I looked closer. Right at eye level, and right where I was staring was a place name—Graignamanagh, and just up from it was another place name—Kilfane.

G'managh and Kilfane! The place names on the transparency!

I swung round to the others, pulling off my backpack. "The transparency! That's why Dad drew this cupboard!"

"It *is* a map!" cried Boges, peering closer at the lining of the old cupboard. "I see what you mean! C'mon, dude! Hurry up and find the transparency!"

I rummaged through my backpack and carefully lifted it out.

My fingers were trembling with excitement as I held up the transparency against the map, lining it up against the inside of the cupboard door, until the two names written by Dad—G'managh and Kilfane—were perfectly superimposed over the names on the old map.

Between them was the black dot.

"Wow!" breathed Winter.

"Will you look at that!" Boges spluttered.

I stood back, holding the transparency to see that now the black dot sat right on top of another name.

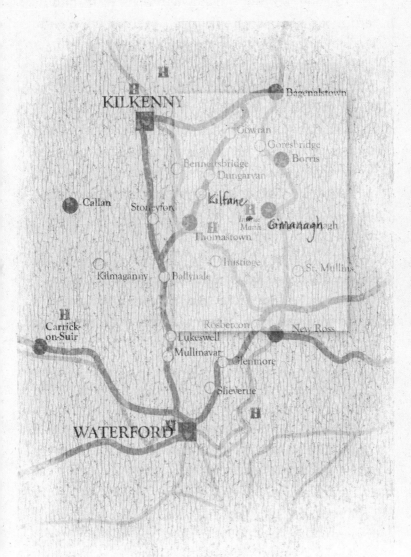

"Inisrue Marsh!" cried Winter. "Your dad is telling us that we have to go to Inisrue Marsh! This is incredible! Now we know where to go!"

"I wonder what's there!" said Boges. He traced a finger along from our present location on the riverside at the edge of the village of Carrick-on-Suir, moving up to the black dot. "Across the river and north," he said, pointing. "It's not that far away."

The sound of scuffling and thudding, topped by a woman's scream, shocked us away from studying the map.

"Mrs Fitzgerald? You OK?" called Boges, racing to the door and sticking his head around it.

Footsteps pounded down the hallway and Boges jumped back, slammed the door shut and turned the key. I'd never seen him move so fast.

"Sligo!" he hissed, horrified. "And Zombie Two! How did they find us?"

"Sligo?" Winter repeated, nervously. "He's *really* here! I guess that means he's definitely cancelled his New Year's Eve Ball!"

I grabbed the transparency, shoved it in my backpack next to *Lives of the Saints*, whipped it over my arm and hurled myself across the room, knocking the yellow roses to the floor in the process. I wrenched the window open and gestured to Boges and Winter to climb through.

As soon as they'd landed on the other side, I heaved myself halfway over the sill, ready to leap into the dark drizzle of the oncoming night. From somewhere outside I could hear Mrs Fitzgerald calling for help and neighbours responding with alarmed shouts.

"Call the Garda!" I heard someone scream.

Sligo and Zombie Two were battering on our room's door.

"Jump!" shouted Boges from below.

I pushed off and thudded down. I scrambled to my feet and followed my friends over the back fence, heading for the quay.

"They've escaped out the window!" Sligo's voice boomed from behind us. "Get the car!"

"Run for your life!" Boges shouted to me. "Don't follow us—we'll do what we can to steer them away from you!"

"But—"

"Just go!" he ordered, slowing to wave his arms and grab Sligo's attention.

"Boges!" I shouted, worried about my friends. "Winter, you have to run!"

"Go!" she shouted.

4:46 pm

I shot away over the back fence, down the quayside

and then towards the low stone bridge that crossed the river.

Freezing rain started pouring down in sheets, drenching me as I bolted over the bridge. It was almost impossible to see where I was going—everything ahead of me was a wet, grey blur.

Suddenly something glowed in that grey blur. Headlights! A car skidded and swerved towards me, flying recklessly along the quayside.

I ran out of its wild path, but it jerked and twisted after me, tires squealing on the slippery ground. It spun and screeched to a halt.

Seconds later Zombie Two had kicked the front car door wide open and was barrelling after me on foot, pounding down the cobblestones, eyes locked onto me.

I was sure I could get away because he was so big and lumbering and I was faster, but my sneakers skidded on a slippery stone and I went flying, crash-landing on my stomach.

I scrambled to my feet and looked back, but couldn't see him.

The car started again—he must have run back to it! I was frantic, I couldn't let Sligo get his hands on me, let alone the transparency and everything else in my backpack.

I ran alongside the river as it curved around a bend. Pulled up on the stones was one of the canoe-style boats that Mrs Fitzgerald had called a Carrick cot, almost completely covered by a canvas tarpaulin. Quick as a flash, I wrenched my backpack off and flung it perfectly into the opening in the skiff, and then I took off in the opposite direction.

I could hear the car coming behind me, accelerating, and I knew I had to find a thin lane where a car couldn't follow. A narrow bridge crossed the river a little distance away, and I pelted across it.

I'd hoped the narrowness would stop Sligo's car, but all it did was slow it down. They forged ahead with only centimetres on either side between their vehicle and the bridge's brick walls.

There were fewer houses on this side of the river, and between two of them was a grassy paddock which led to a dense forested area—my chance of escape. I ran for it.

In seconds, I was sinking up to my ankles in boggy marshland. I struggled and staggered unevenly, slowing down to a snail's pace. I wrenched my legs out of the bog and ploughed ahead, desperately aiming for firmer ground.

When I finally felt solid ground under my feet again, I kicked mud off my legs and ran again, straight for the forest.

A blow on my left sent me flying to the ground sideways.

Zombie Two had tackled me down. He must have seen that I was heading for the forest, and worked out a way to grab me from the other side. I struggled and kicked, but he had me in a painful wristlock, twisting my arm behind me.

He yelled and spat at me with what I was sure were foreign swear words, as he dragged me by my feet over to his car. I clawed at the muddy ground, trying uselessly to break free.

Once we reached the car, Zombie Two picked me up and tossed me inside, then climbed in and practically sat on top of me to keep me restrained.

A shadowy figure in the front seat turned around.

Sligo was sitting at the wheel.

"We meet again," he growled, his cravat crooked and crumpled around his thick neck. "I'll make this simple for you. If you want to live, you'd better start talking. You tell me about the Ormond Singularity in exchange for your life."

I gulped, trying to get my breath back and clear my head.

"Speak!" he demanded. "What do you have for me, boy? Do you want to live? Where are the Ormond Riddle and the Ormond Jewel?"

"Back home where you'll never find them!"
I yelled, wriggling under Zombie Two's stifling
mass.

"*Home*? A delinquent like you doesn't have a
home," he sniggered, sending shivers down my
spine. "Neither does that little viper, Winter. Don't
you worry, I'll find the Jewel and the Riddle.
I'll track down your buddies, too, including my
precious ward—I know she's here with you, and
I've read the notes she wrote."

"Then you know as much as I do!"

"Did your father find something here?"
Sligo snapped. "Tell me what you are doing in
Carrick!"

"They say travel broadens the mind," I
wheezed.

Zombie Two pushed his weight down on me
even more, clearly not finding my joke very
funny. I groaned in pain.

"You obviously don't value your life, Callum
Ormond," said Sligo, viciously reversing the car,
then accelerating forward. "Winter didn't give
me any trouble until she met up with *you*. This
is personal now. This *ends* now," he said with
severe finality.

The car sped along, driving through the mist
and rain.

"We're about to go to a little-known local

attraction. Have you ever heard of the Dundrum Oubliette?"

I hadn't heard of it, but whatever it was, I knew it meant trouble.

"I said, have you heard of the Dundrum Oubliette?" he repeated.

"Yes. You just mentioned it a second ago."

"Think you're funny, eh?" hissed Sligo. "I'll be the one having the last laugh."

My blood turned ice-cold as I considered the fact that this was also the man who had left me to die in an oil tank. This was also the man who had left *Winter*—the girl who was supposed to be in his care—to die.

5:23 pm

We drove for another twenty minutes or so, passing the dark Irish countryside. I tried to sit up a bit better to see where we were going, but it wasn't easy—Zombie Two kept pushing me, face-down into the backseat.

I caught a glimpse of a Y-intersection and could just make out a row of big stones and a signpost pointing to the road on the right that read something like "Roland's Tower." Sligo wrenched the steering wheel to the left and the car rattled and jerked its way down a dirt road instead.

Eventually he pulled up at a gate. Zombie

Two eased off me and I sat up a bit. "Dundrum Oubliette," I read to myself. "Open June–October."

Sligo climbed out of the car, stepping into the pouring rain. He dragged a pair of heavy-duty bolt cutters out of the boot, stalked over to the gate and cut right through the chains woven through them. I peered ahead, trying to see through the rain drumming on the windshield. Some distance ahead, I could make out what looked like a half-fallen wall.

Sligo lumbered back into the driver's seat and drove the car through the gateway and up to the stony structure.

"Get him out," he ordered Zombie Two, cursing the rain as he lifted his heavy body out of the driver's seat again. "Destroy his phone!"

Zombie Two hauled me out into the cold night air and patted me down. My phone was in my backpack that I'd chucked into one of the Carrick cots, so I didn't have anything on me for them to destroy.

"No phone," he yelled out.

Sligo shone a flashlight ahead of him while Zombie Two dragged me along after his boss, my arms twisted up behind my back. I was led down some stone steps and into what must have been a courtyard hundreds of years ago, but was now more like a flat, crumbling rock.

I noticed Sligo was also carrying a grappling hook on a chain.

What was an oubliette? I wondered, panic rising.

Maybe it was good that I didn't know what I was in for . . .

In the middle of the courtyard was a round drain, covered by a heavy iron grille. Sligo knelt beside it. He put down his flashlight and wedged one of the barbs of the grappling hook under one of the bars on the grille.

His flashlight sat in a puddle, directing light onto a plaque that had been attached to the ground near the drain.

"Hold on to the little scumbag while I get the cover off," Sligo yelled out to Zombie Two.

Zombie gripped me while Sligo went back to the car. With the other end of the chain attached to the front of the vehicle, Sligo jumped in behind the wheel and revved it up. He slammed the accelerator and the car reversed, ripping the cover off the drain opening. It rolled and landed a few metres away.

I struggled vainly against Zombie Two, as horrifying images of the inside of the oil tank came back to me. Was Sligo going to shove me in a drain? Drown me in stormwater?

Sligo returned and scowled at me, an evil leer on his pudgy face. "As you can see from the sign, this is an oubliette," his voice boomed over the easing rain. "I trust you can read, but maybe if you listened better in school, you'd know that the French word 'oubliette' means 'place to forget.' You might also have learned that an oubliette is a medieval prison, made for those who had displeased the local noblemen. The offender was dropped into the hole and, well, *forgotten*! They were abandoned in these deep underground dungeons, sometimes knee deep in water, sewerage, rats . . . but this one has an extra attraction of another kind." Sligo paused and grinned. He turned to Zombie Two. "Drag him over so he can see."

Zombie Two followed orders and pushed me towards the hole. It gaped like nothing but a black circle until Sligo shone his light down.

I croaked in horror!

I was staring down into a seemingly bottomless pit, with a *huge* spike spearing up from the darkness. Its wicked point glinted in the light.

"You should thank me for it, really," mocked Sligo. "Being impaled on that spike, as excruciatingly unpleasant as I believe it will be, means a much quicker death than starvation. The treacherous bogs have already proven to be a great place for dumping a troublesome body, but this is far more gruesome, don't you think?" he said to Zombie Two.

Zombie Two bellowed with laughter.

"Although it was fun," Sligo continued, "watching Rathbone struggle in the mud."

"You murdered Rathbone?" I screeched.

"Enough!" he screeched back. "Throw him in!"

I shouted and screamed and struggled uselessly in Zombie Two's iron grip. He began lifting me up and I kicked out as Sligo grabbed my other shoulder and upper arm. Together they were about to hurl me into the black hole! I would be speared like a piece of meat on a spit!

This couldn't be happening—but it was!

I fought with all my strength, but slowly, inevitably, they hoisted me over the edge. I stretched my legs out wide, making it impossible for them to drop me into the narrow passage. Zombie Two saw what I was trying to do and he kicked my feet back together and into the hole—leaving me with nothing to keep me above the surface.

Then they let go.

Instinctively, as I fell, I swerved like a diver in a sideways twist, trying to curl my body around the spike.

I crashed down painfully, the flesh on my thighs and arms grazing right off as my clothes tore and I collided with the jagged, stony walls. I landed with a back-breaking thud.

I was hurt, but I'd avoided being impaled on the spike!

Stunned and winded, I looked up at the pale circle of night sky above me. The grille had already been returned to its original position—the straight lines of the bars drew shadows over my battered body.

I was trapped, bleeding and soaking wet, in the bottom of an oubliette, in the dead of winter, somewhere in Ireland.

As if to push my despair just that little bit further, a clap of thunder sounded, and the rain began pouring down again in buckets.

I tried to get to my feet but slipped in the pool of water. I wanted to scream out, but I stopped myself, thinking it would be better if Sligo and Zombie Two thought I was already dead.

The sound of Sligo's car disappeared into the night and I was alone. Abandoned. *Forgotten.*

He'd killed Rathbone.

Was I about to die next?

6:29 pm

I slumped against the wall and looked up, the rain relentlessly pelting down on my face.

There had to be a way out of here. I could climb up the wall somehow. Maybe—if I could get up to the top and find a strong enough foothold—I could push the grille off.

The numbness wore off from my shaking limbs and I was aware of how uncomfortable I was, sitting on the stones or rocks or whatever it was that covered the ground of this hole. I struggled to sit up and twisted around to see what I was sitting on.

I jumped up in horror.

What had cushioned my fall were piles of dead leaves on top of old, broken bones! The bones of other prisoners who had lived and died down here, forgotten centuries ago!

Stay calm, said a voice in my head. *Think, Cal, think.*

I tried to control my breathing and let my eyes adjust even more to the darkness. I shielded my face from the rain and looked around. I could see I was in a circular space, slightly wider than the opening many metres above, with sloping stone walls covered in thick, slippery moss.

Over the bones and the dust, I felt my way around the walls. They were wet and slimy and worse, they were funnel shaped, so that the opening at the top part of the oubliette closed over me like the neck of a bottle. There was no way I could climb out.

I moved my legs to check that they were OK, sloshing them around in the water that was building up like a well. Next I checked my arms and remembered the distress beacon Boges had given me! My watch!

I squinted at it on my wrist, but could hardly see anything. I rubbed its face with my fingers and almost choked when I realised it was completely shattered—the glass had been crushed in my fall. The insides of the watch were destroyed and saturated.

The beacon was not going to save me.

With trembling fingers, I pressed the winder of the watch anyway.

Nothing happened. I stared at the watch-face. There was no sound. There was no pulsing, blue light.

Again and again I pressed on the tiny winder, until the whole watch fell away in pieces and all that was left on my wrist was the band.

Nobody knew I was here and the sign on the gate said that this place was closed until June. I was done for.

I grabbed at the slippery, moss-covered stone walls again, trying to find any possible hand grips. I made several attempts to climb the wall, but just fell crashing to the ground, drenching myself over and over again.

No matter how hard I tried, it was impossible—I wasn't getting anywhere. My hands were scraped and cut from trying. The small indentations that I managed to hook my fingers onto crumbled away under my weight, weakened by constant water erosion.

After about two hours of useless clawing, I crouched in the damp darkness, exhausted. I made a pile out of the broken bones to sit on, above the rising water level.

It was freezing. I felt as cold as I was when Three-O locked me in that seafood shop freezer. I was on the verge of death then, and I was pretty sure I was on the verge of death now.

Sligo's gloating words returned to me as I stared at the spike. Maybe he was right. Maybe it would have been better *not* to have avoided it.

30 DECEMBER

2 days to go . . .

Dundrum Oubliette

11:30 am

I spent hours yelling out, begging someone to come and help me out of this death trap. I shouted until my voice was hoarse.

More hours passed and I tried to soak up the few weak rays of winter sun that made their way down to the bottom of the oubliette, trying to get my clothes dry after the intense rain of last night. The icy water had risen past my knees, and even though I was doing all I could to stay out of it I just couldn't get completely clear and dry. I was worried about what another sub-zero night down here would do to me—I didn't think I could take it.

I shuddered as a faint beam of light shone on the bones of the others who'd perished here before me. I wondered if they had remained hope-ful until the very end. Or if they had just given up. I was in Ireland and so close to solving the Ormond Singularity, but every second I felt more and more convinced that this was it for me. I was going to die a horrible, slow, lonely death.

3:17 pm

Could I make a rope out of my clothes? I wondered. If so, maybe I could wrap it around the spike and shinny up, closer to the grille. Maybe, once there, I could loop the rope around one of the bars and somehow haul myself up, kick the bars and swing out . . .

I had to give it a go. My hands were shivering as I slipped out of my T-shirt and undershirt, pulled my tattered sweater and coat back on, and started ripping the material into strips.

When I guessed I had enough length of knotted fabric, I wrapped it around the spike and made a start on shinnying up. I grabbed the spike tightly in my hands, clamping my muddy wet sneakers around it, like some crazy climbing frog. My hands and feet slipped painfully down again, and I smacked my chin on the spike. My skin scraped off from the sharp flakes of rust under the slime, and I fell back, wincing in pain.

Over and over, I threw myself up the spike, trying to grab it and haul myself up. But over and over I found myself painfully slipping down again until the palms of my hands were skinned raw and the fabric on the inside thighs of my jeans was torn and ragged.

It was no use. No way was I going to be able to get up this deadly giant needle.

I was freezing, bleeding, hungry and exhausted. I collapsed on top of the pile of bones and started trying to send telepathic thoughts out to Winter and Boges. I hoped they were OK and somewhere safe. It was like I was back at the cemetery, when they were searching for me, not knowing where to dig. I knew they'd be going out of their minds with worry.

Even if they sensed I was still alive, somewhere, the odds of them finding me were about a million to one.

10:37 pm

Another night in the oubliette. I was faint and dizzy. My body was jolting with shock from the cold, and my teeth chattered constantly, desperately trying to shake me into some semblance of warmth. My hands were swollen and painful and I was having trouble thinking straight.

I thought of how this journey had begun with a drawing of an angel. The Ormond Angel was supposed to come to the aid of the heir in his time of need.

"I need you now!" I screeched into the air, willing him to swoop down and save me. "Where are you?"

All I could hear was water dripping.

"I'm the heir! Come and save me!"

Again, all I could hear was dripping.

"There is no Ormond Angel," I muttered to myself.

Right at that moment I thought I saw something move in a fresh circle of light above me. I shook my head, convinced hallucinations were starting.

But then something moved again. The shadows over me definitely shifted.

I stared up. It seemed like a figure was standing on top of the grille.

Then I swore the figure bent down and peered into the hole. White light shone around the figure's head like a halo, and what looked like a huge, folded wing peeked over its shoulder.

I blinked. Was I hallucinating? Had the stress and fear sent me completely around the bend?

The figure shimmered above me.

Was it the Angel? Just in time?

"H-h-hello?" I murmured.

I blinked as light suddenly fell on my face. "Cal?"

A voice! A voice I knew!

"Cal? You OK?"

Relief flooded my body.

"Rafe," I wailed, like a baby. "Uncle Rafe!"

It wasn't the Ormond Angel above me, but my uncle Rafe. What I'd thought was a rounded wing was now revealed as a huge coil of rope, backlit by powerful lights—probably his car headlights.

"Hang on, boy, I'm going to get you out of there," he said, moving the grille away with something like a crow bar. He lowered a rope with a loop at the end which I quickly fixed around my waist.

"I'm r-r-ready!" I called out, and immediately he used all his strength to haul me out of the dreaded oubliette.

Once he could reach me, Rafe grabbed onto my arms and pulled me all the way out and onto the ground. I lay there, numb and shivering, unable to move. He wrapped a blanket around me, picked me up and carried me to the car. He sat me upright in the passenger seat, slammed the door then ran around to the driver's side, turning the ignition and cranking the heat, full blast.

"Look at you," he said, leaning over and rubbing my hands. He passed me a bottle of water. "Lucky I found you when I did. Any serious injuries?"

I shook my head and sipped from the bottle. "Just c-c-cold," I stuttered. "H-h-how on earth," I said, barely able to control my words through my freezing lips, "did you find me?"

He took a deep breath, seeming unsure where to start.

"It's a long story," he began, turning all the air vents of the rented car in my direction. "As soon as we were notified that you'd been arrested after ramming the police station, back home, your mum and I rushed in to see you. But," he said, driving us away from the oubliette, "it wasn't you we found there, was it?"

I shook my head gently, picturing Ryan Spencer, and smiled with dry, cracked lips.

"I'd heard that the authorities believed you were a flight risk, so as soon as I realised an 'impostor' had been arrested, and that the whole thing had been a set-up, I knew you'd flown the coop."

"So you saw Ryan?" I asked, finally starting to recover my speech.

"We sure did," he said with a wide grin and a sparkle in his eyes. "I never thought I'd see the day, Cal. I never thought we'd see Samuel again."

"And Mum?"

"Your mum was extremely overwhelmed," he said, firmly.

"In a good way, right?"

"Certainly, Cal," he said hesitantly. "This year has been one long, emotional roller coaster. The highs *and* lows just keep on coming."

"What's wrong?" I asked, sensing he was holding something back. I knew I should be slowly warming up, but my body was still shivering, and I was finding it hard to understand what Rafe was saying.

"Your mother and I had a very serious argument," he admitted. "I discovered that she'd been secretly dealing with the family lawyer, working on finding the Ormond Singularity."

I coughed, almost choked. "What? Mum? Working with Rathbone?"

Rafe looked surprised that I knew who he was talking about.

"Look, I don't know how involved she is," he said, "so don't go jumping to any conclusions, OK? But after she told me Rathbone had left for Ireland, and then your missing twin was arrested, I started piecing things together. As soon as I realised Bodhan had gone on some mysterious 'excursion' I figured you'd both come here together. When I heard that Vulkan Sligo was on his way here, too, I knew you were in terrible danger—more than ever before."

"You were right," I said. "I survived Sligo, but Rathbone wasn't as lucky. He's dead."

Rafe looked shocked.

"Sligo murdered him," I explained. "Tossed him in the bog."

Rafe just shook his head. "I knew Sligo would be tracking you," he continued as he drove, "so I tracked *him* to Clonmel Way Guest House, where I discovered all hell had broken loose. Your friends Winter and Boges filled me in on what had gone down."

"So they're OK?" I asked, relief hitting the deep frozen organ that was my heart.

"They're both fine. They chased after you for a while, but lost Sligo's car. Winter had even borrowed a horse in an effort to keep up, but she simply couldn't."

"Borrowed a horse?"

"She found one in a paddock belonging to the Travellers and jumped up and over the nearest fence to chase after you."

I pulled the blanket around me, starting to thaw out, trying to imagine Winter "borrowing" a horse like that.

"They haven't been able to go back to the guest house. They're actually huddling down with some gypsies."

"The gypsies Winter borrowed the horse from?"

"Yes, they're camped out in some tents and trailers, by the river, a few kilometres south of the guest house. We're heading there now."

"So how did you know I was down in that pit?"

I asked again, my teeth finally easing in their chattering.

"I didn't. Not at first. But I started following the tracks on the road—the rain had washed the top layer off—but the road Sligo had taken only forked off to two places."

I remembered the Y-intersection I'd spotted as I struggled with Zombie Two in the back of the car.

"I wound up at Roland's Tower first, searching for you there. Once I'd exhausted that possibility, I backtracked and headed towards the oubliette. I was standing there, thinking it was a dead end, when I realised I was standing on top of you. The rest is history."

I let my head fall back into the car seat, still struggling to believe I'd been saved. By my uncle.

11:52 pm

As we turned back into Carrick, I asked Rafe if he'd stop the car near the river just before the row of houses started.

Rafe waited in the car, while I staggered out and down to the skiffs on the riverbank. It took me a little while to find the right Carrick cot that I'd thrown my bag into. I was shivering with cold when I pulled back a canvas cover and saw with great relief that my backpack was still safely stowed there. Soggy, but safe.

I was just about to haul it onto my back when a shot rang out. The sound sent a shockwave through my body.

My eyes darted up to the car.

I stumbled back up the hill to my uncle, as fast as my legs would take me.

The driver's door was open.

I hurried around to the driver's side and fell to my knees in horror.

Rafe's body was lying half out of the car. His head had fallen to the cobblestones, his neck was twisted and his arms were hanging lifelessly from his body.

"Rafe!" I screamed, grabbing at him. "Rafe!" I screamed again, but he wouldn't respond.

I opened his coat, scared at what I would find.

I was dizzy. Everything was spinning.

All I could see was a big red blur.

He'd been shot in the chest.

Thudding feet approached me, and I shook my head, trying to focus.

"What's happened?" a voice cried.

"I heard a gunshot," cried another.

"Out of the way," said another, as I was suddenly pushed back by the small pyjama-clad crowd that had gathered.

Then I heard the two words I was dreading.

"He's dead."

31 DECEMBER

1 day to go . . .

12:30 pm

"Cal, you're OK!" cried Winter, as I opened my eyes. She was looking down at me—I was lying in a sleeping bag inside a tent.

"Where am I?" I asked.

"It's OK, you're safe. You've been unconscious for hours—since the Travellers brought you back from the accident."

Winter said the last two words so softly, they were almost a whisper.

Everything flooded back to me. Rafe had been shot.

I couldn't speak. I was numb.

"I'm so sorry, Cal."

I shook my head and fought back tears.

"We wanted to go with him," cried Winter. "We wanted to help him find you, but he wouldn't let us—said it was too dangerous. I can't believe it. We only just saw him yesterday. He only just got here!"

A woman with long, dark hair handed me a hot drink in a chipped mug, and gently touched my shoulder.

Winter smiled at her, gratefully.

Boges sat down beside me. "What happened?"

"He saved me," I said, finally finding my voice. "Sligo had thrown me in an oubliette—a deep dungeon. I was minutes from death, praying for the Ormond Angel to come and save me, and then Rafe appeared. It was a miracle. He drove us away—we were headed here—but I'd thrown my backpack into one of the cots by the river when Zombie Two was chasing me, so I asked him to pull over so I could get it. Then I heard a gunshot, ran back to the car and found him lying there, bleeding." I was dizzy again at the thought of him lying there so helplessly. "Locals started running over. I don't know what happened after that. I must have blacked out."

"You were practically frozen, Cal. You were in shock. You'd lost a lot of blood, too. We're lucky to have you back so soon," said Winter.

There was a pause while we listened to the quiet gypsy camp around us. A fire crackled nearby and I noticed a couple of kids looking our way, peering out from behind tent cloths.

"What about Mrs Fitzgerald?" I asked.

"Mrs Fitz was fine," Boges said. "We figured we

couldn't stick around. Not with the Garda asking questions. Winter stole—"

"Borrowed," she corrected him.

"*Borrowed* one of the Travellers' horses, and when we came here to return it, they welcomed us in and offered us a place to sleep. Ashling and Quinn said we could stay as long as we wanted. They said they're always more than happy to help out good folk on the run from the Garda."

I was hearing some of what Boges and Winter were saying, but Rafe's face wouldn't leave my mind. I buried my head in my hands.

"What are we doing here?" I asked my friends. "People are dying! For what good reason? Why? For the sake of the Ormond Singularity? I don't even know if I can trust my own mother, so who am I doing this for? Why does it even matter any more?"

"You have to keep going, Cal," insisted Winter.

"Why should I?"

"For the rest of your family. For Tom and Rafe. For your great-uncle. For your great-aunt." She stopped and shook her head. "For all the people who've helped you along the way—Jennifer Smith, Lachlan, Melba Snipe, Repro, Ryan Spencer, Sharkey . . . For us," she added, grabbing hold of Boges's hand. "Me and Boges. We've both been here with you for almost all of this insane journey.

We believe in you. We want you to see it through to the end. If you quit now, everything will have been for nothing."

"You know she's right," said Boges. "Today's the last day, dude. You can't give up now. You have to keep it together for just a little bit longer."

My body was aching. Rafe's murder was consuming my thoughts, and the pressure of having only hours left was sending me into a sweat. But they were right. I had barely one more day to get through. A matter of hours left to find the answers.

Everything Dad had left me was pointing to Inisrue Marsh. Was this where I'd find the ruin he'd photographed? Would there be an inscription around the walls as we'd seen in the faded sketch?

For a moment I thought I could hear my dad's voice again, telling me to keep going. I had to find the Ormond Singularity. I *had* to.

"The map in the cupboard pointed to Inisrue Marsh," said Boges. "Winter and I have directions. We're going there whether you want to or not, and we're going to find out why it was marked. Now see if you feel strong enough to get up."

"OK," I said as I began to shakily stand. "Did you just say you have directions?"

"Sure do, thanks to Ashling."

"Ashling?"

"The woman who brought you here," explained Boges. "She had a book listing all of Black Tom Butler's land holdings in Inisrue in the sixteenth century. The bad news is that Inisrue is a swamp, but the good news is that it is home to the ruins of *three* of Black Tom's buildings—Slievenamon Castle, Cragkill Keep and Ormond Tower. One of them *has* to be the one your dad took the photos of. One of them *has* to hold the secret."

"I hope you're right," I said, feeling my strength returning.

"So do I," admitted Boges. "Winter made a copy of their location, so we don't get lost."

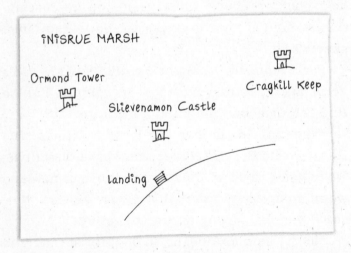

"The buildings were originally on an island in the middle of the river," Winter added, "but that was hundreds of years ago. They're still there, but now the island has turned into an unpredictable swampland. We'll have to be really careful."

"At least we don't have to worry about Rathbone any more," I said. "Thanks to Sligo."

"What?" asked Winter, suspiciously. "He killed him?"

I nodded. "Said the bogs have already proven to be a great place for dumping a body."

1:50 pm

My hands were sore, red and swollen from the failed attempts to climb the deadly spike, so Boges helped me slowly shuffle into warmer clothes. I was getting worried. We'd come all this way, I'd survived almost a year, despite the dangers of the Ormond Singularity. One of these ruins *had* to be the place.

I could feel Boges and Winter looking expectantly at me. Whether the ruins were rubble or not, we needed to search them.

"So we have three ruins to search," said Winter, as she shoved bits and pieces back into her bag. "We have about ten hours left. Before midnight. Before the Ormond Singularity runs out."

"Even if we *do* find whatever the Ormond Singularity is before midnight," I said, "how do we prove it? There'll be no one there to witness it except us."

"Relax, dude," said Boges. "I'll film it on my mobile."

I was moving awkwardly, in pain, as I gathered my things. I had been counting on everything falling magically into place over here, but I was still unsure of the basics. How was I going to clear my name?

I didn't see *Lives of the Saints* on the floor until I skidded on it, twisting my ankle, and falling hard.

I yelped in pain. "Useless book!" I shouted, picking it up and throwing it at the wall of the tent. It made a slapping sound on the tarpaulin-like fabric before hitting the ground.

"Take it easy," said Boges. He picked it up from the floor. "This is a valuable old book, man. *Was* a valuable old book," he corrected.

The cracked leather on the spine of the book had come apart, and the front cover was left hanging by a few threads.

I looked closer. Where the binding had come away from the book's spine I could now see a narrow strip of vellum that had been wrapped around under the spine's binding. Some kind of reinforcement for the stitching?

I snatched it from Boges and peered even

closer. The piece of vellum was familiar. It had been sewn into the underside of the cover, but was now loose because of the torn stitching.

Carefully I pulled it out.

"Unbelievable," I breathed, mesmerised, smoothing it out.

"What is it?" Winter asked, coming over to see.

Slowly, I held up the piece of vellum.

Winter blinked, amazed. "It's the missing part of the Ormond Riddle! The last two lines!"

"Dude! Let's have a look!" said Boges, leaning over her shoulder, staring at the strip that I was holding up.

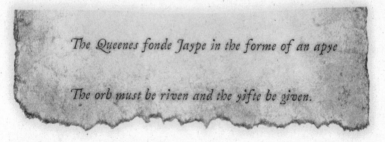

The Queenes fonde Jaype in the forme of an apye

The orb must be riven and the yifte be given.

Winter read it out, slowly, but instead of reading "yifte" she said, "gift."

"I can't believe it, Dr Brinsley was right!" she said.

"But what does 'riven' mean?" I asked.

"I think it means 'split apart,'" replied Winter.

"Grab the rest of the Riddle," said Boges. "Let's put them both together."

The ORMOND RIDDLE

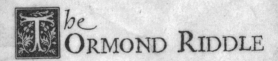

Eight are the Leaves on my Ladyes Grace

Fayre sits the Rounde of my Ladyes Face

Thirteen Teares from the Sunnes grate Doore

Make right to treadde in Gules on the Floore

But adde One in for the Queenes fayre Sinne

Then alle shall be tolde and the Yifte unfold

The Queenes fonde Jaype in the forme of an apye

The orb must be riven and the yifte be given.

"'Apye,'" I quoted. "The form of an ape! The monkey! Winter! The white monkey in the portrait you saw of young Princess Elizabeth! It's holding an orb, and Dad drew a monkey holding a ball."

"I still don't get it," said Boges. "What does it mean? What's the 'Queenes fonde Jaype'?"

We both looked to Winter.

"Shakespeare uses that word," she said. "A 'jape' is a trick of some kind. A joke. Or some sort of deception. And in those days, the word 'fond' actually meant 'foolish.'"

"A foolish joke," I said, thinking aloud. "What do these last lines mean? What foolish joke is Black Tom playing? He's supposed to have written these lines, according to Dr Brinsley."

"Quick!" hissed Ashling, suddenly storming into our tent. "Get into the trailer, the Garda are here!"

"What?" I asked, panicking. "They're here?"

"You need to go and hide in the chests in the trailer. Now!"

Winter, Boges and I grabbed our bags and ran out of the tent, following Ashling into a trailer. Once inside, she started pulling books out of three separate chests, making room for us to climb inside.

"Get in!" she ordered.

The three of us awkwardly squashed ourselves

inside, then the heavy, dusty books were piled back on top of us.

"Don't move until I come back!" she hissed before leaving.

2:27 pm

Cramped in a box of books, the minutes were flying by. Every minute passing meant less time and less daylight to get out to Inisrue Marsh and search the three potential locations.

Being found would hold us up at a time when *time* was as crucial as air. I was petrified we'd be caught by the Garda with our fake passports and be unable to answer their questions about Sligo's raid on Clonmel Way Guest House the other afternoon . . . and about Rafe's body left lying in his car on the road.

I wondered if my mum had been notified yet. She'd be devastated. Again.

I also couldn't help thinking about what Rafe had told me before he died—about Mum's involvement with Rathbone.

At least for now it was quiet in the trailer. I hoped Boges and Winter were holding up in their hiding places OK.

2:38 pm

We were wasting so much time and my body was

killing. I couldn't help lifting the lid of the chest and peering out.

"Boges? Winter?" I hissed.

"Stay down," I heard Boges reply. "No point getting caught now. Surely they can't hang around for too much longer."

3:04 pm

"We just use this one as our library," I heard Ashling's voice as she entered the trailer, followed by heavy footsteps. "The children come in here to grab a book and quietly study."

"Uh-huh," an unknown voice replied, tapping what I suspected was a baton on top of the chests. "Books, you say," she added.

The sound of one of the chest lids opening sent chills down my spine. I heard some prodding and gritted my teeth, praying my friends weren't about to be sprung. I prepared myself to launch out of the chest and run, but in moments, Ashling and the unwanted guest had left the caravan. For good, I hoped.

3:20 pm

"It's OK, you can come out now," said Ashling, finally lifting up the lid on the chest I was in.

I stretched out my aching limbs and saw Boges and Winter also emerging, looking like dishevelled, broken jack-in-the-boxes.

"I thought they'd never leave," said Ashling. "They were very thorough, investigating the Clonmel Way raid and the shooting. Checking our camp, making sure we weren't harbouring any *fugitives*. Are you all right?"

Clearly, by the light-hearted way she said "fugitives" she thought we were just kids who'd been caught up in the wrong place at the wrong time.

"We're fine," I said. "Thank you for everything you've done for us, but we really need to get out of here. We must go to Inisrue Marsh."

Ashling shook her head. "I don't think you should set off now. It's far too dangerous to go there. There's not enough light and you only have to wander a little way off the path and you'll never be seen again. The Marsh has claimed a lot of lives over the years. Why don't you wait till morning? It'll be much safer then. You can stay here and celebrate the start of the new year with us!"

Morning would be too late, party or no party.

"What about by river?" I asked, thinking we could take one of the Carrick cots along the river to reach it. "That would be safer, right?"

"It will take you longer, but it probably would be safer. Have you ever handled a boat?"

"Of course."

Ashling thought about it then shook her head.

"You don't know how dangerous the bog lands can be," she said, trying again to talk us out of it.

"That won't be a problem," Winter interrupted, confidently. "How will we know when we're nearing Inisrue Marsh?"

Ashling could see there was no point in trying to make us stay. "You head north from Waterford," she began, "and follow that direction for some time. When you reach the old St Mullins Bridge—it has six stone arches—you'll know you haven't too much further to go. And when you're close to the marsh area, you'll find a stone landing. You can pull up the cot there."

"Thanks, Ash," I said, already out the trailer door and heading for the tent, while my friends rushed alongside me.

3:30 pm

"OK," I said, back in the tent. "Make sure you have everything."

"But we've gotta try the Caesar shift on the last two lines," said Boges.

I shook my head. "Not here, we don't have time. Let's do it on the way."

The flap on the tent was suddenly pulled open

once more. "Someone else is here!" shouted Ashling. We stopped dead. "Hide! There's no time to get you back into the caravan!"

I rushed to the opening to peer out. A huge wave of relief hit me when I saw who the camp intruder was.

"It's just Sharkey!" I said to my friends. Boges and Winter instantly relaxed. Winter even giggled. "He's with us," I explained to Ashling.

"Sharkey!" I said, rushing out to see him.

"Cal, my boy, I heard you had a close call last night. I'm so sorry to hear about your uncle," he said, uncomfortably stepping forward to give me a hug.

"Thanks," I said, awkwardly stepping out of his embrace. "We have to get going—we have three ruins to search and time's almost out."

"I know, I know," Sharkey said.

Boges and Winter had joined us now. Boges shook Sharkey's hand, and Winter leaned in to give him a kiss on the cheek.

"I just wanted to let you know," continued Sharkey, "that I've spoken with Mrs Fitzgerald from the guest house and I am going to accompany her to the police station now. I feel confident she'll be able to identify Vulkan Sligo as her attacker. I also believe I have found something that will prove he was responsible for not only Theophilus

Brinsley's murder, but also your uncle's. I will do what I can to ensure he's found and arrested."

"You found something? Evidence?"

"Sure did," he replied. "Just call it the luck of the Irish."

"He murdered Sheldrake Rathbone, too," I added. "Admitted it to me himself."

Sharkey exhaled loudly and cocked his head to one side before continuing. "The truth will come out, Cal. With Oriana de la Force behind bars, and only a matter of time before Sligo joins her, I promise your name will be cleared and you'll have your life back."

5:20 pm

Boges, Winter and I crouched low in one of the Carrick cots. We pushed it out in the icy water and paddled the narrow skiff along the river. The tide was behind us, helping us towards Inisrue Marsh.

It was well and truly dark, except for the glow of lights in the sky above a distant town, and the heavy-duty torch Boges had managed to borrow to help guide our way.

As soon as we'd settled into a steady rhythm, Winter began working on the Riddle by flashlight.

"I'll start with a one letter shift," she said, struggling to hold her pencil, paper, the Riddle and flashlight all at the same time. "I have a good feeling about this. A lot of trouble went into hiding these two lines—I'm sure they're going to tell us where to go next!"

As Winter worked, we glided past villages built along the watercourse, and the wide barges moored beside them. Fairy lights dotted some of the houses, reminding us again that it was New Year's Eve—a time for celebration. Rafe and I had both almost died on a small boat in Treachery Bay, exactly one year ago. I didn't know if it was possible, but I could tell we were all silently hoping we'd be celebrating on the stroke of midnight too.

With a bit more luck, now that Nelson Sharkey was going to present evidence against him, the Garda would hunt Sligo down before the night was out. Then Winter, at least, could resume a normal life, with him safely behind bars.

Further along, the tidal water rattled over the stones on the banks, as we passed a small village and smelt the fragrant scent of wood fires burning in the cottages. Stars twinkled through clouds.

A milky mist hung over the water, and the sound of the tide moving to the coast was all I could hear. The skiff followed the course of the river. We couldn't really get lost—there was only *up* river or *down* river, and we knew we were heading in the right direction, looking out for the old St Mullins Bridge.

A chill, different from the frosty air of the night, shivered through my bones, registering a sudden danger alert. I shuddered, uneasy. As the countdown to midnight ticked away, danger was increasing, tensing like a coiled spring.

"How is it going, Winter?" I asked, as a distant town clock chimed six o'clock. We only had six more hours before the Singularity ran out.

Here we were, *still* trying to decipher the Riddle when we had three locations to search. Three! Slievenamon Castle, Cragkill Keep and Ormond Tower. The secret of the Ormond Singularity *had* to be in one of these ruins, but we didn't have time to search all of them.

Winter's voice interrupted my thoughts. "It's worrying me," she said, her face half lit by flashlight. "This misspelling of 'ape.' I mean, I'd expect 'aype' just like in 'jaype,' not this 'apye' with the P before the Y. Scribal errors happened in copied texts, but you wouldn't think it would happen in this Riddle. I can't believe the scribe wouldn't have picked it up. It's so obvious that it should be spelled the other way."

I caught a glimpse of Winter's face. She was smiling.

"What are you getting at?" asked Boges, pausing over his oar.

"What if it's *not* a scribal error?" I began, picking up Winter's excitement. "What if it was *deliberate*? Is that what you're saying? That the misspelling of 'apye' *is* the 'jaype' of the Riddle? Black Tom's *trick* is that word itself?"

"That's *exactly* what I mean," Winter nodded vigorously. "That the scribe intentionally made the error, so that the code would work! I'm going to check it right now!"

With the piece of vellum on her knees, Winter continued her work, focusing on the word "apye," starting as she'd begun with the first words, with just one shift along the alphabet.

"Don't forget," began Boges, breathlessly heaving on the oars, "to look for 'apye' in both lines of the alphabet. Apply it to the top line as well as the bottom line. "

"You're right," said Winter. "It could go either way. I'll check both and see what they give us."

ABCDEFGHIJKLMNOPQRSTUVWXYZ
ZABCDEFGHIJKLMNOPQRSTUVWXY

"From the top line, 'apye' becomes 'zoxd,'" said Winter, shaking her head. "From the bottom line it becomes 'bqzf.' No good. I'll try two shifts along."

ABCDEFGHIJKLMNOPQRSTUVWXYZ
YZABCDEFGHIJKLMNOPQRSTUVWX

"OK, so with two shifts, from the top line, 'apye' becomes 'ynwc,'" she sighed. "From the bottom line it becomes—"

"It's 'crag'!" I yelled. "It's Cragkill Keep! Winter, you're brilliant! Maybe the 'double-key' code also hinted at the double shift needed to decipher 'apye'!"

"Careful," warned Winter, "you're going to tip over the boat!"

Winter wrote out the last of the letters and now it was clear to see:

a – p – y – e
c – r – a – g

"Bridge coming up! Six arches!" yelled Boges, triumphantly. "The St Mullins Bridge! We're almost there!"

7:00 pm

Louder now, I could hear the clock chiming seven o'clock. We had five hours left to make it to Inisrue Marsh, find Cragkill Keep and search it. Winter's map showed that Cragkill was on the right of the stone landing.

Ignoring my stinging hands, I hauled on the paddles as Boges and I swung back and forward in long pulls, sending the light cot scudding up the river. On my right, a low stone wall rose from the river bank, leading to a stone wharf.

"We're here," I said, swinging the skiff towards the banks. "This must be the landing Ashling told us about."

Inisrue Marsh

7:21 pm

We worked hard, cutting across the tidal surge, then jumped out, dragging the cot up onto the stones, running it aground.

Boges swore at the cold but I was too excited to even notice it myself.

We hauled ourselves up the bank and onto

the landing. A small, sinking stone house with darkened windows was the only intact building I could see, but just past it, blocking out the night sky ahead, was the looming mass of a great ruin.

"OK, we have to make our way along the bank to Cragkill Keep," said Boges, "which is further up on the right. Quick, follow me!"

Boges led the way with the sharp light from his flashlight.

Stay on the track, Ashling had warned. None of us wanted to end up sinking helplessly into the marsh like Rathbone had, but we dared to walk quickly along the narrow strip of firm, slightly raised ground that formed what we hoped was the safest path. On both sides of us, the quick-sand of the marsh endlessly oozed into the dark, with only the occasional bare and struggling tree jutting out of its surface.

8:00 pm

The chiming clock, louder still, rang out eight o'clock—it must have been in a nearby town. We'd been struggling along the muddy track through the marsh for over half an hour, and now we only had four hours left.

I paused. I'd heard something. I put up a hand to stop the others behind me.

Boges immediately doused his light. "What is it, dude?"

"Listen."

The darkness and silence of Inisrue Marsh surrounded us.

"What are we listening to?" whispered Winter.

"I don't know. But I get the feeling we're not the only people on this track."

I steadied myself and strained to listen again. "I swear I can hear footsteps," I whispered, as quietly as possible. "Ahead of us, coming this way. Can you hear it?"

This time, the others heard it too.

Flickers of light from flashlights in the distance became visible ahead of us. Low voices drifted along the chilly air.

We crouched low, unsure of what to do and where to go. I didn't want to backtrack and lose ground, but I was worried we didn't have any other option. Winter suddenly gasped beside me—now footsteps seemed to be coming from behind us as well! We were stuck in the middle!

Not knowing who was closing in on us was the worst part. I couldn't even imagine who it could be; all I knew was that the intruders would be hostile. Hostile and desperate to stop us from uncovering the DMO first.

Then I recognised the loud voice ahead.

"*Sligo!*" Winter hissed, before I could.

What was he doing here? Wasn't he supposed to be in the hands of the Garda? If Sligo found us this time, we could kiss our lives and the Ormond Singularity goodbye forever.

"We have to get off the track!" I told my friends. "We can't let anyone see us!"

"Where should we go?" asked Boges. "We can't go into the bog—we'll be sucked down in seconds!"

Desperate, I swung round, trying to find a hiding place. Against the night sky, I spotted a gnarled and witchy-looking tree half-submerged in the marsh near the edge of the track a few metres ahead of us.

"That tree," I whispered to the others. "Let's climb in there and hide. Grab a branch and hang onto it for your lives. Whatever you do, don't let go—we have to stay above the surface."

The footsteps behind us crept closer.

I ran and leaped off the pathway, seizing the low branches of the witchy tree, throwing myself behind it, while gripping it tightly with my raw hands.

Whack! Winter slammed into me as she did the same, almost making me lose my hold and my balance. Seconds later, Boges banged into us, almost sending both of us sprawling into the surrounding marshy mess.

I hated to think what might happen if any of the branches snapped. I could already feel the mud closing over my feet. I hung onto the bough even tighter than the day I was hanging from a tree with those dogs, Skull and Crossbones, snapping at my heels.

Boges and Winter were also straining to keep themselves up in the tree, the pained effort obvious in their shadowy faces.

"They haven't arrived yet," I heard Sligo say as he wandered along the path nearby. "We can grab them and force that Psycho Kid into giving us the last piece of information. He won't be able to keep quiet if he has to watch you use your 'special techniques' on his stout friend and that repulsive little traitor! I know he'll talk if we grab them. And then we'll finally get rid of Ormond. For good, this time!"

Sligo must have returned to the empty oubliette, and realised I'd escaped.

Tension choked the air as we huddled in the branches, trying to keep our nerves and chattering teeth under control.

The figures of Zombie Two and Sligo finally emerged from the murky air, mere metres away from where the three of us were clinging. They both stopped and stared into the darkness of the path leading back to the river.

"Vermin coming now, boss," Zombie Two growled. "I hear them coming."

Zombie Two clearly thought that it was me and my friends making our way down the track towards them. I held my breath.

The heavy pounding of whoever it *really* was who had been trailing behind us came closer.

A single silhouette, black and round, grew larger with every footstep. I knew that silhouette all too well.

I waited for him to step into the soft beam of moonlight that shone in between him and the unsuspecting pair ahead on the path.

I heard a wheezing roar as Sumo suddenly became visible, head down on his massive chest, powerful arms raised in a fighter's stance. His flashlight pointed at Sligo and Zombie Two, standing side-by-side, who'd been expecting the three of us to appear, not Oriana's loyal sidekick.

Before Zombie Two and Sligo could react, Sumo doubled over and powerfully barrelled into them both, knocking the wind out of them, and sending them flying out over the marsh just metres from us! They flew through the air in a big black blur of tangled bodies!

The three wrestling bodies splashed into the treacherous swamp.

For a few seconds, they didn't realise the

serious danger they were in, and we heard them, swearing, shouting, struggling, swinging and kicking. Every twist, every turn, every defensive move was condemning them to a suffocating fate.

I should have known that Oriana's jail sentence wouldn't have meant the end of her pursuit of the Ormond Singularity. She must have sent Sumo to Ireland to finish what she'd started.

"C'mon," I said, trying to refocus. "Now's our chance to get out of here!"

I carefully swung myself out of the tree and planted my feet on firm ground. I held my arms out to help guide Winter and Boges to safety.

The shouts and curses of the battling trio in the mud changed to cries of fear as they realised their threats were useless and they'd encountered an enemy that they couldn't beat. Finally they were facing a force that was greater than all three of them combined.

"Help!" came Sligo's terrified voice. "Somebody help me! Please! Get me out of here!"

For a moment, Winter moved towards the bog, but both Boges and I stopped her. We weren't about to let the marsh take her, too, for the sake of a man who'd tried to destroy her life. It was out of our hands now.

"Get off me!" shouted Sumo, from the darkness.

"Get off *me*!" shouted Zombie Two.

"Stop it, you fools!" cried Sligo. "You're both pushing me under!"

We could hardly see anything as they all sunk lower and lower in the swamp, their struggles and violence only making it worse for them, quickening their relentless descent into the marshes.

"There's nothing to see here. Let's go," I whispered to my friends. I took Winter's hand and led her away, as the desperate cries from out of the unforgiving mud were slowly muffled.

And then even they were gone. There was nothing but silence behind us.

8:51 pm

We hurried along the final stretch and my heart pounded harder with every step. Sligo had boasted about ridding himself of Rathbone in the mud, and now he had suffered the same demise. Maybe there was some kind of justice in the world.

I gripped Winter's hand firmly.

The silhouette of Cragkill Keep finally emerged from the dark, wet mass of Inisrue Marsh. At one time, I guessed, the river would have flowed close to the Keep, but now it was a hundred metres or so away.

9:00 pm

The clock sounded over Cragkill Keep, reminding

us that we had only three hours to go. The Keep stood alone in a field, its fragmented shape etched against the rising half-moon sky. Even by moon-light, and despite the whorls of mist around its crumbling towers, I recognised the ruin from the photos on my dad's memory stick.

We flashed our lights over the stone ruin. Only the central section of the building remained partly intact, with crumbling towers at each end like a giant's four-poster bed.

"No!" said Boges as our lights also revealed that Cragkill Keep was completely surrounded by a tall security fence and locked double gates. Inside this compound I could see earthmoving equipment—a huge bulldozer and two cranes sit-ting idle. We were locked out. "Man, what's all this about?" asked Boges. "Why is it fenced off like this?"

The huge bulldozer with its immense jaw-like scoop squatted on a rise a little way from the massive ruin, next to what looked like flood lights. Piles of numbered stones were stacked nearby, awaiting transportation.

I turned to Boges and Winter. "Mrs Fitzgerald said that one of the ruins here was being boxed up and shipped back to the USA."

"It *would* have to be this one," said Winter in frustration. "What if somebody has already stumbled on the Ormond Singularity? What if they've already been in there and taken it?"

"Relax, Winter. You should know by now that the Ormond Singularity isn't something that people can just 'stumble on,'" said Boges. "I don't think it'd just be sitting in there waiting for someone to walk in and find it."

"I know that," Winter said. "But they might have been digging around. They might have accidentally lucked onto it."

"Come on guys," I said, mentally measuring up the height of the wire mesh. "What's a little fence between us and the Ormond Singularity? We're going over."

I threw my backpack over the fence, and bit down on my flashlight, ready to scramble up and over the security fence.

"What about this?" asked Winter, pointing to a small sign.

WARNING

FOLEY SECURITY, WATERFORD

Back-to-base electronic surveillance

UNAUTHORISED PERSONS KEEP OUT!

YOU ARE BEING MONITORED ON OUR SURVEILLANCE SYSTEM

"I can't see any cameras anywhere, can you?" I said, jumping the fence and landing on the other side.

Winter followed me, throwing her bag over the tall wire netting and throwing herself up on it.

Finally, Boges took a running jump and threw himself up and over the fence too. He dropped to the ground on the other side, puffing.

9:33 pm

The three of us stood inside the grounds, examining the decaying ruin. Weeds grew wildly through cracks in the rubble and over large blocks of stone. We navigated around them, stepping cautiously through the wet grass, avoiding tripping on the uneven ground.

Starry sky peered eerily through the empty window arches of a collapsed tower. Dead grass and plants speared out of the broken walls. The second, less damaged tower stood opposite the first and I could just make out some kind of statue standing on a perch within it.

"What is that?" Winter asked.

Eroded and hidden by the jut of a stone corner, the figure was impossible to make out.

"Not sure," I said, flashing my light through an archway to the interior.

Some of the original roofing remained at the furthest end, and this had protected a section of the stone flooring of what I guessed would have once been the Keep's great hall.

A tremor of fear and apprehension filled me. I couldn't shake the feeling that even though Oriana, Rathbone, Sligo, Zombie Two and Sumo were out of the picture, trouble was very close. We were right where we were supposed to be, I reminded myself. Cragkill Keep. The worst thing that could happen was that we'd run out of time.

Winter guided her light along the mossy stone walls of the interior and up to the sections of the first-floor roof that still remained. Remnants of the plaster patterns that had once decorated the ceiling were now stained and broken, with dead vines drooping from them.

I lowered my light, moving it over the uneven floor of the long room. Under the debris and dead leaves, I could see the remains of mosaic tiling.

"What are we even looking for?" Boges asked the question we were all thinking.

"We won't know what we're looking for until we find it," I said.

10:00 pm

I started panicking as the chimes rang out again. We had two hours to midnight.

"Spread out," I urged, "and look for anything that might give us a clue. Anything familiar."

After a lot of frantic searching, we all stopped and stared back at each other hopelessly. Was this the end of the road? Had we reached another dead end?

"Come over here!" Winter suddenly shouted. "Look at this!"

Boges and I hurried over to her. She was shining her light down to where the corners of a huge fireplace met the broken stone of the floor. There was something carved on the stone. It was only small and worn by the weather.

"It's a rose!" I said, squatting beside it. "Like that one in the drawing of the little kid!" My heart beat a little faster. "And look! Just above it!"

"The pattern on Gabbi's ring," said Winter, pointing to the silver ring on my finger. "The Carrick bend design!"

Just above the rose, the Carrick bend had been carved along the stone wall. It too was eroded and almost invisible.

"Maybe the rose means something like 'X marks the spot,'" I said. I shone my light up and around, searching the darkness in the corner under the collapsing roof.

You were here, Dad, I thought to myself. You

found something. You noticed something—why can't I see it? *What were you trying to tell me?*

As I strained to make out more of the rotting designs in the crumbling plaster, brilliant lights suddenly came on, flooding the interior of the ruined Keep.

Boges and Winter blinked in astonishment, quickly turning around, bracing themselves.

I freaked out. It was now as bright as day. Who was here?

"Get out of sight!" I ordered, ducking into the narrow corridor we'd first come through and peering around the corner of the wide archway.

Someone had switched on the floodlights. I could hear the generator humming outside.

As I crouched out of the light, I nearly jumped out of my skin as outside some huge piece of machinery revved into life. I craned my neck further around the corner. Some distance away, near the fenceline, the massive bulldozer I'd seen earlier had come to life! A hunched figure sat at the controls.

I raced back to the others. "We have to hurry. If we stay out of sight, the guy in the bulldozer might not even realise we're in here. Looks like he's loading stones onto a pallet or something."

"At this hour?" Winter asked. "Nearly midnight? On New Year's Eve?"

"I've heard of overtime," said Boges, "but that's crazy."

The bright light shone on the stained and discoloured plaster of the ceiling above the corner, and for the first time I could see traces of words. As more of the damaged plaster of the corner came into focus, I gasped.

AM R ET   VRE
TOSJO S CEL R

"Wow!" yelped Boges over the sound of the bulldozer, following my line of sight and spotting the words on the wall. "The words inscribed on the Ormond Jewel!"

"And look up here! You can see where they are repeated high up on the wall!" cried Winter, carefully stepping across the uneven floor to see the faint words better. "They would have run all the way round this section of the gallery! Just like in the old sketch you found in Dr Brinsley's study!"

The spot we were standing in looked like it had once been a small room, just off the main long gallery.

"Now I *know* we're in the right place," said Winter, "even in the right corner! The rose and inscription are showing us the way!"

My exhilaration surged as did the sense of danger. I was *shaking* with mixed emotions. To be so close . . . so close to *what*?

Boges twisted to look at the roof and tripped over something on the floor. The contents of his backpack flew out and his water bottle hit the ground, popping its lid and spraying water everywhere. He swore, climbing to his feet.

Winter went to help him gather up his things, retrieving his bottle. Most of the water had spilled out onto the ground, making a slippery mess on the mud-covered mosaic flooring.

"Hey, look at this—there's some kind of pattern on these tiles," said Winter, squatting down to take a closer look. "Underneath the dirt."

"We don't have time for appreciating tiles," said Boges, getting back on his feet.

"You'd better make time for this," scoffed Winter, her voice shaking with excitement. "Cal, get over here and check this out!"

She dropped to her hands and knees, and wrenched off her scarf, scrubbing the ground with it. She grabbed Boges's bottle and splashed more water over the tiles. "Don't just stand there, help me!" she urged us both.

We joined her and started clearing more of the tiles—me with my bare hands, Boges with his cap—pushing aside leaves and debris, wiping dirt away.

Outside, the bulldozer seemed to be getting louder.

"Luckily they're only here to dismantle the place," Boges said, "not destroy it."

I stood back up, shining my light onto the area we'd been working on. Although smeared and dirty, parts of the original mosaic floor of the gallery started to become clear. More and more was being revealed with every sweep of Winter's wet scarf.

"Get up!" I shouted excitedly to my friends. "Look!"

A pattern in the tiles of intertwined leaves of faded yellow surrounded what once would have been a huge, dark green oval. I dug around in my backpack and pulled out the Ormond Jewel, holding it up over the remnants of the pattern on the floor.

There was no doubt about it.

"It's the same design as the front of the Ormond Jewel! The Ormond Jewel is a *miniature*!

It's a tiny replica of the floor design of Cragkill Keep!"

Stunned by this revelation, the three of us stood immobilised, staring at each other, then at the tiled jewel on the floor beneath us.

Feverishly we dropped back to our knees to clear more of the area of rubble and grass, revealing more patches of coloured tiling.

"Look!" I said. "There's the pattern of red and white tiles! The same pattern as the alternating rubies and pearls surrounding the emerald!"

Little by little, the clues were falling into place!

"Hurry," I said to the others. "If that guy in the bulldozer comes any closer, he'll spot us. We mustn't be seen. The clock's ticking!"

I could hear Winter reciting the words of the Ormond Riddle under her breath as she cleared enough ground to start examining the alternating red and white tiles.

"There are thirteen white tiles," she said. "The same number as the pearls on the Ormond Jewel."

"Thirteen teares! Thirteen tiles! Thirteen steps!" said Boges, excitedly. "The numbers in the Riddle relate to counting out the steps on this floor." Boges suddenly stopped, looking deflated. "But the thirteen steps we need to take have to start from 'the Sunnes grate Doore,'" he said.

"Is there some sort of grate or door around here? I can't see anything like that."

With the grinding of the bulldozer becoming louder, I risked running down to the other end of the gallery and back again.

"There's nothing on the floor near the arch where we came in," I reported.

"We don't need to look for a grate," said Winter. "That's just old-fashioned spelling for 'great.' We should be looking for something big that lets the sun in—a great door, or something."

I looked around. "'The Sunnes grate Doore,'" I repeated.

A mix of moonlight and floodlight shone on the rough floor of the ruin. I tried to follow the beams of moonlight, and imagined sunlight pouring through the gaping arches of the three-tiered window in the tower rearing above us.

A wave of vibrations shuddered through the stone walls as the rumbling from the big earth-mover outside became louder. What was left of the roof of the main gallery trembled visibly.

"Something that lets the sun in?" said Winter, suddenly beside me. She was looking up at the moonlight again—the crumbling arches of the empty windows.

"Them?" I asked, staring at the arches. "The sun would have come streaming through those windows. Onto the floor. Just like the moonlight is trying to do now!"

Winter raced over to the crumbling stones beneath the ruined windows, and stood there directly against the wall. "If we take the thirteen steps as starting from here, under the big triple window—the sun's great door—we might find something."

I ran over to join her and we walked the steps, counting aloud over the drone of the bulldozer.

One, two, three, four, five, six, seven, eight, nine, ten, eleven, twelve, thirteen . . . We could go no further. We had already come up hard against the opposite wall of this smaller, ruined room we were in. I stood there with my nose almost touching the cold stones as disappointment drained me.

There was nothing beyond the thirteenth step.

"The tiles don't lead anywhere," I said bitterly. "They end right here at this wall. It's not working. The Riddle isn't right."

"'Thirteen Teares from the Sunnes grate Doore,'" Winter chanted, "'Make *right* to treadde in Gules on the Floore . . .'"

I paused. "Make *right*!" I shouted. "I've gotta take a step to the *right*."

"Of course!" cried Winter.

I stepped to the right and kicked away the leaf litter and debris at my feet.

"You're standing on a red tile!" said Boges. "*Gules!* Gules means red! Gules on the floor!"

"But there's only one of them. Hard up against the wall," I said.

At that moment, the sound of the bulldozer outside roared at top speed and the wall opposite us, under the gaping hole of the ruined window, started to crack in a thin, jagged black line.

Boges yelled. "We'll have to show ourselves, dude. That guy's going to kill us!"

"We can't!" I said. "We're so close to the deadline!"

"You have to 'adde One in, for the Queenes fayre Sinne,'" recited Winter, who seemed unaware of the danger we were in. "That means there should be one more tile! There should be *two* red tiles. The Riddle says so!"

"But there's only one here," I argued.

"Can we have this conversation about how many tiles there should be somewhere else please, dudes?" yelled Boges over the noise of the bulldozer outside. "That crack's getting bigger every second! The wall's going to fall and we're going to be crushed!"

He was right. The crack in the wall now ran all the way down from the window and almost the entire length of the gallery. It was getting wider, deeper and blacker the longer I stared at it.

A shower of small stones from around the three-tiered window above dropped dangerously close. It was about to come down. The entire Cragkill Keep was about to come down.

As I stood there, immobilised with frustration, unwilling to just walk away from the Ormond Singularity, the wall next to me cracked wider with a sound like a gunshot.

Bigger stones tumbled and crashed to the ground, peppering me with stinging fragments.

"Cal!" urged Boges. "I'm serious, we have to move! We have to get out of here!"

"We can't," cried Winter. "We can't leave now! We're so close! There's gotta be something else. The Riddle talks about the orb being riven and the gift being given. There should be something here to show us. Something's wrong! Where's the orb?"

Boges grabbed me and Winter by the arms. "You betcha something's wrong! A lunatic in a bulldozer's bringing the house down around us! We'll be flattened if we don't get out!"

Everything was trembling violently. Boges's fingers dug into my upper arm, wrenching me away from the wall.

"Come *on*! This whole place is about to come down on top of us!"

"No! We can't leave now!" insisted Winter, a crazed, fearless determination in her eyes. "If we leave now, the Ormond Singularity is lost. Cal will never find out what it is!"

The crack in the wall next to me suddenly shifted, and another ominous zigzag crack appeared, spearing down its entire length. More stones and rocks cascaded down.

"Watch out!" I lunged at Winter, knocking her out of the way as a huge rock fell, narrowly missing her.

The close call shook me out of my stupor. Boges was right. "We'll die if we don't get out now!" I shouted.

"That's what I've been trying to tell both of you!" screeched Boges.

I grabbed Winter's arm and pulled her along, following Boges. We were about to run across the shaking floor and get outside when a huge crash made me turn back to see the wall I'd been facing moments ago collapsing. If we'd still been standing there, we would have been crushed by its bulk. Like a line of dominoes, the length of the wall crumpled in a cloud of dust.

And then something amazing happened.

The collapsed wall revealed a black cavity behind it.

"It was a false wall!" Winter shouted. She too had stopped to witness the collapse. "That's why the tile steps suddenly stopped. See? There's a space behind it!" She ran back through the dust cloud to peer into the space that had opened up—it was about the size of a backyard shed. "And there's the other red tile! See? Just here, where the wall was stopping us before! I *told* you there'd have to be another one. The Riddle said so!"

Winter pointed and another huge rock fell from above and shattered on impact just centimetres from her. It sent up more murky dust, acting like a smokescreen.

I heard Boges swear as he was struck by something on the side of the face.

Now we really did have to run for our lives. I thought I heard the clock chiming again—eleven o'clock—but I couldn't tell over all the rumbling and panic.

I grabbed Winter's arm once more and started dragging her out. But as I dodged another rock crashing close behind us I caught a glimpse of something colourful within the dark cavity. Something on the floor, just beyond the last of the red tiles.

I squinted. Protected for centuries from the elements by the fake wall, was a perfect mosaic!

In it was a white monkey holding a ball—an orb—just like the monkey in Dad's drawing!

"Boges, Winter! Wait! Look!"

As my friends and I stood mesmerised by the amazing tiled image, the floor cracked before our eyes and the monkey mosaic began to destruct. The mosaic was buckling up and then collapsing apart, like in an earthquake.

"It's a prophecy!" cried Winter. "The whole thing's breaking up!"

"The orb must be riven," I whispered, as the image of the white monkey holding the orb seemed to lift up momentarily, then subside, breaking up and draining downwards in a waterfall of puzzle pieces. It vanished into the darkness under the floor like being swallowed by a sinkhole.

Masonry and stones pelted down around us, while outside, the bulldozer revved again, making another assault on the walls that surrounded us, attacking what little remained of the structure.

Fearfully we made our way to the edge of the hole that was getting larger by the second. More and more of the floor collapsed and disappeared into the cavity.

Any moment, I thought we would join the rest of the floor, and be drawn down into the darkness of the foundations of the Cragkill

Keep. Then suddenly, the sound of the bulldozer stopped.

The shower of rocks and stones eased.

The floor shuddered to a halt.

I seized the opportunity and crept right up to the widening hole and peered into it.

Under the piled-up earth and broken tiles, I could see the corner of a wooden chest.

Boges and Winter teetered over beside me, dodging falling debris.

"Dude, that must be the treasure!" Boges shouted.

With that, the three of us reached in and started digging away like mad dogs, trying to free the wooden chest from the rubble that had fallen in on top of it.

11:08 pm

"Cal?" came a voice, approaching from outside. "Cal, are you in there?"

"Sharkey!" Boges shouted out. "We're over here! Come and see what we've found!"

Nelson appeared in the crumbling archway.

He strode over, looking up and around, overwhelmed by the disaster zone inside the Keep. "I've stopped that crazy guy in the bulldozer, but this place is dangerously unstable. You need to get out."

As he spoke, a huge stone from the top of the wall crashed down behind him, making us all jump.

Sharkey stopped when he saw what we were all staring at. He whistled. "Seems like you've found what you were looking for!"

"We found it, all right!" I said, almost exploding with happiness. "Can you give us a hand?" I asked, indicating the pile of rubble in the cavity under the floor. I was shivering with excitement. Adrenaline was pumping through every muscle in my body.

Eventually the four of us were able to haul the extremely heavy chest up.

Puffing and panting, we dropped it near the archway. As it settled on the ground, one side of the ancient timber box split open, and a stream of gold spilled out! A steady flood of golden coins, lit by the brilliant generator lights kept spreading in a gleaming pool!

It was like a dream come true. I could feel the excitement of the others. I realised I had a huge grin on my face.

Another heavy stone from the ceiling crashed straight into the top of the chest, splitting the lid into jagged pieces, sending more gold and precious jewels cascading out.

We all stepped back, speechless. Through

the split timber I could see the gleam of more gold, the flash of gems, and what looked like an ancient document, partly obscured by the broken rock. But before we did anything else, I needed proof.If the contents of this chest turned out to be the Ormond Singularity, I needed proof that I'd found it before the deadline. Before time was up at midnight on the 31st of December.

"Boges!" I said, turning to them all. "We did it! Get the camera out and start filming!"

"While you're doing that," said Sharkey, "I'll get some big canvas sacks I have in the back of my car."

I barely heard his words as I threw off bits of the broken rock and splintered timber until the contents of the chest were clear to see: a collection of amazing jewels and gold coins, gold chains, ropes of pearls and, most importantly, the signed document that sat on the top of it all.

"We did it!" I yelled again. I threw my arms around my friends and the three of us jumped around with excitement. "Let's have a look at what we've discovered."

My hands were trembling as I carefully lifted out the document. I knew from the touch that it was vellum. I smoothed it open so Boges could film it more easily.

Codicil: The Ormond Singularity

I give you this charge, my beloved 'black husband,' as I gave you the charge years ago when our honest nurse and servant, Kat, conveyed to you, with utmost secrecy, the gracious fruit of 'amor et suevre tosjors celer.'

I trust you will not be corrupted by any manner of gift, and that you will be faithful with respect of our declaration of mutual and eternal secrecy. I am already bound to a husband, which is the kingdom of England. For me, this end must be sufficient: that a marble stone shall declare that a Queen, having reigned such a time, lived and died childless.

Therefore I charge you to guard our own great secret work, and do assign these rights, privileges and titles to that same secret. This is to be known henceforth as the Ormond Singularity, benefiting the male line of Piers Duiske, so that he and his heirs shall never be wanting.

By the love you bear his mother, when he attains his majority, give him this mantle of black velvet, well-jewelled, and this psalter, broidered by my own hand, complete with rights, privileges and titles as set out herein.

Given under our signet at our honour
at Hampton Court, 1573

The Queen and Black Tom had a baby together. A baby who no one could know about.

Carefully, I picked up a small book, the cover decorated with coloured silk stitching of flowers, Tudor roses and tiny pearls surrounding the central initial E on the cover.

"Hey!" I said, recognising it. "We've seen this before—in that portrait you discovered, Winter, in the Sotheby's catalogue. Hanging from her waist in the painting."

I put it down, my attention taken by something else. Tucked down beside the pile of gold coins lay an embroidered leather satchel. Carefully, I opened it. It contained something made of really fine material, beautifully embroidered with pearls and gold. I picked it up. For a few seconds it hung in my hands, a precious silky robe, made for a tiny baby. But then it fell into shreds, dropping away from my hands into dusty fragments.

"The silk has perished!" cried Winter. "What a shame! But look at the beautiful trimming! Gold embroidered Tudor roses and tiny pearls! How sad for the princess—and later the queen. She could never acknowledge her baby. She'd have been in huge danger if people ever found out. She would have been killed over it. And look at this!" she said, picking up another locket. "It's a bit like the Ormond Jewel!"

She passed it to me. The locket, with a yellow crystal surrounded by diamonds and gold on its top lid, opened to reveal a miniature of the young Princess Elizabeth on one side, and on the other, the portrait of an infant boy, in Tudor finery, holding a rose.

"The boy with the rose," breathed Winter. "Like your dad's drawing!"

"The boy," I repeated. "It wasn't just the secret love between Black Tom and Princess Elizabeth. The greater secret love was their son—the child they had together."

A shower of stones falling over us reminded me that the situation here was pretty dicey. We needed to get this gear secured somehow and then get out.

Winter attempted to pick up the shreds of rotted yellow silk, gathering them into her hands together with the embroidered borders of gold and pearls. "The Princess made this for her baby. The baby she could never share with the world. Black Tom was the dad, and the Queen was the 'great unknown lady' who sadly couldn't name herself."

"This little guy is the reason for the Ormond Singularity. He grew up and became Piers Duiske Ormond. All this," I said, pointing to the treasure trove and documents signed by the Queen, "was supposed to be claimed by Piers Duiske Ormond, for his family and his heirs, but something happened and it was never retrieved. Maybe his dad, Black Tom, died without ever revealing where it was hidden exactly. We'll never know why it wasn't claimed. The descendants of Piers Duiske Ormond kept the line going. The line that started with Black Tom and Princess Elizabeth. My ancestor, Piers Ormond, was gathering information about this secret when the Great War interrupted him. Dad took over and somehow got hold of the Ormond Jewel, but then he got sick and . . ." My voice trailed away. I hoped that somewhere, somehow, my dad could see what I'd done and be happy about it.

"The line came right down to you," said Winter. "It would have all belonged to your dad if he'd lived—he was the older twin. But now it falls to you. You're the older twin. It's been here for centuries, just waiting for whoever could decipher the Ormond Riddle and read the Ormond Jewel."

I wanted to say something but it was hard to talk. Thoughts of Dad and Rafe were making me simultaneously overjoyed and sad.

"How much do you think all this is worth?" wondered Boges, his eyebrows almost jumping off his forehead with excitement.

"Millions," answered Sharkey, who had

reappeared carrying some big canvas bags. "At least. Something like this," he said, coming closer to look at the book, "is worth a fortune in itself. The Queen embroidered it with her very own initial."

"What about all these parchments written in Latin?" asked Winter. "The titles and deeds to different properties?"

"Millions more," said Sharkey. "Enough talk. Start loading everything into these bags."

I straightened up, puzzled at the change in tone of his voice.

"Shouldn't we call the authorities?" I said. "I want to do this properly. I've discovered the Ormond Singularity before the deadline and I want this acknowledged. All legal and above board."

Boges and Winter nodded in support.

"We can do all that in the morning," said Sharkey. "As soon as the banks open, you should deposit all this. You won't be able to take it out of the country without Customs clearance. In the meantime, we really just need to secure it all."

"I guess you're right," I said, but deep down inside me, I couldn't help thinking, *something is wrong. Danger is close.*

Nelson gave each of us one of the bags and we started loading them up with the contents of the treasure chest. I filled my bag with the heaviest stuff first—gold coins and chains. On top of that I placed ropes of pearls and shining rings, and then finally I added the book and the embroidered leather satchel with the Ormond Singularity inside.

"OK," said Nelson, nursing his canvas bag, into which he'd just squeezed one huge ruby ring before securing the flaps. By the time our four bags were filled and sealed, there wasn't much left at the bottom of the crumbling wooden chest. The rest could be collected later. "OK," repeated Nelson, "let's load up my vehicle."

With the walls still shaking around us, and stones still crashing down, we staggered with the weight of the treasure in our bags and, finally, the four of us emerged from the ruins of Cragkill Keep. We continued across the uneven ground to where Nelson had parked his rented pickup —he'd driven right over a section of the wire fencing.

I noticed that the bulldozer was sitting quietly nearby.

"What was that?" asked Winter, pointing into the distance, in the direction of the bog that had taken Sligo, Zombie Two and Sumo. "I swear I just saw someone over there!"

"I think I saw it too," added Boges. "Movement over by that tree. You don't think one of them could possibly have—"

"Come on, let's get this stuff onto the truck already," said Sharkey, swinging his own bag into the tray.

We heaved our bags onto the tray and Sharkey quickly roped them down. Once everything was loaded up, the three of us climbed into the front of the cabin, and squashed up together, waiting for Nelson to take his place behind the wheel.

I sat back, exhausted and happy.

Winter sat between Boges and me and gripped our hands tightly. We couldn't believe it. We had cracked the mystery of the Ormond Singularity.

All that remained now was bringing it home safely and getting our lives back.

11:32 pm

The driver's door swung open and we waited for Sharkey to climb in. I looked back at the ruin, grateful for everything it had given us. Then I turned around and saw the snub of an automatic pistol.

It was pointed at me.

"Nelson, what are you doing?" I asked, thinking this was some sort of sick joke.

"Get out. All of you," he ordered, gesturing with the pistol. "Right now."

"What?" came Boges's shocked cry.

"Nelson?" Winter demanded. "What are you doing? What's going on?"

He didn't answer, just menaced us again with the business end of the pistol.

"Do as I say. Get out. *Now!*"

I was too stunned to move immediately.

"Do as I say or I'll fire."

Fire? At us?

"But, Sharkey—" I began, completely shocked and confused.

Slowly my brain registered what was going on. I cursed myself for not having seen it sooner. It had been there all along and I hadn't seen it!

Rathbone's list.

Deep Water. *Sharkey. Sharks swim in deep water!*

Nelson Sharkey was "Deep Water"!

"You pretended to be on our side!" I shouted at him, pushing my friends out of the pickup and standing in front of them. "All this time you were lying to us! Pretended to help and now you are completely betraying us!"

Rage was pouring up through my spine, shooting down into my arms and fingers. My fists were ready to strike out.

Another vicious movement from the gun stopped me in my tracks.

"Don't do anything stupid, Cal. Just do what

I say. You too," he said, gesturing the gun in Winter and Boges's direction. "It's turned out just as I hoped it would. All I had to do was tag along, lend a hand so I'd earn your trust, and ride your coattails until you tracked down the secret of the Ormond Singularity. For me."

"But Sligo? You said you had proof."

Sharkey laughed. "Proof? How could I have proof? Just add it to the list of lies you fell for," he scoffed. "And Sligo didn't shoot your uncle, *I* did!"

Anger surged through me. He killed my uncle! I picked up a rock and pelted it at him.

He deftly ducked it, standing upright again with a crooked smile.

"But your kids? Your old job? Was none of it true?" pleaded Winter.

"I hate kids! I don't have any offspring skipping around. I don't have an ex-wife, either!"

"But what about the reunion?" Winter continued, tears streaming down her face.

Sharkey laughed again. "I've been here following you three this whole time—I don't have family in Dublin! I haven't been at a reunion! I'm not even Irish!" He shook his head and grinned. He was enjoying this. "I *was* a detective, I didn't lie about that. Had quite an undercover money ring going until my partner in crime—that she-devil

Oriana de la Force—hung me out to dry. We could have been an incredible pair."

"What about the clover?" Winter pleaded.

"Nice touch, eh," scoffed Sharkey. "Had a tracking device in it! I was particularly proud of that one."

"Brinsley?" I asked tentatively.

"Old fool wouldn't give me what I needed."

"You killed him? But I—"

"But, but, but," mocked Sharkey.

Every lie, every reveal, every betrayal hit me in the gut hard. Desperately I looked at my friends. Winter looked heartbroken; Boges looked ready to attack.

"The passports," whimpered Winter, "the clover . . . It was all just to fool us. How could you?" she asked him. "We *trusted* you."

"That was the idea," Sharkey scoffed, before forcing us at gunpoint back to the Keep, back through the archway and into the central gallery.

From the corner of my eye, I noticed that the light in the bulldozer had come on again.

"How many lives does that guy have?" Sharkey muttered to himself, looking back and noticing it too. "I should have hit him harder. He thinks he can pay me to do all his dirty work, and then he can take all the glory! Not a chance!"

What was Sharkey talking about?

I had discovered the truth of the Ormond Singularity before midnight 31 December, and I had the proof of this on Boges's mobile, but none of that mattered if Nelson Sharkey was about to get away with my colossal inheritance.

It was just the three of us now. Mum, Gab, me. I needed all of the treasure so I could get my family back to where we were before. Buy back our house, buy back our old lives.

With a last flourish of the pistol, Sharkey cornered us, then ran back to his truck. We glared at him in disbelief as he climbed into the cabin in the distance and revved up the car. Mud skidded out from underneath the tires.

All of a sudden the bulldozer thundered and charged into view, scoop raised high.

Stunned into silence, we watched as the bulldozer drove right up to Sharkey's truck, blade hovering directly above the driver's seat.

"What's going on?" screeched Boges, breaking the spell. "Sharkey's about to get flattened!"

We heard Sharkey's screams as the bulldozer shifted gears, sending the menacing, heavy scoop pounding down on top of him, crushing the entire front end of the truck, like a half-squashed bug.

"He's dead for sure," said Boges. "Sharkey's dead."

"Who's driving that thing?" asked Winter, completely bewildered.

"I don't know," I said, still in shock at what we'd just witnessed. "It must have been someone who knew Sharkey was a bad guy. Let's go find out."

But as we ran towards the bulldozer, the driver revved it up, lowered its huge blade, and came straight at us, lights blazing.

"Hey!" yelled Boges, as we scrambled backwards. "Stop! What do you think you're doing?"

Winter ran over to the cabin, reaching up to bang on the glass, but the crazy driver took no notice and continued powering straight towards the archway—and me and Boges!

If he took the archway out, I knew that the teetering tower nearby would come tumbling down in an avalanche, with all of us under it!

"Hey! Stop!" I yelled, waving my arms madly in the headlights.

I knew he couldn't hear me over the noise of the big earthmover, but I was right in his line of sight. Surely he could see me. I came closer, waving my arms. Boges and Winter joined me, flapping and shouting.

"He's not going to stop!" I shouted. "He's trying to kill us too!"

It was then that the driver put his head out of the cabin, revealing his identity . . .

But it couldn't be!

He was dead!

I'd seen him slumped, lying half out of the car. I'd seen the bullet wound.

Then I saw his grin.

Had it all been staged?

Him!

It was as if the world stood still and a whole lot of loose strands that had been twisting and turning in my mind suddenly fused together. The bulldozer revved up again, and despite the falling shower of stones, I had a moment of diamond clarity.

As I focused on his determined face, the smell that I'd been trying to remember came clearly into my mind.

It wasn't one of Mum's perfumes.

It was the smell of cigars.

I realised who had been behind almost every bad thing that had happened since the crazy guy, Eric Blair, had tried to warn me.

I now knew the identity of my archenemy.

He was coming at me now, deliberately targeting the wall, intending to push the whole ruin down on top of us. With the speed of light, the missing pieces in my mind slotted into place.

My enemy was an ex-botanist whose special area of interest was the *toxins found in bracken ferns*. I remembered the boxes of botanical textbooks and notes in his office.

Mrs Fitzgerald thought Dad had been acting strange the night she'd interrupted him at the Clonmel Way Guest House, unexpectedly cooking up some rotten-smelling herbal stew.

Except it hadn't been Dad at all. Someone else had opened that door. *Someone else who looked exactly like my father.*

Was he preparing the nerve toxin to give to my dad and his friend Eric Blair? Either secretly placed in food they would eat, or more brazenly, at a friendly meal for the three of them?

Rafe.

Rafe had flown to Ireland while telling us he was on holidays interstate. He'd impersonated my Dad at the guest house, brewing up a toxin, to poison his brother.

A poison that destroyed my dad's brain, mimicking a virus. That was what Dad had been trying to tell me all the time—he'd been trying to warn me against his own brother. Rafe.

My uncle. My dad's twin.

Double Trouble. The last of the nicknames.

Rafe's head disappeared back into the cabin and the bulldozer accelerated towards us.

If we didn't take immediate action, we'd all be crushed.

"Sharkey," I shouted to my friends. "He was the private detective *Rafe* had hired to track me down! Rafe and Sharkey were in this together! But then Sharkey must have doublecrossed his employer—my uncle!"

As the bulldozer came crashing through the archway, I pushed Boges and Winter out of the way.

Now the wall was bulging inwards, stones falling inside, sandy mortar pouring out. It would only be a matter of seconds before the entire western wall of Cragkill Keep fell, bringing the towers down.

I looked around for a way out. The other exit at the end of the long gallery was too far away for us to make a run for it.

Somehow, I had to stop him! I had to stop the bulldozer.

I charged for it. As I ran, ducking the stones that were falling from the archway, I was forced to leap to one side, to avoid the bulldozer's scoop which was raised in an attempt to bash me down.

I was faster than ever. I picked up a heavy stone and jumped on top of the housing of the caterpillar tracks. I smashed the window with the stone, wrenched open the door then hurled myself on him, knocking him into the corner away from the controls!

"You murderer!" I yelled. "You killed my dad! How could you murder your own brother?! Your own twin! You've tried to destroy my whole family! And *I* thought you'd come to *save* me from the oubliette! I thought you were the Ormond Angel coming to the aid of the heir! But you just wanted me alive a bit longer so I could lead you straight to what you wanted!"

My assault took him by surprise: it was the last thing he was expecting—he winced in pain and I saw that his shirt was bloodstained—he *had* been shot. I threw myself on top of him, pinning him down. The rage that I'd felt earlier simmering up through my body now exploded into homicidal fury. I wondered where the terrible growling I could hear was coming from, until I realised it was me. I crashed him as hard as I could against the side of the cabin.

But now he'd recovered from the initial shock and was fighting back, enraged by the pain I'd inflicted on him. Blood trickled from his nose. He managed to free his arms and he grasped me round the throat, starting to strangle me!

Instinctively, I lashed out and his hold around my neck relaxed. It was just loose enough for me to twist sideways and, with all my strength, pull myself away from him. I launched out of the cabin, hit the ground hard and rolled over, getting to my feet again with intense speed. I ran back towards the Keep.

Rafe came after me, jumping out of the

bulldozer snarling. His lips were pulled back to show his teeth, deadly, like a werewolf in a horror movie. Behind us, the un-piloted bulldozer rose up against a pile of stones, crashing down again closer and closer.

Boges and Winter raced towards us.

Then Rafe charged, falling on top of me, trying to hurl me back in front of the bulldozer, barely centimetres from the crushing tracks. I thumped the ground, winded. Getting my breath back, I fought as hard as I could, but I couldn't get any momentum behind my punches.

Again he had his hands around my throat. I rolled over the rough terrain, away from the tracks, twisting his hands, wrestling and gouging. Boges tried to help, trying to land a blow, but whenever he went to hit Rafe, somehow I was in the line of fire.

I could hear Winter yelling in the background, trying to wrench Rafe off me. Then I felt something thud hard on my lower legs. That's when I saw what Winter had been trying to warn me about. A large piece of splitting beam had fallen across my ankles, and for the moment I couldn't move.

Through my dazed vision, I saw Rafe jump up and pick up a huge rock. Winter tried to tackle him down, but he shoved her away, hard, sending her flying. I spotted Boges starting to charge him, but Rafe shoved him away, too, with unbelieveable strength.

My uncle stood above me, the crushing rock held high above him, the evil grin twisted into a snarl of demonic fury.

I tried to get up, but my legs were jammed under the beam.

Rafe was about to smash the rock down on my head.

Any second now, I'd be dead.

Goodbye Ormond Singularity. Goodbye everything.

A roaring sound caused Rafe to hesitate. He turned to look up as the massive second tower of Cragkill Keep finally caved and came crashing down. The huge, indistinct carving we'd noticed earlier separated from the crumbling tower, falling and swooping down to land . . . right on top of Rafe.

The rock he was wielding flew out of his hands and skittered away as the oddly shaped stone from the sky obliterated him.

11:50 pm

Winter and Boges rushed to free me, lifting the beam from my ankles. As they helped me up, Rafe lay motionless under the massive stone formation that had fallen on him, missing me by just centimetres. Beyond him, the bulldozer churned away, uselessly turning in a slow circle, jammed up against the pile of stones that once had been part of the walls of Cragkill Keep.

"Can you walk?" Boges asked me, helping me to my feet.

"Not sure yet," I said, trying. I looked down to see blood seeping through my jeans. I tried to walk, but almost fell.

"Dude, don't try to move. Just take it easy for a moment."

"You might have broken something," said Winter, kneeling beside me.

"What about Rafe?" I asked, alerted by a groaning noise and looking over at the outstretched figure under the massive stone.

He was alive. Just. Half of his face was pulped and unrecognisable. He made a sound—a hoarse, harsh noise in his throat.

"Cal," he was trying to say. "Help me."

"I want the truth," I replied, still trying to stand up.

My uncle groaned again.

"Film this, Boges," I said. "I want a full confession."

Boges whipped out his mobile and selected the video function. "Start now, dude."

"Tell me everything," I ordered. "You killed my dad. You tried to kill me. Tell me everything. It'll go better for you in court."

"I don't think he's going to make it to court," Winter admitted, looking at his flattened body.

"Admit it *was* you who sabotaged the fishing boat that night out on Treachery Bay. It *was* you who sabotaged my life jacket."

"I did," he murmured. Boges leaned closer, making sure his words were captured on the recording.

"So that you could swim to shore safely with a story about how you'd tried to save me but I'd tragically drowned," I continued.

Again, Rafe tried to nod and say yes.

"But you didn't take the storm into account. Then you set me up by attacking Gabbi and inflicting injuries on yourself as well. Making it look like I'd shot you. Admit it."

"Yes," came the weak response. "Sharkey helped me. Please. Call an ambulance."

"Sharkey helped set it up?" murmured Winter, still in disbelief.

"And long before any of that, you hired Toe-cutter," I accused him, sick at the thought. I recalled the house plans I'd found in his house, with an X marking one of the bedrooms. "It was you who organised for both me and Samuel to be kidnapped, wasn't it?"

I could hear the sound of sirens coming our way. Had someone else alerted the police?

"Is that true?" I shouted at him.

"Yes," came the hoarse voice.

"What about my mum?" I asked him. "What really happened to start that fight the other day? Tell me!"

Rafe's eyes blinked. His chest barely moved up and down. His breath came in long, slow heaves. "She discovered that—"

"That what?"

"That I'd been replacing her herbal teas with—something else." His voice was so weak I strained to listen. "Something that made her more *obedient* . . . made it easier for me to—"

"—to control her!" I finished for him. "You were poisoning her!" My face twisted in disgust. This man had been drugging my mum with one of his botanical toxins! No wonder she'd turned against me. "Is that all? There was something else she discovered, wasn't there?"

Rafe could hardly speak now. But I was merciless. "Tell me!"

"She found them. Where I'd hidden them away." He was struggling to breathe—his voice came in strangled whispers. "The Ormond Jewel and the Riddle. Rathbone and I stole them from you. Please Cal . . . get help."

"How could you do that to us? To your own family?"

"I just . . . wanted . . . out of the shadow . . ." he said.

"You let me think my mum hated me! That she believed I was a monster!"

"Your mother loves you . . . you fool."

And with that his head fell to the side, lifeless.

11:39 pm

I stared hard at the oddly shaped statue that we'd finally managed to roll off Rafe.

Winter was staring at it too. "It has wings," she said. "Look."

She was right. It was the crumbling figure of a huge stone angel, worn almost unrecognisable by four hundred years of rain and wind.

"The Ormond Angel," I whispered, looking up at Winter.

"Came to the aid of the heir," she whispered.

"Awesome, dude," Boges said, staring at the fallen angel. "The stories were true. The Ormond Angel saved you."

In the distance, a village clock started chiming the hour. The chimes came slowly, the sweet sound of the bells echoing through the night.

One, two, three . . .

I had rightfully claimed the Ormond Singularity, just in time, and we had proof that Rafe had been behind the crimes I'd been accused of. I could go back to my country, and there'd be no more running, no more hiding, no more watching my back.

Even going to school seemed like a great idea. *Four, five, six* . . .

I thought of what I could do with the treasure I'd inherited. I could buy back our house in Richmond and Mum would never have to worry about money ever again. I could pay back Boges for everything he'd done for me. I could give Repro some jewels to add to his collection, and maybe even help him reunite with *his* mother.

Seven, eight, nine . . .

I slipped my arm around Winter's waist as the three of us turned back towards the floodlit ruins. Winter looked up at me with sparkling eyes. I really wanted to kiss her, but before I could, she hooked an arm around my neck, moved in close and, on tiptoes, kissed *me*.

I'd make sure she would never have to think about Sligo ever again. She could go back to her family's house in Dolphin Point, and start over. I held up her left wrist and softly kissed her bird tattoo. We could both start over. We were both finally free.

Ten, eleven . . .

Boges grinned and draped his arms over our shoulders. We all smiled at each other. Battered, filthy, exhausted and proud. I had two of the best friends a guy could ever wish for.

My team. My friends.

The last chime—twelve—echoed across the marsh and then all was still and quiet. Midnight of the 31st December. We'd done it. After 365 days, we'd finally done it.

I pictured Ryan, my lost twin. Now we had the rest of our lives to look forward to, together.

I pictured Mum, back to her old, happy self, free from Rafe and his poisons. She was in front of our house, welcoming me back, Gabbi beaming widely at her side. We'd be a family again.

Lastly, I pictured my dad. He was nodding at me.

"It's freezing," I said. "Let's go home."

Epilogue

31 JANUARY

Boges, Winter and I are home. It's January again, but a very different January from the last one.

I've reunited with Gab and my mum—who's almost her old self again. We plan on buying back our Richmond house and can't wait to settle in and start getting to know Ryan Spencer. We're all looking forward to telling him stories about Dad, and showing him the drawings that led me to the Ormond Singularity.

My new lawyer, Belinda Quick, is working on having all the charges laid against me over-turned.

I've looked after Boges so that he, his mum and his gran, have everything they'll ever need. Boges is keen to get stuck into his studies—specialising in biometric systems and micro listening devices. He's also keen to ask out

Madeleine Baker, from school . . . but might need some tips from Winter.

Winter's staying with us. She's delivered evidence to the police, proving that Sligo caused the accident that killed her parents. Everything that belonged to her family will soon be returned to her. She's relieved, but convinced someone made it out of the Inisrue Marsh bog alive . . .

I returned to Repro's hideout with a jewel-filled pouch for him. He was speechless when he saw what was inside.

The Ormond Riddle and the Ormond Jewel are in a secure, secret location.

These days, I'm still being chased, but by people who want to know more about my life and the incredible DMO.

This is my story.